THROUGH THE TWISTED VINES

THROUGH THE TWISTED VINES

The Canviant Trilogy
Book Two

by Jess Layne

To the survivors, of all sorts.

AUTHOR'S NOTE

Through the Twisted Vines contains certain content that a reader may wish to avoid. This includes sexual desires and actions, explicit sexual content, emotional and verbal abuse, prejudice to disability, threats of violence, suicidal ideation, scenes of torture, sexual assault, and murder/death.

Your mental health is first, always.

Spice Rack

T3V is quite a bit spicier than IBOF, in both frequency and level. To those who enjoy spice in their books: I love this for you. To avoid possible spoilers, do not read any further into this note.

For anyone who does not want to read the spice (referring to items which surpass kissing, physical attraction, as well as thoughts of and the recognition of arousal) in this book, please note that the following chapters will contain such scenes: 43, 46, 48, 52, 59, 60, 64, 66, 68, 69, 70.

Please know that skipping these scenes may result in a subsequent loss of understanding of the emotional growth and change in certain characters.

PRONUNCIATIONS

Pronunciations listed as spoken in the Ceraschen dialect.

Characters:

Althea / Thea Cardenia: Al-th-ay-uh / Thea: Th-ay-uh Car-dén-ee-ah

    Adathan Evestre: Ad-uh-then Eh-vest-reh

    Dion Evestre: Dee-on Eh-vest-reh

    Ciaragen / Ari Vey: Kyā-ruh-gen / Aa-ree Vey

    Olin Evestre: Ah-lin Eh-vest-reh

    Emelina Dove: Em-el-ee-nuh Duv

    Atlas Malik: At-lass Mal-eek

    Javi Kahale: Ha-vee Kah-ha-lay

    Talia Kahale: Tah-lee-uh Kah-ha-lay

    Sione Natia: See-oh-nay Nah-tee-uh

    Oleander Gervan: Olee-an-der Jeh-r-vah-n

    Melisan: Meh-lis-ah-n

    Oksana Mikhyala: Ox-ah-nah Mik-yah-lah

Amedeo Monserre: Ah-meh-day-oh Mon-seh-ř-eh
Hielo / Hiela: He-el-oh / He-el-ah
Nuria Bentashi: Noo-ree-uh Ben-tah-shee
Jolie Mikhyala: Jo-lee Mik-yah-lah
Bayani Emoral: By-ah-nee Em-or-ál
Deimos: Day-m-oh-s
Ymeda: Ih-meh-da
Acacia: Uh-kay-shuh
Jemage: Jeh-mah-jeh
Lumale: Loo-mah-leh
Nisha: Nee-sh-uh

Places:
   * signifies a capital country, or city

Weaschte: Way-ah-sh-teh
   *Cerasche: Seh-rah-sheh
   *Ebenet: Eh-ben-et
   Jasiira: Jah-see-rah
   Dahlih: Dah-lee

Eshelle: Eh-shay-yeh
   Sabrian: Say-bree-ehn
   *Colina: Coh-lee-nah
   *Oschverre: Osh-veh-řeh
   *Matriel: Mah-tree-el
   Ardhavi: Ar-dah-vee
   *Dekedda: Deh-kayd-dah
   Dremerre: Dreh-meh-řeh
   Obala: Oh-bah-lah
   Parvata: Par-vah-tah
   Sielva: See-el-va

Evredis: Eh-vreh-dees

Divania: Div-on-ee-ah

HIERARCHIES

*In order of rank

Eshelle - Fae and faeries

High King : 1
    Queen : 1
    High Lord / High Lady : 1 per country
    Lord / Lady : children of High Lords / Ladies
    *The mortal status of the parents impacts the title of the children. I.E. An heir (of any gender), once parents are deceased, will take their place as High Lord / Lady (Last Name).

    *Lord / Lady may also apply to those with titles granted to them by the High Lords / Ladies of the country in which they reside.

    Duke / Duchess : rank beneath both High Lords / Ladies, and Lords / Ladies.

Weaschte - Humans / Mages (humans with magic)

King / Queen: 1 of each

    Prince / Princess : children of the King / Queen

    Duke / Duchess : 1 per country

    Lord / Lady : children of a Duke / Duchess

    Lord / Lady : may also be granted title by the Duke / Duchess of the country in which they reside

    Earl / Countess : beneath both Dukes / Duchesses and Lords / Ladies

MAP

For the purposes of Book Two:

Weaschte:

Cerasche is slightly inland, its closest coast composed of cliffs.

Dahlih is northeast of Cerasche.

Jasiira is coastal, and the southernmost country of Weaschte.

Evredis Sea:

The ocean that separates Weaschte from Eshelle.

Eshelle:

Oschverre is the northernmost country in Eshelle. Its capital, Matriel, is a fortified city.

Ardhavi is a peninsula, southwest of Oschverre, northeast of Sabrian.

Sabrian is coastal, and southwest of Oschverre. Its capital, Colina, is slightly inland.

Obala is immediately south of Sabrian.

LANGUAGES

In T3V, the characters alternate between speaking Ceraschen, and Divani.

Divani is the common tongue of the Fae, and is imagined by the author to be similar to UK English; many different accents, under the same language.

Ceraschen is the dialect of Cerasche, Althea's homeland. It is imagined by the author that the languages of Weaschte are akin to the romantic languages: Italian, Portuguese, Romanian, French, and Spanish.

Divani is, however, still taught in Weaschten studies–like Latin. As such, Althea can understand much of it.

Adathan, Ciaragen, and Atlas all learned Ceraschen for their purposes in IBOF. Emelina, however, did not. As such, in any scene where Emelina is present, the characters are speaking Divani unless otherwise stated.

As he had in IBOF, Adathan uses Ceraschen with Althea. Unless otherwise stated, any conversations between the two of them are always in Ceraschen.

Yes, he learned how to say 'sweetheart' (among other things) in her language.

PLAYLIST

(Chapter parts separated by ⇔)

Eternity - Alex Warren (Dion and Ciaragen...you'll see)

Dream Girl Evil - Florence + The Machine (ch1)

Wires (up to 2:34) - Athlete (ch2)

invisible string - Taylor Swift (ch9)

Gale Song - The Lumineers (ch11 & 18)

A Drop in the Ocean - Ron Pope (ch14 & 19)

Wires (after 2:34) - Athlete (ch20)

Rain - Sleep Token (ch29, 30, & 34)

On the Nature of Daylight - Max Richter (ch42 end)

you should see me in a crown - Billie Eilish (Part Two vibes)

Figure You Out - VOILA (ch48)

Even in Arcadia - Sleep Token (ch49 pt.1)

La Llorona - Lucia Flores-Wiseman (ch51)

ceilings - Lizzy McAlpine (ch59)

Castle on the Hill - Ed Sheeran (ch61 pt.2)

Walls - The Lumineers (ch65 pt.2 & ch66 pt.2)

Bow (slowed) - Rayn Hartley (ch68 pt.2)

In My Veins - Andrew Belle ft. Erin McCarley (ch68 pt3 & ch69 pt.1)

Family - Noah Gunderson (ch75)

A Little Wicked - Valerie Broussard (final page)

PROLOGUE
BETRAYED

THEA - 6 WEEKS FROM NOW

SUCH PROMISES MADE THESE PAST WEEKS. I NEVER IMAGINED I would be the one to break them.

It's too quiet as I make my way through the halls. The news of the day weighs heavy throughout, but none so heavy as that within my chest.

I cannot allow any further a burden on those I love. And so, I must decide to go willingly to the fate that has beckoned to me since that night beneath a shattered ceiling, in a castle so far from where I am now.

They would not understand if I shared my plans with them. They've been finding ways around the inevitability for weeks, and that's why this is so hard. Because, all this time, they have been showing me how they love me, too.

I can only hope they will see that this is how I prove my love for them in return.

I find her too easily, as if fate is pushing me, even now,

towards its determination. She turns as I approach, but does not speak. I wonder, though, by the sadness in her brown eyes, if she already understands why I've come.

Still, once I stand before her, I don't so much as allow myself a deep breath to reconsider before I say, "I need you to deliver a letter."

PART I

PRETENDERS

1

SPLINTERED

THEA - DAY 1

I WISH I HAD SUMMONING MAGIC.

That's what I think about as I throw the dagger again at the opposite wall of my cabin aboard the *Burning Rose*. With a *thunk*, it sinks half an inch into the moisture-softened wood. And I walk across the small space to retrieve it. Again.

Aside from me and the dagger, the only other things in here are a bed with sheets that smell of saltwater, and a change of clothes. I still wear the skirt I'd swindled from the shopkeeper in Dahlih, the shirt with its cut-off sleeves, and, wrapped around my head, the plum-colored sash that belonged to a woman named Evie.

The dagger flies once more across the room. *Thunk.*

Yes, summoning magic would be helpful.

Or, *majick*.

My jaw clenches as I wrench the blade out of the wall. I don't know what to call myself anymore. What to call these—

these *things* that run through my blood, and give me the abilities to heal, and to break. Because, as I'd found out just about an hour ago, I am not a Mage, as I've believed all my life. I'm not even human.

I'm Fae.

Kind of.

My grip on the hilt tightens as I remember the conversation. How *she* had slunk back into the cabin she'd emerged from, while Atlas eyed me as though I was some beast about to lose control, and tear into him. With words, or with the blade I hold now, I couldn't be certain. I hadn't even been certain at that moment that I *wouldn't* attack him. That he–nor anyone– had thought to warn me that the woman whose life I'd been born to, and she to mine, was *here*. That facing my true heritage was going to be so immediately forced upon me.

Surprisingly, none of the animosity I held was for that woman. Emelina. If anything, I empathized with her; there was no feigning the shock, and wariness in those painfully familiar eyes when Atlas gave her my name. She hadn't known I would be joining them for their journey back to Eshelle anymore than I had.

No, all of my anger was reserved for those who had kept yet another secret *about* me *from* me. They'd tried to talk themselves out of it, of course. Ciaragen miraculously came down the steps mere seconds after Emelina introduced herself to me to help Atlas explain her presence. From there, they'd just dumped information on me, so many nervous words meant to distract me from the secrets they still kept.

And, damn me, but it had worked. I stood there and listened, my one ally a silent, solid force at my side, while they distracted me with selective truths.

What they chose to share, in their frenzy to tame whatever

they thought I might unleash in my anger, had been about the glamour placed upon me. The majick that has suppressed not only my natural appearance, but also the abilities that I'd been born with. *Everything* is dulled. No super hearing, or scenting, or sight. No Fae beauty, or arched ears. And no Fae-level majick.

That's not even the kicker, though.

No, one of the many reasons why I'm alone in my cabin throwing a knife at a wall, is that not only is this glamour on me—but not one of the oh-so-majickal Fae on this ship has the capability to remove it. The only one who can is the person who cast it. And she's not here. But maybe that's good.

Because one of the other—again, of several—reasons I'm in here by myself is that, when I'd been told all of this, I'd responded that I don't even know if I want it removed. I'd walked into the cabin and closed the door amid the stunned silence in the hallway.

I haven't been able to think about it logically yet. I'm sure that's what they hope I'm doing. Sorting it out in my head, as I have with almost every other damn thing that's happened over the past week. But I don't want to. I want to throw this dagger, and *not* think. Because, for the first time in days, I know what's going to happen next.

Nothing.

The *Burning Rose* cuts through the Evredis, the breeze and the wind majick of the Fae on deck carrying the ship across the sea. I can see the sun-gilded water through the porthole to my right. It splashes against the glass, and leaves behind droplets that then cascade in rivulets back whence they came.

Thunk.

Absolutely nothing will happen, for at least a moment. No life-or-death situations will arise. No life-changing secret will be revealed (I mean, what else could there possibly be at this point?). The ship will keep moving, and I will keep throwing, and that can be it. For at least a moment.

I wish that it could be longer. That I could have hours to myself, and do nothing but watch the sun run its golden course over the sea. Maybe I would sleep for some of that time. Maybe I would change into those stranger's clothes, and out of the ones stained with drops of Adathan's blood.

I might even wish not to be totally alone. But the only person I might have sought, the only one I know would give me that company *and* allow me that silence is down the hall, and my way to him is obstructed.

Obstructed by the two people I came in here to avoid. Who don't seem to be inclined to leave, regardless of the blade I've made obvious use of, and the even more obvious amount of time I've left them out there to argue.

I sigh, and throw one last time. *Thunk.* Then, pulling the blade out as I go and creating a splintered notch in the wood, I walk to the cabin door, and open it.

Atlas and Ciaragen stand there, their bodies facing each other while their faces are turned towards me. In the light streaming through the cabin portholes, and down through the ship deck prisms above us, I can see the surprise in their widened eyes. "Just because I don't have Fae hearing doesn't mean I can't hear you two whisper-screaming at each other out here," I tell them in their language.

Atlas composes himself first, moving to fully face me, his high cheekbones darkening. Ciaragen follows, and it's she who replies to me. "We just wanted to see...how you're doing." She softly clears her throat, and this female, who I doubt very much is prone to blushing, or fits of self-consciousness, experiences both now.

I furrow my brow. "Why should I be anything but alright?"

She sucks on the inside of her cheek, unsure of how to continue. Luckily, wonder-boy is on the job.

"You have no reason to be alright," Atlas says. "Everything you knew has changed, in a matter of days. The better question is, what can we do to help you?"

"Nothing." It's not meant to be rude, or stubborn. I'm not withholding a way they could 'help' me. There just isn't one. And I'm done adding frills to my words for the sake of propriety.

"Aly–"

"*Don't.*" I step into the hallway until I'm just a foot away from him. I look up into the face of the male who might still be my friend with my teeth barred. "*Ever*. Call me that."

Hurt flashes across his features, but he masks it in a heart-beat. He opens his mouth to say something else, but when words come, they're not from him.

"Is there a problem out here?" a familiar rumbling voice asks from down the hall. I don't turn, but Atlas and Ciaragen do, to watch as the male approaches, his footsteps silent despite his size.

"There is now," Ciaragen half-grumbles, half-growls at him.

It's quiet for a moment–long enough that I finally turn from Atlas to look at Adathan. I'd thought his eyes would be on Ciaragen, after her comment, but those irises the color of the sun on water rest on me with the same directness they have ever since their natural shade was revealed. In my periphery, I see Ciaragen shift in annoyance.

Then, he says, "I'm going to get some food. Would you like to come with me?"

It's probably the only question I don't have to think about before answering. I nod, and sheathe my dagger back under my skirt at my thigh. He walks through the male and female that stand between him and me, and they have little choice but to make room for him given the sheer size of him, and narrowness of the hall. Adathan gestures for me to go ahead of him, and I turn without a word or a glance at the others, disliking the coldness of the move, but not knowing what else to do.

Something within me just feels...other. Not one of them, but not me either. And maybe they mean well, but I find myself feeling things too similar to what and how I felt about Adathan three days ago. That until they came along, my life was fine. Great, even. And now it's not. In fact, so damn *not*, that the blonde hair still flowing to my waist in place of the black feels somehow comforting.

I'm not me, and I'm not them. My feelings about that make too little sense to even begin to sort through. The one thing I've been able to establish any certainty over is that I resent Ciaragen, and Atlas. They were in my home, and for what? To protect me? No matter how much I hate myself for it–in a long list of things I already hate myself for–I find myself angry at their failure. They were in my home, and *for what*? I still got kidnapped, and beaten. My friends are still dead. My mother is still *dead*.

In the woods of Cerasche I'd had so much time, trekking through the endless pines. So much time to think about what I felt about Adathan's betrayal, and sort out what it really meant to me. From that thinking, I realized that I blamed him, if only to keep some of the burden from myself. I came to know that, regardless of his position, his work, his very existence, Olin would have found me. The only thing that would be different if Adathan did not exist would be that I would now be on a ship with Olin, instead of without him.

Adathan had allowed me silence. That time to think, without being questioned, or consoled, or pitied. And maybe Atlas and Ciaragen believe the hour I had to myself was enough time to do some more thinking. The problem is, as I recognized before, that I don't want to do it anymore. So, where I could make the same conclusions about them as I have about the male striding up the stairs behind me–that I would be in this position regardless of their action or lack thereof–I haven't. And I don't want to put in the work to try just yet.

My hands clench into fists at my sides as I step out into the mid- afternoon sun. I make way for Adathan behind me, and find Atlas, then Ciaragen following him. My jaw tightens, and bright gold eyes lock with mine two steps from the top. I watch his chest rise as he pulls a breath in through his nose, and then his lips part as he breathes out. I almost roll my eyes, but instead I find myself copying him.

When my exhale is finished, I say, "Your breath still stinks."

One corner of his mouth just barely lifts. "Right back at you, sweetheart," he replies, which has a bit of humor relieving the remaining tightness in my chest. Then a throat clears from behind him, and I remember that the other two are trapped in the stairway, Adathan's frame blocking the exit.

He ignores them, holding my gaze until I nod once. He returns it, then steps up and moves aside. Atlas gives me a slightly wider berth than necessary as Ciaragen comes up, deep blue eyes on Adathan. The male moves first, clearly leading us to the mess hall that I'm sure my walking buddy intended to find with only his super-smelling-Fae powers. But the female doesn't budge an inch until Adathan falls into step behind me.

As Atlas moves through the deck and down another set of stairs, I'm intrigued in spite of myself as I watch the crew make way for him–one even jumps back down the stairs when he sees Atlas about to descend. They smile at him, and greet him by name, which he returns, not stumbling over a single male.

As we approach the mess, I hear the sounds of several deep voices, and forks scraping against plates. But when we reach the bottom of the stairs, me behind Atlas, and Adathan behind me–silence.

The part of me that's been trained to be a princess of a continent lifts her chin, and straightens her already-straight shoulders in the face of the judgment she feels weighing on her. But I don't avert my eyes from theirs, as I would have just a week ago. No, I look at each one of them, leveling cool stares and terse nods to males whose irises are brown, and blue, and even eyes that are wholly black. Faeries.

I keep my expression relaxed, but my stupid human-bred heart isn't as easily controlled. It thumps hard in my chest, and I know that all the keen ears in the room can hear it. Still, I don't lower my chin or my eyes, even as I watch some of the expressions in the room turn mocking.

Then growls sound from both in front of and behind me, and the sources of all those gazes become very interested in the table tops. Meanwhile, the sources of the growls continue with me towards the counter. Observing the perhaps two dozen males currently in the room, I'm able to note the difference between the gazes lowered in deference to Atlas, and in fear of Adathan.

The cook is already pouring stew into wooden bowls, and he sets them on the counter with webbed fingers once filled. His skin is the most interesting combination of dark and light blues, and though his irises are overlarge, they're a pretty silver that's bright even in the dim light provided by the portholes in the wall.

But another set of silver eyes flash in my mind when I open my mouth to thank the faerie for the food. Hanna's face, as it had been when I'd seen it last–pale, frightened, and still–clouds my vision. So, my thanks passes my lips in only a whisper. The cook dips his chin in acknowledgement, his throat bobbing as he takes in the male at my back.

Then I hear some muffled chuckles from the others in the mess, because of course they think fear softened my voice, instead of grief. And, that quickly, all other emotion is chased away by anger.

I will *not* be afraid of these males. I will *not* let them stifle me. Instead, I allow a single ember of the burning rage within me to escape as I turn toward the sound, shifting my expression into a mask of boredom.

At one of the several rectangular wooden tables scattered throughout the mess sit a faerie and two Fae males, still grinning, shoulders shaking with their mirth. My bowl of stew in hand, I stride over to them, the heels of my boots clicking with each step. Surprise takes the place of some of the humor in their expressions, and two of them straighten in their seats on the long benches set on either side of the table. I don't stop my approach, my boots scraping and clicking through the lazy steps I take until I'm just a foot from the only male still slouching.

I take a bite of the stew, and suck on the spoon a bit as I pull it from my mouth. It's much better than I'd dared to hope for—hearty, and flavorful. I chew and swallow the bite, and still their eyes don't leave mine until I ask, "Something funny?"

The faerie shakes his bald blue head, and one of the Fae even lowers his eyes to the table after doing the same. But the other, with closely shorn black hair, and blue eyes paler than the early morning sky, looks me up and down. Slowly.

I hear a shuffling from behind me, but don't turn to see its source, and neither does he. I give him a half-grin, and purr, "What are you looking at?"

The room around us is utterly silent. Not my companions, nor the other males in the hall, seem to be so much as breathing too loudly. I set my bowl down, and take another bite. My cut-off shirt shifts around my breasts as I lean down, and even with my nonexistent experience in the area, I know that's desire that begins to brim in the male's otherwise baleful eyes.

Then he finally speaks. "To answer both of your questions: you."

I smile wider, allowing it to appear real; pleased that this oh-so-handsome male is looking at *me*. "Oh, yeah? And what's so funny about me, sailor?"

He turns where he sits at the end of the bench, opening his legs as he does so. "Nothing, anymore," he replies, his voice low.

"And, why is that?" I lean down further, so that my eyes are only slightly above his.

"Well, because now I'm thinking about fucking you until you forget any of the human filth you've had so far."

I give a throaty chuckle, able to guess what the new Divani word means by the sentence surrounding it, and disregard another small sound of movement behind me. The male smirks, happy to be holding my complete attention. "Mmm," I half-sigh, half-say. "There's only one *small* problem there."

"What's that?" he asks, not even attempting to be inconspicuous as those blue eyes take in my chest. While he's otherwise occupied, I knock my remaining stew into his lap.

He shouts, almost moving to stand up. But, faster than I've ever moved, faster even than Adathan had trained me to be yesterday in the woods, I pull my dagger from its sheath, where I'd been reaching for it as I leaned down, and down. At the same time, I flick the blade he'd kept on the hip he'd so willingly exposed to me out of its holster. The former is at his throat, the latter at his balls, before he's able to rise an inch off the bench.

"Hard to fuck if you've got no balls, isn't it?" I ask, giving him a sweeter-than-sugar smile. "Even harder–no pun intended–if your throat's cut open. Wouldn't you say?" I tilt my head, and let the grin fall.

He doesn't nod, doesn't even dare to speak with how close the blade is to his carotid, though his eyes burn with fury. "I thought so." My brow furrows. "Adathan?" I call, not moving my gaze or my blades from the male before me.

The familiar rough bass says from behind me, "Yes?"

"Our rule on winning weapons–does it apply to all Fae?"

"It does." I think I hear humor in that voice.

A corner of my mouth kicks up in the first real show of a positive emotion since this encounter began. "Just checking." I drop my hands, and the weapons in them, to my sides, and back up a step. As anticipated, the male stands quickly–so quickly he rocks the table, and the bench he sat on rolls onto its side–and his own dagger is once again at his groin before the fist he has half-raised can find its mark.

I click my tongue. "Now, let's not get off on the wrong foot. Finish that move, and I believe you wouldn't be able to get off on much of anything anymore." In emphasis, I press the blade in just enough that it knicks his trousers.

Though the loathing and rage in his eyes persists, he pales. His jaw strains, and he stares at me hard for another moment before backing up, and turning to stride quickly through the mess, and up the stairs.

Once he's gone, I look at his two compatriots. Their eyes are wide, but otherwise they give no response to my action against their friend. So I say, "I apologize for disturbing your meal." Then I turn back to my own companions.

Adathan and Atlas are slightly further from the counter than they'd been when I approached the male. Adathan stands in front of Atlas, looking too much like a barrier to reaching me for it to have been anything else. His smirk is subdued, but those golden eyes are far more bright.

In the gray eyes, however, lies disbelief–like he doesn't recognize the person I am now–which does something to my heart. I turn from him before that look can further harm what I might have dared to give him just days ago.

"I hope that wasn't anyone important," I say to them with false bravado, tossing my hair over a shoulder.

And Ciaragen, who's been still this whole time, tips her head back, and laughs.

2
WORK

*DION - **20.5** YEARS EARLIER*

IT WAS FUNNY, I THOUGHT TO MYSELF IN THE DARK OF MY CELL with only the scents of blood and waste to keep me company. Funny, that a Fae could be so powerful, but all it took was a bit of iron to bring him down.

My wrists, ankles, and neck were wrapped in shackles of the metal. Every three hours, they came and used these strange, long contraptions they called *needles* to inject more of it into my blood. As Olin told me the first time they pumped it into my veins: half a century ago, they had simply fed prisoners foods with dangerously high levels of iron. It was figured that, if they chose to starve rather than eat the poison, either way they'd be weakened.

In the time that I'd worked in a new position for Oleander, and then in an even more recent one against him, they'd made some improvements in their system of imprisonment–and, in my case, torture.

Those *needles* were not painless, but they were the least of my concerns. When a masked male came down with one, I knew that moments later another would join him, and that second arrival would come with instruments that caused far more pain than their associate's.

I'd lost count of the days spent in this black pit of a cell. I hadn't *tried* to count in the beginning–it was just easy to figure out, given their consistent rotation, and my sleep. After the first few days, though, I forgot how many times they'd come; how many sleeps were full, and how many were spells of mercy. Mercy by my own body, of course–none had been delivered to me outside of that.

I guessed that weeks had passed, and moved into months. In my rare moments of reflection on that, I thought of my High Lady. Ninety-seven years, experiencing an entirely different sort of torture, and still she was strong. Still, she was kind.

I only wondered if she would–even *could* still be those things, after her child was taken from her. After she spent nearly a year carrying the baby in secret, delivered her quietly, and then held her for only a moment. The child with black hair through which the smallest of arched ears had poked. Even on her first day alive, she had her mother's lovely face, just in the fairer complexion of her father. And my High Lady had not even gotten to name her before she'd been taken.

Ninety-seven years of torment, and she had still been strong enough to look at her own baby, and turn her into someone else. To take away those arched ears. To glamour the very essence of her heritage, so that even as she grew, she would not know it. She would think herself human, with a small amount of magic–small, in comparison to what she'd been born with.

I sometimes thought that if the human baby had been born without any of the things her parents saw as defects, Lydia would have taken our new Lady anyway. If our Hielo and Hiela had told her that this child would die if left here, she would not have allowed it to happen. I believed the human queen would have taken the Fae babe, and raised her as her own until such time her parents could retrieve her, and remove the glamour from her.

But the human baby *had* been born with those so-called defects. And in the most terrible way, it had worked out that they did not believe the child was theirs, and needed a–replacement. Our High Lady would not have her baby, but her baby would be safe. Living in Weaschte, her new parents and herself believing her to be human.

I couldn't imagine what it had been like for Hiela to have that realization. To peer into my mind as I called for her, and know that her child was going to be taken from her, whether by death or by removal from Eshelle. To simultaneously hear Nuria's beckoning thoughts, and find the saddest of solutions to the situation.

I hadn't been in the room as Jolie made the swap. Hiela told me, mind-to-mind, as I walked up the stairs to the tower with Olin, and with–*her*. She told me that our Lady was now a princess, and a princess was a lady. Arched ears had been hidden for one, and made for the other. Powers had been taken, Fae abilities suppressed. Hiela concealed herself, too, on the chance Olin knew what Oksana Mikhyala looked like. And then Jolie was walking down the treacherous hidden stairs of the tower with the new princess, to bring her to her...parents. The scent of the blood-soaked linens lying over the secret door concealed that of Jolie, and our Lady.

So, we'd arrived to a white-haired, one-armed baby in the bassinet beside our High Lord. This beautiful child, who had never been held by her true mother. Olin took one look at her, and laughed.

"I don't suspect this runt will be much trouble," he said.

"Though, know that if she is, she will not be for long. Whether she's one, or eleven, or twenty-one, I will come. And I will kill her."

Then he turned to me. "You're coming back to Oschverre. Now."

And my heart had stalled in my chest–but not for that. No, as soon as I saw Olin standing in the grand foyer, staring up at the hammer beam ceilings, I'd known that would be my last day in the place I'd come to call my home.

What had made my heart jump to my throat, made everyone in the room but the cooing white-haired babe go quiet–was when Arthur had stepped into the room, and stood beside my brother. A traitor. With emotionless blue eyes, he'd stared over our heads until Olin commanded him to put me in irons, and take me down to the wagon outside.

While I hated the male for his treachery, it was more for the pain it caused those I loved than for myself. I blamed him little for where I was now, chained and tormented. I had been the one hopeful and stupid and reckless enough to believe my brother would let me get away. For that, and for what I did when he finally came for me, I loathed myself much more than I did Arthur.

I suffered so many different kinds of pain in this cell, but the worst was remembering–remembering that separation from my mate. Recalling the way she had screamed my name as both Nuria and our High Lord held her back. Thinking about how she had used her bending of the shadows to escape them, and nothing, no one could stop her. She was going to die trying to keep me free.

And so I struck her. So hard that she had fallen to the floor, unconscious.

I did not kiss her. I did not embrace her. I hit her with my fist so gods-damned hard that I felt it in my knuckles the entire way back to Oschverre. The last image of my mate, my love, my *soul*–the last one I would ever have of her, was of her on the ground, curls spilling around her face, the mark of my fist already red on her beautiful cheek.

That. That was what made me want to scream until my lungs were raw, and there was no more air left. Nothing the masked males could do to my body compared to the pain in my chest when I thought of that image, that moment.

I left her, our court, our family, so that Olin would never go back there. She would be safe. All of them would be; I would make sure of it. The two babies with the same date of birth, and the same story binding them, would live happy and free. And so it would remain, until our Lady realized her true heritage.

That was the last bit of the glamour, of course. It could mask who she was, but it couldn't completely alter something so deeply coded into her genetics as her immortal lifespan. She would reach maturity, just like any Fae, and eventually she would realize–as would those around her–that she was not aging.

I couldn't know for certain, obviously, but I guessed that when that time was approaching, someone would go to her. One of our court would travel to Cerasche, to break the news. Probably observe a bit first, but they would be tasked with telling the falsely human girl–woman, by that point–that everything she knew about herself was a lie. And though I did not wish for anyone I knew to be in my position, I also did not envy them theirs, when that time came.

These were the thoughts, the memories, that I kept hidden behind the wall of night in my mind. A wall I kept up with the last dregs of my power, and would continue to maintain until I died–likely in this cell.

Round, with hatched iron bars in front of, and above me. The stone floor had a slight valley, a drain centered within it.

The chains that bound me were hooked into the walls and the floor with inch-thick anchors that didn't budge, even when I was at full-strength on my first day. Not to escape, of course–but when I strained as they did their work, that strength had not even loosened a pebble of the rock around them.

Those chains remained on me at all hours. When I slept, I sat on the blood-and-waste-covered cement floor, my arms stretched out to my sides, and up, so that they were numb each time I woke.

Then, this morning–at least, I thought it was this morning–I woke to an iron collar around my neck, hooked up to the ceiling bars. A result, I was sure, of my success at ripping out the throat of my tormentor with my teeth when he dared to ask me about my mate. When he talked about her body, and told me what he'd like to do with it when he was done with me.

Suffice it to say he wouldn't be doing much of anything, ever again. But, it had prompted the collar, and my other torturer had promised he would return later with a new second.

Not that I would ever try to escape. No, I was determined to stay right where I was, and not tempt anybody into going back to Sabrian. But I couldn't help but think about how, if my brother were dead, there would be very few strong enough to infiltrate that court. My court.

That was the thing they asked about most, as they beat me, cut me, tore me open. *What treachery is Amedeo Monserre conspiring to commit against our High King?* But no matter how many times they asked it, and no matter what they did to me while asking, my answer was always the same. Whether through gritted teeth, or with blood gargling up my throat, I always responded, *Nothing.*

I didn't try to lie further; to tell them that he was totally loyal to Oleander. We all knew that wasn't the case. It was the reason I'd been sent to Sabrian in the first place. But what was true then remained true now; Oleander would not win a war with Amedeo. Oh, he might have powerful allies, and he would therefore be triumphant at first–but by the end, he would be more hated than ever. And the one thing I was sure the rich tried not to think too much on was that they were few, and the people were many. And if they lost their favor to the extent that the many rose up against them, they would abandon their king to keep their own wealth safe.

That Amedeo hadn't yet marched on Oschverre was a testament to his care of his people. He would not make them fight, not ask them to die, until he was certain of the support of the nation. Until he was sure that they might be scared, but they would stand together for a better future.

I wasn't sure where that stood now. I knew that my imprisonment did not mean that process would change–a fact of which I was very glad. But I did wonder if the loss of their child would do that. If they would strike down Oleander sooner than planned, so that they could have their family without fear. I had learned only so much about their plans in the three weeks after they decided to wholly trust me.

Another thing to be glad of. I didn't know their numbers, their weaponry, the powers they had on their side outside of those our court possessed. The allyships with the border countries had barely begun when I'd been forced to leave. Were they well underway now? Had more been gathered to the cause?

The issue, I knew, was that dethroning Oleander alone would not be enough. Our rebellion would have to become strong enough to take down those with such wealth and majick that they'd managed to keep him there in the first place. Not just that, but also rallying the downtrodden people against the nobility who'd oppressed them for nearly a century. Oleander was not one, but several, and the people may indeed be many, but they were not yet ready to step out from under the heavy, expensive boots of the few. And slit their throats.

I wasn't sure how to change that. Then again, I couldn't change much of anything in this cell. I had to leave that to the court I'd left behind in Colina. I had to believe that the world outside this cell would change for the better, even if I would not be there to see it.

The familiar clanking of keys against the door down my hall of cells sounded, interrupting my thoughts. As much as I hated it, my body immediately seized up with panic. My heart pounded, and my breaths came faster through my mouth—because breathing through my nose had become unbearable.

Then came three sets of footsteps, two much too familiar, and one not at all. They appeared in front of the bars before me. Olin, smiling softly, as the unknown male beside him opened the unlocked door for him.

The male was massive—even for a Fae. Taller than Olin and I by inches, and built like an ox. He wore a mask, just as the now-throatless male had, but, through the holes cut out for sight, I could see the most unusual gold eyes. Like sparkling wine, or the morning sun hitting water.

"Who's your friend?" I asked, my voice rough from screaming, and disuse.

"It doesn't matter," Olin replied, still smiling. Then he gestured with a nod in my direction, and the male came towards me, a needle in his broad hand. Again, I hated the immediate fear that coursed through me, and filled the room with its scent. Even with the rest of the smells in here, they would undoubtedly scent it.

At my side, the large male took my arm with a surprisingly gentle touch, somehow managing to make his fingers look like they grabbed me roughly without actually doing so. The fingers of his other hand, though, were practiced and precise as he angled the needle into the thick vein at the crook of my elbow, pierced it with the metal, and injected the poisonous iron into my blood.

After withdrawing the needle, leaving my blood to flow freely down my arm, drop by drop, he stepped back to stand behind Olin once more. I could see no emotion in those strange eyes as he gazed at the wall behind me.

"I asked him to observe for today," my brother said, his hands clasped behind his back. "I may have told him a white lie, that you get used to the smell in here. While I've enjoyed smelling your fear during our little visits, I couldn't quite deal with your shit any longer. So, I've got a lovely bit of majick protecting my nose as we speak. This one," he turned to the male, and sighed dramatically before turning back to me, "well, he doesn't have enough seniority for that special treatment.

"Once he gets the hang of things, he might get to play with you a bit. But for now..." Olin trailed off, and gave me a wicked grin. On cue, my attendant entered my cell. He had a black piece of fabric under his arm that looked much too innocent, given what was wrapped up inside.

Olin turned to the golden-eyed male. "You will stay here the entire time. You will watch the entire time. Only once Marcys is done may you leave. Understood?"

"Yes, my Lord," the male said monotonously in a rumbling bass.

I chuckled. Once, and softly. And Olin turned ever so slowly back to me. "Do you have to have them all under a blood oath, brother?"

He shrugged with much more casualness than was in his eyes. "Best way to ensure things get done the way I want them to be."

"It must be interesting to know that no one would follow you if they had another choice aside from that, and dying," I returned, and winked at the male. Still, no emotion–but his eyes flicked to my brother, as though he knew him well enough to know a reaction was coming.

Olin huffed a single breath of a laugh through his nose. "You are either an idiot, or a masochist to continue to speak to me so." He turned his gaze to Marcys. "Make today hurt," he commanded. Then he turned on a booted heel, and strode out the cell door. He didn't even bother to close it behind him, just as they never bothered to lock it when they were done. We all knew I wasn't going anywhere.

Marcys laid his instruments on the ground in front of the other male. He played at wiggling his fingers across the many pieces of steel and silver, thinking of which would hurt the most while not causing enough blood loss for me to pass out.

"Any day now," I said.

His dark eyes flashed to me, and filled with hatred and rage. Without looking back down at his toys, he settled on a thin but sharp blade that looked perfect for peeling skin. In fact, it had, several times over the course of–however long I'd been here.

Then Marcys stood before me, and got to work.

3

EXPLANATIONS OVER WHISKEY

AFTER A VERY EVENTFUL LUNCH, DURING WHICH I GOT TO KNOW A little bit more about who Althea truly is–when removed from all expectations, and regulations–I sit in the captain's quarters with Javi and Atlas, recounting the story to our Obalan friend.

"I swear she would have done it. And your blacksmith would have become a eunuch," I say with a shrug, sipping on some of the dark liquor Javi keeps in a personal store in the small credenza behind his desk.

"She disarmed him like he was a novice, and *not* a male who creates and wields blades for a career," Atlas adds, grinning. Though he'd seemed taken aback by her behavior at first, it was clear to me that surprise was the culprit, not any sort of disapproval. I don't think there's anything she could do that would make him abandon her, least of all the act of putting a male in his place.

"I'm going to be a friend before I become the captain," Javi replies, a small smile playing on his mouth. "It's about time someone showed Kent how to behave." Both Atlas and I sit a bit straighter in our chairs set before his desk as Javi's expression sobers. "But we are also stuck on this ship with each other for weeks now. We have to ensure that bad blood stays in veins. Kent will not take the embarrassment lightly, and I'm sure the crew who were there have already spread the news, making that embarrassment worse. And, while he could do with some... humility, we need a cohesive crew to make it to Eshelle.

"Remember that these are the only males who volunteered for the journey. They traveled for a month from Sabrian to Dahlih, then stayed at a port in a foreign continent for much longer than anticipated. The reason for which I am still waiting to hear, since correspondence has been minimal." Though he says it gently, I still feel the weight of the words in my chest. Yes, we'd been in the human land much longer than expected. Kept a High Lord from his lands and people, and a crew from their families, for weeks more than they signed up for. Though they had known their travels would be lengthy, having come for their own purposes of negotiating trade between Obala and some coastal countries of Weaschte, they had since been sitting on the Dahlihan coast for weeks.

Holding his dark gaze, I say, "I hope you know that we never intended to take advantage of your travels to the human continent. Atlas came with you those months ago to spy within Castle Cerasche, as you know, to find out if our Lady showed any signs of her glamour weakening, or of maturity beginning already. And then he heard of that *tradition* they have in place." My fingers clench into fists in my lap, and I see Atlas's jaw tighten in my periphery. Forced marriage under the guise of tradition and allyship.

I take a sip of whiskey, sucking the flavor through my teeth, then go on, "When his message came, I was with the regiment on the eastern border. My High Lord and High Lady then asked me to come here, as even with the few weeks it would take for me to be able to leave my post, I could then shadowalk there, arriving faster than any ship. So, as soon as I was able, I glamoured myself, and left.

"When I arrived, I greeted the King and Queen, explained my disguise, and asked if I could stay; that with such a 'momentous event', I would be honored to act as additional guard for her." A lie, and then a truth, is what I'd told them.

"They agreed, housed me, and allowed me to be around Althea. I used my shadows so that she would not become afraid of a man who seemed to always be watching her. I learned her routines; she was in the training yard every morning. And, over the next few days, I did not...I did not think she needed to be watched there. Her training master and the guards that kept their distance posed no threat to her. If our goal had been to ascertain her happiness, well, she was always happy when doing what she loved, with a person she admired. But then, six days ago, when her training hours had passed...she did not return as scheduled. I went out to look for her, and realized that she had left the castle.

"I told Atlas, of course, and then I followed her trails, old, and new. New, leaving the shade of a tree in a park. Walking into a narrow path through a small wood. And then her scent was not alone. And I knew one of them."

My heart thunders, just as it had in that moment. The fear, the utter *terror* that I felt, knowing that an enemy was truly in Cerasche, and now *had her*–an enemy who she had invited onto this ship with us–

I let out a big gust of air from my lungs. "I followed those scents all the way to a small house, miles from where she'd been taken. I smelled blood that was not hers, and went to inspect further. In the basement, I found two dead Fae males, and a third pool of blood–with no body attached to it."

Javi gapes. "She killed two matured Fae males? Even stuck in a human body?"

I nod. "One had been wounded severely, and she ended his life with a dagger through his skull. The second, she caught in the heart, and he bled out faster than he could heal. And the third...I followed the scent of that blood, and it just–*vanished*. Halfway between the little house, and the castle. I shadowalked back to find her already back in her rooms. Atlas guarded outside her chamber door until Lydia's steps neared to fetch her for the gathering that evening.

"I searched for that scent throughout the castle, knowing he *had* to be there, but he'd concealed it too well." A talented, blood-soaked liar. I set down my empty glass before my fist can break it.

"We told you that the male who betrayed us to Olin all those years ago was being brought onto this ship." It's not a question, but Javi nods anyway. "He, and the male who held Althea in the basement of that house, and lived to betray her again, are one in the same."

The High Lord's eyes widen. "Does she know?"

My jaw flexes. "Yes. She does. But, that's not all." I look at Atlas, a silent request for him to tell the next part of the story, and Javi's eyes move to my godson.

"On the first night of three, where Althea was meant to choose her betrothed by the evening of her birthday," he sighs, and this male who I've rarely seen angry, holds some now in his eyes and his shoulders. "Many men danced with her. I didn't know any of them, and it seemed she hardly did either." Yes, the other bit that we've found out–about just how sheltered she had been from men in order to keep her virtue intact. Ridiculous.

He glances at me before he goes on, but I harden my heart and jaw against his next words. "One of them called himself Dion. We only found this out later, after talking with Lorraine, one of Althea's friends, and her sister-in-law. She was…it took much longer than we would have liked to get her to speak that night, after what she endured." The terror, particularly in her state. The loss of her friends—one kidnapped and one dead. Yes, it had taken us time to get any information from her.

"Before that reveal, we knew who he'd truly been," Atlas continues, his deep voice tight. "After he stabbed the man Althea had chosen—" in the loosest of terms, "—he revealed himself. Olin. Glamoured to appear as someone other than himself to everyone except her."

Javi has paled, not even the tan gathered from months at sea enough to conceal the effect of the shock. "He killed her mother," Atlas says quietly. Not 'Lydia,' not 'the Queen.' Her mother. As she had been, even though it should have been our High Lady with that title. "When Ciaragen and I stepped in, he summoned two men to join him. And their glamours fell, too. One of them, neither of us recognized, but the other was Adathan. He stood there with his father, as he always has until, apparently, very recently.

"And then Althea watched her friends die. Had already seen her mother, lying broken in her father's lap. So…" His lips shift as he runs his tongue over his teeth, and his eyes go distant at the memory. At how powerless we both felt in those moments. "As much as she could with the limits that hold her, she stepped into her power. Put me to sleep just through touch, and broke Ciaragen's bones so that she could not stop her from leaving with Olin. To spare everyone else trapped in that Hall. Including us."

Finished with the portion I needed him to be the one to tell, he turns his gray eyes to me, and I pick up where he left off.

"Olin's majick had us trapped; I couldn't even shadowalk outside of the Hall." I grind my teeth at the memory, but huff a breath, and continue. "When the majick fell at last, we then realized that we couldn't scent her—or any of them; all of them were cloaked. It was Atlas's idea, then, to go to the cliffs first; he guessed Olin would try to keep her from a populated port city, and he was right. In the grasses, we found the body of the third male. Broken neck.

"It was only a guess as to whether she'd gotten away, or if she was already on a ship to Eshelle with Olin. But we just...just *felt* like she was still there." I hadn't had many interactions with the gods over the past two decades, further than asking them *why?*, but on those cliffs... *Someone* had driven us to the land, rather than the sea.

"We made our way to Dahlih, arriving a couple of days before them. And we encountered a woman there called Evelyn, who could see past glamours. She saw us as we truly were, and...was not afraid. She said she'd learned the skill years ago from a Fae customer who was particularly fond of her. So, we asked her if she could keep an eye out for a woman with black hair, and bright green eyes; that she was in danger, and we needed to help her. Evelyn was the one who came up with the next part of the plan.

"She had tracking magic. Strong, particularly for a human. Though Althea had been cloaked so that the castle trackers could not find her with her belongings, and the blood of her... siblings would not work, Evelyn had a different idea. She spelled a sash that she wore, and tied it to us, so that when it made contact with someone other than herself, we would find ourselves to be pulled toward it. When we felt it, we immediately followed the pull, but we were...intercepted. We didn't expect her to take such a personal stake in the welfare of a woman she'd just met.

"She went to them, as they made their way to the docks." A brave woman, to be sure. Standing before a Fae male probably more than twice her weight, all to protect someone she'd known for a few moments. But, it *had* briefly complicated things. "Adathan saw through her then, and ran with Althea away from the docks. It was difficult to keep up with them; even carrying her, he was quick. But, keep up with them, we did. We even got him with an arrow, but she healed him of it." So close. *So close* to having at least part of my vengeance, only to have it taken from me. Again.

I sigh once more, and rub my eyes with the pads of my thumb and forefinger until I see stars. "We're not sure exactly what happened in those woods. She hasn't told us. But what's clear is that, somehow, Adathan saved her from Olin's clutches, and she's decided to trust him for it. The rest, you've probably figured. She knows who she truly is, and she asked that he accompany us, probably out of some kind of debt being paid. We don't know how Olin figured out that Emelina is not the true heir to Sabrian. We just know that when he found out, he planted Adathan as a spy–*again*–and the rest, well...basically cycle the story back, and it's all there."

Javi leans back in his leather and mahogany seat, after having sat forward for the whole story. He lets out a breath in a loud, long gust that smells of mint, and whiskey. At the end of it, he says, "You're not going to like what I have to say."

Atlas tilts his head back and looks at the ceiling, the column of his throat arching over the back of his seat. I just stare at Javi, waiting for him to say it.

And he does. "We need to talk to Adathan."

4

EMELINA

I SET MY DAGGERS DOWN ON THE FLOOR OF MY CABIN, AND THEN join them on the wooden planks I don't think will ever really feel dry. I unsheathe the blade I'd won from Adathan just yesterday from its leather scabbard, and the knife's edge sings as it leaves the tough fabric. The blade glints silver in the afternoon sunshine that streams through the porthole. Long, about the breadth of two fingers, with a black hilt and a matching silver pommel. Sleek. Unassuming. Beautiful in its simplicity.

The dagger I'd won from the male in the mess doesn't have a scabbard–as he'd walked away wearing it, his tail and his balls tucked between his legs. If he has one redeeming quality, it's his taste in weaponry. The dagger is short, but–well, gorgeous. The steel folded so beautifully over itself in the blade, the hilt and pommel carved with whirls that look like waves crashing.

I carefully run my finger along the edge of the longer blade, and as I do, I feel...something. The same kind of feeling I would get during the many times I was watched as I grew up; whispers I couldn't and didn't want to hear following me as I went. Wary, as if fifteen-year-old me would have called them out on it, when I'd been raised to ruffle feathers as little as possible.

But I'm not fifteen anymore. I'm not at court. I'm not even a princess. So, still looking at my won weapons, I say in her language, "I know you're there."

She comes into view in the doorway, all cloud-white curls, and ivory skin. Even not looking directly at her, and in the easy yellow light shining at this time of day, she seems to *glow*. And while my brain tries to convince me that it's just the reflection of that light off of her moon-pale skin, something tells me that she would be a magnet for brilliance even on the blackest night.

When I first saw her, that was my second impression. Of course, following only the gut-wrenching recognition of who she is. I'd shaken the left hand she offered me numbly, struck momentarily dumb by the knowledge–but also by *her*. The human equivalent to a full moon.

Literally. Because as much as her arched ears try to convince me that she's Fae, like everyone else on this ship–she's not. She's more human than I am, and that's part of what had me throwing a knife at a wall for nearly an hour.

I look at her fully now, where she still stands in the threshold. I'd seen her before, yes, but hadn't *really* looked. I took note only of the things that told me who she was, and how she was hiding. The familiar pieces of her make my heart squeeze painfully in my chest, but I look past them for the differences between her and my mother. Her mother.

The long white lashes that would probably brush her cheeks if she looked down. Those familiar, heart-wrenching summer sky blue eyes are set in a lovely heart-shaped face, with berry-pink lips. Though several inches shorter than myself, she is very obviously trained. Toned arms that she doesn't attempt to hide in what looks like a man's undershirt. Strong posture, and I'd be willing to bet that the legs concealed by her trousers are just as powerful.

She allows me to take her in, as I allow her to do the same with me. When she first greeted me, she hadn't known *who*, exactly, she'd been greeting. Then, Atlas had given her my name–since I'd been mute–and her welcoming smile had fallen.

I don't bother to wonder if it's because she never wanted to meet me, or if she'd just been taken aback, like I was. I don't bother to wonder what she might be thinking of me, as she takes in the false blonde hair and unscathed face. Maybe she can see past the glamour.

"You can come in," I tell her finally, then add, "If you want to."

Without hesitation, she steps into my cabin, and helps herself to a seat on the floor, a comfortable distance from myself. The scent of stargazer lilies clings to her, and saturates the air around us, lovely and inviting. She doesn't say anything for a heartbeat, just looks at the daggers lying on the dark wood of the floor.

Then: "Nice blades." Her voice is a bit high, pretty like a bird's, and she looks at the steel with enough interest that I know her compliment is sincere.

And, in the only show of peace I can think of right now, I take the dagger I won today, and flip the hilt towards her. Again, there's no hesitation in her movements as she grabs the blade from my hand to inspect it more closely. Almost as if growing up in a world with a people who think and move and act quickly adapted her to doing and being the same, even if she isn't.

I watch, a bit astonished, as her lips pull up at the corners. She looks up at me from under her thick white lashes. "This is Kent's dagger," she says, and there's definitely humor in her voice.

"Not anymore," I respond, picking up Adathan's, and spinning it absentmindedly in my fingers.

"Good. He's a dick."

The tone to her last word tells me enough about its meaning, and I think–I can like her.

"Seemed that way to me, too." Then we're silent for a moment, but it's not tense. Not tense, even though there are a handful of reasons it could be, the least of which being that each of us hold wicked weapons in our hands. So, I ask, "Anyone else I should look out for?"

She sighs, like I've asked the one question that she's been *dying* to answer, but no one has ever wanted her to before. "*Yes.* I don't know a lot of their names, though. I make up my own, so I'll have to show you for you to know who they are."

I don't think too much on how her statement implies we'll be spending time together. Even if I'd come to terms with the knowledge that the ship is not big enough for me to avoid her for weeks of travel. And even if the direction of this conversation makes me wonder if I dislike that as much as I'd believed I would. "Give me some examples of the made up names."

She flips the short blade in the air, and catches it by the hilt. "Well, there's Weird Tank Top Guy, which feels self-explanatory, but you have to meet him to know. Then there's Peanuts, who leaves his fucking shells everywhere like the whole crew are his maids." She looks up into the air like she's thinking and leans back onto her right elbow before throwing and catching the dagger again in her left hand. "Back Up, who stands too close to you when he talks. Aaand, Swinger."

I toss my dagger at the wall, a few feet lower than the marks from earlier, since I'm sitting. I'm about to lean forward to grab it when she whistles, and the blade suddenly hangs in the air before me. I look over at her as I snatch it out of the air, and she shrugs. "I can't snap for shit with my left hand, and–ope! That's the only one I've got. So, I had to figure out a different trigger for the summoning."

Something about the way she speaks...it reminds me of the way I used to think, when the words I said aloud had to be more proper than the ones in my head. Except better. Not just because she actually *does* say them out loud, but because–and, damn if this doesn't feel pathetic, even if it's true–it makes me feel less alone in who I am.

So, my small half smile is genuine, albeit a bit awkward, when I ask, "Swinger?"

"UGH, yes," she groans, rolling her eyes before setting them on mine. "This motherfucker will wear pants that basically *force* you to see the outline of his dick. Don't get me wrong, it's a nice dick, but nobody wants to be eating in the mess and suddenly be hit in the face with a cock–well, at least not every day."

"Pfffft," is the sound that comes out of me. Not really a laugh, but the closest I've gotten to one in what feels like a very long time. It's a burst of air from my lungs that bubbles through my lips, and I feel a lightness in my chest at the humor I've found in this most interesting conversation with a near stranger. Even if I have to guess that half the words she uses are curses I never would have heard in my studies.

She chuckles, much more easily and freely, then tosses the short dagger into the wall, hitting the exact place I had. A whistle, and it's back in her palm. "I'll show you who they are when we see them, so you don't have to learn the hard way, like I did."

I smirk, and throw my own blade again, striking that same place for the third time. She whistles, and when I grab the hilt from the air, I tell her, "Thanks." And it's nice, because somehow I think we both know I say it in response to her offer, and her summoning.

So, I amend my thought from earlier: Okay, maybe I *do* like her.

5

OATHS TO KEEP

ONE OF THE MOST INFURIATING THINGS I'VE SEEN TODAY—AND there have been many—is Adathan helping the crew on deck with their duties. He's not sitting idly, or plotting murder in the cabin we'd given him. He's up here, being thanked or ignored by seamen. Not one of them so much as looks at him crossly.

But, that could be because he's bigger than every single one of them. Between all those years ago, and seeing him behind Olin four nights ago, I'd forgotten just how *hulking* he is. So, until I am otherwise informed, I'll assume that's why no one is glaring hatefully at him, like I am, and not because he's pretending to be a valuable crew member.

I'm not sure how he does it, since we're downwind and there's so much movement on deck that the three sets of footsteps still several feet away from him should have been indistinguishable, but he turns, bright gold eyes immediately finding us in our approach.

"Lord Adathan," Javi greets him, and I catch myself before I can balk at the title.

The male replies in his menacing bass, "Just Adathan is fine." He ties off a knot without looking at it, and it holds perfectly on the mooring hook. It takes most of my willpower not to roll my eyes at the skill.

Javi nods with courtly grace. "Adathan, then. I have some questions for you, and I was wondering if we might go into my quarters to talk." He doesn't pitch it like a request, but his tone is still more polite than I would be able to manage. But, that's why my sister is High Lady of Dremerre, not me.

Those strange eyes dart to Atlas and I, and then back to the Obalan male. "I'm not sure if they informed you, but I am bound by blood to Olin Evestre. You may ask me questions, but I might not be able to answer them for you."

"Yes, I know he is your father–"

"No. Blood bound by oath."

And Javi is surprised, because, no, we had not mentioned that. *I* had not mentioned that. Like it should be some kind of fucking excuse for *all* that Adathan has done, all that he has *caused*–

But, ever a High Lord, Javi collects himself quickly. "I was not aware. Hm. Well, if you're open to it, I would still like to talk in my quarters. If you cannot answer, then we'll move on to the next."

The male nods once. "Who's going to get her?" he asks. And all brows around him narrow.

It's me who responds, angrily: "She's been through enough– she's probably resting, as she *should*."

Gold eyes settle on me. "She has. But I doubt that." His gaze moves back to the captain. "Some of your questions might have answers. And, if they do, don't you believe she should hear them as well?"

My heart sinks a little, anger quieting, at that. Yes. She should. The princess, the woman, the female–too much has been hidden from her. No more...not if we can help it.

But Atlas is the one who replies to him, his voice as level and reasonable as it has always been. "Will you come with us to get her?"

I think the male's brow *almost* creases. He's much too good at hiding his thoughts and emotions, but it seems Atlas did not miss the near-lapse in his facade of indifference either. "I may not understand it, but whatever you two went through in those woods–she trusts you for it. More than she trusts any of us. If we ask, she might say no, if only so she doesn't have to be near us more than she already does. But if you ask..."

The male stares hard at Atlas for a moment, and maybe it's the dangerous unreadability of his expression, or just because I really fucking want to, but I think about running him through with my sword.

Then he nods once more, and, without another word, begins to walk towards the stairs leading down to the cabins. Atlas follows him, then Javi, then me. I don't miss how many of the crew watch us as we go.

Though we are all light-footed, the damp steps creak ever so slightly under us. Then, over the sounds of the wood groaning, I hear something else. Two familiar female voices. Talking.

Even Adathan slows as we descend. Though we have enough distance between us and her cabin that it's not *really* eavesdropping–when all of us have ears that can't help but hear what they're saying–maybe it's a little closer to it because we're hardly even breathing to listen.

Lina may have glamoured arched ears, but she can only hear as well as a human. One thing about glamours is that they can take away, they can replace–but they cannot bestow abilities that never existed. They could not, for example, give someone the power to bend shadows, as I can; and they cannot give amplified hearing to someone who was born with an ordinary ability for it.

She will not hear us, and, with her own glamour still taking from her, neither will Althea. But we can hear them, along with a strange thunking against the wall that sounds an awful lot like it had when Althea was throwing her dagger at it earlier.

"Okay, six inches to the right," Lina commands, and a thunk sounds again. Her familiar laughter bubbles up her throat, and down the hall. "*Bitch?* I want to live in your world if that's six inches to you."

I have to clench my lips together, though part of me is also horrified for the poor princess. But then I hear the softest, most hesitant of chuckles sound in response.

"Bet you would take that six inches in arm length, too," Althea returns in accented Divani, and my heart drops. Did she just–?

But Lina laughs even louder, and I hear flesh brush fabric, like she's–nudged her shoulder? "Listen, Virgin Aretes, one day you'll see why my version of six–or eight–inches is better than a full arm. Especially when you're as good with the one you've got as I am." Another thunk at that, and then a whistle.

We're almost to her door now, and all I can wonder is when, and *how* this thing that seems damn close to friendship happened. We only finished in the mess a short while ago, and already they're not only talking, but making jokes with each other about things that they would have every right to be insecure about–

But shouldn't be. And I think that's part of it. Lina has been settled within herself since childhood, and I think Althea might have been, too. Might not be self-conscious about her virginity at her age, knowing that her lot had given her little choice. Maybe, of all the things she's had to become uncertain of in her life this past week, that doesn't have to be–*shouldn't* be one of them.

Adathan steps hard on the ground when he's about ten feet from her door, and the talking, the thunking, and the laughter all stop. He continues with the same loud steps until he's standing before the threshold. Atlas, though, holds out his arm to stop Javi and I from continuing to that point with the male.

There's a pause where no one says anything, and then– "Hi, I'm Emelina."

With more politeness than I ever would have thought possible for him, the male dips his chin, and says, his voice not unkind, "Adathan. Nice to officially meet you." From the half of his face that I can see, I watch his eyes shift back to what–or who–they'd been looking at before. And rather than Divani, he speaks to her in Ceraschen. "They have questions for me, and I thought you'd like to be there to hear the answers. They're just down the hall." Even I can hear the implied *so if you say no, I'll tell them to fuck off.*

No answer for a short moment. Then, "Okay." The joking tone she had a moment ago is gone, but it's not angry, or annoyed now either. The sounds of shifting fabric emit from the cabin as she and Lina stand, then a set of lightly clicking boots.

A blonde head wrapped in a plum sash pokes out the door a second later, right next to Adathan's chest. Her face to us, those falsely golden locks brush his arm.

Casually, easily, Althea grasps his palm in her fingers, and gently urges him aside before releasing him. She's not looking, and doesn't have the senses to notice–but I watch as the male's hand flexes at his side. The reaction is so fast, so quickly suppressed back into neutrality, that I might have thought I imagined it altogether. But I know I didn't.

Even in the dimness of this hall, those green eyes are

astounding. Lighter than grass, crisper than an apple, softer than honeydew. Framed in the blackest of lashes, that don't match her new hair color at all. I wonder when, or if, she'll ask Adathan to remove the glamour. It has no use anymore–and yet she keeps it.

Then, of course, there's the glamour her mother put on her. I might not be able to see past Adathan's work, but Evelyn did, and I'm sure others could. However, not even a millennium of training could break through the majick bound so thoroughly by grief and love, cast by a substantially powerful Fae.

I think, though, that part of Hiela had wanted her daughter to guess who she was before she stopped aging. Because past the blond hair, there is still a small point to her left ear. And, something I noticed even back in Castle Cerasche–and see again when she speaks now–is that her canines are like ours. I'd guess the only reason they never seemed suspicious is two-fold. That the rest of the Fae attributes were minimized, or missing. And, that she would never have had reason to believe she was anything but what she was raised to be.

Those stunning eyes take in Atlas, then Javi, then me. And, of all the questions I might have expected her to ask, not one of them was, "Can Li come?"

⇔

The six of us convene in the large sitting area within Javi's quarters. Decorated in Obalan custom with red silk tapestries, and a grand area rug of woven crimson and beige and teal. The orange light of the early evening sun shines through the many windows at the back of the ship, and casts even Lina's pale skin golden.

My goddaughter sits on the carpet beside Althea, the latter having opted out of a chair as soon as we walked into the sitting area. Javi and I sit on the couch with its carved mahogany back, and Atlas sits far forward enough on the matching maroon chair to my left that I almost tell him to just sit on the floor, too.

The other male pulls the second chair from its place at Javi's right, over to a space on the carpet on the outskirts of the circle of us gathered; almost in between us, but just slightly closer to the female sitting cross-legged on the floor, Lina on her other side.

And now is not the time to feel this, but for the briefest of moments, I allow my heart to luxuriate in the sight of them together. The girl I'd seen grow up, and the one I wish that I had–not instead, or in place of Lina. Just there, too. Together, as they are now. Grown, and lovely, and strong.

But, no, now is not the time to feel this. And if Althea knew that my thoughts strayed towards gratitude, even for a second, after what happened to her family, after what she'd endured–she would rightfully walk out of this room, and not speak to me for the rest of the journey. And that, I expect, would be the best case scenario.

Once the male sits, Javi leans forward to rest his elbows on his knees. With no preamble before he begins his interrogation, he asks: "Your name is Adathan Evestre, correct?"

He only nods in response, which boils my blood.

But Javi follows with, "You are the son of Olin Evestre, and a blood oath ties you to his word, yes?" Another nod. "I'll cut straight to it, then: why should I believe Olin has not ordered you to follow Althea, so that you might betray her–and us–to him again?"

The male's eyes do not waver from the captain's. "He hasn't."

Real descriptive. Very convincing, I think to myself. But, though I am a general of the armies of Sabrian, I am not captain of this vessel. And I will not intervene with Javi's questioning, no matter how much I might want to.

Brown eyes bore into gold for a long moment. Then, "What did he order you to do?"

"How recently?" he counters.

"Let's say from the time of your assignment to Castle Cerasche until the day you saved Althea from him." I have to hide my smirk at the way he says 'saved'. Javi might be acting diplomatic, but he's chosen a side–and it's not Adathan's.

"About fourteen months ago, Olin ordered me to be his spy at Castle Cerasche. To communicate to him if any Fae showed up, and to observe the entire family, but particularly the youngest daughter. I came, and observed, and reported to him every three months."

"Why did he want you to watch her specifically?"

"He did not say, and I could not ask."

"What did those reports consist of?"

"That all was well. No whispers of plots, or change, and no other Fae. Until he arrived." The male gestures with his chin to Atlas, who straightens in his seat, his fists clenching. "I notified Olin of it. And he took the fastest ship from Oschverre to Cerasche. He arrived the day after you did, General." He looks at me for a moment, but there's no malice in his gaze, as I would have expected.

He moves his eyes back to the captain. "He brought three others with him. Marcys, David, and Gadsby. He kept Gadsby with him as his personal guard, and ordered me, Marcys, and David to wait for an opportunity to take her. If one did not come, I was...to take her myself." His hesitation is almost unnoticeable, just like the regret in his eyes. Somehow, in spite of myself, I don't believe the emotion is fake.

"But, she left the castle, and so we followed. When we had her, our orders were to take her to the address he'd given us, and restrain her there until he was ready to get her, and take us all back to Eshelle. Which, as I'm sure you know, did not go as planned."

A trick of the light makes it seem like one corner of his lips twitches up for a heartbeat. "He didn't expect that, of course; for her to escape. When he arrived, I was unconscious from the blood loss, though my wounds had healed. He was angry, but, after he was done with me, he adjusted his plan." *Done with what?* I almost ask, but he doesn't give me the chance to. I think I already know, anyway, and it's reinforced by the way the jaw of the female beside him tightens.

"He ordered me to continue my duties as spy, and informed me that he would be attending the gathering that evening as well. Glamoured, so that only she and I would see him for his true self. He approached me after he danced with her, and told me–" His voice abruptly cuts off mid-sentence, and a hand fists in his lap.

"He told you who I am," a quiet but strong voice chimes in from beside him in liltingly accented Divani, her brilliant green gaze on him. "I wondered why you were so pale as he spoke to you. That's why, isn't it?" He looks down at her, and doesn't answer, doesn't even nod–which seems to be answer enough.

"What happened next?" Javi asks.

The gold eyes move back to the Obalan, but the green do not. They stay fixed on the hard face of the male beside her as he answers. "He always planned on taking her prisoner–even if I did not know it until he arrived in Cerasche. On the second day, though, after they danced, he said he realized something, and no longer would she just be that. He'd decided that she could remain unbound as we journeyed back to Eshelle. He was...confident that she would not resist." I might imagine it, but I think his voice gentles then. For the sake of the girl beside him, whose freckles stand out on her now-bloodless cheeks.

The careful blankness in his eyes gives way to something he quickly masks–too fast for me to decipher it. "Then he told me he planned to marry her."

I can't help myself then. As Javi's lips part, whether to ask another question, or just in shock, I practically screech, "*Marry* her?"

"Yes. I will not repeat what he said next." Rage and disgust lace his last sentence with enough fervor to convey the nature of what Olin had said. Large hands ball up, veins popping within them, and then quickly flatten over his thighs when he catches himself in the reaction.

"His order then was to ensure she was present in the Great Hall the evening of her birthday. I was ordered not to use majick nor blade unless it was in service to him; not to speak unless spoken to; and to wait in the back of the Hall until summoned. And you know what happened then." His jaw tightens, and I watch the sun-kissed, freckled skin of the young female next to him lose what little color it had left. I'm not sure she's even seeing him; her eyes are glazed, and my heart strains at the memories she must be replaying in her head. I see Adathan's fingers twitch again, but she doesn't register it. She's seeing the Great Hall. She's watching Lydia die.

"When she fainted after he murdered her training master, he ordered me to accompany her on our journey home. And during that *one* day we traveled together, he had her hurt and broken. One day. I couldn't imagine what he would do if given any more."

Althea does look away then, down to the hands folded in her lap. Lina scooches just a bit closer to her.

"I thought he might have cloaked her, but I couldn't be sure. He loves to play games, and leading you to us only to kill you would have been a game to him. He taunted her with it; acted as if you might catch us. To give her hope, or fear, or even self-loathing as she wondered why you did not come for her. Why *they* did not."

My heart strains as Althea picks at a thread in her skirt's hem, her throat bobbing. Yes, I believe she did feel those things. Wondered if perhaps her own family did not *want* to find her.

"So, the task of freeing her was mine. I worked that day and night to find workarounds to his newest commands; ways to free her which the blood oath would not keep me from acting on. So, the following morning, at the cliffs, I took the only chance we would have, and jumped into the water with her. We walked through the woods until we reached the port city of Dahlih, ate at a pub where we met Evelyn, and you know what happened after that. "

There is more—the story of what occurred in those woods, and why two people who should hate each other seem to trust one another instead. But those tales would only serve to quench my curiosity, my utter bewilderment, at Althea asking him to come with us to Eshelle. However insufficient his tale is to me, I am not the highest-ranking Fae on this ship; not the one questioning him; not the one who really decides if he stays or goes.

Javi leans back, straightening in his seat on the couch beside me. He seems about to say something, maybe put the matter to rest—at least for now—but Atlas speaks for the first time since entering these quarters.

"Which of her injuries did you inflict?" he asks quietly. And this male, who has been gentle and kind his entire life, has menace in his eyes now. The gray roils just as the storms they liken as he glares at the male across from him.

Adathan looks at him, and his jaw feathers. "All of them."

Althea's gaze lifts from her lap, to him, her glamoured golden brows furrowed. "No, you didn't."

He looks down at her, his gaze on her throat. "Everything that has happened to you is because of me."

Althea smoothly moves from her place on the ground, to her feet. She stands, tall and strong, and takes a step closer to him. "Everything that has happened to me is because of *Olin*."

I find the distinction between us, then. She loathes only the male who gave the orders. And I hate the male who carried them out just as much as I do his father.

"Althea, you could have still been at home now, if he hadn't informed Olin of my arrival."

Althea whirls on Atlas. "And if you had never shown up, he would have had nothing to inform him about."

I watch Atlas's eyes shutter, hurt flashing over his features. But she is not done. "The ifs *don't. Fucking. Matter.*" Eyes bright with anger turn to the hulking male to her left. "The things that could be happening to me right now, *aren't*, because of *you*." Back to Atlas. "You would have saved me, too, if you had been there. I know. But the ifs do not fucking matter. He was there. *He* saved me. Freed me."

For the first time, she looks at me. Even being more than twice her age, she somehow makes me feel young in this moment. Small. "Has it even crossed your minds that, if he could see through the glamours to notice Atlas, he knew *you* were there, too? Still, Olin seemed pretty damned surprised when you started throwing your shadows at him."

She raises her brows, and when no answer comes from my parted lips, she lowers them, and looks between the three of us not on her side of the room. "You are wondering why I trust him. I don't give a damn. I am here because of *him*, in more ways than one, and you *know it*. He didn't just keep me alive, and as *unharmed as he could*–" she shoots those words at the male beside her before her gaze slices to me again.

"Because he is with me, I know more about not just the land

we're going to, but *myself* than I would have if you had gotten to me first. Isn't that right?" She glares, but not one of us answers her.

A mirthless smirk curls a corner of her mouth. "You all can keep pretending that you don't have more secrets up your sleeves. Adathan doesn't pretend. So, why I trust him, to me, doesn't seem like the proper question. I believe that would be: why should I trust *you*?" She flicks her hard gaze to Javi. "Are we done here?"

The High Lord composes himself much more quickly than I can, though his voice is quieter than usual. "Yes. All of you," he adds, dark eyes moving to Adathan, "are free to go."

Althea doesn't respond, never mind bow to excuse herself before turning on a booted heel to walk quickly out of the captain's quarters, through the mahogany double doors leading to the deck. The Princess, it seems, gets further from her with each mile and each hurt between us and her home.

Lina quickly gets up from her place on the floor, pecks me on the cheek, slaps Atlas upside the head, and runs after her new friend, only stopping to grab an apple from the bowl of fruit on Javi's desk. Adathan is the last to stand of the three of them. Silently, he picks up the chair he'd been sitting on and puts it back in the empty space where it had originally been, beside the couch. He steps back, and I'm hopeful that he'll just *leave*–but, of course, he doesn't.

Instead, standing before us, just off the edge of the intricate rug, he says directly to me, "I do not expect you to trust me. But, as long as she wants me here, then here is where I'll be." And, with that–with the words I don't believe he would have said if Althea were still in the room–he bows his head to Javi, gives a not unkind look to Atlas, and walks out of the quarters.

6

THE EXISTENCE

DION - 19 YEARS EARLIER

DAYS CEASED TO MATTER. WEEKS WERE INCONSEQUENTIAL. TIME simply passed.

How had my High Lady done it? How did she not lose herself, kept locked in a chamber for nearly a century?

I wondered if it was as simple as having the will to escape one day. The desire to see outside of the walls that were her only scenery for so long. I...I would never leave this place. Would never try to escape.

The difference between us was assuredly not in having something to fight for. I had a mind full of reasons to keep fighting, in the small way that I could still do so: by not giving in.

My most consistent companion was a set of gorgeous, deep blue eyes, looking up at me. So, no, I was not fading because of a lack of things to protect.

I had not broken. I would never break, and reveal the

secrets of my court. But I also was not entirely *me* any longer. Frequently, I felt as though I were only an existence, somewhere between death and life, gazing upon my slowly wasting body. In that form of otherness, I was not me at all–and so I looked down at the male with his many wounds, and felt pity for him.

No one was going to save him, and he did not want them to. When they carved him open, and beat him, his answering screams were never for mercy. They were empty of all meaning but agony. They echoed around the cell, down the hall to be heard by nobody but those inflicting the pain, and the strange existence that watched over him with that terrible pity.

They asked him a question now, and he did not answer. They broke his hand with a mallet, and he screamed. They asked the same question, and he gritted his teeth in pain. They put a nail through one of his feet, and even the otherness covered its ears at the sound he made.

Somewhere within the self he had once been, he knew it had been two years of this. He would not think of it, however.

There were still many to go.

7

———

SHEDDING FALSE SKINS

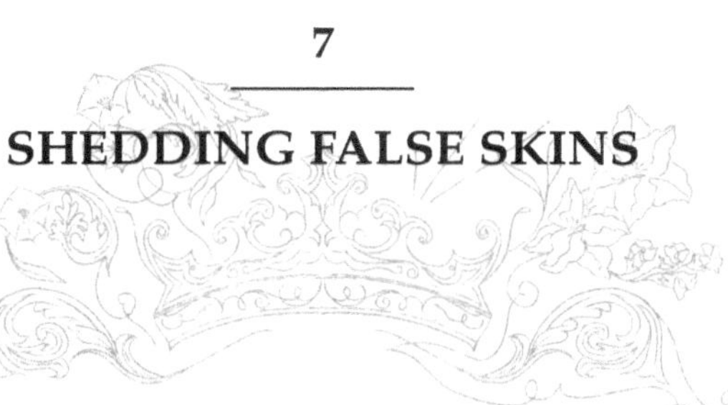

WAKING TO A SHIP FULL OF FAE AND FAERIES HAD NOT BEEN AS jarring as I might have expected it to be. Take away the arched ears and the inhuman features, and they were no different, really, than the human sailors I'd seen in Dahlih. I could not find within myself any of the fear for them that I had just a week ago. When I caught the few who cared to sneer or snarl at me, I only felt certain in myself, and in the dagger at my thigh.

Also in the male who usually got them to lower those looks, just by walking silently at my side, or at my back. I can't even be angry that he has this influence; that they fear him more than they do me. Firstly, because they should fear him; even if I don't, I recognize how foolish a decision that would be for most others. Secondly, because I like being underestimated. It has worked in my favor with their kind before.

Emelina, who I've taken to calling Li–while she calls me Al–has not been as quietly wrathful as us. She caught Kent looking

55

at me on deck after supper, both Adathan and I with our backs to him, and said, "I'd lower that look if I were you. I don't think she'll spare your balls a second time."

And yesterday, after that disaster of a meeting, she'd come into my cabin, and said nothing of it. Only tossed me an apple, and said, "Throw this in the air, I want to see if I can knife it to the wall."

The woman who could have shunned me for living the life she was born to, never even brought that matter up. Instead, not once so much as throwing a contrary look to Adathan as he kept at my side for the rest of the evening, she showed us around the enormous ship. We saw where the crew slept, and where the cannons were. She took us to a large room that had been empty at the time, but apparently when we're well enough underway would be packed with people drinking, playing music, and dancing at night.

I know that Ciaragen and Atlas are probably wondering how we'd become so friendly, so fast. If I were speaking with them outside of when absolutely necessary, I might have told them. Aside from the personality that's bubbly without being bothersome, funny without being cruel, and understanding without being judgmental–she doesn't expect anything from me.

She knows who I was a week ago. But, while the two of them seem to have some kind of idea that I've lost myself, she holds no expectations of me to be any different than how I present myself now. When I say something brash, she laughs. When I ask a daunting question, she answers. Not once has she looked at me with sorrow, with hurt, or like I'm someone she doesn't recognize. Which is the look I've seen in those storm gray and sea blue eyes practically every moment since I boarded this ship.

No, Li is simple, in that she is unapologetically herself. And, unlike them, she doesn't pretend.

She hasn't asked about it, even though I know that she knows. She hasn't tried to make me relive those moments, for which I'm grateful, but it's more than that. She hasn't wondered aloud why I barely smile, or why my laughs are, at most, gusts of air through my nose. Hasn't looked at me strangely when those things happen, either. If she is nothing but herself, then another winning characteristic is that she wants nothing but the same from others. And, as this is who I am now, I find it to be all the more refreshing to not have to pretend, either.

We sit across from each other in the mess now, Adathan to my left. I've intentionally sat at the end of the bench so that no one can sit on my other side, as my being kind to the crew does not mean I'm ready for any more friends just yet. In companionable silence, the three of us eat our lunch of crusty bread, and the same stew as yesterday. And this time I get to enjoy the whole bowl.

I'd spotted Kent again when I walked in, and his piercing blue eyes had followed me and Li all the way to the counter. When I'd turned with her to walk to a table, though, I'd nearly run into Adathan. His back was to me, just inches from my nose, his arms crossed in front of him. After another beat, he'd moved to grab his bowl from the counter behind him. His chest brushed against my hair, strands catching in the fabric of his shirt, and as one hand reached for his lunch, his other accidentally skimmed my waist, lighter than a feather. When I looked out into the mess, Kent's eyes were focused on the table before him, his face as pale as it had been when I'd threatened to cut off his balls.

Now, I'm dipping my bread straight into the stew, no decorum left to care to use a spoon. I'm almost out, though, and have a quarter of a bowl left. I hesitate maybe a heartbeat before dunking a small bit of crust into a large chunk of meat, and then a broad, bronze hand is holding another slice out to me.

I look over at Adathan, my bite halfway to my mouth, and lower it. "How are you going to have the energy for our big, bad training sessions if you give me your food?" I ask him in the Old Language that's apparently called 'Divani', as Li can't speak Ceraschen.

"I'll get more," is all he says. I hold his bright golden gaze for another second, but take the bread he offers. He stands, and swings his long legs over the bench to go back up to the counter, as promised.

"That was nice of him," Li says through a mouthful of food.

I respond around the bite I'd halted for Adathan, my fingers hovering in front of my lips. "Yeah."

"What are you training?" she asks, tearing off another hunk of bread with fingers paler than the dough.

I shrug. "A few things."

"Nice." Finished with the solid portions of the meal, she lifts her bowl to her lips, and pours the rest of the broth into her mouth. When she sets it down, she licks her lips, then takes a long drink of the glass of water beside her left hand.

Because I want to, and not because I feel obligated to extend the invitation, I say, "You can join if you want, but it's probably stuff you already know."

Now it's her turn to shrug. "Maybe I'll come around for some of it. Thanks." She smiles, a true, lovely smile that has a corner of my mouth twitching up in response.

Adathan comes back then, three more slices of bread in his large hands. Seeing as I'd only been given two, and he will be at a total of five when he finishes those, I don't feel bad about taking his other piece now. Not that he doesn't need it–he's got to have a hundred pounds on me, and who knows what a Fae metabolism is like?

"*Al*," Lina whispers, and I look up to find her bright blue eyes alight with humor. One of my brows quirk up in question. "He's coming. Act natural."

I have no idea who *he* is, or how I could act any more natural than I am, lifting my last bite of bread and stew to my mouth–and then I see him. Approaching until he's three feet from my face, then I'm eye-level with it, and he passes without even looking down at me and my definitely-too-wide eyes. All the while, Lina's cheeks puff up with air, her face pinkening.

When he's far enough away, that air comes out in a loud, "Pfff," followed by a cackling laugh that many in the mess turn to. Not that she cares. Her lack of inhibition, and that damn *thing* I was just face-to–well, not face with, has a soft, audible giggle bubbling up my throat.

I turn to Adathan, wondering what his reaction might be to the male who just walked by us, and his sunny eyes are already on me: gentle, and filled with humor. And, to my shock, both sides of his mouth are slightly pulled up instead of just the one, a dimple popping in each of his stubbled cheeks.

Lina's laughter calms a bit, and I turn back to her as she says, "That's Swinger."

"You don't say," I respond dryly, which makes her giggle again.

The air around us is light as we wait for Adathan to finish his lunch. He's finishing his second of the three slices when I see his back stiffen slightly from the corner of my eye. I'm about to ask what's wrong, when I see them. Atlas and Ciaragen, descending the stairs, their eyes finding us much too quickly.

I haven't spoken to them since my outburst yesterday. And, while I've calmed down some, I haven't yet surpassed that mental barrier of forgiveness. I know that I will–forgive them, that is. It's not in my nature to hold a grudge. Just not right now; not when I can't help but remember how they all but admitted that they're still keeping secrets from me.

More than that, though, I'm not sure how to act around them. As I'd just been thinking, Li–and Adathan–don't make me feel like I have to behave in any specific way. Now I wonder, if Atlas had been here a moment ago, would he have smiled at the humor I'd found in Swinger? Or would he have expected me to look away, chaste as the princess I'd been–or, at least, was made and expected to be?

That pressure to behave in a way I *know* is not how I want to anymore, combined with their apparent presumption that I ignore their continued opacity, is what sets me on edge as they approach.

Quiet enough that I don't think even Li can hear right across from us, Adathan asks, without looking at me, "Do you want to leave?"

Without glancing back up at the two approaching Fae, I respond, "No." He only nods the slightest bit, and takes another bite of bread.

Atlas and Ciaragen approach, and I lift my gaze to them. Their eyes are wary, their gaits hesitant, and I know I don't imagine it when I give them a nod of greeting, and their shoulders relax. Ciaragen gives me a tight smile, then an easier one for Li, and ignores Adathan altogether. Atlas, on the other hand, dips his chin to the male beside me, grins lightly–cautiously–at me, and gives a mock salute to Lina, which she returns.

The two Fae stride past us, to the counter, and a moment later come to sit with us at our table. Ciaragen brushes her long braids behind her shoulders as she sits beside Lina, and Atlas takes the spot on the general's other side. There's an awkward moment of silence where they both look like they want to say something, but don't know what, and then–

"Al just met Swinger," Li announces.

They visibly relax, and, while Ciaragen looks sternly at the woman beside her, a smile plays on her full lips. "I believe I told you not to call him that."

"And *I* believe I told *you* that if you expect me to remember his real name, it's got to be more memorable than his–"

Atlas laughs, familiar and happy, as he takes a bite of his bread and stew, while Ciaragen interrupts her, "*Emelina Dove.*"

And, just like that, grief overcomes me. The way she says my new friend's full name is sweet and disapproving, and so *motherly* it makes my heart clench in my chest, and my breaths strain through a throat that's suddenly much too tight. And I know that I just told Adathan that I didn't want to leave, but I can't be here anymore, either. I stand, and all eyes at the table follow the movement immediately, smiles and humor gone from their faces.

And that does something to my heart, too, the way that I take away their joy. If any of that emotion flashed in my eyes, though, it's gone in a heartbeat when I look down at them, forcing indifference onto my features. "We're going to train," I inform the three across from me, Adathan already moving to his feet beside me.

I pick up our empty bowls, and Li's, and bring them quickly to the cook's counter. Jacks nods in thanks, which I return, and then I walk back, past the table, and to the stairs without meeting any of the eyes I feel on me as I go. I know that I only hear Adathan behind me because he wants me to, just as he had yesterday when he'd come to get me before his interrogation.

Without turning to look behind me, I say, "Where?"

He doesn't have to ask what I mean. "That room where they

convene in the evenings." I nod. It's probably the only area big enough to train that isn't the deck, which is much too open and public a place to display my incompetence with Fae combat–on a ship full of them.

We can't risk him blasting a hole in the ship with his wind, so we focus on speed in other ways, within the space allotted. It's a fantastic distraction; my mind cannot fit my grief in with its focus on evading the obvious predator before me. Even if he is taking it easy on me.

When I tell him that, he gets a little faster, sometimes getting near enough that I feel my hair brush him as I narrowly evade him. But–

"You're still doing it," I say through slightly panting breaths. I removed the long sleeve shirt ten minutes ago. Between the summer heat, and the lack of ventilation in this room, sweat has soaked into my tank top, and down between my breasts. Adathan's short-sleeved shirt is hardly better off, but he's kept it on.

"Doing what?" He moves for me once more, so quickly that again the ends of my hair catch on his shirt as I just barely maneuver around him.

"You know what." We repeat the sequence, almost exactly. "You're not being a very good teacher." Again, and I roll on the ground, then spring back to my feet just to make it interesting.

He only stares as he circles me, the flicker of a muscle in his jaw the only sign he heard me at all. When he moves again just a touch more swiftly, I manage to dodge it, this time smacking his arm once I pass it. I look over my shoulder as I circle him in return.

"Adathan–if you don't fight me like you mean it, how do you think I'll make out when someone else *does*?"

He pauses, half in position to pounce again, his dark brows furrowing slightly. "What makes you so sure it's a 'when'?"

I glare at him, more to conceal my fear than out of actual anger towards him. "It's a when. Men–males *will* attempt to hurt me, just because they can. So, it's on me–and on *you*, to make sure they can't. I refuse to be so unprepared ever again."

He straightens, and I do the same, waiting for the regret, or pity. Neither comes, though. Instead, the face I've come to know so well, so quickly, shifts. Brows lower over eyes that shine with ferality, and his lips pull back over his teeth, exposing the canines he so carefully hides with straight faces and tight grins. He sinks into a crouch, all hulking muscle and Fae brutality. My heart thunders, but the terror I expect doesn't rise.

Rather, *my* lips part in a grin that's half a snarl, and I say, "Come and get me."

With unprecedented speed, he springs, and there's no time to plan. Only react. I have to drop to avoid his arms, but he's nearly on me again by the time I've gotten my feet under me. Then I'm on the floor again, just barely dodging him once more, and something begins to change within me. That rage I restrained yesterday in the mess seizes me, and an inhuman roar rips its way up my throat as I push with all the strength in my legs to half rise, violently ram my shoulder into his gut, and take us both down.

My legs straddle his waist, and my hands reach up to pin his to the wooden planks above him. I growl, low and deep in my chest, releasing this strange beast that has been trapped in my body–repressed, however unknown it had been until now. It's an animal that sits back on its haunches in anticipation as Adathan returns the sound, far more guttural and raw than mine had been.

He flips us, hovering over me, and I'm the one pinned. One hand pulls both of my wrists over my head, and the other circles the base of my throat, not so much as brushing the bruises that linger higher up on my neck from when Olin strangled me. My teeth snap near the flesh of his wrist, and it surprises him enough that I'm able to hook my knee around his, and pull it up, throwing him off-balance. He moves to catch himself, and a freed hand finds its mark on his cheek. My knuckles ache gloriously from the blow against the angular bone.

"Nice job, sweetheart," he grits out, wicked delight shining in his eyes as his cheek turns red. "How are you getting out, though?" He lowers himself–his body still hovering over mine, only his warmth touching me. But, with the shift, it's still that much harder to do what he's wondered after, and escape him.

Beyond words, a hiss rattles through my teeth, and that animal seizes complete control, sending a burst of power through my body. It travels into my limbs, and when I push my palm against his shoulder, and hike my legs up and around his, I flip the entire mass of him onto his back once more, my hair falling in a curtain around his face.

Quick as an adder, his hand reaches up, looping my hair around his broad hand, fingers knotting at my skull so that the pressure isn't painful on the strands. The gold of his eyes burning like the sun I've likened them to, he pulls my head down, just inches above his. Through bared teeth, he growls, "Tie this up next time. It's been driving me fucking crazy."

I don't answer. I just drive my forehead down the rest of the distance, and hear a crunch as his nose breaks. He releases my hair as blood gushes from his nostrils, and my fist, half-cocked to swing for his other cheek, stalls at the sight.

Breathing heavy, I drop my hand, and it lands gently on his shoulder. My heart calms as I hold his gaze, the human retaking control of my mind and body. The bleeding has already slowed, but I don't believe even Fae healing will save him from a crooked nose. So, without a word, I plant my hands on his solid chest, and stand. After I move to the side, I hold my hand out to him. His own animal is being reined in as I watch, though his pupils remain wider than usual, his bleeding nostrils delicately flared. But he takes my offered palm without hesitation.

I step into him, and reach a hand up to pinch the bridge of his nose between my thumb and forefinger. He winces ever so slightly. "You were going easy on me." He knows I mean the whole time, even the past few moments; if he'd been giving me his all, I'm certain I would have been pinned in less than a heartbeat. And he knows the implied question that follows.

So, he answers, "It won't happen again." He grasps my wrist just as it tenses to set his nose, keeping it from moving. "But know this: when I struck you under Olin's command–that was the *last* time I will ever do so. If you want somebody to train you like that...you will find someone else."

He holds my eyes with his until I nod, then releases me. Another crunch sounds as I straighten his nose, then heal the fracture and the inflammation until all that's left is the blood. It's on my fingers as I pull them away, until I wipe them on the fabric of his shirt, skimming them across the dense expanse of his upper abdomen, before dropping them to my side.

8

FORGIVEN, INDEED

I STAND AT THE STERN OF THE SHIP, BY THE HELM, LOOKING OUT at the ocean around us. We're far enough out now that not even my sight can make out the Dahlihan coast past the expanse of blue that I'd once been told is the exact shade of my eyes.

My heart tightens painfully–so painfully–in my chest, and the waves become blurry; clouded. I clench my jaw, but a single tear escapes from my left eye and trails down my cheek before I can stop it. I only hope that Javi, at the wheel, and Atlas beside him, cannot separate the scent from that of the salty water surrounding us.

I allow that tear the peace and dignity to travel all the way down to my jaw, where it hovers for a moment before falling onto the wooden railing between my hands. The air off the sea dries my face and lashes, just before I hear a familiar set of footsteps approaching.

I turn, and can't help it when my eyes widen. Althea, her

cheeks flushed, cotton shirt disheveled and sweaty, her waving hair tied up messily in her plum-colored sash. It might have painted a very different picture than what is true, if Adathan, walking behind her, wasn't covered in his own blood.

Many of the crew stop to stare at the pair as well. It's likely only their captain at the helm, overlooking them all, that has them getting back to work quickly. But, just because their eyes and hands are otherwise occupied, does not mean that their ears are giving us the same respect. So, when the two of them begin to walk up the steps, I throw up a sound shield–because, based on the blood on Adathan, and the set of Althea's shoulders, I don't believe this is going to be a simple chat.

"What happened?" Atlas asks as they clear the top step. Standing together, the difference in their heights is dramatic. Althea is not a short female–probably only a couple of inches shorter than me–but Adathan towers over her; the top of her head only just clearing his collarbone.

"I broke his nose," Althea tells him, her lovely accent trailing through the Divani words. Her voice, her expression–they couldn't be more casual, or matter-of-fact.

"It doesn't look broken," Javi says, though I think I hear humor in his deep voice.

"Yes, he has me to thank for that."

"But...you also broke it in the first place," Atlas says, and that's *definitely* humor I hear in his words.

She shrugs, waving a hand, and briefly switches to Ceraschen. "He didn't mind." Behind her, the male smirks, a dimple popping in his cheek.

"*Why* did you break his nose–and then heal him?" I chime in.

"It would have been rude to break it and not fix it." Her brows scrunch together a bit, and her nose crinkles in a way I'd seen her do at Castle Cerasche when she's being intentionally obtuse. A thing I saw her do a few times on the dance floor, talking with the lords who attempted to court her.

"Anyway," she says, still having not really answered a single one of our questions. But a serious air comes over her, and I watch her already-straight shoulders pin back even more. Behind her, the male's jaw clenches, his eyes on her profile. "We need to change our route."

I can't see Javi or Atlas's faces, but I'd be willing to bet their brows furrow at the same time as mine. "Reroute?" Javi asks.

Light green eyes move to the captain. "Yes. To Sabrian."

Again, if I had to put money on the movement of the eyebrows of my friend and my godson, I'd say they're raised now, like mine.

Althea doesn't wait for us to ask her to explain. "I need the glamour removed. I cannot face Olin with its limitations. And, you said the woman–female who placed it on me is there." Her almond eyes are tight around the edges, her normally full lips pursed. And I may not be an expert in how she displays emotion, or how she hides it, but I can tell that while this is her idea, she doesn't like it.

Javi, one hand on the wheel, observes her. She takes it levelly, her expression unchanging, gaze unwavering. Then I watch my friend's head nod, his topknot bobbing slightly. "We need to port in Ardhavi for a day or so. Replenish supplies, and help the males to decompress after the time at sea. We should get there in about four weeks, if the winds and the males' powers hold. We can set sail to Sabrian from there, which will be another week, more or less."

Althea nods once, and then almost turns away to walk back down the stairs. But she pauses, one slender hand on the baluster, her back just a couple of inches from Adathan's front.

She turns back around, and flicks her gaze over the three of us, landing on Atlas. Her voice is surprisingly soft when she says, "I forgive you, Atlas. I know you never meant to hurt me. It's just..." Her gaze flits, a bit uncertainly, between Javi and I before returning to Atlas. "It was easier. To be angry. To blame someone else."

Without another word, she turns once more, this time all the way, and Adathan follows her down the steps to the main deck. Leaving Atlas standing there, watching her go.

When they pass the bubble of my sound shield, I keep it up around the three of us. "Nice job pretending like we weren't already planning to take her to Sabrian," I say to Javi, shame coating each word. Forgiven, indeed.

"She's had very few choices in her life that have not been made for her. I'm glad that this did not have to be another one of those cases," he replies, his tone solemn. It weighs on my heart, too, and by the way that Atlas continues to stare after the young female, I know he feels the same.

"When do we tell her everything?" he asks quietly.

I follow his gaze now, to where the two of them are striding across the deck. Althea stops suddenly to point at something on the ship, and turns her face to Adathan, her brows scrunched in question. Though the sea and the crew are too loud for me to hear what either of them are saying, I watch the male's jaw move as he answers. Her head tilts, arm lowering, and she asks him something else, brow still creased. When he's responding to her third query, I finally breathe my own reply to Atlas's question. "I don't know."

9

KITE STRINGS

THEA - DAYS 2 & 3

THE NUMBNESS HAS SET IN AGAIN. MY CHEST IS VACANT, EVEN though my mind is full. Too many thoughts and unfelt things swirl there, so contorted and confused that instead of settling on one and going from there, I've succumbed to the same emptiness that I felt when I saw my mother dead in my father's lap. A memory that I have seen too many times this past week, but which I have still not allowed myself to feel.

Adathan hadn't objected when I'd walked past my cabin after dinner, and down until I reached his. I'd stepped inside, sat down on the floor with my back against the bed, and curled my knees to my chest. My arms are still wrapped around them, as if physically holding myself together will keep me from mentally or emotionally falling apart.

He sits beside me, one leg bent up, his arm resting on it. His other leg is down on the floor, long and muscled, his hand resting on his thigh. He's been just as silent as me; has not asked anything of me, or of my well-being. Not since I told him down in that makeshift training room of my decision. And I'm glad of it. The silence allows me some strange semblance of peace within the chaotic numbness.

It only makes sense, I'd thought to myself. If Adathan, who does not want to hurt me, and therefore reins in his abilities–if he can still easily catch me, then I don't want to imagine what Olin might be capable of. What he might do, if and when I move to take his life.

It only makes sense. I cannot face Olin, cannot *kill* him, with my glamour-inflicted limitations. Whatever happens as I take my vengeance–whatever I suffer, is unimportant. Because, what I know, but have only thought to myself–not willing or able to share it with Adathan–is that my only concern is ensuring Olin's demise. I don't have any attachments to where my own life ends up in the process.

And that only makes sense, too. What I'd told Adathan yesterday is true: everything that has happened to *me* is Olin's fault. But I didn't specify who's responsible for the things that happened to my loved ones. That, I know, is all on me. On my silence after I was taken. On my move for Olin's blade in the Hall, rather than figuring out a way to stop my mother from charging at him. Her blood is on my hands, just as much as his had been after I'd plunged the dagger into his leg.

My mom. Hanna and Gregor, and their unborn child. Amahd. The innocents in the Great Hall who'd been unlucky enough to be in range of the raining glass. Olin may have killed them–but would he have? If I had been smarter, faster, *better*?

I don't even know, have been too frightened to ask, if Iris is alright. If, when she fell down the dais steps and hit her head, she only had a minor injury...or not. I can only hope that one of the other Weaschten healers surely in attendance had been able to heal her.

I'm not even sure that they'll know either way. They've made it clear that their only focus was me. Maybe they paid no mind to my sister, the human woman who might have been bleeding into her brain as they worked to free themselves from Olin's majick around the Hall.

It's the numbness that saves me from feeling that wholly, though both my jaw and heart clench at the thought. As angry as I had been at Ciaragen and Atlas, even Adathan–it's nothing compared to what I feel towards myself. The absolute, soul-shredding, world-obliterating rage and contempt I have for my own continued existence, when so many whom I loved are dead and gone.

And while I have processed my anger towards Adathan, courtesy of those days in the woods, and who I've found him to be as a person, much of my desire to be near him stems from his understanding of me. A comprehension of how my mind works that enables him to be silent beside me for hours, rather than interrupt my thoughts with questions whose answers would either be obvious, or painful. If I'm completely honest with myself, what negativity I felt towards him had faded not with each passing day–but with each hour. To this point, here and now, where I don't have any left, and don't think I have since I poured water through his lips, and stole pain from his shoulder in a forest of pines.

The anger I had for Ciaragen and Atlas is gone, too. They're going to continue to keep their secrets, regardless of how I feel about it. And, being angry at Atlas...I found that, as he grinned while I brushed off the act of breaking Adathan's nose, it was impossible to be angry with him. Especially when his stormy eyes shined like that.

The rage I have for myself, however, cannot and will not fade until I do. When my life is a memory, and my bones bring new life to the ground–then, perhaps, I'll have begun to compensate for what my existence has done to the world.

After that thought, I settle into an even deeper silence. I bring my cheek down to rest on my knees, my hair spilling over them. I face Adathan, but don't really see him. My eyes find the jagged, star-shaped scar on his neck from Atlas's arrow, and that's what they hold, even when my mind ceases to recognize that I'm looking at him at all.

Hours that feel like minutes pass, and I realize we've missed dinner when the only light in the cabin comes in the form of the silver moon reflecting off the sea. Adathan hasn't complained, has barely shifted in his position on the floor beside me.

Looking at him now, I have a new thought–one that doesn't hurt. And even while I wonder if I deserve to leave that pain, my heart and mind hold tight to the question, unwilling to let it go. Knowing that, once I voice it, things will start to feel just a little bit better.

So I say, my voice rough from disuse and unspent emotion, "I have a question."

Adathan turns his face to me, his expression steady. Patient. Constant. "Yes?"

"Why didn't you use my name when telling your side of the story yesterday?" It occurred to me last night that he hadn't; only said 'her', or 'she'. Actually, I don't believe he's spoken my name since he was Artur and I was a princess.

"I didn't think you wanted me to say your name," he replies, and, somehow, I think I expected the answer.

Still, my brows furrow. "Why?"

His eyes darken. "For many reasons, which I'm sure you've already pieced together in that mind of yours. But, most recently because you asked Atlas not to."

I blink, lifting my head from my knees. "Yes, I suppose I

have." I sigh through my nose, and close my eyes before continuing. "Atlas called me Aly. And he can't. Nobody can. Not now." I open my eyes to find his still on me. "But I don't want you to call me nothing, Adathan."

He's silent for a moment, dark and light shifting in his gaze. "Okay. What do you want me to call you, then?"

I think about his question; contemplate asking him to call me by my middle name, as I'd pretended to be in Dahlih. But, for some reason, my mind rejects the name we'd used in our ruse–when we were hiding. Doesn't want him to speak a name that isn't me; isn't mine. Not really.

"Thea," I answer. A corner of his mouth curls up, and I find my own mirroring it. "What should *I* call *you*?"

His eyes flick down to my lips, and back up. "You can call me whatever you like, Thea."

The sound of it on his tongue softens my mouth and my gaze at the same time that it makes my heart beat a strange, hard *thump* in my chest. I reply, "I think I'd like to call you Adan."

And though, even in the dimness of the moonlight, I can see many thoughts in those eyes, he only gives me a smirk that's just a beat too late, and says, "Then call me Adan."

⇔

The next day passes with ease in comparison to those before it. The morning flies by, between breakfast, glamour training with Adan, and tossing daggers with him and Li. The afternoon is spent on the ship deck: Li steering with Atlas monitoring; Adan, actually helping the crew, just slowing his movements so that I could follow along; me, doing my best, but only just getting the hang of the more intricate knots before dinner.

Li meets us in the mess, her cloud-like curls roped into a thick plait over one pale shoulder. On her way to our table, she flattens the pocket she made with the bottom of her shirt, dumping a pile of peanut shells on a separate bench. Peanuts, it seems, is getting on her nerves.

Ciaragen and Atlas join us, too, though the former glares at Adan so much it's hard for me not to start holding it against her. The two males get along fine, though they rarely talk directly to each other. Somehow, with my minimal experience with men—males, I'm not surprised. Not as I remember a kiss to my neck eight days ago, and a glance at my mouth while his spoke my name yesterday. But, I've got enough going on in my mind without worrying about how all that is going to work out.

Now, I lay in my bed, unwilling to shut my eyes. I know that, regardless of the relative ease of the day, the nightmares will come. They will come, and they will remind me that ease is not something I deserve to feel. Yet, even knowing that, I can't help but keep myself awake, just to feel it for a little bit longer.

I've considered getting up, and walking around. Looking out into the dark sea until my lids are heavy enough that it's a struggle to make it back to bed. Until exhaustion weighs so heavy on me that perhaps I will not dream at all.

I'm about to get up to do just that when there's a soft knock at my door. Then, a female voice whispers, "Al. Are you awake?"

I half-whisper back, "Yeah," and my door opens. Li walks in, bright and glowing even in just the moonlight reflecting off the ocean, and through my window. She's holding items under the top of her right arm, clenched tight to her side to keep them from falling as she uses her left hand to open the door. She closes it behind her, and walks forward as I sit up on my mattress. She takes a seat at the foot of it, and places the items between us.

"I thought you might need these," she says, spreading them

out so that I can see them a bit better. "A book, a nightgown, a brassiere just in case you're not a nip gal, and a change of clothes for tomorrow."

I run my hand over the items, and a lump rises, unbidden, in my throat. I clear it before responding. "Thank you." She waves an ivory hand, dismissing me, and I take the first piece of fabric my hands find, and hold it up. And I raise a brow, as any lingering sentiment about the kind gesture leaves me. "*This* is a nightgown?" The silky thing is open-backed, and its skirt will likely only fall inches below my rear.

"Gown might be an exaggeration," she concedes. "But, it's too hot for anything else. Just look at the other stuff."

I sigh, but place the *nightgown* back onto the bed, and look at the rest of the clothes. The brassiere is a bit small, but well-made, and should support me fine enough. A tan pair of trousers, and a shirt that has the same short sleeves Adathan had worn today–but much smaller, to not swallow me up, as I'm sure his would.

Finally, the book. In the darkness, I can't read the title. "It's called *Night's Beating Heart*," Li tells me. "A romance."

I set it down, brushing my hand over the well-loved binding. "Thank you," I say again. "I'll have to start reading it tomorrow–or, do you have candles, too? I wasn't given any." At night, with only the silvery light of the moon and stars streaming through the porthole, and the ship deck prisms above, it's too dim to read comfortably.

"Candles, and rocking, totally-made-of-wood ships don't go well together. But–maybe you can make faerie lights? I can't, but maybe you can?"

My brows furrow, and my heart clenches a bit in my chest. "Me? Make–what even are faerie lights?"

"They're basically little balls of majick. I never asked how they work, but I've seen my mums make them a bunch. You just...like, focus on your power, and instead of pushing it out the usual way, you concentrate it into this external thing that just, well, glows. And then you'll be able to read after eight in the evening."

Though part of me remains apprehensive, and another wants to reject anything to do with *majick*...I remember how powerful I felt while training with Adan yesterday, when I'd slipped the leash I hadn't known was wrapped around my throat all my life. Rejecting this part of me isn't something I'll be able to do for much longer, anyway, and feeling that strong, that...*free*? I can't deny that I want to feel it again.

And, in my cabin, alone with Li, is probably the best time to try my hand at–majick. I know that, even if I fail, she won't be disappointed in me; she'll just shrug, and move on.

So, I take a deep breath, and focus, like she said, on my mag–majick. I bring the healing light to the surface, and that tendril that looks like sunshine passing through fog rises from my palm. Li breathes, "Wow," and touches my palm with her forefinger. Her skin burns a luminous yellow as my light shines through it, and she giggles quietly. "It's warm."

I smirk, but continue to focus on...pushing it out of me? And the light glows brighter, revealing Li's smiling face. She looks so incredibly awed, and joyful–and I feel something. Like a tether to my power that I've never noticed before. A kite string, almost–but a million of them, all tied between it, and me. And I can see that, if I cut one, it would be released into the world. Not taking from me–the kite is still tied with the rest of the million strings. More like when I heal somebody. An expenditure, but one that's gained back quickly.

I cut one of those strings in my mind, and from my palm arises a kernel of sunshine. It floats in the air between me and Li. Even when my hands dim, it hangs there, warm and bright.

"Awesome," Li breathes, blue eyes transfixed. "At home,

they have these majicked glass orbs that can contain the light, and keep it glowing for days. We used the last of ours while ported in Dahlih, but we'll probably get more in Ardhavi. Out in the open, the lights are usually good for half an hour, sometimes more."

"Awesome," I agree, and let the feeling wash over me. Let it settle some of the lingering unease over my decision to get the glamour removed. It doesn't resolve the true reason for the repulsion I feel for that change, but it does make the knowledge of who I am beneath it just slightly more tolerable.

10

WATCH & LEARN

HE COULD NOT REMEMBER WHAT IT WAS THEY WANTED FROM HIM.

He knew that there was something...*important*. Something that needed to be kept secret. But he could not remember what that secret was. They cut him, and beat him, and made him sit in his own filth. And they asked him, again and again, what he knew about the High Lord and High Lady of Sabrian.

He didn't know anything, he told them. He thought that those words used to be a lie. Now, though, the truth only came to him in his dreams, and it slipped away from him as soon as he opened his eyes to see his chained, filthy ankles. While he slept, his wrists and feet were still bound with them. He did not remember what it was like to live without them.

Just as he did not remember a time where his tormentors did not come to hurt him. They shared this cell with him twice between his longest sleeps–the ones which they did not cause by pain or by loss of blood. Sometimes it was thrice if they were very angry with him.

It was always the same ones who came. A male with dark eyes, and a male with gold eyes. The dark one would hurt him, and make the gold one watch. "And learn," he would say to the gold one. Though, what he was supposed to learn that he had not already, the male in chains did not know. He thought that, perhaps, the dark one enjoyed his work too much to let somebody else do it.

Sometimes, he used to see the gold one cringe, or flinch during the ministrations of his comrade. There was a time, he remembered, that the dark one caught him doing so. Later, he was woken from a long sleep by another male's screams echoing through the hall. They paid more attention to the gold one than they did him for a bit after that.

When he returned, he no longer cringed. No longer flinched. The gold eyes were blank, as he watched. And learned.

11

THE HEART'S WANTS

ADAN HAS BEEN WORKING ON THE RIGGING AND SAILS FOR HOURS. I'm sure, like I have the past two weeks, I will need to heal him of the sunburn that will surely grace his scarred and inked skin by the time he descends before supper. To do so is practically second nature at this point. Though he consistently dons his shirt before coming down, my senses are so attuned to him that, even though he would heal within the course of the evening, I can't give him the chance. Like an itch that needs to be scratched–if my hands were bound, it would drive me just as mad to not attend to it. To him.

I, on the other hand, have spent most of my afternoon weaving a fishing net. Like making the backpack in the woods of Cerasche weeks ago, the task gives me the ability to zone out all that's happening around me. I only pause occasionally to stretch my neck or flex my fingers. By the time the afternoon sun is cresting into its evening position, the giant net sits in my lap as I check it for any missed loops.

"You're going to have a really interesting tan line if you keep doing that," a familiar baritone voice says.

I look up to find Atlas standing a few feet away, smirking, his dark brown arms crossed over his chest.

These weeks have been healing for our friendship. I remember that he keeps his secrets, but have come to view them similarly as I do Adan's. Perhaps a blood oath does not hold Atlas's tongue, but his honor does. If there were not some promise to bind his words, he would have given them to me by now.

I smile back at him, huffing a chuckle through my nose. "Well, then, make it go faster and help me check it to spare me of that embarrassment."

His grin widens, revealing white teeth, wicked canines and all. He moves around the edge of the net to sit beside me, and immediately gets to work.

We pull at the net in companionable silence, occasionally passing the large crochet hook between us to fix any openings that would allow fish to slip through. I notice how our fingers brush when we do so, and how our knees bump together when we shift the net, but it's an easy sort of contact. Not demanding, or daunting; just there.

When we're done, he takes the whole thing from my hands, and easily folds it, flicking the heavy mass of rope so it snaps against the deck into the position he needs to make the next fold. Finished, it sits before us in a square that will be easy for either of us to carry to the hold.

"Show off," I mutter, which gets a laugh out of him. It makes me grin a little without thinking about it.

"I think you mean to say, '*Thank you, Atlas, for saving my legs from looking like fish scales.*'"

"My Divani is a little rusty–did the last part of that mean *'for being an absolute pain in my ass?'*"

"You're clearly learning your Divani from Lina more than the rest of us," he says with a chuckle, leaning back on his hands, and stretching his long, muscled legs out before him.

I shrug. "They're valuable words. How else would I tell Kent to fuck off when he's being a dick?"

But, rather than laugh at my use of two of Li's favorite curses, Atlas's expression sobers. "He's still bothering you?"

In an attempt to salvage the conversation, I pull the short dagger out of my waistband. "He probably just wants this back," I reply, twirling it in my fingers.

Atlas grabs my hand, stilling it before letting me go. "Seriously. Do you want me to talk to him?"

I restrain my sigh. "I appreciate you offering, but no. I don't want him to look at me and see my guards. I want him to see me, and what *I'll* do to him if he tries anything."

Atlas nods, but his jaw is tight. He turns from me, but I see his gray eyes darting around the deck–looking for someone.

Again, I try to distract him. "I like what you did to your hair."

He looks at me again, and touches the shorn back of his head. His thin locs grow only from the top now, currently bundled at his nape with a strip of leather tipped with silver. The style was much more effective when he had longer pieces in the back to tether as well. Now, I have to restrain myself from tucking an errant loc behind his ear.

One side of his mouth pulls up. "Thanks. The whole lot were getting too hot to keep."

I twist my own hair, tied up in Evie's purple sash, around my hand, bringing it forward over my shoulder. "You think I should do the same?"

He huffs another chuckle. "If you want. I'm sure you could pull it off."

But, then he turns away again. Scanning.

Now I do sigh. "Atlas."

A muscle in his jaw flickers, but he doesn't return his gaze to mine. Instead, still staring out at the crew working on the deck, he says, "Do you remember that night in the garden?"

My heart stumbles. Partially because that was the last place I expected this conversation to go, but more so because yes, I do. And have recently been avoiding the memory almost as studiously as I have those of the following days.

When I don't answer, he looks at me at last, his stormy gaze roiling like that which it likens. "I would never be the one who limits you, Althea."

My heart stutters again, remembering. Words spoken against my skin, in a star-flecked night, the scents of flowers and whiskey surrounding us. *But, you are infinite, Althea. And I will not be the one who limits you.*

He goes on, "I know how capable you are. But I want *you* to know that you're not alone. I'm still here."

Then, so hesitantly, his hand lifts. I freeze, but, when I don't object, or move away, Atlas brushes his fingers against my cheek. Along the scar that's invisible to him thanks to the glamour; the slice that first opened when I rolled us on the floor of the Hall, to try to save his life by forgoing mine.

It's warm, and calloused, and sweet. It makes my lips part, and my breath catch. His eyes, and those arched ears notice both, and Atlas smiles softly. And my stupid, indecisive heart asks me if I truly *have* to choose–

Atlas's hand drops, and he stands without another word, grabs the net from the deck, and makes his way to the hold. He looks over his shoulder at me at the same moment that a familiar figure drops onto the deck, pulling his shirt down his torso.

I can shove them down all I want, but those feelings from a night-bathed garden aren't gone. It would be so much easier if they were. Because the feelings that began at a pool of water in the Ceraschen woods are beckoning to me too strongly to ignore much longer.

12
OFFENSIVE DEFENCE

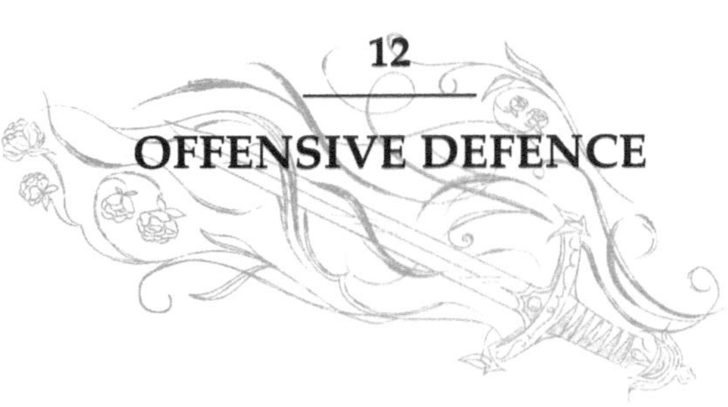

TWELVE DAYS HAVE PASSED SINCE ALTHEA SPOKE OF FORGIVENESS with Adathan at her back, reeking of his own blood. Twelve days, watching that male interact with some of those most precious to me, and with my Lady. My only consolation was getting to watch *her* with *them*, too.

The two females had become fast friends, Lina frequently managing to free the pieces of Althea I'd learned about when she thought no one was watching at Castle Cerasche. The female has been true to her word of forgiveness, and I can tell how much this means to Atlas. How much he enjoys spending time with her, even if Adathan is frequently with her, too.

Between them, though, there seems to be some kind of understanding. However unaware of it the young female might be.

Regardless of that, I refuse to leave my godson and goddaughter in *his* grasp, so I accompany them whenever my own work allows it–which is often, since shadowalking home, or to my division on the Sabriani border, is too dangerous on an ever-moving vessel. Adathan does a good job of pretending he's not uncomfortable in my company, while Althea has not *allowed* herself to be comfortable around me. No, for some reason, she seems to regard me almost as she had back at Castle Cerasche, before we danced. Perhaps with a harder jaw and more steel in her eyes than there had been then.

The nonsensical part is that she does not need to go through all of that formality. I don't need her to be considerate, or to weaponize her learned politeness to keep me at arm's length. I would rather her be brash with me, as she is with Lina. But, I've realized over the days that the respect displayed, no matter how I feel about it...it is just a method of control for her.

She has many, I've come to know. Sometimes, she'll get quiet at seemingly random moments, and I can almost feel anger boiling within her. She does not scream, or cry, or rage. She only sits in simmering, loathful silence. But it stopped feeling like those emotions were directed at me, or Atlas, after she claimed to have forgiven us–with only those blips of tight eyes or flickering jaw to show she remembers our secrets at all.

But that's somehow worse, the repression inwards. Because the only other person that hateful quiet could be for–is herself.

That control, that silence...it's internal rage. She is holding it within her, a punishment for her own imagined crimes. So, when I catch the looks she sometimes aims at me, usually after I am not...particularly kind towards Adathan, I sometimes think of asking her what the issue is. Because I think that single pin prick will cause an explosion; shattering each piece of control that she's built around herself like armor.

The only reason I don't...I'm not strong enough. I am not strong enough to listen to her tell me all the ways I've failed her. I will lash out, as I had when she confronted me back in

Dahlih, and I will say something I regret, and then two things will happen. She, my Lady, will go from simply being on her guard around me, to not trusting me at all. And I will be beside her in spirit; in that self-loathing silence.

So, while I cannot speak to her in those moments, nor can I accompany her in the ones which she directs all animosity inwards, I've watched these twelve days as her three friends took turns going to her during the latter. Always giving her time to think first, and never speaking until she did. Just there, by her side, for whenever she finally would break free of the chains her grief has on her.

They have learned over that time, too, that she responds to touch. I watched the first time, when Lina tentatively reached her hand out to hold Althea's. Watched, as the female came back to herself in just heartbeats. The next time, my goddaughter leaned her white-blond head against the sun-tanned, freckle-dusted shoulder, and a moment later, those falsely blonde waves tangled with the ivory curls as Althea's head rested on Lina's.

Atlas noticed, too. And, though his touch was even more hesitant than Lina's had been, I've caught them with his knee, or his arm resting against hers.

Adathan...the bastard has even more control than Althea, it seems. Because he's only touched her once, that I saw. When the emotions within had paled her, and her eyes were not just distant, but *haunted*. He had gripped her chin, forced her to look at him, and taken a deep breath. The next, she followed. By the seventh, her color had returned. And with it, his self-control, as he dropped his hand.

Other than that, if they aren't training, or she isn't healing him (the male constantly, infuriatingly, volunteers for the dangerous jobs on the ship, and she insists on healing him of any of the injuries he gains from it), they hardly touch. Instead, they just have the most absurdly deep understanding of each other. After I'd broken down to ask her about it, Lina had told me it was Adathan who suggested to her and Atlas that they take turns comforting her. And I hate how that grates on my rage towards him; how he comprehends her mind so well that he could very well do all the comforting himself, as he had those first few days. But he doesn't; he's chosen to give them that opportunity.

That's not even the most annoying part, though. It's the way he treats Althea–the way he knows her, the way he's so obviously worked to ensure she has other people to rely on besides him, when he could have easily added fuel to her anger for us instead. I've watched him be kind, even when she's nowhere to be seen. I've seen him help Lina in a perfectly indifferent way that allows her to get past her own stubbornness at what she is or isn't capable of–something that even I struggle with at times. I've seen him nod in greeting to Atlas, when all signs should have pointed to them being adversaries.

All of that, and then some, has me wondering if he's truly as evil as I've believed him to be for so long. And what makes me want to dive into the sea, and swim the rest of the way to Ardhavi, is how I remember having the same sort of thoughts about–about Dion, all those years ago.

Life is not fair. I've known that since before I met my mate. But, it's particularly cruel, too.

Tears fall from my eyes, and trail down my temples and into my hair. I lay on my bed still, though the soft blue light of the early morning sun has started to glow through the small window of my cabin. There are more mornings like this than not. I will wake up with grief in my heart, so heavy and complete that I don't remember how to move. How to lift my head from my pillow, and then go about my day without him, as I have for over twenty-one years.

Just as with anything, there are good days, and bad. Sometimes, when I'm busy enough, I can almost forget. When the pain is a dull ache, and I can work, and talk, and eat. But always, the worst day is the day he was taken from me. And as Atlas and I had scoured those woods for Althea, my heart had broken even further by the knowledge that neither one of us would ever be able to enjoy her birthday again.

I wouldn't dare compare our griefs. I only wish that neither of us had any. Our hearts unbroken; whole, and lovely.

A knock on my door sounds, quiet and tentative. With decades of mastering my voice, my response comes out evenly, as the tears continue to cascade down my temples. "Yes?"

"Aunt Ari, it's time for breakfast," Lina says, her own tone a bit husky with sleep.

"I'll be out in a minute, sweet girl. You go ahead with Althea." I close my eyes, allowing my lids to squeeze out the final tears.

"Okay, love you."

"Love you, too." As my temples dry, I hear her steps trudge away from my door, and then another knock thuds down the hall. I hear Lina say, "Time to get up, you lazy slut." When there's no answer, she knocks again. And again. Then–

"If you knock one more time, I'm gonna cut off your other arm," comes Althea's voice, probably muffled by her pillow. A pause, then:

Knock, knock, knock.

My lips twitch up at the corners, and the small humor gives me the will and the strength to sit up in my bed. Still, there's no sound of movement from the cabin a couple doors down from mine. So Lina croons, "Jacks made potatoes."

A beat of silence. "Give me two minutes."

I hear her rise then, and I follow suit. I dress slowly, so that Althea will have clear access to the washroom first. Any time I get to it at the same time as her, she always steps aside to permit me first. And no amount of, 'please's or 'no, you go ahead's will convince her to do so. That damned measured, controlled politeness.

I'm ready to be back on land for many reasons, not the least of which being access to a hot shower–though the plumbing Javi rigged with his water majick is pretty spectacular for a ship. But, I've also worn the same two sets of clothes for the past two weeks, since my journey hadn't been anticipated. It's only lucky that Lina's had been, and her mothers had packed her a trunk full of clothes, toiletries, and books. Otherwise, I'm sure both Althea and myself would have fared very poorly, both of us in clothing we'd gotten from the port town in Dahlih. Hers a bit bloodier than mine, courtesy of the arrow we'd put through Adathan's throat.

That moment occurs to me almost daily. The way she'd screamed...So loud and desperate that I had to throw up a sound shield so any human who heard its first beat would think it had been their imagination, or convince themselves it had been the caw of a gull. When Atlas had reached for her as her own fingers wrapped around the gushing wound in her friend's neck, and she shattered his bones. The look in her astonishingly green eyes when she'd risen, before the recognition set in.

All that rage. So at odds with the humming I can hear as she gets ready now. A habit of which I truly believe she's not aware most of the time. She has a lovely voice–husky, and sweet. I think if she were to actually sing, there would be a soulfulness to it that could bring a crowd to its feet, and tears to their eyes.

Dressed, I walk out of my cabin, my gaze instinctively darting to the end of the hall. His door is open, which means– yes, as I turn to look in the other direction, there he is. Leaning against the wall adjacent to the open washroom door, head tipped back and eyes closed. His face is peaceful–this male who I've almost always seen with no emotion in his eyes, the lines of his face hard. Serenity coats his every feature as Althea's humming fills the hallway.

It's only for a second, because he's heard me open my door, but I know what I saw. Now, bright gold eyes open, and flick to me. His expression settles into one of boredom, as one would expect for a male waiting in line to use the washroom at six in the morning.

Without a word, I move to stand at the opposite side of the door. His eyes track me as I move, as if expecting me to shout to the world that he had been soft for a moment, and who caused that softness. I hold his gaze until I lean against the wall a few feet away from him. Seeming to realize that my silence is assured, he turns away to stare at the wall across from us.

A moment later, at the same time that Atlas's door opens, the humming ceases, there's the splashing of water, and she walks out–Lina right behind her. Althea's still-blonde hair is tied into a loose braid, the thick mass of it hanging to the small of her back, tied off with a thin strip of leather. Shorter locks frame her face, waving to her jaw and collarbone, both exposed by the tank top which reveals more of her upper body than she was ever allowed in that castle. Her sash is around the waist of her skirt instead of her hairline, and I know it's in respect to the plait Lina undoubtedly worked hard on as her friend brushed her teeth.

I'm not the only one who notices the way this accentuates her figure. Atlas looks awed, his eyes darting around her ensemble and her face, as if unsure of what he most wants to take in. Adathan's gaze, on the other hand, travels slowly from her feet to her eyes, and I look away before I have to see whatever emotion might be in them.

I'm not sure if just one or both of those gazes cause the

blush that rises to her cheeks. But I do know whose eyes she holds as it spreads across the bridge of her freckled nose.

"You've struck them dumb, gorgeous," Lina says, linking elbows with her. "Come on. If we don't leave now, we'll slip in their fucking drool. We'll wait for you all on deck." She directs the last part at us, then tugs her friend down the hall, and up the stairs. Both of the males in the hall with me watch them go– at first. After a heartbeat, I see Adathan's jaw feather as he turns away, and he steps into the washroom, closing the door behind him.

⪥

The mess has stopped quieting when the two glamoured women walk into it. They had done so initially out of either wariness or examination of our seemingly human newcomer. Now, chatter continues in its same tone and cadence–though some eyes still watch the pair until they meet a pair of gray, or gold eyes.

As the two walk to the counter, Lina waves, and Althea gives polite nods to some of the sailors, both ignoring others (those whom I've also found to be unpleasant) completely. Althea, though she has plenty of reasons to be afraid of and distrust these males, does not let those emotions show, if she feels them at all. Her shoulders and chin do not waver, and her gait doesn't stutter.

She just so *happens* to have a few guard dogs at her back, too.

Atlas has known some of these sailors for years, and even stops at a few of their tables to speak with them before sitting down. But I don't think for one second that the eyes of the males who I've seen leering at Althea lower to the tables as we pass solely out of respect for him.

No, it seems that Adathan's working on the ship has gotten him a measure of respect from many of the seamen surrounding us as well. That he deserves it, after long days in the sun, doing the hardest jobs whenever he's available to do so, is not something I like to think about. He deserves many things in my mind, none of them good.

It's easier for me to recognize their fear of him. Larger than any other male on the ship, in height and in bulk, though even that I could have written off as genetically lucky, ignoring the amount of work I know it takes to get bulk like that. But then there are the scars.

I'd seen them for the first time a few days ago, when he was assisting Swinger with something on the rigging. Shirt off in the heat of the late morning sun, I could see them even as high up as he'd been. On either side of his spine, and one beside each shoulder blade. The amount of times those must have been reopened, how *deeply* they must have been carved for him to have such substantial scarring, made my stomach turn. And I know, as does everyone else on this ship, that if he is still living, still training, and climbing ropes as easily as he walks across the deck–he is not somebody anyone should cross.

He has other scars on his chest, and abdomen. Smaller, and comparatively superficial. I can tell the difference between those which were doled out in previous years, and those which had been inflicted upon him in the past few weeks. And I get a savage sort of satisfaction knowing that, while we'd delivered the one to his neck, Althea had given him the rest.

So, does she need the guard dogs? No. But she has them.

We all sit at 'our' table, though sometimes the individual seating shifts. Atlas, or Lina sit on Althea's right, and whoever doesn't sits beside me on the opposite side of the table. Sometimes the three of us are on one side. But always, Adathan sits on her left, no one on his other side.

"I have a question," Althea says in Divani, after her first few bites of today's breakfast: bacon, eggs, and toast.

All at once: "Yes?", "Yeah?", and, "What?"

"How does the meat not go bad here?" She takes another bite of bacon, looking around the table.

"Jacks. His majick keeps the icebox cold, and he takes the meats out ahead of time to let them defrost," Atlas answers from her right.

Her brows scrunch together. "So he makes the ice? Or does he freeze the box itself, and *that* keeps it cool?"

"A bit of both," Lina answers around a mouthful of toast, with a shrug of her pale, defined shoulders.

A small frown pulls down the corners of Althea's full lips, and she directs her next question to the male on her left. "Is ice majick like water, or wind majick?"

"Water," he says simply.

"But why can't someone with water powers just...make ice?"

"That's a good question. I've never thought about it before."

"Well, think about it now. I'll wait." Althea straightens, turning back to her plate to take a bite of her eggs. But after a beat of chewing, her eyes move to look sideways at Adathan, causing Atlas and Lina to chuckle, and even I crack a smile.

A smirk pulls up one corner of his mouth, that cheek dimpling. "I suppose it's like...a sink. A sink can run warm, or cold water. But, no matter how hard you turn the handle, the cold water would not become ice. Majick works similarly. A person born with one power could not transform it into another, simply by will."

She nods, bright eyes a bit out of focus as she thinks. Sometimes, in these moments, she finds she has enough knowledge, and continues with whatever she'd been doing before her questions began. And sometimes, her thinking leads her to a new set of queries. Never, however, has the male beside her seemed impatient with either of those processes. And neither have Lina or Atlas ever seemed anything but delighted to explain something to her that she wished to know.

Her brow scrunches again. "So, it's not the same as glamours? Is it the amount of will you put towards the majick, or the level of power in the individual?"

"It's both, I think," Adathan answers her, and Atlas nods in agreement, my chin dipping once–reluctantly–as well. "You can be as strong majickally as you'd like, but if you can't commit to the aim behind the glamour–whether it's for their safety, or for ulterior motives–then it likely won't hold against those with more scrutiny."

There's a look that passes through her honeydew eyes that I don't quite comprehend as she listens to his answer, but she masks it behind more curiosity. "And do you think ability to see past a glamour is about power, too, or more so what you told me in Dahlih? That some don't want to see past comforting lies?" Her final question is quiet, but not weak.

"Both," he repeats. His voice is so gentle, it grates on my stomach, and I hardly restrain myself from curling my lip. As it is, I can't hold back my retort, "No one can see past the glamour her mother placed on her, while Evelyn was able to see past yours."

Althea's jaw tightens, just before a familiar blankness fills her gaze. Adathan's arm grazes hers as he shifts in his seat, and he starts before I can even think on which part of what I said might have triggered the reaction. "Evelyn had more reason than any to see past glamours, serving our kind in the way she does. She doesn't have the luxury of blinding herself. And, as for the–" he grits his teeth against the blood oath, and the pain which accompanies a near slip in obedience. I manage to hide my smirk, but the urge to do so vanishes when he continues.

With more anger in his eyes and in his tone than he's ever

directed at me, he says, "We both know your High Lady's gifts have aided in its retention. And, before you can assume that only the blood oath influenced that title, let me be clear: you disrespect both Thea and the memory of Lydia Cardenia by assuming any other title for her. It will not happen again." He holds my gaze for a couple of heavy heartbeats. Though I refuse to nod for him, he must see the remorse in my eyes for her. He turns to look at the female, his voice and expression markedly softer. "Let's go, sweetheart."

Amidst the utter silence of our table, she stands, then makes her way towards the stairs. He quickly grabs their dishes and stacks them on Jacks's counter before following her.

When I turn, I find both Lina and Atlas giving me disapproving looks, and my hackles raise at first. Then, I huff a sigh, half-rolling my eyes. "I know, okay?" Even over twenty years ago I wasn't very good at thinking before I spoke. It got better with–with *him*, but then...then changing felt too hard, too heavy on a heart and mind already bearing so much.

Atlas's eyes gentle, as if registering all that, but Lina only shrugs, too stiffly to be nonchalant, and resumes her meal. I sigh again. "I'll apologize to her later." And I will. I hadn't intended to hurt her, but I did. "He just..." My knuckles pale as I squeeze my fork hard enough it bends.

"He just cares about her!" Lina shouts, startling me enough that I jump in my seat, and drop my fork. Its clattering on the tabletop is the only sound in the instantly quiet mess until she goes on, her usually happy blue eyes angry, and–and sad. "I know that he is part of your pain, Aunt Ari. I *know* that. But Al was right, that first day on the ship: *none* of this would have happened without Olin. And what those scars I know you've seen, too, tell me–what that blood oath he so obviously loathes tells me, is that he may be just as much a victim of Olin as anyone. And I think you know it, too."

Conversation slowly picks back up throughout the room as I stare at my goddaughter, my heart aching. Her eyes soften as she takes in the devastation in mine. "Hating him isn't helping you. And now it's hurting her. She's our friend, and, whether she's accepted it yet or not, she is our Lady. And she has asked that he remain with us. I'm not asking you to like it, but I am asking you to start trusting her, and her judgment. Maybe... maybe let yourself see that she wouldn't have brought him if she thought, for even a second, that he's like his father."

I know she's right, deep down.

It's just that blocking that depth is the nearly impenetrable wall that has not fallen since I lost my mate. It will take more than the words Lina just spoke to knock it down.

13

NOT EVEN A LITTLE; NOT EVEN AT ALL

ON STIFF LEGS THAT MOVE ONLY BY WILL, I GET TO THE STAIRS leading to the cabins, and keep going. I keep going, because I will not fall apart where anyone can see. Through a haze in my mind and the blur in my vision, I find my cabin, barely hearing the intentionally loud footsteps follow me in.

The agony begs to be released, but I don't know how. While breaths gasp in and out of my too-thin throat, and my spine and hands shudder with the all-encompassing desire to surrender, my body finds one solution. One thing it can do, when I will not allow it to cry, or scream.

My fist swings for the wooden wall. Pain, in an entirely different form than that in my heart, explodes through my knuckles. And it's such a relief compared to the feeling in my chest that I do it again. And again.

Before I can strike it a fourth time, my fist is clasped in a far larger hand, a hulking figure slipping between me and the wall.

99

I growl, trying to wrench it free, and swing my other hand into a hard torso.

"That's right, Thea. Hit me," he orders, releasing my fist.

I slam both of my palms into his chest with a snarl. When I repeat the assault, this time throwing all my weight into it so that his back hits the wall, I scream, "*I hate you!*"

"I know you do," he replies, his voice rough. I shove him again, and in my proximity, he slips my dagger from its sheath at my hip, then holds the hilt out to me. "Hit me, cut me, kill me, love. I won't stop you."

I take the dagger, hardly hearing him over my own roar. "*NO!*" Then I thrust the blade, hard, right into–

The wall. The sides of my fists pound his chest twice before my palms open, and then one hand is around his throat, and I feel his pulse thudding beneath my fingers. Pounding, and my magic syncs mine to it so that my vision shudders with the force of my trembling veins–

Then the short dagger I'd hidden in my waistband is being held before me. Breathing heavy, I at last look up into his golden eyes, even brighter than usual now with the emotion in them. I recognize this offering for what it is: one more chance. After failing to take his life in that basement; after removing my knife from his throat in that clearing between the pines; after saving him when an arrow shredded through his neck. One more chance to kill him.

I take the dagger, and press its tip against his carotid, between his jaw and my hand, holding his gaze all the while. "You would let me slit your throat?" I ask lowly, trailing the edge along his skin.

"Yes."

I continue the route of the blade down to his chest, over his heart. "Or stab you in the heart?"

I can sense its continued hammering, but his face holds no fear. "Yes," he breathes.

I push the blade in just enough to pierce his skin, and blood immediately stains the fabric of his shirt over the wound. The scent of him strengthens, saturating my every breath. "Why should I give you what you think you deserve?" He doesn't so much as wince as I push harder, and the dagger sinks in a few more millimeters.

"Because *you* deserve to do whatever the fuck you like for the rest of your days," he answers, and that's anger that brims in his expression. Not at the fact that I've got a dagger half an inch in his skin, but at the injustices of my life thus far.

I step into him, so close now that I feel his heat against my skin. "You want to know what I hate about you?" I tilt my head to the side, my chin high to hold his gaze.

"Tell me." Still, his heart thuds beneath the knife, as if trying to move closer to the surface; to be pierced by the wicked blade, like even it believes its end would be justified.

My voice is barely above a whisper as I obey his command. "Your kindness. Your strength. Your smile. The way that you're *always* there for me, even when I didn't know that I needed you. Your very existence. I *hate*," the word rasps through my teeth, "that those things make it impossible to hate you."

Surprise burns through the grief in his eyes, but I'm not done. My voice is as gentle as the hand around his throat as I finish, "I hate the way that *not* hating you has opened up more room for me to hate myself." I withdraw the dagger from his chest, and it clatters to the floor. As I place my hand over the hurt I inflicted, his blood covers my hand, as warm as the scarred skin around it.

I heal the wound beneath my palm, and release his throat to trail my thumb across his cheek. Amidst the utterly silent room, even Adathan's breathing having stilled, I drop my hands, and walk out of the cabin.

14

BLUE

DION - 15 YEARS EARLIER

WHEN HE WAS CONSCIOUS, MANY OF HIS BREATHS WERE thoroughly entwined with a pain so exquisite, he wondered if he would ever feel anything else again. If there would be, in his immortal life, any sensation that was not an agony which tormented him until–

When he was unconscious, he did not see the images of his own body being cut open, or ripped apart. He did not see the faces of anybody he'd ever known. He could not even remember what they might have looked like. All he knew of faces now were two pairs of eyes: one dark, and one gold.

No, he did not dream at all. Rather, when he closed his eyes, and the sweetness of sleep found him, the strangest thing happened. Instead of a blackness, complete by his own shut lids and the dark of the cell he lived within, he saw–blue.

A deep, calming blue, the shade of the bottomless sea, or the sky right before night swallowed it whole. It held him, like driftwood on the easy waves beneath the moon and stars. It sometimes lulled him into a rest so lovely that he woke feeling content, rather than frightened.

He was so often that: scared. Of what those males were going to do to him today; of what they would ask him, which he would not answer; of what they'd already found out, that had them silently carving him open, no more questions spilling from their masked lips.

He hoped for little, but when he remembered that hope was something he could do, it was for the source of that blue. He prayed that she was all of the things he could not be. Happy, and fierce, and beautiful.

He could not remember her face, had shoved her name so far back into his mind that he dared not bring it forth. But sometimes, he would hear her voice, saying his. And it sounded like what he did in his mind as he thought of her: a prayer.

15

GONE IS THE INNOCENCE

MY BREATHING IS RAGGED, HISSING THROUGH MY TEETH AS I PULL myself another foot up the rope. My wrapped hands–courtesy of the shirt I'd gotten in Dahlih–ache with the effort, but I barely recognize it past the determination in my mind. I look up at where the rope attaches to the highest crossbeam of the mast. Just three more yards above my head.

I allow myself to bring my body against the rope, curling my thighs and chest around it to take some of the load off of my back. It hardly does any good, given the full body work I've been putting in to get this high up, but it does allow me to take a deeper breath with my diaphragm in a resting position.

Despite the fact that the sun has barely risen, sweat coats my body. I wear a tank top to keep the rising temperature at bay, but not even the early morning breeze off the sea cuts through the heat surging through my temples, down my neck and chest.

I've been doing this every other day since my conversation with Adan. The first time, I'd only made it halfway up. The second, about ten feet higher. I've made it past that point now by several feet, and have a hard time believing I can't pull myself up just ten more times.

With that in mind, I take one more steadying breath, and keep going, ignoring the screaming in my back and arms. *It's just one more minute, you can do anything for a minute*, I think to myself. And when it passes, and there are just a couple of feet left, I find no reason I can't get those last couple of feet.

My hands find the wood of the mast, and with every last bit of strength I have, I wrap my arms around it, then curl my lower body up to do the same with my legs. I maneuver into a sitting position, and then I'm just...there. Breathing hard and heavy, body aching, sweat dripping from my every pore. I unsling the waterskin from around my back, and take a long pull from it. Wiping my mouth with the back of my hand, I look out at the sea, gilded a soft yellow by the rising sun. My lips pull up in a small smile.

Even as I imagine that I can see all the way to Cerasche, it stays. I'd finally mustered the courage to ask Ciaragen and Atlas about Iris and the rest of my family a couple of days ago. A healer had, in fact, gotten to Iris quickly after we left. No, they do not know what I am. That will be on me to tell them, if I choose to.

I suppose I'm glad, just a bit, that I have another week or so before we arrive in Ardhavi. That I have no way to get a letter to them before then. I have time to think about what I might say.

I hear a slow clap from below that breaks me from my heavy thoughts. I look down, my stomach swooping a bit at the height. Even at this distance, I recognize the breadth of him; that short mop of dark hair.

I hadn't talked to Adathan for the rest of that day after we'd spoken about my hate, and it's utter lack thereof, for him. Hadn't known what *to* say. But, the next morning, when he'd brought my breakfast to the table, both of us arriving before the rest of our group, I'd thanked him, and then we just...*were*, again. But–different. Deeper. And not altogether innocently.

Between him finally not just hearing but understanding that I don't loathe him as he believed I did–only keeping him around out of debt, or for the knowledge he has–and me having finally voiced what's been in my head since our final day in the woods, things began shifting after that conversation. That desire I'd almost allowed myself to recognize in Dahlih, only suppressing it for *him*, took shape–a blurry, ill-formed one, thanks to my inexperience, but still. And for him...

"Nice job, sweetheart," he calls up to me.

The grin returning to my lips, I reply, "Care to join me?"

"I have a better idea." And the tone, the way I can *hear* his smirk...

I'm already shaking my head. "No. No way."

"Get out of your mind, Thea. You know you can do it. What's the alternative?"

I know he means having to make the climb all the way down the rope, but I answer, "The alternative is I become a pancake on the deck."

"You think I'd let that happen?"

A blush rises to my already heated cheeks, and my lips twist to the side. "Didn't think so," he says to my silence. "Come down."

An order if I've ever heard one, and something about it has my blush spreading, and my slowed heart rate picking back up. I bite my lip against the strange thrill. "Or what?" I call back.

There's no response for a moment, and, even though he still yells a bit for his voice to reach me, he somehow makes his voice sound low. "You want to find out?" And my heart bursts into a gallop, because I'm the most interesting sort of terrified to say yes.

Instead of answering at all, I get my feet under me, and stand up on the beam, bracing a hand on the mast. My already-hammering pulse pounds through me, but I take a steadying breath, and another as I close my eyes.

Get out of your mind. The mind that withholds my true abilities. My true strength. A fact I'd only learned, once again, because of Adan. Though he couldn't tell me about who the High Lady of Sabrian is to me, thanks to the blood oath, he had never been barred from speaking about her majick.

That talk had resulted in us agreeing on two things. First, that I had to learn how to escape the block in my mind. Not just momentarily, or in fits of emotion–as I had with the faerie light, and tackling him to the ground–but long-term.

And second, that I must also learn how to build my own shields *within* my mind. Because, regardless of the fact that it had been done for my safety, I didn't want the High Lady of Sabrian to be able to influence my mind ever again. Nor anyone else, for that matter.

So, not only is Adan still training me in swordplay, majickal and hand-to-hand combat, and in glamours, he is now also teaching me how to build those shields, and how to escape the one put upon me.

The last isn't hard, per se. It's just...annoying. Like trying to see through fogged glass. Just as, if not more annoying, is how it only *truly* helps my strength. Adan says it still blocks my sight and hearing because I can't 'picture' the Fae capacity for those things. But, since I *have* seen what Fae bodies are capable of...

I open my eyes, and, while Adan is no more clear from this distance than he'd been a moment ago, I can almost *feel* it as he grins, knowing I've done it.

Then I step off the beam as easily as I would take a step

across the floor, and free-fall until the deck is just feet away. I soften my knees, and land in a crouch, my braid falling over a shoulder. When I look up, I find Adan still grinning, a heat in his eyes as powerful as the sun they liken. It's gone in a heartbeat, but it was there. I'm certain of it.

His expression settles into one of pride, and it makes my heart squeeze in my chest; a warmth that combines with the thrill that still has it racing. My body reacts before my mind can stop it, and then I'm leaping from my crouch, onto him.

He doesn't so much as sway at the unexpected contact, the weight I've thrown utterly to his mercy. When my arms wrap around his neck, my feet hovering off the ground, I think, at first, his arms wind around my waist out of instinct. But, when they tighten, the thick muscle of them warming and waking me...that's intentional. I turn my face into the space between his neck and shoulder, and murmur, "Thank you," into his skin, greedily breathing in the scent of him.

"I knew you could do it," he says quietly, the gravel of his voice skittering along my bones, the breath that caresses my neck raising gooseflesh in its wake. I pull my face back enough to look into his, closer than it has ever been, and am shocked into stillness at what I see. The gold of his eyes, flecked with silver so bright it burns; the shallow lines of old scars; the deep tan of his skin that otherwise smoothly stretches across such strong features.

It takes only a second for me to absorb all of this, and he's gently setting me down when I finish. My hands stay at his traps, his far more tentative at my waist, and I must look as enraptured as I feel, because he says, "What?"

I don't force myself to consider my answer before telling him, "You're just very handsome, that's all." Shock colors his expression, and I bite my lower lip before retreating out of his touch, dropping my own arms to my sides. "Breakfast?" I ask, hitching my thumb over my shoulder, towards the steps to the mess. I don't wait for his answer before turning and walking that direction.

He follows me closely enough that I can feel the charge between our bodies; an awareness of his existence that my skin revels within, anticipating his nearness as much as if he were actually touching me. And I know I'm truly in trouble when I only wish he was doing just that.

16

SCENTS & SENSIBILITIES

LINA - DAY 20

I ROLL MY EYES AT MY BEST FRIEND, AND TALK PAST MY toothbrush as I look at him in the mirror. He stands behind me, leaning against the doorframe of the washroom. "Just because they hugged once–"

Atlas gives me a withering look, but the condescension in it is minimized by the pain he's trying hard to conceal. "She hasn't let me hold her like that since Cerasche, Lina. I'm not so naive to believe that the first time she lets anyone do so, it's accidental."

I sigh, and hold up a finger so that I can rinse my mouth in the small sink powered, like the shower, by the water system Javi rigged for his ship. Once done, I turn to face him, tilt my head, and ask, "So, what are you thinking, then?"

His lips tighten, and he gives me a look that has brought many males to heel since he hit his maturity. I only raise my brows, waiting.

His jaw flexes, and his gaze hits his boots. "I'm thinking that, if I ever had a chance, I just lost it."

My expression softens, and I step closer to him, so that he's forced to meet my eyes. And when he does, a soft breath escapes me, my heart clenching in my chest. "You love her."

Agony lances through his eyes, and he doesn't answer–doesn't *need* to answer. "Atlas..."

Some of the pain is replaced with anger. "No."

I huff a breath through my nose, and mirror his posture, crossing my arm over my chest. "Why not?"

He straightens, filling the small doorway and towering over me. Not hard to do, but still. "Because she deserves the dignity of her decision. So much has been either decided for her, forced upon her, or both. I won't make her see me when she's already decided to let me go."

I purse my lips, because he's being gallant. He's being the kind, wonderful male he's always been. But, the thing is, that male has a tendency to be selfless to a fault.

Enter Lina.

"Listen," I say, and, though his jaw tightens again, he does. "She hugged him first. But, I bet you he won't be the last. Atlas, maybe...this is her healing. Maybe this is her *accepting* us. Letting us in, after all she's been through. Don't you think she *deserves* the chance to let *you* in, without you deciding beforehand that she won't?"

He sucks on the inside of his cheek, considering. It's when the pain in his eyes eases that I know I've succeeded. "You're right."

I rest my hand on his arm, and give him a small smile, then pat that same spot with not a little patronization. "I know."

The corners of his mouth tilt up, and the rest of the sorrow and pain in his face give way to humor. Then, with that damned

Fae speed, he hooks his arm over my shoulders, and pulls me close to his chest, smooshing my face and hair with one large hand. I swat at him with my hand and my elbow, but he only lets me escape after planting a wet, smacking kiss to my temple.

"*Blech*," I groan, wiping it away with more force than necessary before quickly swiping out to rub his own saliva on his cotton-covered torso. "Next time you do that, I'll punch you in the dick."

"You'd have to catch me first, shortstack."

And then he's running up the stairs, me behind him, my roar of fury marred by the laugh that echoes his.

⇔

No one would ever know the sort of conversation I just had with Atlas by the way he talks and acts at breakfast. He is doing, and will, I'm sure, continue to do his damndest to be the friend to her that she deserves, even if he wants more. Even if I catch the way he looks at her while she speaks, or when he thinks no one else is looking.

Still, if he's going to act, then I'll be his bloody co-star. Not once do I glance at him sideways; no assessment, or questioning stares. I eat with just as much enthusiasm as usual, and talk with the other members of our little group.

Al, on the other hand, has barely spoken. Her head is leaned into her hand, and those fingers fiddle with the earring in the top of her left ear while she picks at her food with her fork. I've caught Adathan looking at her with a furrow in his dark brows a couple of times, but he hasn't asked her about it yet. Which I think has something to do with the fact that, as she leans into her hand, the top of her arm has maintained contact with his, like it's grounding her.

Then, in a lull in the conversation we've been having since sitting down, she says, "I have a question."

It's fucking adorable how she leads with that preamble every time. I also don't miss the fact that, whenever I'm present, she speaks Divani, even though the rest of the table can all speak the Ceraschen that's native to her. And, it's way prettier—flowing and elegant, where I feel like Divani is choppy and harsh in comparison.

Adathan answers her for us all. "Yes?"

"Do all Fae have a scent? Faeries, too?"

Adathan audibly confirms while the rest of us nod.

"What do *I* smell like?" She blushes as she asks it, but I did the same over ten years ago. Pretty much when I had my first crush on a female who worked in a bakery in Colina, and decided I cared about it.

Her blush deepens when everyone hesitates, thinking. "Is it bad?"

"No, no, just...complex," Atlas reassures her quickly. "Your scent is like...walking through a meadow in the sunshine. Grass, and flowers, and bark, and soil. Like the earth, I guess you could say." My friend's high cheekbones have darkened, but he licks his lips and goes on. "It's layered with...it's hard to explain."

"The breath you take after you're no longer in pain," softly comes Adathan's voice from across the table. Al turns her gaze to him, the small smile she'd given Atlas as he answered falling. Her breathing goes shallow, and the intensity with which he looks back at her, combined with the gentle words of his answer, is so intimate I almost avert my eyes. "The taste of peace after agony; fresh, and warm."

The table is silent, the three of us exchanging glances while the two of them seem to forget we're there at all. And, for the sake of the male beside me, I say, "Well, all I smell right now is bacon," and take a bite of the crispy piece Jacks gave me.

They turn to me, a sort of daze clearing from their expressions, and becoming near-twin smirks. Still, I know I don't imagine it when Al moves a touch closer to Adathan.

When her eating slows after a moment, though, I also know why. "What's your question, gorgeous?"

She looks up at me from her plate, a grateful half-grin lifting her full lips and lighting those insane eyes. "I was wondering if all powers also have scents."

Ciaragen's and Atlas's brows furrow, and Adathan shakes his head. Her gaze sliding to him, her own brow scrunches slightly. Before she can voice her confusion, he says, "Only certain powers."

Despite how she has calmed that angry part of her over the past week, I expect Ciaragen to snap at him in some way. Whether for the vagueness of his answer, or for yet another thing he appears to know more about than her. But, she doesn't.

Now, it's not anger, but contemplation that fills her gaze. "You know, I only ever could scent Dion's power...but I never thought about it. It always just seemed a part of him. But then– then, in the Hall, Olin's power had a scent, too."

Al opens her mouth to speak, but a loud crash sounds in the kitchen, followed almost instantly by a gut-wrenching scream of agony. Al is out of her seat in less than a heartbeat, Adathan behind her, the shock that has seized the rest of us having no impact on a trained healer–and the male who, I think, will follow her anywhere; through any danger.

I rush from the table a beat later with Atlas, Ciaragen shoving us behind her so that she enters the kitchen ahead of us, her arm remaining out at chest height, barring us from entering until she clears the space.

Once through, I see what the commotion was; a huge pan

lies on the floor, bacon scattered around it. And then there's Jacks, heaving gasping breaths through his teeth, and his *skin–*

Al kneels beside him on the ground, and he stares up at her with agonized silver eyes as she lays a palm gently on his cheek. Her other hand hovers over one of his seared and blistered arms. I gasp softly as the ethereal yellow light passes from her, to him, and burnt skin begins to heal. And, maybe I imagine it, but it almost...almost looks like her irises, the veins in her hands–they glow, too. She hardly seems to notice any of it as she murmurs, "You know, when I was a girl, I used to run all around my home.

"There was a library, and so many rooms, the Great Hall... but my favorites–my favorites were the gardens." One arm healed, she moves toward his torso, shooting such a quick look to Adathan that it's hardly there at all. He mutters a quick apology to Jacks before unsheathing the dagger from Al's thigh, and slicing through Jacks's shirt, revealing more burns. Still, she speaks as she moves her majick to them, her voice so melodic that even the males who gathered behind the counter and the doorway to examine the commotion seem enraptured.

"We had three at the castle. One was enormous; sprawling with trees and flowers and trellises. Another was small, but with so many carefully manicured bushes, and jasmine that climbed pillars of the same marble we had in the Hall. But there was a third one, even smaller than the last."

She moves onto his other arm. "It was a bit forgotten, I think. The flowers grew over onto the pathways, and there was a little iron bench that had been there for so long that whatever protection magic upon it had expired, allowing it to rust. I only found it last year, to be honest; just before my twentieth birthday. But, almost every day between that one, and my last, I would go to that garden, and I would sit on that bench for *hours*, finding this strange sort of..."

With all that's left to be healed are some shallow, small burns on his neck and face, Jacks asks quietly, "What?"

She gives him a soft, lovely smile, and brushes her thumb along his cheek as the final burn seals and the skin is back to its usual blue. "Peace."

Adathan slides her dagger back into its sheath, and holds out a hand to help her to her feet. She takes it, and rises gracefully. She reaches to help her patient up, too, but Atlas beats her to it, quickly stepping around Ciaragen and I to offer Jacks an arm. Once up, the male bows to Al. "Thank you. Thank you, Lady."

She dips her chin to him. "You're welcome."

I turn to watch them walk back to the table, finding much of the crew doing the same. A grin pulls at my lips. How easily she wraps everyone around those pretty fingers, without even trying. I love watching it happen, especially to these sea-hardened shits.

The rest of the meal is far less eventful, and the remainder of the day follows suit. We're probably about a week away from Ardhavi at this point, and I can't wait to arrive at the port city, and be that much closer to my home and my parents.

When we left Sabrian on this Obalan ship, it was under the assumption that the entire trip would be less than twelve weeks. Then, Atlas had learned of that *tradition* they had in place. And of course, we couldn't leave, allowing the Lady of Sabrian to be married off. Not because of the marriage itself–though it wasn't *not* that, I guess. From what his letter had said at the time, though, Atlas believed she didn't want to participate in the tradition, but she was made to think that it was imperative for her nation's peace, so she was doing it anyway. Desire and happiness be damned (his words, after just two weeks, the sop. How blind had I been to not know it was love until this morning?).

Well, anyway, the forced marriage of our Lady was definitely a good enough reason to stay. For what a certain Lord-turned-server had to say about it, and for the fact that it could very well keep her from returning home within the next decade, it could not come to pass.

So, stay we did. For three weeks of the month, traveling down the coast and back for Javi to do his High Lord trading thing, and the rest spent in Dahlih, we received reports from Atlas from within the Ceraschen castle. I explored where I could during that time, usually either having Javi glamour me, or just pulling my hair over my ears, but found it...unsettling pretty quickly.

The way they *stared*. I don't know if it was my skin, my hair, or my arm, but I felt eyes on me everywhere I went, and not in a good way. So, I decided to spend the majority of my time on the ship. Now, with about thirteen weeks on board and two more to go, I can't fucking wait to step foot on not just land, but a land I know and trust. The land I was born and raised in.

Mama had told me who and what I truly am when I was eight. I'd always known I was adopted–she and mum are both females, and even majick hasn't figured out a way to allow procreation outside of male-female relationships. But, even when I saw that I was slower than the children my age; when I learned that I couldn't hear or smell or see as well as they could...I never thought it was because I was human, and not the Fae I'd been raised to be.

Part of me has always felt inadequate because of that. Being the slowest, the weakest. But also for not being good enough for my birth parents.

I would never tell any of that to my mums, of course. It would only hurt them, and nothing they could say would change my mind, anyway. That I'm loved, and strong, and kind–I know all those things. And I still feel: *not enough*.

Those thoughts came bursting through my head the moment I'd shaken Al's hand in the hall her first day on the ship, and Atlas told me her name. I was meeting the daughter my High Lord and High Lady should have had. My Lady, yes, but also the woman–female who my birth parents had deemed as good enough. Better than what had been born to them.

I'd considered avoiding her. Maybe even hating her. But then I saw the muted agony in her eyes. Learned that she not only lost the life she'd always known, her entire *identity*, but also her mother. Her friends. And I couldn't hate her, seeing that. She was innocent of the hurts her parents had inflicted on me, after all.

And then, just hours after arriving on the ship, hours after she could have decided to hate me, too, instead she invited me in. Something just...clicked. An ease which I've only felt with those I've known my whole life.

I'd obviously recognized that she's beautiful. Stunning, even, with that face, supple curves, and strong lines of muscle. And yet I hadn't looked at her as anything but the friend she's turned out to be. Not just because she's only interested in males, but, well–I don't know. It was like my brain and body, my very *soul*, recognized what we both needed to be to each other. A female friend and ally, with perhaps the best understanding of the loss of identity that came with learning what we now know about ourselves.

"All done, gorgeous," she says now, her Ceraschen accent lilting the words as she pats my shoulders, interrupting my thoughts. She grips me there, and turns me towards the washroom mirror. And, in spite of myself, my eyes widen at what they see.

"You like it?" Al asks hopefully as I stare and stare at the way my curls are defined as they never have been before. She didn't style it otherwise; didn't need to. The usually cloud-like mass of it shines in wide spirals down to my waist, and looking at it, I hardly notice the way my arm ends there, too.

And, though I mean for it to come out irreverently, my voice is as soft as I've ever heard it when I reply, "I fucking *love* it."

Behind me, she does her best approximation of beaming: a tilt to both sides of her mouth, and a light brightening her lovely eyes. "I used to do it for my sister."

My own grin turns a bit, but I quickly distract both myself and her from the change by asking, "Are you sure you don't want to come with us later?" Referring to our little group hanging with the crew in the common room after dinner. Drinking, dancing, laughing. All things she would enjoy–

If she let herself. Her lips drop, a forced pull at the corners keeping them from going completely flat. She busies herself with putting away the oil Ciaragen had let us borrow. "Not tonight."

I manage to stop myself from asking when. I know it's so much more complicated than her not wanting to come dance in the common room with the rest of us. It's her not believing she *deserves* that sort of joy, that sort of *fun*. And I may have only known her for less than three weeks, but I know that if I bring it up, if I tell her how wrong she is–she will both shut it down and shut me out. At least until she believes I won't bring it up again.

"Althea? Lina? Are you in there?" Atlas's voice calls from the other side of the door. Damn my stupid human ears for not hearing his approach.

"No," I tell him, and humor lights Al's features.

A pause. "Can I open the door?"

"Sorry, no boys allowed," I reply, releasing my own tension to tease him, in favor of the relief it brings her. "What do you want?"

"It's dinner time, genius. I came to get you guys to eat."

"You're gonna eat *us*? Atlas, I'm sure whatever Jacks has cooked will be fine, you don't have to resort to all that."

A sigh loud enough that even I can hear it through the door. "I'll see you both there."

A moment later, on the deck of the *Burning Rose*, the evening sun pours over us. Some males still work, waiting until their counterparts finish eating to take their turn. I catch a few of them looking at me, and the stunner at my side. Al, ever demure, gives them polite nods and waves, ignoring or not noticing the desire in their eyes. I'm not so mature; I send a couple of them winks. I may have a preference for females and non binaries, but males get the job done fine, too.

Al pauses a few yards from the mast to look up, shielding her eyes from the sun with a hand. I follow her gaze; he's not hard to find. Up, as he almost always is, on the rigging, so high that my chin is tilted completely vertically when she calls his name. I wonder if she realizes how her voice caresses the shape of it.

"It's dinner time," she tells him.

He holds a rope, leaning at a dangerous angle to call down to her, "I'll be down in five minutes. Save me a plate, sweetheart."

"I'm going to eat your bread if you're not down in ten."

"That's fair."

I grin at that, and find her doing the same. I wonder if she realizes how easily she does so around him.

17

IRREVOCABLE

DION - 13 YEARS EARLIER

HE SCREAMED AS THE DARK ONE SLICED INTO HIM WITH A THIN knife. Wondered, as it happened, if he would ever become desensitized to the pain. How long that might take, and how long it had already been, he did not know.

"You just have to say the words, brother," a male said from the doorway. He leaned casually against the stone of it, unaffected by the noises of the cell before him.

He could not look at the male. Something about his face, the wholeness of it and the body beneath it, struck him in a way the tormentor's fists never could.

Instead, he looked at the golden one who, even after all this time, had yet to do anything but push the iron-filled needle into his flesh each day. He saw nothing but those uniquely bright eyes, dulled by the time spent in this place. Nonreactive to him, on his knees, screaming, as he had been ever since *he'd* been the one screaming in a cell.

When no words followed the end of the scream, the male in the doorway strode forward. With a disgusted expression, he stepped into the filth on the floor, and crouched, forcing their gazes to meet.

"Swear the blood oath to me," the male murmured. When he only panted in response, those familiar green-gold eyes flicked up, accompanied by a slight nod.

The knife once more opened him up. He'd stopped paying attention to where long ago.

The male tilted his head. "If you do not answer to me, you will know nothing but this place, and this pain, for the rest of your days. Is that what you want?"

No. He did not want that. But he also knew, for reasons which had long since abandoned him, that he did not want to bind his blood to this male. That perhaps this sort of pain would end, but another would begin. And he was too frightened to face whatever that might be.

So, rather than give the answer that would be a lie, he spat in the male's face. Red splattered across a clean-shaven cheek, and those terrible eyes closed for several too-fast heartbeats.

When they reopened, the cold in them rivaled that of the cell. Not breaking eye contact, he said to the dark one, "Remember what I said about *no irreversible damage*? Forget it. Just don't kill him."

And with that, he stood, and walked out. The golden one's gaze followed him until something was irrevocably severed, and the scream that echoed in the cell brought that golden focus back to him, on his knees.

18

ALWAYS

I IGNORE THE INTENSE RELUCTANCE IN MY HEART AND IN MY GUT, forcing all the courage I have in this moment to the surface as Adan and Li gather the dishes from our table. Muster it, and then look at the male across from me, and say, "Atlas, can you come with me for a moment?"

Those storm gray eyes widen slightly with surprise, and then his brows narrow in concern. "Of course."

He stands from his place, and I use the last ember of bravery to flick my gaze over to the hulking male by the counter. And wish I hadn't when I see how tight his back, the only part of him facing me, is. When, even as the dishes are so carefully set down, he does not turn.

I wish I could mind-speak like the Sabriani High Lady, or that it wouldn't hurt Atlas for me to shout, *It's not what you think* to Adan, as the nothing that may be becoming something between us demands. Since neither of those options are possible, I instead turn from that something, and walk towards the steps out of the mess, Atlas at my side.

He behaves with me now *almost* as I have seen him interact with Li these weeks. Not quite as familiar, but just as friendly. And I might have been able to continue to call it that until the all-but platonic way he'd touched my face.

I'd considered it as I'd done Li's hair again last night. With how much of it she has, it had taken over an hour, giving me time to think. And with my fingers, practiced as they are from doing Iris's hair once a week from the time I was fifteen, all the way until she married and moved away, I had been able to focus on what I might say to Atlas. What I *could* say, to make things clear.

Because we might have been something once. Before heartbreak and rage and grief seized me. Before *he* existed for me.

For the man and woman we had been weeks ago, alone together in a garden, whispered words of wanting between us; for that 'once', and for this male who has been nothing but kind to me since, I felt a choice had to be made. I could not self-ishly linger between the two of them any longer; the week between his touch and Adan's had been cruel enough.

I can almost feel his confusion growing as I continue towards the steps that lead to the cabins. But I don't stop until we're in mine, and I shut the door behind him. When I turn from it to look at him, his expression is wary, but with dawning comprehension.

Then, pain fills his eyes, too quickly for him to conceal, though he looks down at his boots anyway. "Ah," is all he says, a choked sound.

My heart strains. "Atlas…" I manage to get out, my throat tight. All that thinking of what I might say, and the words are stuck right above my heart. This reluctance isn't fair to him, though. I cannot give him all of me, and he deserves someone who can.

He looks up, his eyes shining even in the dim evening light. Silver lining that captivating gray. And he gives me a tight smile. "I know."

I don't bother clearing my throat. "I'm sorry," I tell him, because I am. Sorry that I'm hurting him, sorry for the loss of something that could have been, but never got to be.

"Don't be. I..." he takes a quick, heavy breath. "I just want you to be happy."

I clench my jaw against new the wave of emotion that rises in me. "I want the same for you."

"I am happy, Althea. Just sad. I don't mind being both for a little while." A tear passes the uptilted corner of his mouth, as if emphasizing his point.

Why does my heart splinter? Why can't it stand by me in this choice I've made, regardless of how I'd like to not make it at all? To it, and to him, I say, "I changed that night, Atlas. If I hadn't..."

"The ifs don't matter," he interjects softly. The words I'd shouted at him that first day on this ship in Javi's quarters. A quiet exhale escapes me, and my shoulders drop.

"No. I guess they don't."

We stand there in silence for a moment. His tears fade, leaving only their tracks to be seen in the light coming through the porthole. My own, unwanted but there, choke me, unwilling as I am to release them yet. I tighten my jaw against them once more, and hope he can see in my eyes that the movement is anything but angry.

He gives me a small smile. "I know it's cliche, but...still friends, yeah?"

A short chuckle huffs thickly through my nose, the sound anything but joyful, but I nod. "Yeah. Always friends."

He dips his chin, that smile sad–but happy. "Always," he repeats, and touches his fingers to his brow in a mock salute.

My own tiny grin tilts my lips, though I put as much force behind it as I'm sure he did his, and I return the gesture. With that, he only says, "Good night, Althea," then turns back to the door. I just get the chance to quickly say it back before he's through the threshold, and I hear his footsteps creak up the stairs.

After a long moment where I stare through the open doorway, my heart heavy and light all at once, I walk to the door with only the intention to close it. So, I'm not sure what makes me do it, but once there, I look out into the hallway, towards the stairwell.

At the foot of the steps stands the familiar figure of him, his head turned towards the stairs, as if still watching someone walk up them. I place my hand on the doorknob, and the metal clicks softly at the contact.

That face whirls to look at me, and the final dregs of daylight allow me to see the confusion, and the shock there.

I look back at him, not breaking from the intensity of that gaze. Only when the surprise fades from his expression, steadily replaced with a hesitant realization, do I slip my eyes away from his. As he had with me last week, I rake my gaze up from his boots to his eyes, taking in every inch. Each curve and line of powerful muscle, imagining I can see the scars and skin beneath. And I know that by the time my eyes meet his, they hold the same sort of heat his had then.

I let him see that for a few pounding heartbeats before I step back into my cabin, and close the door.

19
THE DAY

I ROUSE FROM THE NIGHTMARE, TEARS ALREADY STREAMING DOWN my temples, and into the soft down of my pillow. Quickly, I clap a hand over my mouth, stifling the sob that breaks past my nonexistent control, searing its way up from my chest in a burst of pain greater than any physical blow I could ever receive.

It's the same one, the same day, every year. The day my mate, my love, my *soul*, was truly taken from me.

The years without him had been unbearable, and yet I'd borne them. For the sake of my High Lord and High Lady, who had made a sacrifice of their own ten years prior. For their still-building rebellion; not yet mighty enough to take on the brutes who supported the male on the high throne. For them, and for our people, I'd waited.

As long as I was able. But my will is not steel. I'd never claimed it to be so.

No rationality could keep me from going to him any longer.

Ten years, I'd lived, knowing the torment he must be enduring for us. For me. And I was to–I was to *let* him? To be unwilling to make my own sacrifice, and remain satisfied with the one he made?

No longer, I had thought. And I knew exactly who thought the same, felt the same. Who would come with me on the suicidal mission to save the only part of my soul I still valued.

The sobs wrack me in earnest, and only my shreds of dignity have me erecting a sound shield around my room as I remember.

20

FOR

WHEN HE HEARD THE CELL DOOR GROAN OPEN, HE HARDLY restrained himself from making a very similar noise.

There was no difference between the exhaustion he felt just after they finished with him, and the kind he experienced at all other hours of the day. Only a small difference remained in the level of pain–something he feared they were coming to know. For, if their current methods ceased to draw lasting, sufficient results, he couldn't help but wonder what they would do to ensure his suffering was brought anew.

There was a permanent agony that seemed to pulse through his organs, his skin, his blood. Sleeping or awake, he felt it. And still, he could sleep. Still, he was ready for them when they arrived the next day.

His reaction therefore could only mean that they had either bled him too much yesterday, or that they were back early. He could not tell– had no sun to inform him of the time. And they did sometimes forget that, with the amount of iron in and on him, if they made him bleed too much, he was hardly of any use or fun to them the next day.

He thought *they*, even though the two that had overseen his torment over the years had specific roles. The dark one did the cutting, the breaking, the carving. The golden one, even after so much time to learn, still only ever watched after injecting the iron into his veins each day. Still, he would find himself gazing at the golden one as the dark one tore him apart. He didn't do it to make the male uncomfortable, though surely it did. Strangely, though there was no emotion in his bright gaze, holding it made him feel more connected to his life than he usually did.

Usually, in fact, he had little concern to whether their ministrations would end his life one day. He sometimes felt an ache in his chest–an ache which felt like it was half within him, and half without–at the thought. But, most of the time, he knew that the part of him which lived outside of himself would live on–and would be far happier there than he was in here.

But here that strange golden gaze held him, when he was awake. When he slept, it was that deep sea blue that kept him company, while dreams and memories could not. He knew that the color, and the half of him which was not here, were of the same origin. He knew that the little purpose he had left in his life was for her.

He heard noises that were unusual for their preparations as he thought about all of that. But his eyes still ached a bit from whatever they had done to them last time, and so he kept them closed, and only waited. They would get on with it soon enough.

He heard them approach, and prepared for the stab of the needle as they delivered the iron into his blood. What he felt instead was as foreign to him now as that needle had been years ago: a pair of small, trembling hands against either side of his face. Gentle. Warm. And, through the horrific smells of his cell, he scented from the wrist right under his nose a soul-twisting combination of vanilla and bergamot. With the slightest hint of white oak twining with it.

His eyes opened, and he realized then that he must be asleep. Must be having his first dream in years. For there, before him, was that blue that captured and cradled him during his few moments of peace. The bottomless sea, and the night sky before blackness consumed it.

"Dion," she breathed, and her fingers stroked along his cheekbones, his brow, a thumb running across his chapped lips. Her voice, too, he knew. Used to hear it say his name as he slept, just as it did now. He wondered if it was kind or cruel for his mind to summon such realism into the touch he had not felt in a lifetime, the face he had tethered to the back of his mind to keep it safe.

"Dion, my love," she whispered, and her fingers moved again. New. Those words were new to his mind as it had been in this cell.

And a word he had all but forgotten in his effort to keep it protected rose to his lips: "Ciara."

His voice sounded terrible. Rough, and hardly audible, but she smiled, and a choked sob escaped her. Real. This was real.

His eyes widened, and he moved to stand, rather than hang from the chains on his wrists as he had been. His knees buck-led, and the pain as blood coursed into his arms might have been distracting if he weren't so used to that sensation—pain.

She caught him, strong arms wrapping around his waist, and when he was steady, she touched his face again, her lovely eyes shining. "Yes, Dion. It's me."

That's right. He was Dion. *I* was Dion.

"Ciara," I said again, and my voice was thick. My heart

strained, and my very soul reached out to her while no other part of me could, shackled as I was. She must have felt it, as her tears overflowed, and the hands on my face gripped it still as she rose up to press her lips to mine.

The kiss was a kindling to my heart. It awoke my very blood, and I hadn't even the decency to care about the conditions we were in as I slanted my mouth over hers, and felt the soft warmth of her lips on me. Starved and beaten and broken as I was, I felt whole in that moment.

After a moment that felt much too short, she broke the kiss, and looked behind her. It was only then that I realized we were not alone. There, in the doorway to my cell, stood another familiar face. Another person I hadn't ever thought I would see again.

"Good to see you again, my friend," Jolie said as she strode forward, a key in her hands. I wondered how she acquired it, but in the next second thought it very likely that the dark one would have been cocky enough to leave it right outside. In however long it was that I'd been here, I'd never tried to escape. He probably figured it was better to leave it close, simply so that he wouldn't have to go fetch it if ever it was needed.

Jolie set to unlocking the chains around my wrists. The one that sometimes tethered my neck hung limp from the ceiling already, and she made quick work of the irons around my ankles. As they came off, I felt an odd numbness overcome me. I didn't think I would have moved if Ciara hadn't taken one of my sides, Jolie the other, and the females led me out of the cell that had been my home for so long.

I'd been awake when they'd taken me here, had seen the empty cells pass as I walked down the stone hallway. It felt, all at once, like I'd seen them yesterday, and like I'd seen them a lifetime ago. I supposed that was what happened in the monotony of endless torment. It was both infinite, and nonexistent, because nothing ever changed.

Now, something was changing, and my mind was struggling to catch up, even though my feet moved beneath me, taking as much of the burden as I could off of the females who held me. I should not have been surprised to see that there were occupied cells now. Some of them were awake, their mouths open as they surely shouted for help, but no sound emerged. By the time I saw one, there was another, the females beneath my arms carrying me too quickly, unwilling and unable to stop.

At the end of the hall, into a circle from which stretched six additional arms, there was a long column of stairs. Two hundred, at least, but they would take us directly to the outskirts of the Parvatan border of Oschverre.

Oleander didn't like conducting his business within the castle, or even within his fortified city. There were plenty of dungeons within it, but they were used for short-term imprisonment only, and ended with either exile, or execution. But those who would suffer for years–they were brought here.

I thought that might have been Melisan's doing. Queen she may be, and I had no misconceptions about her being completely oblivious to her husband's actions, I still didn't believe she would want the sort of things that had been done to me to occur in her home. So, this prison on the border of Oschverre had been constructed for the torment of Eshellens– so the queen might sleep at night.

Ciara and Jolie carried me up and up, and, for the first time, I was glad for all the weight I had lost since Sabrian. They panted softly on either side of me, and did not falter, did not stop until we were nearing the top, and there were Nuria and Bayani, swords out and coated with red. The bodies of four guards strewn around them.

I damned my useless legs when I stumbled, nearly bringing

Ciara and Jolie down with me. They only murmured consolations in my ears, the former saying my name over and over, as if she never believed she would do so again; as though she were making up for all of the times she could not say it these past years.

When we reached the hatch door at the top of the stairs where our friends waited, Bayani extended long, muscled arms down for me, and hoisted me up onto–grass.

Grass, so soft and wonderful against my bare skin. I couldn't even care that I wore nothing but a loin cloth as I laid back, panting.

"Dion, up, please my love. We have to move," Ciara whispered to me, and I knew she hated the words. But she was right. Though something in the back of my mind was telling me *no*, this was *not right*, I couldn't remember why that voice would say those things. What possible reason past some sense of self-sacrifice might exist that would have me doubting, for even a second, that I should be leaving with my mate.

So, I pushed myself to sit up, noting in a detached sort of way how many open wounds I had on my legs, my abdomen, my arms. With the iron, the quick-healing nature of my blood had not worked in so long, it was only a wonder that there weren't more. That my limbs, though markedly thinner than they had been the last time I'd been able to fully take them in, still retained any muscle at all. They had been feeding me more in recent times than they had in the beginning, and I remembered being scared of why that would be.

My damned iron-logged and sleep-deprived brain could not figure out what had my heart wrenching in fear every few seconds. By the bodies of the guards around me as Ciara helped me stand, I knew it wasn't being recaptured. In fact, capture seemed somehow alluring. Safer. Not for me, but–

There it was. The second the thought held, I stopped in my

tracks, and not even Ciara's strong arms could budge me. "Dion, we have to go now," she whispered urgently, and I felt the urge to smile at the impatience in her tone. The sass I had not allowed myself to miss, for it would have made me think of her. And I couldn't do that. I had to keep her safe.

"No," I answered, my voice rough, my mouth a flat line against which that joyful impulse tugged. "I can't. You have to leave."

She stopped pulling me at that. "What are you talking about? I'm not leaving without you."

"Yes. You are." I looked down into those miraculous eyes, and reached up to cup her cheek. My resolve nearly crumbled at the feel of her skin against my hand. How pristine and lovely it was within the four fingers I had left. I stroked the space on her cheekbone on which, so long ago and just yesterday, I had struck her to keep her from fighting for me. "I am so sorry, my love," I told her, meaning it for then, and for now.

"We are *leaving*. *You* are *leaving*," she said through her teeth, though her eyes shone. I could only wonder then at the small company we had. How many of our court had advised against this, that she had only the three with her whom I had been closest with in Sabrian? What orders had she disobeyed to come here, what *logic* had she ignored from them to decide to attempt to free me anyway?

"I'm not. You know that I'm not. My being here keeps *them* from going *there*." I ran my thumb—my dirty, nail-free thumb—against the silken chestnut skin of her cheek again as a tear fell. My touch smudged the saltwater along, pulling it to her temple.

I heard it then, and I knew they could, too. The pounding of hooves against the earth. Not many; it sounded like only two sets. And I knew, if it were up to her, the odds would be in her favor. Four against two. But I knew who one in the latter party would be.

"I love you," I told her, and knew it might make me the worst sort of selfish–but damned it as I kissed her anyway. This time, knowing it would be the last. Hoping she accepted it, too. In time.

When I forced myself to pull back, the taste of her lips and her tears on my tongue, I tore my eyes from hers, unable to stand the devastation there. Instead, releasing her and the part of my soul within her, I looked over her head, to my friends.

"Thank you all. For trying. Please, go home." I held Jolie's eyes as I said the last part, the bright blue shining with such pain. I knew she could convince me to go. Would only need to draw upon that desire within herself, and within me, for me to leave this place. Amplify it to a degree which I wouldn't be able to fight. I held those ice-bright eyes, and told her *no*. And I knew she understood when she lowered them.

I turned my gaze to Ciara once more, to see her crying in earnest now. The sight brought a painful thickness to my throat, and tears to my own eyes. "I love you," I said again, wishing it meant anything. But those hoofbeats were getting closer. So, with an agony so different from that I'd experienced over the years, I turned away from her. She only needed a second. To grab Nuria and Jolie, and Bayani, and bring them somewhere. Anywhere but here.

I watched as the two males astride black stallions rode closer and closer, and listened to Ciara's sobs behind me. I waited for them to stop, and they did–for a moment. They came back, and I whirled to her, to find Bayani still here, and she beside him. She must not have been strong enough to bring all three of them together, and now the horses and the males upon them were only yards away–

"Lady Vey!" I heard Olin's voice shout as Ciara moved to grip Bayani's arm, and halted midstide. I turned back to my brother stiffly, silently urging her to *go, GO.*

"I heard of your mother's passing," Olin continued as his horse stopped, and a large male with familiar golden eyes dismounted beside him. "Terribly sorry for your loss, though I hope you don't mind I adjusted for your title myself."

My heart ached again for my mate, for the grief she had experienced, on top of the pain that would always be present for the loss of the person she'd claimed. That she loved me was because I hadn't been able to tolerate her hate for me, and now she had immeasurable suffering because of it.

Still, that he spoke to her meant that he'd succeeded in sparking her anger. And I therefore only felt more petrified when he was able to go on. "So valiant of you, to try and rescue your mate. I'm afraid he's too self-sacrificing for all that. Tell me, would you like to accompany him?"

A snarl the likes of which I'd never uttered barreled its way up my throat, through my teeth. Olin only smiled–an expression which quickly dissipated as a knife-sharp edge of shadows hurled for him. He missed it only by diving two feet to his right, towards the other male, at the last possible second.

"*Shadows?*" he nearly shouted, his eyes alight with a sickening joy. "Oh, Dion, you didn't just get a pretty face, did you? Those powers haven't been seen in centuries!"

Another wave rose to meet him, and he dodged it more easily this time. I didn't dare move my eyes from the males before me, but I could only hope that if she wouldn't move to escape, Bayani would do what he could to get her to leave anyway.

"Oh, what a *prize*. My brother has your heart, but I wonder if I might have the rest of you." A terrible grin twisted his mouth, and though those words were spoken to her, they were meant for me. His eyes, *our* eyes, moved to me, a silent confirmation in them. More words, which said: *your move, brother.*

And so, swallowing my fear and rage, I said, "Let them go, and I'll swear myself to you, brother. I will take the blood oath."

"*No!*" came Ciara's voice, and then the sounds of struggle. As if Bayani knew this was their one chance at leaving here not just alive, but intact. He was choosing her, choosing himself, over me, and I could not be more grateful for it.

I ignored her protest, though my heart ached at the sounds of her struggle. "Let them leave, unharmed, Olin. And I will bind myself to you."

Olin's responding smile was the stuff of nightmares, but I bore it. I stared at it, at him, and prepared myself for the absence of my mate–

A breeze blew, we downwind from it, and I felt my prayers fall flat then. Because I knew Olin's scent. And, finally free of some of the iron, and the stenches of blood and shit and piss that had occupied my cell, I knew the other male's, too.

"Arthur," Ciara and Bayani breathed from behind me, their struggle having halted as soon as that wind hit them.

"Good noses!" Olin exclaimed, clapping his hands once, a huge grin spreading across his face. "Yes, this is *Arthur*. The very same I had spying on you all in Sabrian for seven *months*. We glamoured his scent a touch when he was there, so I'm glad the similarities are apparent enough for this moment. I still–"

But I interrupted him, my gaze on the male as I asked quietly, "Who is your father?"

Those golden eyes darted to Olin, then back to me, but still he managed to look indifferent. Even as Olin laughed, delighted. "An even better nose, Dion! Yes, this is my son. Though, I believe you two are *well* acquainted from your time in that cell together."

I heard more scuffing from behind me, and could only assume that Bayani still restrained Ciara, for another wave of shadows did not come. Olin chose his words with care, and *wanted* her to hurl her power at him, at them, for torturing me; that the hulking male had never hurt me would not occur to her.

Olin might even kill Bayani for sport, so that he could see Ciara unleashed. But I was not willing to be the cause of his death, for his sake, nor for hers. "Ciaragen, *go*," I told her through my teeth, still not taking my eyes off Olin–off the hands he needed only raise to take a life. "Or Bayani's death will lay on both our souls."

The struggle stopped, and I heard one last choked sob that was half-scream before only the wind ruffling the grass sounded behind me. And as my heart ached more than I'd allowed it to in years–I didn't want to know how many–my brother kept on talking.

"Very valiant of you, Dion. And I want you to know that I recognize that, had you not fought them, you would have been gone before Adathan or myself could arrive. Perhaps your time in a cell has brought some of your wits back to you."

I didn't respond. In fact, I wasn't even looking at him. "How old are you?" I asked the golden eyed male.

"He passed three quarters of a century not too long ago," Olin answered for him. "I didn't know about him at first. But his mother had raised him with our surname, and so when she died, he knew where to find me. Gods, how long ago was that, Adathan?"

"Seventy-one years ago," the male replied, his deep voice quiet in this open plain of grass.

I nearly asked him another question, but Olin spoke first. "Well, let's not drag this out." He drew a dagger from the scabbard at his hip, and walked towards me. When only feet separated us, and I could see with even more painful clarity how whole he was compared to my decrepity, he stopped. "On your knees."

For Ciara, I knelt.

"Give me your arm."

For my friends, I did.

Olin sliced me open, and I barely felt the pain of it. "Do you, Dion Evestre, swear to always obey me?" Simple. To the point.

For my home, I agreed.

Olin licked the blood from my arm, then cut his own and held it out to me.

Forgoing all, I drank.

21

WALLS

"AL, HOW DOES YOUR POWER WORK?"

A bite of eggs and cheese halfway to my lips, my eyes widen at the sudden query. We arrived late for breakfast today, leaving only the sailors who'd been too drunk from the night's revelry to dine with us. Still, when I look up at Li, heat rises to my cheeks as not just those at my table, but the few around us look to me for my answer. I straighten under those gazes, though, and tell her, "It's like a sixth sense. I can feel when a person is hurt, but not viscerally. More like...scent. I can distinguish it, just like I could tell you from Ciaragen even if I were blindfolded."

"So, it doesn't hurt you to heal people? To take their pain?"

I shrug, and begin to gather our dishes to busy myself. "Those are two separate questions. It doesn't hurt me to heal someone, no. But, if I take their pain, it does."

Li's head tilts as she hands me her plate, curls spilling over a pale shoulder. "What does it feel like?"

"Which one?"

"Both–if you don't mind."

I stand, and Adan joins me, taking all the glasses. "Healing is...warm. Like stepping out into the sun in perfect weather. To touch someone, and watch their hurt stop because of you–" I use the excuse of placing the dishes on Jacks's counter to face away from them as I finish, "To be able to help people is...a wonderful sort of gift."

Adan's arm brushes mine as he puts the glasses down, and I take a breath before turning around. "For taking someone's pain, it depends. On the level that the person is experiencing it, on how much I'm taking from them. I've found that the closer the injury is to the spine, the more it hurts, probably because of the proximity to the spinal cord."

"Spinal...cord?" Li's white brows raise as she and Atlas meet us at the edge of our table.

"Yes. It's like a rope of nerves, that all pass through spaces in your vertebrae–" I have to use the Ceraschen word for this, but explain, "–the bones that make up your spine. All the way from your skull, to your tailbone."

"That connection–those nerves, I guess," Atlas begins, dark brows furrowed above his storm-gray eyes. Surprisingly clear of any emotion but curiosity after our conversation last night. "Is that how you were able to render me unconscious?"

My heart tightens painfully in my chest, but I don't allow myself to think further into the memory his question brings. "Yes. I have to establish the connection to the brain, though, otherwise the most it would do would be to make your legs fall asleep."

"You seem to need contact, or at least closeness to be able to heal," Li says. "But I've heard that's not the case for your other power?" From Ciaragen. She would have heard that from the female whose bones I broke weeks ago–who has yet to join us for this meal.

Again, my heart strains, but then Adan's solid arm touches mine once more. This time, I push my weight into it, a silent thanks for the quiet support. We have not spoken about the look we shared last night, nor the talk I had with Atlas. But he is here, beside me as he has been since he jumped with me off the Ceraschen Cliffs. Solid. Dependable.

Dependable also in his silence thus far, allowing me to work through these nerves and hard things while I can. "No," I answer Li, and start towards the stairs, the three of them following. "It seems it holds regardless of the distance. Of course, I've not tested it much." My accidental breakings outnumber any intentional practice.

"Why do you think that is?"

I shrug again as we make our way up the stairs. "It seems to me that one power is offensive, and the other defensive."

She opens her mouth to ask another question, but the deep, rumbling voice cuts across her, "I think many of our powers are mysteries to us at times."

I wish I could express my thanks again, but only say, "Exactly. After all, I'm sure there are healers in Eshelle who experience their power differently than I do." That had been the case in Weaschte, at least.

"There are no healers in Eshelle," Li replies matter-of-factly.

My brows furrow, and I look over my shoulder at her as I reach the top of the stairs. "What do you mean there are no–?" I begin, but don't get to finish as I bump into a male on the deck.

His hands grasp the tops of my arms and roughly move me aside. "Ymeda's fucking tits, watch where the fuck you're going."

I'm so surprised between the physical shift and the words

that I only gape at him for a heartbeat. I recognize his thin but muscular build, and closely cropped sandy hair, but don't know his name. He's one of the few crew members whom I'd pointedly avoided since my first day here, knowing in my gut that he was not someone I wanted to know.

I feel rather than see Adan and Atlas come up behind me. The male only rolls his eyes, and even in my shock I recognize how idiotic a move that is. "Oh, and her guard dogs, right on cue. Tell me, *Althea*, how many times a day do you let them fuck you to get them to act like that?"

I don't see it happen. It's too fast. I only feel the air around me move, and then Adathan is in front of me, his hand around the male's throat, lifting him off the ground.

"Don't say her fucking name," he growls, and, while I've never feared him, some part of me does tremble now. Just not with fear.

The comparatively small Fae scratches at Adathan's wrist, but he hardly seems to notice. Any of the trepidation and shock I'd felt a moment ago leaves me, replaced with a sort of feral contentment as I watch it.

"Know that it's only for the sake of the hospitality of your captain that I don't snap your neck now for speaking like that to her. For *touching* her. For saying her name, *as if you deserve* such a thing. But if you so much as *look* at her wrong after this moment, not your captain, nor your crew, will be enough to stop me from *ending* you.

"Now, I'm going to put you down, and you're going to apologize to her. Understood?" Bronze fingers tighten, and the male's head bobs while the veins in his temples pop and his mottled red face begins to take on a bluish hue.

Adan drops him, and the male falls to his knees. He coughs and wheezes, and I can't find it in me to care for the pain I know comes with that feeling. I stand beside Adathan, lift my chin while peering down my nose at him, and wait.

Finally, the male composes himself, tears pooled in his eyes and streaming down his cheeks. Those eyes meet mine, red from bursted capillaries, and, in a voice like sandpaper, he says, "I'm sorry."

I crouch before him, the warmth of Adathan's leg close to my back. "For the record," I say, loud enough for Li to hear, "the reason they rise to defend me is because they're good males. That you make any assumption on their honor says far more about yours than theirs. In fact, I think I'd like to hear you apologize to *them*."

And when his lips open, I know more vitriol is about to spill forth–until we both see the half step Adathan takes towards him. "I'm sorry, I'm sorry!" he practically squeals, cringing away. I rise, and feel the tension still radiating from Adan. I turn my back to the cowering male, and look up in an attempt to meet his gaze.

His jaw, now covered in a dark beard, is tight, the muscles in his neck strained. He seems frozen, like a single movement will cost him his composure. I know how that feels. And I know, like me, it's for the sake of his own control that he keeps still.

He needs to get out. Now.

"You're okay," I whisper, so low he will be the only one to hear. Li's voice is loud as she says something to Atlas, and they both leave to give Adan the space he needs. I only look at him, while the male behind me continues to wheeze.

Finally, sun gold eyes pierce mine with their brilliance, rage visibly roiling behind the wall I can see him erecting. My heart thuds, because I have never seen that carefully constructed exterior crumble before, unless he's allowed it. Seeming to realize this, too, he makes for the stairs to the cabins. The only thing that surprises me about it is that he grabs my hand to bring me with him.

We're down and in my cabin in seconds. He releases me to clench his fists hard enough that his knuckles crack, the muscles in his forearms flexing. Staring out at the Evredis through the porthole, his voice still not as tamed as it typically is, he says, "I almost killed him."

I swallow. Not out of fear, but because I saw that intent in his body, in his eyes. I swallow because fear was the *last* thing I felt when I beheld those things. "I know," is all I can think to say.

But where my words fail me, I hope my actions will not. I find his hand, and bring it up to be level with my chest as I unfurl his fist. My fingers run over the smooth expanse of the back of his palm, his scarred knuckles, the thin gold band of the ring on his forefinger. His eyes widen by a fraction, watching its progress with bated breath, and *I* watch as goose-flesh rises on his forearm. But when my thumb moves towards his pulse, he halts its progress with his other hand.

"Don't. Don't try to take it from me."

And as he holds my gaze, a realization dawns on me, bright and sudden. A memory, of him tearing out of my grip as we stood amongst the pines weeks ago. A shadow that held, regardless of how few or many casual touches he's allowed since then.

It had never been about the touch. But about me slowing his pulse; taking his fear, or, in this case, his anger. Things that he...he *wants* to feel, this male who so often shuts down his emotions.

"Okay." My voice is just a breath; barely loud enough to hear over the waves lapping softly against the ship. And finally, I think I know something, think I'm *ready* for something–

But the gentle way he pulls his hand from mine makes those thoughts shatter, in shards as plentiful as the sunshine scattered across the surface of the sea.

22

TRAINING & TRUTHS

LINA - DAY 23

ATLAS CROOKS AN ELBOW AROUND MY NECK, AND BRACES HIS hand against his other shoulder, effectively locking me in. Al and Adathan, training on deck with us, fade into the background as all the lessons my mum instilled in me rush in.

Let them underestimate you, my darling girl, she would say when frustration would get the better of me. When I would recognize how weak, how slow I was, in comparison to her and mama, who watched from the sidelines, working to unknit the worry from her brow. Pretending that she wasn't concerned for my safety in this world I hadn't been born for, but lived in nonetheless.

I can't do it, I used to cry when she would get me in a hold I couldn't escape, or have me attempt to outmaneuver her to evade capture in the first place.

You can, is all she would say, because the comfort and affirmations she spoke when she would do my hair or put me to bed would do no good here. Not when the dangers she was training me for wouldn't give quarter if I ever faced them. Wouldn't give me time, or consolation, or help.

Reaching only the noses or chins of most females, never mind males. Unable to run as fast as them as a child, and still now. Not strong enough to fight them.

Smaller, slower, weaker. Those are not the things she and mama raised me to be, but the things I'd been born as.

Atlas feels it when my clawing at his arm becomes frantic, rather than a measure of fight. His grip loosens, but doesn't leave me. Instead, he leans in to murmur, hopefully too low for the ears around us to pick up, "Don't give up, Lina. How did your mum teach you to get out of this?"

"Let me go," I grit through my teeth, yanking at his arm.

"No. How do you get out?"

"I don't know!" I yank on his arm, and thrash, but the only thing that accomplishes is me choking myself for a beat.

"You do. You–"

My foot comes down hard on his instep at the same time that I send my elbow back into his gut. One alone wouldn't be enough for me to hurt a full-grown Fae male, but the combination is. With a rough exhale at my blow, Atlas releases me, and, if he were a true attacker, I would turn and bash his nose in with my palm.

Not born strong enough to fight them. But made.

Sometimes it's just harder to remember than others.

Hands on his knees, Atlas looks at me, and grins. "Nice play," he says.

"I know," I reply with a shrug. The look that comes into his gray eyes has me second guessing that move, though. I can tell he's about to pounce on me, and brace myself–

"*Damn it!*" Al's voice is a growl, and we both turn to the sound. Locks of her falsely blond hair stick to her sweaty face and neck. The rest, in a loose braid, pools around her on the deck. And above her, his hand resting on the base of her throat, is Adathan. Some silent battle seems to pass between them as they pant, Al otherwise unmoving beneath the grip. Then, with a force that even makes *my* legs come together a bit, she sends her knee up into his groin. Atlas sucks a sharp breath in through his teeth, a fist coming up to his mouth as he cringes.

Adathan wheezes, and manages to shift his weight to fall to the side, avoiding crushing her beneath his massive frame. She's on him in a heartbeat, straddling his hips–actually, a bit higher, and I don't think it's accidental. Whether to avoid contact due to the pain he's experiencing, or something...*else*, I don't know. But when she does it, she has the dagger that's always sheathed at her thigh at his throat in the next second.

The male needs a moment to recover, his eyes closed as he takes a few long breaths through his teeth. Though some regret shows in her expression, Al doesn't remove the blade from his neck as he struggles. Instead, she asks him something quietly in Ceraschen–likely about his welfare after that blow. Opening his eyes, Adathan somehow manages to ask her something through a groaning breath. It makes her head tilt, just slightly, and then a corner of her mouth pulls up as she purrs something back to him.

I look at Atlas questioningly. He'd learned Ceraschen for his mission months ago, but I hadn't. Honestly, I hadn't even thought about it until my first day in Dahlih, when I realized that, not only was I different enough from the people around me to set them muttering as I passed, but I couldn't understand what it was they were muttering. Then, I'd thought it might be a blessing that I hadn't learned the language. The looks on their faces were enough.

Atlas leans into me to whisper, "He asked if she enjoyed that, and she said 'Payback's a bitch'."

My brows scrunch. "Payback?"

He shrugs, and looks away from the pair starting to rise from the deck–the male perhaps a tad slower than usual. When Atlas's eyes meet mine, though, the lingering pain in them dims, shifting into concern. "Did Ari shield you this morning?"

My hand flies to my cheeks, feeling the unusual warmth. "No." I ran out of the oil that protects my skin from the sun while in Weaschte, so the entire voyage, my godmother has been using whatever majick her shadows possess to do so instead. But she wasn't up when I rose this morning, and when she didn't show for breakfast, I assumed she was tired from the revelry in the common room last night, and wanted to leave her be.

My skin will be paying for it now. Under the sun, so strong over the sea, it must be at least pink at this point. The only mercy is that, with Atlas's superior sight, he might have caught it before it would have left me suffering for days, as my sunburns have in the past.

"Althea," Atlas calls suddenly. His gaze lifts from my face, and I watch his own tighten. So infinitesimally that I only see it because of how well I know him, but it's there. "Lina's sunburnt. Can you help with that?"

"Of course," she replies in accented Divani. She strides over, hips swaying in that way she has of being both graceful and tantalizing all at once. I try, not for the first time, to see through at least one of her glamours–to see what she looks like with the dark hair I'm told she has, and maybe even glimpse the Fae ears–but can't.

She gives me a small smile, her honeydew eyes soft. She lifts her hands, and hovers them inches from my cheeks. "May I?"

I nod, a bit struck by how gentle she becomes when the healer in her is needed. So simple, just a little sunburn, and yet that smile remains a quiet thing on her lips as she rests her hands with the weight of feathers against my skin. It warms briefly, and I feel...*light*. Like any pain I've ever had is being leeched away. Not into her, but just shrinking, and shrinking, while she runs that touch over my forehead and nose, down my neck and across my shoulders.

When she finishes, I can't help but breathe, "That's amazing."

She blushes, the color born from the heat of the day darkening further across her cheekbones. "I'm glad you feel better."

"No." I shake my head, and her brows scrunch in confusion. Does she not know her own power? I look at the males beside us. "Have either of you felt that?"

They both nod, their eyes on her. She meets their gazes, then mine, her expression still perplexed. "Felt what?"

"When you heal, Al. I don't feel *any* pain anymore. Not an ache in my back from sleeping wrong, or the twinge in my knee from tearing a ligament when I was twelve." When her eyes only widen, I ask, "Did you not know you were doing that?"

"No, I–" she looks at the three of us. "I only focus on healing what hurts, and my majick does the rest."

"No, Thea," Adathan says, his voice the sort of gentle it only ever is when he's speaking to her. "It's doing exactly what you ask of it: healing what's hurt."

"But when I healed you–I mean, after the arrows, or even after the pack–" She cuts herself off, seeming unsure of how to continue.

"It does what you ask of it, sweetheart," he repeats, that nickname sounding even softer than usual, too. Genuine, rather than casual or teasing. "When you healed my eyes, and my back, you wanted to heal only those things. But when you healed me after the arrows..." He swallows, his eyes flicking down before meeting her own once more. "Your intention was clear."

She's still looking at him when Atlas says, "It's true. I felt it when you healed my burns in the kitchens at–at the castle."

Al glances at him, then me, her bottom lip pulling between her teeth. Her following query is quiet, like she doesn't want to ask it, but can't not know the answer. "Why doesn't it work on me? And my–my Fae healing?"

Adathan shifts towards her, slight enough that it might not have been noticed if he weren't so huge. "I think it's the same, Thea. Your power is so intrinsic that it must be able to stifle even that part of you. Before, it was likely a part of the mental glamour, combined with the amount of iron in the soil and infrastructure of Weaschte. Now..."

When he hesitates, her gaze hardens. "Say it."

Not a heartbeat passes before he obeys, his own voice tighter. "Now, you're doing it to yourself. And you know it."

Here we go. This sort of honesty, I've learned, is always followed either by an acknowledging kind of silence, or a glare-off that usually ends, or continues, with them stalking off to have at it privately. The last time, I barely restrained myself from yelling after them to just bone already.

I wonder, also not for the first time, if either of them knows that they *both* want to. I don't think so; I think if they did, it would have happened by now. But they're both too self-sacrificing to try to take something from the other. Even though *I* know that there would be far more giving than taking, just based on what I've come to understand about the two of them.

Now, I refrain for the sake of my friend. Who stands beside me, seeming like he wants to say something to interrupt their tension, as he had a moment ago. The pair of them don't seem to realize that, especially in these moments, anyone around them feels outside. Other. Their eyes hold, their wills match, and I think the rest of the world disappears for them.

For Atlas, and maybe a little for me, I say too loudly, "If you two are going to have a pissing contest, take it to the railing at least. Atlas and I don't need to watch."

They blink, Al's cheeks flushing. Adathan sees it, sees the shame and the lingering, poorly hidden pain at the revelation she's just had, and some anger–anger at *me*–marrs his remorse for their behavior. I don't back down from the glare I'm sure many males have heeled to.

Instead, I look at her. *Her*, because I can be annoyed at the two of them, and Adathan in particular, and recognize it's partially out of jealousy. After all, Atlas and I have those 'just the two of us' moments, too. The difference is that I would never fuck Atlas, and vice versa.

Do I *want* Al? No, not since my decision from weeks ago. But I do want to make sure she knows she has more than one person to turn to for honesty on this ship. "You're powerful, gorgeous," I tell her, softening my voice. To help her see that I'm not mad, not really, I give her a wink. "Get over it, yeah?"

A corner of her mouth pulls up in a smirk, and I can *feel* the tension leave Adathan at the expression. I flick my gaze to him. "Anyways, you're probably not feeling too hot after that move, huh?"

He shrugs, crossing his arms, though I know for sure that it still hurts. "I deserved it, and she needed to do it."

"Why?"

"Because if anyone else had had her in that position, I'd hope she'd do the same to them."

It's not lost on me that he didn't answer the why of him deserving the blow, but maybe it's as simple as him still feeling as though he has to make up for all the hurt she's experienced these past weeks. But I agree with Al: what happened to her would have happened even without Adathan. Because Olin always would have existed, and would have always ruined so many lives as a result.

And because I know he's training her not just to survive in Eshelle, but to fight Olin, I nod once, and say, "Good." Then add, "But you should probably ice it. She didn't exactly take it easy on you."

"No, I did," Al replies before he can, and we all look at her. "Didn't want to do any permanent damage."

Ope.

Atlas coughs, and Adathan makes a similar noise, both at the same moment that she seems to realize what the implications could be to what she said. Her cheeks positively flame, and mortification crosses her features, but then–

She squares her shoulders, looks up at Adathan, and just says, "You're welcome." Then she pats his arm, and her fingers trail down a few inches of the muscled length before she turns back to me. "Hungry?"

My responding grin must be as wicked as it feels, because her eyes flash when I respond, "Starving."

We leave the males on the deck, though I brush Atlas's arm as I pass. And, maybe I'm imagining it, but I don't think I am...it looks like the two are about to have a chat. After watching the back of the female ahead of me, their eyes meet, and hold.

My remaining willpower goes towards following Al down the steps to the mess, rather than remaining to hear what they might say as this inevitable truth comes out at last.

23

UNREQUITED

CIARAGEN - DAY 23

I DON'T KNOW HOW MUCH OF THE DAY HAS PASSED WHEN I FIND the will to get out of bed. I hadn't been able to fall back asleep after my nightmare woke me. Still, I'd kept my lids shut against the view that would not have him in it, and I relived that day. Over and over again.

Eleven years, I've thought of that day, that moment. About what I could have done differently. How I could have shadowalked with both him and Bayani, and it would have taken Olin at least a few weeks, if they rode all their days, to reach Sabrian. How that could have been enough time for us to shore up our defenses for a battle.

But not a war.

I know, after over a decade, that taking him would have resulted in war. Olin has had his claws in Oleander for too long for him not to be able to manipulate the king into it. To twist Dion into a dangerous rebel who needed to be chased and put down, lest he single-handedly rally a force to our cause. Lest he lose his crown because of it.

And I know, after all that time, that we would not have won. We had allies already, yes, but Oleander's were wealthier, and far more vicious. Too many innocent lives would have been lost, and so even if we had beaten their armies in the battlefields, we would have lost the one thing that truly mattered: the faith of the people. For, if we cared not for their lives, then we were no better than what they already knew. It was, and is, something our court is not willing to sacrifice.

I had known that, and gone for him anyway. I suppose a desperate heart will do anything. Especially with what feels like only half a soul; the other half taken and tormented and twisted out of the beautiful thing it once was.

He was right to stay. He'd done right by our court, our people, despite all that had been done to him in that cell. He had put them, put the world we lived in, ahead of himself. And, though I miss him more and more each day, the pain of his absence only growing, not lessening with time, I cannot fault him for that. The agony of that is not what keeps me in my room.

What keeps me lying in my bed, feeling all but paralyzed to move is that, on that day, I did not tell Dion that I loved him.

He said it to me. Twice, he said it. Why did I not say it back? Why did I not take the one final chance I might have had, and *say it back?*

It's that thought that makes the sobs come once again. My body aches with them, and there are no tears even left to fall; they have been spent throughout however long I've laid in my cabin.

I've managed to live with the pain, a constant companion through all days and tasks. These past weeks, it's been almost dormant, despite the time of year. I'd been so busy finding

Althea and then beginning this voyage, and contemplating all that was about to come. And I'd been grateful for it.

Grateful.

To be with less pain than I had been for over two decades, when my mate's surely had done nothing but worsen. What he's facing now, I don't know, but it is far more dreadful, I'm sure, than being on a ship headed home. A home he has not seen since he was taken from me.

Grateful, when my mate had seen nothing but a cell for ten years. *Grateful*, when I'd left him to an even more terrible fate. And had not even bothered to give him that last piece of my heart as I went.

I don't know how much longer I cry. How much time passes as I grieve for a male still living, and the life we could have—*should have* had together. Sacrificed for the cause of our nation. For our Lady, who is likely spending time with one of the males who sits in the memory which festers within me at this very moment.

I know that she cares for him. It is the only thing that has stayed my hand these past weeks. But each day that I do, each day that he walks this earth because my Lady has a place in her heart for him, I will remember. And I am not sure which of us I will hate more for it.

⇹

When I finally gather the courage to rise, the sun shining through the porthole in my cabin indicates it should be about lunch time. With a sigh that feels as heavy as my pounding head, I sit up.

The motions come without thought. Stretching. Running oil over my braids. Brushing my teeth. Washing the past hours off of my face.

When at last I'm walking up the steps to the deck, slowly enough that even the moist steps are silent beneath my feet, I look up in time to see Althea and Emelina make way for the mess. Leaving Atlas and Adathan standing on deck. Alone. Together.

I am not so courteous as Lina, who I can tell has noticed this stand-off. I pull the shadows of the stairwell around myself, becoming one with them. They wouldn't see me if they were feet from me.

It's when, I assume, the forms of the females who left them are out of sight, that they turn back to each other. Not realizing that I lurk in the shadows, awaiting a conversation that perhaps isn't my business, but feels like it is. Today, it feels like anything to do with the male and my memory is meant for me.

My godson will have to forgive me. Though I may not forgive myself for intruding when I hear his first question:

"What are your intentions with her?"

I tell myself I need to know for my High Lord and High Lady. For this, which concerns their daughter.

Adathan's response is flat. "Excuse me?"

"Don't pretend with me, Adathan. I can see it. Everyone can fucking see it, except apparently *her*." It's the gruffest I have ever heard Atlas be in his life, and my heart aches when I realize it is not just out of care for Althea; of what happens to her. But to cover his own pain. Only, so young, he's not yet mastered that; I can still hear the ripples of it beneath the hard words.

He is watching another male love the female he loves. And I, too absorbed in my own agenda and my own pain, have not even spoken with him about it. A near son to me, and I have let this topic go undiscussed. Why? Because my own selfish heart cannot stand that the adversary in his story would be the same as my own? Because one of the males who took *my* love from me now has his–however unrequited?

I have to push down the emotions that rage within me–so conflicting, and so many–as I watch the male assess Atlas. Weighing the benefits of telling the truth against remaining infuriatingly emotionally infallible to all but one person on this ship. Finally, he replies, "My intentions are the same as yours. To keep her safe. To make her happy, if possible, after all she's endured."

"That's not what I meant," Atlas grits out, his fists clenching at his sides for a moment before relaxing. This gentle male–I had been willingly blinding myself to all that he's been experiencing these weeks. Days and days, holding these feelings within his ever-calm exterior. I can only hope he's opened up to Lina, with me being so preoccupied.

"I know what you meant." Adathan's voice is hard, but his posture remains calm, with the exception of a flicker of a muscle in his jaw. "It's none of your business. None of Emelina's, or Ciaragen's, or Javi's, or the whole damned crew. The only person I may discuss this with is *her*, and only if ever she wanted to know. Until then, even if it is never, I will keep her safe. Make her happy. However I can."

Atlas takes a deep breath that I have to commend him for. "Listen, I know how you feel–"

"You don't know *anything*," he growls, the last word forced through his teeth. I watch as Atlas blinks at the outright hostility, and then stares at the male–

And takes a step back.

My hand is on my dagger not a second later, but I don't get the chance to step out from the shadows, to confront whatever danger my godson saw before he asks, "How long?" so quietly I hardly hear it.

Adathan's jaw tightens again, but he doesn't answer. Atlas

waits, but when, even a minute later, one doesn't come, he scoffs. "It's a good thing she forgives us our secrets."

And with that, Atlas turns, and follows the females down to the mess. I wait for Adathan to follow, only knowing he will because Althea is down there, and we both know she's waiting for him. He might have avoided her after that conversation, but he is not in the habit of disappointing her. Not again, at least.

So, I wait, planning on following him down after a minute to join our table–

"I know you're there," he murmurs, and turns to look right at me. I don't know how, but he sees me, here in my pocket of shadows. Senses me, even in their embrace. So I let them fade, and stare back at him. My hand doesn't leave the hilt of my dagger as he walks towards me until just feet remain between us.

Then he says, "I'm sorry," and I'm so surprised that I actually let it show before I'm able to force it behind the hate I'm sure he can see in my eyes.

"For what?" I ask, my tone hard.

"I know what this day is to you."

Unwanted emotion sticks in my throat and clouds my eyes, but more surprise comes, too. He must be lying; must only know something is wrong because of my absence at breakfast. I straighten my shoulders and glare at him. "Do you now?"

"It's the day you came for him."

I can't respond, and he doesn't deserve one anyway– certainly not an acceptance of his apology–so I continue to glare, unwilling to be the one to walk away.

"If it were not for her, I would offer up my throat to that dagger you hold." It must be a trick of the light, the slight shine in his eyes. "Blood oath or no, I helped to take something...so precious from you that day. And years before. You deserve your vengeance.

"But she does not. I cannot understand why she wants me around, or how she seems to value me, but she does." Indeed, that usually so carefully blank exterior reveals confusion, and–and *pain*. "I fear that I've become someone she would miss, if I were gone. And we both know she has already lost too many people.

"So I only hope you can believe me–not forgive me–when I say that I am sorry for the part I have played in your suffering."

He seems to understand that I won't–*can't* reply. Rather than wait for what won't come, he only nods once, and turns to start towards the mess.

I need to say it. Just once. "You don't deserve her," I call after him.

He doesn't turn around. Only calls back, "I know."

24

THE TEST

Adan is quiet the rest of the day, and I don't think it's because of the hit I'd gotten in during our sparring.

He'd asked me to do it, after all. Had given me a look while he braced his weight above me with one arm, the hand at my throat only tight enough to keep me from escaping without making some kind of maneuver. I'd known right away which one I would use with any other male. And he'd gotten a sort of gleam in his eye that told me he knew exactly what I was thinking, and to just *do it*.

Still, when we'd switched positions and it had been me atop him, dagger at his throat, I hadn't been able to ignore the pain in his face. The only thing that had stopped me from healing him was, well...the *location* of the hurt. Though, I guess I know now that I could have touched him anywhere and aided that pain.

I'm sure he realizes this, too, but I still don't think it's the reason behind his unusual silence. He hasn't been this quiet with me since we were in the woods together weeks ago.

When dinner is past, it's just the two of us walking down the steps to the cabins. Li had asked me again to join them in the common room for the evening festivities, but I'd declined, trying to ignore the disappointment in her familiar eyes. Atlas and Ciaragen had joined her, the former giving me a mock salute, the latter an oddly strained smile, which I returned respectively.

Now, alone in the hall outside our rooms, I almost let him get away with the silence.

Almost.

"What's wrong?"

He turns toward me, but his eyes are as carefully blank as they have been since lunch. As they had been amidst the pines, before we got real with each other. Before things started... shifting between us, even if I'm not sure how or even in what direction. Even if him pulling his hand from mine sticks like a weight in my gut every time I think of it, but the memory of his arms banded around me in our embrace creates a far different feeling within me.

He doesn't answer my question.

I cross my arms, taking a step closer to him so that he has to look down his nose at me. "You're not answering because you don't want to lie. But something is wrong."

A muscle in his jaw twitches as it tightens, almost unnoticeable beneath the beard he's grown these weeks and in the dimness of the hall. Despite my thoughts from before, I ask him quietly, "Is this about earlier? I can heal you, Adan, if you're still in pain." The last part comes out too quickly, and heat rises to my cheeks.

His eyes soften around the edges, and I feel my shoulders drop a bit in response. The corners of his mouth twitch up, but it's partially forced. "I mean, it didn't tickle. But I'm not upset with you, Thea, if that's what you're worried about."

My brows furrow, and I take another small step towards him. This time, his chin shifts down so he can hold my gaze. "Will you tell me what's bothering you, then?"

His head tilts to the side slightly, contemplating leaving me wondering, or giving me an answer he would rather keep for himself. His deep voice is low enough that the rasp of it skitters over my skin, leaving gooseflesh in his wake as he says, "You are a better friend to me than I deserve, Thea."

It could be an answer, but it's not *the* answer. But if he's not ready to share, I can give him the space he deserves. Even if *friend* has started to feel like a term that doesn't quite encompass what he could be to me anymore.

So, I shake my head. "You deserve far more than you allow yourself to believe, Adathan. I am not some paragon. And you are not my villain. So, stop with the silent treatment, and let me be the–friend you deserve to have."

Adan blinks slowly, his full lips parting in surprise. Feigning nonchalance, I say, "Don't pull away for a second, okay?"

His dark brows scrunch in confusion, but I don't wait to take one of his hands in both of mine. The light of my magic shines through the gaps between our flesh, illuminating the dark hallway as it seeks out any and all hurts within the male before me. And so I can see, with perfect clarity within that light, as he tilts his head back, his eyes close, and his mouth opens by another millimeter in a quiet sigh. Something about it, about the exposed, strong column of his throat, and such a pleasured expression on his face...

I'm the one who pulls away, and his head snaps back down, those golden eyes so bright they're almost glowing. With false bravado, I give him a half smile, and ask, "Better?"

A step has him closing the distance between us; so close

now that if I took a deep breath, my chest would brush his stomach. "Sweetheart," he practically growls, and a shudder works its way up my spine, suppressed by sheer will. "You have no idea."

And even though this back-and-forth is confusing, and damning, and all sorts of shifting at all times, I tip my head back to look at him. My lips in direct line of his, less than a foot separating them, I breathe, "Good night, Adan."

His eyes flit down to my mouth for a heartbeat before meeting my own once more. "Good night, Thea."

I'm the one who steps away first. And my door isn't quite closed when I hear him mutter oh-so quietly, "Void damn me, I can't fucking help myself."

And something about it has a grin pulling at both sides of my lips as I slip into the nightgown Lina gave me, and into bed. Something about it has me sleeping with only the barest of nightmares for the first time in weeks. Something about it has me waking in the morning, feeling charged with a buzz that I can't, and don't want to shake.

⇻

I knew things had irrevocably shifted when my nightmares were interspersed with dreams.

Of bronze, scarred skin. Of bright golden eyes. Of slow, soft smiles. The horrors of my memories were interrupted by them in sleep as they have been during the days.

So, I find myself waking feeling more rested than I have in weeks. And even though I just saw him in my dreams, the first thing I want to do upon waking is not to wallow in the misery of the nightmares I did have...but to see him.

I roll out of bed, and gather my things to wash, hoping the room will be free. The ever-damp floors of the ship are chill beneath my feet as I pad to my door, hoping not to wake the keen-eared Fae in the surrounding cabins, if they're still sleeping. Out in the hall, I can see the door to the washroom is ajar, and I make my way for it.

But, only a few inches in, the door bangs against something. No, some*one*. A very large someone, who steps aside to pull it open the rest of the way, and faces me. A toothbrush held between his lips with a broad hand, eyes still a bit heavy-lidded with sleep. And shirtless.

"Sorry," I say quickly, making sure to only look into the sun-gold depths, and not any lower–which is damn hard considering I'm eye-level with his chest. "I thought everyone would still be sleeping..."

I trail off because, while my eyes have studiously remained up, his do no such thing. And I remember that I'm wearing Li's sorry excuse for a nightgown when his gaze slides up the bared expanse of my legs slowly enough that my core tightens, and my heartbeat picks up the speed his stare leaves behind.

He brings his eyes up to mine, and that beat thrums even faster at the hunger he lets me see within them. It has me pulling my bottom lip between my teeth, and then a blush flares through my cheeks when his eyes catch the motion, and take a good few seconds to look away.

Then Adathan bends over the sink to rinse his mouth, giving me the opportunity I needed to take him in. I haven't seen him shirtless since we were in the woods together, whether by his design or coincidence, I'm not sure. But I look at him with a far different intent than I had then.

Now, I see the mass of him, the muscle that only sheer dedication could have brought, and marvel. Every inch, artfully carved from the shape of who he'd once been, covered in the warm, deep tan of his skin. Then carved again, by the blades of those who wished to harm him, and failed.

Including me.

He straightens, and I don't try to pretend I hadn't been taking him in as unapologetically as he had me. I watch his tongue run along one of those sharp canines, and wonder what it would feel like if it were *my* tongue tracing the shape of them.

"Good morning, Thea," he says, not acknowledging my compulsive apology. Do I imagine it, or is his voice rough with more than just sleep? And did my name always sound that good from his lips?

"Good morning, Adan," I return, and feel–without me thinking about it–a smile pull at my mouth. And I *know* I don't imagine it when his gaze softens.

"Come in." He steps back, leaning against the wall so I can pass. The command that so easily could have been a request if he'd wanted it to be sends a thrill through me. So does the feeling I get when I intentionally brush his thigh with my hip as I do as he said.

"Nice dress," he tells me, and I look at him in the mirror. That golden gaze grips mine, but I wonder if he'd been looking at anything else at my back before I met it.

"I'm glad you like it," I say, and, even though it sets my heart thundering, I reach up for my own toothbrush and paste, knowing it brings the hem of the '*dress*' to the space between my thigh and bum.

Only once I'm brushing my teeth do I glance in the mirror again, curious about his silence. Adan's head is tilted back, his eyes closed and jaw tight. My own jaw flexes, because I suppose the sleepiness of before has worn off enough that he's decided to try to bring things back to the way they have been for the both of us.

Okay. I'll meet him there.

Until he lets that *almost* infallible guard down, that is.

After I rinse my mouth out, I turn to him. "Get out," I order, gesturing with my clean toothbrush towards the door.

His eyes flash open, and he looks down at me over his cheekbones, his head still leaning against the wall. I raise my brows expectantly. "Well, you're either going to turn around while I change, or stand outside for a minute. Based on previous experience, I know you're not prone to peeking, so I'm fine with either."

He sucks on the inside of his cheek, and then straightens. "See you in a minute, then." He exits the small room, its size making it clearly intentional that he doesn't so much as accidentally brush me on his way out, and closes the door behind him.

Still, I smirk, as I strip off the nightgown and the underthings Li had given me–things she had bought for the trip but hadn't found occasion to wear. In fact, she gave me a few sets of them.

But that's not the reason for the half smile on my face. No, that's there because of two different things. One, because, while I'd given him a choice, he'd done as I commanded just as readily as I had with him. And two, because I know he can hear each slip of fabric from the other side of that very thin door. And maybe, just maybe, he might imagine what those sounds are leaving bare, and then slowly covering.

Once dressed in my usual trousers and tank top, I tie Evie's purple sash around my head, and then weave the ends into a braid of my still-blonde locks. As I plait, I come up with my plan, and I only allow myself a quick breath to prepare before I open the door, and stick my head out.

He's there, of course, and unfortunately decided to cover up his previously bare upper body. Still, I give him a small, easy grin–and feel a rush of relief when he returns it. Shielding me from himself, yes, but no forced blankness that would make even my plan moot.

So, I lean against the door jam, and ask, "Are you growing the beard for aesthetic reasons, or because you secretly hated being clean-shaven?"

He raises a hand to his face, and strokes the hair there. "Obviously the former. Jacks hasn't been giving me extra bread for no reason."

That gets a genuine chuckle out of me, but I go on. "Obviously. Makes your eyes pop, and all. Downside is, you lose the dimples."

He drops his hand only to cross his arms instead. "You want me to shave it?"

I look at him, to examine the face above the beard. Wide cheekbones, the straight line of his nose. His hair has grown a bit in the past few weeks, too, but not as noticeably as the beard. It only curls a little now over his forehead, and at his nape. Still a beautiful male, but too much of the face I've come to care for is covered, so I answer, "Yes."

Again, his tongue runs over a canine, but this time I see it even better in the grin that parts his full lips. "Alright, sweetheart. Do you know where Lina keeps the fresh razors?" he asks, and I grin back at him, not bothering to hide the victory in the expression.

We search for the razors for probably one whole minute before giving up, and resorting to the short dagger strapped to my ankle. I have him use what he calls a small majick to reinforce the sink so I can sit on it, and then have him stand before me, pretending to be innocent of the way this forces him to stand between my legs. Even if he does so with as much distance between our hips as possible.

He looks over my head in the mirror to put the shaving cream on, and once he's satisfied with the coverage, he puts the container of it away, and meets my eyes. I flick my braid over a shoulder, and say, "I don't know why you're letting me do this. What if I slice up your pretty face?"

He rolls his eyes, like he's trying not to let each one of my compliments stick. Every one a truth I'm hoping he'll remember when he tries to push us back to where we'd been before.

"I'm sure you could heal me right up," he replies, bracing his hands on the sink on either side of my hips. "We have a mutual interest in Jacks giving me extra food."

I chuckle again. "That, we do. Alright, then. Ready?" I quirk a brow, and he nods once, lifting his chin to give me access to wherever I decide to start.

I take a beat to steady my–luckily practiced–hand, and angle the blade just so, before running it down his cheek. His eyes close as I hear the scrape, the many tiny snaps as the hairs are shorn. The dagger comes away with plenty of cream, and beard, but no blood, and none flows over the now-bare skin either. So, after wiping it off on a towel to my right, I continue, leaning closer to him. To see what I'm doing, yes, but also because I really fucking want to. All the while, he breathes long, slow breaths through barely parted lips, keeping his eyes closed.

When I get to his lips, I have him clamp them between his teeth, and I'm so close to his face as I make the minute cuts that I can see each infinitesimal pore, each tiny freckle. The urge to press my lips to some part of the surface I've so intently worked on these minutes is strong enough that my voice is husky when I murmur, "Tilt your head back for me."

His eyes open by half, but he obeys, baring his throat to me. "I see why you're doing this," he says, his deep voice quiet, its gravel running along my skin.

Though my heart stutters, I don't so much as pause as I raise the blade to his neck. "Do you?"

He hums his confirmation. "You just wanted an excuse to hold a dagger to my throat."

My laugh is a low thing I've never heard myself emit before. "As if I've needed an excuse for that before." I brace my other hand in the crook of his neck and shoulder, and make the first run down his neck. He opens his mouth a fraction, and I interrupt, "No talking now. I like having you around too much to end you in a shaving accident."

Adan remains silent for the minutes it takes me to finish shaving his neck. Once I'm done, though, and grip his chin to turn his face this way and that to see if I've missed a spot, he says, "Is there a way you would prefer to end me, then?"

I set the blade down on the towel beside me, and my other hand falls from his chin to his chest. I trail it to the side, and when I find the ridge of the first scar I'd given him, I stroke my thumb over it. The only sounds are our heartbeats and breaths, each of his thrumming faster and faster in the air between us. I bring my gaze back up to his, and tell him, "I would prefer many things with you, Adathan. None of them to end you."

My plan only had two steps.

One was to get him to agree to this task, this proximity.

The second is now, and more of a test than a step. As I draw my hand away from him–

His strong, broad hand catches mine before I can remove my touch from him. So quickly, his pupils dilate, and I watch his nostrils delicately flare. A growl that's more of a groan rumbles through his chest, vibrating against my palm while his lashes flutter. "Do you have *any idea*," he grits out, "how good you smell right now?"

Not what I thought he was going to say.

I answer him honestly: "No...?"

My heart stutters as he leans in and down, his nose just inches from my throat as he inhales. "Your desire, love. I can scent it on you. And it's driving me out of my fucking mind."

Also not what I was expecting him to say, but I am definitely not complaining now. My heart pounds at his closeness, at his words, and if he can indeed scent that sort of thing, then surely more of it is spilling from me now.

It seems I'm right when that noise comes again, almost like the purr of a big cat, while he inhales in the air near my neck. The speed of my pulse causing even my voice to tremble, I dare to ask, "If you can smell it, then why..?"

I can't think of the words to finish, not with how near he is, nor the sounds he's making, and certainly not when I breathe through my nose, and scent from him something musky; warm and inviting and raw. Not when I realize that I've smelled it before, and never knew what it was.

His desire.

And, as he always has, he seems to understand my mind now, and doesn't need me to be coherent to answer my unended question. "Because lust is common, Thea. And you deserved to feel it, even if it was for me. You deserved to *want*, and not have me expect anything from it. But lust is common," he repeats, his lips so close to my skin I can feel the separation of the air of each word. "What we have is not."

I'm about to ask what he thinks we have, and what his restraint is for–this resistance he's apparently cast upon himself–if we both so obviously want this, when–

Knock, knock, knock. "Al? Are you in there? I have to fucking pee," comes Li's voice through the door.

And Adathan moves to pull away, but no–no, I grip his shirt, and growl through my teeth, "Don't you dare."

His still heavy-lidded eyes flare, then the heat in them burns even brighter. He halts his step away, and instead steps back into me, that warmth urging me to go on. So I do. "You don't get to pull away from me, not again. This conversation is not done. And I'm not going to go the rest of the day pretending that it is. Because you're right; what we have is not common. So I'm going to fight for it, even if it's you I have to fight."

His brow furrows, some of the fire in his eyes banking, and morphing into a sort of gentle devastation. "Okay, sweetheart."

I take a breath that shakes slightly, and nod. "Okay." I release his shirt, and brush a palm over the fabric, the muscle beneath it. Then I hop down from the sink, not giving him any warning so that he doesn't get to avoid my body as it slides down his for a heartbeat. I look up into his face, and give him a little smile. "Yup. Still handsome."

25

THE BURDEN OF BEING A FRIEND

LINA - DAY 24

THE WASHROOM DOOR OPENS, AND NOT ONLY IS AL IN THERE—BUT so is Adathan. And I might as well not be there for the way those bright gold eyes rest on her. Like she's the sun and the moon and the stars, and yet also like she's his last gods-damn meal, and he can't wait to devour her. A look he's hidden from everyone before, including her, and so has me wondering what in the Void happened in the past twelve hours to change that.

"Heyyy," I say slowly, my gaze flitting between the two of them.

"Morning," Al says, her voice bright, but not forced. "We're done here, so you can pee in peace." She steps out, Adathan right behind her, only looking away from her to give me a nod of greeting, which I return. Considering he and I have been pretty friendly since their first day on the ship, I know whatever just happened in there has to be big. Otherwise, he would have bid me good morning, as he has done for weeks.

Are we the best of friends? No, and I don't think we can be until or *if* Atlas's heart heals. It's bad enough that I like him when his very presence here hurts my godmother. But not once has he made me feel less than or other because of what and who I'd been born as and to, and even those closest to me can't manage that sometimes.

Not on purpose, of course. But they do it nonetheless.

Anyway, how he behaves around me is almost beside the point. It's how he is with Al that made me like him, made me *trust* him in the first place. Only seeing how completely dedicated he is, not just to her, but to her safety, to her happiness, got me to see past the prejudice I'd cast upon him for my godmother's sake initially.

I did wonder, at first, how it mattered enough to me that he treated Al so well that I overlooked the stories I'd heard of him in the past. Her words in Javi's quarters that day helped, sure; I agreed with her about Olin's fault in all that had happened to her, and my loved ones in Sabrian. But, more than that, as I'd recognized before, I had this immediate feeling of belonging with her. It felt impossible, after that recognition, to *hate* anyone so fiercely devoted to her.

Adathan is surely that. Being friends with him therefore feels like a betrayal in one sense, and utterly right in another.

The betrayal has taken the forefront now, though. Because I can see clearly that Al's choice has been made, and it's not Atlas. Meaning that my best friend, and my godmother are both suffering in the presence of the male who now walks up the stairs with Al.

The thing is, neither is *truly* his fault. With Ciaragen, the entire blame lies with Olin; in his actions, and in the commands he'd given his son, whose choice was to obey, or die. And, with Atlas...it's Al's choice. To expect her to choose him because, a whole lifetime ago for her, she would have done, is unfair. She's not the person she was when I first met her, never mind when she was a human princess in a castle. Her biggest fear is no longer that she *has* to marry a man.

If she does eventually marry, it should be with someone she chooses herself. Uninfluenced by the past, or expectations. Even courtship, fuck, even a damned *kiss* should be in her complete control. And if she decides that none of those things will be done with Atlas, then...

I know my friend will accept her choice. He won't make her feel badly for it, though it will hurt him. He is a good male, through and through. I believe she will not be the last female he loves. He has an entire immortal lifespan to find someone who chooses *him*.

As though my thoughts summoned him, a knock sounds on the washroom door, and he says, "Any day now, Lina."

I roll my eyes, luckily already done using the facilities, and just finishing brushing my teeth. I open the door, and stick my toothpaste-covered tongue out at him.

"Classy," he remarks, reaching over me for his own things, crowding me into the sink. I shove him back with a shoulder, and by the smile I can see in the mirror, I know he did it intentionally to bug me.

I try to read any other emotions behind that grin. He refused to tell me what he and Al talked about two nights ago. Every time I asked that evening in the common room, he would say, "Mind your business, shortstack," and then take a sip–or gulp–of whatever he was drinking. So yesterday, I'd given him his space.

Given what Adathan and Al had looked like coming out of the washroom moments ago, though...

Gods, being a best friend is the worst sometimes.

With a sigh, I say, "I have to tell you something."

Those gray eyes meet mine in the mirror, and his toothbrush pauses halfway to his mouth. Then his jaw flexes, and he finishes the motion. Speaking around the brush, he mumbles, "It's him, isn't it?"

My brow crumples, but I nod slowly. He does, too, and is silent for a couple of minutes. Once his mouth is rinsed out, he gently closes the door. He rubs a dark brown hand down his face, and once it falls, he speaks. "I thought it would be soon, but..."

"Not this soon?" I finish quietly, and he nods again. Though his eyes remain downcast, I can see the silver lining his lower lids.

"She..." He clears his throat. "She deserves that. I...I wouldn't want her to put off her happiness for anything, especially not for me. It's just..." He takes a deep breath. "Loving her is easy. Stopping...is fucking impossible."

I turn to him, forcing him to meet my eyes. "Did she say she wanted nothing from you any longer?"

He shakes his head with a male-like sniff, and crosses his arms over his chest. "No. We agreed to remain friends."

I place my hand on his elbow. "It's not what you wanted. I know that. And I am so sorry for how this is hurting you. But... is that kind of love not enough? Is it so unsatisfactory that you might rather not be in her life at all?"

"Of course not," he replies immediately, but doesn't shrug out of my touch. "That's why I was the one to even suggest it. I would *always* rather be a part of her life, than nothing at all. We were just friends once. We can be again. I just...it'll take some time. For me."

Not for her. Because, though she may have wanted him once, I don't think she was ever in love with him. Then, to follow that relationship with betrayal and secrets...she would not have had to work to revert back to a friend to him. To no longer look at him as she had when he was with her in the castle gardens.

There is nothing I can say to comfort him, not really. So I don't try. "This is gonna suck for a while. But one day it won't. And through it all, she will be your friend, and you'll be hers. And I can tell you from experience..." I smirk at him, and pinch the skin above his elbow. "That you're damn good in that role."

Atlas returns my smile, and throws an arm around my shoulders. With a kiss on top of my curls, he says, "Right back at you."

⸙

"A storm is coming," Javi announces from the quarterdeck after breakfast. Which wasn't nearly as awkward as it could have been, but definitely not chummy either.

Still, I stand between Atlas and Al as I listen to the Obalan High Lord, Ciaragen and Adathan respectively on their other sides. "It should arrive tonight," Javi continues. "To avoid it would be to sail northwards, which we are avoiding at all costs. You all know your duties. Don't shirk them, and we will be just fine. You'll just be a bit more damp than you might like."

I join most of the crew in a chuckle at that, and even hear a huff of air from Al to my left. "Let's not greet it unprepared," Javi finishes, and taps the railing with a hand before heading to the helm.

"Short and sweet," I mumble.

"Hey, take away the sweet part, and that's you," Atlas says, which gets him an elbow to the stomach that only gets another laugh out of him. This time, all in our little group echo the sound–in varying volumes, of course.

I bump Al as punishment, and she has the decency to budge, as if she's not half a foot taller than me, and solid muscle. Honestly, it's probably more so she has an excuse to sway into Adathan than it is to placate me. The two had been surprisingly–and thankfully—chaste at breakfast, and I can only believe it was in respect to the male at my right. Possibly to the female beside him as well.

Javi's first mate, a male named Geoffrey, begins shouting orders as the captain steps back, and the Fae and faeries around us immediately get moving. Atlas gives me a mock salute as he's ordered to do something near the bow, and Adathan takes Al with him to work on the mainsail. Ciaragen is called to the helm, likely for a chat with the captain, but, alone beside me on the deck, she turns towards me instead of going right away. I feel her majick wrap around us, the sound shield keeping everyone else out of whatever she wants to say to me.

"I heard you talking to Atlas this morning," she says, her deep blue eyes hard.

My lips twist to the side. "Okay."

"You two are just...going to let *that* happen?"

My brows scrunch, and I cross my arms. "It's not up to us, Aunt Ari."

"In the Void, it isn't! I know what you said, I *heard* what you said, but *this*?" She gestures grandly up, towards where Al and Adathan are scaling the netting towards the mainsail. "I can accept that she wants him around, even if I don't understand it. But for them to be–*together*? When he took that from me?"

My heart softens at the conclusion of her argument, the rebuttal that had been building with the ire in my expression dying before they can come to fruition. Another counter comes to me, though, and I speak it as gently as I can. "And what about her?"

Her nostrils flare as she exhales, her lips tight. "What about her?"

"You may not believe he deserves her. But does she not deserve him, if she wants him?"

"She shouldn't want him! He hurt her!" Her eyes widen with her anger, her chest rising and falling with her quickened breaths.

"She's forgiven him for it, as she has forgiven you. Only you never apologized."

She blinks, and takes a step back from me, but she needs to hear it, even if it hurts both of us for me to speak it. "You said you would, but you haven't, have you? You've just accepted that she no longer openly dislikes you, despite the way you treat the male she values so greatly. Whom she has decided is not to blame for what happened to her.

"She doesn't know why you hurt, Aunt Ari. Not really. All she knows is that he is there for her. *Constantly*. Unfailingly. And you haven't been. So, I'm not saying you should apologize, or tell her your side just to get her to come over to it," I clarify. "But as a general to the armies that will one day be hers, and as a *friend* to her and her parents...you need to make that peace. It's not on her."

I step forward slowly, giving her the chance to back away. When she doesn't, I wrap my arms around her waist, laying my head on her chest. "I love you," I tell her. Not as a consolation, and definitely not out of pity. But a reminder; I'm not choosing Adathan, or even Al, over her. I'm not on a '*side*.' I love her as she has loved me all my life, and love sometimes means being more honest than you might like to be. Caring enough to not let that person continue on with lies–even the ones they tell themselves.

She heaves a shaking sigh, and winds her arms around my shoulders, laying her cheek against my hair. "I love you too, sweet girl."

26

THE VOW

WHEN THE SKY BEGINS TO DARKEN WITH THE IMPENDING STORM, and all the crew have finished their work in preparation for it, I find Althea.

She's with him, of course. Both of them sweaty from working on the mainsail, they lean against the starboard railing as they share a skin of water, not talking. Definitely standing closer to each other than they used to, though.

I steel myself as I approach them, taking a breath and straightening my shoulders. He senses me first, and I try not to bristle–too much, anyway–when instinct has him straightening, and his arm reaching to the side. When he sees that it's me coming up to them, he drops the hand that would have put her behind him, leans back once more.

I make myself give him a nod of acknowledgement, which he returns, no wariness to be found in his face, despite our conversation yesterday. Then I turn my gaze to Althea. "Could I talk to you for a moment?"

She is not so careful with her expression. Her brows furrow, and her lips purse as her honeydew eyes scan me, probably trying to anticipate what I might want to discuss with her. I don't know what she sees, but, after a minute, she replies, "Okay." Then she looks up at Adathan, and gives him a dip of her chin.

I barely restrain my growl when he returns the gesture, then reaches hesitantly to run the end of her braid between his fingers. Her breaths stop while he does so, and she stares after him for a few heartbeats when he walks away.

I step up beside her, and lean my elbows on the railing, staring out at the now gray-blue sea. I close my eyes, and take another breath while the rustling to my left tells me that she's turned towards the ocean, too.

When I'm sure there will be no lingering animosity in my tone, I start quietly. "I see a lot of myself in you," I say in Ceraschen. I open my eyes to look at her, and find her jaw tight. Not really surprising, but it does something to my heart to have her react negatively to that statement, so I move my gaze back to the water. "Or, rather, I see what I could have been. Not if fate had been kinder, because the one that's found you has shown me that's nought but an excuse I've made for myself all these years."

An excuse. To continue to be stubborn, and angry, because of the pain I endured. It might have continued to restrain me from changing, from believing I *could* change. Until her. Of course, that's just another reason why I've avoided this conversation. It didn't hurt as much, to live in my comforting lies.

My throat thickens, and tears spring in my eyes as I go on. "When I met my mate, I hated him. Loathed everything I believed he stood for, believed he had done. All the while, he'd done nothing but show me and mine kindness. Still, I hated him." Wasted time, such precious time, doing so.

The tears fall, and I do not stop them. "When I learned how little of what I believed was true, I recognized myself for what I'd been. Not strong, not smart. I was rejecting the evidence of my eyes and ears in favor of the opinion of my own mind. I held onto my views, even as I *saw* him, forcing myself to think he was nothing but a good actor. *I* was nothing but stubborn. And, when I realized that, I promised myself that I would do better, that I would *be* better.

"I was, for a time." I look down at my hands, clasped together on the railing, and watch a tear fall like the coming rain onto the skin of my wrist. "I was kinder, as I became friendly with him. Smarter, as I beheld the facades erected, not out of indifference, or cruelty, but of a need to protect his own heart, and the ones that cared for him. Wiser, as I learned what it meant to rebel for justice, rather than revenge. And happier, as I fell in love with him."

A choked cry breaks from my chest, and I give myself several seconds to allow it to pass before going on. "We had two weeks together. Just two. And I *was* better, during that time. But not long enough. Not *enough* time before he was taken from me. You know who did that, and so that is not what I wish to tell you right now. But that I stopped becoming that person when he was taken. It was too hard to change, while also grieving him, and what we had. I instead became content with regression, to the point where I might as well not have begun to change at all. And I thought that was reasonable. That my grief and pain and loneliness were righteous justification for my shift back to the self I'd been before he came.

"And then I found you in Dahlih." I turn towards her at last, and find her eyes shining as she continues to stare out at the Evredis around us. She doesn't let the tears fall, but there they sit, at the edges of those light green eyes as she listens to my story.

"I found you with one of my worst enemies, and your first action upon that was to save his life. Again, and again, you defended him, and stood by him, and I couldn't understand it, even after you spoke so candidly in Javi's quarters that day.

"Again and again, I have watched him be kind to you, and help you, and stand by *you*, and yet I once more have rejected what I see and hear, in favor of my beliefs. All the while, watching you be smarter, wiser, kinder, despite what he and his have done to you. So, I convinced myself that I could go on hating him as long as I supported you. But that's not the case, is it?"

She turns to me now, her lips tight with grief. For her, or me, or perhaps what both of us have endured, I'm not sure. But she answers me quietly, "No. It's not."

I nod, pressing my lips together, then I straighten, lifting my arms from the railing. She follows suit, turning to fully face me, and I finally give her the words she's deserved for weeks. "I apologize. I've hurt you with my words and with my actions these past weeks, and I am sorry for it. I cannot promise that I will ever like Adathan. But I swear that I will not dishonor you by striking at him, nor will I ever again doubt your judgment."

Her brow furrows. "No," she says, and my shoulders droop—but she goes on: "I don't need blind allegiance, or whatever you may present when you doubt me but might fear speaking. The honesty you exhibited just now...that is the quality of a—a friend I would like to have."

Her grace sends an ache through my chest. But this time, I do not turn from it to protect the walls I've built to defend who I've become in order to keep the rest of my heart intact. I let the blow to them crumble a few bricks, and bow my head to her.

She blinks, and that lovely face, which has been so hard

when facing me in the past, softens. "I do not expect you to like Adathan," she begins. "I could not ask that of you, not understanding what you lost. Our texts on Fae never spoke of mates. But, know that, at this point, if *I* lost *him*…you wouldn't want to know me, would not wish to follow me, if that were to happen. I know what I am to you." The child of my sovereigns; my Lady. She pauses before the order I know is coming.

"Keep him safe."

I steel my expression against any ire at the command. It is the first my Lady has given me. Regardless of how I feel about her male, I will not disappoint her. Not any more.

My smile for her is small and sad while I offer up another piece of honesty. "Mates are a soul bond. More than lust, more than love. So strong that, when accepted, you realize you were never truly whole until you had them. So strong that, when lost, it is then like losing a part of your soul. Part of your self." I take a deep breath, and interrupt the sadness that comes into her eyes: "I will keep him safe."

Her mouth tightens, the emotion remaining with her; she *lets* me see it, as she has not since we were both concealed, in whatever manner, at Castle Cerasche. And she says gently, but not weakly, "Thank you, Ciaragen."

27

THE STORM

THEA - DAY 24

AFTER HOURS OF WORK, AND A SHOWER THAT WILL LIKELY PROVE inconsequential with the coming storm, the entire crew are shoveling dinner into their mouths. Well, with a few exceptions; those who have more sensitive stomachs are readying for the storm by abstaining from the meal.

I am not one of them, and nor are any of the others at our table. The fish stew may stir in our bellies as the waves thrash us in what the skies indicate could be any moment now, but I'm too hungry to give much of a damn about that. Perhaps future me will regret it, but that's her problem, not mine.

Javi, who usually dines in his quarters, stands from his place between Ciaragen and Geoffrey, who also joined us—and his captain—for this meal. Noticing the movement, the crew falls silent in seconds.

"The storm approaches," Javi announces in a voice hardly louder than what one would use for ordinary speaking. Of course, all around him can hear it. "If my majick proves true, the rains should begin any minute. To your stations."

Spoons and bowls clatter, and are deposited with extreme efficiency at Jacks's counter. The seven of us stay put for a moment, allowing the crew to move about as they must. Once they're all filing towards the steps leading to the deck, we move to stand.

"You are staying in your cabins," the captain says quietly. I look up from gathering my dishes to find his eyes flicking between me and Li. But while I feel indignant, my friend seems to have expected this. The tilt to her lips is unhappy, but the rest of her expression is resigned.

I almost open my mouth to argue but...but, something tells me that they would never allow Lina to be out on the deck in this storm. And that maybe, even if my exclusion makes my blood boil, they're *asking* me to stay with her in the only way she will not despise even more. A command, from a captain to a crew member; a request, from one friend to another.

So, when I open my mouth now, all I say is, "Fine." Then I link my arm through Lina's, and give her a conspirator's grin. "What say you and I grab a bottle of something from the common room before all the Void breaks loose?"

Her answering smile is as bright as the full moon she likens, and she replies, "I say fuck yeah."

I squeeze her arm in mine, and turn back to the rest of the table, and I know that's gratitude in each of their eyes. My heart clenches in my chest. "Be careful, okay?"

They each nod, giving me small, kind smiles. Atlas salutes the two of us, which we return. I'm even more grateful than usual for his constant understanding of me when Adan hangs back, standing by the bottom of the stairs, his eyes on me. I look at Li, and she rolls her eyes, but nudges my shoulder with hers, towards where Adathan stands.

I walk to him, and only stop when barely a foot remains between us. Those sun gold eyes track me the entire way, lighting and warming me in the absence of their namesake. "Our conversation is still not done," I tell him quietly.

"I know, sweetheart." He reaches and holds the end of my braid between his thumb and forefinger, twirling it around them. Just as it had earlier, the action makes my heart stutter.

I lift my hand to cover his, brushing lightly over the back of his palm. Satisfaction washes through me when I sense his heart skip as well at the simple touch. "Don't go doing anything heroic, then. You stay safe, and you come for me when it's through."

His eyes heat, and he tugs a little on my braid. "I wouldn't dare disobey such a command, even if I wanted to."

"Good," I murmur, and pat his hand before making to move away–but he doesn't release my hair. Instead, he winds a few more inches of it around his fingers, and pulls me back to him with it. Not hard enough to hurt, but enough to make the animal that had once tackled him open an eye...and purr.

"It goes both ways, Thea. I will come for you when the storm is done. But you will stay safe until I do. Understand?" His brows raise slightly, and there's another gentle pull on my hair.

"Yes," I breathe, and the smallest of smirks tugs at his full lips, denting his freshly shaven cheek.

"Good," he says lowly, its rasp raising gooseflesh along my arms. His fingers unwind from my braid, and then tuck a stray lock of hair behind my ear. "Go with Lina. I'll see you soon, love. And we can finish that conversation."

⇥

As it turns out, it's not that easy to drink from a glass bottle

190

while the ship you're on is doing its absolute best to throw you into every wall of a cabin.

About ten minutes ago, we braved the hallway, and the rain and seawater that somehow managed to make it inside, to get to the washroom. Li and I are now back to back in the tub, with our feet braced against its sides to keep from budging. I've never been more grateful for the strength I've trained into my legs for nearly a decade than I am now.

The bottle slides across the bottom of the copper surface, into my hand. I take a swig of the amber liquid, letting the stinging, smooth warmth of it slither down my throat and across my chest. It helps with the chill of the water still drying on my skin and in my hair.

"I never knew it could be this cold in the middle of the summer," I think out loud, passing the bottle back to her.

"Quit whining," she responds over the noise of the storm that rages just outside the inch-thick door. Her words are slurred a bit, while my head and speech remain clear, though we've had the same amount to drink. I wonder if it's part of the Fae in me, or as simple as the difference in our sizes.

"Don't be grumpy just because you don't get to play in the rain with the rest of them."

I can almost *feel* her roll her eyes at me. "I'm not grumpy."

"You are. And the more you drink, the worse of a job you do at hiding it."

She takes another sip, and I huff a chuckle through my nose.

Then she sighs, forgetting to pass the bottle back to me. "It's just...it's *always* been like this, Al. And it'll always *be* like this. I'll always be the one who's too weak, too small, too slow. I'll always be the one who needs protecting."

I scoff. "Bullshit."

She almost takes her feet off the side of the tub, but the ship rocks to the right, and when she keeps her footing, all we do is sway within the basin. "It's not bullshit! It's how I feel."

"Oh, I'm not saying you're not allowed to feel that way. I'm just saying that it's bullshit. Li, did you not see the way you kicked the ass of a Fae male with, what, a hundred pounds on you yesterday? And don't say it's because he let you win, because I saw the hold he had on you."

"I only got out because I used his expectations of me against him," she mumbles, and brings the bottle back to her lips.

"And that's probably how you would get out if a real opponent ever attacked you. What's wrong with that?"

"It's what they *expect* of me, Al!" Pain and anger mingle in her voice, loud enough that I'm momentarily stunned into silence. "They *expect* me to be weak. And as long as that's what they expect, I will always be the human girl sitting in a tub with whoever they pretend also needed to be here with me."

With the exception of the pounding storm around us, it's quiet in the washroom for a moment.

Then I sigh. "You are not weak because you're human. You are not weak because of your arm. *They* are weak. Because they are so blinded by their expectations of you, that they don't see how you continue to defy them. Li, you have been stronger than them since the day you were born. They don't know what it's like to live in a world that is and yet isn't your own. Adapting to that...becoming strong, and fast, and wicked as you are–that is *strength*."

Silence once more.

Then, a sniffle.

My heart strains, and I reach behind me. Not for the bottle, but to hook my elbow around hers. We tense as the ship violently rocks again, and water pours in under the door. When it settles, however briefly, we relax back into each other.

"It was my mum who taught me to fight like that," Li confesses quietly.

My own voice is cautious when I ask, "The High Lady?"

"No." Surprise colors her tone. "One of my mums is her sister, so she's my aunt. But my other mum is the one who taught me how to fight."

"The Sabriani High Lady didn't adopt you after–after what happened?" I had just assumed that would be the case. That my mom took me, and the female who birthed me took Li.

"No. She only wanted you." The surprise is gone, and in its place is a bitterness I can practically taste.

If not for the damn storm, I would turn to her, but I'm forced to remain back to back with Li when I ask her, "Are you angry with me about that? You know I had as little say in all that happened that day as you did."

"I know that." I hear her take another swig from the bottle.

When she doesn't elaborate, I raise my brows, and follow up with, "Then what are you angry at?"

"I don't know, Al. Maybe the fact that the reason I don't feel good enough for this world I was forced to live in is because I wasn't good enough for the woman who threw me into it like the trash she thought I was."

My heart thunders in my chest, its beat heavy in my throat. It thickens my voice, and heats the blood in my cheeks with indignance. "That's not what happened," I say through my teeth, trying to detach myself as much as possible from thinking about *her* while defending her...Defending her, even as something in Li's words rings true.

Another wave thrashes the ship, spills under the washroom door, and it feels like the sea is expressing the roiling that's beginning within me.

"Isn't it? She took one look at me and decided I wasn't hers.

How could I be? I was *defective*." Another pull of the amber liquor.

I take a breath, trying to calm the anger and desolation brewing within me. "It's a superstition. All Weaschtens believe it."

"It wouldn't have mattered if she actually loved me."

My hands fist on top of my knees. "She didn't think you were hers."

She scoffs, a harsh, cruel sound. "And yet she took one look at you, who was *truly* not hers, and took you right home. She didn't care for her daughter. She just wanted a perfect princess."

I spring out of the tub so fast that Emelina falls onto her back with a shout, and spills the rest of the liquor all over herself. My chest is heaving with the force of my breaths as I glare down at her, the tears in my eyes blurring her edges. The crack in my heart is threatening to fracture, its racing beat splintering the line.

Emelina looks up, her brows furrowed in annoyance and anger, and then her expression flattens in shock and–and *horror*. "Al..." she breathes, and already her voice is shaking, her own eyes, my *mom's* eyes, filling with tears.

But I don't want to hear whatever she might come up with to say. I don't want to be in this room with her at all. And since even the storm has seemed to pause for us to look at each other in this moment, I take the opportunity it gives me.

I throw the door open, exit in one stride, and slam it behind me. I'm instantly dampened by the rain and seawater falling around me, but I don't want to just be standing here for her to open the door again and try to talk to me.

I dart down the hall, my shoulder colliding with the corner of the entryway to the stairs when the ship sways. I don't know where I'm going, but I emerge on the deck, now utterly soaked, hardly able to see from one side of the ship to the other. I hold my hand up to shield my eyes from the water, but it comes from all sides. I stumble along the deck, ignoring the figures that aren't familiar enough.

I'm spinning in place, or trying to; trying to find him, to stop this pain in a way only he can. But the ship is rocking, and my mind is spinning and my heart is *hurting*, and–

"*Thea!*"

I whirl to the name only he calls me, and find him, knowing the shape of him even in this storm. And maybe it's the set of my shoulders, or maybe his sight is good enough that he can see my face, but I can tell when he realizes I'm not up here for nothing. I see him take me in, and a tearless sob breaks from my chest.

His long, powerful legs move to close the distance between us. Even though it's the span of a breath, he's fast–so he's only a few yards away when a huge wave descends on me, and pulls me back into the endless abyss whence it came.

28

THE MONSTER RETURNS

THE PRISONER STOOD ON THE WOODEN STAGE, BEHIND THE ornamental gallows and before the pristine stockades. A burlap sack covered his head, but I could see his family prematurely grieving for him at the front of the crowd of people gathered to watch the execution. A female clutched a girl to her, tears streaming down her face, as a boy who couldn't be more than fifteen held his mother, his face set with determination to be strong for the remainder of his family.

This publicity had only begun one year ago. Before that, my work was done either in the castle dungeons, or in the night as I snuck into the homes of those speaking ill of the king. He had decided that the reason there was still any palpable displeasure to his reign, was because the people were not scared enough. The continued gossip about his insufficiencies, and the possibilities of new rulers, even over ten years after he believed those rumors should have been quashed, had been enough for him to decide on a change of direction.

Before, he had at least pretended to care if Eshellens wanted him as their king. Now, it was either *they* pretended, or they died. And it was working as he'd intended.

There was no hope in the faces I saw in the crowd. No fire that shone through, indicating that a rebellion would be imminent. The vast majority of them looked only either concerned for the loss the family of the male was about to face, or stood with utter blankness in their expressions. Desensitized to the violence they saw here a few times a week.

The worst, though, were the faces of excitement. Those with money on the death—on who would be beneath the burlap sack—or who generally took pleasure in the suffering of others. Those were the only faces I couldn't bear to look at.

As I observed the rest, I ignored the words Marcys was saying to the people. The justification for this execution. How the people should be thankful that their king cared so much about the welfare of his nation. That what they should fear was treason ever going unpunished.

I hadn't seen the male between my time in the dungeons, and two years ago, when these displays began. The first time, the terror the sight of him struck within me made my power go haywire. For a heartbeat, I hadn't been able to get it to work. Then, when it did, I obliterated the prisoner with a force greater than ten cannons.

Marcys had smirked at me after, either knowing or scenting what his appearance had done to me. Now, we neither spoke nor looked at each other as we stood on this stage. I was able to zone out his words, and he managed to look unimpressed by the power that could have him dead in half a second, if I just shifted the direction of my majick past the prisoners. If I were not ordered to leave him unharmed.

He at last finished his speech, and something within me withered further when many in the crowd applauded. Whether it was for belief in the words, or for fear of being identified if they did not, I couldn't be fully sure. I hoped it was the latter. Because if they truly thought Oleander had their best interests at heart, then Eshelle was lost.

Before Marcys stepped back, he ripped the sack off the male's head. I watched him meet the eyes of his family, and saw their sobs deepen in turn. As I was no longer permitted near the king, it had taken some doing, but eventually one of my letters for him had convinced Oleander that we should show the prisoners' faces before they were killed. That knowing their friend, their spouse, their neighbor, had been caught, they would be less likely to whisper after watching that person die.

Really, it had been for this. This one last glimpse they could get of their families, or friends. The final time those loved ones would be able to dedicate the prisoner's face to memory.

I moved to stand just feet from the male, but he did not turn to me, as some of them did. He stared down at his wife and children, and as I raised my wretched hand, he said to them, "I love you."

I could only do them the mercy of granting them enough time to say it back to him before my majick flared. I felt my skin heat, my eyes burn, and smelled the embers and flame. Then, with a flick of my wrist, the male standing behind the gallows turned into a pile of ash.

I listened to it hiss through the boards of the stage before the heartbeat of shock wore off, and his wife screamed. I locked my jaw, and deadened my eyes before I looked out at the people, Marcys striding to stand beside me. As one, we said, "Long live High King Oleander Gervan, the one true ruler of Eshelle."

And the crowd repeated after us.

Or, most of them did.

The son of the male whose remains trickled down to the ground beneath the wooden boards stared at me. He had the same white-blond hair as his sister, and fury burned within his violet eyes. As he held his sobbing mother and keening sister, his lean, not yet matured face held a hatred so deep that I could feel its energy in my bones.

When I'd seen such emotions on the faces of the Sabriani all those years ago, as I paraded into their city with the royal crest on my chest, I'd been ashamed. Had not been able to meet their eyes, for the knowledge that they were right to feel as they did. I had been so loathful of myself that seeing my own emotions reflected in their gazes had been unbearable.

Now, as I stared at the hatred on that boy's face, even as I hated myself just as much, if not more, I did not look away. I held his gaze, and added fuel to his flame with it. And I hoped that one day, he would use it against me.

⇔

I no longer ate dinner with Olin, Oleander, and Melisan, as I had all those years ago. Now, I was forced to dine–for both breakfast *and* supper–with Olin's cronies.

He had plenty of them, but his favorites were here at this table every morning and night. Marcys, David, Gadsby. And Adathan.

I remembered, from the depths of what my mind had been in that dungeon, how Marcys had caught him flinching once as the blond male doled out Olin's punishment upon me. How, afterwards, I hadn't seen him for a few weeks, but I'd heard him. Listened to him scream as they tore him apart.

And I remembered how, even after their ministrations on him, he had still always been gentle as he'd pushed the iron-filled needle into my veins. Considering these factors, it was hard for me to resent anything about him. Except the blood oath my brother had him under.

Whatever else I might have remembered, I kept shrouded behind that wall of night within my mind, safe even from myself.

I realized, as I mindlessly ate the meal before me, that I'd been staring at him as I contemplated all of this. He held my gaze, that same mask of indifference not cracking, even under the awkwardness. The scars beneath the fine clothing he was made to wear by Olin—now that he was of a 'deserving rank,' as my brother so lovingly put it—must be far more than skin deep for that kind of skill.

I was the one to drop my eyes first, not wanting him to see how badly I felt for him having experienced that pain because of me. Because he was so obviously cursed with the soul Olin did not have, even if he tried to hide it.

Though I held no animosity for him, I hadn't gotten any closer to him, either. Two years, and we'd shared only a pleasantry here and there. Even that, however, was far better than my dealings with the other males at the table.

I did not speak with them if I could avoid it. David, while not overtly cruel, was dumb as a rock—but that made him the perfect puppet for Olin, whom he idolized. Gadsby *was* cruel, but I learned years ago that, while he too was bound by blood oath to Olin, my brother also kept him as a lover. Olin had always favored females, but had never really been one to turn away anybody who might want to get his cock wet.

Marcys, well, I tried not to think about. While my fear of him had passed over time, I still could not see him without remembering all the ways he'd torn me apart for ten years.

Then, of course, there was their blood-bonded ruler. He kept no secrets from me any longer, for he knew that, no matter how much I hated my role and myself, I could never leave nor disobey. I knew he still called himself by my name in all areas but his private quarters. It was he who told me about his tryst with Gadsby. He who informed me about how the nations surrounding Oschverre had been completely subdued, and even those *'further south'* no longer stank of rebellion.

Yes, he had no reason to hide these things anymore. My situation was just as it had been in that dungeon. Leaving, or betraying in any other manner, would only serve to jeopardize my court–my *true* court. And so there was no other option for me.

It would have been funny, were it not so devastating, that I could remember this time twelve years ago, when I'd thought along similar lines. How naive I'd been, to how much worse it could get.

29

WITHOUT THE 'IT'

THERE IS NO WAY UP, AND NO WAY DOWN.

Everything is blackness and cold and fear.

I open my eyes and try to make sense of it, but the water is pulling and pushing me relentlessly. My body is spinning and it's taking everything in me to remember to keep my mouth closed; that all screaming will do is drown me faster–

Then strong arms catch me. But they're not the arms I'd been expecting.

My body is turned, steadied by lithe hands, and I have to resist screaming again at the creature before me.

She could have been a woman. The face shape, the features, the curves of her torso. Unmistakably female, but there is nothing human about her.

Her blue skin is flecked with freckles of bioluminescence that make her look ethereal. Her eyes have long, angled webs above them, the shape of an arc of lashes, and the eyes beneath them are a bright lavender. Her skin and scales are such that she would nearly blend in with the sea if not for the hair that floats in the water around her, and crests over a pointed pair of ears. White–as white as the teeth she flashes now. Not in a snarl–but in a grin. It would probably be more disarming if not for the canines from the top and bottom of her jaw that look sharp enough to tear my hand from my body with one bite.

She takes a webbed hand from my shoulder, and points up. Maybe it makes me foolish, but as she just saved my life, I don't think too long before following her gesture.

We're much farther from the surface than I would have thought, and the ship is just a big black spot several dozen yards to the right.

Then the webbed hands are on either side of my face, bringing my gaze back to hers. "Your male comes now," she says, her voice echoing like an undersea bell around me, loud and soft all at once. Then, in a flash of skin and scales, and a powerful tail, she's gone.

I look around, still oriented as she'd set me, and–there. A familiar, large figure swimming for me with a speed nearly equal to the sea creature who had saved me.

His golden eyes are open, and as he closes the last of the distance between us, I have a memory of another moment with him under the waves.

My, how things have changed since then.

Before I can think more on it, his arm bands around my waist, pulling me against him. I wrap my arms around his neck, and then we're moving with preternatural speed towards the surface, and the ship.

When our heads break into the air, I gasp in a lungful of it. "I've got you, Thea," Adan is saying, his voice shaking. "Hold onto me, love."

I nod into the crook of his shoulder, and feel the looming,

swaying mass of the ship approaching. Males are shouting our names, heard even over the remaining sounds of the waves and the rain, which have softened since I was swept from the deck. In fact, the moment that female creature's hands had touched my skin, the storm had seemed to calm. I just hadn't realized in the immediate chaos and fear.

"Legs around me," Adan commands, and I obey, bringing them around his waist. I have no inclination to tell him I could climb the rope and wood ladder on the side of the ship myself as he hauls both of us to the deck easily.

"Out of the way," he orders the bustling males, and even Ciaragen and Atlas, as he swings his powerful legs over the railing. Once his feet touch the wood of the deck, his arms wrap around me. I note with surprise that he does not move to set me down, even with all the eyes on us. Instead, he continues to the steps leading to the cabins. All the while, until my door closes behind him, I can feel his body trembling against mine.

"I'm okay," I whisper against his sodden shirt. Then, for a long moment, the only sounds are our ragged breaths, and the water dripping from us onto the floor.

He takes a shuddering breath, and finally bends to set me on the feet I lower from behind his back. Slowly enough that it feels like he has to force himself to do it, he unravels the hold his arms have on me, and instead places his hands on my shoulders.

I pull back enough to look into his face, and find his head bowed, and eyes closed. "What," he says, his deep voice quiet and rough, "in all the gods' names were you doing on deck?"

I swallow the emotions that rise to block my throat, now that the danger has passed. But when they lodge there, leaving me no room to speak unless I finally allow them release, I shake my head.

Not yet.

Adan takes another breath, slightly more steady than the last, and opens his eyes. Fear, sadness, and anger mingle within them, and the last takes the forefront as he asks through his teeth, "Do you realize that you could have–*died*, Thea?"

Yes. Anger is better; his and mine. It keeps me together, shoves that lump out of my throat and instead my pulse thrums there now. I hold his gaze for a few pounding heartbeats, and ask, far too calmly, "What do you care?"

His hands drop from my shoulders, and he asks with a quiet that makes a shudder race up my spine, "What do I *care*?" He steps into me, and my only choice is to step back in turn, until my back is against the wall, and the solid mass of him is so close I can feel the heat of him along my skin. His hands brace on either side of my head, and I hear wood groan as his hands flex against it. "What do *I* care, Thea?"

I watch the question I'd known was ridiculous rouse this reaction in him. Watch his eyes heat with temper–anger that I can tell he's intentionally giving power to, just like me. Forcing it to rise over the fear and panic I know he felt as he held me in shaking arms.

I lift my chin, though his height makes the motion barely helpful. And, ready to finish our conversation from this morn-ing, I ask again, this time softly: "What do you care, Adan?"

His breath stalls, and the fury in his eyes banks. They flit across my face, and that anger begins to fade into a different sort of heat. A kind that has my pulse spiking in an entirely different way, and has me forgetting how drenched we both are; forgetting all that happened moments ago. And only recalling here, and now, with his mouth just inches from mine, and his body close enough that even with the space between us, my skin warms because of him.

His voice is a low rumble that vibrates through his chest and across my skin. "Stop looking at me like that."

I shake my head slowly, and his jaw clenches. "Thea, you *want* to stop looking at me like that."

"No, I don't," I breathe. And maybe it's that I truly could have died, or maybe it's the fire in his eyes, but the words I've kept inside for days–weeks–come out now. Not rushed, or scared. But quiet, and certain. "I want to keep looking at you, just like this. I want to see what happens when I do. Because, most importantly, I want *you*, Adan. And I know you want me, too."

Disbelief and hesitant hope coats his features, and those bright, lovely eyes take all of me in, as if he'll find some chink in the armor; my expression of desire. My heart pounds as I continue, and I can sense his racing just the same. "Tell me I'm misreading things. Tell me you don't want this; don't want *me*. Tell me, and I'll never bring it up again."

Silence. Only our hearts, our breath, and the pattering rain.

Then, though I'd spoken with ease what lay in my heart, his words are forced through jaw and teeth. "I am not a knight in shining armor, Thea. Not a gallant lordling that might kiss your lips gently for a heartbeat, and call it enough. I am not good; I am Death with his scythe, and I would take from you whatever you gave me. And, if you give me this...I would never fucking let you go."

All I say, my voice a savage whisper, is, "*Good.*"

All he says, his tone half prayer and half damnation, is, "*Fuck.*"

And then his lips are on mine.

30

CHOSEN

THEA - DAY 24

WILDFIRE.

Untameable. Magnificent. Terrifyingly intense. Lightning could strike the ship, and I wouldn't notice.

Adan's hands, calloused and strong, grip me with a need that rivals my own. Long fingers, threaded into my ocean-soaked hair, and more gripping the small of my back, pulling me flush to him. He doesn't try to be gentle with me, his lips crushing mine and his hands tight on my body. That mouth that has cursed at and comforted me now moves in beautiful, unfamiliar patterns, and mine moves with it; not stumbling or unsure. But a dance that was always meant to be with him.

His tongue traces the seam of my lips, and I open for him without hesitation. As he swoops in, the feeling that had been building in my core since his arms caged me against the wall heightens even more. A moan escapes me, and my hands, which had initially found their way to rest on his chest, now rise to wrap around his neck, and I arch against him.

A growl, low and guttural, sounds from deep in his chest, and his hand in my hair tightens, pulling my head back to give him better access. His other arm is a vice around my waist, tight enough that my already panting breaths are shallow, and yet I just want him to hold me *tighter*.

As if reading my mind—or just feeling the same, Adan uses that arm to hoist me up. My legs go around his waist, feeling far different than the position had only minutes ago, and he pins me to the wall. One broad hand finds the back of my thigh, while the other hooks around my neck, his thumb resting against my cheek. My hands are not so well-behaved.

They rove through his hair, even softer than I imagined. They travel down his neck and across his traps, my nails scratching. I hear the fabric of his shirt tear, and don't even care that I did it as it gives me access to the scarred skin of his back.

He pulls his mouth from mine, and I make a noise of protest that's quickly cut off, morphing into another moan as his lips find my neck instead, and suck on the skin over my thundering pulse. So many firsts in such a short time, and, if he's taking, as he said he would, I just want to keep giving them to him.

"Adan," I practically whimper.

"Thea," he groans, his hand squeezing my thigh, and then loosening to stroke it, from my knee to my hip. This time, it's a sigh, "Thea." His mouth trails along the hollow above my collar bone, and I hear him inhale, breathing in the scent of me. "*Thea.*"

Like a prayer. Like I am the goddess he's chosen to worship. Like the more he says it, the more he believes I'm real.

The frenzy of a moment ago shifts with that reverence. I trail my hands gently back over his shoulders, up his neck, and frame his face between them. I lift it until he meets my eyes, and marvel at the adoration in his. And the hunger, which makes my belly tighten.

"Kiss me again, Adathan," I whisper, stroking my thumb along a thin scar on his temple.

It's tentative this time. The way he leans in, and his lips brush over mine, from corner to corner. Back and forth, twice, before he settles in the center. I sigh against his mouth, and my fingers are soft as they run over his jaw. Through touch, I memorize the feel of its edge, then the tip of his arched ear on one side, the column of his throat on the other. He lets me explore, kissing me all the while, his hands on me still; letting *me* decide if they should move now.

"Yes," I murmur over his lips. A low noise vibrates within his chest, and he seizes my consent. He brushes my hair back, then trails his fingers down my neck, brushing over my collar bone. At the same time, the hand on my thigh runs down to my knee, then my calf, and back. It's hesitant as it reaches my hip, just as his other fingers don't travel any lower, and I nod, but he shakes his head in return.

Pulling back by a hair, he says quietly, "I want to take my time with you, Thea. I don't want to do this all in one night." When I open my mouth to argue, a calloused thumb brushes it, silencing me. "More importantly, I want to give you at least some form of the courtship you deserve. I may not be a knight, or a lord, but I am a male. And I'm going to make sure you know that, that you *feel* that, in more than one way."

His thumbs stroke my thigh, and my pulse over my clavicle. "I am not worthy of a single piece of you. Let me do this. Let me do anything, *everything*, I can to at least begin to deserve you."

I would speak, would tell him he already deserves me; that it's *me* who isn't worthy of *him*. But he keeps me quiet with another kiss, setting me down.

And I use every ounce of strength I have to spin us, catching him completely off-guard, until he's the one with his back to the wall; hitting it with a loud *thump* with the force with which I shove him.

One of my hands rests on his chest, the other reaching up to wrap around what I can of his throat, right under his jaw. "You listen to me, Adathan Evestre. You can court me. But let me make something very clear: my choices were made for me once before. I've lived hiding my desires. I am *not* going to let that happen here. Not with you. You don't get to pull away after this, even for the sake of gallantry."

A lazy heat turns the gold of his eyes molten, and he reaches to tuck my wet hair behind my ear. "What is it you desire, then, love?"

Warmth rises to my cheeks at the question, at the name, and I move my hands to stroke over the solid muscle of his chest. "I don't know where to begin," I tell him honestly.

His eyes soften, and the fingers by my ear caress my cheek, grazing over the scar the glamour hides to all but him. "How about with right now?"

My lip pulls between my teeth, and his gaze is drawn to it. I sense it when his pulse stutters, and can't help the small grin that comes as a result. Though I could ask for all manner of physical things I desire, my first request is: "I want to know why your heart just skipped."

"Because I'm fucking obsessed with your mouth."

The utter lack of hesitation, combined with the answer...my step into him is involuntary. "I want to know what else you're obsessed with."

"Every gods-damn inch of you." Finally, his hands roam. The one by my face runs down the side of my neck while his other latches onto my waist. "Every word that comes out of your mouth. Every smile you give me. Every bit of your very existence."

Emotion rises, far different from before but thickening my throat all the same, and I have to take a deep breath before my next request will come out. "I want you to promise me that when we leave this room, so does this. No hiding."

His brows furrow, and he strokes my cheek once more, the calloused pad of his thumb gentle along my skin. "I promise."

He doesn't ask me if I'm sure; doesn't second guess this choice. *This* choice, where not long ago there hadn't been one. My feelings surrounding that time, those days, are tangled in a knot. Threads of rage and grief and regret that have twisted together to form this thing within me, not easily, perhaps not ever, undone. But this...this one thing. It may not unravel the knot, and maybe I don't even deserve to have it, but...Adan does. And that can be enough of a reason to let myself have it, too.

I slide my hands up his chest and around his neck, leaning into him to indicate my intent, my desire. He shudders beneath my touch, a sigh escaping him as he bends to meet me. When his lips are a hairsbreadth from mine, I whisper, "I want you to know something."

"What's that?" he murmurs, tracing the shape of my cupid's bow with his mouth.

"I'm obsessed with you, too." Then I tilt my chin up so that our lips slide together, and feel his heart skip the same beat as mine.

31

THESE THINGS OF OURS

LINA - DAY 25

I'VE HAD SOME SERIOUSLY LOW POINTS IN MY LIFE. RIGHT NOW, though, none of them feel as shitty as I do as I remember the look on Al's face.

I'd stayed in the tub after she left, and even when the storm calmed a moment later, I couldn't find the will to so much as rinse the sticky, reeking liquor from my skin. My anger, combined with the alcohol running through my veins, had loosened my tongue. And I'd decided to spew the thoughts I had of the woman who birthed me, to the one that she'd raised.

The one who had knelt beside her when she died.

The woman was *dead*, and Al had lost her, and my first words about it weren't to comfort her, but to hurt her. To slice and maim with the hateful thoughts that nagged at me in my worst moments. That both females presented with her had wanted *her*, and rejected me.

As if that was her fucking fault.

I know at some point she returned to her cabin. And yet, in all the hours since then, I haven't been able to muster up the courage to go to her. To apologize.

I'd bathed, just so that whenever I did find that strength, she wouldn't have to stand there inhaling the stench of me. My time is running out, though; the light through the porthole is turning gray, and she will be up within the hour, if she's not already. I'm pretty sure today is a rope climbing day, since she missed yesterday for...whatever that was with Adathan, and she's dedicated enough that she'll make the climb even if the rope is wet. Honestly, she'll probably look at it as a challenge.

With the heaviest sigh I think I've ever heaved, I sit up in my bed. I probably slept about two hours through the night, thanks to the alcohol and complete exhaustion from the constant stress of the storm. The rest, I'd spent thinking; sometimes pacing, sometimes staring at the wall of my cabin. Either way, thinking about what I might say to her. How I would apologize.

After all that time, I know I've got as much as I'm going to get in that department. If she's going to forgive me, it'll probably be because of the type of person she is; my pretty words will have little to do with it.

I make quick work of getting dressed for the day, my hair in its usual cloud around my shoulders. The washroom is free, and I gather the nerve to look at the other doors in the hall. Of course, I was right. While all other occupied cabins are closed, their inhabitants still sleeping, hers is wide open. Empty.

Another sigh, and I brush my teeth, and take a look in the mirror. My eyes are rimmed in pink, my lips wan, and that's good. I don't want her to think I slept well, or am *doing* well after what I said to her.

Gods, her face. She had looked so...devastated. So close to shedding the tears she's been holding in for weeks. It could have been just the words I'd said–the things I spat about her *dead mum*. But I have a feeling that pain was also because the words came from *me*. She decided to let me in, to trust me, and I went and twisted both of our pasts, the pasts we are *both* healing from, and used them against her.

If she's up on that rope, as I believe she is, it's not just because of discipline, or routine. It's to rein back in that emotion, so that she doesn't lose the careful control she's had of it so far. Something I almost took from her with my carelessness and cruelty. Which she only has, I think, because she hasn't felt safe enough to release that hurt, that grief, yet. Hasn't wanted to 'break' when so many things around her are already out of her control.

Well, I sure as the fucking Void didn't make her feel any safer last night.

Steeling myself, I take a single breath before leaving the washroom, and go up the stairs to the deck. I spot the rope she's been climbing, and follow it up–

She's about fifty feet high, her blonde braid swaying with each foot she pulls herself up. I watch her make the last dozen or so feet with such ease, it sends a familiar ache through my chest.

No, I think to myself. *None of that, not right now.*

Al makes it to the last crossbeam, and uses her core to swing her legs up over it, straddling it like one of the sloths they have in the wilds of Sielva, the southernmost country in Eshelle. Then she hoists herself atop it, sits down, and looks out at the sea.

I give her a minute to breathe, and to allot myself with another moment to gather my thoughts. I'm about to call up to her with my remaining courage, when I see her look down. Right at me.

Whether she sensed me even as she climbed, or it's just a coincidence, I don't know. I only stand there mutely, my mouth still open, as she stares down at me for several pounding heartbeats.

Then she stands on the beam, and my shoulders drop with some relief; she's willing to climb back down to talk. My stance relaxes by a fraction to wait–and then tenses in terror as she jumps.

But she lands in a crouch, as graceful as any Fae I've seen, even with the glamour still upon her. When she straightens, her expression is carefully blank. It makes my heart clench painfully in my chest, that blankness. Empty, as she has never before forced it to be around me.

It has the tears pooling in my eyes before I even start speaking. When I do, my voice breaks, cracking through the little room it can find out of my throat. "I am so sorry, Al."

Her jaw flexes, full lips thinning, but she doesn't respond. So, I go on, "I was so cruel, and thoughtless. I let my anger get the better of me, and I didn't *think*, I just spewed my bullshit. I was already so upset about them shoving me away for the storm, and it brought all these thoughts of not being good enough too close to the surface. All of it–*all of it* was my own problems, and I put them on you. I'm *so sorry*."

Her lovely face is still tight, but her eyes aren't completely blank anymore. There is...understanding there, but beneath it is the hurt I've been afraid to see again all night. "You meant what you said," she tells me quietly.

I swallow, because I don't want to lie, but... "I–I feel those things, but I never intended to say them to you."

"But you did." Those bright green eyes take on a shine, and my tears finally spill at the sight of it.

"I did," I rasp, knowing apologizing again won't do me any good. Since we both know my remorse is for hurting her with my words, not for the words themselves, I just have to hope that she will forgive me, even knowing that.

Her gaze is unwavering, despite the silver within it, as she stares at me. Then, after a moment that feels like an eternity to my pounding heart, her expression softens, and her voice with it. "These past weeks, I've considered us the same. We both grew up in places not meant for us, and we've both experienced hardship because of it. I didn't..." she swallows, and shifts on her feet. "I didn't think about how it must have felt to be rejected by your–your mom. I could make an excuse, tell you how I've avoided thinking about...about *her* at all–"

Her jaw tightens against the emotion that comes with that, but my tears aren't as steadfastly restrained. As they flow down my cheeks, she clears her throat to continue. "But, you deserve more. So, while I still can't talk about her, and be that friend to you, I hope–I want you to know that I understand what you said. What you feel. Li, I am so sorry for how you hurt." Her lips tremble before she pulls them between her teeth, choking back the tears that want so badly to spill.

I nod emphatically, unable to speak. To verbalize what her words mean to me. She scans my face for another moment, and then she's closing the distance between us, her arms out.

We've never truly embraced before. Only one-armed hugs to the side, or a head on a shoulder. She never seemed open to or ready for it. So now, when she's asking in the silent way she does best, I don't hesitate to step into her, and wrap my arms around her waist.

Her lean, muscled arms wind over my shoulders and my hair, and her cheek presses against my forehead. There is no dampness there, meaning she's yet again succeeded at keeping her tears at bay.

I'm not so controlled. My tears continue to spill, falling onto her collarbone, her chest, and she holds me through it. And I hold her back.

⎄

When dawn is truly upon us, we're standing at the railing, watching the sun begin its ascent. We've been standing in comfortable silence for several minutes, each of our hearts lighter than they'd been when we woke up.

Now, though, Al turns to me, and her voice is wary when she says, "I have to tell you something."

I look over at her, and find her biting her lower lip. "Yeah?"

It comes out in a rush, like she won't say it at all if she doesn't say it quickly. "I kissed Adathan last night."

My eyes widen, and my mouth falls open. I'd known it would be a matter of time, after the way I saw them yesterday morning, so the expression isn't out of shock.

No, it's something far more girlishly-inclined.

"How was it?" I ask, leaning in a bit for the details.

Her lips stretch into a small grin that's perhaps a *little* bigger than it has been in the past, and relief shines in her eyes. I don't know if she expected a negative reaction just because of the prejudices others have had against him, or because she knows how close I am with Atlas, but I am so damn happy to defy her expectation regardless.

"It was...fucking fantastic," she replies, a blush spreading across her freckled cheeks.

I shake my head. "Nope. Not enough. I need *details*, Al. Was there tongue? How far did it go? Are you guys together now?"

The blush spreads, but her eyes sparkle with elation. "There was tongue, and we are together now. It stopped at the kiss, but because of him, not me."

That *also* doesn't surprise me. "Why?"

She rolls her eyes, but the gesture is halfhearted. "He wants to court me. Said I deserve that. But, Li, I don't know how long I can wait." She bites her lip again, and her blush spreads to the tips of her ears. I can tell she's not used to talking like this, at least about herself. The light in her eyes, though, tells me she's anything but embarrassed about it.

"You've waited twenty-one years already, is a little bit longer gonna kill you?" I nudge her arm with my shoulder.

"With him? *Yes*. I want him so badly it hurts–which I always thought was just a thing people say, but it's *true*."

I laugh again, and her lips tip up. "I don't blame you. He's hot."

Her nose crinkles adorably. "He really is, isn't he?"

I snort. "Please. You could fry an egg on his abs. Or on that ass."

Her giggle is surprised, but delighted. Afterwards, she sighs. "It's hard."

I know she means the waiting, but I say, "Yeah, probably everything about him is right now, Al."

And her laugh bursts through the air just as the sun crests over the edge of the sea.

⇛

Together, we go back to the cabins to get the rest of our little group for breakfast. I, however, pause for a minute outside Atlas's door, while she walks further down the hall, to Adathan's room. And screw shame over being nosey, because I'm basically standing guard for her, so I lean against the wall to watch.

She lifts her hand and knocks, and then bounces on her toes a bit as she waits. The door opens after a second, and I can't see him yet where he stands beyond the threshold, but I see her. And I watch her profile as the biggest smile I've ever seen her give lights up her face. "Good morning," she greets him, her voice *excited*. Just to see him in the morning, without any pretense between them.

Then, in a blink, large, tan hands are slightly ahead of the rest of him as he grabs and steps into her. One grips the back of her head, the other her waist, and he pulls her body flush with his in the same instant that his lips come down onto hers.

It's only a few seconds. Three or four heartbeats where her hands barely have the time to settle on his chest. Then he pulls her face back by an inch, and says, his voice a rumble that even pebbles the skin on *my* arms, "Good morning."

She smiles again, a lazy, hazed sort of thing. He kisses the corner of that smile, and her already pinkened cheeks deepen in color. I see his mouth tilt up on *both* sides–which I think I've seen two or three times, though all of them were in response to her–a dimple denting each cheek. Then, he slants his mouth over hers once more, and only when I can tell she's completely forgotten about anyone and everything else, does he nip at her bottom lip, evoking a small gasp that's *definitely* not pained.

He releases her slowly, and she actually *sways*, just a little. And, not out of any begrudgement or jealousy, but for the joy of it, I wish to have that sort of love for myself someday. In this moment, though, I can be glad that she has it.

Even if she doesn't realize it yet.

32

THE EMPRESS

The days following the storm were relaxing in comparison to those before it.

So many hard conversations have been spoken, no longer festering between our group. The storm itself has passed, leaving a day or so until we reach Ardhavi, since Javi's majick kept us on course through those treacherous waves.

He had been at the helm, of course, but I'd been ordered there simply because the High Lord had questions for me. About our arrival, and what I would do once there, no longer bound to the vessel.

I will be shadowalking to Sabrian, of that much I'm sure. Though my Hielo and Hiela have received our missive of who would be joining us–the daughter they'd thought they would not see for a few more years yet, and *Arthur*, in his true skin–I need to go to them. Explain more thoroughly than the length of the letter I'd rushed to send before the two of them had boarded our ship in Dahlih had allowed.

As I had told the captain, though, I would not be staying there, even for the night. I'll be returning to the ship as soon as possible; returning to my goddaughter and godson, my Lady, and the charge she ordered me to protect. The last, I've become nervous about, however. Not because of him, interestingly enough. But because I'm not sure him remaining on this ship will be the best way for me to fulfill that vow in the long run.

Which, of course, I haven't yet figured out how to share with my Lady. Something tells me she's not going to take it well.

For now, though, I'm at the breakfast table with all of them, even Javi. Geoff, his first mate, is steering the ship in his stead, so the captain sits on Atlas's other side, scarfing down the oatmeal Jacks made for breakfast.

Everyone ate the bland breakfast without complaint, but Althea stares at her freshly empty bowl with slightly furrowed brows. I'm about to ask what's wrong, when Adathan stands, grabs the bowl, and walks it to the counter to be refilled.

Jacks is able to scrounge up another scoop for her, and the male thanks him before striding back to the female who didn't take her eyes off him the entire time he was up. He lightly places the bowl down before her, and then retakes his seat to her left.

"Thank you," she tells him, and, for both myself and my godson, I'm grateful that she restrains herself from any physical expression of gratitude. "I don't know why I'm so hungry lately."

"It's the majick, love. All the training is draining you more than your body is used to, and it's telling you to keep yourself fueled in whatever way you can."

Her brows narrow once more. "But I only healed minor things yesterday, and we just worked a little with glamours and wind. Are you saying that I'll be even more hungry when I use more power?"

His voice gentles, because that's apprehension in her expression. Not about eating, which she had no problem with even in Cerasche. But in what her Fae body demands of her. "I'm saying it's a good thing we'll be making birth soon, because there's no way you'll want to eat this many plain oats every day until we get to Sabrian."

One corner of her mouth tips up, and I watch his profile as he sees it, and his own mouth softens in response.

No, he doesn't deserve her.

But she deserves him.

That's the mantra that has been running through my head ever since he emerged with her from the storm-ridden sea. Every time I catch them touching whenever they think Atlas and I aren't looking. Each moment where she seems *happy*, just because of something he's said or done.

Happy, when weeks ago it had seemed possible that she might never be that again.

Yes, she deserves that. No matter if it pains me whenever he seems happier in turn.

That light green gaze flits to the captain. "Is that why you're with us today? To announce that we're arriving in Ardhavi soon?"

Javi nods, swallowing his bite of oatmeal. "Though, of course, I thought I might also grant you all the pleasure of my company regardless."

A laugh huffs through my nose. "You might as well be a mer for all the attention you like to seek, *Captain*," I tease him. "You know very well how aware each of the crew are of your presence. They're practically ready to trip over themselves if you need someone to take a piss for you so you don't have to get up."

His hearty laugh echoes around the mess, and a few chuckles sound from the eaves-dropping tables around us. "My sea legs are tired, Ari. You try standing to piss three times a day on open water."

"Three times a day? Does your desalinator not work, or have you already been using your crewmen's services?"

"A captain never tells."

After the beats of laughter end, a familiar husky voice asks, "What's a mer?"

She's looking at me as she asks it, so I answer, "A mermaid; a species of faerie that lives in the oceans. They have the upper bodies of humans and Fae, but their bottom halves are like that of a fish. Fins, and all, only far more grand. They like to show them off, to see if they can lure you with them."

Her eyes are wide, and Lina, with an air of telling a ghost story to a child, continues, "My mum told me all about them when I was little. Apparently, they get vicious when they mature. Lose principles, and whatever humanity born within them from their Fae side. They give themselves to the sea and its darkness, and become creatures of *terror*." She grins as she says it, and then fingers one of her glamoured canines, baring the rest of her teeth exaggeratedly. "Their teeth–they sharpen one when they make a kill of a Fae. Take rough coral, and carve every one to be like a shark's by the time they're a few centuries old."

The female's skin has paled a bit beneath her freckles at Lina's tale, but confusion far outweighs any fear in her expression. "I saw one."

All at the table freeze, and Javi asks, "What do you mean you saw one?"

"When I was pulled into the sea during the storm. She caught me in the water, and held me steady, but swam away as soon as she saw Adathan coming for me."

All eyes move to the male, who's looking at Althea with horror written on his features. "I didn't see her," he says, golden eyes darting across her face, as if looking retroactively for any hurt he could have possibly missed.

"She blended in with the water; I only saw her because she was so close. And she had this white hair–even more white than Li's."

"Purple eyes?" Javi asks in a growl from my side, and we all turn to him, finding his dark eyes intent on Althea.

Her brows scrunch. "Yes," she answers, surprise lacing through the worry in her tone.

Javi scoffs. "Congratulations, my Lady. Your life was saved by their gods-damned Empress."

⇔

"What the fuck do you mean, their Empress?" Adathan asks, the consideration he usually has absent now in the face of the danger Althea unknowingly faced. The Fae male coming out through the carefully constructed exterior; when their partner is threatened, they become more beast than anything else. Even if the danger is passed.

Luckily, Javi understands that, and keeps his tone calm. I may not like Adathan, but I'm not stupid enough to believe that he wouldn't win in a fight against any at this table, even the High Lord of Obala. Right now, speaking about Althea's life having been in the hands of someone so powerful and dangerous, all he would need to do is use one wrong word, and Olin's son would have him on his back.

"She rules the mer. Not just of the Evredis, but of all the waters of Divania; commands the waters themselves, too. It's said that her mother was the one who ended her father's life, using her sharpened teeth to rip out his throat. And, in retribution, the now-Empress killed her own mother. For that act of brutality, the mer bowed to her without hesitation, despite the fact that she has an elder brother.

"It would seem that the Empress known for her savagery took a liking to your–Althea. I had wondered at the storm stopping so suddenly. Now, I believe that the Empress stopped it *for* her."

"Why?" Althea asks quietly, but not weakly. "Why me?"

Now, with Adathan's wrath tempered, Javi does look at the female to reply to her. "That is the question, isn't it?"

It's my turn to keep my expression neutral. Because I'm pretty sure I know the answer. But that is one part of the story I don't mind keeping secret.

33

WILLA

Thea - day 27

Adan's been quieter than usual since breakfast.

To see him so feral...a side of him I haven't seen–that he hasn't *let* me see before. All because of a danger to my life that had already passed.

I'd found myself bothered by the territorialism of the questions, of the *tone*, but also, in a different way...very much *un*bothered by it. Paradoxically wanting to throttle him and straddle him.

Feral, indeed.

The longer I spend with my mind open, that mental glamour wiped away like fog on glass, the more I learn about the Fae in me. The more I come to *like* her. She is strong, fast, and powerful. And while each new thing I learn about her throws me, just a bit, I'm starting to find that I am undaunted by it. That it's not the me I am now who fears her, but the human princess I still cling to.

I know why I hold onto her. The reasons tangle together, in a sister knot to the one which holds my rage and grief. That I have not yet freed her, have not yet begun to unspool those twisted skeins, is the same as it had been in the pines. She is not safe. Not yet.

I am closer than ever with the one person who brings me that feeling of security, but that is not enough. Not him; he *is*. More than enough, in fact. But, even with him, I am not safe.

Not from what releasing her will do to me.

It will *hurt*, more than even the nightmares do. And there will be nowhere for it to go, because the sources of that pain—that grief and rage—will still be *gone*. No amount of tears shed nor roaring screams or shattered knuckles will bring them back.

And it will still be my fault.

So the lovely, easy thing I once was, who then became wrapped in embers and glass—the coals of her heart still flaring, forging that broken glass into the weapon it is... She is still locked within the ferocious thing I am becoming; that which will take one of those horrid shards, and use it to slice apart the only other person to blame for destroying all she knew, and was.

Until then, the male who has stood by each version of her, of me, will help us both to continue that becoming. As he is now, sitting across from me in my cabin as I hold the mental shield up against the invisible onslaught of his unknown majick.

He has barely spoken through our lessons thus far today. Not through combat, nor swordplay. Not as I practiced my own wind wielding, except to congratulate me when I was able to billow a sail. And certainly not while practicing glamours and mind shielding, which demand the most concentration.

So, to distract myself from the heaviness of my own

thoughts, I decide I've had enough of his quiet, and purposely let my shield drop. Those miraculous eyes fly open and hone in on me, but before he can either chastise me or make butterflies tumble through me–I can't yet tell which will be which–I say, "If you can't read minds, how can you test my shield?"

Ever ready and willing to answer any question he's not bloodbound to keep, he immediately replies, "They're not so different from physical shields. I can sense them, even if I can do nothing about the mental sort. You could, too, if you wanted."

Deterred from my original query by a new line of questions that occurs to me, my brow furrows. "And the physical shields are individual, just like mental ones, right?"

"No; depending on the power of the Fae wielding it, a physical shield can cover a single person, or an entire army."

"So that day in the woods–you could have shielded both of us?" Because he hadn't; he had chosen me over himself as hunters aimed their arrows at his head and heart, just barely missing. Had chosen me, long before I chose him.

The edges of his eyes soften in understanding. "No," he replies quietly. "It might have demanded too much power, with how weak I was from lack of food and water. And Olin could have tracked it to us. To you."

Without another word, I roll onto my knees, and then move on them to close the few feet of distance between us. Once there, I maneuver my hips to the side, to sit on one of his crisscrossed legs. His hands brace my waist without hesitation, and my heart strains at the ease of the contact.

I raise a hand to his cheek, and stroke my thumb across the stubbled expanse. "What did I ever do to deserve you?"

It was the wrong question to ask. Though he doesn't pull away from me, as he said he would not any longer, his eyes shutter. "You did nothing to deserve me, Thea. You will always deserve far greater than me."

"Why?" I whisper. "Why do you believe that?"

"Too many reasons to count, love. But you offered yourself to me, and I took you, anyway." His jaw tightens beneath my hand, and he gently, but effectively, moves me from his lap, and helps me to stand as he does. He takes just two steps back and turns from me. And I know that if it were not for his word, he would be walking away right now.

"Then tell me," I demand, no longer quiet, but angry. Angry at whatever he believes about himself that makes him *literally* turn from me. "Tell me why you don't deserve me. Tell me why you're trying to take from me the *one good thing* I've found since my world was flipped upside down."

"Because *I'm not good, Thea!*" he yells, and whirls back to me. His sun gold eyes are bright with self-loathing, and tight with desperation. *Desperate* for me to understand the lies he thinks about himself. "I told you that two nights ago, and I put a gods-damned exclamation mark on it by devouring you like a male starved as soon as you let me."

"Because I wanted you to!" I shout back at him. "Does that not matter?"

"You want me because you don't know the whole story. And I have been too much of a coward to tell it to you."

I seethe through my teeth, "Then stop being a *fucking coward*, and tell me now."

He straightens at my words, and I don't take them back. My chest heaves and my eyes burn, but I don't take them back.

Then resolve hardens his gaze, and he says, "One more, then." He closes the distance between us, and seizes me, holding my body to his and crushing his lips to mine for a heavy heartbeat, then again with the weight of a feather. I damn the instant want and wildfire that blazes through me at his touch when I lean into the kiss, my anger at the back of my mind.

But he pulls back, and strokes the calloused pad of his thumb slowly along my cheek, his eyes unreadable as they hold mine. Then he releases me altogether, steps back, and without preamble, he begins:

"I am Adathan Zale Evestre, but I was raised under the surname Mykel, for my mother, Reina. She died when I was seven. She was a seamstress to Melisan, the Queen of Eshelle, but we lived in the lower hills of the city, too poor to either move up towards the castle, or out towards the more open spaces. My grandfather and I were the only ones at her funeral, and he was a drunkard. Still, he took me in, and tried to find work to attempt to make enough to feed and clothe me. His reputation was known, so his two days of searching brought no results.

"Then, on the third day after her funeral, a male came to our home. He said he was Dion Evestre, that he was my father, and offered my grandfather one hundred gold marks to take me. I like to think that my grandfather would have said no, if he hadn't given his name.

"As Ciaragen told you, Dion is the brother of Olin. His twin, in fact. But, because Olin's work for the king was darker than his brother's, he used that name. I'm not sure if it was meant initially to make Dion suffer, or because he didn't want the bother of people knowing him truly, but he did it, and still does.

"So, Olin took me after giving my grandfather the gold, but did not bring me to the castle. He brought me to underground dungeons on the outskirts of Matriel. And he told me that if I did not swear myself and my power to him, he would stick me in one of the cells, get my grandfather, and make me watch while Marcys cut him apart."

My stomach plummets, though it had been dropping since he started speaking of his mother. He only goes on, eyes and jaw tight. "I agreed, of course. When we swore the oath–an exchange of blood–I felt power I didn't even know I had be ripped from me. I dropped, screaming at the pain of it, and he locked me in the cell without food or water for two days for being weak. When he returned, he gave me those things only after he made his first command: that I never harm him.

"I spent much of my time for the next few decades either in those dungeons, or at his personal estate. I could not use my power, and I was glad of it." His eyes drop from mine for the first time, but raise before he speaks again. This time, though, the pain in them is enough to make my heart clench, and my fingers ache to reach out to him. "Because, one moment of lost control, and not knowing my own strength...it killed my mother. I killed my mother."

Silver lines his eyes, and I feel my own eyes fill at the sight. At the broken-hearted words that make me want to hold him, and finish this conversation another time, my shouted statement from a moment ago be damned.

Adathan only clears his throat once before continuing. "I did not resent what Olin did to me, and had me do to others in those dungeons. I deserved the suffering; I wanted nothing to do with the power that stole her from me. So, though I hated the work I did, I also hated myself enough to do it. I was glad the blood oath forced me to; that it ensured my pain, while I caused theirs.

"I tortured people, Thea, since the time I was nine." My heart cracks. *Nine.* "With blades and blows, or with my weakened power. Some of them deserved it, and to them, I eventually–I found that I *enjoyed* my work on them." He swallows, as if waiting for an expression of revulsion on my part. None comes.

So, he doubles down, like he's trying to force me to see the monster he sees in himself.

"I cut them apart, and *liked* to hear them scream. I would leave their cells covered in their blood, and savored the fear I could scent from new prisoners when they saw me coming. Then, believing I relished only the cruelty itself, Olin started assigning me to the innocents. When he realized that wasn't the case, he would command what I was to do to them. And I chose my life over theirs. Over, and *over*, Thea, I put innocents to the mercy of my hands, rather than die myself.

"Until twenty-one years ago, when Olin commanded that I only oversee the torture of my uncle. The true Dion Evestre.

"Even though I never laid a hand nor blade on Dion, I was there; I helped to *bring* him there from Sabrian in the first place, and was responsible for Olin taking him. I spied on him and them for months, and then I watched him get tortured for almost ten years. Every single day, without exception, I stood there while Marcys cut him apart.

"Then, on the day Ciaragen finally came to free him, I was there to stop her. That was when she realized who I was. Made the connection between the male who had swapped shifts with her as his guard in Sabrian, and who I really am. And rather than kill me, as she probably could have then, she spared her friend's life by leaving with him. Leaving Dion with us.

"After that, he–" he gasps, his fists clenching, and I understand immediately what's happening. Knowing not to touch him, I say softly, "You can't say, because of the blood oath. It's alright."

He nods, and the pained expression fades after a moment. He takes a deep breath, then goes on. "We all worked together for years after that. I was always the one in those dungeons, though. I was the one ordered to make males scream in those cells, as I had for decades. Until one day, Olin told me he had a new assignment for me. You."

His sun gold eyes are bright and intent on mine, and they flicker over my face like this might be the last time he gets to see it.

"I have borne the blood oath nearly my entire life, Thea, but I never resented it until you. Not as I tore males apart, nor even when I watched my uncle receive the same torment. It was always something that I deserved. But you...you have *always* deserved better, and so I did my best to give it to you, in the small way that I could. I was near you, as assigned, but I didn't watch you. I didn't even *look* at you, and still... "

Again, his gaze sweeps over my face. Then he sets steady eyes on mine, and speaks softly. "Eleven months, and fifteen days ago, I was posted near the kitchens. There was a loud noise, and then a scream. So like those I'd heard in the dungeons, and...it did something to me. I ran inside, because I hadn't been ordered to be the one to inflict pain, and I thought maybe, just maybe I could help instead of hurt for once.

"There was a girl, perhaps fifteen, screaming on the floor, her hands and forearms so red, peeled in some places and covered in blisters. No one, including me, knew what to do with burns that bad. I couldn't understand why–they were in the kitchens, surely they should know how to treat almost any level of burn? Until you burst through the doors."

Yes, I remembered this. A girl called Willa dropped a pot of boiling oil, and rather than let it fall and make a mess of the stove, she tried to catch it, resulting in half of it pouring over her arms.

"You shoved everyone out of the way, including me, your focus wholly on the girl. Then you reached for her arms, blisters and all, and I watched as the redness vanished. The burns and blisters healed. All the while, your teeth gritted, like you were fighting against a scream yourself, even though hers had quieted almost immediately once your hands were on her. And once the worst was healed, you scooped her into your lap, cradled her head, and you sang to her as she cried.

"You traced your finger over pink marks on her face I wouldn't have even known came from the splattered oil. You didn't lose patience when she was fully healed, and still her tears ran for the memory of the pain. When they slowed, and she began to sit up, you helped her. And, my eyes on your hands, I still saw it when you looked up at me.

"My heart was thundering, but I left, though I could feel your eyes on me all the while. Still, you followed me out, and you said my name–or, what was supposed to be my name. I turned to you, and I watched as your hand slowly reached, and grabbed my arm. And though I had never so much as looked you in the eye, or said a kind word to you, you squeezed my arm, and you said 'Thank you, for going in there to help Willa.'

"That, Thea," he says, his voice rough, his gaze not wavering from mine. "Was the day I fell in love with you."

34

DEEPLY, TRULY, IRREVOCABLY

MY HEART POUNDS TO THE RECURRING BEAT OF SIX WORDS: *eleven months, and fifteen days ago.* In love with me.

Adathan is in love with me.

His eyes don't move from mine; no hesitation, no doubt within them. His voice only turns more certain, more passionate, as he continues, like if this is the last time he will ever speak, this would be the one thing he would wish he could say again and again. "I was falling for you by my second month at Castle Cerasche, and no amount of talking myself out of or around it could stop my fall. My plummet into being so godsdamned in love with you that it consumed my every thought. My dreams were of you, and my nightmares were about Olin coming for you.

"Still, I was happy. *Happy* to love you, because it would be the best thing I ever did, and you could go on and live the life you deserved, never knowing you held my heart in your beautiful hands.

"Then Atlas arrived at the castle." His hands fist at his sides, but he does not stop his story. "And again, I hated the blood oath. Never had I loathed it so much as I did when I saw past Atlas's glamour. Because it damned my will; forced me to write my letter to Olin of a Fae's arrival in a zombie-like state, where my actions were not my own. Writing a letter that I realized in that moment would end with him coming for you, and breaking you in any way he knew how.

"I was about to take my own life to stop it—my disobedience shredding through my veins, minutes away from the end—when you bursted into my room in the staff quarters. You'd sensed my pain from all the way across the castle, and come to help, just as you had with Willa.

"You ran to me, and rested your hands on my chest, and then I wasn't in pain anymore. You healed what I'd begun to tear apart, and it took hold once more. You offered to stay, or get me water, and I didn't even acknowledge you as I left to send the letter in that same half-dead state. When I got back to my room, you were gone, and I vomited all over the space where you'd knelt to heal me. And if I ever thought I hated myself, in all of my deeds I've now told you, it was nothing compared to what I felt then." His voice breaks for the first time since he revealed the cause of his mother's death, and it takes everything in me not to reach for him.

"I counted on Atlas to get you out. I tried to emanate a danger that he might sense, but he either didn't, or just didn't tie it in to danger past an unwilling marriage. Whether it be him, or some other man who took you from the castle, I didn't care. The agony of never being near you again was nothing against the thought of what Olin would do if he ever got you in his clutches. I prayed as I hadn't in years that he would not arrive in time to see you. To want you, as he wants anything he thinks he can mold and break. To want you, when he saw that I did, too.

"So, even as I tried to signal Atlas, I distanced myself further from you. Stopped saying 'you're welcome,' though you always thanked me for holding open doors for you anyway. When he finally did come...you know what happened then. When we kept you in that basement, I spent an hour trying to think around my orders. When I could find none, I offered to check on you, and planned on releasing you, and giving you my dagger before my blood could kill me for it.

"Then Marcys went downstairs..." His eyes darken, and his fists clench tight at his sides. "I would have easily taken my own life to slit his throat before he could touch you. In a second, I planned to do so, and to make sure my dagger was close enough to you when I died that you could free yourself.

"I should have known you wouldn't need my help. But when I came down with David, it was to enact that plan. Then I saw you–and I froze." Yes, I remember thinking he was in shock at the sight of the dead male on the floor behind me.

Adan's voice loses all the violence within it after speaking of Marcys, and becomes reverential instead. "For the first time, I'd looked into your eyes. And I was yours. I was happy for you to kill me then, because it was enough. To have loved you and to have been yours, even if you would never be mine. It was enough, because you should never be tied to someone like me.

"But I didn't die. By a small healing majick that had abandoned me after what I did to my mother, I lived. When Olin finished his work on me for failing him, he put the glamour back on, sent me back, and said he would see me later that night. So followed three nights of torment, waiting for him to strike at this beautiful, precious thing that was your life before me."

His voice begins to tremble, as it hasn't at any point yet in his story. "He–we were supposed to *leave*. He swore he would take you from the gardens, alone and unharmed. Nothing–*none* of that was supposed to happen, Thea. And, I know I've said it before, but not clearly. Not well. So, please hear me now when I tell you that I am so–*so* sorry for what happened that night. For what I had a part in. For the pain it caused you then, and ever since. *I am so sorry.*"

A tear falls from his eye, the first since his story began. Tears of my own blur him in my vision, my will barely enough to keep them from overflowing. I don't have it in me right now to tell him it's okay; I'm not sure I could even get the words past the thickness in my throat. It's not okay–but I forgave him long ago.

He takes a deep, shuddering breath to steady himself, and though the shine in his eyes doesn't dissipate, he goes on. "After you woke in the woods, I was so cold to you. I held you back, I was harsh, and I *helped* him hurt you. I injected iron into your veins while you slept that first night when Olin asked which of us would do it. All for the ruse that I didn't care for you. Because Thea, if he knew...he would have done everything and more than he threatened. He would have broken you, just to spite me for wanting what he saw as his.

"When I figured ways around his final orders, I knew again that I would die to protect you. If he took my life in the process, at least you would be free. Of me, and of him. That I lived in my attempt to free you from him was unexpected, but when I did, I only hoped you would let me help you survive. To get back to Castle Cerasche, or go wherever in the world you wanted. *Anything* you wanted, as long as you would live. So, when you told me you wanted to kill Olin...I knew I could only help you in that task by staying with you, even if you hated me for it.

"But then came our days in the woods. Where I couldn't

keep you warm, couldn't get you water past a drop every few hours. I stayed awake until that last night, just watching to make sure your teeth didn't chatter, and your brow didn't furrow. When they did, I took the shirt off my back and laid it on you, only putting it back on when the sun began to rise, so that you wouldn't know I'd done it.

"I don't know if it was how calm I was after you healed me, or the conversation we had, or a combination of the two, but I fell asleep that final night. Crashed, with only enough wherewithal to lay closer to you so that I might hear you if you woke.

"Only I didn't hear you. And when *I* woke, to find you no longer there–I'd never felt fear like that before. I went mad, crashing through the woods, hoping to draw anyone nearby to me, not to you. And I knew that if you had been harmed, I would turn back into a monster to kill them in ways I'd learned all men feared.

"But there you were. Unharmed. More content than I'd seen you in days, standing by a pool of water. And you touched me, so gently. Like–like you *wanted* to. You know why I pulled away now, and I would be sorry for it, if not for those men."

Rage glints in his eyes, and his hands fist hard enough that his knuckles crack. "We escaped the trap they tried to lay for us–which might have succeeded, if I'd been distracted by your touch. When we had to run again in Dahlih, I could only think of two things: of keeping you safe, and of how disappointed you would be, to be further from the justice you deserved to take. And then an arrow went through my neck."

I shudder at the memory; the way he'd fallen to the ground, like a puppet with its strings cut. "I heard you scream. A sound so desperate and afraid, they might as well have shot me in the chest, too, for what it did to my heart. I can't explain to you what it was like to not be able to protect you from whatever threat had shot at me. But then I saw you there, above me like a goddess of the Heavens. I heard you shout something to me, and only wanted to tell you to run, but there was so much blood in my throat; in my mouth. When you began to clear, I saw and felt you siphoning my pain. And when you touched my cheek, your hands covered in my blood, I connected your scent with that feeling. Like the breath you take after you're no longer in pain. The taste of peace after agony.

"Then, at every turn, you continued to ask me to stay with you. For as long as you want me to stay, I will be with you, Thea. But, I want you to know now that if that's no longer what you want, I will leave. You don't have to worry about seeing me on the ship, or avoiding me, or think about any of the things you said before you knew all of this. If that's what you want, you will be free of me, and I will go as far away from Olin as possible, so that you'll be safe. If there is anything you can trust me on after all I've told you, please let it be that."

He takes a deep breath now, and holds my eyes as he waits.

Many thoughts race through my mind, as plentiful as the emotions that whirl through my heart. He would, I know; he would leave, despite his words from the other night. He would let me go, if I asked. So, my question for him is: "Are you done?"

Devastation he tries hard to mask fills his gaze; trying not to let me see that the imminent dismissal he's sure I'm about to give him will be agony. He manages it, though, this male who has spent a lifetime unable to feel truly and freely for fear of what it would do to him, or those he loved. Loves.

When his face is a mask of calm certainty, he nods. "Good," I say. Then, with the two paces between us, I bound to him, and leap, my arms closing around his neck and my legs around his waist. And I crash my lips down onto his.

Adan is frozen for all of a heartbeat before his arms wind around me, so tight I can feel his relief in my bones. There is no space between us, his unspoken words no longer there to separate his desires from his actions as he holds me to him, and kisses me like he thought he never would again. With recklessness, and abandon; tongue and teeth, and gasping breaths.

I kiss him like words fail me, and I hope he can read them in my lips now. Read the way I open for him, understand the prose of my fingers twining through his hair, and my legs tightening around his waist.

It seems he does, as he groans into my mouth, one hand traveling down my waist, my hip, to grip my thigh. The other moves up, skimming over my ribs, my shoulder, to latch onto the hair at my nape. He fists it there, somehow managing to pull without pain, tipping my head back so he can kiss his way down my throat, sighing my name.

I turn my face to kiss his temple, my fingers trailing down his chest. He shudders beneath that touch, and then his mouth is following the path of my hammering pulse back up to my own.

Softly, he presses his lips to mine twice before pulling back to look at me, releasing my hair only to brush it back from my face. We're both breathing hard, our hearts pounding in unison. Within the silence of all but our passion for each other, I reach up to stroke the hard, beautiful line of his cheek.

"You love me?" I ask quietly, and that's wonder filling my tone.

Those burning golden eyes turn molten. "I love you, Thea." A kiss to the apex of my cheekbone. "Deeply." Another to the corner of my jaw. "Truly." Open lips travel across my jawline. "Irrevocably."

My breath stutters, and he pulls back enough to look at me fully. When he sees my eyes shining, his brow furrows, his thumb caressing the ridge beneath my bottom lip.

"Yes, you do," he says.

Now *my* brows scrunch, confusion loosening some of the tightness in my throat. "I do, what?"

"You deserve to be loved as much as I love you. You deserve someone better than me to do it, but as of the moment you kissed me rather than curse me, I'm no longer willing to let anyone else try."

I swallow my doubt, and, even though it gets stuck in that knot in the center of my chest, I lean in to softly brush my lips against his, hoping he again reads the words I'm not yet ready to say.

35

LEFT BEHIND

WE ARRIVE NEAR THE COAST OF ARDHAVI SHORTLY BEFORE DUSK. The usually-bustling port city of Dekedda–a peninsula, jutting out from the main land–glitters in the distance with its faerie lights lining the streets. By now, the only things open are probably pubs and brothels, the shops either closed or about to be. Still, as I look at it, my heart beats the words to me: *we're home, we're home.* Because, though it isn't Colina, it's *Eshelle.*

I stand on the quarterdeck, practically bouncing on my toes as the males on the main deck weigh anchor. Javi is leaning against the helm, his face more calm than it has been these past weeks; hardly noticeable until now, when every line of the High Lord's handsome face is relaxed. I can practically feel the relief from Atlas beside me, and the rest of the crew as they do the work necessary to make birth.

There are only two people who don't seem to share our contentment, or excitement.

Ciaragen, on my other side, looks at the land before us with a clenched jaw and tight eyes. My hand has rested on hers for the past few minutes, and though she's grasped my fingers within her own, her expression hasn't eased.

Al, who I see now from the corner of my eye, is striding for the railing facing the city, her posture tense. Her hands are in fists at her sides, thumbs rubbing nervously along her forefingers, like she's trying to keep the fidgeting contained, but stillness isn't possible.

I'm about to go to her, with Adathan being occupied by work on the ship. But I should have known he would notice her, and drop everything once he did. In the light of the moon and stars, I see his massive frame approach her back, and even though she isn't facing him, whatever she senses already has the movement of her hands slowing.

When he's less than half a foot from her, he gently rests his hands on her shoulders, and I see them visibly relax, even from this distance. She leans back into him, and his arms move to wrap loosely around her shoulders. Al's hands, no longer fisted, rise to hold one of his forearms, and she takes a long breath, closing her eyes.

I know I'm not the only one who watched the encounter. Ciaragen's hand is tense within mine, and Atlas is staring studiously out at the land before us, his gaze too intent.

"Almost home," I say to both of them, quiet enough that it doesn't startle them, wherever in their thoughts they've gone. Atlas looks down at me, and smiles–small, but genuine. Ciaragen's hand slips from mine, and instead she puts that arm over my shoulders, and leans in to kiss my temple.

Geoffrey ascends the steps to the quarterdeck, his bald head covered with a bandana, even with the sun hours away. "All tended to, Captain. The gents request leave to take the longboats to the city for the night."

Javi nods once. "Back by sunrise for their work, then all can have the day. We make sail again first light following."

"Aye, Captain. In the morning, then." The male salutes his captain, and Javi dips his chin in response to the farewell.

But as the first mate goes to the deck, and the sailors begin to gather to the longboats, Javi calls out, "No whoring on my ship. Keep it to the city, or find yourself without a way home."

A chorus of chuckles and aye's, and the males pile into the boats. I know without asking that I won't be allowed to go with them, but for once I'm not resentful about it. I have no interest in mingling with drunks set on finding a wet place to keep them company for the night. Once I've eaten breakfast tomorrow, and the longboats have returned, that'll be a different story.

As soon as the males depart, Ciaragen straightens, and says, "Come with me." I send a wary glance back to Atlas, who shrugs. We, along with Javi, follow my godmother to the main deck. She strides straight for the couple still embracing, looking out at the sea and the city.

Sensing or hearing her, they turn, and Adathan pulls his arms back–in favor of putting one behind her, his hand resting on her opposite hip. I swear I see her lips tilt up at the possessiveness of the touch, but she rights them into neutrality quickly, her eyes flicking to the male behind me for a heartbeat.

Though even that small touch undoubtedly pains Atlas, I'm also glad she doesn't step out of it for his sake. Yes, he's hurting at her choice, but we both know she deserved to be able to make it–and to enjoy all that should follow it.

Without any greeting, Ciaragen says to them, "Now that we're settled for the night, I have business to attend to. And I believe it would be helpful if Adathan were to come with me."

Al blinks, and then looks up at the male in question, her brows scrunching. His hand tightens on her hip, a soothing gesture, but he doesn't look away from Ciaragen. When Al moves her gaze back to my aunt, she asks, "What business?"

A quick sigh. "I'm going to Sabrian, to inform my High Lord and High Lady of our upcoming arrival."

Surprise strikes me, pulling my shoulders back, and parting my lips. Home, she's going *home*, and this is the first I'm hearing of it–

Al's tone hardens. "And why do you need Adathan for that?"

"Because I think not giving them notice will be the most effective method in ensuring they are not prepared to...*do* anything about his arrival. It will give both of us time to explain, and therefore get back here with as little incident as possible." Her fingers bunch, the only indication that she's nervous about this at all.

And Al doesn't miss it. "You think they'll try to take him prisoner anyway. For being a part of what happened." Seconds pass, and Ciaragen doesn't deny it.

Al scoffs, backing into Adathan's arm, and laces her fingers through those still on her hip. "No."

"Althea–"

"*No.*"

"Love."

She looks up at him once more, and those gold eyes are settled on her, resigned. Her jaw tightens, seeing it, but he speaks before she can. "They will take me now, or later. At least in this way it gets to be up to us."

She's already shaking her head, and she pulls away from him when he finishes. His hand falls slowly to his side, like the absence of her takes a moment to process. "No," she says again. "I–I thought we were *done* with all the self-sacrificing *bullshit*. You can't–you don't–" Her breaths are coming too quickly, and she turns–but not fast enough to hide the shine that's come to her eyes.

He steps around so that she's facing him, though still away from us, and holds her face between his hands. "It's only a week. You will travel back with everyone else, and in a week I'll see you again."

Adathan leans down, tilting her face just a bit higher, and presses a soft kiss to her lips. Her hands reach up to grasp his wrists, and when they part, he moves again to kiss her brow, his eyes closing as he inhales.

Even I can hear the breath Al takes before they release each other, and she turns back to us. The silver glint still lines her eyes, but they're steeled as she directs them to Ciaragen.

The female nods, and her voice is a solemn oath when she says, "A week."

It seems enough for Al, though she takes another breath. And that, too, seems enough for Ciaragen, because she looks over her shoulder at me now.

I know the question in her eyes. She might have neglected to tell me that she's going home, but she's asking me if I'd like to come with her now. She's strong enough to carry two, even with Adathan's significant size. She can take me to the castle in Colina, and I could be seeing my mums as soon as the morning.

But my gaze slips over to Al. I can see how hard she's trying to build up her walls; to not crumble when Adathan, her greatest support, is no longer there. Maybe even to keep him from seeing how much this is hurting her.

I may not be him, but I have a feeling that if I leave, too–especially with the state of her relationship with Atlas right now–she will close herself off. All the progress she's made towards accepting joy into her life after what happened to her will vanish. The smiles, the laughs, as small and quiet as they may be, will cease. Unwilling as she is to face her pain, she will only exist, waiting for the people she's chosen to let in after losing so many others.

A week is too long for her. And more than doable for me.

I shake my head minutely to Ciaragen, and swear I see gratitude in her eyes. She would have taken me, yes, but it seems she knows as well as I do what our Lady and friend needs.

Atlas and Javi start bidding farewell to Ciaragen, the latter promising to make the remainder of their journey as swift as possible. It's not a mistake that he says it loudly enough for Al to hear.

Adathan kisses her again, and then pushes a lock of hair behind her ear. "I love you," he tells her, not bothering to keep his voice low.

She only leans up on her toes to seize his lips once more, her hands fisting the fabric of his shirt. She says nothing at all when they part, those hands dropping. Quiet, when he caresses her cheek, and walks over to Ciaragen. Silent, when Ciaragen grabs his wrist, and they disappear into the shadows of the night.

I move to stand beside her, and tentatively grab her hand. With a face like stone, and just as voiceless, her fingers grip mine with enough force to break.

I don't pull away.

36

DEJA VU

CIARAGEN - DAY 27

ADATHAN AND I APPEAR AT THE GATES OF THE CASTLE OF COLINA. While my intention is to give myself as much an opportunity as possible to keep my vow to Althea, I also don't wish to give my High Lord and High Lady heart attacks by slipping out of the shadows right in their entrance hall.

Now, Hiela will at least have some notice when the guards who let us in—with not altogether unconcerned glances at Adathan—call to her mind-to-mind to inform her of our arrival.

She, nor Hielo, know the male's true face. But, like me, it's probable that the instant they scent him, they'll recognize that it's Arthur who stands before them. I suppose that my goal is to keep them as calm as possible upon that realization. Especially because, after being in physical contact with her so consistently these past few days, his skin and clothes smell of their daughter, too.

Hiela will know it. Through the new baby scent she'd

inhaled at the top of her child's head after she was born, Althea's current scent existed. I'm not naive enough to believe that she will not recognize it because of how little time she'd had with it.

Adathan and I walk in silence through the doors, but I don't have even a moment to appreciate being here. Being *home*. To look at the hammer beam ceilings, and the mosaic floors, and breathe in the constant scent of dew on clovers, and freshly baked bread. No time, because the entrance hall is just feet away, and I know who will be there when we turn the corner.

I am surprised as we do so to hear that Adathan's heartbeat remains steady. He knows who and what he is about to face, and is not daunted by it. I wonder if it's the face of a green-eyed beauty in his mind that keeps him so calm.

My heart, on the other hand, skips a beat when we round through the threshold, and see them. On their thrones, even their sleeping clothes grand. Hiela's keen eyes take Adathan in, curiosity and wariness mingling in the face so like her daughter's, only in a darker hue.

His shoulders tense, and now I wonder if he perhaps forgot how alike they are. Althea's eye color, freckles, and glamoured ears are all that separate her from the female before us. The straight line of the nose, the full lips, even the almond shape of her eyes—she got them all from the female who carried and birthed her.

Several paces from the dais, I drop to a knee, silently urging Adathan to do the same. The airflow in the hall is such that their scents are being carried to us, not vice versa, and kneeling would be one step in the direction of them trusting him before they know him.

Of course, he doesn't, though. He bows his head until his eyes hit his boots before looking up at them once more, but his long legs remain unbent.

"Please rise, Lady Ciaragen, and introduce us to your companion," Hiela says in her strong, gentle voice, using my first name in my title. After the altercation with Olin eleven years ago, I had no longer been able to stand the proper usage of 'Vey,' and had therefore rescinded my status as second-born. My brother now holds the title of Lord Vey, our sister his High Lady.

They are well-suited to it. Dremerre is my birthplace, yes, but it is a small country on the border of Sabrian, without enough might to have armies of its own. After following in my father's footsteps and becoming a general to the armies of Sabrian, my home of over twenty-three years, my place would always have been on the battlefield, not in the ballroom.

I stand per my High Lady's command, and take a quick, but deep breath. "High Lady, High Lord, this–is Adathan Evestre." Their brows shoot up at the last name that burns its way up my throat, but I force myself to continue. "Son of Olin Evestre, and once known as Arthur Evans."

Hielo shoots to his feet, his hands fisting, but Hiela is frozen on the edge of her throne, her sienna eyes wide as she looks at the male once more. I had told them in my brief letter of his accompaniment for our journey, but had not told them what he looks like, nor that I would be bringing him here now.

"I beg you both listen before you call your guards," I go on quickly. Without my word, they would surely call upon their males to seize my Lady's, and take him to one of the cells he would not come out of alive. I look between the two of them, perhaps a bit longer at the still-standing High Lord. He does not sit, but his fists move behind his back. Hiela has not taken her eyes off the male, as though, if she did, he might disappear once more.

I open my mouth to begin, but she interrupts, "Why is our daughter not with you?"

The question is surely for me, though she continues to stare at Adathan. "She...High Lady, she did not wish to come." I knew this without having to ask Althea at the ship that she was not ready to meet her birth parents. Especially not after the way she reacted to seeing Ardhavi. She needs the coming days to prepare herself.

In any case, she would not have allowed them to arrest her male, and he needs to be. These people, who suffered so much because of a missive sent over twenty-one years ago...they deserve to have him in their grasp, even for just a little while. And, while I vowed to keep him safe, I hold no qualms for that particular justice for myself, either.

Hiela's eyes fill with the hurt of my answer, but she sets her shoulders, and asks, "Well, then, my Lady, please share the story of how it came to be that this male has traveled on the same ship as our child for her journey home."

"You will want to avoid that sort of talk when she arrives, High Lady," Adathan says quietly, and I whip my head around to him, widening my eyes in warning, but he does not look at me. He stares at the High Lady, as she does at him.

"You *dare* speak to my mate, after the pain you have caused her?" Hielo booms, his gaze filling with malice and fire.

"The child you birthed is also in pain, after all she has endured. She will not take kindly to Eshelle being referred to as her home, nor Lydia and Aron Cardenia as anything but her mother and father. She will be here in a week." The hands behind his back clench, the only indication that this means anything to him, and they can't see it. "I thought only to prepare you for who you are about to meet."

"It is because of *you* that she is in any pain in the first place. That she does not call *us* father and mother, and has lost those whom she does. Do not think to *lecture* us about her." Hielo has moved to stand beside Hiela, placing a comforting hand on her shoulder even as he looks with hatred upon the male beside me.

"My letter brought Olin here, but as Lady Ciaragen knows, it only informed him of Lord Dion's neglect of duty. I, as your other staff, did not know you were with child–and learned only weeks ago that Th–Althea is that child, not Emelina."

"Your intent, along with your ignorance, is meaningless. We have not had *our daughter* for over twenty years because of your actions. And now you will pay for them."

"High Lord," I interject loudly enough that his call for the guards halts at his lips, my vow forcing my own speech. "He is also the reason Althea is on our ship, and not Olin's."

A beat of stunned silence, then: "Explain."

"Atlas and I were not fast enough to reach them. Upon the coast of Cerasche, where Olin would have forced Althea onto a ship to Oschverre, Adathan fought his father, and freed her." They seem set to listen, at least for another moment, so I rush on. "He traveled with her to Dahlih, and, by her own claim, saved her life on more than one occasion."

Another moment of quiet before Hiela asks, "And how did he come to be in Olin and Althea's company?"

For my High Lady, I don't hesitate to answer, though my honor stirs in my gut. "He had worked as spy for Olin in Castle Cerasche. But, Hiela, he did not know the reason. As he has said, he only learned that the female he was ordered to watch was the daughter he never knew you had on the first day of their nation's traditional ball. He, as Olin had for so long, believed Emelina to be your trueborn."

"It sounds, Lady Ciaragen, like you are defending the male who helped to take your mate from you," Hielo observes, his tone hard enough that I flinch.

Then I pull my shoulders back, and lift my chin. "My Lady ordered me to keep him safe." In my periphery, I see Adathan look over at me, likely surprised by this news, but I ignore him. "My aim is to keep my vow to her; to keep him living, unharmed, if in a cell, until she arrives."

"And why," Hiela near-whispers, "would she ask this of you?"

It's a conscious effort to keep my hands from fisting at my sides. "They have grown quite close since he freed her from Olin."

Sienna eyes move to gold, and through bared teeth the question is asked, "*How close?*"

I might have answered that he has become her best friend. Maybe that she trusts him more than anyone else. But I don't get the chance to, because Adathan answers, "Take a look, High Lady, and see what she means to me."

Her gaze unfocuses as he lets her into his mind–to see what, I'm not sure I want to know. Then, after just a few heartbeats, Hiela jolts back in her throne, and breathes, "*No.*" Hielo looks down at her, but she must not even have it in her to mind-speak to him of what she's learned, because his brows are still furrowed in confusion when she stands. "*NO.* Guards!"

Immediately, four males enter through a panel in the wall, faces set, and swords out. "Put this male in a cell. Lady Ciaragen, for your admirable honor, you may keep him company as guard outside his door."

My heart stutters at the dismissal, but her eyes and tone leave no room for argument, especially not before an enemy. Jaw tight and eyes burning, I bow deeply as the guards seize Adathan. One to each arm, one at his back, and the last leading the way. He doesn't so much as struggle, though I can see that they grip him with bruising force, and the male behind him prods him hard enough with the sword to get him moving that blood blooms on the back of his shirt.

Past the threshold, when he moves to do it again, I grab his arm to halt it. Though my throat is thick, I say, "That's enough. He bleeds already."

The guard takes me in with a grimace, but, though his face is new, he must know my name and my rank. He stands down, his sword at half-ease.

Minutes later, that guard locks Adathan into his cell. The other three give me dips of their chins as they depart, but he only gives me a cool glare as he passes. When I hear the door at the top of the stairs close, I turn to Adathan.

He leans against the back cell wall, looking completely at ease. His eyes are closed, arms crossed over his chest, and even his pulse is steady.

"You should have kept your mouth shut," I hiss at him.

His eyes open a crack. "They were going to arrest me no matter what you said. At least now they know. Now, she doesn't have to be the one to tell them."

I huff an impatient breath, and turn away from him. There's a stool a few feet away, but I'm too anxious and aggravated to sit. Instead, I stand outside his cell door, my back to the wall.

Settling in for a long, awkward night, I mindlessly weave tendrils of shadows through my fingers.

37

THE NEXT

THEA - DAY 28

LI STOOD WITH ME ON THE SHIP DECK LAST NIGHT UNTIL WE BOTH were nearly sagging against the mast. When we finally went to our cabins, she wordlessly grabbed her pillow, and came into mine.

She didn't ask anything of me. Not if I was okay, or if I needed anything. Only read *Night's Beating Heart* beside me in silence for the ten minutes it took for me to pass out with the book in my lap.

I hadn't been so exhausted as to not have nightmares since my first night in the woods of Cerasche, but this morning, I'd woken to the yellow light of the dawn, with not so much as a memory of a bad dream from the night. The book was resting on one of my shirts, safe from the constant dampness of the floors, and Li was snoring softly in the bed beside me, her back against the wall, and one of her legs thrown over mine.

We ate breakfast with Atlas and Javi as the crew ambled in

from their night in the city. The captain watched them, possibly making sure none of them were about to vomit in his ship without a bucket present.

It's after lunch that the matter I'd been dreading was broached. "Would you like to go into the city?" Atlas asks.

When I saw it in the distance last night, I'd frozen. Of course, I had known we would reach our destination soon. I just hadn't been preparing for it–hadn't thought I would *need* to prepare for it after faring so well with the majority of Fae and faeries on the *Burning Rose*.

But, seeing the land I might never leave... Seeing, in the distance, a bit of the place where I was born, and will make my final stand, had set my heart thundering, fear seizing me.

He'd sensed it, of course. Had stopped the work he'd been doing, and came to me, without hesitation. Those heavy, warm hands had settled on my shoulders, and his scent of embers and leather and oak had wrapped around me just as surely, each of them granting me the ability to take a deeper breath.

Now, he's gone.

A week.

It shouldn't feel so long, having only known him less than five times that, but it does. But, when he disappeared with Ciaragen into the shadows, it felt like he took half of me with him.

So, really, I have no interest in going into the city. Already, I feel like I've retreated back into myself, so like I had been my second day on this ship. When I try to reason with myself, that I perhaps should not be so dependent on him, it does little but make me feel worse about the fact that I do. I *do* depend on him; how do I act like nothing's wrong when the first person I let in after losing so many has also been taken from me?

I would like to sit in my cabin for the rest of the day, the rest of the week, only emerging at meal times, and when we arrive in Sabrian. No, I don't want to go into this port city of Ardhavi.

But Li does. She won't say it, but I can see how badly she wants to set foot on her home soil. And, since I've become quite practiced at putting on masks, I can don this one for her.

I make my eyes light, not too much—just enough to show intrigue, if not excitement. "Sure. We can explore, maybe even eat dinner there, if you're all up for it?" I look at Li, Atlas, and Javi. I'm not sure if the High Lord will be interested in the venture with us—though he looks to be in his early thirties, he just *feels* older than Atlas and Li—but it feels rude to exclude him. And, honestly, over the past few days where he's joined us at our table, I've grown fond of the captain. His severe demeanor drops easily and frequently, replaced with self-deprecating humor, booming laughs, and smiles that light up his dark eyes.

Li squeals, and throws her arms around my shoulders. Her happiness lightens some of the heaviness in my chest. So, when Atlas smiles at me, I find myself able to return it.

Javi nods, wiping his mouth with a napkin. "I'll have Geoff mind the ship. I'll have to be in town for an errand after dinner-time, anyway."

"Ooo, what errand?" Li asks, gathering her dishes.

There's a twinkle in the captain's eyes as he replies, "I'll be fetching Talia and Sione, and they will be taking the remainder of the journey with us."

Li's jaw slackens. "Are you serious?"

He nods. "I sent a message to Tali when we arrived last night. Sione will be flying with her. If they left after breakfast, they should be in Dekedda before dusk."

Li actually *screams* with delight, and rushes to put her dishes on the counter. She runs past me, shouting over her shoulder, "Al, I'm going to get changed, you can have the washroom after me."

Once she disappears up the mess steps, I turn bemusedly to the males opposite me. Javi only gives me a knowing smirk, but Atlas says, "Li has a thing for Sione."

My brow furrows, though I feel a little bit more happiness creep in at the joy of my friend. "I thought she prefers females?"

He shrugs. "In comparison to males, yes, but Sione is nonbinary. They used to go by male pronouns, but when they were sixteen, they asked us to stop calling them 'he' or 'him,' said they didn't feel male nor female. And that was that." Another shrug.

I frown appreciatively, and finish my last bite of the thin fish soup Jacks scrounged up for lunch. He left to go food shopping after the crew ate, and only asked that we leave our own dishes on the counter when we were finished before departing. Atlas takes care of that, snatching both my and Javi's bowls before we can, and stacking them on the cook's counter, as requested.

Li is still in the washroom, but I got ready before breakfast, as always, and don't particularly feel the need to freshen up. There's only one thing that needs tending to, and I take a deep breath before attempting it.

My eyes close, and I remember all of Adathan's training. How to visualize, and shape, but also the *goal*. To keep me safe in a city full of Fae. I don't know for certain that I would be targeted just because of my human features, but I'm not willing to find out.

The majick is warm, tickling the tips of my ears. When the sensation ceases, I tentatively lift a hand to finger them. Somehow, even though it was my intent, feeling the pointed arches surprises me.

A glamour, I remind the painful twinge in my chest. *Just a glamour*. Easily removed at the end of the day, when I don't have to worry about the heat which necessitates my hair being pulled back in a plait.

With a sigh, I leave my cabin, and make my way up the steps. The sun is positively scorching today, possibly due to the nearness of the land; no more open water to cool its fire. Not for the first time, I'm grateful Li and I are similar in size. Her tank top already begins to cling to my back with sweat, but it's better than the sleeved alternatives.

I wonder if there will be a shop where I can get my own trousers, though. To hide how short they are on me, the ones she lent me have to be tucked into my boots. Another thing I might like to replace, since these are the same boots Olin packed for me in that horrid case all those weeks ago.

I wonder about these things for all of a moment–before I remember that I have no money.

I hear heavy steps coming towards me, and turn to find both Li and Atlas coming up the stairs from the cabins. Atlas's eyes go to my hands, and I stop picking at my callouses, having not even noticed I'd started. Lina's brows scrunch in worry, and she asks, "What's wrong?"

My cheeks heat as I answer her. "I don't know if I can come with you. I–I don't have anything to pay my way."

The concern clears in a heartbeat, and she waves a hand, scoffing. "Oh, we know that. Don't worry about it."

"I don't know if I'll ever be able to pay you back, and–"

"Althea," Atlas interrupts, an amused glint in his eyes as he smirks. "Li and I are the children of Lords and Ladies. Javi is a High Lord. We have the extreme privilege of being able to buy whatever we want for our friends, and not bat an eye over the cost."

"Besides, did you think we expected you to have Eshellen coin? That makes no sense." Li's brow furrows again, but this time it's mocking. Then she jerks her chin to the longboat. "Let's go, gorgeous. Day's wasting."

And that's that.

The captain climbs in with us, having emerged from his quarters at the end of that conversation. He and Atlas lower us to the water, and the former's majick renders the oars within the boat unnecessary. We make it to the coast so fast that my nerves barely have time to set back in.

They're gearing up to do so as Javi holds a hand out for me to exit the boat, while Atlas helps Li. Trying to ignore the unease that sets my heart on the beginning of its racing course, I take the offering, and let him assist me over the lip, and into the sand.

And I'm grateful for his continued grasp when my knees buckle.

Because the second I set foot on the land, power, the likes of which I've never felt before, rushed into me with crippling force. It radiates over my skin, spears through my bones, fills my lungs. So intensely overwhelming that a scream begins to build in my throat–

And then it's gone.

Wait, no, not gone. Just condensed. Settled. Like one of my twisted knots, but this one is loose, its crevices not filled with darkness, but with golden light. Its threads are softly coiled, with tendrils that flare with the gentle to and fro of a wave on the shore.

"Are you alright?" the High Lord asks, his other hand having moved with preternatural speed to grab under my other arm before I could fall. His straight black brows are narrowed, his eyes tight with concern.

I notice all of this, while still reeling from the unprecedented feeling of all that power, and its tapering. Looking around, Li and Atlas are just as worried, gathered closer to me than they had been a moment ago.

Are they just used to the sensation of their homeland? Is it only so intense the first time?

I refuse to acknowledge the questions that whisper in the back of my mind: *What if they don't feel it? What if it's just you?*

"Sorry, I..." I begin, straightening. Javi's hands lighten, but don't leave me yet. "I must have stepped wrong."

I ignore how my lie makes it obvious which set of questions I truly believe the answers to. None the wiser, Javi releases me, but Li takes up residence at my side instead, hooking her elbow around mine. I give her a small smile, shoving those queries and their terrible answers into a chest in my mind, locking it as I go.

The smile freezes while Atlas and Javi lead us off the beach, and into the Eshellen city. As we walk, I let Li's confidence seep into me; let it strain through the unwanted nerves and lingering apprehension while we enter this place of faeries and Fae. The place of my birth.

Faerie lights hang on either side of the road ahead, glowing dimly in the daylight. Shops of brick, and brass roofs line the sidewalks, their doors open even in the oppressive humidity. Carts with vendors calling about their wares sit within feet of stores with signs which do the same. And every single one of them is being patronized by the many people of Dekedda.

Thanks to my weeks on the *Burning Rose*, I'm used to the kind of faeries that are more sea-fairing. The land-dwellers, however, must not choose the sea as their career, because they are utterly unfamiliar but for the descriptions Adathan gave me when I asked about them as we trekked through the woods. Dryads, who can only be out of the woods for twenty-four hours, or else they lose their affinity for the places in which they were born and bred. Faeries with wings, the feathered being Lumale and the leathered being Jemage. Those two seem at odds with each other, somehow—the Lumale glaring at the Jemage when they pass each other.

I'm distracted by it too easily. By the sprites that flutter overhead, the size of my palm. By fauns, which, like mermaids, have the upper bodies of Fae, but instead of fins, they have legs like deer. Katari have serpentine features, ranging from slitted pupils to scaled tails. We don't see any of those spirits or wraiths he told me about, and for that I'm glad. Based on his tales of them, I'm not sure I ever want to meet one.

It's overwhelming, all of it; the city and the people. But I've been overwhelmed all day. First by the absence of Adan, then by that burst of power. This...perhaps it can be a welcome distraction. If I let it be.

I turn to Li. "Where do you want to go first?"

Her responding grin is brighter than the sun above us.

⇎

Li brings me–and a slightly reluctant Javi and Atlas–everywhere her heart desires. Reluctant, on the males' part, likely due to the countless clothing stores she pulls me into.

The *clothes* here–I no longer have to wonder how Li procured such a scandalous nightgown. The females around us walk around in states of dress from coverage for all but their eyes, to coverage of only their chests, and hips.

In this heat, I admire the commitment of the former, and understand the bareness of the latter. Still, when Li hands me things to try on, even she seems to understand my limits lie north of them. I end up with two pairs of 'shorts,' which are trousers that end a few inches down the thigh, and a 'sundress,' which is like a day dress, but less fancy. When I'd tried the dress on, Atlas's bored expression had shifted to awe before he could hide it, so, my heart squeezing and cheeks heating, I'd moved my gaze quickly to Javi to give him a moment. The High Lord had only looked at me with a father-like softness that had made my chest ache, and said, "Very pretty."

I hear Li flirt with the faerie who owns the shop as I change. When the female weaves two daisy stems into the twine-bound packaging, my friend smiles brightly at her, and kisses her cheek in farewell. Both girls are blushing a bit–the faerie's skin glowing a deep lavender over her cheeks–when we depart.

From a lean-to stand set to the side of a busy avenue, Javi buys us some kind of dessert that's fried a golden brown, and coated in cinnamon and sugar. I eat mine so fast that he walks back the few yards between us and the stand, and buys me another. I munch on that, strolling next to him while Li drags Atlas along by the hand, looking for a specific type of shop.

The inside of the parlor is dark, and teeming in places with a sweet-smelling smoke that reacts beautifully with the dimly glowing faerie lights. Many leather-winged Jemage, and a few serpent-like Katani work within, tattoos covering their exposed arms, throats, even faces. In less than ten minutes, we're walking out of the shop; me with a stud in the shape of a sunburst, the yellow diamond glittering just below the amethyst earring, and Li with an aquamarine crescent moon in the same ear. We'd even been able to convince Atlas to get a couple of silver hoops in the same spaces where my studs are in my ear. Javi had taken a little more doing, but I don't think anyone can successfully say no to Li.

"My daughter will never let me hear the end of this," he'd mumbled, and the Jemage female chuckled softly while she pushed the needle through his earlobe.

Dinner is just as relaxed, and I realize upon thinking it that, at some point, I had successfully allowed Dekedda to distract me. From Adan, the surge of power, from the teeming city itself.

I became *relaxed* in this foreign land with these varying peoples, as I'd walked through the streets with–with my friends.

I don't notice I'm fiddling with the point of my ear until I catch Atlas's eyes watching it. They move to mine when I drop my hand, and he gently says, "It will take some getting used to."

My lips twist to the side, and his head tilts the same way. His deep voice is even quieter when he speaks next. "You still don't want to get the glamour removed."

Javi and Li turn to look at me then. I clench my jaw, swallowing, and my fingers find my glass. I don't pick it up, though; just trail my finger through the condensation it's left on the table. "No. I do."

His own glass is near his lips when he raises his brows and says over the rim, "I thought we were done lying to each other."

My finger stops its motion. I hold that stormy gaze as he takes a sip of his whiskey. Then, slowly, I raise my own glass, and shoot the last bit down, letting the fire burn away my hesitation. "I want to get it removed so I can kill him." I don't dare say his name, with so many listening ears around. Who knows where he has spies? "But, I wanted to kill him as my mother's daughter. And, once I get the glamour removed, I won't be."

Li leans her leg against mine beneath the table, our understanding hanging in the air between us. Javi manages to keep his sadness to just a small frown, and sympathy in his eyes. Atlas sets his glass down with a soft *clink*, then leans forward, bracing his elbows on the table.

"You have been Lydia Cardenia's daughter for twenty-one years. You will be her daughter for a thousand more. The skin you wear will never change that. It's your heart, Althea." My eyes lower, because his words are bringing tears to them, but then a dark brown finger is under my chin, lifting it so I have to look at him. "That vital, beautiful heart of yours is what makes you *you*, darling."

I bite the inside of my cheek, and his hand drops to the table, leaving my chin feeling a bit colder than it had been a moment ago. Li wraps her arm around my shoulders, and I lean into her, unable to speak.

"If I may," Javi interjects hesitantly, and when I move my gaze to his, the softness there makes my chest tighten. "I have a daughter. And nothing she could ever do would make her any less mine. Nothing she could ever be would make me love her any less."

I swallow again, this time against the thickness in my throat, but nod, knowing he's speaking the truth, even if it will take more than a single conversation for it to stick in my heart. Li presses a kiss to my temple that makes my lips tilt up, and Javi orders us another round of whiskey. With the glass, the company, and the words I'd finally released from my mind, I feel even lighter than I had walking the streets an hour ago.

The High Lord insists on paying for all of our meals, and tips the server handsomely enough that he runs out after us, and breathlessly thanks him. Javi only smiles kindly, and wishes him a good night. I find myself glad for this time to get to know a little more about the male who, without hesitation, took me and Adathan aboard his ship weeks ago.

Except, as the sun casts the last of its dregs into the navy sky, he turns to us and says, "I have to go meet Talia and Sione, but it's getting late. Head to the longboat, and take it back to the ship before these streets fill again. I'll see you all there shortly."

He pats Atlas on the shoulder, and to whatever words are written in his dark eyes as he holds that touch for a beat longer than necessary, Atlas nods in confirmation.

Then he turns to Li and I, his expression far gentler. She hugs him without him even needing to reach for her, and he returns it with an arm over her shoulders. He hesitates after they part, his eyes on me, and I am just as hesitant as I step closer to him, and tuck my arm around his waist, the top of my head against his jaw.

"Thank you," I whisper to him. For his generosity today, and many days ago.

His warmth seeps into me as he embraces me back, a calming scent of sandalwood and rose weaving through the hair that tickles my nose. "No thanks needed, dear."

He parts with a squeeze of my shoulder, and a nod to Li and Atlas before turning to walk further into Dekedda.

I look at my friends and ask, "Why go to them? Could he not have asked them to meet us somewhere?"

Atlas answers, his voice a serious sort of quiet that has my brow furrowing before he even fully answers. "Javi is–*protective* of his daughter. His mate...she died giving birth to her, and he's terrified something will happen to Talia, too. So, the fact that he sent them to a location outside of the main city is not out of character."

As he speaks, he begins walking towards the ocean several blocks away. With me sandwiched between him and Li, she says, "Tali *lets* him be overprotective. But Aleki and Elei have been overseeing Obala for months now. She probably got sick of watching them do it, when we all know it should be her."

"It would put her under too much scrutiny, in his mind. And if she's coming here with Sione, they must be doing a good job of it, anyway. She wouldn't leave otherwise."

I listen to these unfamiliar names and situations, while understanding completely what the plight of the Obalan Lady would feel like. And hearing Atlas speak of her, how *well* he knows her, makes me wonder...

"She's gonna be High Lady some day. Even if she mates or settles with Su to rule beside her, she will *always* be the one under scrutiny." My wondering stops, replaced with a strange pang of relief.

"*Some day.* Javi is only five hundred or so; he still has centuries left, maybe even a millennia."

A thousand years *on top* of five hundred? I'm practically gaping, though I continue to swivel my head back and forth between them as they argue, keeping pace with them down the darkening alleyways we're taking to shore.

"He's not gonna rule the *whole* time. And Tali is over fifty years old. Don't you think he should have...cooled off by now?"

"He lost his *mate*, Lina. I don't think you realize–"

But I don't get to hear Atlas minimize Li's human experience with what mates are. Because one second, Atlas is talking, and the next, there's a cracking noise, and he's on the pavement of the alley, unmoving. The next, Li is grabbed by a large set of arms, her scream muffled by the palm that covers her mouth. The next, an elbow is hooked around my throat, and something thin and sharp stabs into my carotid.

That ball of power within my chest disappears. The sixth sense of my healing evaporates into the thick, humid air of Dekedda. And Kent says into my ear, "Lord Olin sends his regards, *Princess.*"

38

SHATTERED CELLS

I'VE HAD QUITE A FEW HOURS TO THINK ABOUT THE PARALLELS OF today, and twenty-one years ago. Standing outside Adathan's cell with nothing to do but play with shadows and count the bricks on the opposite wall, I hadn't been able to avoid the recognition.

It has resulted in a constant ache in my chest which accompanies the one that is always there, in the fissure of my fractured heart. Remembering a time when it was Dion who was on the other side of the door I guarded. And a time when I found him in a cell, too, far darker and filthier than this.

Adathan is just as silent as his uncle had been on his first day in this castle. He does not speak to me, which is more than fine, as I would probably ignore him, anyway. The difference here, in this time, is that I don't feel any sort of obligation to keep my thoughts from him, should he force me to voice them.

Althea made no such demands of me, and my High Lord and High Lady would *certainly* not object.

He either knows that anything from him would only result in quiet or vitriol from me, or he doesn't feel inclined to speak to me at all. Perhaps to anyone. Not when his thoughts, like mine, are hundreds of miles away. On the people we are being forced to live without.

And, since mine is a result of him, I do not mind in the least returning the favor.

If it weren't for the fact that I know Althea is suffering his absence as well, the victory might feel more complete. As it stands, I can only feel half of the satisfaction I am owed, standing before a cell with him inside of it.

There was only one point in the day where *I* spoke to *him*. A little past lunch, our empty trays already disappeared by the majick of the kitchen staff, likely deposited right into their bathtub-sized sinks. He had jolted from his place against the wall–the only other position he'd taken had been to sit in the same spot to sleep–loudly enough that I'd turned and looked at him through the cell bars.

His eyes were wide, nostrils flared, staring out into the hall where I stood, but not looking at me at all. His jaw and shoulders were tense, hands flexed, as if readying to grab something, or some*one*. My brows furrowed, I asked, "What's wrong?"

He didn't look at me or answer me for a moment. Then, the tension had left him along with the first breath he'd taken since starting away from the wall. His eyes at last met mine, and he replied, "Do you actually want to know?"

What little curiosity I had was not worth listening to him speak. "No." I'd turned away, and resumed my counting of bricks.

It's dinner time now, and I sit on the chair that had been left in the hall, my tray in my lap. The soup I practically slurp down is light and flavorful, the bread served with it topped with cheese which had been baked into it. I'd noticed, not without a little satisfaction, that Adathan had been given only plain bread, and a grilled slab of some kind of bone-in meat. Not so much as a pat of butter to moisten either.

We aren't starving him, the meal says, but we certainly aren't wining and dining him either.

He eats both without complaint, or even a contrary look, though. When he passes the tray through the slightly wider opening between the lowest bars of the cell, only the bone from the meat and a couple of breadcrumbs are left.

Then, he speaks his first unasked words of the day. "You should inform the cooks that it's unwise to give prisoner's bone-in meat." I look up at him from under my brows. "It can be sharpened against the stone. Turned into a key. Or a weapon."

I set the tray down beside mine, and respond too calmly, "You would know, wouldn't you?"

"Yes."

His gaze doesn't so much as flicker, no twitch of his mouth. I tilt my head. "It *almost* doesn't make sense."

I think I spot some confusion in his eyes, but otherwise his expression remains still. "What doesn't?"

"You, apologizing." When he doesn't shift, or reply, my lips twist up into a cutting grin. "You apologized for my suffering, but never for his. It almost doesn't make sense–*almost*, because I can only conclude that you're not sorry for it. I wonder: as you sit in your cell, do you remember what you used to do to him in his?" The grin is gone by the end, replaced with a hateful frown that bares my teeth.

"It is one of the two things I have been thinking about all day," he answers quietly.

An unsmiling chuckle barks its way up my throat. "Does *she* know?" I don't have to clarify who or what I'm talking about.

A long breath. "Yes."

I take a step back despite myself, truly not expecting that. The shock wipes the fury from my face, and its cold splits my heart further, like fracturing ice. "And–and she still–" I hate how small my voice is, but can't yet find it in me to strengthen it.

He ignores my words, and continues his answer. "But you don't."

I'm grateful for that sentence. It's the line I needed to pull me back to the safety of my rage. "I *saw* him. The open wounds, the starved state of him. He was missing a *finger*. What the fuck do you mean, '*I don't know*'?"

"I was in the cell with him, as Olin implied that day. But I was never allowed to do anything but inject the iron into his blood. Those wounds, the finger..." He swallows, and it must be a trick of the shadowy light of the cell that makes it look like *disgust* fills his expression. "That was Marcys. Thea killed him the day we took her from the city gardens in Cerasche."

I'm reeling, and my doubt must be showing through my anger, because he continues, "I would never have told you. I was still there; still watched those things be done to him. Hate me for it; I will not and have never blamed you for doing so. But I will not allow you to think less of her." His jaw sets at the end, and it's his turn for anger to flash through his eyes. Not for himself, but for the sake of the female he cares so deeply for.

It takes me several minutes to process what he's told me. The images that have plagued me, of him, this male before me, tearing my mate apart. The male who actually did those things, killed by my Lady; vengeance rightly taken, and yet I mourn its loss for myself. Then, something snags at the edge of my mind, incomprehensible. "What do you mean 'inject the iron'?"

His eyes, which did not leave mine throughout all my thinking, harden. "An invention of Oleander's regime: an instrument called a needle. It can be filled with the component of iron in a liquid form, and the sharp end of it is stuck into a vein. A plunger is pushed, and the liquid flows into the veins, just like their blood. It doesn't just dampen powers, as chains or even food can. It negates them completely."

A chill runs through me. Not just at the description, or the action of something so...*invasive*, but at the implications for the battles to surely come as our rebellion builds. When it comes to fruition, as it must when our Lady takes up her mantle.

"So..." I say slowly, "you would use this *needle*, and then Marcys–he did the rest?" The rest: the cuts, and bruises, the missing pieces. All of the things Dion endured for his court. For me.

Adathan nods, and I pretend that I don't see the remorse in his eyes. It doesn't change the fact that he played a part in taking my mate from me, therefore *causing* the torment he endured for ten years, if not *committing* it. It doesn't take away my pain, or Dion's.

But it does make *keeping him safe* a little more bearable.

As I'd thought those things, my eyes had remained on him, unseeing. I refocus now, and, when I do, my heart stutters a hard beat in my chest.

His eyes are again out of focus, as they had been after lunch. But what makes dread pool in my stomach, without knowing why, is how bloodless his face is, and the horrified expression on it. That cool, calm mask has shattered, leaving behind this blanched, terrified thing with wide eyes, and parted lips, through which one word comes in a breath: "*No.*"

Hesitantly, my pulse racing, I say his name for the first time. "Adathan...?"

It's alarming, how quickly his gaze flicks to mine. I can scent the intensity of his fear; it mingles with a petrifying fury in his eyes. "Let me out."

My head jerks back, and I frown. "I'm not letting you–"

"*LET ME OUT!*" he roars, and slams his palm against the wall so hard that dust and small bits of stone rain down from my side of the wall.

"Why?" I shout back at him, because even in the depths of my loathing for him, I know there is a reason for this. That he may be a villain in my story, but he's not a monster without cause.

"*Someone is* hurting *her!*" He snarls as he grips the bars, and *pulls*. More dust, and larger bits of stone fall. He does it again, and the metal jerks towards him by an inch.

"How do you know?" I yell, my own terror seizing me, not at the dangerous level of strength, but at his words.

"*YOU FUCKING KNOW HOW.*" Another pull, and whole bricks clatter to the floor. One more, and a deafening crash sounds as the bars are freed from the walls, and those walls crumble. He throws them to the side of the cell, and steps out, his eyes burning as he holds out a shaking, red hand. "Take me to her."

My heart beats so hard it can surely be seen through my clothes. "I don't know where–"

Through his teeth, he says, "You don't need to. Think of her, think of your *gods-damn Lady*, and *take me to her*."

Though my pulse thunders, I can do nothing but believe him in the face of Althea's life; even more precious to him than it is to me, he would not steer me wrong in this. So, I don't hesitate to grab his hand, and do as he said. I only note how, despite his rage and terror, his hold on me is gentle, before we disappear from the dungeons of Colina in a puff of shadows.

39

OPEN YOUR EYES

I ALLOW KENT TO HOLD ME, THRASHING WEAKLY AS I ASSESS MY surroundings. I could make an excuse, say it's the healer in me that watches Atlas's back rise in a breath before I look around the alley. But, even as that sharp is pulled from my neck, and replaced with a dagger, the relief in my chest is too great for me to lie to myself like that.

Including Kent, and the one who holds Li, there are eight males in the alley with us. Only Kent, and the sandy-haired male Adan attacked days ago are familiar. Every one of them is larger than me in height and stature, and armed with at least one blade. Yet, the only fear that has settled insidiously into my gut is that which is attached to the vulnerability of my friends.

"Don't bother screaming; I put a sound shield up around this alley before we even grabbed you," Kent says, then chuckles. "You know, I didn't know it was you, that first day on the ship," Kent says, and I feel the hard, cold edge of his dagger run along my neck, beneath his arm. "We're not allowed to fuck you, so good thing I realized, because Olin's wrath against your cunt…it's a close call, but easily made."

"As if you would have gotten the other," I growl through my teeth, giving another partial-strength tug on his arm.

I feel his anger tighten his grip. Good. If he's not thinking rationally, he's an easier opponent. And target.

"Fuckin' bitch," he spits, and I restrain my cringe at the saliva that spatters on my cheek. Instead, I look from the corner of my eye at Li, then down at her ankle. I don't dare meet her eyes again, but hope she understood. "You'll get what's coming to you."

"As will you," I reply. Without an intake of breath to give him notice, I knock his lower arm up, so that his own knife slices his other arm. It's a nice, deep cut that forces him to let go of me with a hiss of pain and rage, but I don't take so much as a heartbeat to assess it. I reach for the dagger he was too cocky to remember to disarm me of, and slash across his unprotected abdomen.

The others are reacting now, but Li managed to escape the one that held her, and has the knife I'd given her before leaving the *Burning Rose* in her left palm. One tries to grab my arm, but he's sloppy, and loses his hand instead. My next maneuver puts metal through a place where metal should not be, and his scream is cut off abruptly when he drops, dead before he hits the pavement.

I don't look, don't process it, only move onto the next. Li is still free, still fighting, and that's all I let myself assess before ducking to evade the arms of another male. He takes my dagger across his shin, not deep enough for it to catch on bone, but certainly enough to make him shout in agony and fall like his companion. My dagger finds the soft skin of his throat in the next second.

I whirl looking for the next, as they begin to come in from all sides–

"*Stop*," a deep voice commands, and I dare to spare a glance at it because it halts the males as well. My heart stops dead in my chest when I see Li on the ground, her face turned towards me, a blade pressed under the line of her jaw. The male is kneeling *on her*, one pressed into the backs of her thighs, and the other beneath her shoulder blades. The hand not holding the knife holds hers behind her back.

Tears are running across the bridge of her nose, and down her temple as she looks at me. Her voice wavers so painfully that it feels like a fist has reached within me and pulled at my guts when she says, "*I'm sorry.*"

I reply, as gently as I can, "It's okay, Li. Are you–?" I'm about to ask her if she's hurt, my gaze flicking around the remaining males. The two I'd felled are lying in pools of their own blood, and the one on Li has a nasty slice from his brow to his jaw, but the rest are unharmed; breathing. I curse internally when I see that Kent is still writhing on the ground, his skin steadily knitting back together from the wound I'd inflicted on his belly.

But, I don't get to ask, because the sandy-haired one cuts me off with a "Shut up!" Then cackles, looking around at his companions. "I told you, I told you if we kept the freak awake she'd be useful." Then his eyes zero in on me, and his smile twists into something even more cruel. Predatory. "Drop the knife."

I look around as quickly as I dare, calculating my odds. The one on Li would have to be the first to die, but the only way I might do it fast enough to keep his blade from beating mine to its destination would be throwing mine into his temple. Would he really spill her throat on the pavement, though, knowing it could be the only way to control me?

I'm not willing to risk it, and I know Li sees the resolve in my eyes when a choked sob bursts from her. *"Don't."*

I listen to the male's command over hers, my dagger clattering to the ground, raising my hands. Not a permanent surrender, but one that might buy me time until–

A fist hits the side of my face so hard that I feel my cheek split, and I stagger back, my head ringing. "Not so high and mighty now, huh?" I vaguely hear through the sound. I don't answer, and can't when another blow lands in my stomach, and I nearly vomit up my dinner.

It's just the one male; the others only stand there, some of them looking away, as if convincing themselves that if they're not *doing* it, they're not a part of it.

But I'm aware now, even through the haze of pain, and when his arm swings again, I catch it, and use it as leverage to send my knee into *his* belly. He wheezes, and with a feral grunt, I fracture his jaw.

And then we're moving around each other, the others standing by, not caring enough to get involved themselves, or to stop it. All the hand-to-hand training from Amahd, and from Adathan is not kicking in–it's hard-wired into my system. Each movement isn't a thought, it's instinct. Block, swing, absorb the blow, and start again.

The male has worked himself into a frenzy; his eyes are wild with rage. I'm panting, bleeding, my ribs throbbing with each breath, only saved from complete agony at their breaks because of the adrenaline coursing through my system. But, I'm calm. Only the blade still at Li's throat, and Atlas's prone body give me any sort of pause.

"How does it feel to know you've drugged me, and you're still losing?" I ask, my voice thick courtesy of the blood clogging my nostrils.

It's a tactic, to make him even more unhinged, less coordinated, and it works. He snarls, and swings with a strength that would break my jaw, but I evade it, and in my duck I send my bruised fist into his kidney.

He whirls, his teeth bared, and a wicked backhand catches my other cheek. Li screams, as she has every time he's landed a blow, but it's alright. It's how I know she's still alive without having to take my focus off my opponent.

I don't realize that this scream is different, that there are words to it, until the dagger is already in my chest.

A choked gurgle escapes my throat, my arms falling limp to my sides. The male's eyes are filled with savage delight as I meet them, and the blade *twists*–

Now the other males shout, and in the tunnel my vision is becoming, I see Kent yelling, his stomach apparently healed enough for him to rise. Then the dagger is ripped from me, and plunged into his throat, and then Kent is gone. It's only him, and he–

I'm on the ground, and it's wet. My blood is warmer than that, and it adds to the pools beneath me, while the male climbs atop me. Amidst the other voices, he says, "She's dead, anyway," and I only truly realize what he's doing when I feel fingers pulling at my belt.

I move then, through the agony, and blood pours from my chest, but good. It's good because either I will fight him and win, or the blood loss will kill me before I have to experience what he wants to do to me.

I never strayed far from my discarded dagger. Now, my hand travels, searching for it, and he is so intent as one of his hands grabs my breast and the other continues to undo the buttons of my trousers that he doesn't see it. And he certainly doesn't see it when I send the dagger straight through his eye, into his brain.

I hear some kind of roar in the second that he freezes atop me, his brain flickering with the end of his life. The other males are screaming, likely due to the unexpected death of their companion. I wrench the blade out of his skull, and blood rains down onto my neck, my chest. Finally, he falls, his weight crushing me–

And then it's gone. I feel cold in its absence, despite the humid night, and I know it's from loss of blood, internal and external. The analytical healer in my brain thinks about that with a sense of otherness, like it's not *her* but her patient experiencing these symptoms.

The rest of me listens as I hear strange and sickening splatters and crunches and breaks, and, one by one, the ends of terrified screams. I hear all of this, but don't see, and not like before, when my vision had tunneled. At some point, as I listened to the noises around me, and I realized I was no longer the one being harmed, my eyes had closed. Even the sound of Li's voice, much nearer than it had been a moment ago, can't get me to find the energy to open them. She sounds so scared, and I want to get up, I need to protect her from what's frightening her, but I can't move. Even when I feel a slender, trembling hand tentatively rest on my throbbing cheek, I can't reach up to cover it with my own.

"Al, please open your eyes. *Please,*" Li's voice sobs in my ear, and I want to do as she asks. I try to find the muscles to do so, but they feel so far away.

When only her cries are heard, and the sounds of men dying end, another voice comes. "*Thea,* open your eyes right now," he demands, and familiar, large hands reach around my face, thumbs stroking my eyelids. "Thea Maria, *open your eyes.*"

With the touch on my lids, and with the desperation in his voice, I find the muscles and the will to do as he says. They feel so heavy, but I force them into slits, to find that sun gold gaze on me. So much shinier than usual, and beautiful even in this near-death whose inescapable edge I'm getting closer and closer to tipping over.

"That's my girl," he says, and his voice is rougher than usual–filled with pain and panic. I try to raise a hand to comfort him, but I can't. The only thing I can move are my lips, and I open them to say, "Adathan," but it comes out garbled and slow.

"It's me, sweetheart. I need you to tell me where you're hurt. There's too much blood, I can't–" His voice breaks, eyes darting over my face, my body. Agony is written on his every feature, only overshadowed by rage for a heartbeat when he notices the open buttons of my trousers. When his eyes are on mine again, waiting for my answer, I open my mouth...but my tongue feels heavy, and all that comes out is a pained moan.

Then, a small, pale hand reaches past my face, shaking hard as it points at my heart. Adan's eyes freeze on that point, and any remaining color in his face drains as he stares at the fatal wound.

Then, in a blink, the frozen panic is gone, replaced with determination. He rips off his shirt, balls it up, and holds it with a heavy hand against my chest. It hurts, that pressure, and I must make a noise for it because his face crumples. "I know, I'm sorry. I'm so sorry, Thea, but I need to slow your bleeding."

And I wish I could say that it's okay, at least nod, but I'm still fighting with all my might to keep my eyes open for him, and for Li. They need me to do it, they need me...

"*THEA*," Adathan yells, angry, and desperate, and scared. "Open your damn eyes. *NOW*."

I try so hard, but even his voice is fading. The sounds of sobs are softening. Things are starting not to hurt as much, and that lack of pain is so comforting; so easy to drift further into.

"Al, please open your eyes," Li begs again, but it's so quiet, like I'm hearing through a wall. And I don't know how to do what they're asking of me anymore. These two people who I didn't know just weeks ago, and yet have latched themselves so thoroughly to my heart.

"You. Will. Not. Die," Adathan growls, his voice hardly recognizable. Then a light, brighter than the sun, bursts around us, burning even behind my closed lids, and warming my insides. It shocks whatever sense is left in my brain, and my eyes fly open of their own accord. That light sputters out after only a second, and he roars an oath into the alleyway.

The shape of him is blurry, and I wish that it weren't. That I could see those sun-like eyes, the line of his nose, the twist of his lips with clarity. Instead, I can only make out dots of gold, above red-splattered cheeks. At least when he caresses my face, I can feel that. Otherwise, I can't feel much of anything anymore. Not in my body.

My soul, on the other hand, is shredding apart as I hear the thickness, the agony in Adan's voice when he speaks. "You *promised*, Thea. You promised back in those woods that you would take me with you if you die. You going to break your oath, sweetheart?" He tries to force his tone to hold a challenge, but there's too much pain there for it to stick. My heart aches as I try to use that pain like an anchor to life, to hold onto *him* while darkness beckons so strongly.

Sensing that, or perhaps hearing the too-slow beat of my heart, his lips lower to my ear. His breath is warm, comforting, as he whispers brokenly, "Thea, stay with me. I need you. Please, stay with me."

As my head tilts towards him, my lips brush his cheek. The breeze of death, my final exhale, dries the saltwater of his tears on his skin, and mine.

40

THE ONLY THING

CIARAGEN - DAY 28

THE BODIES OF NINE MALES LAY SCATTERED AROUND US, SOME OF them in pieces. Atlas's heart is the only one left beating. Its sound is even louder when one of the few remaining beats... stops.

Stops.

Lina's breath on my shoulder stutters, then ceases, when the hand that had loosely held hers opens.

The last kiss of a lover hovers in the space between Adathan's face, and *hers*. Still. Blank. Unseeing.

The world is frozen, even the earth beneath and around us seeming to halt. To watch, and remain, disbelieving.

"No," is the first sound, whispered more quietly than the waves that lap at the shore a mile away. They must pull at the sand; take it from this place that has just taken so much itself.

Then it gets louder. "No, no, *no, no, NO.*" Large hands move from a blood-soaked shirt, and overlap beside it. Pressing, pressing, pressing.

A scream, desperate and terrified: "*Thea, PLEASE.*"

Lina's shock morphs, and her silence becomes gasping breaths.

Breaths; he gives them to her, pinching her crooked, bloody nose with one hand, and opening her mouth with the other. Then the compressions begin anew, the begging raggedly whispered.

It will not work. The blood on and around her is too great. If her heart were to restart, her veins would scrape together, empty. Empty as the brilliant green eyes that stare up at the stars over Eshelle. Where she was born.

Where she has died.

My own tears flow down my cheeks, while Adathan continues his fruitless efforts. If I had taken his hand when he first requested to be let out, would it have been enough? Would those few seconds have caught the dagger before it found its mark, or made that burst of light from his palms take hold?

Those palms push and push on a chest that doesn't move on its own. Covered in blood; her own, and others'. Hers has stopped leaking, the cuts on her face darkening as they dry. The blood on those large hands, too, is caking. From the males lying in pieces around us.

Lina is sobbing, true and broken and raw, against my shoulder. Somehow, somewhere, it reaches Atlas in his unconsciousness, and he begins to stir.

I wish he wouldn't. That he might sleep, just a bit longer, before facing this.

Adathan's movements at last slow, then stop altogether. Panting, tear tracks cutting through the spattered crimson on his cheeks, he looks down at Althea.

He whispers, his voice like gravel on broken glass, "I'm going to bring you back."

My brows furrow, and my lips part. To ask what, I don't know; I don't end up making a sound. I watch him place one hand across her forehead, and lay the other over her heart, and close his eyes.

It's not like Olin's. His veins don't instantly blacken as his power flows through him. Rather, steadily, darkness creeps its way through the vessels in his hands, then his forearms. Up the thick vein in each bicep, and then shattering over his shoulders, blending with the tattoos there. His throat, and temples; the capillaries around his eyes.

Like Dion's, and Olin's, and Althea's, his majick has a scent. As whatever he's doing flows from him, into Althea...I smell earth, and fire, and wind. Freshly turned soil; ash, and the air that carries it.

Then I *feel* it. The pulse of power shudders through the alley, out into the world around us. The world that ceased to exist these past few minutes. Even Lina tenses beside me, her cries having quieted when Adathan spoke. Watching, as I am. Waiting for the impossible.

Majick thrums around us, and when Adathan's jaw is tight enough that his teeth might break, the blackness in him spreads once more. Over his chest, it creeps, and pools over his heart.

"*You cannot have her,*" he growls. Speaking to the gods; daring them to try.

Atlas is rising now, and I can't look at him. Not just for the agony which will surely ripple across his face when he sees Althea; hears that there is nothing to *be* heard from her. But because I can't look away from the power before me, and the female it's surging into.

"She is *mine*," Adathan snarls, and those blackened veins

pulse, somehow darkening further. A black so deep it swallows up the light around him, casting him and Althea in shadow from which my own majick repels. *Other*, it says. *Darker*.

The faerie lights in the nearby streets dim enough that the stars seem to brighten in the sky. The world quiets again, along with the people of Dekedda, who sense the thrumming power without knowing it comes from this alley of death within their own city.

Then:

Thump thump.

Thump thump.

The darkness fades, lights brighten. Slowly, the black of Adathan's veins retreats, in the same way it came. So, when Althea's chest rises, and her eyes blink up at him blearily, the veins in his face, down to his chest, are still filled with whatever dark majick–dark, *incredible* majick–he has.

No fear gleams in her gaze at the still-black veins of the male before her. Slowly, his hands move, and the fingers over her brow push a lock of hair away from her face. Her eyes blink twice more, and her lips part, then twitch. But her lids must be too heavy, and the words too hard, because when she blinks again, her eyes don't reopen, and whatever she wished to say turns into a sigh on her lips.

Adathan's throat moves harshly with the force of his swallow. Keeping whatever emotions he has down, and favoring one more gentle stroke under her cheekbone, avoiding the split skin at its apex. Then his face moves in my direction, but his eyes don't leave her.

"He will know we're here now."

He doesn't need to clarify who '*he*' is. My heart, aching and exhausted after these past minutes, gives a painful stutter, but I only nod my acknowledgement.

With infinite care, Adathan's arms slip beneath Althea's

shoulders and the backs of her knees. Easily, he lifts her from the blood-soaked pavement, and stands. Her falsely blonde braid is dyed crimson, her hands coated with the blood of the male who had been atop her when we arrived.

The male closest to Adathan had been the first to die, losing his head in an inhuman rip of muscle and rage. His companions had been frozen in terror for all of a heartbeat before trying to escape their certain deaths.

But I'd seen Atlas on the ground. Lina, too. And the scent of her fear had whetted my own rage into something viciously sharp. So, when the remaining three males had attempted to flee, I'd thrown up a wall of impenetrable shadow. Blocking them in, lambs for the slaughter.

I did not blink when Adathan tore them apart with his bare hands. Did not cringe at their screams. When the male atop Lina had dropped his blade, attempting surrender, I did not wince as Adathan relieved him of his head. And I remembered my own thought, from back in the Sabriani dungeons:

Not a monster without cause.

We, two monsters, now only stand with our charges. Lina grips my waist, still shaking. Atlas rises alone, his bloodless face slack with delayed terror and current, knee-wobbling relief. As Adathan turns to continue down the alley, towards the shore, Althea in his arms, I hold out my free arm to my godson. Wordlessly, he comes to me, only pausing to pick up the shopping bags so close to where he'd been laying, and the dagger a few feet from where we are now. His gait wavers here and there, courtesy of the mostly-healed wound to his skull.

The three of us follow the two of them, the expanse of Adathan's heavily scarred back shifting so that the female in his arms does not so much as jostle with his steps. He somehow manages to keep us to darkness and deserted alleys, leaving the people of Dekedda temporarily unaware of the bloodbath behind us. I hope to be on the ocean before someone discovers the scene.

I've had enough of screaming for the night.

⇔

We reach the sea, the long boat, but Adathan does not stop. He walks into the water, and keeps going until it's past his knees. There, he kneels, setting Althea in his lap. With one arm, he supports her, the other hand reaching for the tie at the end of her braid. He lets her head tip back, her blood-caked hair falling into the water, and begins to gently run his fingers through it. Washing out the gore of this night.

He continues until her locks are clean, her face and hands, too. Such care he takes around the cuts and bruises on her cheeks, her knuckles. But, once done with those, he hesitates to move on.

Lina separates from me, and pads into the water. So pale and lovely, she likens the moon above us and its reflection before us as she turns in the water, facing Adathan. Then she drops to her knees, too, and cups water in her hand, spilling it onto Althea's chest. She rubs that space, ridding it of blood— hers, and her attackers'. Slowly, she pulls a small dagger, and then cuts through the thin tank top, and brassiere. Adathan's head tilts back to stare up at the stars, Atlas turning to look at the city behind me as Althea is bared from the waist up. They avert their eyes while Lina washes Althea's torso, so hesitant around the vibrant scar over her heart.

When her skin is clean of blood, Lina buttons up the mostly untarnished trousers. My dinner stirs seeing it, at what that male had been about to do, after inflicting a death wound. When her trembling fingers leave the buttons, Lina takes off her own shirt, a tank top underneath left to cover her. Gently, she threads Althea's arm through one of the short sleeves, and Adathan helps then. Without looking down, allowing my goddaughter to guide the movements, he lifts the female, supporting her weight while Lina maneuvers the shirt over her breasts and belly.

But she is not done. My heart stops in my chest as she reaches for Adathan's free hand, and dunks it in the water. His fingers and palms are mostly clean, thanks to his efforts with Althea, but his forearms are still covered with the blood of those males.

She cleans it for him. The rest of his arms, and his torso, were covered by his shirt as he did his work, so all that's left when she finishes the other arm he allows her to take is his neck, and face.

He jerks back when her hand reaches for him, and she hovers it in the space between them. "I know," she murmurs, so softly. "But she shouldn't have to see it when she wakes."

His jaw tightens, but when she tentatively extends her hand once more, he allows it. She rinses off the red spatter on his cheeks, his brow, down his throat. But when she moves for his hair, he pulls back again. Seeming to understand that is the limit of touch he will permit from someone who is not Althea, she drops her hand. He folds over Althea's unmoving form to dunk his hair in the water, roughly tousels it for a moment, then straightens, seawater dripping down onto his shoulders, and Althea's stomach.

Only once the male is physically free of the gore of this night do they stand. "Thank you," he whispers, his voice rough. With emotion, or from his screams earlier, I'm not sure.

But Lina dips her chin. "You're welcome." Then, she pauses, and looks at the female in his arms. Silver pools in the rims of her eyes.

"It's not your fault," he says, and my heart clenches

painfully. Yes, that's what she must be thinking right now. And I've been too lost in my shock and relief to say it first.

"She disarmed herself for me. Because I got caught," she argues, and the tears fall, cascading down the same paths they had in the alleyway.

"And I *left her.*"

Agony ripples through those words. Of course, he would see it that way. Not that I had taken him. He sees it as his choice to leave; his fault those males had the nerve to attack.

Because they would not have, if he'd been with Althea. Atlas was one thing, and he is strong, and powerful, yes. But, even before I saw his power, I'd known Adathan was different. Whether it was the scars, or the mass of him, or even just an air he gave. I'd hated him even more for it; the unapproachability he garnered without trying.

No, they would not have dared to try anything if Adathan had been in that alley with them. Which makes me wonder: how did they know he would not be?

Lina's brow furrows. "You went so that she wouldn't have another week to get closer to you before you were taken away. You left *for* her."

"And you fought for her. It was eight against two, Lina. Do not blame yourself for the actions of cowardly males." His tone does not leave room for discussion, and the fact that my goddaughter, the most argumentative person I know–second only to myself–actually heeds it is astonishing. "Now, we need to get back to the ship."

At last, he turns, and his eyes are on mine as he walks out of the water, Lina a pace behind him. "Fuck the longboat."

I realize immediately what he's saying. Another test for my power, as finding Althea had been. I don't allow myself to swallow before nodding. "To my right. Atlas, hold tight to Lina on my left." Both males do as ordered without question. I grasp

Atlas's hand, and Adathan's arm. Close my eyes. Focus. Feel the vastness of the water, and the ship within it. Picture the deck, its features; the swirls within the wood, the measure of the mast.

Then I draw the shadows of the night around us. More, and more to cover the breadth of those I carry with me. All encompassing; no light may pass through. I grit my teeth, a bead of sweat running down my temple, and tell them to take me with them, into the darkness I steal from the hollows of the swaying wooden ship.

I feel its constant surge beneath my feet, smell the moist wood and salt and the canvas of the sails. Four other scents register; complex, woven through skin and bone and blood. Hearts that I can hear pumping beside me.

I open my eyes, releasing the males beside me. The *Burning Rose* rocks gently in the ever-lapping waves, and the females, though they hadn't touched me directly, are on it with me. Atlas lets go of Lina, but Adathan only walks towards the steps to the cabins.

I could ask them what happened, but I won't. Atlas's shame hangs heavy on his shoulders, and Lina's guilt does the same to hers. So, instead, I gather both of them in my arms, my chin on top of Lina's head, and my own brow near Atlas's throat. They embrace me back, arms winding tightly around me, hands fisted in each other's clothing.

"I love you both so much," I whisper to them, because, of all the things that could be said right now, it's the only one that matters. Because, of all the things I *have* said, it's the only one I wish I'd said more.

41

2,118

DION - 4 YEARS EARLIER

TWO THOUSAND, ONE HUNDRED, AND SEVENTEEN.

That was how many people I'd executed over the past seven years. Yes, to the day.

Seven years since my scars and starvation had been covered in a pristine suit, and I'd killed my first rebel. I was no longer physically starved, but in every other way that mattered, I was hungry. For any sort of happiness I could find; I longed for it more than food or water. Yet I knew with complete certainty that I would continue to go wanting.

I contemplated ending it, as I had so many years ago in the same role. However, when I had those thoughts, I would find myself unsatisfied with them. That I might go quietly to the Void while my people, my court, my *mate* would have to go on fighting? It had become inconceivable. To abandon life for my own sake would be the most selfish of deeds, more even than stealing that one last kiss from Ciara on the border of Oschverre.

No, I would not succumb to my selfish, starving heart. A beast, after all, is all the more feral when hungry. And the people of Eshelle have been without food for too long.

For over these new, changing years, a shift had occurred in the gathered crowd before me. In place of applause as males and females became ash on this stage, there was silence. Rather than avert their gazes, they would stare at me and Marcys with hatred in their eyes.

There had been three attempts on my life. Each one would have succeeded, if not for Marcys. I'd stood there, and waited for the sword to fall, or for their power to grip me. This, I thought, was not self-sacrifice. Not done by my own hand, my death would be a catalyst. For, if they could take me down, why should they believe they could not take down the king?

Instead, because the dark-eyed male had been given the same order to allow no harm to me as I had to him, the blood of the brave had coated the platform on which I now stood, prepared to once again deliver the king's justice.

There had not been another attempt in over a year, and I damned myself for it. I wasn't deluded enough to believe it was for lack of want. Rather, during that time, I had seen some of those loathing looks change. They considered...why I had not fought. What it meant that I was never the one to deliver the king's speech. And, worse, I saw them understand.

Worse, because it meant that spark may take a while yet to ignite. Because, yes, there was less applause and there were angry looks, but too many whispers were being silenced. The plot our High Lord and High Lady had conspired all those years ago had been successful in that; word had indeed spread about prosperity under other rulers.

And so many had died for it. For the better world they believed in, and would never get to see for themselves.

I held out hope in the heart that belonged to a female of that same court that the whispers had not died, as well. That, instead, they had become smarter. Quieter. I had to hope for that, because the people I loved in Sabrian and those I did not know at all on the pavement before me deserved to live in that world they breathed about. In the world they held close to their starving hearts.

But, today...when no one so much as twitched as I raised my gloved hand towards the prisoner on his knees before me—it seemed today would not be the day they moved to seize it.

Two thousand, one hundred, and eighteen.

42

THE MAELSTROM, AT LAST

IT FEELS UNREASONABLE THAT WE'RE STILL IN THE EARLY HOURS of the night. That the summer sun had only set minutes before all that occurred in that alley. I've lived an entire life since then; one where I died, and returned, right beside the female who'd given her own life for mine.

Weaker, slower, smaller. Over and over again, the words play in my head. Because even with iron in her blood, Al had killed two of those males in just *heartbeats*, and I had barely scratched the one who had held me, and then recaptured me so easily.

I'd seen it in her eyes, the instant she decided my life was worth more than hers. And had thought that I had never been more scared than when her dagger had clattered to the pave-ment. Thought it again when that male had hit her for the first time.

I know now that I will never be as terrified as I was when

his blade sunk into her heart. When he'd climbed atop her, while her lifesblood flowed so heavily out of the wound he'd inflicted.

I had added another term to define myself with in that moment: helpless.

Then Adathan had arrived. His hands had seized the male nearest him, and ripped his head off his body before the others could blink. When their screams began, he'd spotted Al, and done the same to the male atop her. The one who held me had been next to die, his body lifted off mine, then relieved of its head, just like his friends.

So followed two more, unable to escape through Ciaragen's wall of shadows. As solid as the brick around them, they were clawing at it when Adathan snatched them, one by one, and killed them with nothing but his blood-coated hands. I'd seen it as I knelt beside her, begging her to open her eyes.

Foolish, blind hope had filled me when he'd fallen to his knees on her other side, the bodies of eight males scattered around the alley. Surely, if anyone could get her to remain here, if anyone could *save* her, it would be him.

I was right, in both ways. Could see the shift in her when she realized he was there. She had more fight; more will. But her body was failing her, between the iron and the blood loss and the shredded state of her heart.

When that heart gave out, I'd known it. In the stillness of the Fae beside me, and the way her hand released mine, though I don't think she had realized she'd been holding it in the first place.

And in that moment, *my* heart...it had broken. Fissured down the center, my soul with it.

The next minutes were a blur. I don't know how Adathan brought her back. All I know is that debt will never be repaid.

He blames himself for what happened to her, so he probably thinks there is no debt between us. That's okay. I will spend the rest of my short, human life trying to repay it anyway.

At least I have good company for it.

Atlas stands beside me, leaning his elbows on the railing facing the city of Dekedda, his jaw as hard as it's been since Ciaragen left us to go find Javi. Another one of us who believes they are at fault for what happened.

He hasn't spoken at all, but I know what he's thinking. That he should have sensed them. Shouldn't have taken us through alleys to get back to the ship. Should have been awake, healed faster, to maybe help Al before her heart stopped. Whatever.

I haven't spoken, either. Unable to comfort him, while feeling so miserable myself. That's the saying, though, isn't it? Loving company, and all.

Something catches his attention, too faint for me to notice first. He turns slightly, and his gaze zeroes in on something out in the water. I follow his eyes, and my heart squeezes in my chest at the approaching longboat. More accurately, the people within it.

With Javi's majick, the boat reaches the *Burning Rose* quickly. In a minute, they've tied up the boat, and are climbing the ladder up the side of the ship. Well, all but one.

Once everyone else is scaling the ladder, they spread their wings, and, with one mighty flap, they're in the air above Atlas and I. In the second it takes me to turn around, they've landed smoothly. Cocky as ever, their wings give a *snap* as they pull them in tight, and a lopsided smile tilts their mouth.

Maybe earlier today I would have been more inhibited. More cool, and collected. But, after tonight...

I run towards them, and catch the way their eyes flare with delighted surprise before I leap. Lean, strong arms wrap around my waist, mine around their shoulders, so in sync one would think we've done it a hundred times. When, really, I haven't allowed myself this sort of embrace with them ever since I grew old enough to no longer see it as the hug of a child—especially when they still did.

"Hey, moonshine," they say into my hair, that grin still in their voice.

My own is choked; broken, and thick with emotion. "Hey, mountainside."

Silly nicknames we've called each other since I was eleven and they were sixteen. I'd gotten mine earlier; have been 'moonshine' since I can remember. But they'd only gotten 'mountainside' after that trip they took to the mountains of Hart, when they came back somehow more free than they had been before, despite years of flying with the wind. They'd told me they would still go by Sione, but I'd wanted to give them a name to christen that new beginning. And, whether they had simply accepted the nickname from a kid to avoid arguing about it, or because they actually liked it, it stuck.

I'm sure, to them, it has stayed a silly, easy thing to have with a childhood friend. For me...things changed for me that year. And even as we grew, and I became of an age where they might see something other than a friend in me, I know that things have not changed for them.

Still, however platonically they intend it, when they hear the strangled sound of my voice, their arms tighten around me. "Hard night?" they ask in a murmur. Ciaragen must not have told them. Maybe thought it best to wait until we were on a ship, with no one to see or hear but for those she wanted to know. With the rest of the crew enjoying their last night in the city, she'll surely have that privacy.

"You could say that."

So they can't do it first, I start to loosen my arms. They set me down, and I indulge myself in a moment to look at them as I pull back. The straight lines of fine features; uptilted red-brown eyes; dark hair that parts over their horns, but otherwise flows uninterrupted to a lean, sculpted chest, partially covered by a thin leather vest. Those unique russet eyes are tight with concern as they take me in, too.

"Want to talk about it?"

I open my mouth to tell them no, but don't get to. From a few feet away, Ciaragen asks, "Are they still in the cabin?"

I have to assume so, so I nod. Then she starts towards those steps, and curiosity has me following her. I feel Sione follow behind me, and I'm sure Atlas, Javi, and Talia join them. But then my aunt stops in her tracks, and turns back towards us, something like guilt in her eyes.

"Sione, Talia, I missed you very much, but you'll need to stay up here," she tells them. "Tonight...it hasn't been easy for the people down there, and neither of them know you well enough for your presence to help."

The two of them nod, albeit a bit slowly, and Ciaragen sighs. "Thank you." Then her expression heats. "While up here, keep an eye out for returning boats. You both know the crew. If there are any faces you don't recognize, stomp three times on the deck. Got it?"

Their brows are scrunched with concern and confusion, but they nod again nonetheless. My aunt dips her chin to them, then turns and proceeds towards the cabin steps. I dare a glance over my shoulder at the winged faerie, and pretend it doesn't do anything to me when I see them watching me go.

I'm sure Adathan's heard everything the past couple of minutes, but we still walk with loud steps towards Al's cabin. There, Ciaragen raps softly on the closed door. No response comes, though I don't think she expected one. "It's me. Javi, Atlas, and Lina are with me. We need to talk about what happened tonight, and I thought–I thought you might want to be included."

After a tense, silent moment, Adathan's deep rumble comes from the other side of the door, "It's unlocked."

Ciaragen opens the door and walks in, and we file in behind her. Adathan kneels at Al's bedside, one of her hands in both of his. He doesn't turn as we enter; just keeps staring at her, waiting for her to wake.

Between him, and the not-insignificant bulk of Javi and Atlas, the cabin is at maximum capacity, but I don't think any of us intended for this to be a sit-down conversation, anyway.

"You wanted to talk," Adathan says, still not looking at us. "So, talk."

My godmother looks at me. Right. Because Atlas was unconscious, I'm the only one who can recount all that happened in that alley.

My hand fists, my throat thickens, and my heart begins to race as I force myself to remember. Atlas shifts a bit closer to me, and I take a deep breath that's saturated with the scents of thyme, vanilla, and sandalwood. I find a little extra strength in the reassurance of their presences, and manage to unclench my hands.

I look at Al. Her chest moving with her breaths. The tips of her fingers curled around the edge of Adathan's hand. Alive. Still, tears pool in my eyes, and fall as I begin: "We were walking back to the shore from dinner. They–they came out of nowhere. All I heard was a crack, and then Atlas–he was on the ground, and I barely got to look over at him before two of them grabbed me and Al. Then...something dimmed. For a second, I stopped struggling, because I thought she might already be d-dead. Because it felt like this–this force of her, that I didn't know was there until it wasn't...it was gone.

"But she was there, baring her teeth at Kent. Letting him

think whatever he did to her had weakened her. And she looked at me, just for a second, but the look...she told me to *fight*. So, when she struck, so did I. I had to watch my own opponent, but could see the way...she killed two of them in *seconds*, after wounding Kent enough that he couldn't recapture her. Even after whatever he did to her, she was that good."

All of that, though true, I say for the benefit of Adathan. To tell him that he trained her well; that the blame is *not* on him. He doesn't look at me, but his hands tighten around Al's, and he bends his head to press his lips to her fingers. He straightens after a couple of seconds, and I go on, so that he can fully understand who *is* to blame.

"But, I...I wasn't fast enough. I only wounded the one who'd held me, and not enough to keep him from doing so again. He threw me to the ground and kneeled on me, and he was too heavy–" My voice cuts off in a sob, and I can't look anywhere but at the figure that has become blurry on the bed, but Atlas moves to put his arm around my shoulders.

I don't allow myself to sink into the embrace, but I don't pull away, either. I wipe the back of my palm under my eyes and nose. "He told her to drop her dagger, and she did. For me, she disarmed herself. And then she fought the–the one who shoved her when we were leaving the mess. She was so strong. Didn't fall when he hit her, or even scream or cry, though it had to hurt." Full-strength blows from a mature Fae male? I hadn't fathomed it then, and barely can now, how she didn't succumb to the bone-cracking blows he delivered.

"Then...she didn't see it. He'd just hit her across the face, and she was still straightening from it when he pulled his knife. And then–" The look on her face. The shock, and pain. I can't restrain the next sob, and Atlas's hand tightens on the top of my arm. "Kent started yelling at him, something about how they needed her alive, and he pulled the blade out of her and killed him with it. When she fell, he tried to—he was grabbing at her, and he didn't see that she was so close to her dagger. And she put it right through his eye, into his brain. Then you two were there, and…"

I take a shuddering breath, and wipe my eyes once more. I can feel the others, except for Adathan, looking at me, but I can't look at them. The room is silent but for my sniffles for a moment.

Then, his voice gentle, Javi begins, "Did they say why they needed–?" but he doesn't get to finish. Cutting through his question, a quiet, pained moan comes from the bed.

Lashes flutter.

And then open. Not all the way, at first. Blearily, she looks up at the ceiling, moaning again. The male on his knees begins shaking, and tentatively reaches a large, bronze hand towards her cheek. "Thea…" Adathan whispers roughly, a knuckle caressing a patch of unmarked skin. The cuts are still a deep red with dried blood, and the bruises have worsened, but he must have straightened her nose while she was sleeping; though black and blue, it's once again a straight line.

She blinks, a groan working its way up her throat. "*Hurts,*" she rasps, and her breaths become irregular.

The four of us are frozen, though I'm sure mine is not the only heart aching at the word. Adathan is the only one apparently capable of moving, of responding to her, his voice thick and desperate. "I know, love, I know. I'm so sorry."

She turns her head by a fraction to look at him, and seeing her fully sends a sharp lance of pain through my chest. Her other lid is nearly swollen shut, the split in her lip deep. Breaths wheeze a bit, and stutter on the way in and the way out, the blows to her ribs making normal respiration impossible.

"Adan," she moans, and then her face works. Her lips pull, setting the split bleeding again, and her cheeks and eyes bunch painfully. Her brow, also cut through on one side, furrows in the middle, and I don't fully understand what's happening until a short cry breaks through her teeth.

It's only the beginning of the storm. The thunderclap before the downpour. Because, in the next instant, a tear careens from her intact eye, and falls into her hair. Then, the maelstrom she has held within her for so long...at last, she frees it.

And I watch in heartbreak as she closes her eyes, and begins to cry. The emotion runs through her slowly, at first. Her shoulders shake, and small, pained breaths escape her. Then, her mouth opens, and she screams.

Not a shout of pain. Not a cry of rage. It could never be described as something so simple as that. The desperate, broken noise rips its way from her lungs, her neck arching under the strain of it. Tears flow in steady streams over her face, into her cuts and bruises, onto the pillow beneath her.

Again, Adathan is the first to break the shocked stillness of our group. He sits back on his haunches, bowing until his head rests beside hers. His free hand is clenched over the bed frame, and I swear I hear the wood splinter beneath his hold between Al's first scream, and her second. His face is turned slightly towards me, his brow nearly touching Al's shoulder. His golden eyes are closed, and, like hers, tears leak out of them, falling in rivulets down the planes of his face. My own cheeks are wet, and I can feel the tension within Atlas at my side as he tries to rein in whatever noise or emotion he might otherwise let out.

Though quieter than the last, Al's next screams still hold more pain than any one person should have to manage. She rolls slightly, gasping through her sobs and through the pain in her ribs, to turn into Adathan. With that–with her permission to be touched and held after what she endured–he moves, encompassing her. One arm winds so carefully under her shoulders, the other over her, the fingers of that hand threading into her hair to hold her close to his shoulder without actually pressing her bruised, bloody face into it. Her hands, red and black and blue at the knuckles, fist against his still-bare back, shaking as hard as the rest of her.

There, she begins to shudder, the screams morphing into heavy cries. And, within them, she says two words: "*They're gone.*"

My breath hitches, and Atlas pulls me to his chest, which trembles against my cheek. Adathan's back curves around her, getting as close as he can without hurting her further. He says nothing in response–what is there *to* say to that? 'I know'? 'It's okay'? It's not and will never be okay that she lost so much, so *many*.

Then, spoken with the agony of something held in for too long: "It's my fault."

This time, the response is immediate. "It is *not* your fault," Adathan whispers, stroking her damp hair.

"If-if I had just *gone* with him– If I hadn't fought–" She gasps around the words, the pain in them more raw than the knife she'd taken to her heart.

"He would have done it anyway. Just to hurt you, he would have done it. Nothing you said or did would have changed the evil in him, Thea. And," he kisses her temple, closing his eyes once more, "nothing you said or did would have kept your mom from trying to save you. Or Hanna from trying to help you. Or Amahd from trying to free you."

His voice quavers as he continues. "And one day, you'll see them again. But I couldn't let it be today, Thea. Selfish as it might have been, I *couldn't*–"

"I know," she murmurs, her cries softer now. Then she begins to reel herself back in. Not to the extent as she had before today, but still–this will not be the last time she cries for them.

Adathan's shoulders rise and fall with a heavy breath, and Al sniffles against him, breathy hiccups the only remnants of the wracking sobs. Quietly, Javi moves between us and them. The captain's dark eyes are shining, but he looks at Atlas and I, and then gestures with a jerk of his head towards the door, shooting a glance at Ciaragen after.

Leave. Yes, we should leave. Maybe should have left minutes ago, but we'd been frozen, watching such terrible grief unfold. Now, without a word to the couple on the bed, we shuffle out. Javi closes the door behind us.

43

MYSELF, FREED

*THEA -DAY **28***

I HAD THOUGHT I WANTED TO DIE. IT'S A PRIVILEGE TO BE ABLE TO realize that I was wrong.

That, though I loathed myself for causing the deaths of my loved ones, I'd begun to...love the life I'd found, anyway. The people in it–who would never replace those I'd lost. Only make their absence bearable.

So, when I breathe, "Thank you," into Adathan's chest, I mean it. I try to let the words he'd spoken, the truths I've been too blind with grief and rage to admit to, sink in. That my mom, Hanna, Amahd–they never would have let me go without fighting. Just as I would not have, if the roles had been reversed.

The fact is, even before then, I valued the lives of others over my own. To imagine that they were gone because of *me*, because they put *me* above themselves, had been incomprehensible.

That part of me hasn't changed. In the line of lives I would

306

save if I could, if ever they were in danger, mine is still last on the list. But, now...I can begin to accept that they might have felt the same.

Thanks to the male who holds me now. Who brought me back from that death I'd thought myself to be ready for.

"How did you do it?" I whisper into his skin, my voice hoarse from screaming, rough with emotion.

He hesitates, and I let him. I let him, because I know he carries hatred for himself on these scarred shoulders, and I hope that with even another moment within my arms, he begins to loathe himself less and less, as he has done for me these past weeks.

He pulls back after that moment, but gently. I try not to wince as he lays me back on the bed, but the pain in my ribs is too great to manage it. I can't feel so much as a whisper of my majick to heal myself of it, or the bruises and cuts that ache, if less fiercely.

"I should have brought him back, too. Just to kill him more slowly," Adathan growls, his hand contrastingly gently on my face. I realize that not only have I failed to hide my pained expression, but I've also been holding my breath, my teeth bared behind my lips to keep any sound from slipping through. I look up at him through one eye, the other swollen shut, and find his expression to be darker than the sea beneath us.

I don't answer, because I wish for that, too. Not for the beating, or even for the death blow. But for the touch I can still feel on my breast, and the memory of his hand undoing my trousers.

My legs pull tighter together and curl a bit towards myself, and Adan notices. Rage flashes through his eyes, but he tempers it quickly, concern taking the forefront as he removes his touch from my cheek. "I'm so sorry, Thea. I'm sure the last thing you want right now is a male's hands on you," he says hurriedly, looking like he might even back away from my bedside.

I reach my arm out before he can, and grab his wrist. He halts immediately, and meets my eyes again, still uncertain. "You are not *a* male, Adan," I say softly, pulling him so that he's just a few inches from me once more. I put his hand on the side of my face that's the least sore, and move my other to rest against his cheek. "You are *my* male."

He closes his eyes, and covers my hand with his free one. A turn of his head has his lips pressing into my palm, and I feel his breath run over my skin. After a few heartbeats there, he curls his fingers around mine, then brings our joined hands to rest on the mattress by my head.

The knuckle of his forefinger grazes my jaw, the cool metal of the gold band there kissing my skin. "You asked me weeks ago what my power was. At the time, I was too afraid to tell you; that you would hear it, and fear me. I knew that you hating me, even asking me to leave–both would be painful. But you fearing me? I wouldn't know how to deal with that. Because even after I helped to take you twice, even when you were forced alone into a tent with me, and as we traveled together in those woods with no one else for miles...you didn't fear me. And I couldn't lose that."

I feel the noiseless hum, the pulse of his power, before it begins. Before the veins in his hands, his arms, blacken. They travel up, intricate and sharp as tree branches in the winter. They catch and splinter over his shoulders, up the strong column of his throat. A dark spiderweb of capillaries forms around each of his eyes, *into* them so that the gold of his irises stands out as starkly as the sun in a night sky.

My free hand moves of its own accord, a trembling finger tracing those vessels in his temples, stroking down his jaw. His eyes track my touch, watching it run over the vein in his bicep when he continues. "I've learned how to control its many parts over the years. How to look like this, without inflicting my power; only to incite fear into whoever Olin was having me question that day. How to use the majick in pieces, to kill *parts* of a person. So they would have to watch their arm, or their leg, decay and blacken before them, only for me to bring it back, and start again.

"I only brought someone back from true death once. Marcys had done his work, excitedly. Olin had just revoked his order to not inflict permanent damage, and he...he was a monster, even before then, but the things he did that day–" Adathan pauses, his jaw clenching as he swallows. Only the still-gentle touch of my fingers on his forearm, his gaze still on that traveling hand, seems to give him the will to go on.

"It was too much. The prisoner was still breathing, so Marcys left, believing it to be a good day's work. But I could tell...he was dying. Too much blood had been lost, and with the iron in his veins, he wasn't healing nearly enough to compensate for it. And I was right. He died, just minutes later.

"And I just...couldn't. I couldn't let it happen. He had been so kind, and would be missed so much, and maybe it was cruel to steal that end from him, but–I had to do something. I don't know what gave me the idea, what insanity had come over me to think it possible, when Olin had leashed the darkest part of my power decades earlier, but...I knelt in his blood, and just *tried*.

"And it worked. His lungs filled, and his heart beat. I know it must have been that Olin never knew I might have such an ability. He'd stolen the bringing of Death from me with the blood oath, but would never have imagined that I could reverse it, as I could with the bits and pieces of his prisoners. Or, if he did, perhaps he'd thought I would just never have the inclination."

At last his eyes rise to meet mine, the silver lining them bringing out the burning stars within the sun-gold shade. "But, I did. With him, and then, tonight... If it was selfish, I will wear that description proudly. If it was cruel to take that end from you, as I had from him, then cruelty is my badge of honor. Because I could not live in a world where you don't exist, Thea, and wouldn't want to even if I could. And maybe me living isn't something that matters, but until the gods-damned Void takes me, I will make sure that *your* life–the beautiful thing that is your fucking existence–goes on."

The brief thanks wasn't enough, then. Not enough to tell him that I not only don't hold his act against him, but that I am *grateful* for it. I suppose I will have to explain it to him differently.

"Can I ask you a question?" It's tentative, and I run my thumb along his knuckles to add to the calm I want to bring to my query.

Surprise cuts through the fervor in his expression. "Always."

"That healing that you did for me in Cerasche...you tried it tonight, too?" Pain lances through his eyes, and a muscle in his jaw flickers, but he nods. I stroke the back of his hand again. "Do you have enough strength to try again now?" I don't know how much power it takes to bring a person back to life, but I'm sure it's significant.

His brow furrows, but he nods again. I take his hand, and flatten it, ignoring the ache in my knuckles at the movement. I place the broad, warm expanse of his palm against my ribs, my breath hitching in spite of myself. "Here first," I tell him, because, while I'm the smallest bit self-conscious about how my face must look right now, that's the top priority.

Adan's black and gold eyes close as he focuses, and, after a beat, I feel the familiar warmth of healing majick roam over my skin, into my muscle and bone. It's more hesitant, less confident, than my own, but it finds my hurts, and begins to seal them. And, just as I'd thought it would, it does so over more than just my ribs. I feel their fractures knit together, and take my first comfortable breath since waking.

He feels that movement beneath his hand, and opens his eyes–and then they widen, upon seeing me. I can feel it; the lesser aches in my cheeks and jaw. Can see clearly through an eye that's no longer swollen, just sore. I smile at him, and my lip is whole, doesn't split open again as I do so.

He looks confounded by what he's done, but I'm not surprised. I sit up a bit, bracing on an elbow, and take his hand from my ribs, curling it up so that I can kiss the back of it. I breathe him in, the embers and leather and oak, the salt of water and sweat. Feel his pulse under my fingers, a bit faster than usual, but beneath it: that strong, constant beat that has become one of my favorite sounds.

How wasteful it would have been, to die so soon into loving him.

I release his hand to sit up on the bed, the movement only slightly stiff. I lower my legs to rest on either side of his kneeling form, and drape my wrists over his shoulders. Adan rests his hands lightly on my hips.

"I never would have imagined someone like you for myself," I murmur, playing with the hair at his nape. "I couldn't have pictured a male who could see the darkest parts of me, and treasure them. I never would have thought I would find someone who could bring me joy, when I believed I wouldn't have any again. Who gives me passion, when I'd only been able to hope for contentment. Who made me want to live, even after weeks of contemplating my end."

The black has begun to fade from his veins, but even in the pitch surrounding his iris, I can make out the adoration in his eyes. His brow crumples softly as he listens to these words of my heart, but I have more to give him.

"You are everything and more that I could have wanted, if I'd dared to. You are beautiful, and kind; strong, and vicious. I see your darkness, and revere it as your light. I see *every* part of you, Adathan Zale Evestre, and..." My heart is pounding, and I can see in his eyes that he's wondering about it. But, hours ago, I had known what it felt like to die without him knowing I love him. And, though I have no intention of leaving this world again any time soon, I also refuse to go on without telling him—

"I love you, too." His lips part, though no breath comes, and he stares into my eyes as if committing to memory exactly how I look in this moment. "I love you, Adan, and I don't care how long it's been, I only—only wish I'd been brave enough to say it sooner." In time with the racing of my pulse, my next exhale shakes on its way out.

"Thea..." It's a breath, ragged and raw, and in the next, his lips are on mine. Warm, and somehow both soft and hard at the same time in the passion with which he seizes the kiss. One of his hands spears into my hair, the other latching onto my waist to pull me to him. I grab onto him just as fiercely then, the fingers of one hand knotting into his loose curls, the nails of my other digging into his back.

It's the first kiss where my hips are not above his as it progresses. So, it's a gasp of something new and—and *exciting* that rips its way out of me when I feel the length of him begin to press into my belly.

He pulls back by a fraction, tilting away from me, panting. "I'm sorry, I—"

But I won't know how he was going to apologize for his body's reaction to the wildfire that consumes us when we allow it to, because I use my grip on him to tug him back into me before he can say. I push my belly against him, and he groans into my mouth, hardening even more. And it's my turn to moan against his lips then.

He devours the sound, the kiss somehow, impossibly deepening. Whatever restraint he's kept to be what he thinks I need has snapped, and more than even the kiss after I accepted him and his past, Adathan unleashes himself upon me.

Broad, calloused hands run over me, one down to the small of my back, the other to my thigh, right beneath my backside. He holds me with bruising strength, his tongue sweeping over mine with languid strokes that are counterintuitive to the consumption of wildfire, but which have my core clenching each time.

It's painful, this need for friction, a need to be *filled*, and I whimper with it. The hand on my leg loosens, and I'm about to make a sound of protest, tell him that it wasn't out of pain of his grip, but–

He only brushes over my hip in one long, fluid touch that screams *possession*. When he hooks a thumb into the waistband of my trousers, I think I might burst into actual flame. He uses that hold to pull me, and suddenly he's sitting back on his haunches, and I'm in his lap.

"I'm not usually one to give up control, love," he growls against my lips. "So understand that if you use me right now, I will let you. But when you let me put my fingers and tongue on you, when you take my cock, I'll make it so you'll never wish to come again unless I'm the one making you do it."

I'm not sure what sort of sound escapes me at that, but it makes him nip at my lower lip, and hold it between his teeth. There, the hand encompassing my hip *yanks*, and–

High, breathy, a bit of a moan. Another new sound, when I feel him against my very center. I don't know what I ever expected, but I don't think anything could have prepared me for it, for *him*. My hips move of their own accord once, feeling the thick length of him against the softness of me.

"That's it," he breathes. "You'll come if you keep doing that, sweetheart."

I do it one more time, and know that he's right. There's this tightness curling up within me, at the base of my spine, and I can tell that when it snaps, I will unravel with it. Still, I gasp, "What about you?"

His lips move back and forth over mine as he shakes his head. "This is not about me. Take back your control, Thea."

I understand fully, then. That he's trying to give me this experience, so that it will replace the one I had hours ago. So brief, and yet the memory of the intent of that male makes dread and nausea pool in my gut.

Adathan...he's giving me the chance to replace, or at least supercede that memory with this. With *me* on top, *me* in control. My choice, my wants.

With all of those in mind, I take his hand from my hip. He lets me, seeing what I might do, but by the halt of his breath and the twitch of his cock beneath me, he wasn't expecting me to place his palm on my breast.

"Please," I whisper. In response he slants his mouth over mine once more, and his hand contracts around me, my nipple pressing into his palm.

The rumble from his chest is punctuated by a groan, and those sounds, from something so simple, fill me with a power even greater than majick. And somehow, him taking what I give...it makes me feel more in control than the opposite; than what he's offered me.

"I want–" But, I'm interrupted by another gasp as he slides the peak of my breast between two of his fingers, and gently pulls.

"What do you want, Thea?" He repeats the motion, and my hips rock involuntarily against his.

"You, in control. I want you to take everything I give you." As he said he would, before the very first time he kissed me.

He doesn't ask me if I'm sure, doesn't hesitate on the basis of time. Time we've known each other; time that I've let him into my heart. I've waited long enough to feel this sort of pleasure, and I've never been more certain of anything than that I want to experience every bit of it with him.

Instead, as he had those days ago, in a tone of mixed salvation and damnation, he grunts: "*Fuck.*"

In an instant, I'm on my back on the mattress, Adathan atop me, settled between my legs. Wanting, *needing* to feel them, my hands find the scars on his back, and rove over them in reverence to him, to his strength. He shudders, and his cock jerks against me once more, just a bit off the center I crave.

Then he rolls us to our sides, still hovering slightly above me, and presses a single kiss to the side of my throat before saying, "Look at me now, love."

I open my eyes to find his, heated and hungry, yet softer than I might have expected. He pushes a lock of hair behind my ear, and his thumb travels across my cheek to snag my bottom lip. "I'm going to make you come, Thea. I'm going to touch you, and taste you. If at any point you want me to stop, you say so, and I will stop. Do you understand?"

"Yes," I breathe, my heart hammering.

Adan leans in to press his lips gently to mine. The hand on my face travels down my neck, and his fingers trace my collar bone. Slowly, they rove over the slope of my breast, eliciting another breathy noise from me. Over my shirt, his fingers tease the hardened peak, evoking new and intriguing sparks of pleasure, and the length of his cock presses harder into the space between my thigh and my core.

His hand continues its path, raising gooseflesh over my ribs, making my belly and hips writhe. "So responsive," he growls, and I prove his point when the vibration and the words hitch my breath, and my hands grip his back tighter.

"Give me those eyes, love," he orders, and I do, not having realized I'd closed them again. "Gods, you'll have me on my knees just for those eyes. Worshipping at your fucking feet like the goddess you are for even a glimpse of them."

My nails dig into the skin of his back, and I hold his gaze because I know that's what he wants. What he'll command, if I look away again. And, though something about the authority makes my core tighten, behaving for him feels even better.

I'm even more glad for my eyes on his when the first button of my trousers comes undone. He pauses, gauging if I'm alright, and I nod to tell him *yes*, to *keep going*. The rest follow in quick succession after that, and then his fingers are right–

A low, coarse sound rises from my throat, and I'm not even completely bare to his touch. Adan kisses the corner of my mouth, fingers trailing back and forth but *not* up and down. "The next time I move my hand down, I'll touch your clit. I'll put my fingers inside you. But, before I can do that, I need you to tell me yes, Thea."

"Yes, Adan," I reply immediately, and a noise emits from his chest, rough and deep. His fingers slide into the band of my underwear, and that sound gets louder as he feels how slick I am beneath it. And when the pad of one circles over my clit, I arch off the bed, a shout of pleasure ripping its way up my throat.

"Sweet gods, love. I told you I'm obsessed with every word out of your mouth. But the fucking sounds you're making for me give them a run for their money," he grits out, his eyes as heated as the fire that blazes through me as his fingers move down, only his thumb remaining on my clit.

Then, so slowly, he slides his finger inside. I clench around him at this new feeling, and he grunts. "Fuck, you feel so good, sweetheart. So wet for me." I moan at the praise, my eyes rolling back while he pulses that finger in and out of me, accustoming me its girth before joining it even more slowly with a second. The two of them together stretch me, the sensation of being filled quickening my breaths.

"Now, be a good girl and ride my hand. My mouth is about to be occupied." And I don't even get to ask him what he means by either before his mouth is on my nipple, over the fabric of my shirt. My body begins to rock against his hand without me commanding it to, and I take from his growl against my skin that it's what he'd been talking about. He's learning my body as he goes, figuring out what I'll want and ordering me into it, and I don't have room or time to think about my inexperience because of it.

Adan moves his hand in tandem with the push of my hips, and his mouth moves from one nipple to the other. I can't and don't want to control the sounds that come out of me almost every breath. I keep thrusting against his hand, and the pace and force with which he moves his palm and fingers is so perfect I might have thought this was it. But I can feel the pleasure, the tightness in my core building, a culmination so exquisite that I know the shattering of them will utterly undo me.

When my breaths are heavy and stuttering, my hips even more insistent, I can feel it approaching. And so can he. Right as I'm nearing the ledge I'd never known existed until now, he says, "Come for me, Thea."

And, like a good girl, I listen.

As my climax takes me, I shout Adan's name, over and over. His hand doesn't stop, stroking and filling me through the throes of it. I can feel my inner walls clenching around his fingers, and he curses under his breath as they do.

It takes longer than I would have expected for the throbbing of my clit, and the pulsing in my core, to ease. When they do, I'm breathing hard, and Adathan gently removes his fingers from me. I open my eyes, my head spinning, and find him already looking at me. He holds my gaze as he puts his fingers in his mouth, and sucks on the taste of me–then his lids flutter closed as he hisses, "*Fuck.*"

Then, he's not there, and I'm being yanked to the edge of the bed by strong arms. I yelp, half sitting up, and I can't help but notice the extremely prominent impression in his trousers. He clicks his tongue, his finger lifting my chin so that my eyes meet his once more. "I'm not done with you."

His fingers go to the waistband of my trousers and underwear, and as they begin pulling them down, his mouth goes, too, trailing open-mouthed kisses across my ribs, and down my hips. I lay back, sighing, and feel his teeth around my hip bone as he grins, and slips the garments off my legs.

I expected to feel nervous, and at least a little self-conscious, being bared to him. But, as he kneels before me, my knees open, his breaths caressing the wetness on and between my thighs, I don't feel either of those things. His gaze moves from my sex to my eyes, and I'd swear the heat in his could burn the world down. "Beautiful," he says.

Still with his eyes locked on mine, he grips my calves, and puts them over his shoulders. His hands, warm, strong, and calloused, travel to the very tops of my thighs, raising gooseflesh in their wake. He bows his head, and then I feel a kiss on the skin of my inner thigh, so close to my core that I gasp. He bites the skin there, then licks gently at the hurt that's not truly a hurt at all, and his lips travel along that line of flesh, and then over to the top of my labia. My breathing stutters again, the anticipation so lovely–

A long, laving stroke over my center sends a lash of pleasure through me, so deep that I don't know what words I say, only that his hands squeeze me tighter in response.

I gasp, and then moan as the warm, wet point of his tongue circles my clit, and then travels down to plunge deep into my core. The instant it's inside me, he groans, his hands tightening on my thighs. My fists clench in the sheets, a high, soft sound coming out of my throat as he pulses in and out, the feeling somehow so different from his fingers.

He says, his mouth against me, "You taste even better than I imagined you would." He slowly laps up my wetness, and growls deep in his throat. The vibration does something interesting, and I moan again in response. "Fucking paradise. You taste like the Heavens themselves."

He delves back in, and then out, up to my clit. And sucks.

I shout, and my hands move from the sheets to his hair. Adathan alternates between suckling and licking, his tongue moving in skilled patterns. He somehow manages to draw out the pleasure, never lessening it in a change of motion, only making me feel new, different things with each shift.

When I think I can't bear anymore anticipation, he devours me. Sucking and licking in tandem, like he's ravenous for my taste, for my climax. I move my hips, and he growls in approval, that same vibration making my head swirl, nothing but pleasure in my thoughts. So I do it again.

Gripping his hair, I move against his face. "Fuck yes, Thea," he says against me, and my name on his lips into the most sensitive part of me makes my eyes roll back in my head. He continues his pattern, because he and I can both feel that this is it. I thrust, over and over, as he sucks and licks and groans, and I feel it approaching, so, so close...

If my first orgasm shattered me, this one obliterates me completely. I shout his name, and the noises he makes against me as I take the last dregs of my pleasure from him make me want to do wild, animal things to and with him in return.

He kisses my swollen clit, breathing heavily against the sensitive flesh. His lips trace my labia, then the crease of my thigh, up to the crest of my hip, his hands following all the while. His breaths warm each bit of skin he reverently passes until, with one more kiss to the base of my throat, Adan rises.

He says, "Open." Lazily, still reeling from both orgasms, I open my mouth. Adathan leans down, and, his lips so close to mine that their movement brushes my cupid's bow, he says, "So you know how gods-damn good you taste." Then he sweeps his tongue into my mouth, leaving behind the essence of him and the taste of me.

His lips still on mine, I reach blindly towards his trousers, but before I can so much as graze a finger over him, one large hand circles both my wrists, and pins them against my stomach. I feel his lips tilt up, and he says, "No."

I don't fight him, not after that word, but I do pout. He chuckles against my lips, and pulls back. "Do you realize that you've undone me, Thea? I'm a grown male, and yet the feeling of *you* taking control, something I've never allowed with a partner before...I'm unraveled." His expression has softened, the smirk no longer there, leaving a lingering hunger in his eyes, along with an adoration so deep it feels like my very arteries tighten at the sight of it. "I wouldn't let you touch me yet, regardless, but you don't even have to. If I thought your self-control to be greater than mine, I would let you feel the evidence for yourself."

He doesn't let me contemplate that before he leans in and kisses me. Easily; slowly. Like we'll be doing it forever.

"Will you stay?" I whisper before either of us can pull away.

His eyes open, meeting mine, and his smile returns, this time dimpling both cheeks. "I will. But, first, I have something to attend to." A quick peck against my cheek, and he extricates himself from my grasp, and is out the door a second later, just as "What?" passes my lips.

He returns in less than a minute, holding a rag in one hand, and a pair of trousers and a shirt in the other. "You," he answers, dropping the latter on the floor, and striding over to me.

I'm still utterly bare below my navel, and can't find it in me to even be surprised that remaining so with him in the room is *comfortable*. He kneels by the bed once more, then gently pulls my knees apart, pressing a kiss to the inside of the one closest to him. He wipes my own wetness off the insides of my thighs, off my center, then uses the opposite side of the rag to clean his face. Then it's tossed into the corner of the room, and he stands.

When I see the wet spot on the front of his trousers, I understand what he meant a moment ago. Slowly, raking my gaze over every scarred, muscled inch, I raise my eyes to his, and I find him looking down at me already. "Turn around," he orders, his voice gruff. But, a bit more directly in my line of vision, I see his cock begin to strain against the fabric around it. I don't really realize that I'm staring until his hand is under my chin, lifting my attention back to his face. I expect a scolding, or for him to just repeat himself, but instead he murmurs, "You are so beautiful," then brushes his lips over mine. "But you need to turn around, because I still have the taste of you in my mouth, and if you look at my cock like that again, the combination will snap what little is left of my restraint. And, I would like to have this memory. Separate from the next."

I nod, but close the distance between our mouths for a few

thudding heartbeats before turning onto my other side, facing the wall. I hear the hurried sliding of fabric over skin, and then a hand is on my hip, rolling me back. "Had to make it quick, because the other side of you isn't exactly easy to resist, either."

I chuckle, and he climbs into the bed beside me, trousers changed but still shirtless. It's not large by any means, but I don't want space between us, anyway. We fit like puzzle pieces as he lays back, my head resting in the space between his shoulder and his chest. That arm wraps around my waist, and his fingers begin to trace patterns along the skin over my hip. One of my legs straight beneath me, I throw my other over both of his, and his free hand latches onto the back of my knee. I rest my hand on his bare chest, and my fingers trace one of the scars there.

My eyes close of their own volition; I'm suddenly so tired, where just a moment ago I felt like I could go another round with him. The events of the day pull at me, but those which might have added to my nightmares tonight fail to take hold. Far more pressing, practically all-encompassing, is this. Here, and now, with Adan's heart beating against my palm, his pulse in my ear. I breathe in his scent, letting it seep into my lungs and flow with the oxygenated blood through my arteries.

And, I feel happy. Happy, after all that occurred tonight, and so many nights before. All because of this male I love. Because he gave me this chance to live, and the desire to do it in the first place after weeks of contemplating my end. Because he understands me so deeply that my need for this new form of release after what that male tried to take from me did not trouble nor daunt him. He saw it, as he sees all parts of me, and gave me this experience that molds to my heart, just like the rest of him has.

"I love you, Adan," I mumble, and turn my head to press my lips to his chest, my eyes still closed.

"I love you, Thea," he replies, his hands and voice tightening with the emotion. He says something else, I think, but unconsciousness seizes me before I can hear it.

44

THE BEGINNING

THEA SLEEPS SOUNDLY AGAINST MY CHEST, AS THOUGH SHE hadn't just flipped my existence over on itself, and made everything I knew before her meaningless.

I love you, Adan. It runs through my head, over and over, and each time the heart in my chest thuds so forcefully, I worry it might wake her. This woman, this female who is the center of my being, the purpose of my life, loves me.

I would have taken any piece of her she was willing to give me, and lived forever with that most precious belonging tucked safe and close to my heart. Forever, I would have lived beside her with only the knowledge that I somehow added happiness to her life. That somehow, she came to me for comfort. Sought me out to ask me one of the million questions that buzzed inside of that beautiful, brilliant mind. Asked me to train her, even with so many others on the ship who would be willing and capable of doing so.

I planned to be by her side until she sent me away. And I prepared for that moment, steeling myself for the inevitable time when she would finally realize what I was. Darkness, and death; blood, and torment. Evil incarnate, regardless of how unwilling.

But, at every turn, she asked me to stay. In an alley, my blood coating her hands. On a beach in Dahlih. In a captain's quarters. In this very cabin, after hearing my whole truth. She reached for me, again and again, and I'd been so blinded by the impossibility of her ever feeling for me even a fraction of what I feel for her, that I hadn't seen what she was trying to show me, when she didn't have the words to tell me.

I love you. That sentence had mangled my mind, heart, and soul almost a year ago. For weeks before, I listened to her speak and laugh, never looking at her. I would catch glimpses of the skirts of her gowns, the delicate yet strong healer's hands. I didn't realize that I waited with bated breath for her to speak while she conversed with others. That I listened for her voice, not out of duty, but because it had become the highlight of my day to hear it. The sweet sincerity, contrasted with alluring snark and easy humor when she didn't have to don the mask of the princess.

I didn't realize that my lips would twitch up when she joked. That when she laughed, my heartbeat would skip. That I found myself wanting to laugh, and smile, for the first time since I was a child.

I didn't realize these things until it was too late. Until that day when she ran to help a girl with burns. Took her pain, and held her when she cried afterwards. When I heard her sing for the first time.

I'd had to run out, because I felt it then. The inevitability of what was not happening, but had already happened. A male who did nothing but lie and deceive the gift to the world that was Thea Maria, had fallen in love with her. She didn't, could never have known it, and had sought to thank me in that sweet way that she always did, and touched my arm.

How could a simple touch ignite my fucking soul? How could I not ever have looked into her face, and still feel, in that moment, that I burned with love and desire for her?

For months, I continued to deceive her, the blood oath binding my tongue. There was a constant pain of thinking about disobeying, of telling her who I was and what might be coming. I didn't know yet who she truly was–only that I loved her, and, for whatever reason, Olin had an interest in her.

Even the pain of my very blood feeling as if it were being pulled out of me when I contemplated disobeying did not compare to the agony of betraying her. The fresh order Olin gave me that gods-forsaken morning, having arrived with the carriages of the other suitors. That I was to wait until a moment where she left the castle, and follow her. Let Marcys knock her out, and then take her to that wretched basement.

I'd carried her there, my heart feeling like it was being torn from my chest. Marcys had been given the order to bind her, and he did. I'd already wanted to murder him for the blow to her face, and the rough ropes he chose to tie her arms. And then he threatened her.

When he started down those stairs, I was already preparing to kill David, who sat beside me. Doing so would have begun the process of taking my life, but this was not like the letter to Olin. There was the same self-hatred, but, so much more than that, there was *rage*. I would slaughter them for even considering doing her harm, and then I would die knowing my last act had been to protect the woman I loved.

But, of course, my Thea could handle herself.

When I heard Marcys shout, I knew she was fighting. I just didn't know how well. The dagger I'd slowly drawn, readying to kill David, remained out, ready to assist her. Down those damned steps again, to find Marcys, bleeding from his thigh, and a knife through his skull.

And then she looked at me.

If she shattered my world when I loved her, she rebuilt it in that moment. My existence was no longer tethered to the earth, my past, or even to myself. I was hers. My body, my heart, and my soul, all belonged to the woman who looked at me with murder in her bright green eyes.

I stood frozen while she attacked David. Killed him with a swiftness that should not have been possible. When she whirled on me, I would have let her kill me, too. Belonging to her seemed the best possible end I could have hoped for, even if she didn't know it.

I expected the knife through my skull when I fell, as she'd done with Marcys. But it didn't come. As my blood flowed, I listened to her breathe, heard the racing of her warrior's heart. She whispered, "Enough," and I didn't think she meant to say it.

I waited to die. But that small majick within me that had slumbered since the day I killed my mother woke again. It healed what even my Fae blood could not stall. And I knew what the return of that power meant. Even as Olin tortured me afterwards for losing her, and then sent me back to the castle, I felt hope.

She gave that to me. As she has given me purpose, and joy. Laughter, and beauty. Things I had lived without for nearly my entire life. And, now, she's given me her heart.

I love you. I hear her say it again in my mind, and when my heart tightens this time, my arms around her do as well. She hums a soft, satisfied sound in her sleep, and her hand on my chest strokes blindly over my inked and scarred skin.

What we'd done tonight...I had dreamed about it for

months, even as I never believed it would happen. Had learned the Ceraschen words for all I might tell her in those fantasies. When she said my name for the first time in those woods, it took remembering how she hated me to keep myself from reaching for her, and having her say it again against my mouth, to memorize the feel of it on hers. And then she gave me my nickname. Hers, and only hers, as the rest of me is.

Just as everything about her only makes me love her more, it also drives me wild. A frenzied, mad sort of lust that could only ever be quieted, so that she would never think her body is all I seek. One look from those eyes, one hint of a smile, one time of her saying my name, and I'm ready for her. Just thinking of her now has my cock hardening.

I can still taste her on my tongue. Still feel how tightly she was wrapped around my fingers. I want to listen to the noises she made like a fucking song, over and over. Feel her ride my hand and my face every day, as many times as she can take.

My body reacted as she took her pleasure from me, her fists in my hair, and her Heavens-sent taste in my mouth. Without even a touch from her against my cock, I'd come while she did, spilling into my pants like a young male who'd never had a female before. The pleasure so intense, I don't think I ever truly knew what the word meant before tonight.

There will be time for the rest. I know how much she wants to touch me, to feel me inside her. Denying her what she wants—far more than denying myself, that is proving to be more difficult by the minute. But I refuse to make her first time anything less than perfect. I already dread the pain I know I'm going to cause her, until she adjusts to me.

And then, when she does, I don't want there to be even a second of question or doubt in her gorgeous head about how she wants me. Hard and fast, or slow and languid. No thought of anybody but us, in a space where she can let the wildness I saw tonight free.

She took back the control that male had tried to steal from her. My jaw clenches so hard that it clicks, and I have to focus on keeping my hands relaxed on her as I think of it. That he'd tried to take her choice, her autonomy, her body for his own... I've thought multiple times if it might be possible to put his head back on his body, and bring him back. Just to kill him over the course of days, weeks, months. Only coming up to see her, and figure out more about the body attached to the mind I've known and loved for so long.

It will have to be enough, that he's dead, and she–isn't. *Alive*, her warmth around me says. Two syllables thumping with each beat of her heart against my ribs, with each inhale and exhale over my chest. She still has minor bruising on her face, but the healing that loving her brings out in me erased the worst of what the male's fists had done to her.

His hands...if I hadn't smelled her blood in the alley, enough to whet the rage I'd already felt into something more sharp and wicked than any blade, I might have taken the time to rip them off, too. For what *they* had done. I'd felt her relief as she placed *my* hand on her breast, heard the plea in her voice. Every plan I'd had to wait, to court her further before taking any more physical steps, vanished. I ceded control to her, as I had never done with a partner before, ready to do whatever she wanted. Whatever she needed.

Which turned out to be me doing what I promised her I would do before I kissed her for the first time: taking. Her consent was her control, and anything else was mine. And, while I've been the dominant party in any coupling I've had before, this felt different. Ordering her into finding her pleasure, and then her seeking it out on my tongue...

Anything to do with me can wait. Though not being buried

inside her tonight had been, and currently fucking is, damn painful, it's a pain I can and will endure. She doesn't deserve to have her first time be on a too-small bed in a ship full of sailors who would smell me on her, and make it known. And, though I may not know when we might have any better accommodations...I will wait.

As it is, just a week ago, this, *us*–it had been an impossibility to me. My love for her still secret, my lust, too. I could scent her occasional desire, saw the way she sometimes looked at me, but forced my mind from it each time. Chalked it up to attraction in close proximity, without many other options available to her. And she could have that; could have whatever she wanted from me, and I had no right to expect anything further from it.

That had been what I'd held onto after our first kiss. She wanted me, and so she would have me, because I was too selfish to say no to the taste of her, even just once. I prepared, over the night, for her to regret it, despite what she'd said when lost in lust. But, then, the next morning...she was so damn *happy*. Happy, just to see *me*. So, I'd taken from her again. Hated myself for it, for devouring her so easily, when there were still so many things about me she didn't know.

Then, as we've done for each other since even our first night together in Cerasche, she called me on my bullshit. Rightfully called me coward, until I spilled my soul on her feet. Told her *everything*, everything I could that was not bound by my father, and then prepared for her to finally ask me to leave. And I would have done it. She could ask anything of me, and it would be done. Leave for her, kill for her, die for her.

I hadn't expected her to ask me to stay again, with her body and her words. And I certainly hadn't expected her to love me, too.

I would have lived alone in my feelings for the rest of my days, if she had me stay but couldn't love me back, at least not in the way I love her. *That* is what I'd anticipated. Agony, yes, but a far lesser one to not being around her at all.

I prepared myself for her to choose Atlas. I let him touch her, though it ignited a murderous hatred in my gut as I watched him so much as caress her cheek. I knew—and know—him to be a good male, who would treat her well, and so I'd shoved that part of myself down. Her happiness is before mine, always.

Only she hadn't wanted him. Had looked me in the eye after closing that door for them, with so much intent in her gaze as it raked over my body that my cock had hardened by the time her eyes met mine. I'd needed to go to my cabin for release afterward, those eyes still staring at me in my mind.

I know he still harbors affection, possibly even love, for her. I can't blame him. I wonder how anyone *couldn't* love her. Brilliant, and kind, and heart-stoppingly gorgeous.

And mine.

I must have fallen asleep to thoughts of her, because when my eyes open, the bit of sky showing through the porthole in her cabin is dark blue, instead of black. My first sleep without nightmares in...I can't even remember how long. Decades, maybe.

I tilt my chin down to look at the female who still clings to me. Her face is utterly serene. Pink colors the tanned expanse of her cheekbones, freckles dusting her cheeks, her nose, her eyelids. Her full lips are parted slightly on my chest, as if she pressed them to it in the night in the midst of her dreams. The black hair that I'd been too selfish to hide from myself when I placed the glamour on her in Dahlih spills behind her, over my arm, its waves still tangled from all we did last night.

Void leave my fucking soul right here, so I can keep looking at her. The most beautiful creature I've ever seen.

She is also still bare from the waist down, her left leg bent across my waist. I feel at once an emotion that tightens my throat at the trust explicitly stated in her openness–both in posture, and in her exposed skin–and a burning desire for her that has me hardening, just below where her thigh rests over my hips.

As if she senses the shift in me, Thea begins to stir. Her breaths change, and her eyes move behind her lids. A deep breath pulls through her nose, and the exhale is a long, contented hum that makes my soul soften, and my cock harden further.

I lean in to press a kiss to her forehead, and she makes the noise again, this time accompanied by her hand moving slowly, leisurely, across my chest. Even with her eyes still closed, her fingers find my deepest scars, and caress them gently. "Adan," she murmurs, her voice husky with sleep. I nearly shiver with pleasure at the first word from her lips upon waking being my name.

"Love," I greet her in turn, my own voice rough.

She hums again, this time a small smile curling the corners of her mouth. "I missed you," she mumbles, still not opening her eyes.

"I've been here all night," I tell her, kissing the top of her head. Something so simple, yet I still can't believe I get to do it.

"Noo." She pouts, nuzzling even closer, her nose finding its way into the crook of my neck. Practically on top of me now, she says into my skin, "Yesterday. I missed you all day."

I tighten my arm around her, trying to calm the response my body is having to hers, so close and so open. "I missed you too, sweetheart." I did. All day, I'd thought of her, and wondered how I was going to make it through another six.

She hums again, and presses her lips to the side of my throat. I spent so long thinking about them, dreaming about them, and now she puts them on my skin without thought. I called her responsive last night, but my entire body feels fucking electrified now. And that energy surges through me when she opens her lips, and I feel the warm wetness of her tongue as she sucks gently at that same spot.

All of my restraint goes into not flipping us and finding out how ready she is for me. Instead, just muting the growl that vibrates through my chest, and extending my neck.

Then I feel her canines scratch over my pulse, and it's for her that I quickly spear my fingers through her hair, and pull. I look down at her, at the incredible eyes that are heavy lidded with sleep and lust. "No biting," I mock-scold her before kissing the tip of her nose.

She pushes out her bottom lip, and if it weren't so fucking sexy, it would be adorable how needy she's allowing herself to be with me. "Why?" she asks.

I should have known she would. That she'd wonder why, of all the things we've done and will do, that's the line drawn. But, for only the second time, I intentionally don't answer her. I use my grip on her hair to bring her to me, slanting my mouth over hers, and sliding my tongue through her parted lips.

And the gods curse me for my silence, because it takes all of two seconds for her scent to heighten, and for me to feel her get wet, marking my hip with the sweetness that was on my tongue just hours ago. She moans into my mouth, as if I could have forgotten the sounds she makes, as if I don't want to evoke them from her until the sun is fully up, and even after that.

I make myself pull back, and smirk. "What, you're not going to tell me my breath stinks?" I joke, harkening back to our very first morning alone together.

She sees right through me, that brain of hers working behind eyes that flit over my face. I don't know what she's looking for, or what she sees, only that whatever abilities I've had for decades to keep my thoughts and emotions hidden seem to be failing me now, as they always do whenever it's her eyes that are looking.

I wait for her to get rightfully angry at me for my selective silence, to tell me to stop keeping secrets, but she doesn't. I watch those incredible eyes soften, and she says, "I have a favor to ask of you."

It's hypocritical, after the past few moments, to say, "Anything, love," but it's what comes out, regardless.

"Can you remove your glamour?"

She asks it so quietly, my hand that's still on her leg opens, stroking the skin of her thigh with only affection, not a hint of heat to it. I kiss the scar on her cheek that only I have been able to see for weeks, and as I do so, I cut off the constant flow of my majick that has kept her concealed. I pull back to look at her, and caress her leg again. "Done."

Thea's hand lifts from my chest, and she fingers a lock of her hair, pulling it forward to see for herself. She stares at it for a moment, and then I watch as her bottom lip trembles, and her eyes fill.

No more hiding behind it. No more illusion. She wears the face and hair she had as a Princess of Weaschte, as Lydia Cardenia's daughter–with a scar across her cheekbone, and a new one through her brow to show what she has been through since. When she steps out of this cabin in the light of the morning, both as the female she has become, and the woman she once was, the next beginning will truly start.

But it can wait a moment. I let go of her hair, and wind that arm around her shoulders, the other over her hips, and hold her close as she cries. And when she finishes, with a grateful brush of her lips against my chest which I return upon her forehead, she rises.

Too early for the others to be awake, we take advantage of the open washroom. We talk as she bathes, and as I do after her, all the while telling me things that nearly make me forget that I'm naked, barely stopping myself from snatching back the curtain. Around our toothbrushes, we discuss the next steps. Now, dressed and ready, her hand is on her doorknob. She pauses, and looks over her shoulder at me.

So much has changed since the last time we left this hallway. Since we left Dahlih. Since we left Cerasche. And things are not about to stop changing now.

As if I said the words aloud, she takes a breath, and nods. Then she holds out her other hand, one side of her mouth tipping up.

I take it without hesitation, then step into her. Not a follower, or bystander, but a partner. By her side for this, and all that is to come.

Thea opens the door, and I walk with her into the next beginning.

PART II

REALITIES

45

ONE MORE TALK

THE LETTER WAS SIMPLE. OR, AS SIMPLE AS IT COULD BE, GIVEN all that happened last night.

Hiela,

I am sorry for the state in which we've left the dungeons, but not for the act of leaving them. For the sake of your daughter, we returned to Dekedda; it was a matter of life and death.

Adathan Evestre's majick is far greater than that of his father, even tempered by the blood oath.

We will arrive in Colina within the week.

Ciaragen Vey

I'D SENT IT UPON RETURNING TO MY CABIN, INTO THE POCKET realm where they would sense its presence, and hopefully understand after reading it. I would never have let him escape, would never have left with him if it were not the only choice available.

I didn't lie; I'm not sorry for it. Though, my mind has since made me regret being so blunt. Between nightmares of the typical sort, interspersed with images of my dead Lady, the torn bodies around her, and the way she'd screamed upon waking, I've barely slept. I hadn't been able to muster up the will to welcome Sione and Talia after witnessing Althea's cries. I'd only walked out of her cabin, and into mine. Written and sent the letter. Then, still fully clothed, I'd lain my tear-stained cheek against my pillow, and closed my eyes.

To no avail. The light outside has gone from pitch to navy, and I wish that sleep would seize me for just fifteen minutes, so that the ache in my chest at the color would ease. So that I wouldn't be forced to remember my favorite voice telling me that it is the same color as my eyes. Confessing that, in the days before our mating, he'd woken early to witness it, because I would still be hours off from that point, and he missed me.

I'm not the only one awake. By the sounds of her footsteps, and the contrasting silence, Adathan and Althea are readying for the day ahead. After leaving her cabin, Javi closing the door behind us, the sound shield around it had kept me from hearing any continued cries, or words of comfort. Or anything else they might have done, for I never heard his door shut down the hall.

The sky is a bit lighter by the time the sounds of washing cease, though the crew in the city are still about half an hour away from returning. Sighing, deciding that sleep is a lost cause, I sit up, and rub my hands over my face until it feels like I might not look like the dead when I step out of the room. But, before I can, there's a knock at my door.

Brows furrowed, I stand and walk to open it. And I don't know who I expect to see, but it certainly isn't Althea. With black hair, a scarred cheek, a fresher-looking one through her left brow, and only a few yellowing bruises remaining from last night.

"We all need to talk," she tells me, at the same time that another knock sounds across the hall. Her bright green eyes are steeled; a command, under the guise of a request.

I bow my head slightly. "I'll need two minutes, and then I'll be on the deck."

She nods, then hesitates. I might not be as close with her as Adathan or Lina, but I still understand immediately the reason for it. "No thanks are needed, my Lady," I tell her gently.

Her lips pull up in a tight smile, and she nods again. "Then, would you mind waking Talia?"

I blink, surprised by the inclusion of the newcomers in the upcoming conversation, but grateful for it, too. To not have to ask after them, or keep any more secrets than I do already. "Of course."

"Thank you." And, though I'd told her they were not necessary, I can tell by the tone of her words that they are for more than agreeing to this small favor.

I give her a small grin, and another bow of my head before she turns back into the hall, and I into my cabin. A quick application of oil onto my braids, the remnants onto my face, and then I'm in the washroom. Adathan woke Atlas, my Lady roused Lina, who did the same for Sione. My teeth brushed, I leave the small washroom, and I'm not surprised to find the winged faerie leaning against the wall of the hallway, talking to Lina with a smirk on their face.

There's only one more room in the hall, and I knock on its door. Either she's been awake, like me, or she heard the movement of all the people outside her cabin, because Talia opens the door within a couple of seconds of my knock. Her uptilted cinnamon-brown eyes are sleepy, but she still smiles warmly at me.

"Morning," she greets me. "What's up?"

"Meeting," I answer with a shrug, my own smile sincere, if little. "Not sure what about yet. Meet us on deck in five?"

She rolls her eyes. "I'll be up in two, because if anyone but me wakes my dad after just a few hours, he's gonna be an asshole for the rest of the day."

That gets a chuckle out of me, and I tell her, "Thanks," before turning to walk up the steps to the main deck. The morning is still dim, even the lights of Dekedda few and far between as its people sleep. While the *Burning Rose* gently sways in the sea not far off the coast, I wonder if anyone has found the scene we left behind last night. I hadn't heard any screams, but maybe I'd been too deep in one of my nightmares to hear.

"Where did you even learn how to do this?" I hear Althea ask as I round the threshold, her voice relaxed. They're sitting on the stairs to the quarterdeck. Too narrow for them to sit side-by-side, he sits a couple of steps up behind her, his fingers working her hair into a long black braid. Her eyes are closed, and he doesn't stop, though I know they both sensed or heard my approach.

"I watched you do it, and learned the pattern."

Her brows scrunch over her closed lids. "When?"

"In the woods. You braided your hair each morning." He ties it off, and then brings it in front of her, laying the thick length over her chest. Memories make my heart ache as I finger the end of one of my own braids.

She looks up and over her shoulder at him, but before she can do more than open her lips, the sounds of many sets of feet come from the stairwell. Althea is still looking at him, though, when he holds out his arm; an offer. I turn away before she can take it to stand, and find Atlas leading the pack, Lina behind him, then Sione, followed by Talia.

The female makes her way to the doors of the captain's quarters, and knocks without hesitation–or quiet. "Dad?" she calls, then knocks again. Right away, there's a groan from inside, followed by heavy steps.

The High Lord of Obala is fairly disheveled as he opens one of the double doors. Dark eyes squinting, his long hair mussed. When he sees that it's not just his daughter, but the whole lot of us waiting for him, he gives a baleful look to Talia before closing his eyes and pinching the bridge of his nose.

"Come in, all of you," he says, stepping aside, then muttering something about *ass crack of* and *imbeciles*.

We all file in, following him into the same part of his quarters where we questioned Adathan. He takes a spot on the couch, Talia plopping down beside him, and tucking herself under his arm. Atlas sits on her other side, so I take one of the armchairs. Lina sits on the floor, and Sione leans a shoulder against the wall behind her, tucking their wings.

Adathan once again grabs the other chair, but this time gestures for Althea to sit. To my surprise, she does so without argument, or hesitation. He takes up his usual spot to her left, standing with hands and arms loose.

"Kent was working for Olin," Althea tells us without preamble, and Adathan's previously open hands fist while the rest of us go still. "He intended on taking me last night, I assume to Oschverre. I don't know if any of the males with him were on the same mission, waiting for us to arrive in Ardhavi, or if he recruited them on his own. I suppose it doesn't matter now."

Her gaze had been roving over each of us as she spoke, but she looks at me now. "I need you to go to the scene, and burn the bodies."

Though my stomach rolls, I nod once, already moving to stand, but Javi's voice stops me. "We took care of that last night."

All eyes but the other two Obalans move to him. "I figured the last thing we wanted or needed was for their scent to be tracked to us somehow. Tali burned them, Sione used their wind to keep the smoke and smell contained, and I washed the ashes away. They gather like piles of rot in the surrounding alleys, now." He shrugs, his eyes hard as he looks at Althea. Probably remembering how her face had looked the last time he'd seen it.

Her voice is a bit savage when she replies, "Seems fitting."

"I thought so."

She turns to glance between Sione and Talia. "Thank you."

They, like their High Lord, shrug their shoulders, though both cinnamon and russet eyes are kind as they rest on the Sabriani Lady. Sione replies, "As you said: it was fitting."

Still, she gives them each a grateful look before turning back to Javi. She takes a quick breath, her eyes darting once to the male beside her, then tells the captain, "No one will know what happened last night."

Javi's brows are joined by everyone else's in the room as they furrow. Except, of course, the male beside her. "I don't need to ask to know you had no idea about Kent's involvement. But, none of us knows if he was working alone here. There may be others. If there are, they will see me, and think one of two things: that he failed, and they are found out, or that he's gone on the run, rather than go back to Olin empty-handed. They must not be allowed to believe the former."

Javi's eyes are grave, but he nods his agreement. "You think they will make another attempt if left unchecked."

"Yes. And when they do, we will be ready." She reaches, and takes Adathan's hand. The male had become a statue as she spoke, but still his fingers curl around hers–though his jaw remains clenched. "Adathan will be expected to continue his work on the ship. If he's suddenly by my side at all times, they will either become suspicious, or not attempt at all. Because of that, both Li and I will need accompaniment, whenever it can be spared."

Althea takes a breath, and I can tell that this ask is not for her, but for Adathan. She essentially confirms it with a squeeze of his fingers before she turns her gaze to Lina. "Not because of you, but for me, Li. If they somehow get you..."

But Lina is already shaking her head, her sky blue eyes determined. "You'd turn yourself in. I know. Keep going, gorgeous."

Althea's shoulders relax a bit, and she looks at Atlas. His gray eyes move from hers to Adathan's, and the two share a look that's too quick to say all it must, but does the job for this. Though his jaw is still tight, Adathan gives a stiff, small nod.

Atlas returns his gaze to Althea. "Whenever you need."

She smiles a little at him, and he returns it. Then says, "If anything needs doing on the ship, though, it will be suspicious if I don't volunteer to assist. Especially with..." he trails off, looking at Adathan again. "They'll notice. Wonder why you're letting me around her."

Althea's mouth opens, indignance written on her face, but Adathan speaks before she can. "I don't *let* Thea do anything. I am not her keeper."

"I know that, but *they–*" Atlas grits out, his patience thinning.

"Alright, alright," Lina interrupts as Adathan takes a half step forward. "We don't need to whip out the yardstick right now."

"Yardstick?" Talia asks, her straight black brows raising. "Whose dick are you measuring, fucking Deimos?"

Lina rolls her eyes, but the comment that would usually have no effect on her sets her cheeks ablaze. I try not to look at the faerie at the wall beside her. "Whatever. These two are about to get into it because they're both feeling pissy this morning, and there's no time for that. When Adathan is working, and Atlas is called away, if I'm not already with her then I'll hang with Al, and you two will join us. Okay?" She looks between Sione and Talia, who nod immediately, then all of them look back at the female in question.

She grins at them. "Considering how I've spent the first five minutes of knowing you, I look forward to it."

"Great," Lina says, sitting forward with a clap of her hand to her knee. "Anything else?"

Althea shakes her head, looking up at Adathan for confirmation. "I have a question," I say, looking between them, but settling on him. They turn to me, and I continue. "You said Olin would know we're here, now. How?"

Anger darkens his gold eyes, but it's not towards me; rather, the male so set on recapturing his female that he found a way to place spies on an Obalan ship. "The power expenditure. With the blood oath, he's able to track all of us by its signature, but only if we use enough that it drains our stores."

I nod once, then say to Althea, "So, when we leave this room, it's breakfast as usual, then you'll be with Atlas while Adathan works." I know already why I wasn't asked; we've never spent one-on-one time together before. A fact that makes shame rise in my chest, and which I hope to remedy once we reach Sabrian.

She nods, and Lina stands first. "Sounds like a plan. I'm fucking starving."

Althea grins at her, and stands, too. Adathan releases her to put the chair back in its place, the rest of us getting to our feet as he does so. Javi mutters something about getting a moment to himself to take a piss, sending Talia off with the rest of us.

When we exit the captain's quarters, the sky is just beginning to turn from first light to sunrise. The crew will be back within the quarter hour, though Jacks should already be in the kitchen. It's not unusual for us all to arrive at the same time, so as we file into the mess, the faerie doesn't so much as stutter in his movements behind the counter.

Thanks to his grocery run in Dekedda, the space once again smells of bacon and eggs, rather than oatmeal, as it had the past few mornings. Jacks is already lining up seven bowls for the eggs, sticking two pieces of toast into each one.

"We'll need one more, Jacks," Talia tells him; familiar with the cook who has worked on her father's ship for years. He inclines his head to her, and sets down another bowl in the line. "How's Irene? And Syndra?"

At the pot of eggs on the stove, he replies as he stirs, "Oh, they're fine." He picks up the pot. "Probably will be better once I'm home, though."

Talia's mouth twists to the side while he scoops some eggs into each bowl. "It must be hard to be away from them for so long."

He shrugs, moving to put the pot on one of the low-firing burners. "At least I won't have to leave them again for a good while after this journey."

"It's still summer, maybe they'd like a trip to the beaches, or the countryside to get away from the city for a while."

He looks up from the bacon tray he's now serving from, and gives her a tight-lipped smile. "Maybe."

The word of a tired male, wishing to be home with his family; who has been stuck on this ship for weeks longer than planned at the journey's beginning. Talia's responding grin is a small, understanding tilt of her lips, and she takes two of the bowls without another word. We all follow suit, thanking him quietly before finding our table.

Javi comes down then, his hair much more neatly arranged atop his head, wearing his captain's garb. He takes his seat beside Talia, kissing the top of her head as he does.

"Careful you don't get the ends of your fancy coat dirty on the commoners' bench, High Lord," Lina teases him, and his dark eyes flick up from his food, humor instantly piercing the obvious preoccupation from the encounter in his sitting area moments ago.

"Emelina, please." He takes his napkin from his lap, tilts up his chin, and primly tucks the cloth into his collar. "I have half a dozen more fancy coats in my wardrobe upstairs. Each one grander than the last."

All at the table are openly grinning or smirking, even me. All but Lina, that is. She scrunches her brows, and tips her lips downwards in a disapproving frown. "Only half a dozen? I'd have thought single digits beneath your sensibilities."

"Quite right. But, you see, after that sea storm, I seem to have soiled a few of them." He conspicuously checks the coat-tails of his current jacket.

She sucks on a tooth to keep from smiling. "This is why one should always pack their brown pants when going sailing."

Sione guffaws beside her, and the rest of the table breaks at the sound. Since Javi left, Sione's parents, Duke Aleki and Duchess Elei, have overseen the country's governance. Usually, a High Lord would not leave his sovereignty for such a long time, but, for one, they hadn't known it would be *this* long. And, for another, Javi's exceptional water majick had made him indispensable to this mission. Ever since that court gathering all those years ago, he's been a friend to the High Lord and High Lady of Sabrian. When they asked for his help, his ship, and his time, he agreed. No questions, no holds, and no hesitation. He'd only arranged for his own trade negotiations to take place at the same time, and that had been that.

Althea, of course, doesn't know that. "How do you all know each other?" she asks in accented Divani.

Sione gives her a kind smile, and casually slings their arm over Lina's shoulders. "Our courts have been friends for over twenty years. During that time, either Emi and Atlas would come to Obala, or Talia and I to Sabrian. You should know, Tali's the granny here. Fifty-two in October."

Talia rolls her bright brown eyes. "Yeah, which meant I had to babysit you idiots while the grown-ups talked politics."

"Honestly, cuz, which one would you have rather been doing?" Sione raises a brow.

She shrugs, acknowledging that, and Althea smirks. "So, even with those immortal lifespans, all of you are young by mortal standards?"

"I guess. Well, how old are you?" Talia asks Adathan, brows scrunching in question.

I don't miss–I'm sure no one does–the way his eyes dart to Althea before he answers, "Eighty-nine."

"*HA!*" Talia shouts in triumph, then sticks her tongue out at Sione. "I'm not the oldest." She looks at the raven-haired female, her lips holding the curve of that victorious grin. "But my dad is over five hundred, so neither is he." She tips her head towards Adathan.

"Damn," Althea sighs, and pats Adathan's knee beneath the table. "You almost won. Better luck next time."

A smirk pulls at one corner of his mouth, and that cheek dimples. Even just seeing his profile as he looks at her, I *watch* his eyes soften.

The expression doesn't last long, though. The sounds of male voices emit from outside the ship; the crew are returning. All smiles at the table fall, but one.

"Someone say something," Althea says, too quietly for Jacks to hear from inside the kitchens, a tiny, easy grin on her face. Her bright green eyes are serene; only the elevated beating of her heart gives away that she feels anything at all about their return.

"We'll have to have a party for you, Aunt Ari," Atlas says, his voice light. I look at him, and he's got just as ready a smile on his face as Althea. "I know with me and Lina gone, you didn't have one." He turns to Althea, and jerks his thumb towards me as he tells her, "She turned fifty right before we left."

Althea's eyes widen, so believably exalted by the news of a birthday party, I can't see through it; I only see Adathan's arm move around her, his hand settling on her opposite hip. "A reason to–celebrate. Right?" Her brow crinkles as she stumbles over the Divani word.

I smile at her, not entirely forced. "I doubt I'll have much of a say in it if this lot is involved, but yes."

Green eyes tighten in a barely-perceptible wince as several sets of boots stomp down onto the deck above. Lina, leaning a bit into Sione, her own body tense as she listens to the noise, replies, "At least you're aware."

As footsteps sound from the stairwell, the many voices with them, we all look towards the noise. Many of the crew greet us upon seeing us, only those we'd already been unfriendly with ignoring us. After exchanging nods and "good mornings" with the rest, we turn back to each other. And, even though Sione comes up with our next topic, the thought behind each of our falsely-calm faces lingers:

Which of them will betray us next?

46

TERRIBLE TASKS

*DION - **15** MONTHS EARLIER*

As Ciara rode me, her lovely eyes closed and head tilted back, I could still taste her on my tongue. The way we felt together, whether it be our mouths or our hips joining, should have been damning in itself. I might as well be sent to the Void now.

If not for the way she sighed my name like a prayer.

I looked up at her, utterly entranced by the way her curls bounced as she did. My favorite little line formed between her brows as she found pleasure in the movements, but I knew what she needed.

It was only a bit difficult, as she'd tied my hands to the bedpost after I'd made her come three times on my tongue. I would have gone for four. I wanted to hear her make those noises, hear her breathe and then scream my name, every day for the rest of my immortal life.

Instead, she had flipped us with all that wonderful strength of hers, and bound me with my own shirt. Before she'd jumped on my cock, she put her mouth on me. Slow, and teasing. Driving me wild, until I'd practically begged her to sit on it.

Still, as she rode me, she was focusing on my pleasure. Doing a damned fantastic job of it, too, but I couldn't have it. I needed to feel the way her walls clenched around me when she came on my cock. After all, I'd vowed when our matehood solidified just a week ago to give her as much pleasure as I possibly could. Just because the vow had been internal, did not make it any less binding.

So, with her eyes still closed, I worked to get my hands out of my bindings. She heard it when the thread and fabric tore, and her eyes snapped open, but I'd already pressed my thumb to her clit, and began rubbing it gently, knowing she'd be too sensitive for anything else.

"Gods, Dion," she moaned, the movement of her hips slowing, and changing. Rocking, instead of bouncing. I grinned wickedly before sitting up, wanting to be closer to her. Still, I kept my hand between us, while she put her arms around my neck.

I lightly pinched her nipple between the thumb and forefinger of my other hand, and she moaned again, this time wordlessly. Her walls flexed around me, and I grunted in pleasure. I was close, but so was she. And damn if I didn't love falling over the edge together.

Her panted breaths grew faster, her thrusts more demanding, and I met her stroke for stroke. "Come on my cock, Ciara," I growled at her, and the fire in her eyes brightened even further.

"Only if you fill me with yours, Dion," she countered, and it was my undoing. I pulsed within her, and it was the final match for the spark of her orgasm. She clenched around me, screaming my name as she bounced harder than before, drawing out both our pleasures. When she was still, and we shared heavy breaths in the small space between our faces, I moved my hands to grip her ass, and hold her down on me. Then, I leaned in to press a kiss to her mouth.

That was where the fantasy ended.

Panting slightly, I unwrapped my fist from my cock, and opened my eyes. The canopy over my bed was not nearly as good a view as my mate riding me, but it was the one I had.

I sighed, long and heavy, before sitting up. A trip to the washroom to clean my hands, then wash fully. Shaving the two-day stubble from my face and neck. Dressing in a suit with a cravat. Walking into the halls that might have been lovely, but couldn't be in comparison to those I'd met her in.

Being one of the esteemed High King Oleander's right hand males again, I was back in one of the more beautiful areas of the castle. After my immediate hall, the walls opened up, only a hip-high baluster, and generously spaced columns to hold up the ceiling. Looking through their spaces, one could see a fountain, surrounded by a sprawling painting on the floor beneath it. The fountain represented the Evredis. On its right sat Eshelle; vast, and painted in exquisite detail. On its left: Weaschte.

The human continent was rendered dull in comparison to the land of the Fae and faeries. A splotch of land, depicted only with specifications of when the Fae had been ousted from each country. One thousand years ago, being the most recent. One thousand and seven the least.

I had wondered, when I first moved into this section of the castle last year, why Oleander might have a painting of it at all. He had no nostalgia for his forefathers, who'd put it there. He could paint right over the centuries-old work, and not bat an eye.

I no longer turned from my wonderings, as I once did. So, just like my others, I'd faced this one. And I could find only one reason why the king of Eshelle might have such a constant reminder of the loss of a seven-year war.

He intended to start another. And he meant to win.

And, if I didn't succeed in inciting rebellion, and soon, he might do just that. For, without majick, Oleander had apparently sought to make himself powerful in other ways. With weapons that could decimate a city. Or a continent.

The people were riled–had been so for years, now. They'd become more daring; three rescues for prisoners being led to the execution stage had been successful in the past month. Neighbors were not telling where the rescued had gone, and the city guard were leaving them to their devices after questioning, rather than seizing them for interrogation.

But, things were moving too slowly. As if *knowing* that my presence on stage was somehow inciting the people, Olin had ended my appearances on the execution stage. He could not go himself, pretending to be me; the outward expression of our powers was too different. Instead, Marcys acted alone, simply beheading the prisoners.

He did nothing more extreme, though I knew both his and Olin's appetites could call for it. My brother knew gutting or dismembering, or any other heinous method of ending their lives would only add fuel to the people's fire.

His ambitions had grown these years, too. He deferred to Oleander less and less. Gave him counsel to his own gain, far more than he used to. And so, seeing that painting, I had to wonder after Olin's ambitions, as well. What sorts of horrors did he have planned for the Mage King and Queen–who had taken one of our own back home with them?

Did they know it yet? That the Fae child they'd once dreaded to have was actually in their midst now? Not even twenty years old, the female would not have quite reached maturity. And, even when she did, it would be years still before it would become clear that she was not aging like her friends.

I wasn't sure my Hiela and Hielo could wait that long. Though, I had no idea how they might think to extricate her from the human realm. Surely Aron and Lydia would not be able to shun the woman they'd raised from infancy, even if her heritage became known. They'd been able to turn from a babe, but an adult? I didn't think it would be so simple as that again. If such a word could be used to describe that situation in the first place.

Regardless of that transgression, neither they nor their people deserved an unprecedented war at their doorstep. With another glance at the map below, I lifted my chin, my boots clicking softly along the tiled floors as I made my way to Olin's office. It was close–far too close for my liking–to my chambers, so by the time my contemplation was through, I was there. I knocked, and turned to look once more at the painting before the handle twisted, and the door opened.

Adathan stood there, dressed much more casually than I. I might have frowned, but, just like him, I had extensive practice with keeping my expression neutral and my eyes blank. It was highly unusual for the male to both be here during the day, rather than those underground cells at the border of Oschverre, and then not be wearing a suit, as Olin preferred.

He stood aside so I could enter, and I nodded my thanks, which he returned. I strode across the polished mahogany floors until my boots hit the center of a Parvatan area rug. I turned on a heel, clasped my hands behind my back, and looked at my brother.

Olin gave me a kind smile, his hazel eyes crinkling at the corners. "Please, sit, Dion," he said, gesturing with the pen in his hand to one of the oak-and-velvet chairs before his desk. I took a seat, and crossed an ankle over a knee, which made Olin smirk before going back to his work.

The pen was a newer invention. Ink, in a tube that was reminiscent of a needle, with a small point that carried the words far more easily than a quill. It scratched along the paper similarly, but it was as different as the weapons Oleander created were from a bow and arrow.

I looked around his office as he finished whatever he was doing. Undoubtedly, he could do it later, but was doing it now for two reasons. One, to show me just how important he was; that he was given so many tasks by the king that even a conversation with his brother had to wait. And, two, to do just that. To make me wait, just because he could.

Art from many Eshellen countries hung on each wall. The windows to the west were wide, not covered by curtains, but open to look out into the more tasteful part of the city. The floors were wood, instead of the black marble many of the grand spaces in the castle possessed. Even the velvet of the chairs, instead of leather, gave an air of comfort, rather than rigidity. Olin had decorated his office as though he had a soul.

Of course, I knew that wasn't the case. The way he made Adathan stand, rather than invite him to sit, too, showed just how little soul he had. He cared only for power, and how to get more of it. Pain, and how best to dole it out.

Finally, he set his pen down, and I looked back at him. He made careful work of setting the pages with still-wet ink aside, and then folded his hands over his desk. "I have good news, brother," he said.

"What news is that?" I asked, fighting to keep my tone and expression bland, but mildly interested, instead of rolling my eyes at him.

"Your nephew is going on a trip." He grinned, and looked

up at Adathan, who had moved to stand behind the chair beside my own.

"A trip to where?" I was already getting annoyed with having to ask him for details, and I was only two questions in. Not a good sign.

"Cerasche."

That training to keep my face and eyes blank kicked in immediately, and I worked as well to restrain my heart from racing. "Cerasche?"

"Yes. He is going to act as a spy for me again. A nice break from his time in the dungeons, I think."

"Let us not pretend that you care for his wellbeing. Why is he truly going?"

Olin laughed, and raised one of his hands to point at me. "You always could see through me, brother." He lowered his hand, sat back in his grand chair, and sighed. "Yes, you're quite right. He *is* going to be my spy. But, you see, I've learned some things. Things which...demand my attention to go to the royal humans."

I focused on not swallowing. Not showing or scenting fear. I furrowed my brow. "What things?"

"Oh, Dion. You either know, or you don't. If you do, you also know why he's going. If you don't, then I might tell you once Adathan is well on his way, and you can do nothing to stop him."

Reveal myself, or not? I didn't sense a bluff, but perhaps they knew nothing, and Adathan was going to find out what he could about the humans. Learn about the sovereigns there, for the purpose of the war I was more sure by the moment Oleander–perhaps no more than a mere puppet for my brother–was plotting.

Saying something would only serve to give me more knowledge with which I could do nothing. My correspondences were monitored, and there was nobody in this castle who would carry one for me, rather than turn me over to Olin for a quick silver.

So, I only responded, "Why would I seek to stop him from serving our High King, and his realm?"

Olin smirked again, dark humor sparking in his otherwise cold eyes. "Why, indeed." Then he braced his hands on the arms of his chair, and stood. He walked around his desk to Adathan, who stood a few inches taller than him. I wondered, not for the first time, what power the male had. It was oddly masked. Not glamoured, I didn't think, but repressed. Tempered, most likely, by my twin during their blood oath when he was just a boy.

Perhaps I didn't know what Adathan's power was. But I knew it must have been vast, and fearsome indeed for it to have warranted Olin's leashing of it at such a young age.

"Alright. Can't have you looking like this, you'll draw too much attention." And then I watched Adathan's dark hair turn blond. His bright gold eyes darkened into a dull brown. His scent changed completely. Arched ears rounded, and I would bet that his canines did, too. Then he shrank by several inches, and lost quite a bit of muscle. I understood the reason for the casual clothes when Olin provided him with another, smaller set. And then made the male change in front of us.

I turned away while he did so, but Olin continued to face him. Another measure of control, taking away that small dignity. Only once the sliding of fabric over skin ceased did I look over my shoulder. Adathan now faced Olin as I had when I walked in: straight on, hands clasped behind his back. Eyes and face utterly blank.

"Good. Now, for your orders. Adathan Evestre, you will travel immediately to Cerasche, the capital country of Weaschte. You will disembark in Dahlih, and travel either on foot or by horse to Castle Cerasche. Once there, you will get a job–one where you will have constant exposure to the royal family, but particularly the princess called Althea.

"You will observe them. Observe *her*, at any opportunity. During this assignment, you will not give any indication that you are not who they believe you to be. You will not inform them of your true position in any way. If any Fae arrive at the castle, you will inform me at once. You will remain at Castle Cerasche until I retrieve you, or until I notify you that your service there is done.

"Last thing: throughout your time in Weaschte, unless I say otherwise, you will be named Artur Evani. Do you understand, boy?"

"Yes, my Lord," he replied, his voice a bit higher than his usual bass tones. Even I, with extensive training in glamours and seeing through them, could not make out the male I knew from the man who stood in front of my brother now.

"Good. Be on your way, then. Your bags and your chosen weapons are with your horse at the stables."

Adathan bowed his head to Olin, and then turned on his heel to exit the office. I didn't know what compelled me to do it, especially in the presence of my brother, but when he was about to reach for the door handle, I called to him: "Adathan."

He turned, a bit slowly, until he faced me. I didn't want to wish him luck, not in this journey that could mean danger for so many. So, what came out was both what I could say, and what I meant. "Be safe."

His jaw clenched, but he nodded after a beat. Eyes on the ground, he left the study with a soft *click* of the door.

"How sweet," Olin said, drawing my attention back to him. He was smirking slightly, a terrible, knowing look in his eyes. "Don't worry, brother. He will be fine. I may not care for him, but I would never put my son and heir into harm's way."

"You had him tortured for flinching when Marcys carved me open," I reminded him. Flatly, to conceal the anger.

He waved a hand. "Oh, that. Well, that was to teach him a lesson. He learned it. *This* is for me. You can at least trust my personal interest in what he might learn while in that human castle."

That, I could. If there was anything Olin cared about aside from power and pain, it was himself.

"Now." He sat back in the large, unnecessarily intricate chair behind his desk, and grinned at me over steepled fingers, though it didn't reach his eyes. "For your tasks."

47

WINGS & HEALING THINGS

SETTING SAIL REQUIRES ATLAS'S HELP PRETTY QUICKLY, SO AL hangs out with Talia, Sione, and I at the bow.

Adathan had been reluctant to leave her, to say the least. I could see the argument passing between their joined gazes before he gave in to her logic. She'd gone up on her tip-toes after, and managed to plant a kiss on his still-clenched jaw. Then the three of us had turned away, Sione whistling, as he grabbed her to him, and kissed her lips with enough passion to make a message clear to all the males around us: *mine*.

Now, she's working the curls of my hair into an intricate braid, all because I said I was hot a couple of minutes ago. "How does it look?" I ask Sione, who's leaning against the railing, their wings draped behind it.

"Good," they answer, popping a grape into their mouth from the bunch they'd nicked from the kitchen.

I roll my eyes, and so does Talia, who sits on the deck near their feet. "Ymeda's tits, Oné, you could be a little more descrip-tive." She turns her light brown eyes to me, and smiles. "It's beautiful. Frames your face perfectly."

I lift my chin. "*Thank* you." Then stick my tongue out at Sione, who returns the gesture, clumps of grape on theirs. I make a noise of disgust, and they smirk. "You know, they say absence makes the heart grow fonder, but–"

"I'm very fond of you, moonshine," they interrupt before I can tell them to give me another few weeks to see. With a crooked grin, they toss the next grape in the air, and tilt their head back to catch it.

Hoping the blush on my cheeks is masked by the color already there from the sun, I roll my eyes again.

"Would you quit hogging those?" Tali scolds them, wrenching the bunch out of their hand, and plucking off a few before tossing it to me. They're a bit warm from the day's heat, and from Sione's hand, but still crisp. I put one in my mouth, then hold one behind my head. A second later, soft lips brush against my fingertips, seizing the snack.

"Almost done," Al says, pulling the final lock of my hair into the plait. "You've got a lot of hair."

I shrug. "My mum said I was born with it, and it just never stopped growing from there."

"That's a human tale. A princess locked in a tower, her hair long enough to pull up her rescuer prince from the ground below." I feel Al's fingers tie a bow around the bottom of the braid, and scoot over on my bottom so that she's within our little circle.

Talia's brows scrunch. "Wouldn't that hurt? Why can't he just climb the tower?"

Al snatches a couple of grapes from the bunch in my lap. "Probably, and I suppose he just didn't have the idea."

The Obalan Lady crinkles her nose, then holds her hand up

for me to toss the fruit to her. As she catches it, she says, "Seems like a bad prince. Not worthy of her at all."

Al frowns contemplatively. "I guess not."

"Now who's hogging," Sione grumbles, plucking a grape from Talia's hand. "Anyway, we have some stories like that, too. Remember, the one with the mer? The male didn't even recognize his mate. Let one little glamour fool him."

"He just wanted to get some tail," I mumble, and the three around me stop in their movements.

"You did not," Sione says, a second before Al laughs.

Not a huff of air. Not a two-beat chuckle, or a humored hum, but a *laugh*. Bright, bubbling out of her chest, clear as a bell and lovely as the sun-soaked meadow I would liken it to, if sound could be such a thing. *Laughing*, for the first time since I met her.

Talia joins in, Sione, too, and I'm right with them. For me, my–terrible–joke is only part of it. After a couple of seconds, Al seems to realize the same thing I have, and I watch her allow it to take her. To let the humor deep into her belly, until she's half in my lap as she clutches her side. And it's so ridiculous, the joy she's found in my–again, terrible–pun, that the rest of us are there with her, tears streaming down our faces, and cheeks hurting from wide smiles.

When the laughter calms, coming out in exhales and sighs, Al straightens, wiping her eyes. Then, she says, "That was so bad, Li."

That gets another chuckle out of us, just out of the absurdity of it. As she sighs after the last beat of laughter, though, her brow scrunches, and she looks at Sione, tilting her head slightly.

"What's wrong with your wing?" she asks them.

They look at her with a similar expression, their dark brown wings ruffling a bit. "Nothing, why?"

"I can sense that something hurts," she tells them, standing. "I can heal it for you, if you want."

Their eyes flick to me for less than a heartbeat, then back to her. "Jemage don't let people that aren't theirs touch their wings."

Al's voice shifts; softer, understanding. "I don't have to touch them. Just hover my hands near them. Is that okay?"

They look between the two of us again, and I nod, trying to indicate that it's alright, that she won't touch them if they've asked her not to. And that seems to be enough, because they say, "Yeah." Al closes the distance between the two of them as Sione turns, putting their back and those beautiful wings to us.

I can't see anything wrong with them, but it doesn't mean it's not there. Al confirms that, saying, "A couple of strained muscles. I can heal the inflammation and the small tears causing the soreness, but you should still rest them for the remainder of the day."

"No problem," is their only reply, and Al takes it as consent to begin her work. I watch in familiar wonder as the ethereal light emits from her palms, and that strange glow brightens her veins while she hovers her hands before Sione's wings. After a couple of seconds, their back and shoulders visibly relax, and she lowers her arms to her sides.

They turn to her, eyes wide. "That's fucking amazing," they tell her, wings expanding and contracting fluidly. But she's barely grinned at them before her attention moves to me, and it fades.

She comes over to me slowly, and kneels, the question in her eyes. I swallow, trying not to look up at the faerie who has paused in preternatural stillness a few feet away. Instead, I swivel on my hip until my back is facing Al. Gently, her healer's fingers so swift yet soft, she lifts the hem of my shirt until it exposes the bruise.

I'd felt it last night, and snuck a peek at it this morning, after kicking Atlas out of the washroom to use the facility. Deep purple, and huge, nearly the entire width of my waist, from that male who kneeled on me. His grip on my wrists had somehow managed to avoid such marks, and the side of my face is sore but unscathed from him pressing it into the pavement.

"Who did that to you?" comes Sione's voice, far darker than I've ever heard it before.

I turn my head towards my shoulder, but don't lift my eyes to them. "One of the males from last night. I tried to fight him, but..." Shame at how easily he'd recaptured me colors my cheeks. "Anyway, Adathan ripped his head off as soon as he arrived."

Al's fingers stutter slightly as she rests them on my skin with the weight of a feather, and Talia asks, "Like, *literally* ripped his head off?"

I nod. "Yeah. He didn't have any weapons. Guess he didn't need any." And if there were any one fact that should make it obvious that he's not a threat to us, as I know Ciaragen tried to believe he is, it's in the fact that she's not watching him now. That, even though he could kill his way through a quarter of this ship before anyone could even make him pause, she's with Atlas at the mooring lines.

Sione just says, "Good," while I feel Al's majick radiate through me. The ache in my back and wrists disappears, as does the soreness in my cheek. Al lowers my shirt, and I move back to my original position, criss crossing my legs.

"Thanks," I tell her with a tight grin.

She reaches, and tucks an errant curl behind my ear. "He caught you because you were focusing on me. Not because you're a bad fighter. He took advantage of your distraction. I saw him fake a lunge to me. You tried to stop him, didn't you?"

I tighten my jaw against the thickness in my throat, and look down at my hands in my lap. But, I nod.

"He was a coward. He saw how good you were, and found the easy way out. And when you were brave enough to try to save me, he took advantage of that. He was a *coward*," she repeats through her teeth, and I look up at her through my lashes. She brushes away a fallen tear with her knuckle. "He had over a hundred pounds on you, and he *kneeled* on you to keep you down. That's how fucking strong you are."

My lips wobble, and with silver lining her own eyes, Al pulls me into her arms. My head notches below her chin, and I wrap my arms around her waist. "I'm sorry," she tells me. "I've been so focused on myself, that I just–"

"Al," I interrupt her, sniffling once and pulling back from her embrace to look at her. "You fucking *died*. You were almost...that male would have violated you, even as you were bleeding out. If you *weren't* focused on yourself, I would be fucking concerned."

"I'm not sure how either of you are functioning right now, to be honest," Talia inputs, shrugging her toned, tan shoulders, arms crossed over her chest. "If we were at either of our homes right now, I would be putting you both to bed, and be ready with ice cream when you woke up. Probably some gossip, but that part's for me, too." She smirks, and I find the expression mirrored on Al's face, and my own, the heaviness of the previous moment lifting. "For example," Tali goes on, a gleam in her cinnamon eyes as she looks at Al. "What's going on between you and the fucking giant on the rigging right now?"

It's so like Tali to be immediately welcoming; to not even hesitate to act as if she's known Al forever. To talk as comfortably with her as she does with me or Sione, and not make her feel 'other' or 'outside' of us. Even though she's been in her maturity since before I was even born, she did the same for me when I came of age.

Al's cheeks fill with color at her questioning, and she bites her lip. But the wariness in her eyes is anything but that of a female in love. "I'm sure you've heard about him, but–"

Tali cuts her off, actually slicing her hand through the air to emphasize it. "Stop. He killed the male who hurt Lina, and he's the reason you're still here. So, seriously–I don't even go for males, but I can tell...I mean, he looks like he *fuuucks*."

Sione is the one who shrugs now, in agreement. "He does. So, does he really, or...?"

The blush has spread across Al's nose and into the tips of her ears–once more free of the Fae arches, since the iron negated the glamour, and she hasn't reassumed it. "I wouldn't know, exactly, but..." The bite of her lip now is definitely *that* female. "From what I've experienced so far, I would guess so."

"*What?!*" I exclaim, slapping her arm. "*What happened?!*" Each syllable is accentuated by another slap.

Al shrinks away, grinning like a fiend, holding her hands up against my assault. "Things! Okay?!"

"NO!"

She chuckles, and Tali has mercy on her. "Okay, okay, but it was good?" Black brows raise, and Sione not-so-sneakily snatches the forgotten bunch of grapes from her hand.

"Very," Al says, her face practically aflame, and eyes just as bright.

"I knew it. You can tell, just looking at him."

"Which is fun to do," Sione adds, winking at Al, who smirks back at them, biting her bottom lip to tame the grin. Then their gaze shifts to me, and something within it shifts, too. "What about you, Emi? Any fun since you left the Sabriani shore?"

Now *my* cheeks heat, but I sit back on my elbows, feigning nonchalance. "Unfortunately not. I wasn't about to bring any of those idiots into my bed." I jerk my chin in the general direction of the main deck, and the crew working on it.

They shrug their agreement, that look easing in their russet eyes. "Tali and I have had a boring summer so far, too."

I ignore the useless flutter of relief in my chest, and snap my gaze to Talia. "What happened to Su?"

She twists a silken lock of hair around her finger. "We ended things a couple of weeks after you left. She couldn't deal with the *future High Lady* of it all."

My brows scrunch. "You two were together for *five years*. What, did she think you were going to step back from your title?"

Her tone is hard. "Apparently, yeah. She was waiting for either the mating bond to click, or for me to tell my dad that I wasn't going to ascend. In a few fucking *centuries*."

"So, what, if you had mated–?"

"She thought it would be enough for me to do whatever she wanted. But, when we didn't..." She wiggles her fingers in a twiddling wave good-bye, a sarcastic grin on her round lips.

"Well, she's an idiot. And you're too good for her."

"That's what I've been saying," Sione adds, nudging her shoulder with the back of their hand.

"Saying what?" comes Atlas's voice as he moves towards us. Sweat has soaked through the chest and back of his cotton shirt, and it clings to the muscles there. He's tied his locs back with a thin strip of leather, but I doubt it brought him much relief in the open sun.

He holds his hand up, and Sione tosses him the bunch of maybe five remaining grapes. "How Tali is too good for Su," they reply.

Atlas's brows scrunch, and he moves to stand close to Al, until she pats the space on the deck beside her. "That's over?" he asks as he sits, and we all nod. His brows raise as he hands

Al and I each one of the last three grapes. "You know your dad never liked her."

"I *know*, which is precisely why he hasn't heard we ended things yet. He has the *worst* 'I told you so' face." She leans back against Sione's leg.

"So, your plan is to just never tell him, and hope he forgets you were with her in the first place?" I ask through my chewing.

"Exactly." She winks at me, and Sione rolls their eyes above her. They spread their wings behind the railing, not enough to catch wind, just enough to sun them a bit. And when they tilt their head back, eyes closed against the bright sun, the column of their throat continuing to a leanly muscled chest, I have to force myself to look away, and pretend to have been paying attention to what Atlas has been saying the whole time.

As I do, seeing them straighten in my periphery, I have the strangest feeling that Sione was very aware of my gaze.

48

EVENED SCALES

THEA - DAY 29

THE DAY PASSES IN RELATIVE EASE, ALL THINGS CONSIDERED.

Sione and Talia are two incredibly welcome additions to our little group. Both kind, and witty, with a bit of attitude that keeps me on my toes, and winds up freeing that part of me throughout the day, too. I hadn't realized how much I still kept it leashed, after my time of holding my tongue so often in a human court, and in my grief.

Atlas keeps his word and inconspicuously guards me, even when I continue to lounge with them and Lina at the bow. After lunch, though, I get a bit bored of sitting around, and he shows me a few things with the mooring lines, and even has me help with a sail tie. When I nail a complicated knot on the first try after his demonstration, I earn a wide grin and a high five.

All the while, though, his storm gray eyes flicker over males as they pass us, and he stands just slightly in front of me when they come to converse. I manage to keep my body loose when they do, and not tense up, preparing for a fight. My smiles when they encourage me on my work are their usual slight width, and none of them bat an eye at the small show of gratitude or enthusiasm.

"Can I ask you something?" I ask Atlas in Ceraschen shortly before dinner. We're leaning up against the portside railing, watching the sun on the opposite side of the ship crest over the sea. We're both coated in sweat, hair up–mine albeit more disheveled since Li has my sash–holding water skins that were far fuller a couple of hours ago.

Throughout our work together, we'd talked and joked as easily as we had a month ago. I'd watched his eyes gleam with the joy of it, and I knew mine glimmered the same.

Yet, there had been moments when he seemed uncertain. Where he would hesitate before nudging my shoulder, or teasing me. Or saying my name. And, it's those moments which drove my query.

"Of course," he replies, turning to me, not so much as wrinkling his brow at the query, or the language.

"I suppose it's not so much a question, but...You know that my–well, my smiles and laughs, they haven't been what they used to be. And I just want to make sure that you know that...it wasn't you. That when I told you I forgave you, I meant it, and those small pieces were–they were just all I could manage. For anyone."

His eyes are so tender, it raises some of the heat that's left me since we ended our work back to my cheeks. "Yes, I know that, Althea."

I swallow, glancing down at my feet before meeting his gaze again. "That day...it wasn't because of you, not really. So, if you want–Atlas, you can call me Aly."

He fully turns his body towards me, eyes somber but kind. "I didn't think it through when I said it to you our first day on the ship. I know that's what your friends and family called you and that it hurt to hear it because of that."

My throat thick, I give him a half smile. "Well, you told me you would always be my friend, right?"

He nods, just a slight movement, and his own lips tilt up. "Always, *Aly*."

My grin widens, even as my heart twists, and I bump his arm with my shoulder. He smiles back at me, then bites his bottom lip as he looks up. His expression slightly subdued, he says, "I'm gonna go wash up for dinner. I'll see you there, yeah?"

I know what his leaving means without having to ask. Softly, I reply, "Yeah," then give him one of his mock salutes, which he returns with a smirk before turning and heading for the cabins.

I look away from his retreating form as Adathan finishes the climb down from the mast. His back is to me, shining with sweat from working all day in the sun. The long, thick scars demand for me to trace them with my fingers, and then my mouth, showing him that what he finds abhorrent, I find beautiful. The tattoo across his shoulders, and down to his triceps, so intricate. Strong and striking below the waist, too.

It's a game for myself, to look at him and not touch him, now that I've thoroughly done both. Greedily, and without inhibition. And games can sometimes have wonderful consequences.

He turns, and his eyes find me immediately. And not even the distance between us can hide the love, and the hunger that fills his eyes.

He slides his shirt onto his arms as he walks towards me, his steps intentionally measured. I bite my lip as I watch him, glad that my friends aren't near and the crew aren't watching. Glad they can't see what draws my eyes, below the waistband of his trousers. Glad they can't scent the wetness that pools between my thighs.

When Adathan reaches me, he grabs my hand, and leads me to the stairwell Atlas disappeared down. And I manage to briefly hope that my friend is in the washroom already before Adan's hand seizes my jaw, the other goes to the small of my back, and his lips are crushing mine. He turns us with his body to be within the dark of the threshold, and presses me against the wall. His lips part mine, and he swipes his tongue into my mouth with thorough, tantalizing strokes. I moan into his mouth, and tangle my hands into his hair, more than happy for this fire to consume me.

The hand on my jaw moves down my neck, and skims over the side of my ribcage, not quite touching my breast, but close enough that I arch further against him, pressing them into his stomach. Then it's my turn to swallow the sound he makes against my lips. My hands travel down to his chest, and grip the fronts of his open shirt, pulling him, even though there's no space remaining between us.

The ache in my core builds, and I slide up onto my tiptoes to bring that ache closer to the hardness against my belly. When I feel it rub against my clit, I gasp at the sensation, and press further into it.

His lips curl up against mine. "Greedy," he growls.

"No more than you, devouring me like I'm your last meal," I return, breathless.

A low noise rumbles in his throat. "You should know not to say that idly. Not when I've been waiting to taste you again all day."

I whimper, utterly unashamed of it as his lips take mine again, more gently this time. I feel him pulse against me and my hands spear beneath his shirt to run over the hard, thick muscle of his abdomen, fingers sneaking down...

Adan grips my wrists in one large hand, stopping their pursuit. He sucks my lower lip into his mouth, pulling it slightly as he draws his face away from mine. I open my eyes to look into his, finding his pupils blown wide, their expression half-mad with desire. It's the other half that has him bringing my bound hands to his lips, and pressing soft kisses to my knuckles.

"Are you going to behave if I let you go, love?" he asks roughly.

"Only one way to know for sure."

He smirks, and steps back from me. My eyes travel down the expanse of skin revealed by his open shirt, to the still-prominent impression in his trousers.

He clicks his tongue, and grabs my chin with his other hand, tilting my face back up. "I suppose it's lucky I have enough control for the both of us," he says, his eyes dancing with mischief, and those emotions which make both my heart and my core tighten.

I roll my eyes. "Yeah. Lucky."

Adan chuckles and leans in, only to kiss my forehead. He releases my wrists, and I sigh before moving my hands to do up the buttons of his shirt, reveling in the way my knuckles brush over the scarred skin beneath the cotton. The muscles of his chest expand as he takes a deep breath, my hands by his navel. But, when I reach the button at the waistband of his trousers, his hand grasps one of mine before he pulls me back into the sunshine.

"You did great today, at the mooring lines," he tells me as we make our way to the other stairs that will take us to the mess.

I grin up at him. "Thank you." He returns the expression, his eyes soft and sweet, and brushes his thumb along the backs of my knuckles. When he takes the lead down the narrow staircase, I lean in to brush a kiss to the back of his shoulder.

Everyone but Atlas is already at our table. Even Javi sits beside Talia, and I'd be willing to bet that missing his daughter is only part of the reason. After what Atlas and Li were talking about last night, and what happened after, I would have been surprised if he didn't join us to keep an eye on her, and the crew.

I wind up sitting between Adan and Sione, and we all eat the fried fish and chips Jacks made, with easy chatter between bites. Even Ciaragen doesn't glare at Adathan beside me, and when Atlas sits across from me, the two males only exchange a nod.

But, at the end, as Talia and Ciaragen clear our plates for us, Li turns to me with hesitant excitement in her face, and raises her brows.

And, even though I finally released the worst of my grief, and I feel lighter than I have in weeks...

I give her a rueful half grin. "Not yet," I tell her, hoping she understands.

The look in her blue eyes tells me that she does, and she replies, "If you change your mind, Sione will be playing after the first hour."

I look up at them where they stand behind her, surprised. Not that I believed all Fae and faeries to be fighters alone, but none so far have expressed any interest in the arts. At least that I've seen. "What do you play?"

"Violin, and guitar. I'll probably do a bit of both tonight." They shrug, an easy smile on their lips, then their brow scrunches a bit. "Do you play?"

Before I can speak my answer—that I know only the pianoforte, and the Ceraschen version of what they call a *guitar* —Li pipes in, "She can sing. Like, *beautifully*."

I feel a blush rise to my cheeks, and widen my eyes at her. "But I don't perform! Also, how do you know?"

She rolls her eyes, teasing but affectionate. "You hum a lot. All the time, lately. And you never performed, even in Cerasche?"

"No! I sang my nieces and nephews lullabies, that's it."

"What about that one song?" Adathan asks quietly from beside me. I whirl to him, and there's both challenge and softness in his gaze. *Challenge.* Like, being embarrassed about this hobby isn't doing me any favors, and he wants to see if I'll face it, or keep running.

And softness, because I know what song he means. "It was a special one. For my mom." Of course, he would have heard it; her, playing her pianoforte, while I sang the lyrics for her. Near me, as he always was by assignment and then by need, Adan probably knows the notes himself, with how often she had me sing it for her.

He squeezes my hand beneath the table, and then I feel slender fingers brush through my hair behind me. I look up over my shoulder to find Talia smiling, small and sad, down at me.

A female who lost her mother. I return the expression, and she twirls a lock of my hair around her finger, slowly dropping it down my back. "Well, you deserve the rest," she says gently. Then, the fire that became a little familiar after spending the whole morning with her gives an edge to a dawning smirk. "But if I don't see you down there on our final night, I'll drag you down myself."

A bit nervous and a bit grateful, I grin back at her. Li takes the loss, Sione slinging an arm over her shoulders and not giving her an option but to leave me and walk beside them. Atlas salutes me, which I return, and nods to Adathan again, to which he does the same. Javi gives us a smile, and Ciaragen waves, and then it's just us, walking up one set of stairs, and down the next.

Outside my cabin, Adan halts, his jaw tight. He's not meeting my eyes, so I reach up, and place my hand on his cheek to get him to do so. When he does, I say, "You know I have no intention of sleeping without you tonight, right?"

Relief spills through the apprehension, and he smirks. Something lays behind the easy expression, though, and he's doing a good job at hiding what it is exactly as he grabs my hand from his face. "I didn't want to be presumptuous, love."

"And, what? The alternative is that you would stand outside my door all night?" I raise my brows, and he runs his tongue over a canine, the movement dimpling his cheek. I roll my eyes, and use my hold on him to pull him, not into my cabin, but to his. Once inside, though, he's the one who tugs at my hand. I'm wrapped in his embrace in the next second, his head tucked low into the side of my neck. I hear and feel the slow, deep breaths he takes, expanding the breadth of his torso around which my own arms are so tightly wrapped.

Into my hair, he begins softly, "I spent the entire day reigning in the urge to kill almost every male on this ship. Just for the possibility that they could do you harm. All day, I saw *that* image of you in my mind, and I had to keep looking down to see you, or listen for your voice. I couldn't get lunch with you, couldn't come down at all, because I thought if I did, and I saw anyone even *look* at you the wrong way..." His arms tighten, and then let me go, only to trail up to cup my face.

His eyes open, so raw with emotion as he strokes his thumbs down my cheeks that my throat thickens before he even speaks. "Now, I look at you...you are my entire *universe*, Thea. And you were *gone*. For the minutes that felt like an eternity, I was in a world where you didn't exist. And *now*, now you're here, and every fucking breath you take feels like a dream–like I'm going to wake up, and find that the past day has been–" His voice breaks, my heart with it.

One of his hands pushes my hair back from my face, his eyes scanning, like he can see every mark he healed this morning. "I know we have to figure out if there's anyone else on this ship working for Olin. And your plan–it'll work. But every second of waiting, of not being beside you to hear your heart beating, or to see the life in your eyes...that darkness inside me tries to take over. The power that brought you back is a gift, but its counterpart is a curse. It runs through my veins, and begs me to give in so that you'll be safe. Any other factor–it doesn't fucking matter. Burning the world down for you would be easy. But living with the way you would look at me afterwards...that would not be easy.

"Not when you stand here now, with–with *love* in your eyes. Not when you walk into my room like it's as comfortable to you as breathing. Not when I would live for centuries with the memory of how it felt to have you, only to lose you to the darkest parts of myself."

Finished, his hands move from my face to my hips, and he releases a shuddering breath. His head turns, his lips pressing tightly together, pulling at his jaw. I can tell he's only composing himself, that he's not avoiding continued conversation, or shutting me out. But I don't want him composed.

I lean up on my toes, placing my palms on his chest for balance, and kiss the side of his neck, right over the star-shaped scar. He sighs, and his hands tighten on me. "No amount of darkness could blind me to you, Adathan. Could ever make me turn away." I tilt my head so that I can kiss the column of his throat, and feel it vibrate slightly against my mouth. "If you are Death," I say, quoting his words from a sea-soaked cabin all those nights ago. Pulling back, and laying my hand on his stubbled cheek so that he looks at me once more, I finish, "then I am your scythe. If you ever needed to burn the world down, I would be right there by your side."

"You are not my scythe, Thea," he whispers, one hand moving to the small of my back, and the other to cup the back of my neck, supporting it as I look up at him. "You are my Life." Then he leans down, and covers my lips with his. Gently, at first, the wildfire that consumes us languid as lava, flowing through us slowly. Leisurely, like the way his lips part mine.

Then his arms shift, and I'm lifted off the ground, being carried across the small room. Reverently, he lays me on his bed, then his hands move down my arms, and grab my wrists. Slowly, he lifts them over my head and holds them to his pillow, making my back arch like a cat stretching.

He moves my wrists into one hand, and hovers over me, while his other hand begins a caress at my cheek that continues down as he speaks. "Do you remember when you asked me to call you Thea?"

I nod, beyond speaking as the backs of his knuckles trail over my peaked nipple. "You were in here for hours, and your scent...it stayed here all night. So, I know you want to touch me, love. But, the amount of times I pleasured myself that night alone, breathing in your scent and whispering the name you gave to me as if I were saying it to you...it outnumbers how many times I've made you come. And I'm going to remedy at least that much before I hold you in my arms, so sated that you're asleep before you can think to feel how hard I am for you."

I moan, arching more, his hand now at the waistband of my trousers. "You only get one choice, sweetheart," he tells me as he flicks open the buttons. "My fingers or my tongue?"

I remember each from last night in exquisite detail, and it makes my thighs clench together. I think I know which one, but... "I haven't bathed, Adan," I breathe.

He growls, looping his hand into the hip of my trousers and undergarment, moving them down by inches. "I was hoping you'd want my mouth on you, love. Let me make something clear." His teeth scrape against my breast over my shirt, and I gasp. "If I want the taste of you, the only thing that will stop me is your word. Not your bathing status."

I yelp as, in one swift motion, I'm bared from the waist down—well, for all but my boots. I try to subtly move to toe them off, but Adan stops me. "Keep them on. I got them for you. Never imagined they would look so good on my shoulders, though."

I'd always assumed Olin had bought them, but I should have realized that couldn't be true. That they had fit me so perfectly I could have sprinted in them without issue. I feel like anything but running now, as they rest over the broad width of his shoulders while he moves, trailing open-mouthed kisses down my belly, setting me writhing already.

My breath catches and then releases in a sigh at the first stroke, all the way up my center. Adathan groans against me, and maybe it's how he'd leashed himself all day, or maybe it's just that I'd already been throbbing for him, but after just a few flicks of his tongue over my clit, I come undone, shouting his name with my nails in his neck. I pant out breathy moans as it passes, his mouth soft on me all the while, then expect him to rise.

He doesn't. Steadily, he builds the pleasure back up, and one hand reaches up to my breasts. He pinches and pulls at my nipple, somehow knowing when to alternate with gentle brushes of the pad of his thumb instead. With a growl, a lick, and a tug, I'm coming again, this time with one of my hands pushing his harder against my chest. The noise that vibrates out of him when I do makes this one even longer than the last.

Again, Adan doesn't straighten. My knees are splayed so wide, my legs practically limp over him, but when he sucks on the bundle of nerves at the apex of my thighs, I whimper, and they manage to close a bit around his head. "I know, sweet-heart," he murmurs, kissing the crease between my sex and my hip, giving deep pressure onto my thigh with his free hand. "You can give me another one, though."

I'm shaking my head, but he knows it's not a true denial. "Yeah, you can. You're so good." Then his mouth is too occupied to speak. But mine isn't.

"Adan," I sigh, and push my fingers through the loose curls of his hair. His hand squeezes and kneads my breast, his other arm looping around my hip so his palm rests on my belly. The crook of his elbow tightens, pulling me against his face, and I think I understand his unspoken request. I undulate beneath his touch, and he snarls his approval, so I do it again and again. Then his hand moves off my breast, trailing fire down my body until I feel his finger enter me. He fills me while he licks me, and when he groans–

The gods might hear me call out for him, yet I don't care. My god kneels between my legs, and his name is the one I pray to.

When I move to sit up, his broad hand spreads over my belly, pinning me to the bed, his arm too tight around my thigh to move. "One more for me, love."

"You said–" I pant, tugging, because there's no way I can.

"I said I would be making you come more than I did that night. Seeing as it took me three releases before I was exhausted enough to fall asleep that night alone, you owe me one more, Thea." He kisses the inside of my thigh, pulsing his finger in and out of me. His hand on my stomach tightens. "*Fuck*, you feel good, sweetheart."

I'm already gasping, my eyes rolling back a bit, but even his breath on my sex sets me squirming. "Adan, I can't–"

"You can. Come all over my fingers, Thea." He adds a second slowly, allowing me to stretch around the width of them inch by inch. Meanwhile, he plants kisses on my thighs, my labia, so softly on my clit. When he feels me relax into it, that last kiss becomes a stroke of his tongue. Seconds or minutes or hours later, his long fingers find a point inside me, too exactly and suddenly for it to have been anything but intentional to not touch it until now.

I shudder, and shatter, and my head is weightless, and I'm seeing the backs of my eyelids as he finishes taking me through the throes of it. With one final kiss to the inside of my thigh, he rises at last, looks me in the eye, and places his fingers on my lips. I think he expects only a lick, because when I take them into my mouth instead, my tongue running over the calloused pads of his fingers, he curses under his breath, and his hips buck. Just a bit, a small jerk that slips his control, but I feel the evidence of his arousal against my thigh.

And it must be whatever Fae grace has settled back into my blood with the iron gone that makes me able to sit up so quickly. But, not fast enough for the immortal being between my thighs, because his hand catches both of mine before I can touch him.

"Why?" I ask him through my teeth, my face an inch from his.

"I've just evened the scales, love. Now, you're going to lie down on that bed, and sleep." He kisses the tip of my nose, far too sweet for all that we've just done, and for all the menacing heat in his words. Then he sits back on his haunches, and lets go of my wrists. One hand finds the back of my knee, and the other hitches on my heel, and pulls the boot off. Adan repeats that on the other leg, and presses his lips to the inside of my knee before pushing it back, into me. It forces me down, to submit, and his eyes flash to mine at what his control does to my scent, and my center.

"You're just perfect, aren't you?" he growls, and lays at my side. His arm reaches through my thighs, elbow crooking so that his hand is on my back, and he pulls me to him. My leg ends up hooked over his waist, and when my hands on his chest pull at his shirt, he takes it off with his free hand.

Sated exhaustion weighs on my lids, but I lift my chin. I feel his smirk against my lips as he presses his to them. "I love you," he murmurs there, his arm moving to wrap around my waist.

It's garbled with sleepiness, but I smile and reply, "I love you, too." Then, I nuzzle my face into the space between his neck and his chest. With his scent in my lungs, I only stay awake long enough for my fingers to find the scars on his back before unconsciousness takes me under.

49

OBSESSED WAS A FUCKING UNDERSTATEMENT

I SHOULDN'T BE SURPRISED THAT A DAY WHICH FELT LIKE THE Void had taken me could be followed by a night that the Heavens would aspire to. Not when Thea exists.

Leaving her this morning had been fucking painful, and that had little to do with her being in the hands of a male who had failed to protect her before, and loves her still. No, though the previous night, with her love in my heart and her body in my arms while she slept overshadowed the memories from just hours before, that oversight ended this morning.

As I worked, over and over the image of her unseeing eyes flashed in my mind. The feeling of her heart, unbeating beneath my palms, had been like a phantom limb, agonizing when it wasn't even there. When it was rope or wood or sail in my hands, and yet that was all I could feel.

But, I had to continue to work with the materials, and the males. Males who might wish her harm; who could be working for Olin, and would take her to endure whatever sort of immortal torment he has planned for her. Even those I'd been friendly with these weeks had been enemies in my eyes and mind all day. I'd envisioned faces that had smiled at me in genuine camaraderie still and pale in death.

They'd sensed it, too, as I'd known they would. It's why I had kissed her so thoroughly before leaving her; so they might believe any tension or rage would be of a male unable to rut. And, understanding that, they'd wisely kept their distance throughout the day.

That consistent fury and agony had not left me until I'd heard her laugh.

In its first few beats, my heart had stopped, and I'd hung by an arm off the mast net to look for her. The sound I'd listened to for months at Castle Cerasche, ringing beautiful and clear as a bell through the air after weeks of huffed breaths, or stilted chuckles. A *laugh*, almost as lovely as she'd been as she made the sound. Her cheeks pink with the joy on her widely smiling face. I only wished that I could have been closer, to see how it might look, as I never had before.

That high, that light had reined in my wrath–for a time. And only when I saw her at last before dinner, her eyes full of love and heat, had the relief of her existence set back in. I'd kissed her with that feeling, not having enough mercy to dilute the need in my soul to allow Atlas a moment to get into his cabin. The control it had taken to not claim her on the deck for all to see had been my limit, and it had been for her.

What we'd done since arriving in my cabin, though...that had been for me. I needed my hands on her, to feel her live so thoroughly beneath them. Writhing, her breaths and heartbeat so fast and strong, her beautiful voice calling my name as she came on my tongue, over and over. Its passion was a truth as great as those I'd told her, and which she'd returned.

They were not unfamiliar thoughts to me, the depths to which I would descend for her. I'd been accustomed to them for almost a year now. What I was not familiar with was sharing them with her. Just how far I would go, how little I would care for the world if the choice were ever between it, and her. Slaughter and chaos would come so easily to me, yet because she continues to live, she has only ever seen the lighter parts of me. The *life* that she brings out.

Because of that, I had thought she perhaps heard the stories of my past, and the darkness of my soul, but could not align them with the male I am with her. But, no. *No amount of darkness could blind me to you; could ever make me turn away.*

Thea sees through the blackness that is me outside of her, and still she is my Life.

Your scythe. As if she could ever be a *tool* for me to use for my dark purposes. As if she weren't above me in every way. The sentiment, though, was clear. That, if I descended to those depths I warned her about, she would be by my side for it.

As she has been for weeks, through perils and truths and nightmares both waking and asleep, she has been there. She continued to choose me, through all of it. Even when the time came for the choice I dreaded her to make, she had turned away the male who, by all accounts, would be better for her. She chose me. To believe she did so with any sort of naivety would be an insult to her brilliance.

She chose me.

It still feels unreal. I can't imagine a time when it won't. When her words of love won't feel like a dream. When holding her in my arms will feel like something I deserve.

She's moved in her sleep, her head now resting on my bicep. I look down at her now–

That face. I live and breathe for it. An interesting thing, given how often it makes my breath stop.

That I spent so long not looking at it feels blasphemous now. More sacrilegious than cursing the gods; they hardly exist for me anymore. *She* is my goddess, and her wish is the only one I will answer to. The only command I could never resent–

My thoughts pause.

I feel it before I see it. The dreadsong in my blood rings with it, horribly familiar. Her terror invades my mind as it has since that first night together in the woods of Cerasche.

The outward expression of it isn't as obvious as it was then. As if she'd forced herself, even in unconsciousness, to suffer alone, in silence. It's only a slightly pinched brow, the smallest downward tug to the corners of her mouth. Her breathing doesn't change, only her heartbeat accelerates. Her body within and against mine is preternaturally still.

It doesn't look like much at all is happening, but, even if I couldn't feel it, the scent of her fear would tell me enough. I pull her closer without thought, only instinct. My hand runs gently up her back, though keeping it from fisting is an effort. I press my lips to her forehead, then trail them across, and down her temple, until I reach her ear. "I'm here," I tell her, rubbing her back.

The terror stutters, but resumes; not believing the reprieve. "Thea, I'm here," I try again, and kiss her cheek. Again, the fear halts, this time longer than the last. "Thea, I'm here." I will not tell her she's safe. The images I'm sure she's seeing will contradict that too easily, and I may lose whatever traction I've gained if she decides not to believe the words that come through to her.

"Thea, sweetheart." I curl my fingers, giving multiple points of contact for her to cling to as I continue the path up and down her spine. "Love, I'm right here."

Her hands on my back twitch, and my heart skips. "My love, I'm here for you."

I feel her nostrils delicately flare against my jaw. Then, though I can tell she's still in sleep, her inhale is audible as her nose skims to my pulse. She breathes at my throat, and that terror that had abated dissipates completely. Her fingers relax, and emotion clogs my throat as they find my scars once more, and she sighs, relaxing into me, and into a sleep far more restful.

The way she seeks out the marks, so deep and dark even after all these years. I'd hidden my back from every lover I'd taken since, not wanting their questions, and certainly not their disgust, or pity. With the crew, it's different; they say *'Don't fuck with me.'* Having my shirt off as I work has been part necessity, in this heat, and partially to give that impression.

Otherwise, I've covered them. When Thea had seen them for the first time, healing my back of the allergic reaction to the pine, it had taken all my will not to cringe away from her touch as it brushed over them. I'd waited for her revulsion at their jagged edges, so tense that my body had locked still.

But, she hadn't pulled away. No disgust radiated from her. Shock, yes, and a healer's assessment. Nothing else, though.

Now, she seeks them out, even in sleep. Not repulsed in the least. No, in the moments where she's caressed them, it's felt more like reverence than anything else. Like, if she noted how much effort it surely took to inflict them, she's only glad that I withstood it, to be here with her now.

I release a trembling breath, and allow myself to tighten my arms around her. I kiss the top of her head, inhaling the scent at her crown, and close my eyes. The way my thoughts have run rampant these past two nights isn't unexpected. Neither is the way that, once I decide I'm ready to sleep, my body curls around hers without me commanding it to. Her existence is a beacon to my own; I haven't belonged to myself since she locked eyes with me in a blood-soaked basement.

⊕

The next three days pass similarly to the first. At least, now that the iron is completely out of her system, I was able to train Thea again. To get that small bit of extra time together before I was expected to work.

She's doing spectacularly, of course. She's able to cast and see through glamours with ease. She's discovered a minor gift for wind, and can produce faerie lights like she's been doing it since childhood. The one thing she refuses to practice is her breaking. When I'd tried to order her into it, she'd placed her hands on those pretty hips–already distracting me–and told me to hit her.

Point fucking made.

Her hand-to-hand combat has reached a level where she got me pinned yesterday, even when I was giving my full ability to the fight. I'd rewarded her for it quickly in her cabin, the thighs she'd used for that push of strength around my head. The satisfaction of leaving her, still flushed, my hair mussed from her fingers, had lasted me almost to lunch.

Every night, she's tried to touch me. I had to punish her for it two nights ago, by not giving her the orgasm I'd edged her to. Still, she tried again last night, and so I gave her the opposite; I made her come so many times that tears streamed down her temples, and when I cleaned her up, she'd practically run away from the touch of the cloth over her.

We'll see if she's learned her lesson tonight. Though part of me thrills at how eager she is for me, I don't plan on giving in just yet. All her life, she was led to believe that her desire was something to be hidden away. That her pleasure would somehow make her impure for whatever sniveling husband might take her. The true lesson I hope she's learned by now is that her desire, her pleasure, should be fucking *celebrated*. Gods-damned worshipped, actually.

The intensity of my own desire is painful at this point. It gives me that edge I've needed to keep the other males from getting near me, or her, and therefore keeping their heads attached to their bodies. I came in the shower this morning, just to dull its sharpness a bit, picturing those green eyes looking up at me, at the same height as my pumping fist.

It doesn't help that Atlas gets to spend those hours with her. I know he's respected our relationship so far, but there's a primal part of every male. Right now, his is saying '*unclaimed.*' Even though he keeps his hands to himself–which is good for their current state of remaining at the ends of his wrists–Thea has no such knowledge of our workings. Just as she does with Lina, or even Talia and Sione now, she occasionally bumps his shoulder, or swats his arm. A show of friendship, and yet I know I'm not the only one on this ship finding my pleasure with her in my mind.

Every time I think of it, my instincts scream at me to take her. To claim her, in every way my body and soul demand. I know she wouldn't say no, and that's part of the fucking issue. My claiming would be taking more than she's yet aware of, and there's too much going on already for me to try to explain it to her.

She's wondered after it, and after my 'no biting' rule, too. That the explanations are the same likely hasn't occurred to her. Not for any lack of brilliance on her part, because she has plenty of that, but because she would have no way of knowing what the significance of either is.

She sits beside me at dinner now, her ankle crossed over mine while she eats. As if my self-control isn't already hanging on by a thread, she's wearing the skirt she got in Dahlih, the one that swishes with every sway of her hips when she walks.

The purple sash she'd gotten from Evelyn, the woman who had cared enough about a beaten girl to stand up to a Fae male, is tied just behind her hairline. Those beautiful waves flow around her, past her waist after these weeks of going uncut.

She feels me looking at her, and turns to me. A smile, so easy and bright, lights up her face, albeit closed-lipped with the food in her mouth. I hope the time never comes where my heart doesn't skip a beat at the sight of it.

"I'm calling in our bargain, Aly," Talia says across the table. We look over at her, and she raises her eyebrows at Thea. "You said on our final night, you would come to the common room with us."

Thea's cheeks pinken, but her foot beside mine doesn't so much as twitch. None of her nervous fidgets come as she smirks at the female, and replies, "I am a woman of my word."

Lina, on Thea's other side, shoves her shoulder, pushing her into me. Finished with my food, I take advantage of it, slinging my arm around her waist, my fingers hitching on the crease between her hip and her thigh. "I should be insulted that I asked you to come down for *weeks*, and this bitch is here for a few days, and here you go agreeing to it."

We both know the reason has nothing to do with the female who asked, and everything to do with Thea finally releasing the grief that had shackled her for those weeks, so Lina's tone is light and joking. My sweetheart only shrugs. "Tali told me they'll have whiskey. You should have led with that."

"How would I know that the virgin Aretes's drink of choice would be straight fucking whiskey?" Lina asks, her white brows lifting halfway to her hairline, eyes beneath them wide.

Thea chuckles, and my thumb moves of its own accord across her thigh. "You didn't ask."

Lina groans, and Sione smiles beside her. After what the Obalans and their High Lord did *that* night, I found myself able to warm to them much more quickly than I have with people in the past.

It could also be that the female beside me has made getting close to people not feel like such a pointless thing. Either way, I've had no issues with them, even though both seem to prefer females, being with Thea for hours each day.

The only person I *have* had difficulty with says, "Are we ready?" to which everyone but me nods. Still, when they begin to rise, I do, too, holding my hand out to assist Thea over the bench. Rather than just stepping over it, she steps onto it, and looks slightly down at me.

"Is this what you see all day?" she asks in Ceraschen, her brows scrunching. "It's so high up."

I smirk. "You get used to it after a few decades."

"It doesn't bother your back? The arthritis has to be kicking in by now." Though she keeps her face straight, her eyes are bright with the humor she finds in her own joke.

I suck on the inside of my cheek, and, too quickly for her to anticipate, I notch my shoulder under her bellybutton, and lift her over it, her upper body hanging over my back, my arm hooked around the backs of her legs.

She squeals, and Lina and Sione, the last of the group walking up the stairs, turn to the commotion. Lina laughs, and Sione looks at her, their grin widening. When I stride towards them, they continue on, just a few feet behind the rest of our table.

Thea's hands slap my back. "Adan! Put me down."

"No. You're in air jail."

"Air jail?" she asks with a cackle that makes me smile, but I wipe the sound of it from my voice before responding.

"Yes. Your feet are in the air. Air jail."

She mutters, "I can think of quite a few times this week where I've been in air jail, then."

A growl rumbles its way out of my chest, those thoughts in my head, now, too. As I walk us up the stairs, I lightly smack her ass for the snark, and rein in my groan when I scent what that does to her, so close to my face.

"Fine," she says, and her hands stop their whacking–

Only for me to feel her cup *my* ass.

I set her down with enough speed that her hair and breasts bounce, and she giggles, almost falling backwards, if I hadn't caught her.

"Ymeda's tits, love. You sure you didn't have any of that whiskey already?"

She rebounds forward, jumping from her toes, and lands a kiss on my lips, then twists her way out of my arms, the twirl setting her skirt flaring around her. "Nope," she answers, popping on the 'p'.

I move to follow her, shaking my head with a smirk on my mouth, and she looks over her shoulder at me. The sun tints her tan skin golden, and the green of her eyes alight like that of a driftwood fire. She's still grinning, tiny crinkles forming on her freckled nose and at the corners of her eyes. The breeze on the ship deck lightly ruffles her midnight hair, blowing strands across her chest.

"Gods, you're gorgeous," I breathe, the loudest I can get out in my awe. Thea halts, her smile softening, and she holds her hand out for me. I take it without hesitation, her calloused palm sliding over mine, and I lift our hands to kiss the back of hers.

Down another set of steps, the common room is far louder than it is when we're training. Dozens of male voices boom through the space, the smells of sweat, ale, and liquor strong enough that the scents of the sailors are indiscernible. I bring Thea close to me, letting her lead to the bar in the back of the room while I inconspicuously take in every movement of the males around us.

I remain behind her, senses open, as she puts her palms on the bar. "Are you ever not working?" she asks Jacks as he readies a few pints of ale. I rest my hands on either side of her waist.

"I sleep sometimes," Jacks replies, earning a chuckle from Thea. Sione is beside us for a moment, seizing the pints, and parts with a wink. "What'll you have, Althea?"

"Hmm." She moves onto her toes to lean over the bar, peering to see what's there, like she doesn't know already. Like she doesn't realize she's just pushed her ass up against me. My fingers around her tighten, and I watch the muscles in her upper back shift as she arches a bit. "How about a whiskey, with an orange twist?" She turns her face to me with an overly innocent expression. "What would you like?" she asks sweetly.

I direct my words to Jacks, but knead the small of her back with my thumbs. "I'll have the same."

Jacks nods, and gathers the bottle of dark liquor, and one of the oranges. She straightens slowly, and I lean in until my mouth is at her ear. "Don't ask me what I'd like while your ass is pressed against me, love."

"Or what?" she whispers back, tilting her head to expose the side of her neck to my mouth and my breath.

Fuck I want to sink my teeth into the soft skin there. The desire, combined with the attitude in her question, has my body very quickly answering for me. Close as she is, she feels it, too. And the gods-damn vixen rubs up against me with a sigh.

My eyes roll back in my head for a heartbeat before I still her hips with my hands, grateful for Jacks's back to us, and the strong scents which might mask the lust raging within me now.

My lips still by her ear, I reply, "I'll be thinking on your punishment, sweetheart." Then softly kiss the freckled cheek that pulls in a smile.

50

REVERTED

DION - 5.5 WEEKS EARLIER

THE OSCHVERREN CASTLE WAS CLASSICAL. DARK STONE, MARBLE surfaces, grand rugs and fireplaces.

The Castle of Colina was more modern. Light stone, large windows, a garden filled with life instead of order.

Castle Cerasche was somehow both. It was beautiful, and grand, without feeling stuffy. The Great Hall, even on this night, didn't give an air of pretentiousness. There was a welcoming beauty in its painted ceiling, even the pristine white marble floors not quite able to counterbalance the space into monarchal rigidity. None of this, though, could compare to the sweet, open face of the female before me.

"Princess Althea," I said, bowing low to her. "My name is Dion."

Her responding grin was hesitant, but kind. "Lord Dion," she greeted me with a curtsey, then gestured to the more petite woman beside her. "This is my friend, Duchess Hanna Mayfeld."

"A pleasure," I said to the woman who I could scent had a life growing within her. *Please, stay away from me*, I wanted to tell her. But the blood oath bound my tongue to the roof of my mouth, which was set in a believably content smile.

"Likewise," Hanna replied, her silver eyes darting between me and Althea. "If you'll excuse me, I'm going to get a refreshment." Then, she bowed to her princess, and gave me a dip of her chin.

Althea's eyes followed her friend, but I kept my gaze on her. She seemed pleasantly surprised when she turned back, and saw that. A smile lit up her face–the same face I'd seen on a powerful female across the sea so many years ago, just in a lighter hue. I wondered if the memory was simply too distant for her human parents to recognize that fact.

"I'm sorry, Lord Dion, but I don't believe I was made aware of your attendance tonight," Althea said, more learned in the custom and courtesy of court than some triple her age in Oschverre.

"I was invited fairly last-minute–" I was not invited at all, "–and arrived even later, I'm afraid. I would have liked to be the first to ask you to dance." I looked over her face, waiting for her to call me on my lie, hoping she would–

"Well, my Lord, better late than never," she replied instead. With a grin I meant for this kind girl, but which felt like acid in my gut, I held out my hand to her. She took it, her palms soft, but surprisingly calloused at the backs of her knuckles, and the heel of her hand.

For over a year, I practiced the customary Weaschten dances, so, when the song began, I swept her into the steps without hesitation. I also learned the Ceraschen dialect during that time–so much more fluid, and lyrical than our Divani in Eshelle. Divani was a common tongue, meant to be spoken throughout the continent. Until the Last War, it had been forced upon the humans, too.

Their native languages had never truly left them, though; instead, it seemed that Ceraschen became the most widely-known language throughout the continent, with other countries primarily maintaining their own tongues, with Ceraschen as secondary. How or why Divani had been maintained at all...the possibility that the Fae who fought with the humans remained after the War was the only explanation I could fathom. As Fae majick only strengthened with age, I had no doubt that they could have glamoured themselves for these centuries, with none the wiser.

As it was, Olin and I were considered young in our hundred and twenty years, and still, the dark-skinned male who I'd seen as a toddler in a castle across the sea had not seen through me. Even though, when Atlas's gray eyes lifted from each person he served throughout the Hall, they landed on the female dancing in my arms.

Upon that thought, I realized that we'd been dancing for a whole minute, and I'd yet to say anything since we began. Looking at her now, I noticed her bright green eyes darting occasionally to the crowd surrounding us. "They're watching you," I murmured, meaning it as a warranted compliment to her grace and beauty, and her gaze found mine. Her cheeks filled with color, and I couldn't help but give her a small, reassuring smile.

But, she responded, "They're not."

My brow furrowed slightly. "They are. Why wouldn't they be?"

It could be rhetorical, but I wanted her answer. Why did this obviously kind, lovely female doubt herself? Why did those around her look on with such judgment, as if waiting for her to fail?

I thought I knew the answer to the latter. As in any court, jealousy was an insidious thing. And these humans were surely jealous of the unprecedented grace, and preternatural beauty of the–*woman* before me. To see her fail would confirm for them that she was not better than them. Which she might not have been, if not for that dreadful hope of theirs.

I'd no doubt that she could sense that ferality, if not its source. Knew as well that many looked at her as only a chance to further their own power–a space for wealth and heirs.

She acknowledged none of this, pasting a serene, easy smile on her lips that barely managed to reach her eyes.

"So, Lord Dion," she said instead. "Tell me about yourself."

More lies now. Olin wanted her to know him, not me. "I'm afraid there's not much to tell." I twirled her as the wind instruments lilted into a higher octave, and wished we could keep spinning. Round and round, that smile on her face, more genuine than it had been a moment ago. The daughter of my court, trapped in a moment of happiness which she was yet unaware would be few and far between soon.

But I couldn't stop time–or my brother.

I could only pull her back into the dance with gentle arms, and continue: "I'm the son of a lord and lady, just like most of your prospective partners. I have one brother, no sisters. I was raised to love my king and country, and have served both loyally throughout my life. And, I love dogs, and chocolate. Not together, of course," I added, making a mock-serious face.

She laughed, as expected, the sound bright and happy. I grinned in response, hiding the sadness in my eyes.

Then she grew quiet as she looked at me, and my heart stuttered. Hope, hesitant and fleeting, seized me; she, like her birth mother had years ago, would see through me. She would end this, and she would be safe. "What are you thinking about?" I asked, forcing my voice to be only curious, hiding that hope.

But the final notes of the song sounded, and I tilted her, rehearsed and mandated, into a dip so deep that her long hair formed an onyx pool on the ground. As the people around us applauded, I pulled her back up to a standing position. Another blush pinkened her cheeks, and I wanted it to be due to the sound, and not the success of my order being carried out, but her eyes held mine as the color filled her young, happy face.

So that she might have just one more piece of joy before it was snatched away from her in two days, I bowed, and pressed a kiss to the back of her hand. I felt her pulse quicken under my fingers, and straightened. "Princess," I said, before releasing her hand, and walking off the dance floor. I was both chagrined and grateful that all eyes in the crowd followed me, giving her a moment to herself before she was once again scrutinized.

Another song started, and I sighed shakily. It was done. I completed my task, and–

I felt a force tug at me from my right, more powerful than that which pulled me to the doors. I turned my head, slowing my steps, but still moving so that I might not collapse in pain at disobeying. I saw nothing, no one, but my eyes were repeatedly drawn to a chestnut-skinned man in a general's uniform.

As if sensing my gaze, the man turned his face to look at me, and my heart stopped dead in my chest at the deep blue eyes that found and held mine. Even in a different face, in a land across an ocean, I knew those eyes. The color which had kept me company where nothing else had for years in that dungeon. Belonging to a female who was mine, and I was hers. My Ciara.

Her brows furrowed in the man's face, not recognizing me through the glamour, though surely noticing the intensity of my stare. Rather than feel hopeful that she might approach me, though, I felt dread. No, she could not know what I'd done. What I was doing.

So, I quickly tore my gaze from hers, my heart tearing with it, and walked the last few steps out the double doors of the Hall. The familiar blond doorman gave me only a quick glance before shutting them behind me, him on their other side.

I doubled over, hands on my knees, feeling as though I might be sick, right in this hallway. She was here. My mate, my love who I hadn't seen in over a decade, just a room away. So close, and I could not reach her. Couldn't even want to, with the plan I was participating in.

The only reason she could possibly be here was to keep safe the woman I was helping to hurt. The woman who was not a woman, but a female. Our Lady, whom I was betraying. And her mother and father in the process. I was failing my entire court, after twenty-one years of doing my best to protect it.

I thought I hated myself all those years ago. That feeling was nothing compared to what seized my heart and soul now.

"Well done, brother," I heard Olin say, steps away from me. I looked up, finding him in an identical suit, his hair cropped like mine, and clean-shaven. Glamoured so that all but myself, and the three Fae he knew of in that Hall would see him as someone else. He'd dimmed his power, too, likely so that the *enemy Fae* would not sense him. Though Adathan's missive informed him of the presence of an Eshellen, it made no mention of who that person was, specifically.

I took comfort in that, at least. That the boy, her godson, might be free of a target borne of Olin's hate for the Sabriani court. That he might leave him be, leave *them* be, if he remained unaware of Ciara's presence, and Atlas's loyalty.

"What's wrong?" my brother asked, a cruel smile on his

face. "I've heard your Lady is quite pretty. Surely dancing with her couldn't have been that terrible."

In the last effort I could make to save my court, and my loved ones, I straightened, shoving down the nausea, and the self-loathing. I told him flatly, "I'm fine. You're up."

He nodded, not caring enough to push the matter. "Did Adathan suspect anything?"

"No. He thinks it was you."

"Good." I felt his glamour–camouflaging me from everyone but Althea–disappear. That which hid my scent remained. "Best start your journey back. Go to my ship, and stay there until I arrive." My feet moved immediately to stride down the hallway. "Quickly, now, Dion. I need to get *back* to my Princess."

My jaw clenched, but my steps quickened against my will. Before I knew it, I was running. Through the halls, the grounds, out the gates. Careful to avoid the eyes of any staff, especially guards. My legs carried me unfailingly towards the pine-thick woods, all the way to the wind-blown cliffs. When I crested the hill, I saw the sails, drawn up until the master of the ship arrived.

As I swam, I fully recognized why Olin had me do this. Before, I'd thought it was just payback for my past betrayal. For my lies, and deceit. Perhaps that remained part of it.

I knew now that the reason he gave me this task–to dance with my Lady, beginning a course which would steal her once again from her parents–was so that, no matter what happened, I could never go back to Sabrian. I could never face my Hielo and Hiela. I could never let my mate hold me in her arms.

She will likely reject the bond once she finds out. Turn from it, and me forever. I won't be able to blame her. I will go on, forevermore only half of myself. And I will deserve every bit of torment that comes my way.

51

WHAT IS & WOULD HAVE BEEN

IT'S GOTTEN HARDER, NEAR IMPOSSIBLE, FOR ME TO DESPISE Adathan anymore.

He helped to take my mate from me. Yet, he did not participate in the torment Dion then faced for a decade, further than injecting him with the iron that kept him from fighting back. But, I'd heard Dion that day; understood his meaning. He would not have fought, anyway, would never have attempted to escape. To keep our court, our people, to keep *me* safe, he endured, and would have kept doing so.

Knowing this, it's become easier for me to understand the words Althea said, her very first day on this ship. Everything that has happened to me, to my mate, is because of Olin. Without the blood oath, without his command, Adathan would never have been in Sabrian, nor Cerasche.

Still, I'd held onto that loathing for him, even when I recognized its similarity to how I'd felt about his uncle decades ago.

403

Because, just as it had then, that anger kept me tethered. Grounded, however falsely.

Then, he'd brought Althea back from the dead. My Lady, whom I would have failed even more thoroughly than her parents. That stubborn, hateful part of my brain tried to reason that he did it selfishly. Not for her parents, or even her, but for himself, because he did not want to live without her.

I almost could have convinced myself that his selfishness had hurt Althea. It had made her finally release that grief, after all, and who would have known how long that would have taken to be staunched?

Then, for the first time since I was a man in a castle where she was a princess, I'd heard her laugh. Freely, without inhibition. *Joy*, where it had been absent for so long.

He did that. Did not just bring her back to survival, but to *life*. No longer did she sit in those quiet, raging silences when her heart ached too much for her to conceal it. Instead, when those moments struck, she would turn to Lina, who was most frequently beside her while Adathan worked, and let my goddaughter hold her until they passed.

Does this mean she has stopped blaming herself? Maybe not entirely, given her words in her cabin days ago. But, perhaps she no longer loathes herself, at least not nearly as much. The proof of that is in the happiness she allows herself now.

I see it, standing at the wall beside Javi—who has not lost sight of his daughter at any waking hour since she arrived. Althea sits with Tali and Lina, the others standing around them due to the shortage of seating. Sipping on amber liquor, Adathan's hand on her shoulder, Althea smiles at something Lina is saying, her hand waving expressively before her. That grin is unguarded, and so is the quick laugh that's echoed around the table as Lina sits back in her chair, her shoulder bumping Sione's thigh.

Any minute, the faerie is due to switch off with Geoff, who plays easy music in the far corner of the open floor. Right now, though, they move Lina's hair to the side to rest their hand on the back of her chair. From where I stand, I see three things happen: Lina blushes, Tali raises her brows by a fraction at Sione, who shrugs and takes a swig of ale. Lina, watching Althea as she speaks, doesn't notice the latter two.

"What do you think it's like for them?" I ask Javi quietly, my own drink hovering by my chin.

The High Lord sighs, and drinks his own whiskey before answering. "Probably just like it was for us."

I crest my lips over my pint, and barely take a sip. "I miss that," I whisper.

I don't need to clarify. The hope. The love. The comfort. "Me too," Javi replies just as quietly. He clears his throat. "It's sort of comforting, though, isn't it? To see life go on, after a time."

"Even when it feels like your own has stalled." I nod slightly, understanding his meaning. Looking at the faces at that table, so bright, their possibilities before them. My heart aching, I ask on a breath, "Does it ever get any easier?"

Javi finishes his drink. "Yes, and no. It doesn't hurt any less. You just get a higher tolerance for it over time." Another sigh, and his voice is soft when he continues, "She helps, though."

I look at Tali, whose neck is craned to look up at Atlas as she says something to him. I never met her mother, but her likeness is not that of the male beside me. I imagine, then, that seeing her face must at times feel both like a curse, and yet the greatest gift.

"We never had the chance for that." I would have wanted a child with Dion. However unwise in the midst of the rebellion that had been brewing–and then stalled–I would have stopped taking my tonic after having that talk with him. And perhaps now I might be looking at a child with green-gold eyes at that table with them.

A gift, and a curse, indeed.

Interrupting these heavy thoughts and words, Sione tugs on one of Lina's curls, chugs the rest of their pint, and says something with a wink as they leave. Geoff finishes his final song as Sione is crossing the makeshift, unused dancefloor, and bows to the light applause he receives.

Sione chooses their guitar today, their violin in its case behind the chair they take to play. In the raucous of the room, they lean into the instrument as they lightly pluck the strings, twisting the pegs according to what they hear. Once they're satisfied, they sit up, tap their foot, and begin.

Even the first strums are full of passion, and in my periphery I see Althea turn in her seat to look at them. Adathan moves so she can see better, looking over his shoulders to make sure he's not blocking anyone. The only ones near him, though, are the same seated or standing with his female; the rest of the males on the ship have been keeping their distance from him for the past four days.

I realize I'm watching them again, and can't quite help it. He leans down, and says something, to which she looks up and replies with a smile. He kisses the scar on her cheek before straightening, which deepens the color on the skin there, and then holds his hand out to Lina. She grins, and hands him her nearly empty pint, and he picks up his and Althea's glasses in his other hand before nodding inconspicuously to Atlas, and heading to the bar. Althea watches him go, turning from Sione to do so.

Such joy. Yet, tonight, I can't find it in myself to resent it, even for him. Instead, watching it–seeing these people love, and be loved...a small, sad smile curls my lips.

As the music picks up, I nudge Javi with my elbow, and jerk

my head towards their table. "Let's go," I tell him, and his black brows raise. My grin widens, and I say softly, "You're going to dance with your daughter."

At court all those years ago, he had not. All the Obalan nobility, even Sione, had been on that dance floor, except him. At that point, he would have been without his mate for longer than I've now been parted from mine. I know it's not the same; Dion is alive. My soul is constantly aching, but intact. I don't know what it would be like to lose him to Death.

But I know that Javi feels happiness. Allows himself joy, especially with his daughter. And on this, the last night before we yet again head into the unknown, he should have that.

And I will, too–if he agrees, because I'm certainly not leaving him here by himself. Either seeing that, or just understanding that I'm right, Javi nods, smirking a bit and coming off the wall we'd been against. We walk towards the table, and those facing us look up at our approach. Lina grins and waves, and Atlas, who scooted closer to Althea when Adathan left, nods to us.

Javi steps up to Tali's side, and holds out his hand. Her cinnamon eyes take on a shine, and crinkle at the corners with her grin as she takes it and stands, setting her drink on the table. I raise my brows at Althea, whose lips pull up a bit, and she looks at Lina, and offers her hand. When my goddaughter beams and reaches across the table to grab it, I look at Atlas, who crooks his elbow to me with a smile that I return.

Adathan arrives, and sets down the drinks. Althea looks at him, to which he replies, "Get your ass on that dance floor, sweetheart."

She grins and stretches her arm with Lina's to close the distance enough to steal a kiss from him, and then snatches her drink from the table. Lina does the same, with a quick,

"Thanks, Addie!" and the pair run onto the floor, Althea laughing at the new nickname her friend has for her male.

Atlas leads me to the floor, and each of our three pairs starts in a simple two-step. The girls in the middle start giggling as they switch into notching their elbows, and spinning, alternating sides. Soon enough, we're all looping and chaining, smiles so wide I'm sure mine aren't the only sore cheeks.

Sione alters their music with each change Lina and Althea begin, and then they're the one making the alterations, demanding new steps and stomps and claps. Some of the sailors join us on the floor, but with no females of their own to dance with, they only remain for a song or two before going back to their talking and drinking. I might have felt bad for it, if not for the fact that any one of them could be planning to betray us.

I don't let that thought stick enough to sour my mood; only enough to keep my eyes open, though I'm sure Adathan is doing a fine job of that a table away. Althea and Lina are in constant motion, and the rest of us can only try to keep up with the girlish sort of joy that powers their feet. We're all sweating, both mine and Atlas's hair pulled back with strips of leather. Althea gave Lina her purple sash, and has tucked her tank top up into her brassiere to compensate for the heavy black hair that hangs down her back.

Occasionally the two dart away to get a bit of water, or another drink before going back to their revelry, always bringing enough back to share with us—thereby giving us no excuse to stop ourselves. Each time they do so, though, Althea slides to a stop in front of Adathan to kiss him, her face flushed with exertion and joy, before running on. By the third, he was smiling before she even got to him. On the fourth, that smile was the widest I'd ever seen on his face. Full lips stretched over dimpled cheeks, revealing white teeth, canines and all.

I saw her halt at the sight, but then twirled with Atlas, and laughed hard enough as he almost dropped me that my eyes closed. His deep, happy laughter sounded with mine, and by the time the females were back, Sione had started a new song for us all to keep up with.

Now, the introduction to the next tune they play is unfamiliar. I furrow my brows, trying to figure if I can place it, and then notice the utter stillness of the female a few feet away. I look towards her, but she's facing Sione. Their eyes are on her; kind, and questioning. Lina looks over at me, curiosity in her own eyes, and I shrug–at the same moment that a low, Heavenly hum sounds from the raven-haired female.

Her gaze still rests on the faerie, and they nod to her as her hum changes; shifts into a note that perfectly matches the key change Sione makes in the same second. The room has gone silent, but for the music the two of them make.

And then Althea sings.

I've always found Ceraschen to be far more lyrical than Divani, and it's reinforced now. In this song, it flows with a beauty like a mountain river. And her voice...a goddess would kill for such a voice.

She steps closer to Sione as the notes build, and her voice crescendos with it until the sound echoes through my very soul with its feeling, and ferocity. Chills skitter up my arms, my legs, my spine. When the song works its way into a new verse, the rasp and soul transitions easily, effortlessly into a soprano trill that makes my heart flutter.

Althea turns as she hits those notes. Her eyes are closed, and I can't help but wonder what she's picturing behind them as she sings.

The guitar begins to build up again, and with it her voice. With her facing me, I can see the force of the song. The way her breath works in tandem with it; the muscles in her abdomen expand when she breathes in, and when the notes are belted out, her entire being goes with them.

An intentional pause in the song, where the audience is meant to hold their own breath for the end. And we do. The entire crew, my friends, myself: we are frozen as her eyes open, gleaming with unshed tears. I know who they land on without having to look. Who would have provided the notes for Sione to play, over whatever little free time he had these past days.

As if they'd played together their whole lives, Sione's guitar and Althea's voice pick up in the same beat. The notes are the same as her hums in the beginning, her voice rasping after the way the last words had torn up her throat.

Both musicians quiet, and the room is silent for several thudding heartbeats before the applause sounds. Resounding, and deserved. Tears had started down my cheeks at some point, and they pour still as I stare at my Lady.

She looks down at Sione, and extends her hand. They place theirs in hers, and I watch as she bows her brow to their knuckles. They seem stunned, and the gesture has the red-brown of their eyes shining, just as hers do.

As I watch her release Sione's hand, and accept a hug from Lina, praise from Javi and Talia–Atlas standing, struck at my side–I think of Dion. And I think how happy he would be, to serve in her court as he had her parents'.

52

ARMOR & LUST

THEA'S VOICE HAS WRECKED ME. I'D THOUGHT THERE WAS NO possible way I could be more enthralled, more astounded by her. Of course, I'd been wrong. It was a ridiculous thought to begin with.

Until her, until she loved me, I hadn't allowed myself to cry since my mother's death. I'd hardened myself against emotion, and only failed in it when I was forced to watch a kind male get carved apart. After weeks of being tormented myself for such feeling, that hardness had encased me like armor over the thick skin I'd already been forced to wear.

Then she came along, and softened me. I didn't even notice at first, just as I hadn't noticed the way I would listen for her voice at Castle Cerasche not out of duty, but because it had become my favorite sound. Steadily, though, the anger I'd kept on such a tight leash, which had been a constant fire in my veins, was replaced with a new one. Rather than consuming, blazing through what could have been good in me, this one was cleansing; baring a forest for new growth, or giving steel its shine.

In the days I was made to cage her, to keep her from escaping the clutches of my father, I'd again donned that armor. Regrowing that skin, though, was futile; I'd shed it, let the new flames burn it. And, just like all fabled armor, it had a weak spot. Though I'd kept it on that first day, giving my all to not letting her see what it meant to me to stay with her, all she had to do to slip through was look at me with those eyes. Speak to me with that voice. With no fear, and no hesitation.

It had been easy to reforge the plated metal to fit around both of us. To allow her to use me as a protector from her own emotion. In the moments when she raged against it, I doffed it just as easily. Until one day, one moment, when I never put it back on.

I don't know which it was, exactly. If it was when she asked me to call her by her name. Or when she told me she didn't hate me. Looked me in the eyes and called me handsome, a thing I'd never cared about being until she said it.

Now, with only my skin and bones to keep me solid, upright, she's knocked me out at the knees, as she had when she told me she loves me. Hearing her sing the song I'd heard over the months in a white marble hall, muffled through doors and walls, with nothing between me and the sound of her voice. I realize that I'm crying again, the fourth time since her cleansing fire roared through me. Tears are trailing down my cheeks as her eyes meet mine, shining and bright.

The applause has only just begun to quiet, my own hands loud even to my ears, when she starts towards me. A standing ovation, from these hardened sailors. A few males whistle with their clapping, then chatter starts back up as those noises die down while she nears me.

She looks up into my face, her own so soft. That hardness she had wrapped around herself, which rivaled what I'd had for decades, is gone. With gentle hands, she cups my cheeks, and wipes my tears with her thumbs. Then, at the same time that she goes up on her toes, she pulls my face down, and presses her full, soft lips to mine.

I'd been right to be obsessed with her mouth. Its divinity challenges the Heavens. Though, my year of thoughts of it didn't do justice to what it actually feels like on mine.

"Take me out of here," Thea whispers, her breath smelling of oranges and whiskey. Her eyes open, so close that I can see the yellow flecks near her pupils.

I nod, lifting my chin to kiss her forehead, and grabbing her hand. I keep her close to me, never allowing her to trail behind. The two whiskeys I'd had aren't nearly enough to make me forget that any one of the males around us could mean her harm.

Once on the deck, exposed to the cool air coming off the sea, rippling the black water beneath us, Thea sighs heavily. She tilts her head back, letting the thick mass of her hair unstick from the sweat on her back. The moonlight guilds the shining column of her throat silver, tinting her closed lids and gold-dusted cheekbones in the same hue.

I'd never thought to look at the world, describe it in such a way. Not until she gave me a reason to see it, after decades in the dark. Because the world around us is beautiful, but not as beautiful as she; and since she is my universe, anyway, it's only fitting.

Chin still tilted to the star-flecked sky, she murmurs, "I used to hate the night. The time from dusk til sleep. I remember looking up through the domed window before it came crashing down, and seeing the sky. I remember thinking how she didn't have any stars to keep her company."

A tear falls down her temple as her eyes open. My heart is in my throat watching it, listening to her. "Then the nightmares came, and every night I would stay awake until I was too exhausted to keep my eyes open anymore. Still, they came. And it seemed only right that I, too, had no company for them."

Her voice, which had been trembling but calm, shifts. It breaks through widening lips with a hitched sob, cracking my heart with it. "I hated you then. When I was alone, and scared, and hurting. I hated you for being there when it happened, because all I wanted to do was go to you, so you could make the pain stop. And I couldn't. Because you were there, in the nightmares, and waking to you would have been too hard, and I didn't deserve the reprieve, anyway." Her tears flow, unending, into her hair, and my jaw is clenched against my own.

"Hating you was easier, and then impossible. And when it was impossible, I only hated myself more. And when I hated myself more, I wished for the end, knowing how awful it would make me, to take their lives in vain. Then you–"

Thea straightens, and turns her face to me. Her eyes are green stars, shining more brightly than those above us. Still, she cries, the tracks across her temples becoming mirrored on her cheeks. "Then *you* made me want to live, Adan. And somehow *still* I felt awful for it; that I should get to live, when they don't, because of me. So, when I was dying, when I was dead, and my soul waited to see what I might do when I felt myself being pulled back...I made a choice. I chose to live. I chose *you.*

"And I don't think they would resent me for it. All of them would have *hated* for me to choose to die for them, rather than live for myself. To live, for love and joy."

Her shaking lips tilt up at the corners, and she turns her body towards me now, too. "You've given those things to me. And I tried, once, to make sense of it. To understand how I was able to give you my heart so quickly. But...it doesn't feel like I've known you for weeks, Adan; it feels like I've known you my whole life. Since my soul was this thought within the universe. Does it feel like that for you?"

My voice is a ragged, broken thing, but I nod and get out, "Yes."

Thea steps into me, and wraps her arms around my waist, tucking her face into my chest. I wind my arms tightly around her, holding the back of her head with one hand, and bending at the neck until my lips touch the top of her head. I breathe in the scent of her, and close my eyes, thinking the full answer: Yes, I was made for her.

⢢

After that, we made our way to the cabins. She'd wanted to wash, and though her words had been clear on the deck, her steps stuttered slightly down the steps, the whiskey showing its effect. I'd helped her to the washroom, and she'd either not cared or hadn't thought about it, but Thea began lifting her top and her brassiere off while I was still in there with her. I'd quickly averted my eyes, and told her I would be just outside.

It's been intentional, to not see all of her yet. To wait. Yet, my resolve nearly crumbled entirely when she'd strode out, wet hair turning my shirt–*my* shirt, which she must have taken from the clean laundry bin in there–translucent. My shirt, and nothing else.

Even after the weight and the significance of the conversation on the deck, the sight had made me so hard it was fucking painful. Luckily, the drink and the warm water had thoroughly set in, and she nearly tumbled into the bed, her eyes already closed. She'd only had enough consciousness left to pout, and hold her arms out, waiting for me to join her. Smirking, I'd stripped my shirt off, knowing she wanted bare skin, and laid with her, arranging her hair up and behind her, as she likes it when she sleeps.

Now, the light of dawn wakes me as it comes through the porthole, and she still sleeps; soundly, on my chest. My shirt twisted on her as we slept, and the open collar is pulled over to reveal one muscled shoulder. I can't quite help it when my hand rises to brush over the soft skin.

She makes that humming noise, setting my blood thrumming already. I turn my head to kiss her brow, and she does it again, and stretches against me. Her back arches and her toes point while she shoves her face into the crook between my neck and shoulder. I don't hold back the chuckle that stirs from me, and she lifts her head, eyes slitted with sleep, her own lips turned up at the corners.

"What?" she asks, her voice even huskier than usual.

"You, love," I answer simply, and kiss the tip of her nose, my hand trailing down to her waist.

As I lay my head back down, she touches her fingertips to my cheek, now fully awake. "I love you," she says quietly, but not weakly.

My heart squeezes in my chest. "It feels like a dream, hearing you say that to me. A dream I had many times, and each time, I would wake to find you gone; never there to begin with."

The small grin on her mouth turns mischievous–not what I expected from my confession. "Well," she begins, the hand on my cheek caressing down my neck. "I suppose I'll just have to convince you you're awake." Then she leans her head down to press a kiss to one of the scars on my chest, following her lips with a flick of her tongue.

My breaths stutter, but Thea is merciless. She follows it with a second, and a third, progressing up my chest all the while until the fourth is at the pulse point above my collar bone. She sucks on the skin there, and a groan escapes my throat, my hand clenching around her waist.

I feel those wicked lips curl up against me. "Do you feel awake yet?" she asks, and nips at the same space she just suckled. I know what answer she wants, and I find myself more than happy to give it to her.

"No. If anything, this is more of what I imagined in my dreams."

She chuckles darkly, then licks her way up the column of my throat. My hand tightens on her again, and while I might have been wary of bruising her, her scent elevating in that instant tells me not to loosen my grip.

With force, Thea turns my face to hers, and then presses her lips, contrastingly gentle, against mine. A ruse ruined by the way she slips her tongue into my mouth the next second. She wraps it around my own, to pull it into her mouth. And sucks.

A growl rumbles through my chest, and it's taking everything in me not to grip her hips, roll her beneath me, and plunge my cock deep inside her. It strains so hard against my trousers they might as well bloody burst at the seams from the pressure.

"And now?" she asks, a growl of her own in the question.

"I'm only hoping I don't wake from this dream any time soon."

"Hmm," she hums, low in her throat. "It seems I have to convince you in a different way, *my* love."

And then the heel of her palm rubs down the ridge of my length. I curse, and curse again when her fingers find the tip, and caress it over the fabric.

She nibbles on the point of my ear, and says into it, "I've had enough of you keeping me from this." In emphasis, her hand tightens, wringing another oath from me. "Unless you tell me no now, I am finally going to be the one making *you* come." Her arousal heightens as she strokes me again.

With the hand not on her waist, I plunge my fingers into her hair, and bring her face around to claim her mouth. Her hand holds my cock while I kiss her until she's making those delicious sounds, and then I pull her back. Our panted breaths mingle between us. "Take what you want with your hands. But if you think I'm letting you put your mouth, or pussy on me while we're still on this damned ship, I'll use *my* mouth to make you come so hard, you won't be able to think straight enough to try again for a while. Understand?"

The fire in her eyes brightens, making me pulse within her grip. But then her hands shake slightly as she reaches to undo the buttons of my trousers. And, so easily, so quickly, I shift to what she needs in this moment.

My own hands soften on her, and she stares into my eyes when only my underwear remains. I slip my fingers out of her hair to hold her hand in mine, pausing her progress. "You stop at any point, love," I tell her. "There is no obligation to finish."

She nods, and kisses my lips. "Will you show me how?" she asks there, her voice full of an emotion that has it trembling a bit, and a heat that keeps it low, and sultry.

My heart might have either melted or combusted. I release her hand to stroke her cheek. "What you were doing was amazing, sweetheart. And whatever you do will be amazing. But," I gently bite her bottom lip, "because you asked so nicely, I will show you." I feel her mouth tilt up before she pulls back.

Thea moves to prop herself up on her elbow, looking down at her hand. My hand and eyes both remain on her face, even as an unprecedented pleasure comes from her fingers simply skimming over me as she pulls the band of my underwear down, and I spring free.

Her eyes widen a bit, her lips parting, and, as if in a trance, she wraps her hand around me–and that easily I arch into her, a groan slipping up my throat. She works her fist over my entire length, until her thumb rubs over my tip, and picks up the precum that's already beaded there. It all feels so good that my eyes roll back into my head, and only fix themselves when her hand comes away. I check to see that she's alright, about to open my mouth to ask, when I see her eyes are already on mine. While she sticks her thumb into her mouth, and sucks on the taste of me.

I restrain the voice that wants to snarl out of me to a rough whisper. "Fuck, Thea." She doesn't give me even a second to recover before she puts her hand back on me, and strokes again. Gods, this female will be the end of me. And what a glorious fucking end it will be.

Because she asked, I wrap my hand around hers, and squeeze it tighter, bringing it up and down a few times. A smile plays on her lips, the bottom one pulled slightly by her teeth, like she's thrilled to watch us work my cock together. She keeps that pressure and pace when I remove my hand, the scent of her arousal saturating the cabin–turned on by touching *me*, just as I am with her.

I almost close my eyes, the feel of her hand–*her hand*, of which I've had many dreams of doing exactly this, but until recently didn't believe I would actually feel on me–so exquisite that I might have come so quickly if I didn't want to make this first time last. And, Void fucking take me, the way she looks like she's having so much fun doesn't make that any easier.

I watch her hand run up and down my cock, the sight alone nearly enough to unravel me. Combine that with the way she jerks me like the Heavens sent her to do it, and if I weren't already a goner for her, I would be now.

The noises, the words that escape me as her hand moves on

my cock, taking what I showed her and making it even better, are nothing like I've ever uttered before. When she leans in to suck on the skin over my hammering pulse, I have to rein in the Fae in me, so I don't fuck her hand right before I pull up those pretty hips and see what the rest of her feels like.

Her hand twists around me now, and each time, she brushes her thumb over the sensitive line right beneath my head. Both to rein in that instinct, and because I really gods-damn want to, I thread my fingers through her hair, and pull her face to mine once more. Her tongue works mine in tandem with her fingers working my cock, and sweet, rutting *gods*–

"Thea, I'm so close," I gasp around her lips–a warning, in case she's not ready to stroke me through it; to have her hand covered in my cum.

But she smiles against my mouth. "Come for me, Adan," she says, giving me the words I'd spoken to her that night. And, fuck, do I oblige her.

My release is powerful enough that I have to let go of her to grab the headboard behind me, and I feel it crack beneath my grip. Thea's hand doesn't stop stroking me, pulling every last drop like it's her life's ambition to make me see fucking stars. I'm gasping her name, cursing the gods, cursing her Heavens-sent hands as she draws out a longer orgasm than I've ever had.

When there's nothing left of me to spill, and the intense shudders that wrack my spine subside, I open my eyes and find her already looking at me again. She takes her hand from me, and examines the ropes of my cum between her fingers. Then, she lifts them to her mouth, and licks every bit off. And swallows.

I growl, and remove my hands from the headboard to grab her instead. In one swift motion, I've flipped us so that she lay on her back, me above her, both her hands pinned in one of mine above her head. She grins up at me, and purrs, "Looks like someone's had enough."

The words, the tone–they pull me out of the animal need, and a smirk tugs at my lips. She spoke those same words to me when we were in the Ceraschen woods, only under far different circumstances.

"Of you? Never," I reply. "Of not having the taste of you while you torment me with your hands? Yes." My arm goes around her waist, and I hoist her high up on the bed, her back against the headboard. I bite at the soft skin of her inner thigh, careful not to pierce it. Thea moans, and it only gets louder when I follow my teeth with my tongue.

Without further preamble, I thrust my tongue inside her, and groan at the taste, at the *perfection* of her around it. Her knees splay wider, granting me better access, and I lick all the way up her center, swallowing every honeyed drop. Her fingers spear through my hair, and mine grip her thighs. I listen to her pant, to the fantasy-like breathy moans she makes, to her saying, "Adan. Gods, Adan."

After getting her close to the edge a couple of times, so close that her hands pull at my hair, and she curses me when I ease her *just* far enough down, I decide to end her punishment for her sass last night, and give her what she deserves for this morning.

When I suckle and lick her, growling with pleasure, she moves her hips. *Fuck, yes.* I grip her ass–or what of it I can grab, even in my hands–helping her with the angle given the position she's in. When her moans turn to quickened breaths, her belly going tight, I growl again, and she shatters.

I lick her throughout, and I think I'd like another from her as she says my name, grinding against my face. So, I take one hand from her ass to stick a finger inside her pussy. She gasps, her hands shooting to my shoulders. Once she adjusts, pumping in and out of her wet heat all the while, I give her another finger. And then, my mouth still suckling, I hook them within her.

Her climax hits once more, and her fingers dig so deeply into my shoulders that I feel some of her nails break skin. When the spasms that arch her spine, and tighten the soft, hot inner walls around my fingers cease, I remove them, and lift my face. Hers is flushed, her lips parted, and there is only heat in that bright green gaze. To give her a taste of her own medicine, I stick my fingers in my mouth, and suck off the wetness she left on them. Her fingers on my shoulders contract, and I feel a savage pleasure as she draws my blood.

"I love you, Adathan Zale Evestre," she pants, somehow making my name sound beautiful, instead of monstrous. "But, know that each moment where you deny me of filling me with your cock, especially now that I've *seen* it, and *held* it–I will hate you, just a little bit."

I grin up at her, and move into a kneeling position.

It has the desired effect. Her eyes are nearly level with my still-hard cock, and she licks her lips as she looks at it. Though that look makes me want to do nothing but stay in this cabin, pleasuring each other until the rising sun is setting, I pinch her chin between my fingers. "Althea Maria Cardenia, you are the love of my existence. You have more power over me than you know. But, here, love..." I jerk her chin down so she has no choice but to watch while I fist my cock, and pump it slowly. She has the nerve to *lick her lips*, so I run my thumb over my head then across her mouth to give her something else to taste should she do it again. "You'll take what I give you. In fact, I think that, for the rest of the day, my tongue will only be spent talking with you," I tilt her chin up, and lean down to press a gentle kiss to her cheek, "as had been my greatest pleasure for weeks."

A purr like a cat skitters up her delicate throat, and she rolls to her knees before me. My cock pokes her belly, and she smiles, causing my heart to strain at the sight–so gods-damn gorgeous, put there by joy. Joy somehow because of *me*. Then, that beautiful curiosity fills her gaze.

"Not that I'm complaining, but how are you still hard? My physiology texts stated that after a man is spent, he can't go again for a bit." Black brows lower slightly as she rests her hands at my waist.

I move my hand from her chin to slide it back into her hair, gripping the strands in my fingers while my thumb hovers over the pulse thudding in her neck. I grin enough that I know she can see my canines. "I am no man, my love."

The adoration that shines in her eyes makes my heart stutter, and her own teeth make an appearance in her smile when my cock twitches against her. "No, you are not. You are my male. My love. My Death."

53

ALL SHAPES AND SIZES

LINA - DAY 34

I CAN'T GET OUT OF BED. IT'S PHYSICALLY IMPOSSIBLE. MY HEAD weighs about five thousand pounds, and I don't think my feet work. Even if they did, and even if I was strong enough to lift my five thousand pound head, I don't think my stomach would be happy about it.

I didn't even drink that much last night. Or, maybe I did? I lost track dancing, and I'm not sure how many times I ran to the bar with Al. Maybe it was a mistake to quench my thirst from so much activity with ale instead of water, but I deemed that a problem for tomorrow me.

Well, here we are, and yesterday me is a dumb bitch.

Plus, I'm thirsty *now*, my mouth so dry that I can hardly even smack my tongue against my palate. Yesterday me was also too tired from all the dancing to get a glass of water before falling into bed.

Dumb. Bitch.

With a groan, I twist my head, and crack open my eyes. One person could help me. The smart one of the two of us.

"Al," I croak out, and it's barely loud enough to register to my own ears. I swallow what little saliva is in my mouth, and try again. "Al." It's a little louder, probably something she could pick up if she's awake. But she might not be, so: "*Al.*"

A few seconds later, my door opens, a breeze wafting into what I'm sure is a cabin full of stale, stinking air. She's blurry, thanks to the sleep and crust in my eyes, but I can also make out the unmistakable shape of Adathan behind her. He was already by her side often–with her life in potential danger, I'm surprised he waits outside the door when she comes in.

"Not feeling well this morning?" she asks me, her voice mostly kind, with just the tiniest hint of humor.

"You could say that," I mumble, my voice muffled further by the half of my face still on my pillow. I close my eyes against the brightening dawn light. "Help."

A soft chuckle huffs through her nose, and her gentle, calloused hand lays on my cheek. I feel the familiar warmth of her majick leech the pain from my body. In seconds, my head stops most of its pounding, and my body doesn't ache nearly as much.

I'm able to open my eyes again, and find her still smiling softly down at me. "I can't fix the dehydration with majick, but the glass of water at your bedside will."

My brows scrunch, and I lift my regular-weight head to look down. There, sitting in a small puddle of its own making, courtesy of the rocking ship, is a mostly-full glass of water. "I didn't get that."

Her grin widens, and she stands. "Hm, I wonder who did?" One step backwards. "Maybe a faerie?" Another step, while I sit up. "With wings?" Another, as I reach behind me to grab my pillow. "Who's so fucking into you?" With a squeal, she launches herself out the door, and just manages to close it before my pillow connects with the wood surface.

I look down at the water again, and my own smile widens hesitantly, my heart picking up its pace in my chest.

⬌

Javi informs us at breakfast that we should arrive at the Sabriani port today, and I practically bounce in my seat for the rest of the meal. *Home.* Back to my mums, and my house, and Colina.

I don't even need to ask her before Ciaragen is telling me she already sent a message to Hielo and Hiela–and therefore mama–about our arrival. That they'll meet us at the castle the day after tomorrow, when we should arrive.

To pass the time, I join Al and Addie for their training session. She's a fucking badass, hair sticking to her with sweat as she just *never. Stops.* Every time he gets her in a hold, or his hands wind up in places where blades–which he's refusing to use, despite the excess since Kent is no longer here to hoard his wares–would be fatal, she fights. At one point she even heaves one massive leg out from under him, and pins him to the ground, a dagger–no qualms there–to his throat.

Once they're done with the insanity that is their hand-to-hand training, he invites me to practice seeing through glamours and making mind shields. We both do well, thanks to my mums training me in both since I was thirteen.

When we're done, and Adathan is expected to work, we move to leave the common room, Sione with us. They'd come down a few minutes into our mental work, and damn if it hadn't been distracting. Especially as that glass of water kept flashing through my mind, behind the shield I kept up through practice and will alone.

The sun is hot and bright as we emerge, and I hold a hand up against it to shield my eyes. "You put on sunscreen this morning, right?" Sione asks as they step up beside me, their dark brows furrowed.

"Yeah," I reply with a reassuring grin. "Just still bright to my eyes." I shrug.

Then a massive wing is extended before me, the sun turning the thinner membrane of it a deep red, highlighting the vessels between each juncture. I lower my hand from my face, no longer needing it there, and unthinkingly reach to touch the leathery surface–

Then I remember myself. "Sorry," I tell them, quickly dropping my hand to my side.

"It's okay, moonshine," they say, their voice a bit rough in a way that raises gooseflesh on my arms, which extends down my legs when I meet their red-brown eyes. "You can feel it if you'd like."

And I would. So, I do.

My hand trembles slightly, but I reach again, and this time brush the surface with my fingertips. It's smoother than I expected; leather worn to the texture of silk, stretched tight between the sharp bones. "So beautiful," I breathe, not having meant to say it out loud. I step forward a bit so I can more fully rest my hand against it, and start to trail my fingers across, towards one of the junctures–

But then my hand is caught in a larger bronze one, halting it.

I turn my face to Sione, my cheeks heating, and then burning at the look in their russet eyes. "You'll want to stop there," they murmur softly, though that same roughness lies beneath the gentle tone.

"Okay," is the only reply I can think of, though my thoughts venture into what the reason could be for their statement. They release my hand, and even in the warmth of the summer day, I feel a little cold where my skin no longer touches theirs.

Then they give me an easy half smile, the remainder of that darkened expression replaced with lightness. "You excited to get home?"

I grin back at them, ignoring whatever that disappointment in my gut stems from. "Yeah. My mums are probably going crazy." I roll my eyes, but don't mean it. That they might smother me with hugs and kisses when I arrive at the Castle of Colina actually only gives me the bright thing in my chest that is the feeling of being loved.

"I bet. They probably miss you after just a day." Their eyes shift across my face as they say it, probably scanning for that same longing.

"After a hundred of them, they probably won't let me out of their sight once I'm back," I agree as we begin walking to the rest of our little group, their wing retracting now that my eyes have adjusted.

"Sounds about right," they say as we reach Atlas's side.

"What sounds right?" he asks while Al steps up to his other side, Adathan having departed for his work for the day.

"Our parents missing us after being gone so long."

"Oh, yeah." His head tilts back in a similar unserious display of preemptive dread of our parents loving us as mine from a moment ago. When he rights himself, he says, "They'll probably be waiting at the gates."

"You think they have that restraint, after three months?"

He answers my grin with one of his own. "Definitely not."

"Guys," Tali whispers suddenly from Sione's other side. We look at her, Atlas's brows scrunched in a mirror of mine. "Shut the fuck up." Her cinnamon eyes dart to Atlas's other side–

Shit.

Al is still standing there, but her arms are crossed over her chest, shoulders tight, and I can only see her ink-black hair as she's turned her face towards the sea. "Al..." I start, at the same time that Atlas says, "Aly."

Her head shakes, incapable of answering, but even I hear her shuddering inhale. Atlas reaches a tentative hand to her shoulder, and when she doesn't shake it off, he takes a step closer to her.

"I'm sorry," she says thickly. "You guys should be excited, I don't mean to ruin that for you." She turns towards us, her eyes shining but not yet shedding, her throat working to swallow the emotion while she looks up at Atlas, and gives him a trembling, reassuring smile. Whatever restraint he was exercising cracks at that look, and he pulls at her shoulder to turn her into his chest. She bows into it immediately, her brow against the base of his throat. Her arms are still curled around herself, but his double down on it, winding over her shoulders.

"Nothing to be sorry about, darling," he murmurs, his hand running along her upper back. "I'll take you to your cabin so we can talk, yeah?"

She nods against his chest. He shoots a look up, probably where Adathan is, and then to me, and juts his chin, indicating we all should come. Though his jaw is too tight to express he's happy with what he probably thinks of as babysitters to keep his distance from her.

He tucks her under his arm, and Sione leads, spreading their wings a bit to block Al from view from everyone in front of us. Tali and I are the last to walk down the stairs, and enter her cabin. The female closes the door behind us while Atlas sits with Al on the bed, his arm still around her, and Sione leans a shoulder against the wall. Tali and I sit on the floor, and I'm even more grateful for my friend when she hands Al a kerchief from her pocket.

"Thank you," she says quietly, dabbing under her eyes, which are downcast. Atlas's hand squeezes her shoulder, and she takes a deep breath. "I just...I forgot. I've been so absorbed in who I lost, and in becoming this...this *person*. And I convinced myself back in those woods that he wouldn't want to find me after what I caused. So, I forgot about him. Forgot about my dad." She sniffs again, her hands tightening around the kerchief.

"Darling...I wrote him." Atlas hesitates as he confesses it, and his gaze is wary as Al lifts hers to meet it. "Right before we left Dahlih. Found a page, and sent him off with it."

"You...you wrote to my dad?" A tear leaks from a bright green eye, and she doesn't move to catch it with the kerchief. He nods once. "What did you tell him?"

"That you were safe, but couldn't return home. That...that I would keep you safe, and write him again when we arrived in Eshelle."

"...And did you?" This question is even softer than her last.

Atlas nods again. "While you and Lina were shopping, I sent it with a Jemagen page. If he left right away, stopping at the isles within the Evredis to rest...he'll probably be arriving any day now. Don't worry–he'll glamour himself upon arriving."

Al swallows. "Did you tell him what I am?"

Fae. The daughter of the High Lord and High Lady he visited so long ago. To both, Atlas shakes his head. "No," he answers gently, and I watch Al's shoulders sag with relief. "I thought, if you decided to share that, you would want to be the one to do it."

She nods, new tears budding in her eyes, and pauses for a heartbeat. Then, she reaches up, and wraps her arms around Atlas's shoulders. He freezes for a second–a second where I remember what he said about her holding him, allowing herself to *be* held after all she endured. Then his arms wind around her waist, his head tucking towards hers. His hands are tight enough that I know his will is going into not pulling her flush to him; leaving the space between their torsos and hips. They tighten further, the pads of his fingers paling when she whispers once more, "Thank you."

After a few seconds of quiet, Sione asks, "You have any siblings, Al?"

She pulls away from Atlas, nodding as one hand wipes under her eyes while the other trails off his shoulders. I can see the reluctance in my best friend's movements as he lets go of her waist, and plants his hands on the mattress, curling his fingers around its edge.

"Yes, three," she answers. "Two brothers, and a sister."

"Ymeda's tits, humans just pop them out, huh?"

A startled chuckle bursts out of her, the thickness leaving her throat with it. "I guess. What, is it different for Fae?"

"Oh, yeah. It's a good thing we live for centuries, because otherwise we'd probably have a population crisis."

"It's *because* we live for centuries that it's so hard, dingus," Talia chimes in, rolling her eyes. "Imagine if we could do it like humans? The world would be overrun."

"We have tonics, doofus," he reminds her.

"Tonics?" Al asks, her brows scrunching.

"Yeah," Tali answers, then her own brow mirrors Al's. "You know, something the male or female can take to prevent pregnancy?"

When Al's expression only becomes more confused, Tali isn't the only one whose eyebrows raise incredulously. "Do you not have that in Weaschte?"

"No," she answers, her eyes flitting to all of our faces, a blush rising to her cheeks.

"So, what? You're just forced to get pregnant?"

"I just–I never thought of it like that." The blush spreads across her nose, to the tips of her ears.

"Well, you don't have to anymore," Tali says easily, like it's the simplest thing in the world to reframe the knowledge Al has, thanks to a life within purity culture. "Li, do you have the tonic?" Those cinnamon eyes move to me with her question, and I feel the russet set do the same, only with far more weight to the gaze.

Now my own blush flares, but I answer, "I do."

Tali waves a hand to me, looking at Al again. "There you go."

My eyes flick to Atlas just long enough to see how tight his jaw is as he looks at the female beside me–who is dutifully ignoring him.

I tell Al, "Yeah, I'll give some to you while we're packing. I haven't been using it, anyway."

Do I imagine it, or do those leanly muscled shoulders loosen where they lean against the wall? Does the weight of the red-brown gaze feel heavy in a different way? I'd told them the other day that I haven't been having *that* sort of fun since leaving Eshelle, but did my having the tonic give them doubt for a moment?

Regardless of my feelings for them–as hidden as I hope they are–they have no right to believe me a liar. I add, an edge to my voice as I give Al a smirk, "Only *some*, though. Who knows what fun I'll find now that we're back in my territory?"

Her blush tempered to the usual light glow in her cheeks, she scoffs. "I seem to recall you teasing me about something along the lines of eight inches? Or will you be seeking other companionship?" Her brows wiggle, and Tali chuckles.

I shrug, noting the slight way those wings turn towards me, waiting for my answer. "Why decide now? Fun comes in all shapes and sizes, my dear." I wink at her, and she laughs. The only people in the room who don't seem to find amusement in this conversation are the male whose forced grin is more of a grimace as his eyes flit between Al and I.

And the faerie whose own eyes, when I dare to meet them for a heartbeat, gleam with something like a challenge.

54

BIRTHLAND

THE COAST OF SABRIAN AWAITS BEFORE ME; ONLY A HUNDRED yards of aquamarine sea separating me from it.

I am not afraid. Though my heart beats erratically in my chest, it's of anticipation, perhaps a bit of nerves. Despite what happened in Dekedda, I refuse to *fear* the land in which I was born, and from which I'd been taken. If any who will journey with us to the castle wish to harm me, they won't catch me unawares. And, though I could make them regret trying on my own, I'll grant that privilege to the male who steps up behind me now, and loops his arms over my shoulders, pulling my back to his front.

I'd sensed him approaching, that steady heartbeat as known to me as my own, but Atlas's departure—with a promise to see me shortly—had assured it. Now, I lean my head back against Adathan's chest, raising my hands to grab his forearms.

The muscles there flicker beneath my palms as he tightens his hold.

Scruff, and soft lips press to my temple. "I can hear your heart from across the deck, love."

I roll my eyes, and pinch his arm. "Shut up, stupid, good-hearing broody-male," I return, and I feel him grin against my skin. They come so much more frequently now, and my chest warms with more than his hold and the light of the evening sun at that fact.

"Remember our first day in the woods, when I'd just caught our dinner for the night? I believe you called me a 'stupid, good-hearing turkey murderer.'"

I restrain my smile, and shrug under his grip on my shoulders. "Maybe I did, maybe I didn't. Though, if I did, it would have been an incredibly accurate description, and I would stand by it."

"And if you didn't?"

I look up with an overdone look of offense. "Well, then I would find whoever did, of course, and make them wear itchy pine backpacks."

He laughs, and my heart skips a beat at the sound, and at the way his resulting grin stretches across his face; dimpling his cheeks, and flashing his canines. Then he leans back down to me, and kisses my cheek before murmuring, "You are a fearsome thing, Thea Cardenia. But that backpack was sent to the Void, where it belongs."

I turn out of his arms, and swat one of them, but can't quite contain my smile this time. He easily seizes my hand, and twirls me, crossing my arms over my torso and then dipping me so that the ends of my hair pool on the deck. I laugh then, no longer able to keep it in for the ruse of false indignation.

"I didn't know you could dance," I get out through a final

giggle as he straightens me, drawing me into him and an easy two step.

Now it's his turn to pretend to be offended. "I am technically a lord, you know. Had to learn to keep up appearances somehow."

"Can't imagine why. Your air of 'don't fucking come near me' isn't intimidating at all."

"Apparently not. You were all too near me this morning, love." His voice shifts towards a growl by the end, and his fingers tighten around mine.

My cheeks heat, and I hum as if in contemplation. "I don't know. I think I could have been a lot nearer. Though it certainly wasn't your air that was intimidating." The sheer *size* of him... I'd been able to tell he was large in my all too few encounters feeling it through his trousers against my thigh or my belly, but I'd been ridiculously unprepared for the actuality of it.

A low noise rumbles in his throat, and his voice is even lower when he says in my ear, "You didn't act like a female unsure of herself when you made me come hard enough to see fucking stars."

Desire licks through me, slickening my core and thudding through my veins. "Did I?"

Adan pauses, then slowly pulls back, his hands moving with him. His fingers weave into my hair starting at my temples, bringing it off my face, until they're tangled in a mass of black waves, and he's tilting my face up to look at him. His eyes, perfectly matching the late afternoon sun glinting off the waves, are filled with sincerity, edged with hunger.

"If I wasn't vocal enough for you, sweetheart, I'm sorry. It's not an excuse, but I–" He sighs, and one of his thumbs brushes the apex of my cheek. "I was trying to restrain myself, because having you touch me...it made my every instinct come alive. I worried that, if I told you how good you were doing..." His eyes darken, and dip to my mouth. "How well my cock fit in your hand, and all the other places I've dreamed of it being in you," golden irises rise to meet mine once more, "I would lose control."

I rest my hands on his waist and stroke his obliques, my desire heightening at his words, and the solid strength of him beneath my palms. "I don't understand," I tell him honestly. About the instincts, or his self-imposed restraining of them.

"There's a beast in every male, love. And mine—it has always been more unleashed than most. I'm not sure if it's my power, or just the way I am, but ever since you...Just *knowing* you, Thea, I've felt it, even more than before. It tells me to hold you without care of how tightly I do so, to sink my teeth into you and call you mine. Letting it free...I didn't want your first time pleasuring me to be marred by me behaving like an animal. So, I kept a leash on my words, and my body. Even still—" His fingers tighten in my hair and this time I *see* it; I see him rein in something that brims in his eyes, and then relax his hold. "You jerked my cock like you were made to do it, sweetheart. I've never come so hard in my life."

I feel the brightness of my responding smile as it steadily overcomes my face while his words sink in, settling to thrum within my core. "Yeah?"

He grins back at me, the softness of it contrasting with the fire in his eyes. "Yes, love. I think I made the males around me sick with my scent, with how much I thought about it today."

I close the small space between us, my hands rounding to his back, finding the scars along his spine. His hands compensate for the movement, turning at the wrists to tilt my face further up to still hold his gaze. "Me too. Especially when I thought about how it would feel in my mouth. Inside me."

A growl vibrates through his chest, his lids lower over his eyes, and I feel him harden against my belly. My grin turns wicked, and I keep going, his reaction deepening the confidence in my words. "I liked the taste of your cum on my tongue. And I wondered how it would feel filling me. Which is why I took some tonic from Li this morning."

He goes preternaturally still, his pupils nearly swallowing up his iris. My voice has become this low, sultry thing, and I let it rasp up my throat with all the things on my mind. "But I want you to know something else, Adathan Evestre. Once you take what I'm all too ready to give you, I'll have all of you, too. That leash has no place between us." I pause, considering. "Only perhaps your fingers as a collar."

"Fuck, Thea," he grits through his teeth, his fingers once again tightening in my hair, and the pull sends a whip of pleasure down my spine. His nostrils flare delicately, scenting that, and I feel him stiffen further. I vaguely hear sailors calling for people to start getting in the longboats, but I ignore them from our side of the sound shield I know Adan's had up since he turned me around. I don't really care that it doesn't make us invisible. With how close we are, the only thing it looks like is happening from the outside is an intense conversation. Which I am not done with.

"Because here's the thing, Adan: you would never hurt me. You grip me hard because I like it. If you bite me, it will be because I want you to. Your power is in taking, dominating me, telling me what to do for each of our pleasures. Well, mine is in letting you. In saying yes to everything that I might never have thought of before you lit that fire in me. In knowing that you would never take something that I was not enthusiastically giving. And you know that, too."

The kiss he presses to my lips is hard, fast. Like he feels the time rushing us, hears the males calling for us, but his need is too great to restrain. "Yes," he breathes harshly before seizing my mouth for a few more thundering heartbeats, then rests his forehead on mine. "Love, I–*fuck.*" He's breathing heavy, and his cock is so hard between us it has to be painful against the buttons of his trousers.

I soften my hands, and bring them up to his face. His eyes flash open, his pupils great pools of liquid black, ringed with a sliver of gold. "Do you want help to come back down?" I ask quietly.

"Please." It's actually pained, the way he says it.

I smirk, and his gaze flicks down to the movement. "Okay. But only because you begged."

His chuckle is a sharp exhale, but it gets him to relax a little, too. I close my eyes and let my majick loose, the only intention to send a healing sort of calm through him. He takes slow, measured breaths that warm my face and caress my lips. As I feel both take their effect, his hands relax in my hair, and slip out of the locks. His knuckles trail down my jaw, then move to grasp my wrists as he takes one more breath, and I open my eyes.

Adan's are back to gold, the pupils retracted to normal size. "Sweetheart," he says, and softly kisses my lips. "Begging for you is a privilege."

⇹

It's only when we reach the shore, and Adan, Atlas, and Javi get out to pull us further up on the sand that I remember what happened the last time my feet touched Eshellen soil. My eyes widen, and I look at Adan, his back to me as he brings us ashore. When he turns, his hand already out, only to find me sitting like a stunned dear, his brows furrow.

He crouches to my eye level, and I feel his majick envelop us again as he erects a sound shield. He lifts a hand to gently tuck a lock of hair behind my ear, the concern in his eyes making my heart clench in my chest. "What is it, love?"

I swallow, and his eyes catch it, the concern deepening at the unusual doubt of the motion. Quickly, as the others around us are disembarking, I tell him, "I–well, I'm not sure. But, last time, in Ardhavi, when I stepped on the ground, I...I felt this *surge*. Of power, as if it was coming from the earth, and into me."

His expression is confused for a second, and then begins to shift. His eyes flare, and shock comes to the forefront, but when his lips open, they halt for a heartbeat, and then his face changes again–to agony.

"*Ah,*" he grunts, his eyes scrunching shut, and my immediate instinct is to reach for him with my hands and my majick. I grab his face between my hands, and feel this familiar pain lashing through him.

Familiar, because it's exactly what I felt over two months ago, when I'd barged into his quarters. When he was a doorman named Artur, lying on the floor in agony as he tried to disobey a blood order.

"I don't understand–" he pants through the pain, steadily overcoming it. "I don't remember that command."

"You guys okay?" I hear Sione's voice ask amidst the sounds of a dozen males talking and gathering their belongings, and look up. After getting their things out of the other boat beside us, they must have noticed Adan and I had not moved. Because Li, Ciaragen, Tali, Atlas, Javi–they're all staring at us now with wrinkled brows of varying degrees. Sione takes a step towards us. "Adathan, you alright?"

The pain I can sense has dulled to discomfort, and he nods between my hands before I drop them. The sound shield dissipates, and Adan stands as if he didn't just have barbed wire running through his veins, and offers me his hand once more. I stand in the boat, and when I place my fingers in his, he runs his thumb over the backs of my knuckles in reassurance. *I've got you*, he seems to say as I look into his eyes, and step over the lip, and onto the sand.

My grip on him tightens when that same power from Ardhavi awakens–but it's not like it was then. That ball of energy in my chest hadn't disappeared, I see now; only slumbered. It flares, like a beast opening an eye, and emitting a purr when no danger is found.

I release the breath I'd been holding, and walk with Adan to the next boat to grab our scant belongings. He claps Sione on the shoulder in thanks as we pass. Though our behavior is too strange to remain unquestioned, none of the others do so as Adan takes both of our bags, and we approach them. No, with any one of the males around us possibly working for Olin, they'll let the issue pass for now.

Javi begins shaking hands with his males as they depart, thanking them for their service. Atlas had told me earlier that the High Lord won't yet be returning to Obala; his first mate, Geoffrey, will be sailing the ship back there with the rest of his countrymen, just another day's journey down the coast. Javi will be meeting with the High Lord and High Lady of Sabrian to discuss next steps, and leave with Tali and Sione shortly thereafter.

I'm grateful for it. Aside from Adan, the rest of my friends will likely be whisked away by whatever loved ones they have waiting for them upon our arrival. At least with the Obalans present, I might have an additional buffer between me and the people who'd like to call themselves my parents.

I haven't let myself think of it too much. My mind has been busy enough these days and weeks to call it unintentional, but that hasn't been the case the past few days. Aside from the training hours, and nights with Adan which leave my head blissfully clear within them, any time the Sabriani sovereigns have come to mind, I've shoved them aside.

My feelings about them are too complicated, and honestly? I have enough complication right now, what with the probability of someone trying to kidnap me within the next twenty-four hours. So, for now, I will focus on what I *know*.

I tighten my hand around Adan's, and he looks down at me. Silently, he leans down as we walk to press his lips to the top of my head, his fingers squeezing mine. I don't need his words to know what he's saying: *I love you*. I say them back with a turn of my head and a kiss to his shoulder.

Then, facing forward, that mighty power in my chest looking with slivered eyes at the land before us, we walk with friends and foes alike into my birthland.

55

NO MORE

DION - 5 WEEKS EARLIER

FOUR NIGHTS, AND FOUR DAWNS, I WAITED ON THIS DAMNED SHIP for Olin. For him, Adathan, and Gadsby to bring the would-be princess aboard. I couldn't help but wonder what sort of state she would be in when they arrived. Though she was sweet, the callouses on her palms spoke to years of training. I didn't think she would go without a fight. And I knew that they would hit back twice as hard.

It wasn't fair, that statement. At least to the golden-eyed male. He hid his compassion well, but I'd seen it first-hand. Felt him, even under Olin's command, even after they tortured him for weeks, be gentle when he pushed the needle of iron into my skin. He wouldn't hit Althea unless ordered to. If ordered, he still would pull the punch unless otherwise commanded.

I hated Olin for many things, and yet another was for trying to make Adathan like him. For taking a boy, who might have grown into a great male, and making him into someone to be feared rather than loved. Given the male's obvious predisposition towards kindness, I had to figure his self-hatred functioned the same as mine. The more evil he committed, even under Olin's order, the more he loathed himself for it. Unlike me, however, his first century of life might not be clouded by an unwillingness to change. I had little doubt that, if free of the blood oath, Adathan would set out to do far more amazing things in this world.

I, on the other hand, was well and officially fucked. And in the version of self-hatred that I shared with Adathan, I could do nothing but think I deserved it for what I had done. For my betrayal to my court, to my mate, to my own soul, I did not deserve happiness—not only now, but for the rest of the time I would spend under the service of the usurper king my brother will surely become.

My only comfort was in knowing that I may be nothing anymore, but the people weren't. *They* would bring the change. They would make this continent a land worth living in, as it had not been in centuries. That world would be beautiful, for my loved ones who still lived in it, who, too, would be a part of that change. For my High Lord and High Lady. Nuria and Jolie, and Bayani. For Ciara.

They will be better off without me. As I was now, I could not stand the idea of Ciara being tied to me. I used to mourn that I had never gotten the chance to claim her. Now, I was grateful for it; that I was hers by rite, but she was not mine.

I hoped she had a second mate. That, if her soul missed me, that person might help to fill that emptiness. It was a knife in my gut, and razorblades on my skin to even think about her with another, but, again, my happiness was worth less than nothing. Hers...hers was everything.

There would be war. Battles to be won, once the rebellion began. But, once it was done, she could have a beautiful life.

Olin would have to be dead for the war to ever end, but I would never interrupt her peace simply because I was free. I was sure she would learn what I'd done, and, once she did, she would want nothing to do with me. Perhaps, at that point, I would not have to live with that fact. I hoped, truthfully, that the rebellion would take my life, too. Olin and I were identical, after all; I didn't doubt the people would eradicate both of us, just to be safe.

They said, speak of Deimos, and he shall appear. I thought that was funny, for an instant, when I saw Olin cresting with broad strokes through the water. My humor died, though, when I saw that he was alone.

I met my brother at the top of the ladder against the starboard railing. Dripping wet, his teeth bared and hazel eyes bright with fury, he asked, "Do you have something to tell me, Dion?"

"Where's Adathan? Where is the princess?"

Quick as an adder, he struck my cheek in a wicked backhand, whipping my head to the side. He was strong, to be sure, but I'd be damned before I gave him the satisfaction of knowing it. My head still turned, I spat a wad of blood and saliva onto the deck at my feet before straightening to look at him once more.

"I asked you a question. Did you neglect to mention something to me back at Castle Cerasche?"

I fought against the urge to blanken my expression. Instead, I furrowed my brow slightly. "What are you talking about?"

He snarled with rage, and spittle landed on my face as he growled his response. "I am talking about your gods-damned *mate* being at the castle, Dion. Ring a bell?"

I kept any hope from rising in my chest, and only scrunched my brows further. "No. What, did she keep you from getting the princess?" *Where is Adathan?*

Olin laughed without humor. "You'd like that, wouldn't you? No, I got her. All the way to those fucking cliffs. Until *my fucking son* took off with her, into the gods-forsaken Evredis!" His eyes went positively mad as he shouted. The veins in his temples and throat swelled, and pulsed black with his fury, and his power.

Controlling my expression in response to that was far more difficult. Only a century of training kept the surprise in my eyes to just that, rather than delight. "Adathan betrayed you?" I asked, my heart swelling with pride.

"Probably wanted her cunt all to himself, the cocksucker. I should have damned the sanctification, the ceremony of it that would *give me what I deserve*, and fucked her while I had the chance. By the time he's done, she'll either be used up, or got with *his* spawn."

I restrained my jaw from tightening; kept my hands from fisting. "Possibly," I said, and the lie tasted good on my tongue, for it was not for me. "Would that change your plan?"

In an instant, Olin's switch flipped. The madness was gone from his face, replaced by a serenity that churned my stomach far more. "You would like to know, wouldn't you?" he asked. "Too bad you never will."

His veins flashed black as he raised his hand–

And I knew no more.

56

A PROMISE MADE

CIARAGEN - DAY 34

I MAY NOT KNOW WHAT WAS WRONG WITH ADATHAN BACK AT THE shore, but I think I know why Althea was so hesitant to step onto Eshellen soil. That knowledge keeps my shoulders tight as we walk the mile from the shore to the stables, Javi beside me.

If the High Lord notices anything off in me, he keeps quiet about it, just as we'd all outwardly brushed off the strangeness of our arrival. With the three other males traveling with us, we could scarcely do anything else.

Peanuts, whose true name is apparently Franc. A faerie with blue skin and silver eyes like Jacks called Petyr. And another Fae, named Harris. Are any or all of them employed by Olin? It's possible that none of them are, but that's not a chance we will be taking.

Across the grassy plain which flows on from the sand of the beach, the stablehand spots us coming and waves. The reeds crunch beneath our feet and lightly scrape at our boots and trousers until we reach the dust and dandelions of the immediate area around the stables.

"Evening to ya!" the hand calls to us, just a dozen yards away now. "All o' ya will be needin' horses to the castle, aye?"

"Aye," Javi answers, reaching the male and shaking his outstretched hand. "They'll be returned to you in three days' time."

He waves his other hand, dismissing that. "Isn't no rush. The High Lord and High Lady always send back more than what they owe; I'd lend 'em for free at this point, if they'd let me."

I smile a bit. Just arrived, and already hearing how beloved our sovereigns are. I hope Althea is listening. I hope she hears that those people she may resent...that they are kind. I hope, because I don't want to see the look in my Hiela's eyes if the daughter she's waited so long for rejects her. I don't even think Amedeo could heal the fracture that would cause in her heart.

"We appreciate it, friend," Javi responds. "Would it be alright for us to go in and choose, or do you prefer to assign at your discretion?"

"Och, go on in. That one looks like she won't trust a beast she don't pick herself, anyway." He points behind us with a kind grin on his weathered face, and we look over our shoulders.

Althea attempts to give him a rueful smile back, but it doesn't meet her eyes. Her hand on Adathan's stomach is fisting his shirt, the knuckles pale. And, now that I'm facing her, the breeze having blown her scent away from us before, I can smell her fear.

Undaunted by traveling across the sea to kill the male who murdered her loved ones. Unafraid of the danger she faces now, and of the male beside her, whose power is even darker than his father's.

But scared of horses.

Not wanting to make her even more self-conscious than he's likely just done, I turn back around, and smile brightly at him. Not a thing I typically do around males, but if it spares her the discomfort...

It has the effect I normally wouldn't have been able to stomach. His eyes move to me immediately, pupils flaring, and his responding grin is easy. "Thank you for your assistance," I tell him, to which he removes his cloth hat and tips it to me, revealing small horns. Javi and I once again lead the way, into the dimness of the stables, lit by scant faerie lights and the evening sun shining through the doors and roof slats.

The smells of hay and horsehair are even stronger inside. I hear the others file in behind us amidst the sounds of snuffing snouts, and clopping hooves of the horses, and the faun who just admitted us. A few other stablehands mill about, tending the horses, paying us little to no mind as they go about their duties.

I'm not picky, but I also know that animals are even more aware of us than we are of them, so it might not be *me* who decides here. As I walk past a few stalls, I take note of averted eyes or lifted heads, and pass them by without pausing. A few get my pace to slow, but the Fae creature in me recognizes them, picking up on any shift that tells me: *no*. Until, finally, I reach a palomino gelding. His dark eyes are steady as I turn to face him, and when I lift my hand to his snout, hovering it to ensure his comfort, he remains still.

"Ah, Marengo will treat you just fine, miss!" the stablehand calls from a few stalls away as I lay my hand on the horse's muzzle. "If you'd like to wait in the field out back, I'll have him saddled up for you."

"Thank you." With a final scratch on his snout, I leave Marengo, passing by Tali and Lina as they peruse the steeds with soft smiles on their lovely faces. Sione, Javi, and Atlas are playfully arguing over a stallion, and Adathan and Althea are slowly walking down the center of the aisle. One of her hands is wrapped around his bicep, the other arm looped behind his forearm, fingers twined with his.

And, as I turn from them to walk into the field behind the barn, I find that my lips have curved up slightly in humor.

Not flat in resignation to the two of them together. But *humored*, and maybe a little glad, that in this most interesting fear of hers, he provides comfort to her. I can find no anger in my heart that he gets to have that, *gets* to comfort her and hold her. Only contentment that I will never have to worry that my Lady is protected as long as he's around her.

If not for him, this homecoming would be so dark. So, while my heart still holds that familiar ache, and my ever-wilting stubbornness tells me *that* is because of him...I can no longer find it in me to hate him for it. Only the male who gave the order, and who would have caused such darkness in our court.

I sigh as I lean against the back of the barn, closing my eyes. The evening sun tints the backs of my lids red, and warms my face, and the exposed skin of my arms and shoulders. Standing still after so long at sea, it feels like the waves are still beneath me, constantly pushing and pulling my weight. With that short reprieve less than a week ago, I hadn't taken or even *had* the time to realize how much I missed the land. The smells of grass and soil, and air *not* tinged with the scents of salt and damp wood.

I inhale that air greedily, and as I let it out in a long breath through parted lips, I hear footsteps approaching. I open my eyes, and turn my head in time to see Javi walking out.

I smirk at him. "You got the stallion?"

His brows furrow, as if it's a ridiculous question. "Of course, I did."

I chuckle, and one corner of his mouth pulls up. He moves

to my other side to lean against the wall beside me. As his shoulders thump against the wood, he pulls in a loud breath. "Land, ey?"

My grin widens as I stare out at the gold-tinged field. "Fuckin' *land*."

It's his turn to huff a laugh, and he tucks his fingers into his pockets. We watch the sun make patterns on the waving grasses across the field, the light breeze picking up dandelion seeds from the space before us and scattering them to wherever they might find a new place to grow.

Tali and Lina come out shortly after the males who are journeying with us, now standing and talking slightly to the side of the open field. The females take up the same stance as us on Javi's other side. His daughter hooks her arm around his, and leans her head on his shoulder. My throat tightens when he covers her hand with his, squeezes, and leaves it there.

Sione and Atlas join us a couple of minutes later. The faerie sits a few feet in front of Lina, and spreads their wings to sun them, while Atlas comes to my side, and slips his arm over my shoulders. I lean in, and the sweet boy presses a quick kiss to the top of my head.

Yet another thing to be grateful for, though my capacity for it had been minimal in my aching heart these past weeks. I may not have children of my own, but this boy, and the girl who now moves to sit in the shadow of one of Sione's wings are as close as I'll come to it. That they've grown into such kind, strong, brave people...allowing myself to see it, absorb it–it makes my heart clench in my chest, and tears spring in my eyes. I am not their mother, but I watched them both grow up into these people all the same.

Sitting now, Lina picks a stick up from the dirt, and begins to draw swirls and shapes in the dusty top layer. My lips twitch up at the child-like whimsy she possesses to do such a thing at twenty-one years old, and I swear Sione's wing curves a bit around her, too.

More footsteps, and then Adathan and Althea exit the stables, turning to find all of us just existing amidst the breeze and the setting sun. Althea's eyes catch on Lina, and she smiles softly before moving towards her, dragging Adathan along by the hand. The male beside me lets out a quiet breath as she sits, pulling him down with her so that her back is against his front, between his legs. When she holds her hand out to Lina, my goddaughter extends the stick so Althea can break it in half. Then the two draw together, and I find Atlas's wrist in front of my shoulder, and squeeze it in understanding. His tension loosens just slightly in response.

Several sets of clopping hooves move towards us a moment later, and we all look to see each stablehand walking out with two steeds. Our quiet is at last interrupted by the male who'd greeted us saying with a grin, "Alright, they're all set for ya. Now, we've got ya a mule for belongin's an' such. He don't take kindly to riders, so keep off his back and he'll be quiet enough. The rest of 'em are all ready for ya."

We all straightened or stood from our positions as he spoke, and, closest to the male, Atlas extends his hand. "Thank you, sir."

The male takes it with a laugh. "That'll be a first. *Sir*. Well, I 'preciate ya, son." Releasing his hand, Atlas grins, and the male waves us towards the steeds now tied to the post a few yards away. "You all have a safe journey."

Several thank yous are directed to him as we make our way to the horses. Lina practically skips to a dappled mare, who waits calmly for her. My palomino chuffs as I near him, and I grin a bit before stroking the side of his neck.

Althea and Adathan each chose midnight black mounts. The female at least seems unafraid of those two, though the stallion is large enough to make Adathan look nearly normal-sized. He directs her in how to mount her mare, and she nods at each instruction, her brow scrunched a bit in concentration as she grabs what he tells her to. At the same time that I swing my leg over Marengo, Althea hops off her grounded foot, and smoothly does the same, landing right in the saddle.

Adathan smiles up at her and says something too low for me to hear over the sounds of everyone else clamoring onto their horses. She grins back with pinkened cheeks–a grin that widens and a blush that deepens when Lina and Tali clap and wolf-whistle for her. I don't hesitate to join in, and, though I will be back with my closest female friends the day after tomorrow, I relish this moment of girlish joy with them.

"What's her name?" I ask Althea.

Her hand runs along the mare's neck. "Nisha."

I tip my head towards Adathan's stallion. "And his?"

Something in her face softens when she answers, "Nox." Then, she adds, "Jakob told me they're mates." In the corner of my eye, I see Adathan stiffen, just slightly, in his saddle.

Before I can reply to her, Lina interjects with a tone of delighted surprise, "He said the same thing about Wynonna and Grace." She pats her mare, and points to Sione's, whose coloring is chestnut throughout. "Said it was good the pairs were going, because apparently they're not very nice to be around when separated. I didn't even know horses could *have* mates."

"Everyone has a mate, Emi," Sione says before nudging Grace's sides with their heels, and bringing her to a walk. Her lips purse as she watches them go, and then, securing the reins in her hand, follows them, her cloud of curls bouncing with each shift of the horse beneath her.

The males make to follow them, and I quickly put myself between them as inconspicuously as I can. Atlas joins me at a lazy pace, making my interruption a little less obvious. Javi and Talia follow them, and Althea and Adathan bring up the rear.

I haven't ridden a horse in months, so I'm glad for the low position of the sun in the sky that will enable us to set up camp in just an hour or two. As we enter the forest of oak and walnut trees a few miles off the coast, my inner thighs are already not thrilled with me.

Each pairing of people on the path before and behind us chatters quietly as our horses take us at a leisurely pace down the wide trail through the trees. The fallen leaves of the last autumnal season crunch delicately under hooves, their dry scent mingling with that of the green leaves above us. The last dregs of the sun pour in through the canopy in fat orange beams, which steadily fade as the sun crests over the sea behind us.

It takes us another twenty minutes or so to find a suitable space to set up camp for our group. When we do, I hear more than a few grunts and groans as we all dismount, mine being one of them. Sea legs transitioning back to land like this will definitely leave us all sore by the time we reach Colina.

Atlas goes with Franc to collect firewood, while Petyr and Harris go to hunt. It doesn't take either group long to come back, the latter with a few rabbits hanging from their fists.

As they move to sit, unsheathing their daggers, though, Althea's whispers, "One of them is still alive."

They look up at her from under their brows. I don't miss the dismissive annoyance in Petyr's eyes, though Harris is the one to respond, turning his curious gaze to the rabbits. "Which one?"

She stands, and I see Adathan's hands tighten over his bent knees so hard that his knuckles pale, but he doesn't follow her. She steps until she reaches the animals, and kneels before them. Gently, she lifts one, and sets it aside, revealing another. Its nose twitching, though blood soaks its coat.

"Ah, shit," Harris says. Then he picks up the animal, and snaps its neck.

Althea gasps sharply, and Atlas stands, Adathan at her side in an instant. "You know where your food comes from, don't you, girl?" Petyr asks, disdain written on his face. A bold move, since–

"What the fuck did you just say to her?" Adathan asks. Not a growl or a snarl, but rather a far more dangerous emptiness to the tone. Petyr has the good sense to look afraid as he tips his head far enough back to meet the male's eyes.

"I just–she shouldn't be so put-off by one little rabbit–"

"You ever talk down to her again, you'll find yourself without a tongue. I'll rip it out of your gods-damned throat." That quiet, blank calm even sends chills up *my* arms. Adathan doesn't look away until Petyr gives a shaky nod, the scent of his fear saturating the camp. Then, he crouches beside Althea, and caresses her cheek with a knuckle. She turns away from the dead rabbits, the haunted look in her eyes subsiding a bit as she meets his. In an instant, the quietness of his voice shifts into a gentle, loving sort. "Let's go for a walk, sweetheart."

He holds a hand out to her, and helps her off her knees. Then, twining their fingers, he takes her back down the path we'd just been on.

I turn back to the males, and find I'm not the only one who does so with a glare. In fact, the only person *not* glaring at him, instead studiously tending the fire, is Franc.

It's Atlas's eyes that Petyr meets, though, and holds up his hands. "I'm sorry, okay?"

Atlas's jaw ticks, and he strides forward, and carefully takes the rabbit from Harris's hands. He cradles it in his palms, and walks it further into the woods. By the time he stops, I can just make him out as he takes a knee, and places the rabbit, curled as if in sleep, beneath the canopy of a great oak.

Someone–probably Javi, given the tone of the word–must still be looking at Petyr, though, because the male says again, "Sorry."

But he's only apologizing because we're angry with him, not because he was rude to Althea. In fact, by the way his mouth moves ever so slightly as he mutters under his breath, he's not truly sorry at all. No, he's just an asshole, who also happens to be a coward.

It doesn't make him Olin's male. But it makes it a hell of a lot more likely.

57

AND KEPT

THEA - DAY 34

ADAN WALKS WITH ME INTO THE DUSK-SHROUDED WOODS, HIS thumb rubbing comforting patterns on the back of my hand. I feel it, feel the warmth that accompanies his touch in more than just the physical sense, but can't quite process it.

Once, I'd found a doe in the Ceraschen woods. Had sensed her pain in the silence of first light, and gone to her, heedless of the dangers that might be lurking within the pines.

I'd felt something similar just now, only amplified by ten. I'm not sure if it's the absence of iron in the land, as Adan had implied weeks ago, or if it's the fact that I still have my mind open to my true abilities, but when that rabbit had been suffering...

It wasn't quite visceral. Not like when I siphon someone else's pain. More like...an alarm blaring in my brain and in my blood saying *not right, not right.* And then that male had snapped its neck–

I cringe again, remembering it, and Adan's hand tightens around mine. I know he's getting us far enough away that not even the advanced vision of those at our camp will be able to make us out. Waiting to put up a sound shield until we stop moving, and remaining silent until then.

A few more strides, and he pulls me to the side of the path, putting my back to a tree, and standing, just as solidly, in front of me. His free hand moves to my face and caresses the scar on my cheek. I feel his majick wrap around us, and he says simply, "Talk to me."

I tilt my head back against the bark to look into his eyes. The protective numbness I'd been clinging to these past minutes crumbles as soon as I do so, and my lower lip trembles. "I'm so overwhelmed, Adan," I whisper, because even though we cannot be heard now, it's the loudest I can get out past my heart in my throat.

His brows come together over eyes that fill with devastation, but his hands remain soft on me as my words grow angry. "I'm trying to hold it together, because it feels–it feels like this is some fucking *destiny* that I'm supposed to be ready and strong for. Like every time I'm upset, or scared, or *anything* except 'ready,' I'm failing. Myself, you, *everybody*."

My tears run hot down my cheeks, the threads of sadness and anger in that twisted knot within my chest unfurling too quickly for me to attempt to reel back in. "I feel like I'm not doing enough, and yet like if I try to do anything more, I'll split apart at the seams. It was killing for the first time, and being forced to choose a husband, and then *wishing* my problems were that simple anymore. Because then it was my–my *mom* and Hanna and Amahd, and being choked and beaten, and killing Gadsby. It was ripping an arrow from your neck, and fighting my heart, and then it was Dekedda, and death."

His hands and jaw tense while shadows fill his eyes, and it

just makes my voice thicker, rasping its way up my throat. "And now it's tonight, and then it's to Colina, to *them*, and then Oschverre and Olin and Oleander, and in between *everything* is this power that feels like, when I access it, it will be *endless*. Every step we've taken since leaving the beach, it's like this beast *roaring* at me, telling me to free it, but I don't know how. And it's both a relief and distressing that the High Lord and High Lady will know."

I laugh humorlessly. "Except they want to take *you* prisoner. And *me*? Adathan, how is it possible that I can want nothing to do with them, and yet I'm worried that I'll be–" I close my eyes and lips, shaking my head against the last words.

"You'll be what, love?" he asks, his own voice rougher than usual, softening his hands to stroke my cheek once more.

I open my eyes again, and force out, "A disappointment."

"Oh, sweetheart..." He pulls me to his chest, and I wrap my arms around his waist, burying my nose in the fabric of his shirt. While I inhale the scent of him, my tears slow, and a heavy sigh escapes me, which he echoes, tightening his arms around me. After a long moment, he pulls me back, only to replace his hands on the sides of my neck.

Adan's thumbs brush across my damp cheeks, and speaks as gently as he cradles my face. "You could never be a disappointment, love. Everything you are is exactly as it should be. If you should change or grow, if you should fail or succeed, you will still be *exactly as you should be*. Nothing but *you*." His expression darkens, and each following sentence adopts more of the killing calm he had in the camp a minute ago. "And if, for some reason, they don't see that, it will be their loss, not yours. And if it doesn't feel like that to you, if that is the choice they make, then I will spend the rest of my days making sure you never feel less than ever again.

"I might also splatter them across the walls for hurting you, but seeing as you seem to *not* want me arrested, I would restrain myself for you."

That evokes a thick chuckle from me, and some brightness returns to his eyes, and emotion to his voice. "As for the–you know I can't discuss it, and I hate my father even more for it; for him taking away my ability to comfort and help you through this. But, trust me when I say *they* will know. And, if they try to pad it with pretty words, or try to delay sharing with you another truth about yourself, you don't worry about their feelings when you tell them to fuck off until they feel like talking about what *you* want to know."

I nod between his hands, feeling steadier by the minute within them, the chaotic whirling within my mind from a moment ago calming with each word. "And when it comes to tonight..." He sighs, and his jaw ticks. He's not happy with my plan, hasn't been since I spoke it to him, alone in the stables with a sound shield around us. But, he also was not able to come up with a better one, further than "I could just kill them all."

Still, he continues, "It will be a problem eliminated by morning. And, at the very least, one thing off that stunning mind of yours."

It's my turn to sigh, and I reach up, placing one hand on his cheek, and the other on his chest, over his heart. Its beat, so familiar to me now, pounds strongly beneath my palm. "I love you," I tell him, and feel that heart skip one of those beats.

He leans forward once more, tipping my head back further to press his mouth to mine. It's a warm, whispering kiss that's all too fast before he tilts away to rest his brow against mine, and says, "I love you, too, Thea. So much."

By the time we return to camp, the rabbits are already on spits over a couple of fires. My eyes widen when I watch Tali wave a hand at one, and its flames immediately flare brighter and higher than a second before. She grins when she sees my expression. "Never seen fire majick before, Aly?"

I shake my head; we had a single fire-wielder in Castle Cerasche, but he only tended to the forever-burn candles, and the hearths in the winter, and I never saw him in action.

Tali flicks her wrist, springing licks of vermillion flame to the tips of her fingers. A twitch of each knuckle, and one by one they switch to gold. "You never asked about our powers," she points out.

I shrug, and take a seat on a log beside Adathan, lifting my feet up onto it to get them away from the ground. Though remaining tethered to him–our hands still intertwined–helps that strange power feel more manageable, this is just another measure. "It's not a thing we do in Weaschte, since not everyone has magic."

While Tali replies, "That makes sense," Adathan takes my feet, and swings them over his leg, my knees bending over his thigh, leaving my toes hovering several inches off the ground. The female goes on, "Well, I think you know most of them, but–" She points around the group. "My dad has water, Sione has wind, Ciaragen has shadows, Atlas has lightning, Lina has summoning, and–well, I'm not sure about you guys," she finishes, looking at the males.

Clever. So clever to get them to reveal what they might use against us without arousing suspicion.

It's Harris who answers, "Not as strong as the High Lord's, but I've got water, too. Franc's got wind, and I think Petyr has ice."

Nothing too dangerous, then, but Tali only nods. And none of them bring up Adathan's power. "I think the coolest is between me and Ari, then," she says, flipping her still-blazing fingers to inspect her nails.

Atlas leans forward, a challenging smirk on his mouth, and

holds his own hand out. Sparks dance from one finger to the next, connecting like lightning to a tree, and reflecting across his stormy eyes. "You sure about that, my Lady?"

In an instant, his hand is wreathed in shadow so dark, the lightning cannot even flash through it. "She's sure," Ciaragen says from a few seats down, a half smile on her lovely face.

Atlas moves his hand, no longer alight, and waves it towards Tali. "You could do the same thing to her flame."

"So, you agree. Mine is the coolest."

He rolls his eyes with a laugh, joined by all but the sullen faerie by the other fire. Or, maybe he's just staying silent on Adathan's threat of ripping out his tongue. Admittedly, my male remains quiet as well, likely seeing the same thing I do.

In fact, he stays mostly silent for the rest of the night. Luckily, it's not out of the ordinary for him to be the least talkative of our group. He is quiet through dinner–during which I notice a rabbit is missing, but don't know who ensured that–and while everyone sets up their bedrolls. Until we lay on ours, flush against each other.

Then, one of his hands grips my thigh, the other sliding under my shoulders, and he pulls me on top of him. Immediately, the roaring of majick in my blood and mind calms to a low, easy purr. "Better?" he asks quietly, his first word since he thanked Javi for giving him supper.

We don't put a sound shield up, as it would ruin my plan if the males across the camp were unable to hear us. So, I tilt my chin up until my lips are next to his throat, just under his ear, and whisper, "For a few reasons, yes." Then, I press a kiss to the same space over which my mouth just hovered. He restrains the noise I know he would have set free if we were alone, but his arms tighten around me, and I feel him harden against my leg.

Also lucky, or, more likely, engineered by the male beneath me: we are downwind.

I inhale the rich scent of his desire, the depth it brings to the oak and embers and leather. I'm sure my own heightens as well, and Adathan's hands running up my ribs and down my thigh confirms it. With the full day of training, then work, then deboarding, and then several miles of travel, we haven't been able to so much as kiss for more than a few seconds all day. And, after this morning, I'd like to do much more than kiss him.

I move my leg so that my thigh runs down his length, but his hand stops me. I lift my head off his shoulder to look into his eyes, and find both their edges and his jaw to be tight. My own gaze softens, and I lift my hand to lightly run my fingers down his cheek. Because his expression tells me he can't right now, with what's about to be done, and I need him to know that I understand.

As I brush a loose curl back from his forehead, he lets out a long, quiet breath, closing his eyes. I can sense his heart slowing to its normal pace, the quickness I'd attributed only to lust a moment ago subsiding. When he opens his eyes again, they're a bit calmer, but not much.

And they won't be. Not until our task is done. So, I lean in and press my lips to his other cheek, then move back to rest my head in the crook of his neck and shoulder. He turns his head to inhale at the crown of mine, his broad hands steady on my back and my thigh.

Slowly, his breath evening, one arm falls away, then the other, leaving me perched atop him, only the breadth of him keeping me there. I slide my leg off of him first, then join it with my other. I try not to cringe when I straighten my torso, and all that separates me from the earth is the thin bedroll. Adan must sense it somehow, because his hand twitches. The only movement in him except the even rise and fall of his chest.

I stand, tiptoeing out of the campsite, leaves crunching

lightly underfoot. When I find a particularly large oak several yards in, I move behind it, and take the small water skin out of the top of my boot. Uncorking it, I then lower it just off the ground, and pour some of it into the dirt and leaves. After resting it there, the moisture absorbing the sound it might have made, I shuffle around, scrubbing my hands against my trousers.

I hear them before I see them, and freeze like a frightened doe. My heart pounds in my chest, loudly enough that their keen ears surely pick it up. I pat the empty scabbard at my thigh.

A low chuckle sounds, and then he steps into my sight. "Unarmed, in the woods, at this time of night? You truly are foolish, girl," Petyr says.

The other sneaks up behind me, and thrusts a needle into my jugular. I jerk my head away, but not before there's enough iron in my blood that the roaring beast in my chest once again quiets, albeit in a different, darker way than before.

What I'm not prepared for, is the person who steps out from behind me, dropping the needle into the leaves.

"I'm sorry, Althea," Jacks says, his silver eyes downcast as he takes a few steps back, away from me. "He has my family."

"Now, here's what's going to happen," Petyr continues, as Franc takes up the spot to his right. Franc's expression is dull compared to the smugness in Petyr's. "You're goin' to come with us to Oschverre, and you're not gonna make a peep about it. Else Jacks here will freeze 'em where they stand, and ain't no comin' back from that—not that you could heal 'em now even if there was." He laughs to himself.

"You work for Olin," I whisper the accusation, my voice trembling just like my hands.

"Aye. He's goin' to be High King soon, and best to be on his good side innit? Let's go now, time's wasting." His left hand reaches for me, and he takes a step forward.

But I have a feeling he's too proud of himself–of his cleverness in choosing a side and in capturing me–to keep his mouth shut, so I ask, "Harris isn't with you? And the rest of the crew?"

His arm falls to his side, though he takes a step closer to me. "Nah, couldn't have everybody knowin' what was what with you. Only males he could trust not to rut you as soon as we got you." He sniffs, scowling. "Though he prolly don't know that you've got with that fucker back at camp. Ordered us to kill 'im, but I reckon he won't be too angry if we just take you now, and get oh, about seven hours' head start on the journey." Not blood bound, then, if they're defying an order.

"Are there others?" I flit my eyes around the woods, into the spaces of shadow and dark where anyone might be lurking.

"Aye, but not here. He's got someone in that castle ready if we would have failed. That won't be happenin', though." He looks over at Franc with a shared half smile, then back at me. "Enough talk now, let's go–" His left hand reaches again, and I let him grab my wrist.

With a weak tug against his hold as he drags me a single pace, I ask through my teeth, "What about Kent?"

"Ah, fucker ran off back in Deke–what you know about Kent?" He switches mid-sentence, stopping in his tracks to look at me once more.

"I know he's dead. Just like you're about to be." As fast as Adan has trained me to be, I reach behind me, to the back I've kept to the tree for more than one reason, and slip my dagger out of its sheath. I hold the tip to his heart, knowing he'll see it as the move of a scared female, unsure about taking a life. Easily deflected and disarmed.

By the smug smirk that spreads over his cheeks, I'm right.

"Ah, you think you're gonna kill us? It's three against one, love, and all you've got is that scrap of metal."

I grin back at him, and that makes him twitch with uncertainty. "Oh, *I'm* not going to kill you."

Bone crunches, and Petyr whirls to the noise, dropping my arm. Franc makes a choked sound, his eyes so wide they might come out of their sockets. Behind him, wreathed in shadow which he steps out of like the avenging Death God he is, Adathan doesn't even spare the male a glance as he yanks–

Taking Franc's spine with it, sinew and gore clinging to the vertebrae, Adathan's fist is shining with blood in the dim light of the moon overhead. He drops the bones without even looking at the male as he sags to the ground, dead before he hits the leaves.

Javi slips out of more shadows and gets Jacks in a chokehold. Realizing that he is now alone and surrounded in his already lost fight, Petyr panics like the scared little animal he is. I toss my dagger with a flick of my wrist into his foot the second it lifts off the earth, as if he might try to run. He yowls, bending to remove it, but I'm there first. I pull it out sharply, and thrust the pommel up into his nose.

He falls backward with a thud, and begins to scramble across the leaves, his nose streaming. Thunder cracks as lightning strikes his leg with precision; not enough to kill, but enough to make him convulse in agony for several seconds. A whistle sounds, and then my dagger is in Li's hand. A snarl curls her lips as she spears the blade into Petyr's left hand until the steel is sunk in the earth, and the hilt is flush with his palm.

I go to a knee beside him, and grip his face tightly between my fingers, the movement stifling his shout of agony. "Only one male gets to call me 'love.' If you remember anything in the barrens of the Void, I hope it's the memory of what he's about to do to you for trying to take someone who doesn't belong to you."

I turn his face to look at the approaching male before I release him. Through gasping sobs, he pleads with the Death incarnate taking slow, measured steps towards him. "I-I didn't do nothin' to her! I was ordered to take her–"

"*Silence*," Adathan orders, his voice echoing with the darkness that blackens his veins now. A wet spot grows on the fronts of Petyr's trousers as he sees it, eyes wide with terror.

"W-what are you?"

Another lightning strike hits him in his other leg. When the male stops shuddering on the ground, Atlas says, "That was not a request."

Adathan drops to a knee on the other side of Petyr, and, so slowly, pulls the dagger out of his hand. Petyr's scream grates on my ears, but neither me nor any of our friends in the space around us flinch. Adan cleans the blade on Petyr's shirt, flips it in his grasp, and then holds the hilt out to me.

But, when my hand closes on the pommel, Adan holds fast, and tugs my hand forward until he presses his lips to my knuckles. Only then does he release the dagger, so I may sheath it in its rightful place at my thigh.

Then, looking back at the male, he raises a single finger, lays it on Petyr's cheek, and draws it downwards. In its wake, the flesh turns black–not like Adathan's veins, but like a corpse; desiccated and sunken.

"For the sake of the female you thought you might *take*, I won't draw this out as I would have otherwise. I did make you one promise, though, and I intend to keep it."

Adathan lets the realization dawn on the male, and I'm sure the reek of his fear saturates the small clearing. He only gets out the first syllable of his plea for mercy, then the thing that was Petyr's throat is torn open. Death then lays Petyr's tongue in his own hand, and watches him bleed out through the shredded vessels of his neck.

When the male goes still, his eyes unseeing, Adathan looks up at me with gold eyes rimmed in spiderwebbing capillaries black as pitch. I untuck the tails of my shirt from my trousers, and reach across Petyr's corpse to gently grab Adan's blood-coated hand. I stand, though he remains on a knee, and with the linen I wipe off what I can of the gore. Each swipe reveals blackened veins which steadily recede as my hands tend to his.

Once done, I twine our fingers, and only when I meet his eyes again does Adan rise to his feet. His jaw is tight, but I can see him battling to keep that well-used wall down before me. To not retreat behind it, expecting me to shy away from his darkness. He's taking decades of practiced apathy, and shoving them aside for my days of affirmation.

I raise my hand to his cheek, and say, "Thank you." Before our company, it's all I say, but I know that he can see the rest in my eyes. Thank you for killing for me. For believing in me. For trusting me.

His hand squeezes mine, and he replies, "Always, love."

After a stroke of my thumb over his cheekbone, I drop my hand and turn to our friends. "Thank you. All of you." I meet each of their gazes, now that Ciaragen has let her shadows fall completely. It had been a matter of moments, and of trust. That I would leave and the males would follow, and as soon as they did, Adan had to wake her. Tell her what was happening, and count on her jumping into the role we planned for her.

I hold her gaze, hoping my expression shows how grateful I am since there's still an unattended matter in the clearing with us. She places her fist on her heart, and bows her head, curving her shoulders before straightening. My heart stutters when Lina and Atlas–the remaining Sabriani of our group–replicate the gesture.

I take a steadying breath, then turn to where Javi holds Jacks. The High Lord has water swirling over his hands and arms where they touch the faerie's skin. If Jacks were to use his ice majick, my guess is that water would freeze, right over where one of Javi's hands rests on his heart.

His silver eyes are filled with regret and terror, but no hostility. Pulling Adan along with me–because, even with Javi's majick protecting me, I'm sure being left behind is not something he would tolerate well right now–I stride towards the males.

When I stand before Jacks, I drop Adan's hand, and feel him stand ready behind me. Jacks's silver eyes flick between ours, up and down, until he settles on mine. "I'm sorry, Althea. So sorry." A tear wells up and falls, but I can't tell if it's for the loss he expects from us, or for what his actions could have cost me.

"What did you mean when you said he has your family?" I ask quietly, but not weakly.

"B-back in Obala, months ago, a male named Marcys came to my door with two other males. He asked if I'd been hired as the cook for a ship heading to Dahlih, and when I answered yes, he asked if I would act as spy for him. When–when I said no, the males beat me in front of my mate and our daughter. When they finished, he said if I didn't want the same done to them, and–and worse, then I would spy for him on that ship."

My brow crumpled when he spoke of his beating, and rage lit in my heart at the mention of more violence being threatened against females. Against a *child*. But, I press on. "What did he ask of you, exactly, Jacks?"

He swallows, and another tear falls. "He asked for me to keep an eye out for a female boarding the ship in Dahlih. Said that you would look human, but weren't. If you did, I was to send a message to him in his pocket realm, including where we would be making birth. He said if I did that, and if his males managed to take you from there, they would leave my family alone."

I can feel my male behind me restraining his wrath at the part, however unwilling, it seems Jacks played in my suffering last week. "And when they didn't take me?"

His silver eyes flick up to Adathan's for a heartbeat, probably seeing in his face that careful blankness that has been absent for weeks aboard the ship. Though Jacks continues speaking to me, I'd be willing to bet that he believes he will die regardless of what he says.

"If they failed, I was to stay with the remaining males who were supposed to make sure that it didn't happen again. And... my Lady, I'm sorry for it, but to get them to trust me with their plan, I–I spoke crassly of you."

As darkness flares behind me, and lightning flickers in my periphery, I have only one thought: *gods-damn males.*

"Did it work?" is all I ask.

He nods, though he trembles slightly now. "They told me they were going to try to take you the first night, but that if you didn't give them the opportunity for it, they would send a message in the morning to their lord, requesting him to send more males to ambush our group tomorrow. They would–they would kill whoever they needed to, knock you out, and take you."

Again, power flares on either side of me, and I whirl to them "If you both can't control yourselves, you will wait back at the camp." I look at Atlas first, but settle my eyes on Adan's at the end of my sentence. I see the swirling wrath there pause, and, as he holds my gaze, it's steadily replaced. Not with annoyance, or even indignation at being rebuked by a female, which I've been conditioned to expect in my training for dealing with human men. Instead, what brims in those golden depths now is something that makes my toes curl in the boots he bought me.

Still, I harden my jaw against that reaction, and he nods once in submission. I look back to Atlas, and he does the same.

I turn back to Jacks, whose trembling has now ceased. "Do you have access to this pocket realm?"

"Yes."

"Good."

58

FACTS & POSSIBILITIES

LINA - DAY 35

BY DAWN, EVERYTHING IS SET IN MOTION.

After Tali had burned the bodies of those males and Sione used their wind to blow the pungent smoke up through the canopy of leaves above us, we'd finally gotten some sleep. The female had made her flames burn hot enough to turn even bone to ash; all that is now left of those pieces of shit.

Ciaragen sent a letter to Hielo and Hiela warning them of what Petyr had claimed in his final moments—that a spy is in their castle, awaiting Al's arrival. And now, Jacks is finishing his own letter to Olin–which he addresses to Marcys, as he's not supposed to know who the true master of this orchestration is. Nor that Marcys is dead.

It says that Petyr and Franc were successful last night, and are heading to Oschverre now with Althea. That Adathan is mad with rage and grief, and Ciaragen had to arrest him to keep him contained. He writes the plan Al

472

tells him to: how they're going to Colina to see what the High Lord and High Lady might wish to do about the matter.

After she had asked him if he has access to the pocket realm last night, she had looked to Javi, who still held the faerie male. "I have one need of him in the morning, but otherwise would only like to send him home to his family. However, he's your subject, and your crewmate, not mine. So, come dawn, his fate is yours."

I don't know what the High Lord has decided. He only watches Jacks disappear the finished letter into the pocket realm with lowered brows and crossed arms. When the male turns to him, his head bowed, we all wait in silence for his ruling.

"Harris," he calls, not turning to look at the male as he addresses him. Harris hadn't woken with the rest of us when Adathan roused Ciaragen last night. Heavy sleeper, or maybe just sensed the tension and decided to stay out of it. I'm leaning towards the latter, given that he hasn't so much as asked about the whereabouts of the two males who had accompanied him yesterday.

"Aye, Captain?" he replies now, stepping up, a few feet away from Jacks's side.

"I'll give you twenty gold marks to travel with Jacks to his home, and ensure his family is indeed safe. If not, take five and hire someone to help you dispose of the males keeping them captive. Will the remainder after your travels be sufficient for you to do this task with the honor I should expect from my crew?"

"A-aye, Captain," he repeats, eyes wide at the large sum being offered to him. Even if he spends a quarter of the amount on his way to Obala–unlikely–he will have enough to support himself and his family through at least half a year without work. And that's to say nothing of the wages he earned for the months on the *Burning Rose*.

Javi dips his chin in acknowledgement, then says to Jacks, "You are pardoned for any espionage committed aboard my ship for the sake of your family's safety. As the Princess of Weaschte and Lady of Sabrian has pardoned you as well for any offense to her, you are free to go."

Jacks gasps in a shuddering sob, and bows deeply to Javi. "Th-thank you, High Lord." He pivots, still with his back to the sky. "Your Highness. Thank you."

Al's eyes have a bit of a shine to them when she nods, accepting his thanks. Not ten minutes later, Jacks and Harris are packed and on their mounts. With only a bow from their saddles, they head south for Obala.

As soon as they disappear from view, the rest of us find ourselves standing around the camp. There's a look passed from person to person as we all realize: that's it. The week of stress and uncertainty is done. No one will come out of the bushes to accost us. No one is in immediate danger.

My eyes are on Tali's when I catch motion in my periphery. I look just in time to see Al sink to the ground, and put her head in her hands. Her dark hair falls in a curtain around her, covering her face from view.

Of course. This danger may have passed, but change hasn't. Not for her. Weeks and weeks of event after event, and yet there's more to come. We may be heading home, but she is still in greatly unfamiliar territory, with our final destination being only a stop for her. A stop, where she will be forced to meet the people who want to call themselves her mother and father, when the people who raised her still hold those titles.

Adathan crouches beside her, his expression set with the same compassion I'm sure mine has. The rest of us stand there for a moment, allowing her to gather herself—until footsteps crunch over the leaf-strewn earth. Ciaragen closes the distance quickly, and when she stops in front of Al, she says, "Get up."

The growl that rumbles in Adathan's chest is echoed; Tali and Atlas both finding offense to the gruffness of her words. But Al looks up at my godmother, no anger to be found in her bright eyes.

"You will get up, and you will go on. This moment you're taking to collect yourself will be gone too quickly, and you will still not feel prepared at its end. I know it's a lot. I know how much is left. But you will *get up*, because you *can*, Althea." Then she holds out a hand. Because yes, she can. But she doesn't have to do it alone.

Al's jaw sets, and her eyes harden with determination. She reaches up, and takes the offering to get to her feet. Once there, the females don't release each other. They lock eyes, and when Al nods, Ciaragen returns the gesture, and moves to release her hand.

But Al holds fast, and over the course of a few heartbeats, Ciaragen's brows scrunch, then relax, her deep blue eyes softening. Then, their hands are at each other's backs as they embrace, the general's cheek pressed to the lady's brow.

When they part, the air in the campsite has lightened, along with the area itself as the sun continues to rise. "To Colina, then," Al says.

Ciaragen grins at her. "To Colina."

⇔

By midday, even the trees can't keep the summer from infiltrating the forest. Sweat runs down my back and chest, despite the fact that I'd changed into shorts, along with the rest of the females, during our last break to water the horses. Then we'd done possibly the girliest thing we could do, and formed a braid chain; Al braided my hair, Tali hers, and Ciaragen ended the line. Her already-braided hair is tied back with a strip of leather, though I can see, where she rides ahead of me, that her shirt is soaked just like mine.

I take another sip of water, clenching my thighs around Wynonna to keep from wobbling on her back with no hand on the reins. Luckily, she stays at her steady stroll, not taking the movement to be an indication to pick up her pace.

Sione ruffles their wings, which sends a rush of cool air my way. They'd tried using their wind to cool me earlier, but anything stronger than a light breeze only blows the hot air around, and I'd told them to conserve their energy because I didn't mind sweating.

Now, I regret my earlier confidence in my ability to be uncomfortably hot for an extended period of time. Even if every so often those wings or the air around me will stir, and make the heat bearable for a few minutes. And since I'm too proud to admit I was wrong, instead I occasionally turn in my saddle to look at them, riding beside me, and stick my tongue out.

This time, though, they make a face in response. "Ugh. I just thought about last night."

I quickly reel my tongue back into my mouth, knowing exactly what they're referring to. "Yeah, I didn't know tongues went, like, down your throat."

"The more you know." They tilt their head, then angle it towards Al over their shoulder without looking away from the path ahead. "You'd know about that, though, being a healer and all?"

There's a dark humor in her tone when she simply replies, "Yes."

"Any other weird facts you'd like to share with the class?"

The smile in her voice grows. "Hmm. Well, on the topic of tongues, their prints are as unique as fingerprints."

Sione pauses. "Okay, you followed the assignment, but I don't like the way you did it. Pick another one–*not* about tongues. Weirdo."

She laughs now, and a grin lifts my own lips in response. "Alright. Well, the-erm–" Al says something to Adathan in Ceraschen, and he gives her the word in Divani. "Yes, the stomach *acid* is strong enough to dissolve metal."

"No way," Sione says. "So, if I, for example, ate a tiny knife, I would be okay?"

"If it were entirely made of metal, yes, though you might want to see if you're okay in other ways if it occurs to you to eat a knife."

It's their turn to laugh, and everyone joins in, having stopped whatever respective conversations they'd been having to listen to Al's answer to Sione's question. "What's another one?" Atlas asks from the head of the group beside Ciaragen.

She thinks for a second. "If you laid all the vessels in your body end-to-end, they would be about sixty-thousand miles long."

"Fuck off," Tali scoffs.

"It's true! What else...the body has over six-hundred muscles, but your heart is the only one that never gets tired."

Another pause. "Well, that's poetic as fuck," Sione murmurs.

Al giggles again, this one lighter. "Are you surprised? We compose and write and create. We are poems brought to life."

This silence is slightly longer, everyone thinking, perhaps a little stunned, by something we've never considered. Then Tali says, "Shit, Aly. I think I'm in love with you now, too."

⇔

By the time the sun is setting, my shirt is almost see-through with the amount I've sweat throughout the day. Luckily, given his proclivity for water, Javi was able to lead us to a campsite fairly close to a stream where we take turns washing. No one is allowed to go alone, though, so when the males offer for a group of females to go first, all four of us leave. The only hesitation was in Al stealing a kiss from Adathan before lightly jogging until she was beside me, following Ciaragen and Tali into the trees.

She did seem stunned, though, when we all began to strip at the stream's edge, laying our clean clothes atop a saddle blanket Ciaragen had thought to bring, and our dirty ones in heaps on the forest floor. She joins us slowly, pulling her shirt over her head and her trousers down, folding them neatly before her blush deepens. Fully naked myself now, I go to the stream, knowing Tali and Ciaragen are both keeping ears and eyes out on the woods around us, so she can choose to fully bare herself or not in peace.

The water is only a few feet deep, but it's clean and cool, so I sit on a rock worn smooth by the constant flow. I moan, and tilt my head back at the sensation of it running around me, ridding my skin of the thin layer of salt that coats my every pore. I cup water in my hand, and splash it over my face again and again until even the front of my hair is soaking. That's the last to be rinsed, and when I'm done lathering the water everywhere that needs freshening, I stand.

Tali and Ciaragen are sitting on the saddle blanket, air drying with their heads tipped back, soaking in the orange streams of sunshine coming through the canopy of leaves overhead. Al is wringing out the length of her raven hair into the stream, the sculpted length of her on full display from behind. I move to join my other friends on the blanket, impressed that she forwent her underclothes after decades of forced modesty.

"The males are probably wondering what's taking us so long," I point out as I sit.

"A tragedy," Tali laments, her eyes still closed.

"How ever will they cope?" Ciaragen wonders, crossing her ankles in front of her.

"The world may never know," I answer, shrugging one shoulder, and the other females hum in agreement.

After a few minutes, though, the sun begins to dim by a fraction, and we decide to have mercy on those waiting back at camp. Dressed, we make our way back through the woods, Ciaragen leading the way, likely following our own scents.

They haven't been idle in our absence. A fire is going, with a few rabbits already on the spit. Our bedrolls are set up, our bags laying next to them. Sione is leaning against an oak, their wings flared out on either side as they play an easy tune on their guitar. Javi, Adathan, and Atlas stand from their spots by the fire, and hand us filled water skins.

"Any hot water left?" Atlas asks over his shoulder as he makes his way into the woods.

"Nah. I'd ask Tali to warm it for you, but wouldn't want her to have to gouge her eyes out after."

"That's fair."

I chuckle as he disappears into the trees, and hear Al urge Addie to join him, Javi already on his tail, and Sione moving from their spot by the tree. They come up to me, and hold out the guitar. "Watch this for me, moonshine," they say, pressing it to my front as they pass with a wink, not giving me a choice. Therefore also not giving me a choice but to prod their ass with the butt of the guitar before turning away with enough speed that my still-wet hair flares around me.

I can feel their eyes on me, though, as warm as the russet shade of them. I don't turn back around; instead I hook my elbow under the neck of the guitar, and strum with my fingers to the rhythm of the steps I take away from them. Only when I hear the rustling of leaves underfoot as they finally go to follow the males do I twist to look over my shoulder.

To find them doing the same. In the instant before they disappear behind the same copse of trees as Atlas, the corner of their mouth tilts up, and my pulse with it.

59

EVERYTHING

THEA - DAY 35

THIS JOURNEY THROUGH THE WOODS IS SO DIFFERENT FROM MY last.

It's more than the fact that it's oak and walnut that surrounds us rather than pines. Greater than travelling with several people on horseback, instead of on foot with only Adan. Even more than the power that sleeps in my chest, humming through my veins.

In Cerasche, it had been real; I had the conviction to make this journey to kill Olin, even if it was with a male I'd hated at the time. I had nightmares about my loved ones dying, and dreams about bleeding the life from the male who killed them.

Now, those same images come to me in my sleep, but they are not accompanied with the hopelessness they had been then. I no longer crave my own end after I achieve my goal. I look around at this world, and wish to continue living in it.

Living in it, alongside these people that I hadn't known that first day I'd trekked through the pines. Some of them I didn't know at all, and others not truly.

The general I had misunderstood.

A friend, even through deceit, danger, and desire.

A captain who took me in, no questions asked.

A female who understood my pain. A faerie who made me feel seen in this new world.

A sister in fate.

And the male who's been with me through it all.

In that forest of pines, I'd made him to be my enemy. My angry, grieving mind incapable of understanding that I *wanted* to look at him, *wanted* to heal him. Not out of him being the only person there, or out of some sort of debt. But because his pain was mine; *he* was *mine*.

There is no reason, no logic to how strongly I feel for him. There is no rationality to being in love with him, even though I hated him barely more than a month ago. But, I don't need there to be.

I just need him.

Adan sits on a stump behind me, while I sit on the ground with my shoulders between his legs, and his fingers working through the lengths of my hair. Between his touch, the laughter around me, and my full belly, I'm able to observe the beast of power that occasionally stretches within me like a great cat. To rest with it, rather than battle it. In the time that I stood naked in the stream, my feet planted in the land while the life of it flowed around me, I *felt* the power shift, noting the absence of my fear of and hostility towards it. And, in that shift, we found contentment.

Content. A strange thing to be in a strange land, but easy to understand in this moment. The iron gone from my blood, leaving each of my powers to their devices. Surrounded by friends. And my male's hands on me, his heart thrumming steadily at my back.

Our group sits in a circle around a crackling fire which offers the warmth lost from the sunken sun. Sione strums their guitar quietly, leaned up against a thick tree trunk, their wings spread wide across the ground behind them.

Atlas is telling a story of being a boy in these woods with his fathers, his face alight with the memory. Lina listens to our friend, interjecting at points, since she'd accompanied them for part of that particular trip with her mums. He rolls his eyes when she tells him that he actually *didn't* win the lizard contest–wherein they each caught and released as many of the tiny things as they could, and made their parents keep count. She claims she had seventeen, and he sixteen, and he insists the opposite, grinning all the while. Only when she sticks her tongue out at him do we know who's right.

I manage to laugh with the others. But, in my heart, I ache as I watch the male I turned away speak. Selfish–it's so selfish of me to wish I didn't have to choose. To struggle, even a little bit, with the decision I made weeks ago, and the one I made today. The latter unknown even to the male I've made it for.

He has given all of himself to me. It's my turn to give all of myself to him.

It will make me happy–which is actually an understatement. If not for the hurt stemming from the male across the fire, I would be so overjoyed that Adan would have to tether me to the ground to keep me from flying on the high of my choice. Just as he said to me when he poured his heart at my feet: being his is the best thing I could be. I *want* to belong to him. I want the future I once resented with *him*.

It's only that, in a castle a sea and an eternity away, I had once thought the same thing about the male whose stormy eyes now meet mine over the flames.

I avert my gaze, my cheeks heating, but I feel his linger for a moment, as much as I can feel the warmth of the fire on my skin. When it lifts, its absence is just as tangible. Much colder, though.

Still, I've made my choice. I know what I'm going to do tonight. I'm *ready* for it, in my heart, my soul, in my very bones. It will make me so happy that...perhaps it will not be such a hard thing to add a new grief onto the others. The grief for what might have been, quashed by the joy of what has found me instead.

After a few more stories from the Eshellens around me, scattered yawns have all of us heading to our bedrolls for our last sleep before we reach Colina. I lay facing Adathan while new logs crackle in the fire, almost covering the sound of someone's light snores. He holds me to his chest, and I can tell the even rhythm of his breath is not faked this time. I pull my head back to look up at him one more time before things change again. His face is softer in sleep, full lips parted, and no tightness in the hard angle of his jaw. Soft in one place, strong in others, I find myself transfixed by all of it.

I made a promise to myself, though. And, while my heart pounds at knowing now is the time to carry it out, it's not with nerves, or fear. *I am ready*, its thudding says.

I raise a slightly trembling hand to his cheek, and run my thumb over the stubbled expanse. "Adan," I whisper, because I don't think he put a sound shield around us tonight.

His eyes open slowly, and his arms pull me closer than they'd held me in rest. "Thea, love?" he asks, a little groggy, and I *almost* second guess myself, *almost* tell myself it can wait.

But no. Because we don't know what tomorrow will hold. And, honestly, I don't want to wait.

"I–I need to show you something."

I don't know if it's the stutter, or the otherwise determined tone of my words, but any tiredness leaves him. He nods, and presses his lips to my forehead before standing with far more grace than a male of his size should have. He takes my hand to help me to my feet, then squeezes it; a silent request for me to lead the way.

I let the land guide me. I might not be able to do anything with the power I can feel flowing beneath my feet, but as I'd finally allowed the majick of the land *in* instead of rejecting it... when I'd asked something of it, it had answered.

It leads me now to that place where the world falls away. A cave, about a mile from our camp. I find it with ease, Adan following me without question or hesitation. Leaves and twigs crunch softly beneath my feet until they touch stone instead.

Within, the sound of water trickling. Around a dark bend, still trusting my feet–as Adathan showed me back in Cerasche, and as this land requests I continue to do now. Soft blue-green light emanates towards the end of the curve, and when we emerge, I gasp softly at what I find. Releasing Adan's hand, I walk, transfixed, deeper into the cave.

A shimmering pool sits off left of center, the bioluminescence within it turning the water a deep, glimmering teal. Several thin streams of water trickle into it, all along gleaming obsidian rock. That same otherworldly glitter shines like blue and green stars on the cave walls, interrupted here and there by vining plants, fed by the constant water. Night-blooming flowers grow in lush patches where they were too stubborn even for the rock. They fill the moist air with their gentle, sweet scents.

I don't hear him follow, but I feel him. His presence, and his eyes on me. The curiosity at why we're here, mixed in with the constant love and desire, all mingling with a stunned awe at the space around us.

"You've told me a half-truth," I say softly as I turn to him.

He's just feet away, and in the light I can see a bit of confusion enter his sun-gold gaze. I take a step towards him. "You said you belong to me. But, you left out the second bit." Another step, and I'm just inches from him, my face tilted to look up into his. "The part about how I belong to you, too."

His heart squeezes hard in his chest, and then picks up in pace as his pupils flare, and his lips part. "Thea," he says slowly, his rough voice rumbling even deeper with restraint. "I need you to tell me what you mean."

"You already know," I murmur, but don't touch him. Not yet. "You are mine, and I am yours. Sweetheart, Thea, love–call me whatever you wish, so long as one of the things you call me when we leave this cave is: mate."

I feel a rush of emotion from him, so powerful that it sweeps me up in its tides, carrying me into his black, sun-gilded sea. "Thea–I–how–" for the first time, he seems unable to think of words sufficient enough for the thoughts and feelings coursing through him.

"Ciaragen told me what a mate was last week, and I knew right away that you are mine. I was a coward to not admit to it, holding onto the kind of love that was all I'd known before. But I don't want to love you with limitations, Adan. I want to love you completely, in every way my heart and soul are capable of. I'm sorry I let you be alone in it for longer than you had been already. If you'll have me...it would be my greatest joy to be your mate." I look between his eyes, waiting with bated breath, my heart thundering.

My wait isn't long.

"Thea," he breathes, and then his arms are around me, lifting me from the ground as he crushes his lips to mine. I wrap my arms around his neck, and hook my ankles behind his back, his lips moving urgently with mine all the while. Like my kiss is the air he breathes, my touch his heartbeat, my life his soul, and without any of them, he would cease to be. His fingers thread through my hair, his other hand tight against my ribs. He slips his tongue in my mouth, and swallows the sound I make.

When I lean back, he lets me, trailing kisses across my jaw. They halt when my hands grab the hem of my shirt. He gives me enough room to pull it over my head, supporting me with that arm banded behind my waist, and when I drop my shirt to the ground, my bare breasts gleam softly with the blue-green glow of the cave. He takes them in for a moment, ragged breaths caressing my naked skin. The fingers of his free hand trail over a slope, his thumb brushing over the hardened peak, and I gasp softly at the sensation.

His eyes move to mine, and he cups me brazenly, his hand warm and calloused around my breast. With one arm, he hikes me higher up on his torso, and, still watching me, he sucks my nipple into his mouth. My eyes close, rolling back a bit, and my fingers go into his hair as his tongue circles and flicks the taut bud. When he bites it softly, I arch further into him. I nearly cry out in complaint when he releases me, but he only switches to my other breast, giving it the same devotion.

I'm panting, achy, wet, and ready by the time he trails his mouth from my nipple to my jaw, then sucks on the skin over my hammering pulse. His hand squeezes one more time, wringing another gasp from me.

He reads what I want, though. What I need. And sets me down slowly, my body trailing over his until my feet touch the ground. I grip his shirt, and slide it up his torso, my hands skimming every muscle and mark on their way up, until he needs to take over to pull it over his head, and toss it to the floor. With my fingers, I trace every beautiful scar I encounter as I circle my left hand around to his side. He pulls his arm back obligingly, revealing the two-inch scar from the first time I harmed him. I lean in, and press my lips to it. Next, I find the one on his abdomen, remembering how it had felt to have his blood spill over my hand as I trail my tongue up the scar's length. The muscles of his stomach heave with his breath, and I feel a shudder wrack his spine.

My fingers don't tremble this time when I reach for his trousers. My eyes on his, heart wrenching at the all-consuming love in his eyes, I grip the buttons, working down over the erection that strains against the fabric. As I bend, and he steps out of them, I spot the scar on his hip from when he jumped with me into the sea, and I kiss that one, too. His cock twitches against my shoulder.

I want to move my lips to the left, and wrap them around him–understand how it might feel to pleasure him with *my* mouth–but later. I straighten, and pull the waistband of his underwear out and down, circling until I touch his ass, skimming the flesh with my fingernails. When Adathan stands naked before me, I can't help but run my hands down his stomach, fingertips tracing the vee of muscle at its bottom.

He shivers, but, slowly enough that it's clear he's *still* ready for me to need him to stop, he loops his fingers into my trousers. He's seen me naked from the waist down–intimately so–but this feels different. And so I understand why his hands are measured and gentle as he works them, and my undergarment off.

Bared to each other, I take him in, as he does with me. His eyes are awed, reverent, as they look me over, inch by inch. Such passion in their depths, like I am the very center of his universe; like, without me, his world would be nothing but darkness. I've seen it in his eyes before, but never so plainly as he lets it shine through now. Always, my needs had come first; what he wanted, or even *needed* was secondary.

I know the first time will hurt; by the size of him, probably more than I'm truly prepared for. But I'm not afraid, or even worried about that. I want this, I want *him*. So, I move to my tiptoes, laying my hands on his bare, inked and scarred skin, and kiss him. His cock pokes my belly, and I feel it leave a bead of wetness behind.

"I'm ready, Adan," I say against his lips, and his hands on my waist tighten for a beat. Then, one goes to the back of my neck, cradling my head, while the other scoops below my backside, behind my thighs. He holds me, and I bend with him while he takes a knee, and then lays me gently on a shallow bed of moonflowers. He settles over me, and I open for him naturally, like we were always meant to fit like this.

My eyes hold his, and our breaths collide in the air between us. Braced on an elbow, that hand caresses the side of my face, while the other goes down, between us. I look, to find him adjusting, readying for the perfect angle–

"Eyes on mine, love," he says. I lift my gaze back to his, and feel him nudge against my entrance. His breath stutters, but he waits for me. My needs, always first. My own breath stutters a bit as it leaves me, but I nod, nothing but certainty in my heart.

"I need you to say it, Thea." Adathan's body trembles with restraint, but his hand on my face and his eyes on mine are patient. Gentle. "I can't do this if you don't tell me yes."

"Yes, Adan. I want this; I want *you*. Yes."

A shaking sigh caresses my face, and he gives me a light kiss. Another, and a third even more soft and hesitant; hardly the weight of a feather against my lips. He pulls back by inches to look into my eyes, and then I feel the broad head of his cock slide into me. I gasp at the stretch my body is already forced to make around him, my fingers digging into his back. His pupils take up the whole of his irises, his breathing is labored, but still he waits until my hands relax before continuing. His lids flutter as he takes me deeper, and again he pauses for me to adjust. But I know there is so much left. And I want it all.

I pull him against and into me, and, unprepared, he sinks in further with an oath, the pleasure of me around him making his lip pull between his teeth, even as he looks to see if I'm hurt.

The pressure and stretch of him inside me is intense, and I know that, any further, there will be pain. But, with him...I want that hurt. I want it, because I *need* him. I don't fear the moment's pain, because after, I have an immortal lifetime of pleasure awaiting me.

Seeing that in my eyes, perhaps hearing it from my heart, he pushes past that barrier of resistance within me. I gasp in and cry out, pain shattering in my core, and his brows furrow, such love in his gaze. "I know, I know, love. You're doing so well. I need you to relax for me, Thea." His thumb strokes my cheek, the other hand leaving his cock now to caress my waist. I breathe with him, a slow, deep breath, and on the exhale, I feel my inner muscles loosen a bit. "That's my girl." With a shift of his hips, I shout in both pleasure and pain as that final barrier comes fully undone at last.

"You're doing so good, love." With a kiss to my cheek, he pushes in a bit more, using the tightness of my hands and the looseness of my breaths to guide each inch of him into me.

The pain begins to subside, replaced by such–*fullness*. So full of him–my love, my Death. My mate.

I tilt my hips up, claiming another inch. Adan grunts, and, with one last look into my eyes, into my very soul, he sinks the remaining distance into me until his hips are flush with mine.

I'm breathing heavy, and so is he. He remains still for several pounding heartbeats, allowing me to adjust to the sheer size of him within me. His parted lips skim over my cheeks, my lids, my nose, brushing so delicately that I shiver, and relax further.

Then, so slowly, my name a whisper between us, he begins to move. My hands against his back soften, and a sigh escapes me, because this feels *right*. As the pain clears completely, I realize: him inside me, filling me, isn't good–it's fucking *great*. His next thrust is longer, deeper, and I move my hips with his on an instinct I never would have thought I'd have.

"Gods, that's it, Thea." Another thrust, and I move with him again. Adan pushes a bit harder, a bit faster, and not only do I not feel pain anymore, but I start to feel that now-familiar tightening in my lower belly.

I tilt my chin up, and capture his lips with mine, tracing the scars along his spine with my fingers. His strokes become more languid, no more hesitation or worry of hurting me to keep him any longer. We move together, a whole different kind of pleasure than his mouth, or hands on me. This is *us*, this is him and I, thrust for thrust, sharing breath and heat and sweat. We feel good *together*.

Adan rolls his hips, getting me closer to that edge. "You feel so perfect around my cock, sweetheart," he pants against my lips, and *gods*, the praise, combined with the name... Thrust, "*So–*" thrust, "*fucking–*" thrust, "*perfect.*"

I shatter, my release electrifying me. My fingers dig into his back, and as we continue to move, my hips swirling with his, it draws out my climax around him. It feels so good that I clutch his muscled ass, pulling him and grinding my hips against his. He curses as my inner walls pulse around his length, his hand so wonderfully tight on my hip.

"Fuck, Thea," he groans when my orgasm subsides. "I almost came inside you."

"I took the tonic again while you bathed," I gasp while he resumes his tortuous rhythm. I put as much certainty into the unfamiliar words I say next as he does into every gods-damn thing he says about me. "I want to feel what it's like to have your cum fill me, Adan."

"*Fuck.*" His hips slam into mine, and I'd known he was still holding back a bit no matter how fucking *exquisite* it felt, but I didn't realize how much. Our flesh slaps together, each thrust running so deep, and I feel a strange bliss at knowing how sore I'll be in the morning–knowing I won't want to heal myself of this pleasuring pain. My feet move up from his hips to his waist, tilting and taking him until I can't feel anything that *isn't* Adathan. That isn't his cock ramming into me, his body against mine, my name on his lips.

I feel something else rise then. Infinitely more beautiful and promising even than that edge he's driving me to again. I know he feels it, too, this thing that always was but now threads between us, shining so that I can finally see it. Adathan's eyes hold mine, full of wonder, his thrusts slowing as I seize my end of that bond. Always. It has *always* been there, and at last it's tethered together the souls that once wandered the universe in search of each other. Brighter than a million stars, warmer than the sun, vaster than that very universe.

It is infinite. It is everything. *He* is everything.

Now, it's not just that bond but his eyes that are shining, and I feel my own tears trickle down my temples.

"Mate," he says at last, dipping his brow to mine, thrusting deep and true at the same moment. "My mate."

My heart feeling at once full to bursting, and like it's come undone into a million little pieces that all belong to this male, I tilt my head back to kiss his lids, and the wetness on his lashes coat my lips. He continues to move in me, and I with him, our pace picking up, giving and demanding. That cliff approaches again, different somehow than before; monumental and life-altering. "Adan," I gasp.

"Together, then, love." His hand squeezes my hip, and he

presses a hard kiss to my lips. His teeth grab my bottom lip, and when they release it, he orders, "Get those eyes on mine."

I open my lids, and the combination of his fevered gaze with him pounding within me sends me over the edge again. And, this time, he goes over it with me.

I feel him pulsing inside me, as I do around him, and I know what he asked, but it's not my brain that rules my next act. It is primal, and absolute, and I need to do it right *now*, as he begins to spill inside me, gasping my name.

I lean my face up and into him, and sink my canines into the muscle above his collar bone. His blood spreads across my tongue, and as he growls his approval, his seed filling me, all of it feeling so incredibly and unexpectedly good that one climax leads right into another, his hand cradles my head, holding my face there.

A lifetime and a moment later, he stills, breathing hard, and plants kisses on the top of my head while he curses me, and murmurs things that make me want him again already. I only hook my legs tighter around him in answer, holding him inside me. When I remove my teeth from his skin, I lick the twin puncture wounds, and swallow the essence of him.

I move one hand from his back to grab the edge of his hard jaw, and tilt his face down, until our eyes meet. Then, with a certainty bred of love, our joined bodies, and the taste of his blood on my tongue, I say, "You're *mine*."

60

A THOUSAND YEARS & ON

MY MIND IS SPINNING, THE WORDS SPILLING FROM MY LIPS—PRAISE for her, love for her, everything for *her*—coming without thought. Only the need to somehow begin to express all that runs through me, as she tightens her legs around my waist, and removes her teeth from my neck.

I'm still trying to piece myself together from how she's fucking *wrecked* me when her hand, soft and forceful, grips my face, tilting it to look down at her. Her freckled cheeks are flushed and damp, full lips parted to reveal the pink that stains the points of her canines. Yet none of that compares to the look in her miraculous eyes when she says, "You're *mine*."

My hold on her tightens, and she gasps softly when the movement pushes me more firmly inside her. "I am yours." I always have been. From the moment our souls formed in the universe, to the day I fell in love with her. From a dark basement where *my* soul left my own body and gave itself to her while she stared at me with murder in her eyes. To her asking me, again and again, to stay with her. From the day she told me she loved me, too. And to now, when the other end of the bond that has been within me, billowing in the maelstrom of my life before her, at last was grasped. She bound me to her, undaunted and utterly certain, and pulled me out of the storm.

I dip my head down to kiss her, and her fingers again find the scars on my back, and worship them. "I love you," I breathe against her mouth.

"I love you," she replies, easily and earnestly. "Deeply, truly, irrevocably, I love you."

My brow furrows with the depth of emotion only she could ever evoke from me, and I kiss her again, those words I said to her days and a lifetime ago sealing between our skin.

Because I have no intention of this being the last time I'm inside her tonight, I find the strength to reach behind myself, and unlatch her ankles from my waist. As I pull out of her, I kiss my way down her neck, and pull her nipple between my lips, giving it soft love with my tongue. Her sighing breath heaves her breasts against my face, and I almost lose my motivation to move us from this spot–but not quite. More primal even than the desire to rut is my need to take care of her. In more ways than one, but the first is to find my shirt, and tear off a scrap of it to clean her.

I can tell she tries not to, but when my cloth-wrapped fingers run over her swollen flesh, she gasps quietly at the discomfort. My other hand running up and down her thigh, I work as gently as I can. The fabric comes away with some of my seed, and more of her blood.

"It's okay," she says when my jaw tightens. She moves slowly to her knees before me, takes the soiled linen from my hand, and tosses it into a dark corner where not even I can see it. She takes my face between her hands, and I rest mine on her hips.

"More than okay. That was...more than I ever could have imagined, Adan. More than I could have ever wished for." Her fingers trail down my neck, to rest over my pounding heart. "It was everything. *You* are everything."

I lean into her, bowing my head to press my lips to hers. Soft, warm, and inviting, she sighs and wraps her arms loosely around my neck. Swiftly enough that she squeals a bit, and giggles against my mouth after, I sweep my arms around and under her, and stand with her cradled within them. As I told her to do what feels like so long ago, I use only my senses to walk us into the warm pool within the cave.

The water isn't deep–it reaches my torso, and, when I set her down, the gentle ripples play with the skin below her breasts. I know Thea enjoys this; being smaller than me. I wouldn't have cared if she were my height or taller, but walking the line of making her feel both precious *and* powerful has been one of my favorite balances.

I place my arm behind her shoulder blades. "Lean back for me, love," I direct quietly. With a small smile, she tilts backwards until her hair streams through the water behind her, her breasts arched to the ceiling, gleaming with the blue-green light of this space she found for us. I place my hand on the scar between them, and stroke it lightly with my thumb before skimming my hand over one perfect slope, to her collar bone. Up the line of her neck, knuckles brushing her cheek. Finally, my fingers in her hair, pulling free the leaves and petals of the moonflowers woven through the strands.

She makes that incredible humming sound, her eyes closed and her mouth pulled into a soft, gorgeous smile. "Remember when you did this for me in the woods of Dahlih?"

I gently knead the base of her neck. "It was the first time you allowed me to touch you outside of escaping danger." I remember making the offer to help her wash her hair without thinking–cursing myself as soon as it was past my lips. Knowing she would reject it, and not comprehend what would make me even ask such a thing. But, as she has made a habit of doing, she surprised me. "You bowed back, your body so like this over that pool, and it took all of my willpower to stop when your hair was clean. To let it be enough as the locks slipped through my fingers, and not stroke them down your body, as I wished to."

Her eyes opened as I spoke, and she straightens now, the thick blanket of her hair covering my arm. "It was the first time I realized I wanted to look at you," she confesses, her gaze on her hand while it trails over my chest. "Not just see you, or heal you. I saw your body, and your scars, and I thought how beautiful it all was. I was too stubborn to allow myself to look more, as I wished to. If I had, maybe I would have seen what this was sooner."

I stroke her cheek, trailing it back to tuck her soaking raven hair behind the barely pointed ear. "You had plenty on your mind without adding this to it. I would have waited weeks, months, years. A century, or a millennium. Even if this never became all that it is now, I would have been happy to just be by your side. And, if eventually it came to pass, it would have always been worth the wait–however long."

Green eyes flit between mine, silent for a moment. Then she breathes, "The things you say. I never imagined I'd hear such things spoken about me."

My knuckles skim the smooth skin over her collarbone. "I've never been much of a talker, Thea. I've been silent, or sullen, for most of my life. But, talking with you...it's one of my favorite things in the world–and the rest all pertain to you as well. I look forward to a thousand years of making sure you know it. Of making sure you never go a day without knowing how incredible you are."

Silver lines her eyes, and she reaches to wrap her arms around my shoulders. I hug her to me, burying my face in the side of her neck, and inhaling her scent. The combination of it, with her body pressed so tightly against mine, stirs my cock beneath the water. She hums again, and her fingers twine with the ends of the hair at my nape while she writhes a bit against me.

No further encouragement needed, I scoop one arm under her ass, and lift her off the stone floor of the pool to carry her to a natural bench towards its shallows. When I set her down on it, her legs open for me, her hands skimming over my traps and shoulders, to clutch my biceps. When I pull back from her neck to look into her eyes, I find in them only love and desire, certain and passionate. So, without words, I sheathe myself inside her in one, swift thrust.

She cries out, but not in pain, and the feel of her around me has my hands clutching her thighs, and my eyes rolling back into my head. "Who needs the fucking Heavens when I can have you wrapped around me?" I growl, pulling out to the tip, and taking her again.

"Gods, Adan," she moans, her fingers gripping my arms. My next thrust practically lifts her from the bench, and I feel a savage pleasure in watching her take me so well.

"My mate. Fucking made for me," I growl as I push in again, and I watch her *smile* in the midst of it, at my words. Those lips, those eyes and the look in them have my thrusts going deeper, harder. I palm her breast, and look down between us while I knead it to the sound of her moans. I could have climaxed at just the sight of my cock disappearing into her. "Look at us, sweetheart," I tell her, and she tilts her chin to peer through the clear, illuminated water.

Her walls clench around as she watches me drive into her, deep and slow, and a one-beat, throaty chuckle comes from her when I curse at the sensation. So, of course, she does it again. I grip her hips, and hold her solidly against my base while I bend my mouth to her ear. "If you think I'm going to let you make me come inside you before I get you to come around my cock, you are mistaken, love."

To which she replies: "Prove it."

She clenches around me at the same time that she bucks her hips in my hands. We both moan at the feeling, but matching, wicked smirks pull at our mouths after. Her eyes widen in excited surprise when I lean her back against the wall, cushioning her spine with my hand against the rock. With one knee braced on the bench, her leg thrown over mine, my thrusts are punishing. Fast, and hard, I take her and she takes me, pulsing around me, those delicious sounds ripping their way up her arched throat.

I know I'm winning when her brows furrow, the utter lost bliss replaced by the concentration on the pleasure rising within her. She knows it, too, but doesn't seem about to protest. As a final measure, I move one hand between us, and press my thumb to her clit. I circle only twice, feeling her clench around me, listening to her panted moans–

Her shouts of pleasure and my name echo around the cave. The feeling of her coming around me, the way her pussy works my cock...

Reeling in the gods-damn beast that tells me to forget everything and just *fuck* and *take*, I press a kiss to her temple, and say, "I'm close, Thea. So close. But I need–I *need* to claim you as you claimed me."

Her fingers soften, and move from my arms to stroke my hair. "Sink your teeth into me, and call me yours, Adan," she breathes my words from yesterday into my ear before biting down on the arch.

I shudder, and the primal part of me takes over the male,

only giving me the mercy of holding onto enough sanity that I won't scare her. Still, I *fuck* her now, driving into her with an intensity that I might have waited for until she'd had more time to get used to this, to get used to me. But she meets me, thrust for thrust, and when I feel the edge, she does, too. Her hands move from my hair to my back and, as she moans my name, I feel her nails sink into me and score the skin over my scars.

My release hits, and I bite down hard on the side of her neck as it does. As her blood coats my tongue, and my cum fills her, the effect is so powerful that I think the very earth around us shakes. She locks her legs around me, and my hands grip her, pulling her up and down my cock until every drop of me is spent inside her, and I hold her to me at that moment. Shudders of pleasure wrack my spine, and her fingers stroke down it, so gentle and trusting.

I pull my teeth from her, but can't yet bear to pull my cock out of her. I kiss the puncture wounds left by my canines, the animal part of my brain giving way to the male once more. I loosen my hands, and move them to wrap one arm around her waist, and place the other hand on the back of her head. I part from her only enough to look into her eyes, and give her the words I've held in since I gripped her hands in a training yard across the sea.

"You are *mine*, Thea. My every thought, my very heartbeat. My reason for existence. My mate."

"I am yours," she agrees, her eyes shining once more.

It settles between us, more vividly and forcefully than even before. We are claimed, marked, and taken. And so those brushes of emotion I could always feel from her, and those thoughts that I could make out in her eyes–they come to true fruition now.

I'm swept away by not just *my* love for *her*, but for all that she's feeling for me in this moment. Her mind curls around mine, even with our shields up, because what is the use of them in the face of each other, anyway? I am hers, and she is mine. I will spend the rest of my days with her; loving her, talking with her, being inside her. And, even after a thousand years, it still will not be enough.

I'll never get enough of her. Her smiles, her touch, her laugh, her words. The sounds she makes around me: a spectrum of contentment just in having me near, through the passion of me pleasuring her. Those feelings in themselves: somehow being a person who brings her peace, and joy; her body against mine, my name on her lips, my cock buried in her wet heat. Mad for her is an understatement, but so is everything else. There are no words to sufficiently describe what I feel for her.

"What is this, Adan?" Thea asks softly, awed.

I stroke her cheek, my heart in my damn throat. "This is us, my Thea. Bonded: heart, body, soul, and mind. Right now, it's more potent, because it's new. It's harder to separate my feelings from yours, your thoughts from mine. But, already, I can hear your voice in them. Feel your heart in them. And, of course, we can learn how to mute it. You're entitled to your privacy, and I don't want you to–"

She presses her fingers to my lips. "I'm going to stop you there, handsome, because I know you're not about to suggest I keep secrets from you."

I smirk against her fingertips, and kiss them. She removes them, her brows still furrowed slightly, and I murmur, "Alright, love."

Her expression clears, and I kiss her brow before pulling out of her. Again, the only thing that gives me the strength to do so is my need to care for her. My bite was not gentle, my hands even less so, and the way I'd fucked her...

"Stand for me, sweetheart." I release her body, only to hold her hand to help her up and out of the pool. Water drips from her skin, caressing every silken edge and curve. My heart strains at the sight of her, and then tightens painfully when my eyes find the bruises.

Her neck looks like it was mauled; puncture wounds deep, the impressions of the rest of my teeth already forming purple crescents over the delicate skin. More purple on her hips and thighs, in exactly the pattern of my fingers.

"None of that," she says, her voice filled with more steel than she's used yet in this cave. She crouches down, and puts her hand beneath my chin, forcing me to meet her eyes. "Don't regret me, Adan."

"Not you. Never you, Thea."

"You are. You're regretting being so rough with me. You see these bruises as a loss of control, as you hurting me. But you're not looking past the surface. So, look. Now."

I place my hands on her knees, and do as she says. Enter her heart and mind purposefully–and I'm immediately swept into passion. Thorough, unrestrained fucking. My hands so wonderfully tight on her, my loss of control as orgasm-inducing as my cock moving inside her. When my teeth sank into her skin, and she felt my claiming sing through her, practically wishing she could pour more of her blood on my tongue. Pounding into her, spilling myself inside her, and she reveled in the fact that this was her forever. This bliss, this love–there was no need for control because it was *uncontrollable*. She was mine, and I was hers. Mate.

When the memory releases me, I come back to myself to find my hands on her knees have tightened, my cock hard as the rock surrounding us. "Do you see now?" she asks, her hand still firm, but her voice soft.

In answer, I wind my arms through her bowed legs, and pull them towards me, catching her head in my hand as she falls backwards, more than a foot before it can reach the ground. I set it down gently, and slide her to the edge of the pool. And I fucking *devour* her.

Her hands in my hair, her taste in my mouth, her ass sitting in my palms. I make her come on my tongue in less than a minute, and don't even consider stopping until I wring two more from her. I stare over her body while she writhes on my face, watching the lines and curves of her work and move like the best fucking dance I've ever seen. I reach up to cup her tit in my hand, and pinch her nipple between my fingers.

When her third orgasm shatters her, the way she screams my name could reach the gods in the Heavens themselves. I lick her throughout, ensuring she feels every ounce of pleasure possible until her body falls limp, only her gasping breaths and her shudders of ecstasy moving her.

I move my mouth, and brace my hands on the stone on either side of her hips to pitch myself up and over her. I kiss my mate deeply, and let her feel the answer of what I see for herself.

⇔

Thea and I stay in that cave for some time, knowing that we will have to restrain ourselves once back at camp. I make love to her again on the ground, and fuck her against the wall. Each one evokes different emotions, but neither is less than the other. Slow and intimate, or fast and primal–each brands her so deeply into my heart and soul, I'm surprised her name isn't burned into my skin beside the mark of her claiming.

Dressed and dry, we walk hand-in-hand out of the cave. By the angle of the moon through the branches when we exit, it's nearly one in the morning. Only being able to sense the lateness of the hour had given me the will to leave the cave. Every instinct is screaming at me to bring her back, and fuck her until the sun comes up. To fill her so much that the impossible could happen, and my seed would take root.

When she'd said she had taken the tonic the first time, I'd stilled, knowing what she was truly telling me. That, sometime soon, she would be ready for me, and she wanted me to know it. What *she* didn't know, and still doesn't, is how my dreams since have been plagued with filling her with my cum until the vision shifts, and she's swollen with our child.

An impossibility, and not just because of the tonic, or even because she has not had a bleeding since our third week on the ship. No matter how much the Fae beast in me roars to rut and breed her *now*, now is not the time. We are heading into danger at the least, and war at the most. Whether we complete our journey to go to Olin and kill him, or if he meets us on the battlefield, I don't want to know what I would do if not only Thea, but our baby was in danger.

Even the thought of Thea confronting my father has driven the nightmares that twine with the dreams of our future together. I would never keep her from it, from the revenge she deserves, no matter how I have to fight my mind and body daily to remind myself of that. But, if she tried to do so while pregnant...it terrifies me to know that I might lock her up to keep her from attempting such a thing. That my need to protect her already drives me to bloodshed and murder, but if she were vulnerable? The atrocities I would commit to keep her safe might perhaps encroach onto *her* freedom–the very thing I ensured she would have since the Ceraschen Cliffs.

So, my instincts, my beast, they can roar at me all they like. But, for her, I will continue to keep them at bay. I will continue to walk away from that cave, and to our camp, where our journey as we've planned it will continue come morning.

So she would be prepared, I informed her that the others

would know what we'd done. Once we mated, our scents shifted, accepting a part of the other into ourselves. Thea had only asked what she smelled like now, a lovely, elated smile on her face. I'd told her, added onto that scent of the earth and peace is a ribbon of oak.

She'd still been smiling when she put her nose to my neck. Then said she knew what I meant now, about that peaceful scent. *That* was what my body had taken and she had given as we mated; that warm and bright thing that makes it hard to remember what pain even feels like. My fingers tighten around hers now at the thought, and she looks up at me, and smiles. So unbelievably beautiful. That smile brightens when I say so out loud.

We reach the camp, and I relax a bit for her sake when I see the fire has died, meaning no one has woken to note our absence. She'll be able to get some rest without some busybody watching her with knowing eyes.

I'd warned her, as well, about the probability of me being... possessive of her in the coming days. That I might be more aggressive towards others around her, and my need for her would be more unquenchable than ever. Thea had only tilted her head with a small smile, then leaned up on her toes to kiss my cheek. And damn if it didn't make those possessive instincts sit back, even as I remembered the way *he* had looked at her as we sat at the fire.

I'm sure she's thought about it—about *him*, too. But, honestly, that's the last thing I want to think about right now. We will figure it out in the morning.

Now, we lay down facing each other, as we had an eternity ago. At once, our hands reach out, and our fingers twine between us. I look into her eyes, *my mate's* eyes, and send a thought down the bond to her, stroking the back of her palm.

I love you, Thea.

She returns the soft graze of her thumb across my hand. *I love you, Adan.*

Sleep seizes my sweetheart moments later, exhausted from all that we did, on top of the chaos of the past two days. Could it be just last night that I'd ripped a male open and turned his flesh to rot for threatening to harm her? Just yesterday afternoon that we'd arrived in Sabrian, thinking of meeting its rulers, only to stumble upon a power that neither of us can verbalize?

The last thing I'd shared with her in that cave, she'd felt already. My power is still contained; leashed tightly by Olin's blood oath. But, sharing blood with my mate–something had changed. My soul opening because of her, I'd felt my majick unravel within me, more uninhibited than it's been in decades. Because of that love, whatever I have left outside of the oath *thrives* within me. Dark, deadly, and ready to destroy anybody who might threaten my mate.

And that kernel of light that had hibernated for so long–so long, until I'd looked into her eyes and felt the bond–it had grown. Strengthened not just by this freeing of my soul, but by *her*. And, in exchange, I sensed some of my Death coursing through her Life. In her blood, pumping strong through her heart.

So brave, and fierce, and powerful. Thea is formidable and glorious, gentle and bright. And I can't fucking wait to witness it for the rest of my days.

61

THE CASTLE

LINA - DAY 36

OH, TO WAKE AT DAWN *NOT* ON A ROCKING WOOD BARREL IN THE middle of the sea.

On my bed roll, I stretch enough that several joints pop, and sigh before opening my eyes. I'd fallen asleep facing Sione, and find them still sleeping. Their back is to me, rising and falling with even breaths that shift their wings each time. Dark waves crest gently over wicked looking horns, and fall into the crooked arm beneath their head. Sitting up, I have the urge to feel one of those horns, and maybe it's my sleepy mind or my lowered inhibitions as we get closer to home, but I reach a finger out and do just that.

It's smooth and rough at once beneath my touch, and I continue it, fascinated, around the slight curl in the middle. I'm so engrossed that I don't realize their breaths have shifted until their head turns slowly so that they're looking at me over their shoulder.

I quickly bring my hand back, in the same instant that russet eyes find mine, their grogginess nearly absent in the wake of–of *hunger*. They look at my hand, and, their voice low with sleep, they ask, "Did you like it?"

I stumble over my response, which is an embarrassing, "W-what?"

Their gaze moves back to mine. "Did you like touching them?"

It has to be the fact that the crush started in childhood that causes me to become a bumbling idiot whenever they do anything that could be outside of the realm of platonic. I've been with females, males, and otherwise, and even with my insecurities I never had an issue in *that* department. The thing is, I never *really* cared for any of them. When things would inevitably fizzle out, it didn't bother me.

But, this...if I'm misreading things, or if I'm not, and it ends...I don't think I'll be okay. The child in me and the female would both crumble under the weight of the words *not good enough*.

The struggle is that I've never been very good about respecting the consequences for future me, deeming them her problem, not mine. Living in the moment seems the only logical thing when my lifespan is at least ten times shorter than that of everyone around me. So, maybe future me will hate me for it, but–

I tilt my head, letting a sparkle come to my eye. "And, if I did?"

Whatever heat had been in their eyes positively blazes now, the red becoming more prominent. They turn over, trousers slung low on their slim hips, and roll off their knees into a crouch in front of me, their wings flared wide to not touch the ground. "I would ask if you're finally done hiding from what this is, moonshine."

I tilt my chin up stubbornly, intentionally closing some of the distance between my mouth and theirs. "Tell me what this is, mountainside."

They open their lips to answer, but it's not their voice that comes.

"*Ugh*, get a *room*," Tali says, groggy and annoyed from behind me. I turn to find her vigorously rubbing her eyes, and when she stops, they rest on us, narrowed.

"Where was all that with them two, Tali?" Sione asks. I don't need to look to know who they're gesturing to.

She sits up, pin-straight hair falling over her shoulders. "*She* is possibly the sweetest person I've ever met, and *he's* gigantic and intimidating. You, on the other hand–I don't need to watch my *cousin* get the hots for anybody."

"For your information, I already *had* the hots for her, so you're a bit late on the *getting* part." My heart stumbles over their words, and I whirl to look at them over my shoulder–only to find their eyes already on me. And then they *wink*.

"Yeah, for, like, two years. Everyone knows, idiot. Except her–well, I guess, until now. Still. I watched both of you grow up, so take it somewhere else or I might barf up last night's dinner."

"I'll remember that the next time I find you in a coat closet with your tongue up a female's–"

"Sione, I beg you not to finish that sentence," Javi says, his voice hoarse with sleep. I peer past Sione to find the High Lord staring up at the canopy of walnut branches, and certainly *not* at his daughter.

"–ass. What did you think I was going to say?" Sione's brow scrunches, and I laugh despite the racing of my heart while Tali groans, covering her face with her hands. Atlas's laugh joins mine from the other side of Talia, and Ciaragen cackles beside Javi, her deep blue eyes on the mortified female.

"Have you guys always been this loud in the morning?" comes Al's voice from the other side of the extinguished fire, which gets a chuckle even from Javi.

"Yes," I answer for everyone, and turn to her. "Best get used to it, gorgeous."

Her back to me, she sighs. Adathan's woken up, too, but his bright golden eyes are only for her, a gentle smile that I don't think he's aware of gracing his face. My heart warms seeing it–knowing that kind of love is no less than what she deserves.

Then, Sione says, "Well, look who's got another scar." My brow furrows, and I turn back to look at them. Grinning, they tap the right side of their neck, just inches above their collar bone. I look to see for myself, finding the same space on Adathan to be marked with twin puncture wounds, a very distinctive distance apart.

I gasp. "*No fucking way.*" I scramble up so quickly that my head spins a little, and I practically fall over Al as I lean over her to see. On the left side of her neck is the same type of mark, along with purplish half-moon healing bruises of the rest of Adathan's teeth. I squeal, and now I *do* topple over her, my arms around her shoulders. She laughs against me, the sound so genuine and lovely. "You're telling me *everything* later," I whisper to her, and she nods, another giggle bursting out of her.

I roll off of her, into the dirt, to face Addie, and I shove his shoulder. He doesn't so much as budge, but his responding smirk is full of joy. "*Mated*, my friend. So fucking awesome." Through the excitement, happy tears pool in my eyes. And, though he's not a physical touch kind of male–with one obvious exception–he reaches out to pinch my cheek. Like a friend. Like a brother.

I roll back over, leaves tangling in my hair, to kiss Al on her blushing nose. Then I stand, carefully stepping over her, and find Sione smiling at me. But, even with the brand-new knowledge that hangs between us, I catch motion in my periphery. I look just in time to see Atlas disappear into the trees.

Fuck.

I rush after him, but his emotions have carried him quickly; only that anger weighing his steps enough that I can follow the noise of them allows me to find him. He's stopped by the edge of the same stream in which we bathed yesterday, and even from behind I can see the way his breaths heave his chest and shoulders.

I'm not sure he can hear me through whatever is going on in his mind right now, so I make my own steps intentionally loud, stomping on dry leaves and twigs. His hands clench and unclench at his sides, shaking in between, and, though I'd been so excited for Al–and, damn, even for Adathan–my heart aches now for my best friend.

"Atlas?" I say quietly, just feet from him now.

He whirls suddenly, and lightning shoots across the space, and fractures a tree in two several yards from me. I didn't so much as duck, or dive away; even in this state, he would never hurt me. My eyes are still on him when his power fizzles, and his chest is rising and falling too hard and too fast, but it's not that which causes my own breath to leave me in a weighted sigh.

It's the shine in his gray eyes.

"Atlas..." I start to close the space between us slowly, but on my second footfall, he half turns from me, creating distance with body language if not with steps.

"I just–" he grits out. He sucks his lips between his teeth, wetting them, then shakes his head, his tied-up locs bobbing with the movement. "I'm too angry to not say something I don't mean."

"Then put up a sound shield and give me your worst," I tell

him, crossing my arms. He looks at me then, his brows scrunching a bit as my words catch him off-guard enough to surprise some of that chest-heaving rage out of him. "Tell me, Atlas, because we have at least an hour of travel left, and a fucking lifetime after that, and they–" I sigh, but force myself to finish, "–they will still be mated."

Agony lances through his expression, and the air around us crackles with his power. When he finally speaks, his words are so low that I almost miss them. "It should have been me."

My chin jerks back a little, and my eyes widen as I take a hesitant step towards him. "Are you saying that you...?"

He shakes his head again, and shrugs, though the gesture is anything but nonchalant. "I'm not talking about that right now, Lina. Not when they—" He crosses his arms, and huffs a breath that does nothing to the silver in his eyes. "I knew. That they were mates. He all but told me that day, after we all trained together. I just...I managed to convince myself she wouldn't claim him. That she could want him, and love him, but not wish for the bond. I thought it because–because I thought that might have been us, too."

My eyes are likely dinner plates at this point, listening to him confirm what he began his statement denying. "You think you're her mate, too," I breathe. It's a possibility. Not common, but not rare either, to have two mates. Even three, though that was almost unheard of.

Atlas is quiet for a long moment. Then, "I wanted to give her the choice she deserved to make, and not force her to realize she might not have to make it. She spent her life having her virtue shielded by others. To go from that to not one but *two* males who would...Lina, I couldn't do it to her.

"This pain...I can live with it. Even if my instincts are shouting at me to go back there, and–" He takes a loud, quick breath, stifling the anger that had quickly risen in his eyes.

Another, slower this time, and the gray of them is half as heated. "I won't. Because she loves him. And I love her."

Yes. He would never hurt Adathan, knowing it would hurt Al so much more. What I think, but won't say, is that if he *is* her mate, too...he would also be Adathan's. Not necessarily romantically; matehoods have been known to sometimes be between the closest of friends, which...even that is a long fucking way off for the two of them.

In any case, that logic–what is known of matehoods with more than two people–would not be helpful right now.

Instead, I ask gently, "So, what now?" In those three words are many others. Will you ever tell her–about your love, or your bond? What will you do, now that this is the path she's on?

He looks at me, and I watch the remaining fury cool over several heartbeats, into a calm, sad, determination. "I made her a promise. I'm not about to break it." Again, implied words flow from those spoken: even if I loathe him right now. Even if I have to continue to hide from part of myself.

"What did you promise?"

He looks back towards the camp, as if he can see it, can see *her* through the trees. "That I would always be her friend."

⇔

The air when we returned to camp was not as light as our friends were making it out to be. Though Tali and Sione chattered, and Ciaragen and Javi shoved food into our faces–just a bit of dried meat and a piece of fruit, as a larger meal would await us at the castle–the feel of the camp when we arrived was weighted.

That weight has eased in the half hour or so we've ridden through the woods since. Probably because Atlas leads our group with Javi beside him, the two males as far as possible

513

from the newly mated pair at the back of our group. Tali rides beside me, and Ciaragen and Sione are third. We took this order without discussing it, all of us knowing how volatile a newly mated male could be. Even to two females, for the simple fact that we might also be attracted to his bonded.

Sione, never having expressed nor exuded such attraction, and Ciaragen, mated already, were safest to be ahead of them. And I can almost *feel* those russet eyes on me. Waiting. As, apparently, they have been for over two years.

I try to think back, and see the point where things might have shifted for them. But, at nineteen, I was hardly different from what I am now. Was it during a trip to Sabrian, or when my mums took me to Obala? What had I *done* to make them see a female, instead of the girl they'd played in mud puddles with?

Tell me what this is, mountainside. They hadn't gotten the chance. But, they'd asked me if I was done hiding from it, whatever it may be. And, I sure as fuck am, because as soon as we can get a moment alone together at the castle, I'll repeat my request. And this time I'll get my answer.

I turn in my saddle to look at them, and find their eyes trained on me, as I'd thought they would be. In a look that's just a few heartbeats long, I try to convey my intention to them. Just before I turn back around, their lips pull up in a smirk, and they dip their chin.

And damn if my heart doesn't start fucking galloping.

That high carries me all the way to the foothills of Colina, and I only have the presence of mind to brace myself before Wynonna brings us through the last of the trees.

The castle sits on top of the central hill, the others around it rolling smoothly into the plains, the city, and the forest. Its gates and walls surround the main structure, granting a few acres in every direction to the lands of the castle itself. If I focus, I can pretend I almost smell the flowers of the gardens above, and the bread from the bakeries in the city below.

A broad smile stretches across my face, and I turn again in my saddle, but this time to look at my godmother. She's already smiling back at me, just as happy as I am to be home.

My grin turns mischievous, and I say, "Race you."

Without hesitation, I twist forward, and kick my heels into Wynonna's sides. The mare huffs, and picks up into a trot. My hand tight on her reins, I kick again, and she *flies*.

A hoot of exhilarated laughter leaves me as I pass Atlas just in time to see him urge his gelding into a run. Then it's me, and the other two Sabriani racing as fast as we can to the walls.

I'm breathing heavy when we close the last several yards, Wynonna doing the same as she slows beneath me. The guards recognize us, and Sam uses his majick to open the gates. "The Obalans and the male and female with them are with us," Ciaragen tells him as we pass.

"Yes, General," he replies, bowing his head. He gives a small incline to Atlas and I as well, being a Lord and Lady of his country.

We amble into the front courtyard, with its clover lawn and bustling staff. They smile and wave at us as they go about their work, and we return the gestures. Unfortunately, we can't just go into the castle yet, leaving our horses to graze on the small blooms underfoot. Instead, we urge them to the stables on the opposite side of the grounds from the main gardens.

The stablehand, a female named Jewel, grins as we approach. "Welcome home," she says, patting one of our mares on her rounded belly, and walking towards us. Her short blonde waves are pulled back by a bandana wrapped around her hairline, the blues and purples in its pattern bringing out the chocolate brown of her eyes. They crinkle at the corners as she grins up at us.

"Good to see you, Jewel," Ciaragen answers before dismounting. After fleeing Parvata, and making the journey here, Jewel had been hired just a couple of weeks before Atlas and I departed for Weaschte. Seeing that she's found her place here, as so many others have, has my smile for her softening.

I hop off Wynonna, then give her a few grateful pats while Jewel steps up to take her reins. Her stature is surprising to most, I'm sure, given she handles these beasts all day; just an inch or so taller than me, and with less muscle, too. But, in the time I'd gotten to know her, with the few times my mums and I had come to visit from our estate since she arrived, I learned that the fire in her heart more than makes up for what she might lack in physical strength.

After shooting me a bright grin, she moves into the stables with Wynonna and Marengo, while another stablehand takes Atlas's gelding. A moment later, the rest of our group arrives, and more hands come to receive their mounts.

Al looks around warily as she hops off Nisha's back as if she weren't afraid of horses two days ago. She hangs by the horse, her chest nearly touching the black mare as she looks around. Adathan looks at Ciaragen and me as he dismounts his stallion, and then gestures with his head towards Al.

Immediately, we go to her, Tali following suit without being asked. He spares Al a look, making sure her eyes are on us, that she sees support coming, before halting the stablehand whose path is obviously set for Nisha in his tracks. The male must either scent the mating on Adathan or see the fresh mark on his neck, because he turns and walks back, calling for a female without so much as a wayward glance at Al.

Nisha's body blocks me from seeing any more than Adathan going to meet the female halfway.

Al watches him over the back of her mare, but then Ciaragen is there, intercepting her view. Nisha flips her mane, as if affronted, but makes no move towards my godmother as she stares at the female she seems to take offense for.

A silent conversation passes between blue eyes and green, and Al sighs at its end. I know there wasn't any fear in her hesitation; that sigh *screams* reluctance. She doesn't *want* to meet the two people who have been waiting for her for twenty-one years. I get that. That's a lot of fucking pressure.

Not to mention they might very well try to arrest her mate again when they arrive.

He comes back with yet another stablehand, the other scurrying off, holding something in her hands. The female takes Nisha and Nox, who'd waited patiently by his mate, and then it's just our group once more, Atlas and Javi hovering several feet away.

Ciaragen holds Al's gaze for another second before looking around at all of us. "Shall we?" And then she turns on a heel and makes for the cobblestone path that will lead us back to the main entrance of the castle. Atlas and Javi quickly follow her, then Tali, Sione, and I, with Adathan and Al at the back.

I think, if it weren't for the surely awkward–at the least, terrible at the worst–interaction to come, my heart would have swollen to two times its normal size as we walk through the grand double doors. As the hammer beam ceilings rise high above us, and the mosaic tiles click beneath our feet. But, we quickly pass through the arched doorway of the entrance hall, and find the thrones at its end are already occupied. The High Lord and High Lady of Sabrian sit, so straight and at the ends of their seats that they might as well be standing. Their eyes move right past Atlas, Ciaragen, Javi and Talia, Sione and me. And land on the raven-haired beauty who steps up to my side.

62

HER, AT LAST

CIARAGEN - DAY 36

I CAN SEE THE EFFORT IT TAKES FOR HIELA TO REMAIN IN HER throne as I take a knee with the other Sabriani, bowing to her and her mate. I'm grateful for the Obalans in that moment, as they only bow their heads in respect. Not so uncomfortable, then, when Althea and Adathan do the same.

Atlas, Lina, and I stand after the customary amount of time before guests. "High Lord. High Lady," I greet them, dipping my chin to each. Not because I have to, but because I *get* to call them my sovereigns.

Hiela can't tear her eyes from Althea. I fight the urge to step in her eyeline, to spare my Lady from the weight this moment has to the female on the throne. It was I who challenged her to take this on right away. If Adathan can keep from stepping in for her, I bloody well can, too. She is strong–I don't think I could follow her if she wasn't. She does not need us to make her so.

Hielo responds to my greeting, "Lady Ciaragen. Can—can you please bring forward the rest of your party?" It's the stumbling in his words that makes my heart tighten for the couple. In my decades of serving him, I'd never before heard Amedeo stutter.

I step to the side, and gesture each of them forward. "Lord Atlas Malik. Lady Emelina Bentashi-Mikhyala. High Lord Javi Kahale, and his daughter, Lady Talia Kahale. Laird Sione Natia." I take a deep breath, and wave the final two forward. They take slow, measured steps into our line before the dais. "Lord Adathan Evestre, and...Princess Althea Cardenia, of Weaschte."

Their hands are so tight on the arms of their thrones that their knuckles pale, but still the High Lord and High Lady do not stand. "Princess," Hielo says, with a bow of his head that does not move his eyes from hers. "It is a...a pleasure to meet you."

The breaths of our group stall all at once as we wait for a response. I keep my gaze forward, jaw clenched.

"High Lord," she replies in her accented Divani, her voice strong and clear. "High Lady. I am glad to meet you as well."

Exhales sound throughout our group, quiet and relieved. Followed by a strained silence, where none in our party, nor the High Lord and High Lady seem to know what to say next. Then Hiela's eyes finally move from her daughter to the male at her side. And harden.

"You made quite the exit from your cell," she says.

"I would do so again, High Lady, if given the choice."

Her jaw flexes, but she looks over at me. "Your letter was fairly vague, General. What was the reason, exactly, for your act to free him? Is it great enough for him to remain out of captivity now?"

I see Althea's hands twitch in the corner of my eye, but she reins in whatever emotion causes it, not even allowing them to fist.

A princess indeed, perhaps not born, but raised.

"Yes, High Lady, it is," I reply without hesitation, nor a hint of regret. "As it was the person he'd previously assisted in taking that he saved that night."

The eyes of the High Lord and High Lady flash to Althea, then Adathan, before settling even more intensely on me once more. "Explain," Hielo says, his voice unusually stern. With a huffed breath, he adds, a bit more kindly, "Please."

"If we had not left, if I had not brought Adathan back to Dekedda...the princess would not be standing here today. But, truly, High Lord, it is not my story to tell." I look over at Althea, and I can almost feel the relief from her at not having to rein in her words for propriety's sake any longer.

As she steps forward, I see Hiela's breast halt, as if she's holding her breath while her daughter approaches. So alike; their faces are near mirrors of each other, only in different hues, with distinguishing eyes. Hielo watches her, too, and if it weren't for the possible enemy–in their eyes–present, I think he would have reached for his mate in this moment.

Her chin high, shoulders back, and hands loose at her sides as if she doesn't notice any of this–though I'm sure she does–Althea tells them the story. "The night after General Vey brought Adathan to you, I was attacked in the streets of Dekedda. Males who sought to take me to Oschverre, to Olin, knocked Atlas unconscious, and captured me and Emelina." The eyes of her birth parents widen, their faces paling, but Althea goes on.

"We managed to get free, and I was able to kill two of them, but there were too many for us to take on alone. When they threatened to harm Emelina if I did not drop my weapon, I saw no choice but to follow the instruction. One of them, though, had a–a vendetta," she doesn't so much as falter after finding the word, "against me. We fought while the other males watched."

She hesitates for only a heartbeat, barely long enough to notice at all. "But that was not enough for him. He stabbed me in the heart, and when I fell, he attempted to violate me."

Hiela does stand then, and Hielo is beside her in an instant. Their eyes rake over her, as if scanning retroactively for any hurt.

"I killed him before he could do all that I'm sure he wished to do," Althea says, fury lining her tone. Fury, which shifts into something like reverence in the next sentence. "When he arrived, Adathan pulled his body off of me, and killed the remaining males in that alley. And when the wound to my heart was too great for my body to heal with the iron in my veins...he brought me back."

The brows of both my High Lord and High Lady furrow. "Brought...brought you back?" Hiela nearly whispers.

"Yes. I died in Dekedda." Hiela's hand moves to her stomach, the other over her mouth as her eyes take on a shine that is mirrored in Hielo's eyes. "And, I would have been taken, or worse, several times before that, if not for Adathan. I stand here today because of him. Because, while you have some of the finest males and females I could ever have had the pleasure of meeting in your service and on your counsel, I would have been in Olin Evestre's clutches regardless. If not for *him*."

She takes a step closer to the dais, and a darkness I've only heard twice in her voice saturates it again now. "Without agenda, he has remained by my side, and I by his. And, while I would hope that would be enough for you to refrain from arresting him again, just in case: as a Princess of Weaschte, I claim him. If you attempt to take him into your custody, I will assume it to be an act of aggression against my court."

Pain ripples across Hiela's face as Althea's harsh words. While I ache for my High Lady, I understand my Lady. I would have done the same for Dion, if the need had ever arisen.

Althea either doesn't see it, or ignores it, continuing on: "By both the rites of your people, and mine, he belongs to me. And I to him." She flips her hair behind her shoulder.

Revealing the very distinct twin puncture marks on her neck.

I watch rage fill the eyes of my High Lord as he moves them from those marks, to the male behind her. Hiela's face, on the other hand, has gone utterly blank.

I've known her long enough to know it's not due to shock. It's her containing her emotions. Because, as she's just been told, any act against Adathan will cause her daughter to shun her, and her court. And she's had all of two minutes to go from hating and distrusting the male, to learning that he's saved the life of her child, and then mated her.

Her stillness holds Amedeo in place as well, though he visibly works to move his glare from Adathan to look at his own mate. Then, those remarkable sienna eyes soften, and she tilts her head, just slightly.

"Does he make you happy?" she asks Althea quietly.

Though I can't see her face, I'm sure it's surprise that stalls her response. When it comes, her own voice is far more gentle than it was a moment ago. Whether it's for the sake of the question, or the male she regards with such love and devotion, I can't be certain. In any case, some tension eases from her shoulders when she says, "Very much."

Hiela nods, then turns her gaze to Adathan. "Adathan Evestre, you are cleared of all charges against you. But, know this, my Lord." She steps down from her dais, and speaks as she walks, until she stands in line with Althea, just a few feet in front of Adathan. "If you ever hurt her, there will be no power in this world that will save you from our wrath."

"High Lady, if I ever hurt her, and don't commit myself to the Void directly after, you will likely be in quite the line to send me there. With her at the head of it."

⇻

Everyone is assigned chambers, and granted time to bathe and change. Nate and Bash, and Nuria and Jolie should be here within the hour, and Hiela said they'd been invited to stay the day and night, as well.

I've been leaned up against my closed door, staring into my chambers for a quarter of that hour. Everything is as it had been when I left. And as it had been when *he* left.

I've not been able to bear putting his belongings away. I leave them, mingling with mine, as we arranged them after that first day of being mated. His books on our shelves, his clothes in our armoire. The clothes lost his scent long ago, but sometimes I allow myself to open the pages of a book for a heartbeat or two, and find him amidst the ink and paper.

Not yet. Those moments are usually followed by me laying in our bed, holding the book tightly to my chest, sealing the scent within while mine crawls over the cover. And, though I miss him so much right now that my heart strains in my chest, swelling with the sob I won't set free yet, I care about myself enough to hold it in for now. To bathe, and go have breakfast with my court.

Tonight, I will open those pages. And I will hold close the one thing I have left of my mate.

63

HOME

EVERYTHING HAD BEEN A DREAM.

I knew it, as soon as consciousness took me, and I smelled the inside of my cell. The scents of blood, piss, and shit saturated the damp space. Combined with the way my head throbbed so badly I thought the cell might be swaying, only the fact that I had nothing in my stomach spared me from vomiting when I retched.

It must be early morning, for them to not have come for me yet. Perhaps Marcys was outside the cell door now, waiting only for a shift in breath, or heart rate, for his cue to begin. Depending on his mood, he sometimes liked to start right away, immediately ruining any dreams I might have had about the deep blue that continued to cradle me. Other times, he preferred that I wait in suspense to eventually see his face, the fear rising within me until he appeared, the golden male behind him.

Had I dreamed of him? The boy with eyes like the sun, called Adathan? Was I truly so delusional that I had imagined I might be able to care for somebody in this dark cell?

And why did I feel a wrenching in my chest at the knowledge, as I grieved what never was?

Well, I might as well get started. With a heavy sigh, I cracked my eyes open. And paused.

This was not my cell. There were bars in front of me, but the walls were all made of wood, not stone. And that rocking–it wasn't in my head, though I certainly felt incapable of standing. It was the ship. The damp scent was from the sea, not the earth.

Not a dream. Though, apart from that one factor, I wished that it had been. Instead, everything rushed back, so clear it could only be reality. I was a traitor to my court. To my High Lord and High Lady. To my mate. It didn't matter that Olin claimed the would-be Lady had escaped, Adathan by her side. I'd served my brother in direct detriment to my court, and my continent. Who knew where the pair of them were now, anyway? If they were even alive?

With concentrated effort, I pushed myself into a sitting position, and nearly shouted at the pain in my back. I managed to restrain it by biting down on the inside of my cheek, but my breaths came hard and fast through my nose. Unfortunate, since that also made the smell worse.

I was in relatively clean trousers, but another pair lay just a couple of feet from me. I knew it was a game for Olin, showing me how I'd soiled myself, and letting me remember it. He didn't have to mock me with words; he knew the sting of shame would hit harder without the distraction of arguing with him.

Jaw tight, I lifted one hand from the floor, and reached behind myself. When I touched my back, a breath hissed through my teeth, and when I drew my hand back around, my fingertips were wet with blood.

There was the sound of a door opening, and bright blue light streamed down into the brig. I lifted my bloodied hand to shield my eyes as a figure appeared in the light, and strode down the steps. I wasn't surprised at who it was when my eyes adjusted.

"You've looked better, brother," Olin said, his hands clasped behind his back as he stopped in front of my cell.

"I could say the same about you," I replied. I would have said it anyway, but it was actually true in this case. His hair and beard had grown from their usual respective buzzed and clean-shaven styles, neither suiting him. His eyes were half-crazed, with light gray half-moons beneath them, though he was trying to hide all that.

"Yes, well, it's been a long journey. Not that you would know about any of that. Luckily, we're here now." A smirk that made my stomach flip rose on his face, but it seemed I was better at hiding my feelings than he was.

"Home sweet home." I sighed, and stood, holding back winces and grunts from the pain in my back. Once standing, I stuck my forearms through the bars, and crossed my arms over them, the cold metal a bite to my skin. With how drained and achy I felt, I must have been without food for some time.

"Yes, welcome *home*, Dion. I'm sure everyone will be thrilled to see you." The smirk twitched up a bit more.

"Yes, they're all big fans. I've only killed a few thousand people over the past decade. I think I might only hit their sour spot when I reach a nice, rounded ten-thousand." I kept my tone light, but the self-loathing roiled in my gut.

"Ah, they might have a bone or two to pick with you, when you arrive. But I'm sure their forgiving hearts will let you back in more quickly than you might imagine."

My brow furrowed in confusion. In my belly, however, I

began to feel sick. Something my body was recognizing before my mind dared to. "Let me back? Do you mean to ask them?"

Olin chuckled, true humor showing through the new sort of madness in his eyes. "Oh, no, Dion. I had my fun playing with you all these years, but you are far better suited for this role. For many reasons, all of which I enjoy, but particularly because it's a part you've already played before. You'll be so good at it, now that you won't have a choice but to obey your orders."

My arms fell back from the bars, and I took a step away, further into my cell. "No," I breathed, dread pooling in my stomach, my heart racing in panic.

The smirk turned into a full, cheek-splitting grin. "Yes! You, dear brother, will be taking your part back within your precious Sabriani castle. Only this time, they will believe you to be loyal from the start." He took a step towards the bars, his smile still wide, the eyes above it filled with malice and joy. "Dion Evestre, you will go back to the castle in Colina, and you will spy on them for me."

"*No!*" I shouted as I took another step back, though I already felt the order seal into my blood. I longed to cover my ears, to drown out his words, but all that would do was get more males down here to pin my arms while he continued his list of commands.

"You will inform me of any movement of their uprising, rebellion, or crusade–however they word it, this order applies.

"Adathan is dead." Those three words had my retreat and my heart stopping, and it took all the strength I had left not to allow my knees to give under the weight of my grief. "I would grieve for him if his last act hadn't been to betray me. My spies have captured my princess, and are taking her to Oschverre now, so his treachery, and his life, were pointless. I will have her, glamoured as she is, unable to fight me with the might she was born with. You know, that fun bit of majick, and parentage you conveniently forgot to tell me about for over two decades?"

He sighs, the exhale hissing through his teeth. "You know, if not for that, that might have been your last order. But because of your treachery, you have two more." Olin takes a step which brings his face just inches from the bars, and stares into my eyes with that dead, cruel grin. "Dion Evestre: the next time you see your mate, you will kill her."

The words hit me like a thousand knives, shredding me apart. I feel them course through my blood, binding unto death. Death, I will *die* before I–

"Most importantly: you will forget that I ordered you to do any of this. You will believe I discovered that you knew all along about your lost Lady, and sent you to Sabrian, as I hadn't been able to execute my own brother–let's say for the sake of the mother who bore us. Your body will carry out these orders without any will on your part. Now: forget."

Olin stood before me on a coastline, his jaw hard as he looked out at the sea where a ship waited. "Go now, Dion," he said, the hatred and betrayal heavy in his voice. "Before I change my mind."

I ran.

64

CHOICE & ITS DESIRES

THEA - DAY 36

THE CHAMBERS ASSIGNED TO US ARE STUNNING. ARCHED thresholds part the separate rooms, and without any doors to block it, the morning sun shines brightly throughout. The wood-and-glass doors leading to a small balcony are open, billowing the linen curtains with the breeze that airs out whatever stagnancy had been present before our arrival.

Adan steps in and closes the door behind me, and then his arms wind around my waist, his head dipping until his lips are by my ear. I lean back into him, and close my eyes, feeling the weight of the encounter in the entrance hall leave me with each heartbeat.

He holds me for a moment longer, and presses his lips to my temple. "You amaze me. Every single day, you amaze me, Thea." I turn into his lips, my heart straining, and they skim across my brow. "You are so strong, and brave. And...and no one has ever defended me as you did in there."

I turn further and open my eyes to look into his. "Was that alright? I didn't have the time to clear it with you, but I thought the only way they would allow me to keep you would be to claim you as part of *my* court. Which—we never talked about, and—"

"Let this be the only time I interrupt you, love, and with good reason. You *claiming* me, under *your* rule, nearly had me forgoing all sense and taking you from there so that I could sit you on my face and show you just how well I plan to serve you. As a matter of fact," he twists me around, and one hand finds the small of my back, the other my face, his thumb hitching on my bottom lip. "Take your trousers off, or they'll be a scrap of fabric on the floor if I have to do it myself."

My teeth automatically go for my lip, but with his thumb in the way, they catch on that instead. He hums, a gritty, satisfied thing, when I close my mouth around it instead, and his sun-gold eyes darken beneath his lashes. His other hand gives me only enough room to obey his command, and after I shimmy them over my hips, they fall to the ground.

"Good. Now walk that gorgeous ass of yours over to the bed, and you better be completely bare to me by the time you get there."

Heat rises to my cheeks, and further fills my core, my already wet center slickening more at his words. I turn when he releases me, and walk towards the bed, pulling my shirt up over my head as I go. When I reach the massive thing, its covers so cleanly pressed, waiting for us to ruin them, I stop, awaiting my next instruction.

He's behind me a moment later, close enough that I feel the warmth of his body caress my own. He makes me listen as he doffs his own clothing, and then his arm reaches over me, diagonal over my breast. A quiet growl rasps up his throat when his fingers slide through the wetness at my center. "All of this for me?"

I nod, panting as he pushes the tip of one finger inside me. "Hmm. And yet, nothing to fill you." He retracts that barely-there touch, evoking a noise of protest, and walks around me, to the bed. I'm more than disappointed to see he's kept his underwear on, though his cock tents them so significantly he might as well have removed them.

He moves to lay down, pulling me with him, and it's thanks to the absurd strength of his arms and abdomen that I wind up straddling his waist. "Sit on my face, and give me those eyes when you do" he orders me, tugging at my hips.

My brows furrow, though my heart gallops and my core tightens. "*On* you? How will you breathe?"

"I didn't say question me. I said: *sit on my face.*" He pulls me more forcefully, and I wind up splayed over his chest. "You get comfortable, love, and I'll take care of you. As long as you keep those eyes on mine."

I bite my lip again, smirking. "You know, it wasn't so long ago that I had you pinned like this with a dagger to your throat."

"And I wanted to taste you then. If you make me wait any longer, I'll make *you* beg before I let you come. My tongue will find its gods-damn home on your clit, Thea. So sit on my face now, or wait to come until *I* let you." He squeezes my backside with near-bruising strength, and I feel myself get even wetter in response.

Still with my lip between my teeth, I lift myself off my haunches. Right away, he pushes his arms beneath my thighs, and I wind up with my sex hovering over his chin. He inhales, and his exhale is a moan as he grips the sides of my hips, and without any further instruction or warning, he tilts his face down, and licks my center.

With a sigh, my hands move into his hair, and I sink a bit further down. When his tongue thrusts inside of me, I close my eyes–

They snap open when he pulls out, and I find him looking at me. Right. *Keep those eyes on mine.*

He pushes his tongue in more slowly, holding my gaze with intention. I can practically see his soul within them, aflame with the depth of his desire–

I hope she doesn't make me stop again. But, stop I will if she takes her eyes off mine.

Fuck, I can feel *her. And it makes my cock so hard I have to force myself to focus on the task at hand. I'll be damned if I don't reward her for being so brave, and thank her for claiming me.*

I make her pleasure last, serving my princess, my fucking Queen *as she deserves. I bring her close to the edge without allowing her to fall over it, freeing one of my arms from those amazing thighs to play with one of her dusky nipples, her tit laying perfectly in my palm. Only once she's so wet that it drips down my jaw do I growl, and pull her ass to bring her more solidly against my face.* Grind on my tongue, Thea, *I order her through our intertwined minds. And my sweetheart obeys.*

Her fingers in my hair, she watches my eyes while she writhes over my tongue. Her moans turn into pants, and then into no breath at all, her mouth open in silent ecstasy as she holds herself hard over my suckling lips. With one more growl from deep in my chest at the taste and feel of her, she comes for me.

Thea shouts my name, not once tearing her gaze from mine as her wetness fills my mouth. My own pleasure hangs tenuously in the balance; just from the sight of her taking her pleasure, her body moving fluidly as I drag each drop of her orgasm from her–

I'm breathing hard as I sit back on Adan's chest, and don't give him any warning–physically or mentally–before I reach behind myself and grab his cock. He curses, one hand squeezing my breast, his other arm still pinned beneath my thigh as I stroke him once over his underwear before pulling the waistband up and over his length. I felt how close he was, and so I stroke him the way he showed me, not taking my eyes off his, not even when I graze my fingers over his balls.

In an instant, I slide down his arms so that they're freed, and plant myself on his cock right before he comes. With how wet he's made me, the stretch of him still allows me to sink halfway down. He grips my hips as he begins to fill me.

Then, I'm flipped onto my back, my hands pinned above my head, and he slams his hips to mine, over and over, his other hand fisted with crumbling restraint on the mattress beside my waist. When he's spent, and his gorgeous fucking body stills between my legs, his voice is breathless even within my mind as he says, *Thea Cardenia, you were fucking made for me.* He plants a solid, searing kiss to my lips. *And I was made for you.*

⇔

Luckily, when Tali and Sione come to collect us, we're bathed and dressed. A few minutes earlier, and that would not have been the case.

We just couldn't seem to stop. I can't get enough of him, nor he of me. Especially after the first time our minds came together, well, they were not the only things to *come together* from then on. Lost in pleasure, Adan would speak his words of praise into my mind, urging me on, giving me confidence where I might have otherwise been unsure of myself. The things he thinks about me, during our bouts of passion, and outside of them...I never imagined I would be so loved. So completely worshipped.

After the third time we'd come for each other, and we realized we truly needed to get ready, he'd run the shower for me, but refused to join me in it. Then, over the noise of the water, the glass between us fogged enough that I could only see the shape of him, he'd said, "I have to tell you something, love."

His voice wasn't necessarily subdued, but it was certainly different from the smirking command he'd given me to get in the shower, sealed with a kiss. My brows furrowed at the sound of it, but with conditioner in my hair, I hadn't poked my head out to see him. "What is it?"

"I'm telling you because I want you to know everything in my mind that isn't hidden by the blood oath. Not because I expect anything from it–not at all. But, because I–it's something I thought about last night, and it–all it is, is something that brings me pleasure to think about, and–"

"Let this be the only time I interrupt you," I repeated his words to me from earlier. With the last of the conditioner rinsed from my hair, I at last opened the shower door enough to look at him. He stood, his trousers slung low on his hips, the top buttons lazily left open, leaning against the sink. The steam in the room hadn't been enough to cloud the conflict in his eyes, and the look had made me tilt my head before going on more gently, "Tell me, Adan."

His hands clenched on the edge of the counter, the only indication that he was nervous. Even then, I knew he could have controlled the reaction if he wanted to–but, he didn't. Instead, he wanted me to see it. "It gives me...immense pleasure to imagine that when I come inside you...something might arise from it."

It took me a second to understand what he was saying, and then my eyes had widened, my heartbeat picking up. "Oh."

He continued quickly, "Like I said, I would never expect that from you, Thea. I could live a thousand years with just you and I, and it would be more than enough. I just–when I imagine it...you, growing with our child, because we made love, it–" he sighed, his hands clenching again, and I caught the motion of his cock twitching, too. "It's an image that gives me... great pleasure. I didn't want it to pop into my mind while you were in there with me, and catch you off-guard."

I'd gone back into the shower to turn off the water without a word, having already washed and shaved while the conditioner was setting. I wrung out my hair, and then stepped out onto the mat just outside the shower. "Come here, so I don't track water all over the floor," I told him, and he'd pushed off the counter and walked to me, his jaw tighter than usual.

Once he was in front of me, I'd placed my hands on his waist, and looked up into his wary eyes. "When I used to imagine my life, being married, with children, I resented it. They were being forced upon me, with such intention that I didn't allow myself to truly picture anything different for my future, because I didn't want to *want* something that would never be.

"Much has changed over the past weeks. My life, yes, but also *me*. I no longer feel *obligated* to marry, and have children. But, I also have not given much waking thought to what I might want for our future, because things are not done changing, and I don't want...I don't want whatever I imagine to be snatched away before it can ever come to be."

His brows furrowed over eyes that filled with understanding, but I went on, "But it is *our* future I imagine, Adan. There is no life for me without you. And, that life..." I trailed my hands up his sculpted, scarred abdomen, to his chest, over that strong, beautifully dark heart. "When I've dreamed of it, I dream of what you desire, too. And, I know we haven't–" Then, it was *my* turn to be nervous. "We haven't talked about the ceremonies of humans, but I dreamed that maybe–"

He'd seized me, capturing my body in his arms and my lips with his. Perfectly, we fit so perfectly together, and our mouths moved in patterns made for us, tongues passing with more words unspoken. When he pulled back, only enough to rest his brow against mine, he said, "Thea, calling you my mate *and* my wife will be the greatest privilege I could ever know."

A future I would be choosing for myself. A male who made every possible fate undaunting. With him, I wanted the things I hadn't yet allowed myself to think about, as well as those which I'd once resented. I would continue to take the tonic, as I still had a promise to see through, but after that...

I'd pictured his fantasy in my mind, adding in my personal touches–him, behind me, his bronze hands resting on my rounded stomach–and sent it down the bond. Adan had whispered my name, and kissed me again, softly. Then he'd laid me down on the tile, and made slow, deep love to me amidst the steam.

I didn't shower again after, so I'm sure the Fae and faerie before us can scent the sex coating my body, but I find I don't particularly care. For one, they're probably used to being able to smell those types of things, so it shouldn't be different for us. And, for another...well, if they did have a problem with it, I'm not going to stop fucking my mate regardless, so there's really no point in worrying about how they feel about it.

We make idle chit chat as we walk down the pale stone hallways. Pretty–the castle is very pretty, and I find the fingers of my right hand skimming the wall, over the grooves of the stone and mortar. My left hand is held in the familiar warm, calloused one of my mate, who smiles softly at me, not thinking I notice it as my fingertips roam over the halls.

Though I'm very comfortable now with trousers and tank-tops, I'd dared a look inside one of the armoires while Adan bathed. Now, the skirt of a pale blue summer dress skims over my shins, exposed thanks to the strappy heeled sandals I'd found. They click lightly along the tiled floors, and as I trace one stone corner, I skip a step for them to tap a staccato beat.

It's echoed by feet in front of me, and I turn away from the wall to find Sione looking at me over their shoulder, smirking. I grin back at them, and tap a different rhythm between my steps, which they alter with a few scuffs. Tali laughs as they slide, imitating a cymbal. I tap out another beat, and Adan raises our hands above us, twirling me and setting my skirt flaring.

A giggle turns into a full-blown laugh when he reels me back in to dip me, and his responding smile is broad across his beautiful face; dimples in each cheek, straight teeth and canines flashing. I'm still chuckling, Sione with me, Adan and Tali grinning, when we turn one more corner–

Into a dining hall filled with people.

My laughter dies on my lips, but the unfamiliar faces are scattered among the familiar ones, so I manage not to blanch at the fact that nearly all of the eyes in the room rest on me as we enter. Without me commanding them to, my shoulders straighten and my chin lifts, and I move my hand to the inside of Adan's elbow. His pulse thrums beneath my fingers as he crooks his arm for me, and follows my mental tug towards the males and females near the center of the room.

I feel Adan tense when Atlas's gaze meets mine, but my smile for the other male is too immediate. Whether Adathan feels that through our bond, or just recognizes that I would never be able to omit Atlas from my life–however temporarily– that tension fades with a breath he finishes before we reach them.

"Al, these are my mums," Li says excitedly, tucked beneath the arm of a stunning female with near-onyx skin, whom she gestures to first. "Nuria, and Jolie."

I smile at them, catching myself before it can slip as I note the striking similarities between Jolie's face and mine. Ice-blue eyes look back at me, filled with understanding, and something like...joy.

I hold my free hand out to each of them. "Althea. It's so nice to meet you." Then I turn to the males next to them. "You must be Atlas's dads."

They grin, taking my hand when I extend it. "I'm Nate, and this is my mate, Bash," the fair-haired, gray-eyed male says, gesturing to the dark-skinned male at his side. Unlike Atlas, his hair is shorn close to his head, and his eyes are a brown so dark they're almost black. Still, looking between them...

Nate must be used to the wondering look I'm sure comes into my eyes, because he laughs, and says, "I know, it's uncanny." His smile saddens a bit. "He was my sister's son. I know they look almost the same, but," he places a palm on Atlas's cheek, then pinches it as if he's not twenty-three, and taller than his father, "he's got her eyes, not mine."

"Yeah, just like I've got mum's hair," Li says, lightening the briefly heavy moment, and Nuria tugs on a long white curl.

"Back for an hour, and already disrespecting your mother," she says, to which Li shrugs, earning a kiss to her temple.

I move my now-free hand above my other on Adan's arm. "This is my mate, Adathan." I sense his heart stutter at the introduction; at hearing me so blatantly use the word he'd once feared I would resent.

Whether they know his past, or not, I can't tell. Because all four of them only give him welcoming smiles and greetings, which he returns. I feel his relief. Not for himself, but for me—he's glad that his presence won't keep them from wanting to get to know me.

If it did, I wouldn't care to know them, either, my love, I tell him.

There's a hesitation in his thoughts, emotion barring his words before he replies, *I don't know what I did to deserve you.*

Before I can respond, Jolie says, "Are you hungry?" Her brows narrow with a bit of concern over those glacial eyes.

"Very, actually." We had that small bit of food before leaving camp this morning, counting on the meal we were to receive here. Then, of course, there was the...*activity* Adan and I had been engaged in for an hour.

Jolie's responding smile is sweet. "Would you care to sit with us? It's just one long table, but I–I would like to sit beside you, if that's alright."

The request is quiet. Not in volume, but in feel. Jolie's very presence is...comforting, somehow. So, I find myself answering, "That would be nice."

We find our seats a moment later. Adan is, as always, to my left, Jolie to my right. Lina sits between her and Nuria. Around the curve of the oblong table beside them are Nate, Atlas, and Bash. Ciaragen sits beside him, another male on her opposite side who looks similar to the Obalans, who sit by him. Well, with the exception of Tali, who unexpectedly took up the spot to Adan's left. Sione is directly across from Li, and I don't miss the look that passes between them.

I may have been preoccupied with my mate the past twelve hours, but I noticed the shift between them this morning. I just need a minute alone with my friend to ask her about it, and give her the same giggling elation she'd given me when I'd confessed my feelings for Adathan to her.

Everyone is talking except me, Adan, and Jolie. The female had passed me the nearest dish–pork sausage–after taking some herself, and as the rest of the items came around, she only continued to hand them to me silently. Truly, she seems happy to just sit next to me. And so, surprising myself, it's me who asks the question, "So, you're my aunt, right?"

She blinks, seeming equally unprepared for me to acknowledge any relation to her. Her terracotta cheeks flush a pretty, deep pink that makes the blue of her eyes even brighter. The conversation at the table stutters before resuming, all the keen ears having heard my query, too. But she gives me a small, kind smile. "I am."

65

THE THINGS WE MAKE TIME FOR

LINA - DAY 36

"So, THAT WOULD MAKE LI AND I COUSINS," I HEAR AL SAY, thanks to the lull in conversation.

I wasn't sure she'd acknowledge it, the relationship between mama and her birth mother, so I never brought up how we could technically be related. But, now that she has, I lean around mama, and tell her, "That means, legally, you have to put up with me forever."

"*Legally*," mum scoffs, always teasing me about the way I talk to others, when it was her I watched speak so frankly as I grew up. *Maybe* I make more unsubstantiated comments than she does, but whatever.

"She's right," Tali chimes in from Adathan's other side, then points a sausage-tipped fork at Sione. "I'm stuck with that one for life, and our parents aren't even technically related."

Sione kisses the air towards her. "Love you, too, Tali."

She rolls her eyes while those around us chuckle. Al, smiling, says, "I never had any cousins before."

"You have, like, eighty-seven siblings. You don't have any cousins?"

Now it's her turn to roll her eyes when she replies to me, "I have *three* siblings. My aunt died when she and my mom were both young. My dad's brothers were always mad that he got magic while they didn't. If they had any kids, I never knew, and never met them." She shrugs, biting into her sausage.

Her bite freezes, her eyes focusing on the arched doorway. I follow her gaze, and find Hielo and Hiela standing there, the movement of Hiela's skirts indicating they'd just arrived. They both look at her, and I can see the effort it takes for them to look around the room, and smile at their guests. "Good morning, everyone," Hielo says, and his greeting is echoed throughout the table. They move towards the two open seats at the other end of the table, and I don't miss how Hiela's eyes flick to mama's before focusing on her seat.

Tali, the brilliant bitch, sits on Adathan's other side, leaving the spots between her and Javi open to the Sabriani High Lord and High Lady. Hielo pulls out the chair for his mate, then sits in his own once she's tucked beneath the table. Luckily, mum hasn't stopped talking to Ciaragen and Bayani, having only paused to bid our sovereigns good morning before going on. The two of them return the conversation, all three pretending not to notice the silence at the opposite side of the table.

"All for the best," I finally respond to Al, maybe a touch too loudly, but she looks up from cutting into her fried egg with her fork. "They wouldn't have been able to compete with me, anyway."

She smirks, humor and gratitude shimmering in her pretty eyes. "Obviously not. They never would have introduced me to Swinger."

I cackle, and her own laugh joins in. With it, more conversation resumes around the table. Javi even manages to pull the attention of Hielo and Hiela, probably talking to them about some super-important fellow High Lord business. Whatever it takes to make the stiffness in Al's shoulders ease.

My eyes wander back to Sione, because of course they do. They'd been leaning back in their chair, carelessly eating a large chunk of watermelon, the juice dripping down their fingers a bit. As if they feel my eyes on them, their russet gaze flashes to me, and holds. They smirk a little as they take another bite of the red fruit that makes their eyes look nearly burgundy.

We didn't get to have that talk yet. *What is this, mountainside?* I still don't know. Because as soon as we'd left that entrance hall, Javi had asked Sione to venture out and make sure Harris still traveled north with Jacks. A day's journey for a Fae, but, for a Jemage as swift as Sione, especially with their considerable wind majick and wingspan, only half an hour's flight. I figure that they would have returned carrying Harris by an ankle if he had betrayed Jacks and our High Lord.

But, since they had entered with Tali and Addie and Al, I assume Harris kept true to his word. If a betrayal were to happen, it would have already; giving the male plenty of time to scurry away with the gold, long before Javi would have expected to hear anything from Jacks about his safe return.

I can appreciate all that, while also being annoyed that, because of it, I don't have an answer to a question I've technically been waiting for since dawn, but actually for a decade.

A decade. So much more significant for me than it is for them. The Jemage don't live quite as long as a full-blooded Fae, but still at least ten times longer than the longest lifespan for humans. And, as much as my glamoured ears and canines try to convince people I'm Fae, I'm not. I will die, and everyone at this table will live centuries more.

What kind of life would that be for them? Not only will I be gone long before them, they will have to watch me get old. While they continue to look just as they do now, I will wrinkle and gray. My eyes and ears will go, and even my voice might thin.

My mums know this, have long since discussed with me how they will love me all my life, and theirs. It wasn't an easy conversation, but it's one that had to happen.

Maybe Sione is just into me for now. I can do for now. I can live out my teenage and adult fantasies and be with them, for as long as they'll have me. But, if they're looking for anything more serious than that...it will only hurt them in the end. And that is something I refuse to do.

I'm not sure what emotions passed through my eyes as I thought through all of this, but I know it wasn't the heat or longing or even the mischief they expected. So, when I emerge enough from my morbid thoughts to see the look in their red-brown eyes, I'm not surprised that their dark brows have scrunched over an unreadable gaze. Nor that their smirk has shifted to tilt the corners of their mouth down, and the melon rests half-eaten on their plate, the rest of the food going untouched.

And I wonder, my heart sinking, if I will hurt them no matter what I do.

⇔

I've been avoiding everyone since breakfast, pulling my mums to the balconies, the turrets, anywhere but the library and the gardens, where I'm sure everyone else is relaxing or being toured around the castle. I feel a little bit guilty for taking mama from Al, but I know my friend–my *cousin*–noticed the look between Sione and I this morning.

I can't deal with her asking me about it. Or Tali. I certainly don't want to talk to *them* about it. So, I only hope the two Obalans are keeping Adathan and Al company. Maybe even Atlas, if Adathan was able to handle Al being in a room with so many males–

"Are you going to keep dragging your mums around the castle, or are you gonna talk?" I hear his familiar voice say. I turn to find Atlas walking towards me in the sun-filled walkway off one of the patios.

The mums in question are inside, getting refreshment after walking so much on this midsummer day in Sabrian. But, the table with light pastries and citrus-infused water is only a hallway away, and they've been gone for a few minutes...

Atlas reaches me quickly with his long legs, and interrupts me when I open my mouth. "Don't even think about asking me what I mean. We both know what I mean. So, talk."

My mouth snaps shut so that I can clench my jaw, but my anger doesn't last. It transitions into the same despair I felt at breakfast, and tears pool in my eyes before I quickly turn my head away.

"Hey." My best friend's voice has softened, and he brushes the mass of my curls over my shoulder, exposing one side of my face to him. "Lina. What's going on?"

I take a shuddering breath in, and, still looking away from him, I say, "I'm going to die, Atlas."

I *feel* him tense, though I can't turn to see it. To see the pain I'm sure flashes in those stormy eyes. Indeed, he sounds strained when he replies, "Not for a while."

I do turn then, a bit of that anger returning. Not at him, but at the unfairness of it all. Of the agony my loved ones are going to feel one day, all because they loved a human. Of the hurt I feel now, for not being able to spend more time with them, even if I have decades of it left. "But, I will die, Atlas. Long before you, or my mums, or–or *them*. And my mums knew what they were doing when they adopted me, and you and I have been friends since before we knew what death was, but...But, Sione? They still have an out. They won't have to hurt when I go."

His eyes have taken on a shine, but he sucks on his lips, wetting them, before saying, "Yes, Lina. They will. It's just a matter of how much joy they feel until then. Are you going to take that from them?"

"Take. *Take WHAT?* They'll have another ten years before I start to wrinkle. Another thirty before my back starts to bend. A score, and maybe I start forgetting things, forgetting *people*. And, all too soon after that, I'm gone. In the ground, and their soul not destined to join mine in the Heavens for centuries to come. *Take?* I'm *giving* them an out."

Atlas shakes his head. "You're taking those years from them. You think they want to look back when–when you die, and remember how you pushed them away? Or do you think they'll want to remember seventy years of you loving them, in the incredible way that you love people?"

My tears overflow, and he reaches up to brush one away with a calloused thumb. They just keep coming, though, so his hand slides behind my neck, to my shoulder, and pulls me to his chest. "And you," he goes on, even more quietly, rubbing my arm, "will get to go to the Heavens knowing that you were loved, and loved well in return. By turning from them, you're taking that from yourself, too. I know that doesn't matter to you as much as the rest, but it should. If you only have seventy years left...how do you want to spend them?"

I sniffle, wrapping my arms around his waist. "You know,

you're only two years older than me. You're not supposed to be this wise."

He sighs, and rests his chin on top of my head. "It's a curse, really. How much smarter I am than you."

I scoff wetly, and smack his back, but don't let go of him, allowing the last tears to fall, the rest stopping thanks to his comment. After a long moment where I listen to his heart beat against my ear, I ask, "So, I should stop being a fucking pussy, yeah?"

"Oh, Lina. Always so elegant."

This time, I do push away, swatting at his arm, but he easily dodges my second swing with a twist, chuckling. I dart after him into the small courtyard surrounded by the open patio, and when it's obvious I won't catch him, I whistle. A small pebble hits him in the stomach in its attempt to get to me, and he turns with an incredulous grin. "Nice one."

"I know." But then that grin shifts. "Fuck." I scream as I run away from him, and he chases me into the castle, through hallways. He could catch me at any point, I know, but we've been playing like this since I learned how to run.

I look over my shoulder right before I round a corner–
And slam into a wall.

A warm wall, with deeply tanned skin, covered by a thin leather vest. A wall with hands that catch the tops of my arms before I can rebound off of it.

I look up into Sione's eyes, and they say, "Hey, moonshine."

Motion in my periphery catches my attention, and I look in time to see Atlas glance at me, wink, and then give Sione a mock salute, to which they respond with a smirk and a dip of their chin.

"Well played," I tell both of them. Atlas chuckles as he walks away. Sione doesn't respond at all, only softens their hands on me before letting me go completely.

I don't need to have Fae hearing to know this hall is deserted. I know they wouldn't have allowed anyone else to hear whatever my inner thoughts are. Wouldn't have allowed them to influence what I might or might not say, or do.

We stare at each other for a moment, more silent and straight-faced than we've ever been around each other. My friend for all my life, and most of theirs. Who flew me around when I was small, and joked with me even when our age gap was its most awkward. Even when I could have bet anything that I was terrible at hiding my crush on them.

Until, apparently, they had one on me, too. Two years, Tali had said. When I was nineteen, and they were twenty-four. By all standards, a reasonable thing; for Fae, age gaps after eighteen all but cease to matter. After all, there are couples with centuries between them.

We might not have centuries, but, as I look into their eyes... gods, I decide I'll make the most of the time we have.

Without warning, I jump to wrap my arms around their neck, and crush my mouth to theirs. As Sione's arms wind around me, holding me to them, they kiss me back with smiling lips.

66

WALLS

ADAN AND I DON'T END UP HAVING MUCH TIME ALONE TOGETHER
for the rest of our first day in Sabrian. We're pulled by Javi and
Talia to the gardens, so sprawling that it takes us until lunch for
me to be satisfied with exploring them. Gorgeous–they even
rival those of my home, and of the city square where I would
picnic with Iris, Lor, and Hanna.

After lunch, which we eat on the stone edge of a fountain,
Nuria and Jolie find us. Again, they seem happy to just keep us
company. With them, in the comfortable chatter and silence,
the time flies, even through a semi-uncomfortable dinner. After
which, Adan and I bid everyone good night and retreat to our
chambers, the day of socializing and being relatively chaste
driving us there quickly.

And just as quickly into each other's arms as the door
closes. My mate fucks me on top of the apparently very sturdy
desk, and, as we near sleep, there's a heart-straining tenderness

to the way he moves within me, and then around me once we finish, holding me to his chest.

We end up taking breakfast in our chambers the next morning, delivered with a note in Li's scrawl telling us "You two had better have your scents under control by the time we see you." As he read it over my shoulder, Adan had slipped his fingers inside me, and made me come on them before kissing my cheek, and sending me to wash while he arranged the food in the sitting room.

The skirt of the white dress I'd picked out today—which had rendered Adan speechless when he'd exited the washroom to find me in it—swishes between us as we walk the gardens bathed in mid-morning sunshine. Ciaragen and Bayani find us there, and take us to the training yard, which is open to all at the castle. It's got all the equipment we could want: weights, blades, bows and arrows.

I want to play with all of it, but only make an excuse to grab the latter, saying I haven't gotten to use one in over a month. Which isn't a lie, but it's also obvious; where was I supposed to shoot, trapped on a ship during that time?

The weight is comfortable; not a bow built for a very long range, though one could probably manage to hit something a hundred feet away without straining the wood. I nock one of the arrows, and take my stance. Drawing it to my cheek, I focus, exhale, and shoot.

It hits just outside of the black dot in the absolute center, and I hiss through my teeth. "Try another, love."

I look over my shoulder at Adan, and he pulls another arrow from the quiver near us. Extending it to me, he says, "You'll hit the center this time."

To the other two, it probably just sounds like solid faith and encouragement. Like he knows I'll hit it, without a doubt, and wants me to know it, too. But, I hear the command lacing through it. He's not just believing in me. He's ordering me to hit that black dot.

And, damn me to the Void, but I want to find out how he'll reward me if I do.

I take the arrow, keeping my eyes on his until I'm drawing it. In a heartbeat and a half, it sinks into the target. The dot invisible, with the arrow pushing through it.

Bayani and Ciaragen give impressed applause, and I mock a bow to them before turning to put the bow away. Adan is closer than I expect him to be, though, and he gently takes the bow from my hands, and bends to kiss my cheek. In the same instant comes a thought down the bond: *Good girl.*

I blush, and feel his lips quirk up against my skin before he pulls back, and puts the bow and quiver back in their rightful places.

After that, they take me to the library. Without question, it has more books than I've ever seen in my life. Three floors lined with shelves, each of them stacked with tomes, to the point where some lay on their sides atop those lined up beneath them. The space itself is beautiful, too, though I can't look up at the domed ceiling without a painful pang going through my chest. I would like to explore the space–just not today.

Li finds us just before lunch, hand-in-hand with Sione. Her smile is brighter and more beautiful than the moon she likens, and the faerie exudes such joy that I'm surprised they're not dancing where they stand.

Li, on the other hand, skips as the two of them lead our group back to the gardens for a picnic lunch. Her mums are there, likely having set up the space for us, as bottles of champagne sit in buckets of ice on the corners of blankets. Sandwiches on fluffy bread are pre-sliced, small plates and napkins placed next to them.

As we're sitting, Atlas, Nate, and Bash walk towards our group on the cobblestone path, Talia with them. Atlas is the only one who had been notably absent the past day and a half. At least to me.

I want to believe he avoids my eye now because Adathan is still tense with males around me, but I can't help but wonder how...how much my mating is hurting him. I'd known it would, and had left him with only a look across a fire, too cowardly for anything else. Too scared that his pain, and mine, might take from me this one choice I've made since my life was turned upside down.

I remembered our conversation, his assurances, and forced them to be enough. He agreed to be my friend, told me he didn't mind being happy and sad at once, but...*I* mind.

I think I hear a breath from my left, but with so many voices around me, I could have imagined it. A moment later, though, Adan asks, "Love, could you have them pass that champagne?"

I look up at him and grin easily, even through the heavy thoughts of a moment ago, his face and presence enough to bring the expression. I nod, and look towards the nearest bottle–to find Atlas sitting right beside it. And then I know I didn't imagine that breath.

I squeeze Adathan's hand, and call over, "Atlas?"

He turns immediately, storm gray eyes settling on mine. "Could you pass the champagne?"

He nods, grabs the bottle, and holds it out to me. I take it, my fingers brushing his, and say, "Thank you."

His eyes soften, and his full lips tip up. "You're welcome."

I'm still smiling a little as I pour Adan and I each a glass. Then, Bash asks, "Champagne?"

I look up at him, leaning to hand the bottle back to Atlas, who takes it and places it back in the bucket of ice. "Yes. Why, is it called something different here?"

"Sparkling wine," he replies with a grin.

"Ugh. It sounds so boring," Li groans around a bite of sandwich. "*Cham-pagne.* So pretty." As she goes on, she's too busy dipping her bread into some kind of condiment to notice the eyes of much of the group moving behind us, and up. "Divani is so *bleh* in comparison. Like, you say one sentence in Ceraschen and I'm in love with you."

When that doesn't get the chuckle it should have, she looks up, and straightens when she sees her High Lord and High Lady. Javi is with them, and he says to Tali and Sione, "Make some room for us, kids. Gods, who raised you?" He steps over Li, mussing her curls a bit as he goes, and Tali scoots a few feet over, next to Nate.

"You did," she reminds him, then takes a sip of champagne.

"Ah, right."

She rolls her eyes, but when he gently kisses the top of her head as he takes his seat, she smiles softly as she puts her glass down.

The High Lord and High Lady move to sit between Tali and Bayani, the male helping his mate find her seat so she can adjust her skirts. This puts them directly across from me, and I feel my cheeks heat, uncertainty roiling in my belly.

I consider making an excuse to leave with Adan, but what would the point be? I would only be prolonging the inevitable. At least right now there are plenty of other people around to detract from my presence to them.

So, I take another bite of my sandwich. Though, when I settle, lowering my shoulders and loosening my jaw, my body drifts closer to Adathan's. Because, even if I could have helped myself, I don't want to. I yearn for him so powerfully that to just be next to him feels at once like the best place to be, and not enough. Not just sexually, though even after our *three* bouts this morning, I still want him. But, physically, mentally, spiritually, I want to crawl to him and mold myself to him until I can't distinguish our heartbeats, and he fucking breathes for me.

I can hear your thoughts, mate. Do you intend to have me on my knees before you here and now?

I smile a bit around my mouthful, not looking at him. *Is that meant to be a threat of proposal in front of all these people?*

A dark mental chuckle. *A threat? Never. A promise, though...*

My eyes widen, and shoot to him, only to find him smirking at me. *Don't look so horrified, love. I'm going to marry you. Perhaps with a more intimate proposal, though. I'm not sure I'll want to share you for a while after.*

My heartbeat stutters, but his eyes hold mine, gold and lovely and steady. Even to my mind, my response is a bit breathless. *I'm not horrified, Adathan.* Nervous, perhaps, in a strange way I didn't anticipate. But, otherwise...

His gaze both heats and softens, relief I hadn't been able to sense the precursor for while he hid it from me coming through our bond. And, when he stops hiding it, I see that its only source was not in my previous opinion of marriage. But also in what he can see within my heart.

He swallows, almost averting his eyes, and I lay my hand against his cheek. *I made my choice, Adan. I can hurt for it. But, I will never regret it. I will never regret you. Being yours is the best thing I could be.*

His jaw tightens against a wave of emotion as I say to him what he did to me weeks ago. Then he leans in, and kisses my temple—a gesture that would be more comforting, if he were not hiding whatever reaction my first two sentences stirred from him.

Not hiding, sweetheart. Just thinking. A warm, broad hand rests gently on my hip. I lean into the space this creates for me to rest near his chest, sighing to the sensation of that beautiful black heart beating so near my skin. Thinking is fair. I've done quite a lot of it myself, before the mating bond linked our minds. Adan should be given the same opportunity.

My gaze sweeps over to the male and female across from me. Their eyes flit down to their meals quickly, having obviously been on me until now, witnessing whatever they had between Adan and I. I find that their attention doesn't make me angry, as it might have a month ago. To be honest, I haven't been *angry* with them since arriving, save for the moment I needed to defend my mate. Just...awkward. Uncertain.

Now, in place of any hostility, I imagine how *they* must be feeling to have *me* here. To know that horror and tragedy made it possible, and to feel a terrible gratitude for it, as well as guilt for even thinking such a thing.

I know, because, in the darkest moments since I finally released my grief, I've felt that way about having Adathan. Perhaps, for me, gratitude isn't the right word–more so acceptance. And, while that may be the final stage of grief in its technical format–my heart aching with it at random points in the days and nights since–it feels significant here.

Acceptance. *Accepting* that they have longed for me all my life, even if I cannot embrace their relation to me in its entirety. That they are kind, just rulers who sought vengeance for their lost child for decades, yet gave it up for her, for *me*, in seconds.

Yes, their presence has made things awkward for me. At mealtimes yesterday, and here at lunch, too. But, only because I know who I am to them, yet I'm unable to *accept* who they want to be to me. Who they *are* by all rights but those of the man and woman across the sea who raised and loved me all my life.

But...the two people before me *gave* me that life. Sent me away to try and protect me, though it was surely worse than agonizing. So, sure, now that I'm here, the expectations they haven't outwardly expressed weigh on me. Make me feel like

I'm not doing enough for them, when I'm not prepared to give them all that they're probably hoping for.

It doesn't have to be *all*, though, I don't think. Maybe, if I just...if I just do *some*–maybe that will be enough. Maybe *I*, with whatever I am able to give right now, will be enough.

Adan's hand tightens on my hip a heartbeat before I say to them, "I've heard you like to be called Hielo and Hiela."

Their eyes shoot up to me, a bit wide, certainly not expecting for me to speak directly to them. It's the male who manages to swallow, and replies, "Yes. We find it to be less cumbersome than the 'High Lord and High Lady' business."

The new word–*cumbersome*–takes a second to process, but by his tone and surrounding words, I can guess its meaning well enough. "I have called Javi by his name. Is there less formality in all countries here?" Back home, if I'd ever referred to a Duke or Lord as anything but, it would have been social suicide.

The Sabriani High Lord shakes his head, Javi's dark eyes alight with an easy affection. "Not all. The southern countries are more tolerant in many ways, including a bit of...wiggle room for their sovereigns."

"But, you do not like to be called by your names," I say with a furrowed brow, just pointing out what I've noticed. How even the High Lady's sister refers to her by the interesting nickname.

Now, the High Lord's gaze moves to his mate. I look to her as well, and find her sienna eyes bright, though a shadow lies beneath. "It's not that we don't like it." I feel the familiar majick of a sound shield wrap around us. "My name is a secret to most. Everyone, in fact, outside of this group. If...if you would like to hear it, Althea..." I don't miss the way her voice wraps around my name, nor the look in her eyes when she says it. "My story, and the beginning of yours–they are intertwined."

My heart picks up its pace in my chest, and I straighten, my hand moving to Adan's knee, fingers tight. "Alright."

As she hesitates to take a breath, I realize something strange–I don't hear the rest of our group. Not a voice, not a scrape on a plate, nothing. They're talking, I can *see* them talking, but it's as if the sound shield is double-sided. They cannot hear us, and we can't hear them, either. Interesting.

I'm quickly drawn back to the conversation at hand when, after that breath, the High Lady looks into my eyes. And begins.

Her story is one of horror, and pain. Things I'd once wondered, one night in a forest of pines, if I would endure, but was saved from. She...no one saved her. Not for a long, long time. So, she survived while not wanting to live for nearly a *century*.

My hand hasn't once loosened on Adathan's leg. My nails had nearly pierced his trousers when I finally made sense of words he'd said to me what feels like so long ago. *I knew someone with a similar start to her story.* Yes, I'm sure Olin delighted in telling him everything about Oksana Mikhyala and the child she bore, that first night of the gathering. Allowing his son to realize every bit of the horror he'd participated in.

And, how similar we might have been if Adan hadn't done everything he could to work around the blood that bound him. I have no doubt Olin would have done everything to me that he promised and more. If I'm honest with myself, I wouldn't have lasted the three months she did before trying to take my own life. And I don't know what I would have become if forced to endure decades and *decades* of the same torment that pushed me to that breaking point.

The tracks of my tears cool on my cheeks when she tells me of her rescue. Of her recognizing her mate as soon as she saw him through the gates we walked through just yesterday.

There's some comfort in that; something to be said for a female who had endured enough agony and uncertainty.

"But, Althea...there is more to our story," the High Lady says, and I feel the same dread as I had weeks ago at a table in Dahlih pool in my stomach. The same fear from sensing something about to be revealed that would shift what I knew into something I didn't. It has my heart pounding in my chest, my breaths coming shallow and quick. Adan's hand, which has rested on mine since Oksana's first sentence, tightens.

Her chin and shoulders do not waver, but her eyes are gentle and knowing as she tells me, "When I arrived in Sabrian, I had just endured almost a century of being beaten and raped. Amedeo and I felt our bond, but we did not...we could not consummate it for some time. I was not ready, even with the male my soul felt like it had been searching for, in those darkest moments within my prison.

"Twenty-two years ago, it had been a small number of weeks since the last time Oleander had come to–*see* me. Nuria, who attended me most frequently at that time, had already devised a plan to free me, and planned to execute it as soon as was safe for her family. But, one day, when she came into my cell of a room...she scented it. Scented *you*. And she knew she had to get me out that day, because if Oleander came, if he realized, he would never have let me out of his sight again.

"Not when I was pregnant with his child."

There's a second where time stands still, and I with it, my body feeling outside; other. In that realm of being, Oksana's next words resound in my head like the war drum they are: "Althea, you are the biological child and sole heir of the High King of Eshelle."

⇹

My heart thuds so loudly in my ears that I can hardly hear Oksana hesitantly say, "Please, tell me what you're thinking."

There's an edge of desperation to the request, and when my eyes focus, I find hers full of...*fear*. And it's that expression alone that gives me the strength to break from my own shock and say, my voice strained and cracking, "I'm so sorry that happened to you."

Silver pools in her eyes, the fear dissipating, and I know it was the right thing to say. She had been *afraid* I would reject her because of the male who had gotten her with me.

I have a mom. She lived to love me, and died to protect me. This female is not discounting that, has not once referred to me as *hers*, though I'm sure she yearns to. Oksana survived a century of hell, then did everything in her power to keep safe the child she bore out of rape. And, even after that journey from Oschverre to Sabrian, finding her mate, maybe believing she could at last be *free*, be *happy*, she had given it away. For me.

My tears overflow once more, and I roll onto my knees, holding my skirt to shuffle on them, over to her. She seems to be holding her breath, watching me approach, the High Lord just as still beside her. I sit back on my legs, knee to knee with her, and, for a couple of heartbeats, I hold her silver-lined gaze with my own.

Then I lean forward, and wrap my arms around her waist.

She embraces me back instantly, and her sobs wrack her body, shaking within mine. One of her hands strokes my hair, and I feel her nose press into it, and inhale. Something I had seen Iris do with Cleo, and my mom had once done with me. Breathing in her baby, and holding her close, as Oksana might have imagined she would never get the chance to do.

Into the crook of her neck that smells of lavender and cinnamon, I whisper, "You never hated me? Because of him?"

She pulls back, and frames my face in her hands, brushing

away my tears. "Never, my love. Never." She pushes my hair back behind my ear, and her fingers stroke my cheek, and it's exactly what my mom used to do, and so my tears begin anew. She sees it, this fresh wave of emotion, and her brow crumples. "Oh, beautiful girl. How glad I am that you were loved so fiercely."

I'm unashamed when I fall into her arms, my head tucked beneath her chin, and my shoulders cradled in her embrace. Oksana runs her fingers through my hair and holds me while I cry, her lips against the top of my head.

When my tears have begun to dry, I look up through my lashes. Amedeo still sits beside us, his own eyes shining as he watches his mate hold the daughter she birthed. The baby he steadfastly accepted as his own, so much so that he'd been ready to attack Adan yesterday morning.

I have a dad. But, the male in front of me hasn't done anything to disqualify him from a piece of that role. If anything, what he has done has earned the sliver I'm able to give him, and then some.

So, I reach my hand towards him; an offering. He takes it with the only hesitation stemming from the surprise I can see in his kind brown eyes. I give a light tug, and watch the silver lining his lids overflow before he moves to close his arms around his mate, and me. Amedeo's brown beard tickles my brow as he kisses the top of my head, right next to where Oksana does the same.

Acceptance. It doesn't feel like a betrayal to my heart or my family across the sea, as I'd spent so long thinking it would. Instead, it only feels like my heart has grown; expanded to fit them within its walls, as it has for so many these past weeks.

67

THE GODDESS & THE GOD

MY MATE CLOSES HER EYES IN THE ARMS OF HER BIRTH PARENTS, unaware of how every other gaze from those on the blankets with us watches them with tears in their eyes. Including me.

They'd given their High Lord and High Lady privacy as the latter told her story. While I'd known a piece of who she was, what she had suffered years ago, hearing every part...Thea got her kindness from Lydia, and her patience from Aron, but her strength? That is all Oksana.

I had also known that the only reason I remain free within this castle and its grounds is because of the love she has for the daughter she bore. Still, only upon her finishing her recount, I now understand how that's enough for her because of the love *I* have for Thea. I can't imagine hating anybody that loves her, too, no matter how tempting.

His gray eyes are brightened to steel as he watches them, too, his lips pulled up into a small smile.

Tempting, yes. But impossible.

I look back at them right as Thea straightens, and the rest of the group busies themselves. I can't blame them for watching, especially the Sabriani; they've been waiting for this moment for their sovereigns for twenty-one years. That none of them look at me with contempt, regardless of how unwilling my part was in that suffering, is a fucking miracle. A miracle I'm more and more grateful for each moment, as the female who holds my heart and soul in her healing hands gets to know them, as they've wanted to know her all her life.

The High Lady strokes Thea's cheek once more as she sits up, right above the scar there. When she drops her hand, it's to take one of Thea's within it. I feel the sound shield around us expand to include the rest of our group. "I'm sure you have questions," Oksana says.

Thea smiles slightly, but it leaves, along with the straightness of her brow as she furrows it, and tilts her head. "I think I've worked a bit out, actually."

She stands, and since Oksana shows no inclination to release her if Thea is willing to maintain the tether, she goes with her. Thea puts her bare feet in the grass, her shoes next to me on the blanket. "In Weaschte, there's significant iron sediment in the land. But not here. Yes?"

The female's voice is a little mystified when she agrees, not as used to the intellect we've come to expect. From the corner of my eye, I see Lina sit back and cross her ankles, as if settling in for a show.

"Because of that, the magic in the people and the land isn't as strong. We're assuming, of course, that the story of Deimos and Ymeda is true. That the goddess wished to bless the land as well as the people with her power, and the god saw to it that it was done. But, if iron contradicts magic, then that gift would have been minimal, if there at all, in Weaschte. And so, a people that were supposed to be equal, instead became indentured."

Thea drops Oksana's hand, but only to pace, her fist beneath her chin, that elbow propped on the arm she crosses below her chest. "And the Apotheos..." Her eyes flick to mine. "At what age do Fae hit maturity–when do they stop appearing to age?"

"Around twenty-two," I answer her, and she nods, anticipating it.

"Yes. So, because humans age, there must have been a circumstance wherein the magic they received, if any, seemed to come to an–erm–accumulation point. Now, the odd thing is, of course, that no such point occurs in Fae. I wonder...I wonder, then, if those millennia ago, the Fae sought to oppress the humans so thoroughly that they convinced them that whatever *shift* they felt at twenty-two was the final point of their power. That, just as the gods ceased the aging of their oppressors, so did they cease the magic of the oppressed.

"It wouldn't have been hard to convince a people who likely already felt shunned by the gods that such a thing were true. And, once convinced," her eyes move to Ciaragen's, "they would have self-actualized it. Believed it in their minds to the point where it became true. The mind is a powerful thing, after all."

The High Lord and High Lady watch Thea pace, their mouths parted in awe. My mate, so deep within that brilliant mind of hers, doesn't seem to notice anything but the small nod Ciaragen manages.

She lifts her chin from her hand, and looks around at the gardens, the great tree under whose shade we sit. "And the majick of the land...they would never have felt it. Or, if they did, they would write it off. So, of course, if Deimos and Ymeda had ever been gods to Weaschte, they would have been abandoned, their story discounted. But, here–*here*, Ymeda's gift would have held true. Only..."

Those miraculous eyes find mine again, and she nearly whispers, "*Forever blessing it with her glory, to be brought forth by a ruler given freely, and taken well.*" Her arms fall to her sides, and she looks back at Oksana. "How long has the land slumbered?"

She has to clear her throat to answer. "Centuries. For three kings, including Oleander."

Thea nods, a slight motion that she's not aware of making. "And how long since the healers of Eshelle lost their majick?"

"The same," Oksana breathes.

Again, that green gaze lands on mine. "And they would have been like water, or fire. Varying in strength, as healers do in Weaschte, where Kings and Queens have been beloved since the time of the Last War. But the strongest...in Eshelle, they would have had the power to control it all–the life within people *and* within the land. But, when that power abandoned them, they would never have confessed to it." To Oksana, she does not ask; she only speaks with the knowledge that what she's saying is true, not needing it confirmed: "Oleander has no majick."

Even so, the High Lady shakes her head in affirmation. Thea resumes her strides, but not pacing now; only padding her bare soles into the lush grass beneath them, towards the base of the tree. "But, I...I am new. And I was not raised by leaders unwanted and unloved by their people. Would not have been, in any case. Still, I was brought up in a land of iron. I ingested it in my food, breathed in its essence from the air. As a result, just like it repressed my Fae healing, it kept my majick from being as strong as it could be, even considering my glam-our. But, my body grew used to it. Of course, he never would have prepared for that. Never would have assumed a strength in me."

Those last two sentences are quieter, though certainly not weak. They do, however, set many of the brows around us furrowing, but I know who she's talking about. What she means. And the pride I'd already felt an abundance of swells in my chest at her realization that she had and has something that could take Olin by surprise.

She places her hand against the tree trunk, and speaks again at her usual volume. "That's why I can feel it so strongly here, even with the glamour. And Adan..." She looks over at me, and silver pools within her eyes. "Have you realized it yet?"

She must see the confusion in my expression, because when her head tilts this time, it's in rue. "You're him." A single tear falls down her scarred cheek. *"Know that only the love you bear in your soul might keep my majick alive there in turn,"* she again quotes my telling of the story of the goddess and the god. "You said what little healing majick you had disappeared for decades. That the first time you realized it was back was when you didn't die from the wounds I gave you. The day you realized I was your mate, and you accepted death, without any hatred in your heart for what you had done in life. Adathan...you have the power of Deimos."

⇔

I don't doubt that she's right. My mate is too bright and brilliant, and doubting her would be more blasphemous than cursing the gods. Even so, to think of such power being bestowed to *me*...it's difficult to accept, to say the least. It has my lips parting, and my heart stopping in my chest because how— how could *I* ever have been worthy of this? Not only of a mate whom I've called my Life, without knowing how true the word was, but the power of Death that has complemented her own majick since the time of the gods.

"And that's why powers like ours are so strong," she goes on, as if she didn't just shatter my world only to reforge it with gold, as she has done since a touch to my arm in a castle hallway. "Because they were the only ones freely given by the gods. It's why...why they impact our appearance, and our scents, when no others do. Only, mine is still suppressed by the glamour."

Green eyes move to the sienna set across from her. "Did I miss anything?" It's not snarky, the way she says it. There's genuine curiosity there, but I can hear the undercurrent of wariness. The hope that there's nothing else, if only because there's already so much.

The High Lady shakes her head, that awed expression mingling with adoration. After a heartbeat of silence comes Lina's voice, "Holy shit, Al, if I could clap for you, I would."

The spell she'd cast on the group breaks in the form of breathless chuckles. Thea cracks a smile, but I can tell something still weighs on her mind. And I know she doesn't need my encouragement–she is strong, all on her own. But, that's the thing: she doesn't have to be on her own, even if she can be. It's not about pushing her to see what she's capable of because I *know* how capable she is. It's about being there. That's it.

So, that's what I think to her down the bond: *I'm right here, love.*

I feel her gratitude and love radiate back to me, though she continues to look at her birth mother.

Thea says, "I'm ready for you to take the glamour."

⇔

A few minutes later, we're in a large garden with not a fountain, bench, nor trellis in sight. Completely surrounded only by nature, and it's obvious instantly that this place was made for her. Beds of flowers ranging in heights of a few inches, all the way to my hip; grass and clover, so untended I can feel Thea registering it tickling her bare shins. Trees, small enough to have been planted around her birth, circle the space like nature's pillars, holding the open sky.

Thea stands in the very center, the rest of us following the lead of the High Lord and High Lady, and stopping several feet away. I force the instinct to be near her down, grounding my feet as I watch her slowly spin in place, looking around the beautiful space. If such a word can be used regarding anything when she's there to compare it to.

When she faces us, her eyes land on Oksana, whose voice is low when she speaks. "When I remove the glamour, it will be overwhelming. You'll not only be opened up to the immense power of the land, but you'll have our senses, too. Our sight, our hearing." She looks at me, and nods. "Your mate will keep you tethered through the bond, but must remain physically distant from you, as such power is not without risk."

I open my shields to tell her, *I don't care about risk to me if it will help her.*

She responds, *If she hurts you when her power floods her veins, how willing do you think she will be to use it again?* Dark brows raise, and I mentally sigh. Point made.

Oksana turns her gaze back to Thea. "Are you ready?"

My mate plants her feet more firmly into the ground, and I feel her release that ball of power within her chest so that it floods her limbs, her heart, her mind. "I'm ready," she replies, husky and *volatile.*

Fuck yeah, she is.

Oksana dips her chin.

The outward effect is immediate. Her ears arch, and Thea, already more gorgeous than I knew how to handle, becomes even more so, which I would have bet the soul she owns was impossible.

The power, though...that thrums like the reverberation of a drum, rising and rising in volume as it threads through her veins, steadily turning them a burning gold that filters through her skin. She bares it, eyes closed and breaths heaving her breast, and I'm right there with her. Her mind is wrapped around mine while her body cannot be, and then–

A force explodes within her, and I'm nearly flung from her mind. I grapple her, holding tight to the edge of her consciousness, its core filled with nothing but *power*. Her eyes fly open, the green luminescent, shining out like sunshine through a leaf, and her arms raise from her sides without her commanding them to, light twisting and twining from her upturned palms to her forearms.

In the next heartbeat, she's tunneling down into the earth within her mind, but her body...her body levitates, toes pointing towards the ground, several feet away from it. Still, she goes, through soil and twisted vines and ancient bones. Down and down and *down* until she reaches the core of this world, and–

That world shudders as she breaks the binding of its power. That thing once used on bones cracks the very earth beneath us, and, in a castle that feels so far away in this moment, glass shatters, and people scream.

Grass grows to wrap around our legs, and I vaguely hear Oksana order everyone to remain still. I can feel that; how ravenous this majick is. Ready to pull us down into its belly, if it construes us as enemies. I don't so much as shout down the bond, should that convey a threat while its goddess is so vulnerable. I only maintain the white-knuckled grip I have on her mind, projecting my presence so that, wherever she is in that swirling chaos, she can feel me.

The nature around us grows and grows, tree roots dislodging from the ground and the blooms around us wind together with the grasses. When flowers and blades of green are twining their way over my heart–

The pounding drum stops. The growth ceases.

The people around me are panting as the nature releases them, falling to cover the ground like a thick blanket of life. I don't look at them; can't look away from the female who falls from the air, only to land in a crouch, her midnight hair covering her face.

I step forward, ignoring Oksana's hushed warning. At my first footfall, Thea's head flicks up. But, it's not her eyes that stare back at me. They glow still, with the presence of the goddess's majick that holds my mate in its clutches.

I can feel it recognize me. Who I am to her, and what power I possess that speaks to it. I let it through my vessels, blackening them; let the majick pulse in the air between us. It tilts her head as I approach further, and she stands, more graceful than any Fae I've seen before. Then, when only a pace of swirling grass separates me from her, I drop to my knee.

I take off the ring I've been wearing on my forefinger for six weeks, and hold it in my palm. Once there, I remove the glamour from it, and it grows, expanding to the last knuckle of each finger. And I offer my Queen her crown.

The glow fades from her veins and her eyes as she stares at it, and within the latter spring tears, bright as the overhead sun. My own majick returns to rest as her lips part, and her fingers tremble as she brushes them over the circlet tiara that fell from her head on the night everything changed.

I rise slowly, and her eyes track mine as I go. I lift the crown, and gently lay it on her head. It falls perfectly over her hair, sitting behind the waves that crest over her forehead. I restrain myself from kissing her brow, and her parted lips, from brushing her hair back behind her shoulders. I only get down on my knee once more, and hold her gaze for a heartbeat before I bow my head, my fist over my heart.

I hear rustling behind me, and I know the others are doing the same. High Lords and the High Lady, their people alike, all bowing.

To their High Queen.

68

AS I GO

I WOULD NOT HAVE CALLED THE STORY OF DEIMOS AND YMEDA A prophecy. Its telling was more so an instruction manual; how to maintain the power of the goddess who blessed this world so greatly, so selflessly. And how to get it back, if ever it were lost.

The instructions were the same, in either case. The part that perhaps had two meanings in our time, though, was the bit that decided all: *a ruler given freely, and taken well.*

Thea had willingly offered herself to the people, to the majick. And, without hesitation, those people and their land had accepted her.

No, I would not have called it a prophecy. That makes it sound too...fantastical. As if she hadn't done anything to earn this role. To call it such a thing, to me, would discount all that she had lost and suffered to get here. It would detract from the fucking enormity of her strength, and the bravery it took to accept something she had never known was hers. To stare, undaunted, into a future she would have rejected just weeks ago.

And yet, she sits next to me at dinner now, her gaze intent as she takes the small amount of wilt away from the flowers on the table without laying a finger on them. She glares at one, which managed to slip the notice of the staff, low as it is within the bouquet. It's sagged completely, its petals dry despite the fresh, clean water in the vase.

After a moment, she huffs, and takes an annoyed sort of bite of her mashed potatoes. A dish I'd never seen served here in my seven months as a castle guard all those years ago, but has somehow found its way onto all of our plates tonight.

I can't help the smirk that comes, watching her frustration. The wrath of my High Queen is fearsome, but her annoyance? Fucking adorable.

She senses me looking at her, and turns that face–that gorgeous, Heavens-sent face–towards me. The glamour removed, the green of her eyes is even brighter, the yellow flecks like sparkling stars. They glitter with amusement now, too, as one corner of her mouth tilts up in response to mine. "Apparently, I can't bring it back to life." Her gaze bobs to the flower, then back to me.

I shrug with an overdone sigh, turning back to my plate and picking up a forkful of food. "Pity."

A chuckle from my other side, which escalates into a laugh when Thea's finger swipes through my mashed potatoes, and then wipes it onto the tip of my nose.

"Very queenly, Al," Lina says through her giggles while I clean my face.

Thea lifts her chin with false pomposity. "As a Queen, anything I do is queenly, Emelina." She breaks after saying our friend's full name, her mouth twitching into a smile.

"*High* Queen," Sione corrects, raising their brows.

Thea looks at them incredulously. "What's the difference?"

"Melisan is only called Queen, because Oleander, and the kings before him, didn't believe the female should have an equal title. So, it's a big difference, actually."

My mate frowns appreciatively. "Alright, then. Everything I do is *highly* queenly."

Sione nods once in approval. "Much better."

On Thea's opposite side, the High Lady grins, and quietly continues to eat her meal. I'm sure if I had the gifts of Jolie, the joy and contentment I would feel from her as she sits beside her daughter would be staggering.

I know, all those years ago, the plan had been to become a queen herself, once their rebellion was a success. My guess is that they would get news every so often about the princess across the sea, and, when they heard the majick of Ymeda had flowed true through her veins, that plan shifted. And, now that Thea is here, I don't doubt that the would-have-been High Queen will do everything in her power to see Oleander off the throne, and her daughter on it.

⇔

I'm more than fucking ready to be back in our chambers when everyone parts for the night. My blood is practically boiling with need for my mate, and my soul screams for me to serve her, especially after all she braved today.

The door is still clicking shut when I'm on her, spearing my fingers through her hair, and pulling her to me with my other hand on her lower back. Our kiss is wild, and I'd known she was not breakable before, but *now*...there's a savageness in the way our mouths meet, and our tongues twine.

No more holding back, mate, she growls into my mind, one of her hands twisting in my hair, and the other–

A deep noise vibrates from my chest when she slides her hand between us to grip my already-hard cock through my trousers. *You will not break me. Unleash yourself, Adan.*

And with those words, with her hand on my cock, with the name only she has and ever will call me, I will obey my High Queen in this.

As it will be her obeying me for the rest of the night.

I pull her back from me, and tell her, "Take my cock out."

Her answering grin is wicked, and she does what I said without hesitation. I'm already so sensitive, everything heightened, that when her hand closes around me, my fingers tighten in her hair. I grit out, "Now take me to the bed then bend over it, love."

I release her so she can back towards the bed, leading me. Once there, she again does as ordered, letting me go to brace her elbows on the bed, her ass high in the air. I let my length tease her through the fabric of the dress that's been driving me wild all fucking day as I remove my own clothes. Then, slowly, I pull up her skirt, only to find her utterly bare beneath.

My voice is low and dark when I ask her, "How long've you been like this?" I slide my finger through her glistening center.

Around a whimper, she gets out, "All day."

I slip that finger inside her, and her breath hitches, her walls so gods-damn tight around that digit. "All day," I repeat. Then I get on my knees, and replace my finger with my tongue.

Thea cries out, and I fuck her with my tongue until she comes around it, which happens all too quickly. If I had more patience right now, I might flip her over and see how long I could make her wait before she came again.

Later, I suppose.

Because right now, I stand, and paint my tip with her cum. She's still panting from her release, and she tries to push back onto me, but I stop her with a hand on her hip, and click my tongue. I slide myself through her center to hit her clit, and my name moans through her lips.

I tame the thing within me that begs me to fuck her until she can't stand for a moment to say, "I'm going to feel deeper like this. It's going to hurt at first, and you can tell me to stop if you need to, but you won't. Will you?"

"No," she gasps as I rub against her again. "No, I want it. I want to hurt for you."

My hand circles one side of her ass, then starts to travel up her spine, over the bunched fabric of her dress. "I know you do." When my hand is at her hair, I yank, arching her back and leaning forward until my mouth is by her delicately pointed ear. "But, I don't give a fuck if I'm about to come. You say stop, Thea, and I fucking stop. Got it?"

"Yes," she breathes.

I growl, and pull her hair just a bit more. "If you want me to stop, what do you say?"

"Stop–I'll say stop, and you'll stop."

"That's right. Now twist your pretty little fists into those blankets, sweetheart." I let her go, and she immediately bunches the fabric tightly into her hands. Such a good fucking girl.

I pull back from her clit, and plunge into her. She screams on a gasp, and tightens around me enough that half of me is still out. I run my hands over her hips, and feel her relax immediately. "That's it, love." I knead the strong, thick flesh beneath my hands, my eyes rolling back a bit at the feel of her around me. I still haven't let go of that leash; I just can't seem to consciously put myself into a place where I might hurt her, regardless of her willingness for it, and my...my dark desire for it. Not for her pain, but to be within her so deeply that she aches with it.

Suddenly, she pushes back on me, her ass flush with my

hips, and a gritted oath slips up my throat. She looks back at me over her shoulder, her lips parted with heavy breaths, and her crown glinting in the faerie lights. And my leash doesn't just get released. It fucking *snaps*.

I fuck my mate, slamming into her and pulling her against me, my hands tight on her hips. Our skin slaps together, and she moans and screams, pulsing around me when she shouts my name, coming on my cock. I bend to lick my way up the top of her spine, tasting the sweat of her ecstasy, and when I straighten, I use her dress to pull her up with me. I wrap one hand around her throat, and there's a ripping sound when I use the other to shred the top of that pretty dress, and her breasts spill out of it. I grab one of them, and squeeze hard before pinching her nipple. She arches like a cat, reaching up to twine her fingers into my hair.

When she tilts her head back to look into my eyes, the yellow flecks in them glow with majick, and I only realize then that my veins have blackened. It's the look in those fucking eyes that has release barreling down my spine, and I let go of her tit to press my hand to her belly so that I can come inside her so deep it'll stay there, Void-damned tonic or no.

We're both breathing heavy as our majick reels back into us, and we back into our minds. I press kisses to her cheek, her jaw, the mark of my claiming on the side of her neck. Then I pull out of her, and release her throat to turn her around. She stares up at me as if there's nothing else she'd rather do for the rest of her immortal life, and whatever beast still riled within me sits back at that, and curls up, content—for now.

I kiss her lips, and reach between us to tear the rest of the dress open. It falls to the ground in a whisper of fabric on skin, and then she reaches up to wrap her arms around my neck. On the rumpled bed, I lay her back, and run my lips down her body. The corner of her jaw, the lines of her neck.

The curve of her breast, a lave of my tongue over one dusky peak. The ribs that flare with sighing breaths, to the plane of her stomach. Once at her clit, I kiss that, too, then move my mouth to the side, above her labia. Then I part my lips, comforting her with the flat of my tongue before sinking my canines into her.

The mating bite always scars, but I'll take no chances on this one sealing over without a trace. I take the salt of us from her, and skim the pad of my thumb over the second mark of my claiming.

Mine, I think to her, and, to prove it further, I follow through by getting her to come for me twice. It would have been three, but that new Fae speed and strength took me off-guard, and she managed to escape, laughing hysterically as I chased her to the balcony doors. Snagging her, I dropped us to the carpet that covered the tiled floor before them, and was inside her again in the next second.

She moved with me, her fingers soft on my scars until her nails scored them while she climaxed again. When I came this time, it had been with my lips on hers, and my hands brushing over her body. Only after we caught our breath did we notice the not insignificant breeze on our skin.

"Well, Colina just got an earful," Thea said, looking at the empty frames of the balcony doors, their glass shattered and scattered on the balcony itself. I laughed, and she did, too, looking up at me, eyes sparkling with delight, filled with mischief and not so much as a hint of embarrassment.

Now, our bodies twined beneath one of the thin blankets on this summer night, I kiss the top of her head, and gently remove her crown. The scars of pleasure her nails left over the ones of pain along my spine stretch as I reach to place the circlet on her night table. Her freckled lids barely flicker as I kiss her brow, and whisper to her, "I love you."

⇔

My eyes flash open.

Something is happening, something is coming, though I don't know what. There is no noise aside from the branches of trees swaying, and the beginnings of staff quietly making their way towards their stations for the day. There is nothing that should point to me being woken by this strange sense of dread.

"Thea," I whisper, moving my arms enough to rouse her. She grumbles, her brow furrowing, clearly not feeling what I do, but that doesn't ease my worry. "Thea, love," I say again, and maybe it's my grip on her shoulder, but I think it's the urgency in my voice that has her eyes opening, instantly alert.

"What is it?" she asks as we both rise.

"I'm not sure," I answer honestly, digging through our bags which had been deposited for us at some point yesterday. I toss her her boots, trousers, and one of my shirts that she acquired, and she catches all of it nimbly. By the time she's pulling on her boots, I'm doing the same. I reach my hand towards her, and she closes the distance between us to grab it, and then we're out the door.

"What is it?" she repeats, but her tone has changed. She feels it now, too, and I put my finger on it in the same instant that she does.

Our quick walk turns into a sprint, and we're not alone. Their scents hit me as we make it outside, the wind blowing them towards me, which unfortunately means the scent of whoever is coming is downwind. It can only be one of two people, but one is so unlikely–

Until it isn't. Until, through the gates that are immediately opened upon the demand of the High Queen, I see him.

Dion is still a hundred or so feet away, but the light of dawn makes it clear, even if his demeanor didn't. He doesn't swagger, is trudging like he varied between running and walking here, for at least the distance from the Sabriani shore to the castle. But, it's his eyes that truly set him apart from Olin; there is too much emotion there for it to be my father.

His name is a choked rasp from behind me as Ciaragen recognizes it, too.

Too many things happen at once, then, and yet, time slows as they go. One by one.

Dion sees his mate, and the instant reaction on his face is a heartbreaking mix of devastation and elation.

Then, it changes. To dread so deep it makes my breath stop.

He screams from the depths of his soul as his veins light like charcoal being fired, and his hand arcs towards her, his arm straining against the force that drives it.

And I owe it to her. I owe it to them.

I shove Thea behind me, my heart ripping from my chest with the knowledge that my last action towards her will be one of violence. She collides with Atlas, who catches her.

Good. That's good.

As I dive in front of Ciaragen, my mate screams my name. It tears from her, a desperate cry that shreds through her throat, and my soul.

It hurts. Gods, whatever Dion's power has done hurts.

And then it doesn't. Then, I can't feel much of anything at all.

But for a longing ache as I go, wishing I could have told Thea that I am sorry.

69

LEFT

*T*HEA - *DAYS 38 & 39*

ARMS HOLD ME—THE WRONG ARMS, THE *WRONG* ARMS, NO NO *NO*
no NO.

Something hurts, something is ripping apart within me, it
hurts. Its shreds are grasped, but no they're like the skeleton of a
leaf, withering as I touch them.

No, please, I beg them as they float like ashes. I beg other
things, too, though I'm not sure what.

Please, *please, PLEASE.*

Let go of me, let *go*—not of those shreds but of my body, I
think I say it, think I *snarl* it, and then I'm freed, but it doesn't
feel that way.

The support taken away, I fall, and part of me keeps falling,
falling, while the rest of me is crawling, crawling—

It's gone, that being within me that was not me, it's *gone*, and
I can't understand what I'm still doing here, because what once
housed the rest of me is hollow and empty, why am I not, too.

580

Hollow, empty, just like where his heart used to be. It's not there anymore, I can see through–*through* him, the clover is red though, it's red not green. And my hands are red, too, red where they touch him, and no, I get it on his face, his *face*. It's there, and only spreads when I try to wipe it away, why won't it go away?

His name, I say his name, why are his eyes staring up like that? They–no the sun, it shouldn't come out, not when his eyes...no, they look just the same, they *used* to look just the same, the way they would shine when he looked at me. They're so empty now, empty like his chest and like the bond that won't stop *leaving me*.

You can't leave me, you *can't*, Adathan. Stay, stay, stay. No, I'm *here*, Adathan, you have to be here with me.

It's not enough, not enough time. It's not enough, not enough for me to grasp, it's slipping away, *you're* slipping away, but I'm not done, Adan. I'm not done loving you, I'm not, so please, *please*, Adan, you have to stay.

I can't, I won't–I won't *let* you go. With me, you're meant to be *with me*. Gold like your eyes, so bright, but the sun is still rising, it shines from me, into you. I force it through my hands and sounds through my teeth, *force* it to recreate what was once there.

I know every piece of you, have felt your heart against my palm, my cheek. I've sensed it and heard it, always so strong and steady. I've memorized its rhythm and the way it sounds when your blood runs through it. I know its chambers, and I know your vessels, and your lungs. I've listened to you breathe, I've breathed *with* you, because you showed me how when you loved me and I loathed you.

And your chest, I know that, too. Have leaned against it, slept cushioned on it, kissed it. I know how it rises and falls, how it moves because I've watched it for longer than I used to want to admit. I've kneeled over it with a dagger to your throat, kneeled over it bared to you. I've memorized the breadth of it, every scar, too, but those are gone.

Now wake up, wake *up*, Adan.

Adathan.

ADATHAN.

No no *no no NO.*

I did it, I did it so please wake up. I know I did it, because I can feel it as I push my hands into your chest over and over and over. I know I did it because I feel it rise when I breathe into you, for you, just like you did for me, remember?

I can't do anything else, I don't have that majick, I can't *do* anything else. *I* can't–

"ATLAS," I yell his name, and for a second, just a second, I take my eyes off you to look for him. Just a second, because he's close, kneeling near us. I don't recognize the voice that speaks next, even though I know it's me because who else would say, "Get over here and shock his *fucking heart!*"

Why are his eyes almost silver, so bright? What does he look down at, what–?

No.

No, he *saved* her, he jumped in front of her. No, why are her eyes staring up like that?

Dion, it's Dion bent over her, what's on his back? What's that while he hunches over the space where she's been burned away?

I don't look anymore, I say it again instead, "Get over here and shock his heart." It's low, my voice, but he hears me, looks up at me again, but he doesn't move. My teeth are around his name, but they separate so I can be loud, loud because he needs to *hear* me. "I just made his heart from *fucking scratch.* But I can't–" it chokes, those words, I can't say them, no. "*He* can. So, shock his heart, or they both–"

The rest won't come out, and it doesn't need to. I can see it doesn't need to, in those silvered eyes. Shaky, he stands, and then he's on his knees beside you. Oh, my love, I would caress your cheek, but I can't touch you as he holds his hands above your chest, and sparks light up the space between your skin and his.

"Again," because I can't hear it, your heart, it's *still*.

Those wisps are still slipping from me, what was once a tether that could not be broken–I'd *thought* it couldn't be broken, because I never imagined the hacksaw would come for it. Would shred it, those fragments so hard to hold onto, why don't they want to stay with me, why didn't *you* want to stay with me?

"Again." Stay, stay, stay.

"*Again.*" With me, with me, with me.

"*AGAIN.*" Adathan, *Adathan, ADATHAN*.

Thump, thump.

A pause, then:

Thump thump, thump thump.

The red on my hands is dry now when I touch your face, but *my* face is so wet, and you're so blurry. So blurry, but I still see it when you blink. And I feel it as those wisps I'd been desperately grasping for stop crumbling beneath my touch.

When I fall to your chest, the one that I built, it rises and falls beneath me. And now, now that I did it, now that you're back, I'm shaking again, harder than before. But your arms, they wrap around me, and they hold me together, keep me from falling apart, as you have so many times before.

"I'm so sorry," comes your voice, *your voice*, though I've never heard it like this before. You're crying with me, your arms so tight around me. "I'm so sorry, Thea."

I rise a bit, and grab your face again, and I can't find words, but I don't need them right now. I kiss you, and my tears fall onto your face, and I smell your blood on our skin, but you're here, you're *here*.

We separate, and things start coming back to me, things outside of you and me. I hear a male sobbing and begging, and it's so like what I had felt inside an eternity and just seconds ago that I remember–

"Ciaragen," I whisper, and his eyes flare, and we're up. I don't, can't look at the space where we were, but around us... Around us, the land is withered. The green clover is leeched, the flowers bending towards the earth.

But we're with her now, and it's Adathan who says, "Dion, you need to move."

I don't think he hears him, or if he does, he can't obey. I'm not as kind when I tell him, "You need to move. He can bring her back, but not like this." I don't need to look down the bond that hurts to behold when I say it. I know her wounds are too great for her to return as she is.

When Dion remains hunched over his mate, dark, slender hands grip his shoulders and pull him off. He tries to fight Nuria, but weakly, too weakly. The state his heart and body are in renders him unable to combat the strength of the female that holds him away from Ciaragen, so that Adathan and I can move over her.

I can feel the stores of my majick, low in comparison to what I felt yesterday afternoon, but enough to heal her without jeopardizing my own life. I hold my hands over her chest, and light emits from my palms, and flows up my veins. I build back her muscle and flesh and skin; vessels and bone and tendons. A pair of terracotta hands lays a male's shirt over her once I'm done, covering her breasts.

Then, large, bronze hands take the place of mine, and I can barely look at them, can hardly watch the once-stilled veins blacken. I can feel the strain within him, though, after his life-force was so–so drained, and I know it won't be enough on its own this time.

I don't know why the thought occurs to me, only that, when it does, I know it will work. I look over at Atlas, and I hold out my hand with a flick of my eyes to his hip. Wordlessly, though his jaw is tight as he reins in all the emotion likely running through him now, he unsheathes his dagger, and places the hilt in my hand.

I run the blade over my other palm, and then slice a clean, deep line down Ciaragen's sternum. Those around us make varying noises when I cut her, but I feel nothing but certainty, and a blank sort of calm as I squeeze my fist over her chest, and spill my blood into her.

The wound seals almost instantly, and I feel Adathan's strain lessen. He pulls and pulls at her, and those eyes stare up at the pinkening sky as the heartbeats around us pound so loudly I can hear them over Dion's continued shuddering breaths.

Then, the chest I rebuilt rises in a gasp, and those eyes blink. Those who had not seen what he'd done with me that night in the alley are in shock, only Li and Atlas releasing shaky, relieved sighs at first. Atlas takes Li into his arms, and Nuria does the same to Jolie after releasing Dion.

The male falls beside Ciaragen, barely gaining his knees, but doesn't touch her. He keeps saying that he's sorry, he's so sorry, and I think she comes back to herself fully after the third time, because her eyes finally focus. She says his name, then says it again, tears pooling around her deep blue gaze, then trailing down her temples.

I move to stand, and then I see what had caught my eye on his back before.

The word TRAITOR is carved across the backs of his shoulders. Beneath it is some kind of snake, curving as if wrapped around his spine. They're deeply scarred, though obviously recent.

I'm sure there's a story behind it. A reason he's here. But I don't feel curious, or even particularly...care.

I turn from them, and I hear *that* voice say my name, but I keep walking away. I hear it again, shutting my heart off from the emotion that enters it, but it comes *again*, more urgently when my steps stumble. And then I'm falling.

He somehow manages to catch me before I hit the ground. That's all I know before blackness consumes my vision and my mind, and I descend into its comforting embrace.

⇹

I wake to the smells of flowers, and oak, embers, and leather. To the sun on my face, warming my skin.

I open my eyes, and hear the sighs of relief. Looking around, I find Oksana and Amedeo to my right, Li and Sione, Atlas, and Tali standing behind them.

He's to my left, as he always has been. I look into his eyes for a second, but it starts to hurt too quickly, so I look away just as fast. I feel what that does to him, and I shut that out, too.

"Is she okay?" I ask no one in particular.

"Yes," Oksana replies, and I feel her take my hand. I meet her eyes, and find them silver-lined. "You and Adathan saw to that, my love. She is resting in their chambers now."

"And him?" I don't know how to put inflection back into my voice. There's barely enough to make it clear that I've asked a question, rather than stated something.

"Sleeping, too."

I nod to acknowledge that I heard her, then sit up. He tries to help me, but whatever reaction that gets sent down the bond has his hands leaving my body before I'm all the way up.

We're in that garden from yesterday. Could it be only yesterday? "How long was I unconscious?"

She hesitates, then says, "Twenty-six hours."

That registers; shock permeates my brain, but I don't like the way it feels. Once I have it back under control, I ask, "Have you all been here the whole time?"

Oksana shakes her head. I realize my shields are down when her voice is in my mind. *Just me, and Adathan.* At the same time, she responds out loud, "As much as we could be. We knew you were close to waking when the land around you came back."

My brows furrow. "What do you mean?"

"It was restoring you, my love. All day yesterday, it bled its life into you. It was only at dawn today that it started to brighten, while you gave back to it."

"Oh," is all I say, though the fingers of my free hand unconsciously dig into the earth beneath them.

The following silence is probably awkward. Li breaks it by saying, too brightly, "Well, you scared the shit out of us for a minute there, Al, but we're fucking starving. Ready for breakfast, gorgeous?"

I don't really have an appetite, though my stomach feels hollow. I manage, "Okay," then stand, again on my own, still closing off the emotions screaming at me that aren't mine. Those that are stay locked up, nice and tight. I got pretty good at that not too long ago.

So I notice in a detached way as I brush off my trousers that at some point, someone cleaned and changed me, because there's no more blood on my hands or clothes. I don't look down or back after that, just walk towards the castle. Through the unpaved and then the cobblestone paths, down the halls, into the same place we had breakfast and dinner yester–two days ago.

Almost everyone is there. Nuria and Jolie, Javi, Nate and Bash, Bayani. The first two spring up from their seats, and begin to rush towards me, but stop when their eyes move past me for a heartbeat. Their pace resumes more calmly, but the looks in their eyes are so intensely grateful that I have trouble maintaining contact with them.

They don't touch me, thank goodness, but Nuria smiles gently, Jolie hovering, nearly expressionless, behind her. "Thank you," the female says, her dark eyes shining. "Thank you, both." Those eyes flick behind and above me.

I hate it. *Thanking* him? It's not just for bringing her back, it's for diving in front of her, and thanking him for that–

I slam a cover over the deluge of emotion that threatens to erupt from my chest. Because it's true, it's the only true thing I can say to accept her thanks to me, I reply, "I'm glad she's alive."

Then, I walk past them with a nod that I have to force for decorum's sake, and sit in the same spot I had yesterday–the day before. He hesitantly sits down next to me, slow enough that it's clear he's waiting for me to object, physically or mentally. But, that would be a reaction, and who knows where it would end if I let it begin?

It's too quiet, and I realize too late that I haven't reached for any of the dishes before us. Jolie, on my other side, scoops some eggs onto my plate without comment, and Li's pale hand reaches to put some bacon beside them. I don't miss how his hands fist in his lap, and how strained the movement looks when he serves himself some food, too.

I eat mechanically, even when my body recognizes how hungry it is. I eat and eat, not shoveling or stuffing, but cutting, biting, scooping. Everyone but him and Oksana finishes long before me, and from some kind of cue I don't see, they begin to file out, though at all other meals before it had seemed that no one usually left until the entire table finished.

When I finally feel full, it's just me, him, Oksana and Amedeo. Atlas and Li had seemed the most reluctant to leave, but a look from their High Lord had sent them out.

"Althea," Oksana says, and it's only because it's her that my immediate instinct to lash out or run is restrained. "Will you talk to me, my love?"

My love. She keeps calling me that. But, he calls me his love, too, and he still chose–

I shake my head, both in answer, and to clear the thought from it.

More quietly, "Would you like for us to leave?"

No. Yes. I can't decide, so I stay silent.

After a moment, she says gently, "We'll go. But, if you want us, just call for me, alright?"

I know she doesn't mean aloud. I nod my understanding and agreement, and they get up, and walk out without further discussion.

But, I don't like it here, in this too-quiet space where it's supposed to be loud and cheerful. So, I get up, and start to go I don't know where–

On an oak-scented wind, the arched double doors slam shut in front of me. I stand there, facing them, and even with my newly advanced hearing I have to work to hear his steps towards me. He stops, and doesn't touch me, doesn't say anything.

I turn at last, and force my eyes to meet his. His jaw is hard, but not as hard as they are. A front, not for him, but for me. Because, of course, he's noticed what the emotions of others have been doing to me this past hour.

It feels like longer. But, nothing will ever–*ever* feel as long as that dawn had.

And remembering it, thinking about it–the gates to my grief are too worn out to keep the flood out then.

My mouth trembles and tears fog my vision, and I say in a shaking whisper, "How could you do that to me?"

He falls to his knees before me, but when he reaches for my hands I snatch them away, shaking my head and backing up a step.

"I'm sorry, Thea," he says, his rough voice coarse as gravel as he gets the words out through a throat with his heart lodged within it. "I'm so sorry."

"I *don't. Forgive you.*" The words come through my teeth, and my tears trail over the lips that bare them.

"I would never expect you to. But I will still be sorry, until—until the end of my days, and on, I will be sorry."

I'm already shaking my head again, and I turn my face from him and hover the side of my hand over my mouth. His words come fast and broken: "Thea, *please.* Please look at me, talk to me. Scream at me, hit me, *anything.* Anything but this, even though I deserve it. Even though I deserve to never have your eyes or your voice again, please give them to me anyway."

I still don't, still can't, even when a sob breaks from his chest, and plunges straight into mine. "Please, Thea. Anything, anything you want—"

"*I WANTED TO LOVE YOU,*" I roar, whipping my gaze to look at him at last. "*I wanted to love you,* for the rest of my life. I wanted to mate you, marry you, have—have *children* with you. I wanted to make love to you every night and wake up to you every morning. I wanted to spend centuries learning about every piece of you, growing and changing with you, and somehow figure out how I could love you more each moment.

"And, in an instant, you took all of that away. And it wasn't even without thought." My voice had grown quieter with each sentence, now only an empty, trembling breath. A tear rolls down my cheek, and hovers at my jaw, only falling when I speak again. "I heard you think about what you owed to them. I suppose I had come to think I became enough for you. Enough to show you that you are not evil, and never have been. Enough for you to live without doubting that I needed you. *Enough* for me to be able to count on you always choosing *me*.

"I suppose you took that from me, too."

Tears flow, unending, down his cheeks, but his face has lost the crumple to his brow, the agonized set of his mouth. In their place is a sort of horrified sorrow which flattens his expression so that all of the emotion is in his eyes when his lips move. "Do you not wish to be mated to me any longer?"

I hesitate to answer, and it *breaks* him.

Too many fractured heartbeats later, I whisper, "I *can't* feel like that again, Adathan."

His eyes flash up from where he'd found the floor, had been staring at it with such a *lost* expression. They fill with the same desperate plea that's in his voice. "Then–then take my blood, and order me not to die."

Some confusion bleeds in through the grief and anger, and when he feels it, his heart stutters with hope. "Bind me to you, Thea, and *order* me not to die. *Please*."

Uncertain and slow, I hold his gaze and speak back to him. "You want another blood oath? To me?"

"It's not another, not anymore. It would be the only." His heart is pounding, his breaths too fast. Before, it was with utter terror; now, it is hope so great that its loss…I don't allow myself to think about what its loss would do to him.

My tears halt and my brow furrows at what he's said, though. "What do you mean?"

"I–I died, Thea. And the blood oath was tied to my life." He swallows. "I'm no longer bound to Olin."

My eyes widen, and my heart skips a beat, then another. "You're free?"

He nods. "I'm free of him. So, if you take my blood, and I

take yours, I can swear myself to you. And, if you order me to live, I will never be able to disobey." A great, shuddering inhale, like he'd rushed to get the words out, and only now remembered to breathe again.

"But, would you?" I ask, a new tear rolling down my cheek, and his reckless, tentative hope falters. "Would you, if you could? Would I be taking away a choice you would make, or would it be the only one–would *I* be the only one?" I take a shaking breath that's more of a sob. "Would you take from me the only thing I've chosen for myself? Would you *leave me again* because you hate yourself more than you love me?"

His heart, the heart I made from scratch, cracks, and his knees give out, forcing him onto his haunches. "Would you choose that, Adathan, if you had the choice?"

It takes him a long moment to get to his feet. To get his legs to remain sturdy beneath him. When they do, he stands stiffly, like if he moves too much, he will fall again. He says, his voice soft as I've ever heard it, "No."

I wait for him to continue, but he doesn't. "No?"

That softness steadily leaves him as he goes on. "I could say all the pretty words you like, but they won't matter. I've been telling you how much I love you, over and over, in different ways, through different actions, but none of them will *ever* take away from the action that I committed against you two mornings ago."

He manages a small step, and then another, a fire lighting within his tear-filled gaze. "But I'll be damned to the *fucking* Void before I stop trying." There's no space between us now, and I have to crane my neck to hold his eyes. "Until then, until *you* permit me to leave this world, I will love you with everything I have, and everything I am. I will love you, Thea, until the heart you created stops beating from natural causes, in a millennium, and centuries more. And when my soul is a forgotten wind over the barrens of the Void, even the gods-damned sound it makes will be your name."

My chest is heaving, especially in comparison to the stillness of his; holding his breath, looking between my eyes, his jaw and fists clenched tight. I can hear his heart pounding, the sound so familiar. So agonizingly familiar, when I can remember in such exquisite detail when it was not there to beat at all.

He's right. I will never forgive him.

But, I don't have to.

I reach up to wrap my arms around his neck, pulling him down, and I crush his lips to mine. He takes a gasping breath in, the sound so relieved it splinters along the fracture of my own heart. Adan's arms wind around my waist, and he pulls me tightly against him, lifting me off the floor. My ankles hook behind his back, and his hands move, one cupping my nape, his thumb against my cheek, and the other hitching on the back of my thigh.

"I hate you," I say against him, and I do. I hate him for hurting me, and I hate him for making it impossible for me to deny the inevitability of us, even with a broken heart.

"Good," he growls. "Because I'm about to fuck you like I hate you, too."

Gods, why does that make me even wetter for him?

While our tongues twine and I moan into his mouth, his hands move behind his back, and easily remove my boots. When they go between us next, I don't really care when they tear through my trousers, and pull each leg off separately. I only care about the hardness I can feel pressing against my center, and when he's going to put it inside me.

He efficiently undoes the buttons of his own trousers, pushes my belly away for a heartbeat, and then–

A deep, satisfied groan vibrates through him at the same

time that I sigh on the edge of a moan when he slides into me. Then his broad, calloused hands grip the sides of my ass with bruising strength so that he can lift me, only to slam me down to the fucking hilt.

My mouth parts from his in a scream, and slowly, he pulls me to his tip, and again spears into me with a force that surely gets him into my gods-damned guts. Again and again, faster and faster, until he's bouncing me on his cock. The noises our mouths and bodies make are obscene and lovely and I never want it to fucking end.

I come around him, and then my back is against a wall. Adan takes the backs of my knees, shoves them wide to my sides to pin them to the wall, and pounds into me relentlessly. We haven't been kissing since that first time I screamed for him, our faces just close together, open mouths sharing breaths and sounds, but no words. No fucking words while the scents of our sex and our sweat saturate the air, not until I can feel his release coming.

"Sink your fucking teeth into me while I come deep inside this perfect fucking pussy," he orders, and not one single sliver of my being considers disobeying.

I bite down hard on the side of his neck, opposite to my first claiming of him, and as soon as his blood hits my tongue, his cum begins to fill me. He spills and spills into me, never ceasing his punishing thrusts, not until every drop of him is spent.

Only then does he still, and I remove my canines from his throat. Our panting breaths fill the air between us, our hearts thundering. Then, he gently pulls my legs back in to close around his waist. And it's that tenderness, after such savagery, that has my throat thickening.

Adan meets and holds my eyes, the sun gold silver-lined, and cups my cheek, brushing a tear away with the pad of his thumb. I capture his hand with mine, the fingers of my other hand pushing through the hair by his temple, and whisper, "I love you, Adathan." It's my turn to catch the tear that falls from his eye then. "But, if you ever make the wrong choice again..." My fingers tighten in his hair, pulling at the strands, my next tear hot with rage as it rolls under his thumb. "I will bring you back, just so you can watch me leave you, too."

He nods, and I loosen my hold to press my lips to his once more. And, down the bond that I finally reopen to him fully, he says, *Yes, High Queen.*

70

NEVER AGAIN

DION - DAY 39

I'D WOKEN IN BED BESIDE MY MATE, AND HAD IMMEDIATELY retreated to the chair at her bedside.

Probably here from someone who'd visited us for however long we'd been unconscious–by the scents, almost everyone had been here at some point. It is likely still closer to her than I deserve to be, but I'm not fool enough to leave her. Not selfless enough, either.

I therefore have only been sitting, my elbows on my knees, staring at her. I had never forgotten a single detail of her, and yet she is somehow even more beautiful than my mind had recalled. The most stunning creature in this world, or any other that may be out there, in the boundless universe where her soul had been unlucky enough to become destined for mine.

Someone had thankfully changed her–and me–while we slept. She wears only a shift, albeit a long one, flowing down to her ankles. Gone is the shirt that had been singed away, the trousers which had been covered in blood and ash. Her chest is whole, only the absence of a portion of her tattoo left to show that she had been–that *I* had hurt her. Killed her.

I can't remember the order. I *can't* remember, and that terrifies me. My only comfort is my High Lady; surely she will be able to rip into my mind, and find those orders. I don't care if the process destroys me.

I don't care, not after what I did in Cerasche. I yearn for it, after what I did upon arriving home.

Home. It's wherever she is, but she would always have been here. Dremerre hasn't been home for her since before her father's murder. With her mother gone, too, the title of High Lady will have passed to her sister, and her abdication making her brother Lord Vey.

Too much. Ciara has endured too much over the past twenty-two years. She shouldn't have to be this strong, shouldn't have to be, even if it is a quality she embodies already. Strength of character and of spirit, forced into resilience.

She takes a deep breath in her sleep, and the noise is like music. Her heart beating, this perfect sound I had almost rid from the world. What kind of world would it have been, without those eyes like the night sky, or that voice like smoke over glass? For me, no world at all. For others, I can only imagine that it would have been forever dimmed. Colors less saturated, because she is vibrance; scents less pure, because she is their brightness.

Even when she wakes, and banishes me from her side, from this castle and this country, at least I will go knowing that she has others here to care for her. To love her.

Nuria and Jolie, whose scents are most potent in this chair. Nate and Bash. Atlas, now grown into a male. Bayani. And a white-haired, one-armed female who smells of mortality and stargazer lilies.

I'd only remained conscious for a moment after my mate once again drew breath, but I'd recognized the trueborn daughter of the Weaschten King and Queen in an instant. Between the days of travelling on foot, followed by the near-death of my heart and soul, I had only lasted that long, rather than falling over immediately, because of shock.

Shock, at what had been done, yes. But also at who had done it.

Adathan and Althea. Both here, both *alive*, neither in thanks to me. I had–I had *killed* him. The golden-eyed boy who used to hide his soul away, and the green-eyed girl who seems to have set him free.

Yes, seeing them had kept me awake for a few heartbeats. But, once they'd left...well, the next thing I remember is waking up here. In our chambers, next to my mate.

Ciara.

It's almost as if I said it out loud, when her lids flutter. Her nostrils flare delicately, and then again–and her eyes fly open.

She sits up with a gasp, and I can't help my body's instant reaction. I lunge for her, my heart practically beating out of my chest. She catches the motion, obviously, and whips her gaze around to me, and then I'm frozen. I'm utterly frozen within those deep blue depths, treading their waters as best I can, lest I drown in them.

Then, she whispers my name. "Dion?"

Gods, the Heavens reside in that voice, a choir of bleeding angels singing my name. It takes me out at the knees, where I find them at her bedside, looking up at my goddess.

Her hand reaches for me, and maybe I should pull away, but I can't. I let her touch my cheek, and my heart lodges in my throat at that simple brush of her fingers. "Are we dead?" she asks on a breath.

Instinct that I may not have the right to any longer, but

which has not abandoned my love for her, has me seizing her hand in both of mine. "No. No, Ciara."

But her gaze has locked onto my upper hand. Or, more specifically, the empty space where my forefinger used to be. The fingers of her other hand brush over that knuckle, and then her eyes flash back up to mine, her breaths stalling.

"This is real?" Silver pools beneath bottomless blue.

My own vision becomes cloudy, and I manage to squeeze my answer out through the small opening my heart has left in my throat. "Yes. This is real."

She gasps in a shuddering sob, and then launches herself off the bed, onto me, knocking us both to the floor. Her arms around my neck, she crashes her lips to mine, and I could no more help my body's reaction than I could keep the sun from setting.

My hands find their places in her hair and on the small of her back, and I pull her into me, even if my mind knows I don't deserve to do such a thing.

"You're here," she cries against my lips, her tears falling onto my face. "You're really here."

I brush my knuckle across one of her perfect cheeks. "I'm here." Even though I should not be. Even though I could be a danger to our court.

It's that thought that has me stopping her hands when they begin to descend down my chest. She pulls back at once, that little line forming between her brows as they furrow, her tears pausing, tracks drying on her cheeks. "What's wrong?"

"With you? Not a thing, my love. *I* am wrong."

She pulls back, straddling me, her skirt bunched over her thighs, and I am destined for the Void, because I place my hands on her hips. I manage to sit up so that I can look her in the eye. Of course, that creates the dangerous position of having her centered right over where I ache for her. Ache to sink inside her, and never go a day without doing so again.

Instead, I ask, my heart straining painfully, "Do you not remember–?"

"I remember many things, Dion," she interrupts me, that blue fire lighting in her eyes. Such beautiful fire, unsmothered even after all this time and all these violent turns. "I remember you being taken from me, and striking me so that I would not be taken with you. I remember you choosing our court over your own freedom. I remember watching the way your arm strained as your body made you carry out an order burned into your blood. With power that should have turned Adathan and I to ash, yet you fought so hard against it that we are *both* still here.

"And I remember missing you for *twenty-one years.*" Her tears come again, but they surely burn her cheeks with the heat of the anger that drives them. "Of wishing, every single day, that you were here with me. And, now that I have you, now that I *finally* have you, is your own self-hatred going to be the next thing to take you from me?"

I'm already shaking my head. "You don't know the whole story, Ciara."

"Do you love me?"

I blink, and she stares hard into my eyes, her lips tight. "Do. You. Love. Me?"

"More than anything," I answer, because to lie about such a thing would be far more blasphemous than cursing the gods.

"Then *that* is the whole story. Whatever you did for Olin doesn't fucking matter. The ifs *don't fucking matter.* Wondering what might have happened had things been different is a waste of time. Time, which we have already seen can be taken from us in an instant. So, I don't care if you're still sworn to him, and I don't care what you did for him these past years. All I care about *right now*, is that we finally finish what we started over two decades ago."

Like a phantom touch, I feel my pulse throb beneath the mark of her claiming.

And, who am I to deny this female anything she desires?

Without a word, I slide my hands over the fabric of her shift, then up her bare thighs. Her lips part when I tear through the flimsy undergarment covering her, and pull it out between us. Then, I watch those eyes glaze with lust as I run my fingers over her center, and find her already wet for me.

"Shall I take this, my Ciara?" I ask, sliding through her, then pushing a finger inside of her. My eyes almost roll back into my head, just feeling her tight, wet heat, and I know I'll be a goner when it's replaced by my cock.

"Please," she pants as I pulse within her, then she gasps delicately as I press my thumb to her clit, and gently circle it. Gods, those sounds. My memories of them hadn't done her justice.

"Which are you begging for? My fingers, or my tongue?" I reach my other hand up to grasp one of her breasts, skimming the pad of my thumb over her peaked nipple.

"Neither. Do not make me wait another moment to feel you inside me."

I can't hold back the small grin at the familiar sass within the words. Don't *want* to hold it back, as that line forms once more between her brows. "As you wish, my love."

If I'm already going to the Void, it may as well be for this, too.

Ciara breathes through parted lips as her fingers immediately go to work on the buttons of my trousers. As soon as I'm freed, though, I flip us with what remaining strength and speed I have after whatever time I went unfed.

She is a goddess beneath me, her braided hair laying like

tendrils of midnight, framing eyes of the hours before. I skim my tip through her soaking entrance, and don't need her words to tell me not to prolong this part. So, I don't.

Home. Warm, and wet around me, her walls clench as a gasp rips its way up her throat. My mind is consumed by the feel of her, thoughts of anything but this, anything but my mate, shoved out so thoroughly that I forget what it is that could have possibly abstained me before.

We move together, so well and fluidly that the time between now and our last might as well not have passed. I allow Ciara to pull my shirt over my head, craving my skin against hers, even with the state of me. In her eyes, though, I find no pity; only adoration as she skims her fingers over my many scars, and tips her chin up to seize my lips with hers.

"Say my name, Ciara," I plead, rolling my hips in the way I know gets her close to that beautiful edge. "Let it be one of the words that spills from your lips with me inside you."

Say my name, because there was a time I only heard it in my dreams.

Say my name, because there was a time I forgot it.

Say it, because you are here with me, and I with you.

Her eyes fill with tears as they hold mine, and, when she moves her hips in time with mine, she whispers, "Dion."

I dip my brow to hers. "Again."

A thrust, and a murmur, "Dion."

Another, and a moan, *"Dion."*

One more, and a scream, *"Dion!"*

As she pulses around me, she sinks her teeth into the space between my neck and shoulder. A new scar, which may as well smooth away the rest for all the impact it has on my soul.

When she pulls back, my hips having stilled for this moment, she places one hand on the side of my face, her gaze once more capturing mine. And Ciara says softly, "You're mine."

"I am *yours*," I agree, and begin moving once more. Hers, even if I do not believe I deserve to be such a thing. Hers, because it will always be the best thing I could have been in this life. Hers, because as long as she wants me, the only thing I could imagine doing with that life is becoming the male who might deserve her.

And, if I am going to take one more step towards that in this moment, I know what it will be. What she has wanted for decades, and what my soul desires so greatly that the selfishness of it is as insubstantial as any other excuse I might make not to do it.

In her eyes, I can see the permission, and the plea. I only lean my head down to press a kiss to her lips before obliging her.

When release barrels down my spine, and I begin to fill my mate, I say her name against the skin of her neck before biting into it. Her blood covers my tongue, bright and rich, and as she comes around me again at the feel of it, so is my climax more powerful than any I've had before.

When I am spent within her, I release her neck, and pull back enough to look into those miraculous eyes. "You're *mine*," I tell her, running my thumb along one glowing cheek. Angelic as the creatures said to inhabit the Heavens with the gods.

"I am yours," she agrees, and when her tears fall once more, I kiss them away, then rest my brow against hers.

Our bond finally, after all these years, is complete. It twines between our souls, our hearts, our minds, and I *feel* her, in every sense of the word. I hadn't known, couldn't have known, what we'd gone without for those short weeks we had before I was taken from her.

It is everything. *She* is everything.

Has been, since I first met her eyes in the halls of this very castle. But now, with her thoughts in my mind and her emotions in my heart, I tell her with all the conviction in my ravaged soul, "I love you, Ciara." My quiet voice shakes as I say it, the bond glowing brighter than ever between us.

I could have said it to her mind-to-mind. But, I hadn't gotten to say the words in eleven years. To feel the way my lips shape around them, to taste them on my tongue.

My mate recognizes this, and I feel her savor the words as they flow from her own lips. "I love you, Dion," she whispers, and not even the hatred I have for myself could ever rival the depth of that love she feels for me. And I know, without a shadow of a doubt, which one I will honor for the rest of my immortal life.

Forever.

Forever, our love.

71

THREE CONFESSIONS

CIARAGEN - DAY 39

IT WAS A SIMPLE MATTER TO CALL TO OUR HIGH LADY, requesting for her to bring Hielo, Adathan and Althea with her to the midsized alcove on the same floor as our chambers. A simple matter, after my mate had claimed me at last, and after we quenched our appetites for each other as much as possible within the hours we allowed ourselves.

I can still taste him on my tongue, can still feel him inside me as we walk down the halls hand-in-hand. The absence of his forefinger leaves the strangest of marks on the back of my palm, and every time I feel air where it should be, I consider how lovely it will be to repay the favor to Olin ten times over.

I considered a great many favors for him, in fact, as I had looked at Dion's naked body. As I had worshipped him, showing him how much I missed him with my own body when my words failed me.

So many scars, where there had once been so few. Deep,

shallow, long, short, scattered along nearly every inch of him. The only things untouched were his face, and his groin.

While I'm grateful for it, I can't understand the latter; Olin is monstrous and sadistic enough to have sanctioned it. I can, however, guess the reasoning behind leaving Dion's face intact. Olin is far too vain to cut himself, and how ever would he pretend to be his brother if one had a scar and the other did not?

So many scars, still, but none so terrible as the ones carved into his back. TRAITOR, over the Eshellen kingsnake. I can only hope that with Althea's powers fully restored, she may be able to heal him of them.

If she wants to, that is.

However unintentionally, my mate had killed hers yesterday. And, I know firsthand just how much that sort of hatred can fester in your heart. How simple a thing it is to let it rule over other emotions, the ones that hurt too much to feel.

Rage is easy. Sorrow is hard.

It's a terrible thing, recognizing how well acquainted everyone in this castle is with either one, though. At one point or another, we have all been tested, the measure of our hearts taken, always unwillingly. I had failed my test; had allowed myself to sink back into a place of stubbornness and hate.

I can only hope that Althea takes after her birth mother now. Otherwise, the imminent meeting will hurt my mate more than anyone else yet realizes.

When we arrive, Hielo and Hiela are already there. Dion moves to bow immediately, but Hielo stops him with a hand on his shoulder. My mate looks into the kind eyes of our High Lord, holding his breath.

And Amedeo pulls him into an embrace.

"Welcome home, Dion," he says thickly, Hiela looking on with shining sienna eyes.

Dion returns the embrace, his fingers curling to dig into the backs of Hielo's shoulders. When they part, brown and hazel eyes are silver lined. The male housing the brown set says, "We are so sorry. So sorry that we could not come for you."

Dion shakes his head, pulling me into his side without thought; instinct and need, to have me close after so long so far apart. "I understand. I don't blame you for it. Not at all."

Hielo opens his mouth to speak again, but the sound of footsteps comes from down the hall, interrupting whatever way he might have tried to apologize again. Even when I'd gone to rescue Dion, I'd known it was wrong. Unsafe, to so many. Pure desperation had driven me to Oschverre that day, logic only taking its place when two of my greatest enemies had arrived on the flowing land that covered those horrific cells.

One of those males appears now, holding the hand of our Lady.

Not my enemy anymore, however. Nor is she our Lady.

She is our High Queen.

Her circlet crown glimmers on her head, and she again has donned a summer dress rather than the trousers and simple shirts she took a liking to on the *Burning Rose*. In these soft dresses, with her steady confidence, she continues to display the well-hidden truth of the dying patriarchy: power and femininity go hand-in-hand.

When I drop to a knee, my fist over my heart, Dion follows suit, as I'd explained her power and position to him as we'd readied for this meeting. Oksana and Amedeo bow deeply beside us.

"What are you doing?" that sweet, husky voice asks in accented Divani. Adathan must say something to her mind-to-mind, because she looks up at him, then scoffs, turning back to us. "None of that here. There's too much to discuss."

"You should get used to people bowing to you, Your Grace,"

Amedeo says, and there's an interesting sparkle in his eye when he uses the title.

Althea's brows furrow. "Is it 'Your Grace' here?"

"It is up to you to decide, of course, but that is what the High Kings and Queens of Eshelle after the time of Ymeda were called. They only changed to 'Majesty' shortly before her–*your* majick slumbered."

"Hm." She hasn't looked at Dion or myself yet, her gaze flicking between her birth parents before she looks up at Adathan. "You say it."

He smirks, the kind he has only ever reserved for her, and obliges her in his low voice. "Your Grace."

Her cheeks flush, and then her eyes narrow, not altogether seriously. Then, she lifts her chin, and addresses him, "Your Grace."

Turning back to Hielo, while golden eyes stare at her, she nods once. "I like it. But, you all can call me Aly until we're around anyone who didn't travel across the sea with me."

Though Dion doesn't so much as shift his weight, I can feel his tension and uncertainty. I don't know if Althea–Aly can, too, or if she's just finally ready to look him in the eye, but her gaze moves to him now, and I can't make out the expression in it. Not even when they flick to me.

"Do you understand now?" she asks me.

I swallow, taking her meaning instantly. "Yes."

Yes, I understand how she hated Olin, but not Adathan. Yes, I understand how she only ever truly loathed the male who gave the orders, and not the one who carried them out. Dion's action hurt me–killed me–but I could no more hate him than I could stop the world from turning around the sun.

True, Aly didn't know what Adathan was to her when she decided to forgive him of the hurts he caused her, but some part of her must have. Must have rendered her unable to despise the male, no matter how it might have been deserved according to others.

I wait for her to say something, *do* something to punish Dion for what he did to her mate, regardless of how unwilling and unintended. To blame me, too, because I'd been so blinded by my joy that I hadn't thought to evade the power so obviously coming to obliterate me. That I lost my life anyway is inconsequential; it's the action of it that matters.

The action.

I look at Adathan, and say with all the sincerity in my heart and soul, "Thank you for trying to save me. And for bringing me back."

He blinks, surprised, but dips his chin. "I did nothing, in the end. Your High Queen is the one to thank for your life."

"I have no interest in dwelling on that morning," Aly says sharply, then takes a breath before loosening her shoulders. "I am glad you're all alive. That's that. Now, what are we here for?"

That's it? Not so much as a warning or punishment. Not an adverse look at my mate for what he nearly took from her. But, from her harsh initial words, I don't think all of her anger is reserved for Olin this time. Not towards the male who carried out an order, as I had once persecuted Adathan for, either. No, she is *angry* with her mate.

Dion has managed to gather himself after the surprise of the lack of retribution, though, and looks at her with the same consideration as he always has our High Lady. "A few things, High Queen. All of them too urgent to leave unattended."

She gestures for him to continue, and he nods before doing so. "First, that I have no memory of receiving–that order. Which can only mean that there are others, hidden within my mind. By your leave, I would have my High Lady look into my mind to find them, and ensure I am of no further threat to our court, or our nation."

"Of course, my Lord," she permits. "What else?"

He takes a deep breath, and his eyes fill with regret as he looks between his High Lady and High Queen. I had already told him that they would not blame him for what he is about to tell them, but apparently he remains unconvinced.

"On the first night of your gathering in Weaschte, it was not Olin who danced with you. It was me."

The sienna-eyed female only looks to her daughter, whose bright green eyes have gone blank with surprise. So, it is not her, but the hulking male next to her who steps forward and says, "*Explain.*"

Again, I force my instincts down, allowing Dion to hold his own. Something he is more than capable of, but old habits die hard, and I had made quite the habit of assuming the worst of Adathan. To recognize that he isn't about to rip apart my male for a possible crime against his female is easier said than done.

Indeed, though, without a whiff of fear, nor a tremble to his voice, Dion says, "I was ordered to dance with her, and then leave for Olin to take my place. I had wondered, at first, why he did it, but realized when I saw Ciaragen there–when I recognized her, that he had done it because he wanted me to know I would never be able to return home after that. My shame would be too great, my crime against my court too terrible. For my part, I am so, incredibly sorry, High Queen." He clears his throat, of the thickness that came to it towards the end of his confession, his eyes tightening.

Aly steps forward, her lips parted. "Your eyes," she breathes. I look at Dion, into the green-gold of his irises, my brows furrowed as I wonder what she means. "I noticed the first night–and none of the others. Those wrinkles...they're not from smiling, are they?"

Now, I see what she's talking about. The tiny lines at the corners of his eyes, made prominent by his wince. Lines, put there not by smiling, as they are for others. But by flinching. Crying. Screaming.

My throat thickens, and I press my face into his shoulder, inhaling the white oak and amber scent of him. His arm tightens around me as he answers, his voice heavy, "No, Your Grace. They are not."

And her quiet voice is nothing but kind, no pity to be found, when she replies, "I have had quite enough of good males being sorry for actions they were forced to commit. Unless my– Oksana or Amedeo have anything else to say about it, I clear you of any charges you might have imagined you would face."

I look to find Hiela's eyes exceptionally tender, though I think it has more to do with Aly's near-slip before calling them by their names than it does with Dion's confession. "There is nothing to forgive, Dion."

My mate's jaw works as he swallows, hardly daring to believe their kindness. Seeing that, Aly's tone remains gentle when she prompts, "You said 'a few', my Lord. Is there anything else?"

He nods, his gaze moving between her and Adathan. "There is. The story for it, though, is a bit longer."

Instantly, six chairs appear in the space. Aly looks at Amedeo, who *winks* at her, such fatherly mischief in his eyes, even with the known and unknown weighing in the air of this alcove with us. When she grins at him, he returns it, his mate's hand holding tightly to his own.

When seated, though, all eyes, including mine, rest on Dion. He, however, stares directly at Adathan as he begins.

"I once knew a female named Reina Mykel." Instantly, Adathan goes preternaturally still, his mate beside him doing the same, her hand wrapped around his. "She worked in the castle as a seamstress to the queen. I'd been working there for some years by that point, and she was one of the few who knew who I was, and what I did, and wasn't frightened by it. By me." His mouth curls the smallest bit at the memory, though his green-gold eyes are filled with such sadness that I can't help but squeeze his hand. Gratitude floods the bond, and he continues.

"We began seeing each other outside of the castle. Went dancing, took walks, ate meals in small restaurants where no one yet knew my name. I...I started to fall for her. She became the light of my days, and took away some of my dark dreams at night. It didn't take long for me to decide I wanted my mother to meet her. I *knew* they would get along—and they did. They talked and laughed, joked, even."

Dion's jaw tightens, though his eyes only grow more sorrowful. "My father and Olin were supposed to be gone hunting all day. I had planned to have lunch with Reina and my mother, and then take her home hours before they would return, with them never the wiser. Instead, they returned to find me with a female below my station, my mother entertaining her and very much *not* keeping house for the smallest bit of time."

He clears his throat, and all the comfort I can give him for now is in a stroke of my thumb across the back of his hand. "After that, the only choice I had was to end things. She tried to convince me to leave with her instead, that we could make a life together in the south, where it was warmer, and more tolerant. So...I had to convince her that I didn't want that. That I had no interest in her any longer; I had realized my father was right, and being with her would disgrace my family, and me."

Adathan's free hand fists on his knee, though the rest of him remains terrifyingly still. "I watched her believe me. I saw it in those beautiful, bright eyes that had always looked at me with such happiness. They grew dim, and I–I let them. I could not keep her in a relationship with me. The things my father had said about her, *in front* of her—she should not have to be with somebody who let him do that. Regardless of the fear I had felt for my mother, should I add to his anger by arguing with him, I couldn't forgive myself for that.

"I thought she would be better off. Word was beginning to spread throughout the capital of who I was, and what I did for the king. I had no way out of it, and I could not let her bear the scrutiny of the public eye if she remained with me.

"When I left, I assumed she went to the south, as she wished to do. Olin and my father ensured that I was kept busy with work and gatherings, and I didn't see her again, even in the castle. Even though I missed her, I only hoped she would find happiness."

Dion's jaw works again, and his eyes begin to fill. "Years and months later, Olin came to me, seeming very chipper. I knew enough to beware of that sort of emotion from him, but I...He smiled, and he asked if I remembered the female with the golden eyes I'd been with years back. I nodded, while dread filled my gut. And he told me that she had passed. It took...*all* I had not to fall to my knees. And then–then he told me that she'd had a son. Said, 'He would have been about seven,' that the boy had passed from some illness a couple of months before her.

"Then he left me, with the knowledge that I'd lost a son I never had, and the only female I had ever loved, in one fell swoop. I went to her house, since there are no cemeteries in the lower hills, and there she was. There you both were." Tears flow down his cheeks, and fog my own vision. "The gravestone claimed a date of birth in the spring for the boy, meaning he would have been a little over seven and a half when I finally got to meet him. November the eighth, eighty-two years ago.

"My mother had died a few years prior. And, after this loss that I felt I didn't deserve to mourn, for all I'd said to her that day...I shut down. I stopped caring about much at all, to be honest. Until I came here.

"That I didn't know you, even glamoured as you were, still shames me. I could have saved you from decades of service to him, if I'd only been able to open my eyes and *see*. And I was still blind, even in that damned cell. Every day, looking into your eyes, finding comfort in them without being able to remember why. And then, that day on the field, where I saw and scented you fully for the first time," he takes a deep, shaking breath, "that was when I knew. But, when Olin introduced you as *his* son, Adathan, there was no way for me to tell you otherwise, and know for certain that he wouldn't kill you when you knew. When you learned the truth.

"Olin is not your father, Adathan. I am."

⇔

Dion

THE SECRET I HAVE KEPT FOR ELEVEN YEARS, FREED AT LAST.

Adathan looks at me with wide golden eyes. The eyes I would stare into for comfort during my waking hours in that cell. The eyes I had met eighty years earlier across dinner tables and in bed on late mornings. Eyes I had seen lose some of the life in them when I rejected her, and the child I could not yet scent on her.

I have never wondered why Reina kept the information from me. Even when Olin told me of those deaths, of that gravestone that haunted me for decades, and I saw them for myself, there was never the question of *why* in my mind. As I had stared at it, on my knees in the freshly turned earth, I had understood. And it had been the final nail in my apathetic coffin, while the male I used to be had sunk into the soil to lay with the family he never deserved to have.

Now, I stare at one part of that family, knowing the same. Knowing that, if he rejects me now, it will be nothing less than what I deserve. For how I hurt his mother, whom he lost when he was far too young; for the decades following, when he was forced to serve my brother because I had not been the kind of male she could trust to keep her boy safe.

Her boy. Grown into a male any parents would be proud to have; with a heart and soul Olin tried to take from him, and failed. He's hiding them now, as he became so practiced in doing those years within those cells, but I've seen them before. They did not leave him after Olin tried to cut them out of him for flinching at my torment. However tempting, he had instead held onto them so tightly that he had sacrificed himself for my mate, and had managed to find his own.

The Lady of Sabrian turned Princess of Weaschte, now High Queen of Eshelle, in name and by right, regardless of the male who currently holds the throne. Now is not the time to wonder about what will become of that male now that this female has risen, but I am certain that conversation is imminent. As certain as I am that I will not be allowed to be a part of it.

This, though...this could not wait. *I* could not wait. Not after eleven years, and not after eighty-two. The boy I have no right to call mine, the boy who grew into the male before me–I am his, to whatever capacity he will allow. Father, friend, even a mere acquaintance. Nothing...I can endure that, if only because I will know it will be for him. The one thing in my wretched life I could do for him, if that is what he chooses.

I've been watching him since I finished, have been waiting for any words, any reaction he might have, and so I catch it when he shifts slightly, though that infallible mask remains in place. "If you could do anything over again, if you could change anything that happened to me or to her, would you?"

I consider both parts of his question, and the distinction between them. On the surface, it's an easy enough question, with a simple enough answer: of course, I would.

But he's not just asking if I would spare him and his mother the pain they experienced because of me. He's asking if I would do it differently, with everything I know and have now.

I swallow before answering honestly. "If I could go back and do anything to save you from Olin, Adathan, I would. But...no, I would not change the choice I made that day." I squeeze Ciara's hand, and she squeezes mine back with even more strength, love and sorrow flowing through our bond.

He nods once, his golden eyes unreadable. "I know."

He stands, gently releasing Althea's hand when she does the same, to walk over to me. She remains back, only watching him when he stops before me. I stand, too, letting go of Ciara, and my–my son and I are separated only by a couple of feet, though the top of my head only comes to his brow. After however long I'd been on that ship, I'd lost a decent amount of weight, too, leaving me looking thin in comparison to the breadth of him.

All of that is fitting, though, since I feel smaller than him in every figurative way, as well. Especially when he speaks, eloquently and without hesitation.

"For anything you imagine you might have done to protect me, I forgive you for not doing it. For not finding me when I was a boy in his cells, before I tortured my first male at nine." My heart cracks, and its splinters pierce me, but he goes on. "For not recognizing me here, when you had no way of doing so, and for not knowing me when I looked at you with my mother's eyes. The easiest thing to forgive you for is not stopping me somehow from being blood bound to him. If not for that, I would not have been able to fall in love with my mate before I even knew what she would be to me.

"But for your other choice," he says, and I hold my breath, readying for his dismissal of me. "You should know that my mother was happy without you."

Relief at his words floods through me, and I can't help the fresh tears that spring to my eyes before he even continues. "She sang, and danced with me, and played with me when she came home from her shifts. She was *happy* to be alone with me, rather than with a male who thought so low of her."

My heart threatens to curl in on itself when Adathan's eyes take on a shine of their own. "What I cannot forgive you for, is something that I perhaps shouldn't blame you for, but I do. I do, because I blamed Olin for it, even knowing the type of male he is. But, all this time *this*, this one thing that matters more than the rest, because it was done to her and not me, has not been his fault."

His jaw tightens, and the first few words come through his teeth. "I cannot forgive you for not finding me before she died. For not being there to explain this terrible power that runs through my veins, a power she didn't understand. I cannot forgive you for being absent when she grabbed me while it flowed through me in a fit of temper, trying to console me, and I watched it bleed the life from her in an instant."

My tears fall, though his do not. "So, I remain only *her* son, not yours. You are a good male. I know it. I have known it since I met you in this very castle twenty-one years ago. It's why I brought you back when Marcys took too much from you eight years later. I have never regretted it, and still don't, even if I wish with all of my being that I had known that power when I was seven. Though, I think at that time, not even you would have been able to teach me how to create instead of destroy.

"Yes, you are a good male. But you have not been a good father. Perhaps, when you can prove that you are, you might earn the title. Dion."

With that, Adathan dips his chin to me, then to Ciara behind me. Then, he turns his back to us, facing Althea. Past him, I can only see one side of her; the tenderness in one pale green eye, and the hand she reaches towards him. He takes it, and, as they slip out of the alcove, he lifts their joined hands to his lips, and kisses the back of her palm.

72

TWO TRUTHS & A LIE

THE REST OF THE DAY GOES BY IN A FUCKING BLUR OF uncertainty, the one thing I *am* sure of by my side all the while. Even after what I did, after what I committed against her. Thea spends the hours after my—my *father's* confession granting me the silence I need, her hands soft on me.

No questions. No comments. Just *there*.

I had taken myself from her for him. For them. I took the heart and soul she gave me, and ripped them up before her eyes, Dion's majick burning the pieces. I saw it in her nightmares as she slept; the way she grasped at the shreds of our bond, thinking of them as ashes. Floating away from her. *Leaving* her.

I wish she'd taken my blood. Not because I will *ever* betray her again. But because, to be bound to her in yet another way feels like the only thing I can do to show her what being hers means to me. I wanted her commands to sear through my blood; I wanted her words to be the gods-damn air that I breathe. I wanted to be so thoroughly tied to her that when we do go from this world, not even the rutting gods who gave us their majick can take me from her.

Add onto it that I never–*never* want to cause her that sort of pain again, and binding my blood to her is no longer a mere want. No, after seeing that agony in her dreams, it's a fucking *need*.

Of course, she would not do it. Not then, at least. Not after I'd finally been freed from the oath that had shackled me for over eighty years. What she doesn't see–and I won't make her, hiding my thoughts of it even now–is that giving her the oath wouldn't be a new set of chains. It would be my fucking *wings*.

I would never hide my mind from her for the sake of me. But, for her? I would do anything for her.

It's both of those thoughts that have me leaving her with Lina and Tali in the gardens. Even with Dion's confession, and my own sins weighing on me, a small smile comes to my lips, seeing her with them. Time with fellow females that she deserves, without her mate there. To laugh, and gossip, and just *be*.

It's what I hoped for, weeks ago, when I'd first approached Lina on the *Burning Rose*. Told her that Thea had gone down to her cabin, her heart hurting for those she'd lost. And asked her to go to her.

Then, I had done it because I had seen how she was beginning to rely on me. To come to me in any moment where she sought solace, and silence. And I was convinced that it would not last. That she would, at any moment, realize who she was beginning to trust, and turn from me.

To find no one behind her.

I couldn't bear it. And, even as my instincts raged against it, I knew she would need more than one. She would need *him*.

And so I had asked him, too.

I've known him to be a good male since his first day in Castle Cerasche. As I'd listened to him serve her from across the dining room, still feeling sick from the letter I'd sent hours prior, notifying Olin of his presence. I'd heard him spill the soup in her lap, heard her gasp of shock, and pain at the slight burning.

I've known I am not a good male for eighty-two years. But it was solidified even more when I wanted to murder him for such a simple accident. For the mere fact that it hurt her for all of a second before she healed it–and for the way I listened to his voice soften after she laughed off the event.

Over the weeks between then and her birthday, I still did not look at her. But, I looked at him. And I watched another male fall in love with the woman I loved, but could never tell.

And I listened to her falling for him in return.

I heard the way her heartbeat would flutter when he neared. Scented her on him after they would spend time together in the kitchens, knowing she was touching his arm, bumping his hip. Heard her laugh with him, and the way she hummed in their silences. Happy, as I'd believed she would never be with me.

She was hurt, after his secrets. And she forgave him, as she has forgiven me–for all but one thing. But I don't think she realizes that, when she forgave him, she took back the place where she was in her fall, before her life as she knew it changed so drastically. I *know* she doesn't realize that they're both only steps away from what they would have been if I were not here.

She doesn't, because she loves me. Gods, does she fucking love me. I feel it in every fiber of her existence; it radiates from her, warm and bright as the sun, every time she looks at me. From every kiss, and touch, smile, and laugh. She loves me so much, I sometimes forget how to function when it washes over me. It fills my heart to bursting, and I drown in its flood until I remember how to breathe blood and water. Forces of life, sure, but still not as vital as she is to me.

And yet, I had betrayed her.

No, I am not a good male.

It is only by the luck the universe unwittingly bestowed upon me that she couldn't give less than a fuck about that. That, when I told her that I am Death, and would take from her, she believed me. More importantly, she *liked* it.

It doesn't release me from working to become a male who deserves her. But maybe I can give her someone who does already.

"Atlas," I call to him as I approach. He turns, along with Nate and Bash, and I watch his eyes immediately flit to the space to my right. Where I have always placed her.

"Adathan?" he greets me, a bit of wariness in his tone. I don't blame him. I haven't sought him out since that day on the *Burning Rose*.

I look between his fathers, and something about the edge of concern in their eyes sends an ache through my chest. At the way my presence brings about a worry for their son...and because I remember Dion looking at me like that in Matriel Castle. Concerned for me, but unable to express it but for the two words he said to me before I departed for Cerasche. *"Be safe."*

I clear my throat, and my mind of that memory, and say to Atlas, "Can I talk to you for a minute?"

His brow furrows even more, but he says, "Yeah, sure." He turns to Bash, and gives him a reassuring half-smile, and a dip of his chin. The male returns it, but as he takes Nate's hand, the two of them give me a warning look from behind Atlas.

Yes, they've accepted me in their court. But only because I

love the same female he does. Otherwise, I'm sure their opinion of me isn't very high.

Fair.

When the sounds of their footsteps around the bend of the hall fade completely, Atlas puts his fingers in his pockets. "What's up?"

A good fucking question. I probably should have been thinking about exactly how to phrase this while I followed his scent through the castle to find him. Since I didn't, the blunt question I ask is, "Why did you do it?"

Again, his brow scrunches–then flattens, realizing what I'm asking. Which is: why did he bring me back, when my death would have left her to him?

"Because I've seen her in pain, Adathan. I've seen her scared. Betrayed. Enraged. Grieving. But I'd never seen her broken. Not until then."

My heart might as well be gone again for all that those words do to it. I hadn't just hurt her. I had *broken* her.

"Even if I thought that I could put her back together...even if I thought, for so much as a second, that I could have her with you gone–" He shakes his head, his locs moving over his shoulders. "I would never have been able to convince myself I deserved her after that. I would have taken from her the thing she loves most in this world. Why would I ever want to do that to her?"

"But it wouldn't have been you, Atlas. *I* did it. I betrayed her. I *broke* her." *My* voice breaks on that word, but I don't hide it.

"You did it to save them." He sighs, the indignance that had come into his gray eyes fading. "You had all of a second to decide. You, or them. You chose them." Yes. Them. Because, if Dion *had* succeeded in turning Ciaragen to ash–a thing neither Thea nor I would have been able to repair–I have no doubt he would have assured his own death shortly thereafter.

"Anyway," he goes on. "That wasn't the point. The point is that she loves you. So, I'm not about to let anything happen to you."

"Because you love her," I finish for him. Not angry, or accusatory. But matter-of-fact. Stating what we both know, but he hasn't said. At least not to her.

His eyes shift between mine for a long moment. "Yeah. Because I love her."

I nod at the truth that's finally in the open between us. But, "Anything else?"

His cheek pulls a bit into his mouth as he tongues a canine behind his lips. I feel the air of the conversation change; the open honesty reverting back to what we've been towards each other whenever her eyes aren't watching. Whenever she's not hoping with that beautiful, bright heart that we will get along. That the males she loves–one overtly, and the other hidden, even to herself–might come to care for each other, too.

With a hard jaw and harder eyes, he replies, "Not that I can think of."

I know he's remembering the same conversation–remembering the way I refused to talk about this very thing with anyone but her. I give him a humorless smirk, and say to him what he had to me: "Good thing she forgives us our secrets."

I leave him with that, turning my back on the male whose place might have been mine once. If Thea hadn't forgiven me my sins before we even left those Ceraschen woods. If he had found us before we reached Dahlih—before she realized for the first time that she liked to look at me. Liked to talk to me. Before she listened to me speak up for her, demanding the truths she hadn't known they'd kept from her. Truths I could not share, the oath to Olin binding my tongue.

If not for those things, she might have chosen him first. But, just as she said our first day on the Obalan ship: the ifs do not matter. As constantly astounded as I am that she chose me...she did. Believing she could only have one of us, she looked between her options, grabbed me by the fucking heart, and told me to choose her, too. To stop hiding on the basis of my self-loathing, and give myself to her.

My *mate*. So gods-damn strong, to go with her heart, after all that had been done to it. Stronger than I am. And far more selfless.

Because I saw the way she still looked at him. Almost the same way he looked at her. And I let her choose me. I let her, because I needed to be hers more than I needed air to breathe. And, just as I told her I would, I took what she gave me. Which turned out to be everything she has in that beautiful existence of hers.

But, if I am going to work the rest of my days to be worthy of her—to be worthy of that glowing, golden soul she placed into my hands of pitch—then that conversation with Atlas was the effort of today. Tomorrow...I will do more tomorrow.

73

FLYING

"You're either blind or a liar, Tali. And, last I checked, you can see just fine," Sione says through their panting breaths, bronze chest heaving with exertion.

"I'm no more a liar than you are a good football player. Or loser," she replies, just as sweat-slicked as them, her blue-black hair pulled back into a tail atop her head.

"I only lost if you're telling the truth, which you're *not*. The ball went between the goal posts."

"If the other goal post is that fucking tree over there, yeah."

"Oh, Void take me, just give them a penalty kick," Atlas says, shirtless as the Jemage beside me.

"For what?! And, whose side are you on?" Tali glares at her teammate, her hands finding her hips.

"I'm on the side of whatever gets this over with so we can get back to playing."

"Just ask Emi," Sione says, ignoring Atlas, who rolls his eyes with an overdone sigh.

"I'm not asking your girlfriend if you made the goal."

"Because you know I did."

"I know you're full of shit is what I know."

Atlas lays down on the grass, and puts his hands behind his head, closing his eyes against the sun. I join him, sitting and pulling a long blade from the ground, then watch in wonder as it instantly grows back.

"Atlas," I whisper while Sione and Talia continue to bicker. He opens his eyes and looks over at me. I pull out another blade of grass by his face, and his eyes widen when the same thing happens. Then, the surprise shifts to awe, and something even softer.

"Amazing," he murmurs. Then he turns back to the sun, and seems to relax further into the earth, his chest and abdomen expanding with a deep breath which he slowly releases into the summer air.

I sidle up closer to him, then lay down so that my head rests in the space between his chest and shoulder. I don't say anything, just close my eyes to see the bright red of my eyelids against the sun. His arm comes down so that his forearm bands across my collarbone, his hand hooking on my shoulder.

A few moments later, a familiar voice asks, "Are you two napping?"

I open my eyes and look up towards my forehead to see Al striding for us, Adathan at her side. "I could have a nap in the time it takes Sione and Talia to stop fighting," I reply to her as I sit up. Atlas follows me, then stands and holds a hand out to help me up, too. I take it, and, with a solid tug, he hefts my weight up all on his own.

"What are they fighting about? The last thing they said was that she cheated at a card game a year ago." Al gathers her hair in a hand, and holds it aloft, and I can't blame her. I'm overly warm, and I don't have a blanket of black hair.

Without a word, Adathan takes it from her, and begins to work it into a braid. Atlas, without a hint of jealousy in his tone, responds, "Sione says they got a goal, Tali says they didn't."

"I see," she says with a smirk. "What are you all playing?" Then her eyes flit to the bared expanse of Atlas's chest and torso. Sweat-slicked and muscled, she catches herself quickly, those things considered—but not quickly enough.

My friend's voice shifts a bit, lowers so infinitesimally that I only notice it because I know him so well. "Football. You know it?"

A blush spreads over her cheeks, but so does her grin. "I used to play with my brothers. Iris was never a fan, though. I always played with Ben, while Nik got paired off with whatever guard was overseeing me."

"You two want to join the game?" Atlas looks between her and Adathan, who's tied the braid off with Al's purple sash, and comes back around to her side now. Where I might have expected jealousy, even anger in his expression at Al's attraction, and Atlas's tone, though, I find none.

Al looks up at him, and he gives her an easy smile, which has hers stretching further with excitement. She turns back to us. "Sounds like fun."

She kicks off her strappy sandals, then bends to toss them into the sidelines. Adathan follows her as she walks past us, towards center field where Sione and Tali wait, having obviously overheard.

"You don't want to change?" I call to her as Atlas and I follow them. The lilac dress she wears is stunning on her, but not exactly made for sport.

Al looks over her shoulder at me, then flicks her gaze to

Adathan, saying, "I'm going to kick his ass in a dress. Atlas, I'm on your team, yeah?"

He's already grinning, and takes the ball Tali holds up for him. "You got it, darling."

"Och, Tali, we've got the giant," Sione says as Adathan takes a place on their side of the imagined midline. He's across from Al, Sione from Tali, and Atlas from me. "Game fucking on."

A few seconds of anticipation and exchanging wicked grins, then Sione whistles, and the game begins.

I may not be as fast as the others, but I've got crazy fucking aim, so I do what I can until I'm close enough to the goal posts that their speed won't matter. Turns out, though, that I would hate to see Al play football in proper shoes and dress because the ball soars through our posts less than two minutes in.

"Ymeda's tits, Al, is there anything you're not fucking good at?" I shout as we set up for our kick-off.

"Being humble," she concedes with a wink, and I snort.

We get the next goal, thanks to a pass from Adathan across nearly the entire field to me, and I get it past Tali. We're still neck-and-neck after twenty minutes, and everyone is breathing hard, coated in sweat. Al's pretty dress has grass stains, and she's tucked one side of the skirt into the leather belt that usually holds her dagger at her thigh. She'd slid on it once, and the bruise is still purple, all up and down the side of her leg. It's occurred to me that she could heal it, so she must enjoy the simplicity of being a person who can get hurt and keep going in something enjoyable, rather than something awful.

"That's half!" Tali calls, and I fall into the grass where I stand, panting. Even with the sun starting to go down, the heat is absurd. A shadow comes over me a heartbeat later, the expanse of their wing covering me completely.

We've kissed at almost every opportunity since that moment–the best moment of my life so far–a few days ago, but haven't taken it further than that yet. Honestly...it's nice. To enjoy this part with them. Stolen kisses in halls, laughing around each other's lips, no pressure to be sexy or sultry. My friend since childhood, still making me giggle, only now I don't have to hide or be self-conscious of my blushes. They kiss my cheeks each time, and each night they have kissed me good night and called me moonshine, and I haven't needed anything else.

I want to take that step with them, and I know they do with me, too. Just not yet. Anyway, even if we wanted to take it that fast, even if we cared to skip past this flirty, easy thing our friendship has transitioned into, when would have been the right time for that? It's been days of uncertainty and chaos before today.

I hold my hand up to them now, and they hoist me up easily, pulling me into their sweat-slicked chest to give me yet another kiss. I grin against their lips, and they do the same to me, their free arm wrapping around my waist.

When we separate, they lift our joined hands and extend a finger to push a stray curl out of my face. "I almost want to stop calling you moonshine," they say, smirking the smallest bit, russet eyes alight.

My brows furrow. "Why?"

"Because this face is far too lovely to be compared to the moon." They trace my nose, my cheekbone, my jaw with that free finger as they say it, their smirk growing to show their teeth. Then their wings curl around us, shading me, and giving us privacy as they kiss the blush that blooms, even on my over-heated cheeks.

"Hey, lovebirds, you going to keep making out, or are you gonna put it back in your pants so we can play?" Tali's voice comes, her competitive side clearly still in full swing.

Sione pulls their wings back after one more peck to my lips.

Then they release my hand to turn towards their cousin, though their other hand remains hitched on my waist. "Tali, just for that, my girl is going to score every goal on you until endgame."

"I'm leaving Lina completely out of this when I tell you: get fucked."

They let go of me only to tug on my shirt, lightly pulling me towards center field with them. "That's not very Lady-like of you."

"I'm going to murder you a thousand times."

"With what, the ball? Or your teeny, tiny, Lady fists?"

"I'll tell you what I'll do with the ball–"

"*Oh my gods*, just start the fucking play," Atlas says, earning a laugh from me and Al.

The second half is even rougher than the first. Al tackles Adathan three times to keep him from passing to me, and Atlas is ready at each one to steal the ball and score on Sione. The male even removed his shirt a few minutes in–the thing was basically sheer with sweat, anyway–and his bruises from her hits and the ground pepper his ribs and shoulders, layering over his many scars.

When the game is called, Tali's team wins by one goal, and she screams, and rushes Al. The two jump up and down in each other's arms, laughing while Addie gives Sione a fist bump before doing the same to me. Then he turns, crossing his arms and smirking at the elated females a few yards away.

Atlas stands near them, grinning, and when their bouncing careens them into him, he's solid, chuckling as they jostle him. Finally, exhausted, they release each other, and Al squats before splaying out on the ground, her skirt flaring over her thighs. Her breaths heave her chest, and I could swear that, as they calm, the grass around her body leans towards her.

"You alright there, sweetheart?" Adathan calls to her as

Sione slings an arm over my shoulders, and her hand shoots up, her thumb extended. He chuckles, then runs his tongue along a canine. I watch Al turn her face towards him, her brow scrunched a little. The whole mate-bond-communication-thing is intriguing enough to me that I look between them while he nods, eyes gleaming with something like challenge edged with desire, and hers with that challenge accepted, mingling with the same heat.

"What do you think's going on there?" Sione whispers in my ear, low enough that Addie might not have heard. If he did, he doesn't show it; he walks over, still shirtless, to lay a couple of feet away from Al on the field.

"I don't know," I whisper back. After breakfast yesterday morning, it seemed wise to let the two of them be to figure things out. And hanging out with her and Tali last night, well, let's just say she'd let me talk of little else but my developments with Sione. I can't blame her. I wouldn't want to think about what happened either, if I were her.

Whatever's going on now, I'll either find out from her later... or get closer to them *now* to try and figure it out. I look over at Sione with a grin. "Care to join me in laying down?"

"Lead the way, moonshine," they reply, smiling back, and I do just that until we reach a space near Addie and Al. I lay on my back, Sione on their stomach, one wing hovering over me to shade me. I reach up and follow the path of an illuminated vein with my finger, careful to avoid the junctures which seem particularly...sensitive.

Movement in my periphery catches my attention, and I look over in time to see Atlas coming back with waters for everyone. He hands one to Sione for both of us, another to Tali, and one to Addie. He looks like he's about to find a place on the ground by the Obalans, but Al swiftly grasps his hand. "Lay next to me?" she requests softly.

He seems stunned; frozen but for the fingers that curl slightly around hers, as if on instinct. "If you like," she adds even more quietly.

My best friend's eyes go so gentle it makes *my* heart ache. "Alright, darling," he responds, and lowers to sit beside her before laying down. Still holding her hand.

Adathan reaches to stroke her cheek, and she turns from Atlas to lean into the touch with another smile. Again, I could swear that the world reacts, a cool breeze blowing over all of us, rustling the grass that feels so soft beneath me.

I exchange a glance with Sione, who looks so delighted by this most interesting shift, you'd think they were watching a play in the theater. Only better, because it's real, and therefore really *intriguing*. To say the fucking least.

Adathan is super possessive, and Al loves being possessed by him, as much as she loves her independence. Is that the line? Her choice? Or, is he simply so attuned to her pleasure that he felt whatever emotion accompanied that quick wandering of her eyes earlier, and just wants to give her more of it? Perhaps it's both.

That's not even to bring mention of his dedication to her happiness, something I'd noticed about him almost upon meeting them. Al likes Atlas–in whatever way–and to keep her from him never would have lasted long. Another few days of that freshly-mated territorialism, and I'm pretty sure Al would have had something to say, anyway, potential second bond aside. That it looks like Addie made the decision first–taking away the guilt I'm sure she felt for having any remaining feelings for Atlas–just speaks even more to the kind of male he's been all along.

The kind of male who loves her enough not to limit her heart. We all know that thing is boundless. After all, it took me in, too.

✥

Sione and I lay in my bed, our hands twined above us as they gently play with my fingers. We've been quiet for minutes, each of us unwilling to bring up the topic that got broached at dinner.

"We'll be leaving for Obala the day after tomorrow," Javi had said abruptly, probably trying to get it out of the way as quickly as possible. His eyes had lingered on Sione and I, frozen in our seats, before moving to his daughter.

It was not asked. It was ordered. From a High Lord to his subjects. A High Lord who has been gone from his lands far longer than originally planned; his Lady; and the son of the Duke and Duchess who have been overseeing the nation since Javi left.

They have to go back. I'd known they would, though I'd managed not to think about it since we arrived in Sabrian. Now, it's all I can think about, and my heart hasn't left my throat since dinner.

"I don't have to go," they murmur, weaving their fingers through mine, and bringing the back of my palm to their lips.

I can barely speak in more than a whisper. "Your High Lord ordered it."

They pause, then reply, "He didn't say how long I had to stay. I can fly here in an hour, Emi. I can be with you every day."

I look over and up at them, their hair splayed out beneath their lovely face. "You would do that?"

They give me a small, gentle smile. "Of course, I would. I love–flying."

The feeling of my heart in my throat changes; shifts from a terrible sadness to a sort of elated anticipation. I move onto my side, too, a grin coming over my mouth. "Flying?"

They bite their lip, and tuck their arm under their head,

reaching with their opposite hand to push my curls back from my face. "Yeah. Flying is freeing. Beautiful. Intoxicating." I hum, and their fingers trail down the line of my neck, across my collar bone. "Flying is the best thing I could ever love."

I catch their hand with mine as it moves along my arm, and kiss their knuckles. Then I lean forward to tuck my head under their chin, and, as they hold me to their chest, for the first time in my life, I feel like enough.

74

COLINA

Ciaragen - day 41

YESTERDAY MORNING, I WOKE UP BESIDE MY MATE FOR THE FIRST time in over twenty-one years.

I listened to him breathe, and heard his heart beating beneath my ear. His scent was in my nose, his arms were around me, and I felt *whole.*

He is different. Physically covered in scars, and his body is half-starved, the muscle he'd had decades ago only sustained to the extent that it is now by the grace of Fae blood. Scarred and starved on the inside, too, by so many dark deeds done to and forced upon him, and his soul.

It is not like it was then. When he had closed himself off from it all to keep from feeling and processing all that he had done. Dion feels everything now, and does not hide it. Not just with me, but with everyone. The mask I'm sure he'd worn for years has not appeared once since I woke to him two days ago, and he's had plenty of reasons to don it.

Yet, he didn't. Not as he told me everything about his past; the female called Reina, her son, and their gravestone. Not when he listed all that he'd done since being freed from his cell. And not when he told Adathan his story, and how sorry he was for it.

I wanted to be mad at the male for dismissing Dion, regardless of how I understood his reasoning. I wanted to be angry, because Dion was sad, and he had suffered enough.

Until: *It's why I brought you back when Marcys took too much from you.* The first person Adathan had brought back from Death wasn't Althea.

It was Dion.

He never told me, never tried to get me to hate him less by giving me that information. He let me loathe him, and the most horrible part of that is, I think he did it because he knew I needed it. He had seen me after the murder of my father, and known that I would need someone to hate, because it was easier to do that than to hurt.

So, I could not be angry with him. For giving that to me when he owed me nothing, and for never letting me know how much I owed him.

Everything, I think now, as I look at Dion in the late morning sun as we stroll through the gardens. Hielo and Hiela, Nuria and Jolie are with us, the last female quiet as ever as she looks at the heavy blooms of the midsummer. It could almost be twenty-one years ago.

Almost, I think to myself with a small smile as Lina's curls bounce with her steps ahead of us, her hand in Sione's. Bayani, Talia, and Javi walk with them, and Adathan is behind us with Aly, Nate and Bash, and Atlas. The latter three will be leaving tomorrow morning, as will Nuria and Jolie with Lina, though all of them live far closer than the Obalans who will be going as well.

My mate caresses the back of my hand with his thumb, as he has every few minutes since we began our walk with everyone. As if he needs to assure himself I am here, and this is real.

It doesn't feel real, he says to me down the bond. *I've dreamed of you, of this, for so long, my head is trying to catch up to my heart now.*

I squeeze his fingers in mine. *Take all the time you need. I'll be here through it all.*

Love and gratitude flow into my heart from his, and his hand slips from mine so his arm can wrap over my shoulders. He tugs me into the crook of his elbow, and leans down to plant a kiss on my temple.

Nuria nudges me after another moment of walking, the groups ahead of and behind us quietly chatting. Dion and I look over at her, and she and Jolie are already grinning. "Now that you're back," she says, her eyes so soft as they rest on my mate's, "how would you feel about an afternoon in Colina?"

He smiles back at her, his right cheek dimpling. I can feel his happiness, the joy at talking with friends he once thought he'd never see again. "I would feel pretty damned good about it, my Lady."

"Och, so gallant, even now," Nuria scoffs, turning back to the path. "Are you lot in as well?" she calls ahead.

"Fuck yeah," Lina responds for them, which gets her a prompt, "Emelina Dove," from Jolie, though the tone of it is only half reprimand, my friend's voice far too soft and loving around her daughter's name otherwise.

Behind us come scattered laughs, and Nuria looks over her shoulder at them. "You're all in, then?"

"Of course," Aly replies. I'm sure Adathan looked to her for her answer, and Nate and Bash looked at Atlas, who had done the same. I don't need eyes in the back of my head to have seen that she has those males wrapped around her pretty, powerful fingers.

"Will you come?" she asks then, and this time I do look, Hiela and Jolie doing the same beside me. All to find those green eyes focused on the former.

During her pregnancy, Hiela had remained within the castle. She would not risk her glamour faltering, or being sensed somehow. Afterwards, she had been too grief-stricken to go into the city for a few years. My immediate promotion after Dion was taken had been to guard Hielo and Hiela themselves, and I had been glad to remain cooped up with her. When she finally did go into the city, she seemed happy to speak with her people, but it would drain her quickly; being emotionally open while hurting so intensely.

Now, she smiles with such adoration in her eyes as she says, "Yes, my love."

⇄

An hour later, every single one of us walks down the streets of Colina.

"It's just the same," Dion breathes, his hand tight around mine as he looks around in wonder. The shops with their multicolored bricks and oxidized roofs. The homes down the avenues, a few of them with children playing on the land surrounding them. The people that don't slouch or trudge while they head to their destinations, downtrodden and afraid, but rather walk with their chins held high, so as to look around for where they might go next.

I inhale the scents that saturate the street. The flower bouquets and chandleries, the fresh bread and the fried dough, the plentiful people. All Fae and faeries alike mingling, talking over meals on the shaded patios, showing each other their wares or their purchases.

"They haven't touched this place," Dion whispers, and I can see the images of Oschverre in his mind. The stocks and gallows that have become fixtures as commonly walked past as the buildings. The evil of the king and his most disloyal right-hand male, one thinking of a mutual goal, the other of his own. The only reason it works is because Oleander has not yet realized how many supporters Olin has garnered towards himself, and away from Oleander.

My mate does not know how; doesn't know what he promised them. But, I can guess. I look at Aly's back as she walks ahead of us between Adathan and Atlas, but I keep my thoughts to myself. It can wait. That conversation can wait until this evening, when we're talking with the Obalans about next steps for our rebellion.

Now that we have not just a spark, but the flint, striker, and flame, walking the streets of Colina in a lovely red dress.

So, in response to Dion's statement, I only move my hand up to the crook of his elbow, and lean my head briefly against his shoulder.

We do garner quite the attention, though. Particularly three of the five in front of us.

The people of Colina know their High Lord and High Lady. They greet them with smiles and bows, some of them conquering their unnecessary nerves enough to approach and say hello. That is when it begins. The tear-filled gazes of hope and awe, latching onto the female with goddess power running through her veins.

That hope makes my heart clench in my chest. It is not for themselves; they have lives they adore here. Jobs that don't work them to the bone, yet provide them with enough money to always have food on the table, as well as live a life outside of survival. Families that don't fear if that table will be missing one the next day, taken because they dared to speak against the king. Neighbors who talk openly with one another, never thinking their countrymen will betray them for some sort of morality they have to work to convince themselves of.

That hope is not for themselves. It is for others.

The desire for others to have these things, as well. A city of people who want the best, not just for themselves, or those like them. But, for the people who are not. The poor, the sick, the hungry, the *many* people in other nations who deserve the same sort of comfort and joy our Sabriani have. Because they are us, if we had the same misfortune. If we were born with wings in a land where that makes you less-than, or if we were poor in a place where the people convince themselves to hate that more than they loathe those who hoard their billions.

That hope, that beautiful hope, fills their eyes as they meet their High Queen. As they feel the power that radiates from her, and see her kindness and grace. She does not even wear her crown; they are qualities that she has embodied since she was a princess across the sea. I think they can sense that, too. That she is not these things out of a desire to gather approval nor praise. Rather, she is these things as her heart beats. They could no more leave her than she could end its thudding.

I can feel Dion watching it, too. His own heart is split, seeing the same people who so readily accepted him do the same for her. And seeing his son beside her, while she introduces him to people that don't so much as flinch at his size or his power.

His son. Wrapping my head around that had taken some doing before our meeting with him and his mate. For the obvious reasons, of course; that he has a son; that it is Adathan.

But, also because I had never imagined children for myself until him. Had never had the desire with a lover in the past to create another person with them; to raise them, a little of him, and a little of me. I had only ever pictured such a thing with Dion at my side, and, until these past days, had mourned that we never had that joy together.

Well, it is certainly not the time for it now, with war on the way. I'd recognized that as I had thought through his words, his story of Reina and Adathan, and the gravestone he had not gathered the strength to tell me about when we were together those decades ago. Still, it had taken me a long moment to remember that love is sometimes enough for some; that some never look for their mate, happy to have found a person they enjoy life with. Simple. Easy.

Being a mate is not easy. The love is all-consuming, soul-baring, and agonizing. I knew, and know, that Dion is more than happy that he found me. And, maybe it makes me horrible, that his confession yesterday–about how he would not change his choices, and where they brought him–gives me some comfort. But, I am flawed.

But, I can only become better.

Most of the time, we all go into shops together. Dion had coin left over, stored in his night table, and buys me a bouquet of peonies and a crescent roll that Aly calls a croissant. At some points, a few will go into another building while others peruse stands on the street. The pairings change every time: Nuria and Jolie with Bayani and Talia; Adathan with Lina and Sione; Nate and Bash with Hielo and Hiela.

A few times, we have to send bags and boxes back to the castle. When we finally stop for lunch, it's after the usual rush, so all of us are able to push tables together and sit as a group. The waitress starts at the opposite end of the table from us, so Dion and I talk with our side as they order.

Over the slight commotion, though, I hear, "Oh, you're a natural," and look over to see Aly holding a loaf of bread, broken in two, her hair tied back in that purple sash. The servers are still bringing more loaves, steadily filling each table built for two with a small basket.

"I don't mess around when it comes to bread, Acacia," she replies with a smirk, and the female laughs, the males on either side of Aly grinning.

"You just call out if you want any more, Your Grace."

"Oh, you can count on that," she says with a smile, and Acacia chuckles before turning to take Talia's order.

When Acacia gets to us, her black eyes widen. "Dion," she says, and then beams. "Welcome home."

My mate's voice is rough when he answers, "Thank you, Acacia." The female who served us the very first time we came here so many years ago, and perhaps twice after. Remembering him, and greeting him in such a way. I can feel how much it means to him; how much it means to *me*, too.

Everyone's orders are placed, talk and laughter scatters throughout the table as we wait for the food, drinking sparkling wine and eating bread dipped in oil and spices. Dion is mostly quiet, only watching his friends. Listening to them, smiling as they speak. Several times, his eyes travel to the other side of the table, landing on the golden-eyed male sitting beside our High Queen.

It is like having my heart quadruple in size, feeling my own joy, combined with his. Of course, his is incomplete; I would not expect it to be whole, after all he suffered these years. After all he was forced to see, and do, and be a part of. And not after he nearly lost the two people he loves most in this world.

But, he is still happy. And, as he has not been in over twenty-one years, that is exceptional. Just like the rest of him.

Dion looks over at me from Nuria, who has the rest of the

table enraptured in one of her stories. His green-gold eyes are soft, his lips curled up in a slight smile. He doesn't speak the words, not even mind-to-mind. Only twirls a springy curl at my temple, too short to stay put in the ribbon the rest are tied up in, and presses his lips to my forehead.

75

BOUND

EBENET, THE CAPITAL CITY OF CERASCHE, IS LOVELY. QUAINT, almost, with its old buildings, potted flowers, and gravel streets so worn by hoof, carriage, and foot, that they run smoothly throughout.

Dekedda was loud; boisterous. Its people bustled around with drink and fried food, laughing all the while. Shops were open past the time when the moon rose, and the constant music in the streets combined with the humidity made everyone a little bit looser.

Colina is like both, and yet neither of them. Too established to be considered quaint, yet too quiet to be called boisterous. Flowers and faerie lights mingle along the sidewalks, lining the shops that are open even while the sun sets, though the people inside still conduct themselves well in the absence of too much to drink.

I would never call it boring, though. The Fae and faeries here may be kind, and polite, but they joke easily, and laugh even more so. The shopkeepers love their work, as their patrons do their products. Scents of bread and flowers and the variety of the people mingle in the air, delicious and diverse.

It reminds me a bit of Weaschte here, in that nobody seems to be going without. Regardless of appearance, status, or station, everyone around me looks well-fed, cared for, and happy. Even those rushing to get to work, or seeming distracted by their own emotions or thoughts are considerate as we pass.

A great city, indeed. One to model others after, if ever that is something I'll be able to dictate.

I never imagined it would be. Can it be only a month and a half ago that I was a human woman, too far from the crown to be considered in anything but alliances and furthering the line?

I know that's not how my mom and dad saw it. They wanted me to be happy; I know this to the marrow of my bones. But, they thought I had to find it in the way that they did. Because, gods, did they love each other; gods, did they love us.

I wish they could be here with me now; *see* me now. Even if this was never the role I was meant for in that life, I think they would be happy. That they would be...proud.

I changed, over the course of that voyage across the sea. And I changed again after my life was taken from me, and a new one was breathed into me by the male who holds my hand within his as we make our way back to the castle.

Yes, I think they would be happy I found the love they wanted me to have. Even if it's not in the way they thought I would get it.

Maybe...maybe I could write my dad. I put it off, at first because I believed he wouldn't wish to hear from me after that night, after what I believed I'd caused. Then, because there was danger which, at its end, led to days of changes and shifts that were so quick and plentiful that I could hardly keep up, never mind pause to write about any of it.

Now, though, may be the perfect time to do it. It may also be the only time. To tell him that I have found love, and friends, and not to worry about me. Not to worry that I will remain away for a time, to see this land freed of its tyrant king and his would-be usurper, because that love and those friends will never allow harm to come to me.

I can ask after Nik and Ben, Iris and Lor. My first family. And I will have the second one I found surrounding me when it's sent.

Adathan squeezes my hand, hearing all of this, and I look up to find him smiling softly at me. I return it, and the emotion in my heart is powerful enough that he raises our hands to his lips, and kisses each of my knuckles.

I don't think I will ever not be angry with him for what he did that morning. But, I will also never stop loving him. I believe his promise to me; that he will not leave this world until I permit it. A thousand years, and more. Until our very souls are dust in the wind, and the sounds they make will be our whispered names.

Be angry with me forever, love. But, never be rid of me, he tells me, the male I fell in love with mingling with the Fae beast my heart calls to just as fiercely.

And because I believe his promise, and he believes mine, I respond, *Never*.

We walk towards the open gates ahead of half our group, Ciaragen and Dion a few yards ahead of us with Bayani, and Nuria and Jolie. The castle grounds are beautiful, but something about them at sunset is especially lovely. The sky turns the small clover buds a warm cream, and the pale stone seems to soak in the rich colors, giving the impression that the very sky is inviting us home.

Behind the castle, dusk is taking over, leeching the pinks and oranges and yellows, turning them the deep, calming gray-blue of the end of a fine day. Maybe after dinner I can come back out with Adan, and Atlas, and our friends. Maybe we can lay in the clover lawn we walk across now, and look up at the stars.

The cobblestone path transitions into the mosaic tile, and our steps click softly along them. As we make to pass further into the castle, though, a guard hurries out of the entrance hall and intercepts us.

He bows deeply to me, then angles towards Oksana and Amedeo slightly behind us. "Your Grace. High Lord, High Lady. There is someone here to see you." The group ahead of us pauses, hearing that, too, and they reclaim the steps they took past the hall.

My brows furrow. "All of us?"

He dips his chin. "Yes, Your Grace. She waits within."

Still confused, I gesture for him to lead, and he turns to do so. Adan and I follow him in, Atlas at my other side, and Oksana and Amedeo behind us. Additional footsteps sound as the rest of our group files in.

The female stands before the dais, her brunette head tilted back as if she's admiring the hammer beam ceilings. A guard stands with her, his hand on the pommel of his sword. His eyes move from her to us when we enter, and as she hears us, she turns.

I stop in my tracks.

"Evie?"

Immediately, the woman whose sash I wear at this very moment, the woman who thought to save me from abuse after knowing me for minutes, drops to a knee, head bowed, and her fist over her heart. "Your Grace," she says in that strong, raspy voice, her pretty brown eyes on the floor.

"Please." I start forward, away from Adan and Atlas, and grab the hand she rests on her knee, pulling as I tell her, "Please stand."

She does so, and I give her fingers a squeeze before releasing them. "What are you–" I begin to ask, but I'm cut off.

"Evelyn?"

I look over my shoulder to find Bayani gaping, the steps he takes towards us slowed with shock. The voice that replies to him is not nearly as warm and welcoming as the one she has used with me since we met. "Bayani."

I whip my gaze back to her, and find her chin lifted imperiously, looking down her nose at a male a foot taller than her.

"You two know each other?" I ask, glancing between them.

His shock is replaced with a cruel sort of humor now as Bayani replies, "You could say that."

I follow up with the obvious: "How?"

He smirks, and raises a brow at Evie. "Do you want to share, or shall I?"

She shrugs her delicate shoulders, crossing her arms. "You always have been very good at talking. It's other faculties I found to be lacking."

He chuckles without any of that humor, sucks on the inside of his cheek, then says, still looking at her, "Evelyn and I met twenty years ago in Jasiira."

Twenty years? Evelyn must have been a child. How would he recognize–?

My hair flies over my shoulder with the speed with which I turn my head. I stare, using what Adathan taught me, but...

She waves a hand. "Oh, you won't be able to see through it, hon. Don't feel bad; I saw through his, but apparently not all." As she talks, she jerks her chin towards Adan, then her gaze flicks to my ears, yet to meet my eyes.

"You're Fae." It's a statement, and she nods.

"Yes, she's Fae. Masquerading as a human for how long, again?" Bayani leans forward slightly, raising his brows.

"You might as well tell them, seeing as you're so eager to insert yourself into my life."

Again, that humorless chuckle, a bit louder this time. "Alright, honey." He looks at me, a measure of respect returning to his features and his manners as he does. "Evelyn is of our legends. She fought in the battles of the Last War, on the humans' side. Killed hundreds of loyalists and slavers, jumping through space from one male to the next, and running them through. And, when the War ended, she decided she would stay. Ensure that the humans would have a protector, if any ill-meaning Fae returned to Weaschten shores.

"She played her part well, moving from country to country so that no one would realize how she never aged. But, when I had traveled to Jasiira to negotiate trade, I met her in a run-down pub, and she showed her true self to me. Had no reason not to. Until I dared to ask her to return home with me. Then, what did you do, Evelyn?"

"You know damn well I didn't want to, Bay–"

"She *rejected* our mating bond." Twenty years of pain and anger lace those words, and Evie's lips tighten into a rosebud as she looks at him, her eyes carefully blank. "So, tell me, honey, what in the soul-sucking Void brings you here now? Now, when even after a thousand years, nothing could make you leave that land?" Bayani's angular jaw is tight, a muscle within it twitching, but those black eyes are too hard to be doing anything but hiding. Hiding whatever he still feels for this female, even after decades without contact.

"*My King,*" she spits at him, then turns her eyes to me, hitting somewhere along my scarred cheek. "And my High Queen."

She sighs, releasing some of the remaining anger from her

slender shoulders. "My tracking majick isn't as strong as my jumping, but it held across the sea. You never took my tracking spell off that sash. And, when I heard that the royal family were looking for their princess, with black hair and green eyes, along with the descriptions of who she might be with, I realized who you were. So, I went to the castle. Told them I'd met you, and you on a ship heading here; that you were safe." Her brown eyes flit to the male standing behind me, probably replaying the same words in her head as I do: *Thank you. For caring about her.*

"He was relieved, as none of his trackers had been able to find you." She takes a deep breath. "He then asked me to follow my spell until it stopped moving. To find you, and...and give you this."

She holds out her hand, and within it is a scroll–sealed with wax, stamped with the arms of our House.

My dad, he wrote me before I could write to him. I feel badly about it, but in my response, I will explain everything. I take the scroll from Evie, my heart thumping as I break the seal, thinking of how I might tell him what I've been through, how sorry I am, how–

The first three words have my heart dropping in my chest.

My Dear Sister,

The rest of me drops all at once upon reading the first sentence, my knees hitting the tile with a force I don't feel.

It is with great regret that I inform you of the passing of our father.

He was ill for a time, after that night. In the end, I think it was a broken heart that took him.

I know that you have likely gone to avenge our mother. I have seen you in your training, and know that you will succeed.

I know you will, as, when his end grew near, father told me what you are.

He said he did not know for a long while. And, when he did, he could not say anything. He could not break mother's heart, knowing their babe was being cared for across the sea, just as one of them was being cared for here. And, he could not have let you go, loving you as his own, so fiercely.

We have loved you, too, sister. Iris and Ben miss you. Lorraine has given birth to their daughter, a girl they have named Lydia.

They do not know I write to you. They do not know where you are. They do not know what you are. I will not sully their memory of you.

I will only ask that, when you accomplish your task: do not return.

Without you in our lands, the Fae might have left us at peace forever. I will not risk that they destroy another part of my family for the sake of you.

I hope you find happiness with your own.

Love,

Nik

I READ IT, AND READ IT OVER AGAIN.

Father has passed.

Told me what you are.

Do not return.

The letter falls from my numb hands.

"Leave," I whisper, hardly more than a breath. Those in the hall with me pause, but I can't look at them. Any of them.

"*LEAVE*," I scream, my voice echoing around the space, amplifying my desperation. The sounds of footsteps shuffle out, not one word spoken.

Of course, he doesn't want me to come home. I'd thought about it, back in the Ceraschen woods. I don't know how, when

I finally forgave myself, I imagined that it was only my own self-loathing that made me believe in its probability.

Of course, he doesn't want me to come home. I *am* the reason his family has suffered. Olin never would have come for them, if not for me.

She's dead because of me.

They're dead, because of me.

My heart blocks up, beginning to reforge from its cinders. The coals heating the metal walls that will never again falter. Never, I will *never* hurt–

Behind me, strong arms wrap around my body. I try to shake free of them, but they hold fast. I thrash then, tugging and snarling, growling through my teeth, "*Let me go.*" My hair escapes its sash, tendrils catching on my lashes, twisting over my heaving chest. "*LET ME GO.*"

He doesn't speak, only keeps *holding on*, crushing me. So tight, so tight, I can't breathe, I can't *breathe*–

My shouts become sobs, the sounds of my agony echoing, echoing. Those arms become even tighter, holding the shattered pieces of me together. Banded across my chest, constricting so that my heart doesn't have the space to build the thick, impenetrable walls that might have kept this feeling out forever. Kept *every* feeling out forever.

I collapse into him, my hands gripping one of his forearms so hard that my nails pierce his skin. My head tilts back against his shoulder, and my cries call to the Heavens where they rest in the peace they never could have had in the life where they had me.

I don't know how long I scream, sobbing in Adathan's arms. Only that, eventually, they stop, my head resting on his shoulder as I stare up at the ceiling, my tears trailing silently down my temples, into my hair. He loosens his arms, only to scoop me into them, cradling me to his chest. He stands with me there, and my cheek rests against one of my claiming marks, the top of my head at his jaw. I close my eyes with my hands loosely clenched around the fabric of his shirt.

Scents envelop me as he walks. Thyme and salt; mortality and stargazer lilies; lavender and cinnamon. I can't look at them as we pass, can't bear the tears I can smell falling down their cheeks. I let Adan's steps lull me as he carries me wordlessly to our chambers.

The door clicks open and shut. I'm gently laid down on the blankets. My shoes are taken off my feet. After a few trudging, aching heartbeats, the bed shifts as he slides onto it beside me. One arm slips under my neck, the other over my waist, and his chest is against my brow.

Grief and guilt weigh me down, and I might have fallen through the mattress; through the floors and tile and mortar, until I reached the earth. Sinking into it until it swallowed me whole, soil filling my mouth, flowers spurting years later from the holes of my eyes.

But his arms keep me aboveground. His heartbeat thrums, a noise I would be deprived of in my imaginings. I can't speak to him, though I know he could staunch some of this endless hurt if I did. I don't deserve that reprieve–

"There was a garden in Castle Cerasche," Adan says quietly, his voice vibrating through his chest, against my face. "A small one, that was hardly ever visited, and so the staff maintained it to the minimum. Flower bushes grew onto the pathways, weeds sprouted within the gravel. The vines over the single trellis were so thick, it blocked out the noon sun if you stood directly beneath it.

"The first time I went there, just two days into my position at the castle, I stayed for hours. Something about it made me feel more at peace than I had in decades. And whether I sat on the rusted iron bench where my power quieted, walked around the small pathway, or stood within the trellis, I inhaled the air around me, wondering why the scent calmed me so, out of all of the smells–the flowers, the sunshine, the earth.

"The scent would follow me through the halls; I constantly looked for its source, all the while breathing it in more greedily than a smoker with his durry. I searched for days, until I introduced you at the first small gathering held since I'd arrived. You walked past me for the first time, and I nearly followed you to the dais, only the last logical piece of my mind holding me in place.

"A month and a half ago, right before people started arriving for the gatherings, I saw you in that garden. Though I'd always smelled you there, I'd never seen you in it before. Your back was to me, and you were sitting in the same spot I usually occupied on the bench. Your head was tilted back a bit, and I could hear you taking these soft, long inhales. And I thought... wouldn't that be a thing. If you smelled me, too, and it somehow brought you even a semblance of the peace your scent brings me." His fingers twine with the ends of my hair, and his nose presses to the crown of my head. I hear him inhale, and my aching heart strains.

"I remember," I whisper, my voice cracking and hoarse. "I never smelled it anywhere but in that garden, on the iron bench. As soon as I left it, it was like the scent would disappear."

"My glamour," he explains, his lips brushing my forehead. "It weakened when exposed to the iron."

Fresh tears spring to my eyes. "I would sit there for so long some days, searching for that comfort. Looking for you." The oak and leather and embers scent of him saturates the air I breathe now; the scent that has made me feel safer, calmer, for far longer than I remembered until now.

The arm around my waist tightens, and his voice is thick

when he replies. "I was looking for you, too. My whole life, I was looking for you." Down the bond, he continues, *I will never atone for leaving you after finding you. But, I promise, Thea, that I will never leave you again.*

I lift my face from his chest, and he pulls back enough to look me in the eye. "Would you still do it?" I ask in a breath.

For the briefest of beats, his brows furrow in confusion–but then he sees the meaning in my mind, and his sun gold eyes take on a shine as they grow as soft as I've ever seen them. "Yes, love. Yes." Too overcome to speak aloud, he continues, *I would never have asked you again; never have forced you to bind me to you this way. Are you sure you want this?*

Never. He has never before asked me if I'm sure; has always taken me at my word. That's how I know how badly he wants this. Only his own belief that he would be selfish to allow me to take his blood would keep him from immediately obliging me.

I nod, pressing a soft kiss to his lips, and he sighs there, his relief echoing through his soul, and our bond.

My cheeks are still wet, my eyes puffy a moment later as we stand a step away from each other. He explained the process to me quietly when we were still in bed, and once we were up, he'd retrieved our dagger from my night table, where I'd left it before going into Colina.

I hold that dagger in my right hand, my left cupping his, supinated to expose his palm. I gently squeeze his fingers before I slice the blade over his lifeline, then I look up into his eyes, and ask, "Adathan Evestre, will you bind yourself to me by blood?"

"I will," he says, his voice strong and clear, without a hint of doubt to be found within it. I raise his palm to my lips, and drink, the essence of him coating my tongue. When I lift my face, he wipes away a drop of his blood from my chin with his thumb.

I slice the same space on my left hand next, and he takes it with nothing short of reverence, and softly laps at the wound. I feel the majick of it seal between us in an instant. My throat is thick when I reach for his hand again, but he keeps it fisted.

"Don't. Don't heal it. I want this scar."

I nod, agreeing, tears once more blurring my vision. His uninjured hand finds the back of my neck, and tilts my head back so he can kiss my lips. There, I murmur, "You will not leave this world unless I leave it first."

His lips move up and down on mine as he nods, the order searing through our blood. I step into him, molding my body to his, wanting this closeness. *Needing* it. Not to forget my pain, but to help me through it. As he has since the dawn of my love for him.

My heart thunders as the kiss lingers, and so does his; they know the other's song as we have come to know one another. Without judgment, or restraint. Honestly and truly.

He hardens against me, and my core becomes wet, but neither of us makes a move for the other. I could easily wrap my hand around him, and he could put his fingers inside me. But, when he lays me down on the bed, he hovers above me, his hands soft in my hair, and at my waist. Mine gentle against the scars on his back.

When we break apart, our breaths are heavy, our pulses hammering. I'm not surprised that my tears have once again begun to flow down my temples. Loving this intensely is to grieve a little every day, for the loss of the small amount of the forever we have left between us.

It mingles with the heaviness of the black grief in my chest, and Adan pulls me to his, letting me cry silently into his shirt. I fist the fabric of it, and my shuddering breaths fill my lungs with the scent I had always been searching for. My tears only multiply as I think about what I must do now, and he holds me tighter still, not knowing the reason. I shield this one thought from him—him, whom I'd thought I would never have to hide anything from.

It is not so hard, knowing it will be for him. What is hard is knowing that, after this night, we will each have done something the other cannot forgive.

76

HEAVY POCKETS

ADATHAN - DAYS 41 & 42

WHEN THE SKY IS BLACK, FLECKED WITH STARS, THEA SLEEPS ON my chest. The fabric of my shirt is still wet with her tears; I can smell the salt of them, twined with the complex scents of us woven together by claim and oath.

It had not even been a thought, when she asked me for what I offered three mornings ago. After decades of being sworn to the most vile of people, it only feels like a gift to have taken that oath with the most lovely.

Perhaps freedom would have appealed to some. But, I never wish to be free of her. I want to be so completely bound to her that when our souls part from our bodies, even the universe that once fated us for each other cannot divide them.

That I might have to live for a moment in this world after she leaves it is no less than the punishment I deserve for the minutes she endured the same.

No, I never would have broken my promise to her. But, my

will is a small price to pay for the certainty with which she sleeps now, knowing *that* pain, at least, will never seize her again.

Others...

If I could shadowalk, I would go to Castle Cerasche now. I would hold the new king by his throat as he wrote the apology I would force from his hand. Then, before leaving, I would make *him* a promise: that, when my Thea does return to her home, he will welcome her with open arms, or he will lose them.

That he would know me to be a monster doesn't bother me in the least. I will gladly be a monster; my hackles raised, teeth bared in a snarl as saliva drips through them, hungry for the blood of anyone who would dare to hurt the High Queen resting beside me.

She can fight for herself. To doubt her strength would be as foolish as the decision to cross her.

But, in this...she would not defend herself in this. I felt it from her as she read and reread that letter. As she believed the things he wrote, and began to reforge the beautiful, open thing her heart is, into something I fear even I would have been locked out of forever.

Yes, Thea can fight for herself, and she will when she thinks the injustice or hurts against her are undeserved. But, she will always fight for others ten times as fiercely. Her monster, the glorious, gruesome thing she allows herself to be, only ever comes out for those she loves. My only consolation in this imbalance is that there is unlikely to be a time where she will be forced to release her beast, when her friends will not suffer, too, if she doesn't.

War is coming. It has been for a while, but the release of her majick from its bindings was the final piece. The spark to the flame of the flint and starter the rebellion has been since before her birth. There will be no stopping that fire's consumption of our land. It will burn through the oppressors, all the way to Oschverre. And the king and his would-be usurper will finally tremble to behold the people made of fire they tried to suffocate.

The Obalans head home in the morning to make the arrangements for war. Missives have been sent to the rebel countries, to the High Lords and High Ladies of lands that will rally to the cause which has been building for decades. They will gather within a month, the armies to the eastern border of Sabrian, the navies to the western coast. And our High Queen will lead them all, with me by her side, and her court surrounding her.

Until then, she will rest. She will train. She will bend the very earth to the will of the people. But, tomorrow.

Tonight, she will sleep in my arms, the sound of her heartbeat lulling me to rest with her.

⇔

Not a-fucking-gain.

I bolt upright as soon as I sense it–and my heart stops when I realize that Thea is not in bed with me. The sheets where she laid when I fell asleep with her in my arms are cold, rumpled with the absence of her. In a blink, I've followed her scent out the door, not so much as pausing to put my boots on. Twined with mine, she leads me down halls and stairways, out the great double doors to the gates, and–

She's there, her back to me, still in her red dress from yesterday. Its skirt and the hair bound loosely by her purple sash billow in the wind. I see nothing but her as I run up, barely noticing it when Evelyn appears from thin air, into the space beside her. I skid to a stop before my mate, gripping her shoulders, my eyes darting over that face. Her eyes focus on me, and the look in them...dread, cold and insidious, pools in my gut at the desolation in her gaze.

"Thea, love, what is it?" I ask her through the too-small opening in my throat. I frame her face in my hands, brushing the shorter waves of hair back. She doesn't answer me, and I choke back my plea, the dread only rising as she lifts her own hand to stroke my cheek–

Suddenly, her eyes go out of focus once more, and when she looks at Evelyn, the female's eyes are wide as she says, "That is not him."

Who? I want to ask, but I feel it, too. That thing that had woken me, which I'd forgotten about in the face of finding Thea gone from our bed. The approaching power, vaster than what Dion had emitted days ago as he came upon the Sabriani gates.

Then I hear it, too. The sound...it's a heavy, strange *whoosh*ing that has me looking up to the skies. And, even as far as they are, they are not difficult to spot.

Hundreds of Lumale, their feathered wings bright in the moonlight as they soar southwards, towards us. At the gates, guards begin shouting, the alarm bells ringing to rouse those not on duty. For now, I put that look in her eyes from a moment ago aside. Instead, as she looks at me, anger taking place of the hopelessness, I nod to answer her unspoken, and unnecessary question. Yes, I am with her.

She grabs my hand, gripping it with bone-crunching strength, and then we're running. Evelyn appears ahead of us with the gathered guards, the only piece of the armies we would have had in a month that is here already.

Orders are being shouted, and with this castle still being unfamiliar to her, Thea does not interject as males are sent to battlements and gates, shoring up for the imminent attack.

The only person she commands...is me. I realize it in the

same instant she seems to, as she turns that face to me, her fingers squeezing mine.

"I'm sorry," she says, and the regret in her eyes hardens in an instant as she says, "Go up to the highest turret and blow them out of the fucking sky."

My anger at her forcing me to leave her rivals my pride in her. I would have obeyed my High Queen and mate regardless, but it's made easier as I spot our court running towards us. So, though my jaw clenches, I bow my head, only pressing a quick, crushing kiss to her lips before doing as ordered.

I climb the stone walls like a tree, making my way to the highest tower in under a minute. They're close now, too close for comfort; perhaps five miles out. For my mate, for her court, for the people of Colina, the power I once loathed floods my veins, no longer leashed by blood oath to Olin.

My veins don't just blacken. It starts at my fingertips, pitch seeping through my hands. Gold threads through my arteries, twining with the midnight veins, my goddess's power weaving through mine, as it has been promised since the time of Deimos and Ymeda.

I raise my hand, black sky ribboned with gold, and *release*.

Ash on the wind replaces a third of the Lumale force.

The remainder seals the line just as they make it to the castle–

And they circle around it, four objects dropping to the ground before they head back towards the city.

Through the whoosh of wings comes the almost completely synchronized sound of innumerable *clicks*.

Something falls from the hands of the faeries, and time stands still.

Still.

BOOM.

I have to shield my eyes with my arm against the blast, and

the light that erupts from it. I'm nearly blown off my feet by its force.

Panting, I lower my arm, and my heart drops from my chest.

Colina is burning.

⇻

The High Lady's screams can be heard above the chaos on the grounds.

The Lumale do not retreat. They circle again, and then descend upon the burning city.

This is not an attack.

It is an extermination.

I hit the ground, and when I barrel towards the open gates, my mate is beside me, her hand slipping into my outstretched one. As we pass, I see what was dropped as they flew over the castle grounds.

Four heads. Harris, Jacks, and two females. One of them a child.

Thea's hand squeezes mine hard enough to break, but we cannot stop. Can hardly allow a heartbeat of grief for the innocents lost, while so many more are dying, close enough that we can hear their screams.

We run so fast it's more like flying, Thea's wind carrying us over earth that grips our soles just enough to allow our steps to hold, each bound covering several feet. The walk that took nearly an hour today is covered in little more than a minute, and we arrive to it.

War.

Slaughter.

The death cries of the people vibrate through my very bones. My power still flows openly, and with each direction of my hands, a Lumale becomes ash on the pavement. Broken

664

necks have otherwise intact bodies falling into the dust. Fires are tempered and doused as Talia and Javi arrive, metal reforms as Amedeo forges it so people can escape falling buildings. Whistles summon blades out of hands about to run people through with them. Lightning spears down from the skies, electrocuting the invaders where they stand, cracks of thunder drowning out their death cries.

Still, hundreds remain, and several dozen have found us, the sources of their destruction. While others stay behind, tossing little spheres that send buildings and people blasting to the skies, multiplying the remaining fires, they make for us, snarls of fury on their faces.

They've learned a bit already, not sticking together to make it easy for me to decimate them without risking hitting the people of Colina. I have to take them out one by one, predicting the unpredictability of their staggered flight patterns.

I'm following my next target, about to strike when they all fall to the ground, clutching their heads with agonized shouts spilling from their mouths. Not just the airborne, but those on the streets, too. Echoing screams sound from within homes and buildings.

The High Lady steps forward, her tear-streaked face holding such wrath that even my power checks itself in respect to hers. I don't know what she's doing to their minds, but with the time it took for the rest of us to do what we could to help, she managed to connect to each and every one of them, and bring them to their knees.

I take advantage of it, as I'm sure she intended. They have fear in their eyes when they sense their deaths coming to them; the air reeks with its scent, replacing that of the people's. Some of whom join us now on the streets, blades of their own in their hands.

I'm not fast enough, though, not as I can still only take out a few at a time, with the Sabriani scattered among their ranks. Even with Thea using her dagger to slit their throats, and Bash and Nuria running them through, there are too many alive as the majick loses some of its hold on them. Oksana is powerful, but every Fae has a threshold before burnout, and she is reaching hers. Though still in pain, some begin to rise to their feet.

One of them points at me, another at Oksana.

And that's all it takes.

The earth trembles.

Then it rocks, so forcefully beneath our feet that even I fall to my knees. Only one person doesn't.

She is ethereal. Glowing as she had in that garden that had been made for her. Her eyes are beacons; gold ribbons through her veins and shines like the sun through her hands. The world bucks again, but the Sabriani do not scream now. Not even when roots pulverize the pavement, their trees encroaching on the buildings around us.

Like bludgeoning blades, they impale Lumale, the blood from one still dripping as they find the next. Vines travel across the cobblestones to trap ankles, winding up bodies until they wrap around throats, growing and tightening, too thick to cut through and too unyielding to survive.

When the Lumale attempt to flee, those vines rise, catching them in their tangles. Branches swat them down like flies, breaking their wings and their bodies. Where they fall, still living, I am there to fix that.

I can feel my own power beginning to flag, but there are still too many left. Whenever they can, they're tossing those devices, carelessly slaughtering people within their homes and shops. Talia and Javi are doing their best, but the fires are too many even with Sione suffocating them with their wind, and they just keep fucking coming. Atlas strikes them when he can, but the blasts don't kill anymore. Nate and Bash and Nuria go at them, blades flying, Jolie doing something to the emotions of the Lumale which makes them hesitate to fight back.

Ciaragen and Evelyn are disappearing into burning, crumbling buildings and reappearing outside of them, carrying others with them. Bayani and Dion are there with them, helping those they retrieve to safety. When they're noticed, I take out the Lumale before they gain a step towards the innocents, and our court.

Sweat beads heavily on my brow. I'm now only decaying legs or arms, sometimes barely managing to fell them. Thea's power, however, still rages, killing and saving, and shows no sign of stopping. I know she can experience burnout; I saw it happen after she created two hearts and four lungs and layers of bone and muscle and flesh from scratch. Would she heed it if she felt it, though, when lives are still in danger if she stops?

My terrible wonderings are interrupted as a Lumale launches himself at me—and is grasped by a root as thick as my arm to be pulled back into the earth whence it came before I can turn him to ash.

Feathered wings and piles of dust litter the street, and where the bodies are intact, roots and vines drag them through the earth and stone they upheaved, bringing them down and down, where they will never again see the light of day. I spot one, about to bring his blade down upon Acacia, and his arms are ripped from their sockets by tendrils of wisteria.

I don't know how I recognize it, as I've never heard the sound before.

But, when Lina screams, my heart stops dead in my chest.

I whirl to the sound in time to watch a Lumale slip his blade out of Sione, and hiss, "*Jemage filth.*" With a flick of that sword, he severs something in the faerie's wings which makes them crumple just before the rest of them does, falling to the broken ground.

So, I don't see it.

I don't see, until it's too late.

Until my mate is ripped into the arms of a Lumale, my name a cry on her lips.

Not for her, I realize too late.

But for me, as a sword slides through my chest.

I fall to my knees, not hearing the shouts the others give of her name as the blade is pulled out of me, and the Lumale flees my nonexistent wrath. I only see her eyes, wide and tear-filled, as the last of my majick isn't used to blast the Lumale that holds her out of the sky. But to heal the would-be death wound through my heart.

I can almost make out the apology in her eyes before they're too far to see.

Then, I'm looking up at the empty, star-filled sky, the ring I bought her in this burning city weighing heavy in my pocket.

EPILOGUE
BETRAYED

OLIN - DAY 42

MY BOOTS CLICK DOWN THE DREADFULLY DULL STEPS, ONLY THE promise of what I will see at their end keeping me interested enough to continue.

Within the hall, the Lumalen males guard outside the cell, their wings still flecked with blood. I restrain my sneer of distaste. An alliance worth its prize, but so unsavory. It will be a relief, once this war is won, to be rid of them.

They turn as I approach, and bow their heads. I suck on the inside of my cheek, but not now. The disrespect of the shallow bow will have to be repaid later.

I stop between them, and look through the open door of the cell. It took quite a bit of work to cover every square inch in iron while I was away. Not so much as a crack to show there is earth above and below us.

The chains, too, are newly forged. They extend from the walls and the floor, and already her pretty little wrists and ankles are stained red and purple beneath them. Beneath her bare feet, her blood has begun to dry, along with the sweat on her face from the exertion of spilling it as those Lumalens did as ordered before my arrival.

My smile is nothing but genuine when I meet her eyes. "Hello, beautiful."

My Princess bares her teeth at me. I have to concede, she is even more striking with the glamour removed. Perhaps the exchange is worth the power returned to her. She cannot access it here, anyway. And now I don't have to force down my disgust at having to look at human ears.

Oh, such *hate* shines in those pretty green eyes. Such wonderful passion behind it. A lovely little fruit, perhaps no longer ripe for the picking, but I'm sure she will still be delicious to consume.

I sigh, and step into the cell. It's abhorrent, the immediate stifling of my power. But, sweet gods, does it feel good to watch her lashes flicker, just a bit, with uncertainty. She may not fear me wholly. But, she does fear what I might do to her.

As she should.

I lift my hand, and when she jerks away from my touch, I grab her delicate little neck, holding her still while I run a knuckle over her cheek.

Then, I bring her forward, and press her lips to mine.

She thrashes, and the violent, angry thing even growls before biting my lip hard enough that her canine pierces it.

I laugh, pulling back, and rub my blood over her mouth with my thumb. She breathes heavily through her nose, her lips sealed tightly against my finger, and the air flutters the crimson-stained tendrils of her hair.

"Can you guess whose cell this used to be?" I ask her, pushing that hair back from her face. She doesn't answer, but I didn't expect her to. I like her quiet, anyway. When she speaks, she tends to make me angry. And, I'm too happy with my success to allow that right now. "Within these very walls, I made Adathan scream. And scream. And scream."

Her lashes tremble again, the only sign this means anything to her. My grin widens. "Those scars between the shoulder blades are a bit dramatic, I'll admit. There is no proof, after all, that the gods have wings, however our friends out there believe. But, it was too poetic to resist." I begin to circle her, but she continues to stare ahead.

"I hope you like your matching set," I say as I reach her back, her hair pulled aside to reveal the deep cuts. I press a finger to one, and the muscles in her back contract at the pain, though no noise escapes her. I sigh again. "I could make you scream in this cell, too, you know. After all, I sacrificed my own pleasure for the art of this." I trail my hand across her upper back as I walk around her other side.

Her breaths are heavy, and if I close my eyes, I can picture them heaving in similar passion, in very different circumstances. Either way, hearing them now has me hardening.

Her sneer of disgust as I reach her front again tells me she sees that, and my lips pull up. Then my hand is pinching her cheeks with enough force that her teeth cut into them from the inside. "The next time you see me, it will be when I take you for my own, until your cunt forgets what your mate felt like."

Her exhale shakes through her nostrils, and her jaw tightens against that fear. It's so tantalizing that I can't help but step into her, forcing her gaze up to hold mine while I press into her belly. "I have everything prepared for your friends, when they decide to show up. We had to free up the space quite quickly after I learned of your little trick with the ship's cook. Clever. I'll admit, you're a clever thing, pet.

"Speaking of: let's take a walk."

On cue, the Lumale enter, and link the shorter chains

between her wrists and ankles, untethering those attached to the walls. They put her collar on next, then hand me the leather leash attached to it.

I lead her out of her cell, and her chains clank against the floor as she's forced to follow. As we pass each cell, I name the person it's destined for. "Atlas Malik. Emelina Bentashi-Mikhyala. Sione Natia, if he's still alive. Talia and Javi Kahale–I thought it would be nice for them to be together. Even one for Amedeo and Oksana Monserre. The only people not claiming a spot in this prison are my brother, and my son. I have other plans for them."

"What makes you so sure they will come?" she asks, her first words to me since we spoke of cocks at the Ceraschen Cliffs.

I turn to her, delighted by her question. "They will come. You are their High Queen, even if you are no one else's. You are their friend, their *mate*, their daughter."

Her head tilts, and I like that little angle. Even though I can see the marks of teeth better, I'll replace them with mine soon enough. What I like is the way it makes her look like she's playing with me. Her passionate hate already shifting to a different sort.

"Not only *their* daughter, though. Right?"

I click my tongue, becoming annoyed by her talking. "Yes, you are the daughter of Oleander, as well."

Her head angles further, her brows furrowing a little. "And that's why you wanted me, yes? To wed and bed me, and secure your place as High King?"

I twirl her leash around my fist. "Right, again." But, she is taking a bit of the fun out of my explanation now. Intelligence in females is truly a curse.

No matter. I huff a breath for patience, and open my mouth to continue–

"What would happen to you if Oleander found out?"

My jaw clicks. "He will not find out. Not until it's too late."

She grins.

I do not like her grin.

"I think you will find, Lord Olin, that you'll want me out of these dungeons and chains. My father will be expecting me."

Did you like the mermaid introduced in Chapter 29?

Read her story in my next project:

Tides of Divania

A fantasy romance series
by Jess Layne

Coming soon

Keep reading for a look into a special scene in a different POV.

INSANITY & HOPE

ADATHAN - 18 DAYS EARLIER

THERE WAS NO THOUGHT. NO HESITATION.

There was fear, though. I couldn't remember the last time I was afraid. I knew now, however, that *fear* was a weak word. An underexaggeration for what seized my heart when I saw the wave come over Thea. And nothing at all compared to what I felt when that wave washed away, taking her with it into the roiling depths.

No, there was no thought. I didn't hesitate to run to the railing. I only saw, in my periphery, Ciaragen use her entire body to throw Atlas to the ship deck. As I dove over and into the sea, the last thing I heard was him begging her to let him go.

I was instantly tossed towards the hull, but I used it to my advantage. I brought my legs back behind me as the water carried me, and when my feet hit the wood, I pushed off it with all the strength I had in my legs.

My heart twisted as soon as I did it, though, because what if the same thing happened to her? What if she was thrown by the waves, and, unprepared for any of it, her body was slammed to the wood, her head snapping back with it? I looked down into the blackness, and when I saw nothing but that, I bit back a sob. Even still, it burst small bubbles into the water, each one filled with the noise of my terror.

Maybe it was their movement that caught my eye. Something like a flash of white, which must have been the infinitesimal amount of light coming through the sea to where I was. It made me look up, towards the flash, and–

I was swimming before the sight of her truly processed. Propelling myself even more quickly than I had off the coast of the Ceraschen Cliffs, Thea on my back as we escaped my father. Then, there had been such wariness in her eyes as she looked at me. Now, as I closed the distance between us, I could see only relief.

I pulled her to me, and her arms wrapped around my neck in an instant. Strong and *alive*, and I would have held her closer if I didn't worry the constriction would harm her after this long moment without air. I brought her to it as fast as I could, and she gasped in a breath as we broke the surface.

"I've got you, Thea," I told her, not attempting to hide the tremor in my voice. "Hold onto me, love." The second time I'd called her that, and I knew my overwhelm would eventually be my undoing. It was so much harder to hide when she made it so very easy to *feel*.

But, she nodded into my neck, her breaths warm against my clavicle, and her arms only tightened in response to my words. I swam us to the ship, and though I noted the storm had calmed, I didn't care. Couldn't care about anything but the female trembling in the circle of my arm.

That included whatever a sane me would deem proper, as well as the watching sailors above, as I said, "Legs around me."

Thea obeyed right away once more, her legs wrapping around my waist. I had to let go of my own hold to climb the rope and wood ladder that was lowered for us, but she didn't budge. Not even as I swung my legs over the railing, bringing us to the safety of the deck.

So, I didn't talk myself out of my instinct. I didn't tell myself that she wanted to be put down, or that I should set her down regardless, and allow Atlas, Ciaragen, and Javi to attend to her. As Thea held tight to me, I only wrapped my arms equally so around her, and ordered them all to move out of my way. I did hear, though, in a broken whisper too soft for Thea's glamoured ears, a familiar baritone voice say, "*Thank you.*"

It almost made me feel enough mercy to pause. To let him see her, too.

Almost.

Instead, I walked us to the stairway leading to the cabins. Right into hers, and closed the door behind us. And I just...held her. I buried my face into her soaking hair, took deep, quaking breaths of her scent, and *held her*. Alive.

Alive.

"I'm okay," she whispered. My breath shook against the skin of her neck, and it took everything in me not to press my lips to it next. I was still too uninhibited, though–too mad with lingering terror and staggering relief. So, now, I did make myself put her down. Before I could do something I'd regret.

I couldn't quite let her go all the way, though. I rested my hands on her shoulders, and took one more breath before speaking. "What," I began slowly. Carefully. "In all the gods' names were you doing on deck?"

Through the bond she didn't know existed, I felt a familiar agony brim in her heart. So, I knew what sent her to the deck, even if I wasn't sure how it was broached. Knew, too, that if she wanted to be alone, she so easily could have gone into her cabin when the grief for her mother struck. But, she hadn't. She felt it–and she came for me. She came *to* me.

She was so attached to me that she put herself *in danger* to find me. And I should hate that. I should lash out, and tell her that she was reckless, and foolish. I should storm out of her cabin, and finally give the male who actually deserved her the opening he needed.

There was a reason I hadn't done it yet, though. A reason I let *him* be the one to pull back from her. Because I *couldn't*. She needed me, even if I didn't understand why. How was I supposed to be as horrible as I should be to get her to turn from me, when being myself around her comforted her so much?

The anger I held for myself was in my voice when I asked her, "Do you realize that you could have–*died*, Thea?" nearly choking on the penultimate word.

Those eyes held mine, and I watched them take on a bit of a challenge. "What do you care?"

My hands fell to my sides, and my next words were too quiet. "What do I *care*?" My feet carried me forward, and when I saw her small jolt as her back hit the wall, it wasn't enough. I took her space, leaning into it with my hands on the wood on either side of her head. "What do *I* care, Thea?"

Did she truly wonder that? Though I knew I *should* have been pulling away from her, I'd been doing a shit fucking job at it the past week and a half. Ever since she bled me, and told me she didn't hate me. Ever since she launched herself at me to embrace me, and called me handsome.

I told her this morning I was ready to talk it out with her. Because she finally saw, in all my horrible transparency, that she was so much more to me than what we'd been the past month. Or, at least I thought she had.

It was utterly nonsensical for me to have been preparing to tell her we would never work, yet now be incensed that she wondered why I would care if she *fucking died*. But, my sanity left me when I watched a wave turn the place she'd been standing to an empty Void. I supposed all those breaths of her weren't quite enough to return it to me.

She lifted her chin, unphased by the rage in my voice, and in my eyes. Much more softly than the last time, she murmured, "What do you care, Adan?"

My breathing stopped. Because that was the tone she used to ask me weeks ago if I'd "had enough." Days ago to breathe, "Thank you," against my skin. This morning to say, "I would prefer many things with you, Adan."

If she asked me the first question again now, while my relief at her safety made it difficult to remember what I was *supposed* to do, I would have to tell her: never. I would never have enough of her. But, that was not the question she asked. And the one she did was now edged with a fire in those intoxicating eyes. They might as well be liquor, because as that heat filled them, I felt as though I was about to set ablaze.

I used some of the final dregs of my logical mind to tell her, "Stop looking at me like that."

And she just *shook her head*, and kept on looking at me. Just. Like. That.

Through my teeth, the restraint a visceral thing, near enough to pain, "Thea, you *want* to stop looking at me like that."

She didn't even pause. "No, I don't. I want to keep looking at you, just like this. I want to see what happens when I do. Because, most importantly, I want *you*, Adan. And I know you want me, too."

Fuck.

I was never able to deny her something she wanted. In truth, I'd spent every night for nearly a year imagining and dreaming of giving her *everything* she wanted. And now, she told me what she *wanted* was all of me. And I was supposed to deny her. While every piece of the beast in me roared to give in. To *take* and *devour*. And she only urged him on when she continued, "Tell me I'm misreading things. Tell me you don't want this; don't want *me*. Tell me, and I'll never bring it up again."

Fuck.

It was one thing to give her the generic statement of how we wouldn't work. It was entirely another to tell her I didn't want her. Not just because the lie wouldn't pass my tongue; my final day of being false with her was the day we spent together with my father in the Ceraschen woods. But because I could see in her eyes how that lie would hurt her. And that day was also my last of ever doing *that*.

Still, I loved her enough to give her one final warning. "I am not a knight in shining armor, Thea. Not a gallant lordling that might kiss your lips gently for a heartbeat, and call it enough. I am not good; I am Death with his scythe, and I would take from you whatever you gave me. And, if you give me this...I would never fucking let you go."

I didn't even have a second to regret the truth I'd known had to be said, regardless of how much I didn't want to say it. Regardless of how much I wanted to take what she was offering without a second thought, or word. But, no, I didn't have even a second for that, because within that single beat, Thea only growled, "*Good.*"

I said it out loud this time, "*Fuck.*"

Then I *took*.

I took her waist in my hand, and her hair in my fingers. And I took her lips. And any remaining sanity, anything at all outside of Thea–it was gone. There was only her. Only the brief surprise that had her gasping a little breath through her nose.

Only the softness and strength of her against me, for I pulled her close the instant our lips met.

Those *lips*. I'd only looked at them for a month out of the eleven and a half that I'd loved her, but they entranced me even before then. None of my fantasies, even since then, however, came close to the real thing.

Real. Real as the way she opened for me as soon as my tongue traced the seam of her mouth. Real as the moan that filled my lungs better than air ever could. And, fuck, I'd considered what she might sound like if I wrung her pleasure from her over–and over–and *over* again, but that, too, held no godsdamned candle to the oxygen of that noise.

Call her liquor, call her oxygen–I was just a fire. Ignited by her since day one, and now I was consuming her. Maybe that would have been enough to make me stop, where the scent of her desire and her body in my arms only urged me on. Except, if I was devouring her, she was doing the same to me–eating away at the last shields I had left when it came to her. Because I gave her a sound right back, and I'd never done that before with a partner.

And it felt *so fucking good* to give her one of my firsts, too.

I fisted her hair, tipping her head back further, and I tasted every square inch of her mouth. That *taste*...

I lifted her before what I could no longer hold back would press into her belly. Her legs went around my waist once more, but I wasn't shaking with terror this time. Wasn't in the bloody ocean. So, I felt the heat of her against *my* stomach, and it was good that she was small. Otherwise, she would have felt my cock against the bottom of her ass, harder than the wall at her back.

My hands found their places under her thigh and on the side of her neck, and stayed there, though. Not even my extreme need for her could ever make me forget to respect her. Her hands…I was so fucking glad she did what she liked with her hands. They tangled in my hair, scratched down my neck. Ripped the fabric of my shirt, nearly breaking skin, too, and I wished I could tell her she could take my blood whenever she wanted without frightening her. To restrain myself, I moved my mouth to the sea-coated skin of her neck. I sucked on the space over her hammering pulse, scarcely keeping my teeth behind my lips.

"Adan," she sighed.

"Thea," I gritted out against her, my hand squeezing her thigh. *Her*. In my hands, against my lips. It came as a sigh next, and I felt her neck arch at the caress of my exhale, "Thea." *Her*. Her scent in my every breath, her heartbeat thrumming against my chest. "*Thea*."

Her fingers moved again, gently this time. So soft, a sort of touch which I'd so infrequently received in my nine decades. It made my throat thicken, and that was even before her hands found the sides of my face, and tipped it up. My gaze clashed with hers, and I knew she'd done it. She burned away my final mask, and now saw every piece of my adoration for her in my eyes.

"Kiss me again, Adathan," she murmured, bringing her thumb along one of my many scars. One would think the lines made by my violence or others' were veins of gold for all the reverence in that simple touch.

Kiss me again, Adathan. How could I disobey? This time, though, I went slowly. I brushed my mouth from one corner of hers to the other, barely coming to understand the true detail of them after the second time. But, I couldn't make my sweetheart wait any longer. She sighed as I kissed her fully, like *I* was the one granting *her* a gift. As if she wasn't the one blessing *me*; a living goddess within my hands.

And, all the while as I took her through a gentle kiss, her

hands explored again. Sweet and admiring as I would expect if I were a millennia-old work of art; a beautiful thing, meant to be handled with care. And, though I'd begun this with the desire to maintain the respect of my hands on her, that desire turned to dust in the face of her whispered, "*Yes.*"

I barely managed to keep my hands from trembling as I seized her consent, and ran one down the side of her neck, and the other down her leg. Her skin was even softer than I imagined–and I'd imagined it too many times to count. It affected me, and even if she couldn't feel that, up as I had her, she needed only to breathe in to scent what she did to me.

Still, when I felt her desire respond in kind, I stopped my touch. I'd been fighting my hunger for her for nearly a year. But, *Thea* was hungry now, and I was only so strong. If we kept going, and she gave me her starvation, I would have little control over how desperately I would need to see her full.

So, when my hands stopped, and she nodded her urge for me to keep going–I shook my head. I pulled back from her, as much as I was able. And, however much I would regret it in the morning, when my every pore wasn't saturated with her, drowning out the reasons I should keep the truth in–I gave it to her, anyway. "I want to take my time with you, Thea. I don't want to do this all in one night." I laid my thumb over her lips when she opened them to protest. I was already hanging on by a thread. One 'please' from her, and I didn't know how I would disoblige her.

"More importantly," I continued, "I want to give you at least some form of the courtship you deserve. I may not be a knight, or a lord, but I am a male. And I'm going to make sure you know that, that you *feel* that, in more than one way."

I dared to move my thumb to stroke it over her collarbone, the other moving along her thigh. And I gave her one more honest thing. "I am not worthy of a single piece of you. Let me do this. Let me do anything, *everything*, I can to at least begin to deserve you."

I didn't think that day would ever come. But, I'd made her a promise this morning–to talk to her. Tomorrow, when my sanity reclaimed me, and my selfishness wasn't powerful enough to supersede it, I would talk with her. It was just...now, when she looked at me with those eyes, held onto me with those hands...My insanity allowed me to believe that, even after that talk, she might still want me. And, if she wanted me, and even if she did not, there was no going back for me. I would never be able to return to the male I was before her.

I could only be better. With me or not, she only made me *better*. I only hoped, with more ardor and desperation than I'd yet hoped for anything else, that I would, somehow, never have to be without her.

ACKNOWLEDGMENTS

This novel is the result of many (*many*) hours divided between a desktop and a laptop, my nesting phase–yes, getting some of book two of this trilogy done before birth was absolutely nesting–my baby's naps, sugar-free Monsters, and my village.

Reader, get ready to read the words 'I love you' a bunch.

First and foremost, my husband, Mike. For his support in pursuing this dream, without question, hesitation, or condition. For being the best dad to our son. And for every big, slightly goofy, very handsome smile each time I told him about an accomplishment, no matter how small. I love you.

To our son, for being the best blob of joy, giggles, and more toots than you'd think could fit in such a little body. Mama hopes you never read this book–or, if you do, you're over eighteen, and don't ever ask me about *the* scenes. Don't worry, that rule applies to Grammy, Grandpa, Gigi, and Papa, too.

To my sister, Jess (yes, her name is Jess, too, we met when we were nine and our parents married four years later). I am so proud of you. Thank you for always being there for me, from gushing about my characters, all the way to venting about life as a mom. You're gonna crush it.

My other siblings: I love you all–you too, Jess–but you're not going to read this, so Jess will just have to tell you. Mack, if you *are* reading this, it had better be three years from now. If it is, you can ask me about the scenes–just don't tell your nephew.

To Julia and Brittany. My ride or die TCT girlies from day one. I love you both.

To Erin. Soon-to-be mama of two, and always-baddie. Thank you for being my sounding board when I had no idea what I was doing, and for being excited for my books even though you're not a reader.

Dorian and Yashira. My pookies. My loves. My feral, hilarious, beautiful mini support group. I am endlessly grateful to Instagram for bringing us together. I love y'all heavier than Daddythan's thick ole thighs. P.S. I hope you're ready for me to send you what you've been waiting for as I work on book three *side eye emoji*.

To Katie, Em, Devyn, Morgan, Sasha, Sam, and Sars: bad bitches, all around. Thank you for believing in this story.

To Val, my amazing, talented, beautiful cover artist. Your work continues to astound, and I can't wait until I'm sending you concepts for book three.

To Sam. You took on two rounds of edits for this little indie author. Gave me direction when I needed it, and hype when I didn't. Jumped on board for the most wildin' group chat. And, of course, have been one of my best friends for literally my whole life. I love you!

And last, but certainly not least: to you, the reader. Thank you so much for enabling me to make this dream of mine a reality.

ABOUT THE AUTHOR

Jess was born and raised on Long Island, NY. She may not live there anymore, but she will always talk with her hands, and drive like a New Yorker because of it.

She has a degree in health sciences, hence the partiality towards using that knowledge in Althea's point of view. She has no degree for English nor writing, but she *did* take creative writing in high school, shortly after the Twilight/Hunger Games/Divergent craze. These books are the culmination, therefore, of a decade-old dream.

She now lives with her husband, their baby, and their dog, who wonders when the furless puppy will start playing with her.

For signed copies, and prints of your favorite characters (and soon-to-be scenes!), visit authorjesslayne.com

For deleted scenes, and digital SFW and NSFW (coming soon!) art, visit my Patreon @authorjesslayne